PENGUIN BOOKS

The Call of Cthulhu and Other Weird Stories

H. P. Lovecraft was born in 1890 in Providence, Rhode Island, where he lived most of his life. Frequent illnesses in his youth disrupted his schooling, but Lovecraft gained a wide knowledge of many subjects through independent reading and study. He wrote many essays and poems early in his career, but gradually focused on the writing of horror stories, after the advent in 1923 of the pulp magazine *Weird Tales*, to which he contributed most of his fiction. His relatively small corpus of fiction – three short novels and about sixty short stories – has nevertheless exercised a wide influence on subsequent work in the field and he is regarded as the leading twentieth-century American author of supernatural fiction. H. P. Lovecraft died in Providence in 1937.

S. T. Joshi is a freelance writer and editor. He has edited Lovecraft's collected fiction as well as some of Lovecraft's essays, letters and miscellaneous writings. Among his critical and biographical studies are *The Weird Tale* (1990), *Lord Dunsany: Master of the Anglo-Irish Imagination* (1995) and *H. P. Lovecraft: A Life* (1996). He has also edited Lovecraft's *The Thing on the Doorstep and Other Weird Stories* for Penguin.

D1418639

THE CALL OF CTHULHU
AND OTHER
WEIRD STORIES

H. P. LOVECRAFT

EDITED WITH AN
INTRODUCTION AND NOTES BY
S. T. JOSHI

PENGUIN BOOKS

PENGUIN BOOKS

Published by the Penguin Group
Penguin Books Ltd, 80 Strand, London WC2R 0RL, England
Penguin Putnam Inc., 375 Hudson Street, New York, New York 10014, USA
Penguin Books Australia Ltd, 250 Camberwell Road, Camberwell, Victoria 3124, Australia
Penguin Books Canada Ltd, 10 Alcorn Avenue, Toronto, Ontario, Canada M4V 3B2
Penguin Books India (P) Ltd, 11 Community Centre, Panchsheel Park, New Delhi – 110 017, India
Penguin Books (NZ) Ltd, Cnr Rosedale and Airborne Roads, Albany, Auckland, New Zealand
Penguin Books (South Africa) (Pty) Ltd, 24 Sturdee Avenue, Rosebank 2196, South Africa

Penguin Books Ltd, Registered Offices: 80 Strand, London WC2R 0RL, England

www.penguin.com

This edition first published in Penguin Books 1999
Reprinted in Penguin Classics 2002

3

Selection, introduction and notes copyright © S. T. Joshi, 1999
All rights reserved

The stories in this volume are reprinted by arrangement
with Lovecraft Properties LLC.

The moral right of the editor has been asserted

Printed in England by Clays Ltd, St Ives plc

CONTENTS

INTRODUCTION

Howard Phillips Lovecraft was born on August 20, 1890, at his family home at 454 Angell Street in Providence, Rhode Island. His mother, Sarah Susan Phillips Lovecraft, could trace her ancestry to the seventeenth century, while his father, Winfield Scott Lovecraft, a traveling salesman for Gorham & Company, Silversmiths, of Providence, derived from a line originating in Devonshire, England, and domiciled in New York State since the early nineteenth century. When Lovecraft was three his father suffered a mental breakdown and was placed in Butler Hospital in Providence, where he remained for five years before dying on July 19, 1898. Lovecraft was apparently told that his father was paralyzed and comatose during this period, but the surviving medical evidence makes it clear that Winfield died of syphilis.

With the death of Lovecraft's father, the upbringing of the boy fell to his mother, his two aunts, and especially his maternal grandfather, the prominent industrialist Whipple Van Buren Phillips. Lovecraft was a precocious youth: he was reciting poetry at the age of two, reading by three, and writing by six or seven. His earliest enthusiasm was for Grimm's fairy tales and the *Arabian Nights*, which he read by the age of five; it was at this time that he adopted the pseudonym of "Abdul Alhazred," who later became the author of the mythical *Necronomicon*. The next year, however, his Arabian interests were eclipsed by the discovery of Greek mythology, gleaned through Bulfinch's *Age of Fable* and Hawthorne's *Wonder Book* and *Tanglewood Tales*. His earliest surviving literary work, "The Poem of Ulysses" (1897), is a paraphrase of the *Odyssey* in 88 lines of internally rhyming verse. But Lovecraft had by this time already dabbled in weird fiction, and his first story, "The Noble Eavesdropper" (non-extant), may date to as early as 1896. His interest in the weird was fostered by his grandfather Phillips, who entertained Lovecraft with oral weird tales in the Gothic mode; but it was his ecstatic discovery of Edgar Allan Poe in 1898 that put the seal on the matter: ". . . at the age of eight I saw the blue firmanent of Argos and Sicily darkened by the miasmal exhalations of the tomb!" (SL II.109).

As a boy Lovecraft was somewhat lonely and suffered from frequent illnesses, many apparently psychological. His attendance at the Slater Avenue School was sporadic, but Lovecraft was absorbing much information through independent reading and study. At the age of eight he discovered science, first chemistry, then astronomy. He began to produce hectographed journals, *The Scientific Gazette* (1899–1907) and *The Rhode Island Journal of Astronomy* (1903–07), for distribution among his friends and family. When he entered Hope Street High School in 1904, he found his teachers and his peers congenial and encouraging, and he developed a number of long-lasting friendships with boys of his own age. Lovecraft's first appearance in print occurred in 1906, when he wrote a letter to the editor of the *Providence Sunday Journal*, on a point of astronomy. Shortly thereafter he began writing astronomical columns for both the *Pawtuxet Valley Gleaner*, a rural paper, and the Providence *Tribune* (1906–08). Later he wrote such columns for the Providence *Evening News* (1914–18) and the *Asheville* [N.C.] *Gazette-News* (1915).

In 1904, the death of Lovecraft's grandfather Phillips and the subsequent mismanagement of his property and assets plunged Lovecraft's family into severe financial difficulties. Lovecraft and his mother were forced to move out of their lavish Victorian home into cramped quarters at 598 Angell Street. Lovecraft was devastated by the loss of his birthplace and apparently even contemplated suicide, taking long bicycle rides and looking wistfully at the watery depths of the Barrington River. But the thrill of learning banished these thoughts. However, in 1908, after having finished only three years of high school (he had been absent for nearly the whole of the 1905–06 term), he suffered a nervous breakdown that compelled him to leave school without a diploma. This event, and his consequent failure to enter Brown University, were sources of great shame to Lovecraft in later years, and he rarely spoke in detail of this critical period of his life. In the absence of evidence, one can only conjecture as to the causes of the breakdown; perhaps his difficulty in mathematics was a factor, since Lovecraft knew that his goal of becoming a professional astronomer hinged on his ability to master higher mathematics.

From 1908 to 1913 Lovecraft was a virtual hermit, doing little save pursuing his astronomical interests, taking some correspondence courses, and writing a little poetry. During this period Lovecraft was also thrown into an unhealthily close relationship with his mother, still suffering from the trauma of her husband's illness and death, and who developed a pathological love-hate relationship with her son.

Lovecraft emerged from his hermitry in a peculiar way. Having taken to reading the early "pulp" magazines of the day, he became so incensed at the insipid love stories of one Fred Jackson in the *Argosy* that he wrote a letter attacking Jackson. This letter was published in 1913 and evoked a storm of protest from Jackson's defenders; one of them responded with a brief satirical poem. Lovecraft—whose devotion to the poetry of Dryden and Pope was undying—could not resist making several verse responses of his own in the style of the *Dunciad*. The controversy lasted for a full year, and was observed by Edward F. Daas, Official Editor of the United Amateur Press Association (UAPA), a group of amateur writers from around the country who wrote and published their own magazines. At Daas's invitation Lovecraft joined the UAPA in April 1914.

Amateur journalism was just what Lovecraft needed at this juncture. Greatly learned but diffident of his abilities and out of tune with the modern world, Lovecraft found that he could achieve a modicum of recognition and encouragement in the small world of amateur journalism. He published thirteen issues of his own paper, *The Conservative* (1915–23), as well as contributing poetry and essays voluminously to other journals. He also became President (1917–18) and Official Editor (1920–22, 1924–25) of the UAPA, as well as serving as interim President of the rival National Amateur Press Association (NAPA) in 1922–23. This entire experience may have saved Lovecraft from a life of unproductive reclusiveness; as he himself wrote in 1921:

In 1914, when the kindly hand of amateurdom was first extended to me, I was as close to the state of vegetation as any animal well can be . . . With the advent of the United I obtained a renewed will to live; a renewed sense of existence as other than a superfluous weight; and found a sphere in which I could feel that my efforts were not wholly futile. For the first time I could imagine that my clumsy gropings after art were a little more than faint cries lost in the unlistening void. (MW 452)

It was in the amateur world that Lovecraft recommenced the writing of fiction, which he had abandoned in 1908. W. Paul Cook and others, noting the promise shown in such early tales as "The Beast in the Cave" (1905) and "The Alchemist" (1908), urged Lovecraft to pick up his fictional pen again. Lovecraft did so in the summer of 1917, writing "The Tomb" and "Dagon" in rapid succession. Thereafter he kept up a steady if sparse flow of fiction, although until at least 1922 poetry and essays were still his dominant modes of literary expression. Lovecraft also became involved in an ever-increasing network of correspondence with friends and associates, and eventually became one of the greatest and most prolific letter-writers of the century. Gainful employment, however, did not seem to be much of a concern, even though the family inheritance was inexorably dwindling. Never trained for an occupation, Lovecraft eventually drifted into poorly paying work as a "revisionist" or ghostwriter.

Lovecraft's mother, her mental and physical condition deteriorating, suffered a nervous breakdown in 1919 and was admitted to Butler Hospital. However, her death on May 24, 1921, was the result of a bungled gallbladder operation. Lovecraft was shattered by the loss, but by July had recovered enough to attend an amateur journalism convention in Boston. It was on this occasion that he first met the woman who would become his wife. Sonia Haft Greene was a widowed Russian Jew seven years Lovecraft's senior, but the two seemed, at least initially, to find themselves highly congenial. Lovecraft visited Sonia in her Brooklyn apartment on two separate occasions in 1922, and the news of their marriage on March 3, 1924, was not entirely a surprise to their friends; but it may have been to Lovecraft's two aunts, Lillian D. Clark and Annie E. Phillips Gamwell, who were notified only by letter after the ceremony had taken place.

Lovecraft moved into Sonia's apartment in Brooklyn, and initial prospects for the couple seemed good: Lovecraft had gained a foothold by the acceptance of several of his early stories by *Weird Tales*, the celebrated pulp magazine founded in 1923; Sonia was an executive at a successful hat shop on Fifth Avenue in Manhattan. But troubles descended upon the couple almost immediately. Sonia gave up her position to start a hat shop of her own, but it was a failure; Lovecraft turned down the chance to edit *Weird Tales* (which would have necessitated his move to Chicago), and was also unable to find work with New York magazine and book publishers, in spite of assistance from such colleagues as Samuel Loveman (poet and friend of Ambrose Bierce, George Sterling, and Hart Crane) and Harry Houdini, for whom Lovecraft had ghostwritten a story for *Weird Tales*. Sonia's health gave way, forcing her to spend time in a sanatarium in New Jersey. Lovecraft attempted to secure work—including positions with such unlikely firms as a collection agency and a lamp-testing company—but was unsuccessful. On January 1, 1925, Sonia went to the Midwest to take up a succession of jobs in Cincinnati and Cleveland, returning to New York only intermittently; Lovecraft moved into a single apartment near the Brooklyn slum known as Red Hook. Although he had many friends in New York—this was the heyday of the Kalem Club, so named because its initial members (including Rheinhart Kleiner, Frank Belknap Long, and Everett McNeil) had surnames beginning with K, L, or M—he became increasingly depressed. Lovecraft, who in his letters and essays expressed prejudice against African Americans, Jews, and other minorities throughout his life, was dismayed by his isolation amidst the masses of "foreigners" in the city. His fiction turned from the nostalgic ("The Shunned House" [1924], set in Providence) to the bleak and misanthropic: "The Horror at Red Hook" and "He," both written in August 1925, lay bare his feelings about the heterogeneous megalopolis in which he found himself.

Finally, in early 1926, his aunts arranged for Lovecraft to return to the Providence he missed so keenly. But where did Sonia fit into these plans? No one seemed to know, least of all Lovecraft. Although he continued to profess his "appreciation" for her, he seemed to stand idly by while his aunts barred her from coming to Providence or Boston to start a business; their nephew could not be tainted by the stigma of a tradeswoman wife so close to the region of the family's pseudo-aristocratic lineage. No doubt Lovecraft's sluggish sexuality was also a factor in the dissolution of the marriage. Sonia undertook an action for divorce in 1929, although Lovecraft never signed the final decree.

When Lovecraft returned to Providence on April 17, 1926, settling at 10 Barnes Street north of Brown University, it was not to bury himself away as he had done in the 1908–13 period; rather, the last ten years of his life were the period of his greatest flowering, both as a writer and as a human being. As W. Paul Cook poignantly wrote in his memoir of Lovecraft, the New York "exile" was in some senses a necessary phase of his maturation: "He had been tried in the fire and came out pure gold."[1] Lovecraft's subsequent life seemed relatively uneventful: in spite of a perilously meager income, he traveled to various sites around the eastern seaboard (Quebec, New England, Philadelphia, Charleston, St. Augustine, New Orleans), in quest of antiquarian sites to nurture his devotion to the seventeenth and eighteenth centuries; he wrote his greatest fiction, from "The Call of Cthulhu" (1926) to *At the Mountains of Madness* (1931) to "The Shadow Out of Time" (1934–35); and he continued his prodigiously vast correspondence. He nurtured the careers of many young writers, many of whom he never met (August Derleth, Donald Wandrei, Robert Bloch, Fritz Leiber); he became concerned with political and economic issues, as the Great Depression led him to renounce his earlier conservatism and support Franklin D. Roosevelt's New Deal; and he continued absorbing knowledge on a wide array of subjects, from philosophy to literature to history to architecture.

However, the last several years of his life were filled with hardship. In 1932 his beloved aunt, Lillian Clark, died, and in

1933 he moved into quarters at 66 College Street, right behind the John Hay Library of Brown University, with his other aunt, Annie E. Phillips Gamwell. (This house has now been moved to 65 Prospect Street.) His later stories, increasingly lengthy and complex, became difficult to sell, and his revision work was bringing in very small sums of money, forcing Lovecraft into extreme economies in diet, clothing, and other necessities. In 1936 the suicide of Robert E. Howard, the author of the Conan stories and one of his closest correspondents, left him confused and saddened. By this time the illness that would cause his own death—cancer of the intestine—had already progressed so far that little could be done to treat it. Lovecraft attempted to carry on in increasing pain through the winter of 1936–37, but he was finally compelled to enter Jane Brown Hospital on March 10, 1937, where he died five days later. He was buried on March 18 at the Phillips family plot in Swan Point Cemetery.

It is likely that, as he saw death approaching, Lovecraft envisioned the ultimate oblivion of his work, as he had never had a true book published in his lifetime (aside from the crudely issued *The Shadow Over Innsmouth*, only a few hundred copies of which were distributed in late 1936), and his stories, essays, and poems were scattered in a wide array of amateur and pulp magazines. Lovecraft, convinced that the production of art was a form of pure "self-expression" in which monetary considerations played no part, refused to tailor his work to the crude formulae of the pulp magazines, and was also markedly reluctant to "peddle" his work to book publishers. But the friendships that Lovecraft had forged solely by correspondence proved to be the seeds of a posthumous triumph. August Derleth and Donald Wandrei were determined to preserve Lovecraft's stories in the dignity of hardcovers, and they formed the firm of Arkham House initially for the sole purpose of publishing Lovecraft; they issued *The Outsider and Others* in 1939. Wandrei was also convinced that Lovecraft's ultimate reputation might rest as much on his letters as on his fiction, and he spent decades editing what would eventually become the five-volume series of *Selected Letters*. Lovecraft's work is now widely available, his essays, poetry, and miscellany have been collected, and his tales have been translated into a dozen or more languages. His position as the leading American proponent of supernatural fiction in this century is assured.

Lovecraft's reputation as a fiction writer rests upon a remarkably small body of work: about sixty short stories, three of which, *The Dream-Quest of Unknown Kadath* (1926–27), *The Case of Charles Dexter Ward* (1927), and *At the Mountains of Madness,* might be classified as short novels. And yet, this small corpus of fiction presents a surprising richness of form, substance, and texture.

Lovecraft's fiction must be understood in the context of the philosophical thought that he evolved over a lifetime of study and observation. The core of that thought—derived from readings of such ancient Greek philosophers as Democritus and Epicurus as well as from absorption of the discoveries of nineteenth-century physics, chemistry, and biology—is mechanistic materialism. This is the belief that the universe is a "mechanism" operating according to fixed laws (although these may not all be known to human beings), and that there can be no immaterial substance such as a soul or spirit. Such a view necessarily necessitates agnosticism or actual atheism, and Lovecraft was not slow in expressing his adherence to the latter:

> I certainly can't see any sensible position to assume aside from that of *complete scepticism tempered by a leaning toward that which existing evidence makes most probable*. All I say is that I think it is *damned unlikely* that anything like a central cosmic will, a spirit world, or an eternal survival of personality exist. They are the most preposterous and unjustified of all the guesses which can be made about the universe, and I am not enough of a hair-splitter to pretend that I don't regard them as arrant and negligible moonshine. In theory I am an *agnostic*, but pending the appearance of rational evidence I must be classed, practically and provisionally, as an *atheist*. The chance's of theism's truth being to my mind so microscopically small, I would be a pedant and a hypocrite to call myself anything else. (SL IV.57)

In the mid-1920s Lovecraft was momentarily disturbed by the implications of Einstein's relativity theory and Planck's quantum

theory, both of which were hailed by many as spelling the down-
fall of mechanistic materialism; but his later adherence to the materialism of Bertrand Russell, George Santayana, and others
allowed him to reconcile the findings of modern astrophysics
with his fundamental views.

However, does not Lovecraft's philosophy contradict his
stated motives for writing weird fiction, as enunciated in the essay "Notes on Writing Weird Fiction" (1933)?

> I choose weird stories because they suit my inclinations best—
> one of my strongest and most persistent wishes being to achieve,
> momentarily, the illusion of some strange suspension or violation
> of the galling limitations of time, space, and natural law which for
> ever imprison us and frustrate our curiosity about the infinite cos-
> mic spaces beyond the radius of our sight and analysis. (MW 113)

It is important not to be led astray here. Lovecraft is not renouncing his materialism by seeking an imaginative escape from
it; indeed, it is precisely *because* he believes that "time, space, and
natural law" *are* uniform, and that the human mind cannot defeat or confound them, that he seeks an imaginative escape from
them.

Lovecraft's philosophical position virtually necessitated the
central conception in his aesthetic of the weird—the notion of
cosmicism, or the suggestion of the vast gulfs of space and time
and the resultant inconsequence of the human species. Lovecraft
claimed to have derived this sentiment as early as the age of
twelve, when he first studied astronomy:

> The most poignant sensations of my existence are those of 1896,
> when I discovered the Hellenic world, and of 1902, when I dis-
> covered the myriad suns and worlds of infinite space. Sometimes I
> think the latter event the greater, for the grandeur of that growing
> conception of the universe still excites a thrill hardly to be dupli-
> cated. ("A Confession of Unfaith" [1922]; MW 536)

This led to one of his most resounding utterances, made in a
letter of 1927:

Now all my tales are based on the fundamental premise that common human laws and interests and emotions have no validity or significance in the vast cosmos-at-large. To me there is nothing but puerility in a tale in which the human form—and the local human passions and conditions and standards—are depicted as native to other worlds or other universes. To achieve the essence of real externality, whether of time or space or dimension, one must forget that such things as organic life, good and evil, love and hate, and all such local attributes of a negligible and temporary race called mankind, have any existence at all. Only the human scenes and characters must have human qualities. *These* must be handled with unsparing *realism*, (*not* catch-penny *romanticism*) but when we cross the line to the boundless and hideous unknown—the shadow-haunted *Outside*—we must remember to leave our humanity and terrestrialism at the threshold. (SL II.150)

This statement is sufficient to account for the *outré* aspect of many of his alien creatures—the cosmic entity Cthulhu, the nebulous creature (or creatures) of "The Colour Out of Space," the fungi from Yuggoth in "The Whisperer in Darkness," and the Old Ones of *At the Mountains of Madness*. It also points to Lovecraft's central place in the fusion of traditional weird fiction and the then-emerging genre of science fiction. A late utterance is highly significant in this regard:

The time has come when the normal revolt against time, space, and matter must assume a form not overtly incompatible with what is known of reality—when it must be gratified by images forming *supplements* rather than *contradictions* of the visible and mensurable universe. And what, if not a form of *non-supernatural cosmic art*, is to pacify this sense of revolt—as well as gratify the cognate sense of curiosity? (SL III.295–96)

Lovecraft here is actually renouncing the supernatural for what might better be called the "supernormal"; that is, the incidents portrayed in his later tales no longer defy natural law, but merely our imperfect *conceptions* of natural law. His later work, accordingly, could be said to be fully within the field of science fiction aside from its manifest intent to incite fear. It is significant that Lovecraft's most "cosmic" stories—"The Colour Out of Space,"

At the Mountains of Madness, and "The Shadow Out of Time"—
appeared in the science fiction magazines *Amazing Stories* and
Astounding Stories.

One facet of Lovecraft's work that has exercised many readers'
imaginations is what has come to be called the "Cthulhu
Mythos." This term was not coined by Lovecraft, but rather by
August Derleth, who, while being obsessed by it, failed to grasp
its purpose. In effect, the "Cthulhu Mythos" is a series of plot devices utilized by Lovecraft to convey the essentials of his cosmic
philosophy. These devices—including a wide array of extraterres-
trials (deemed "gods" by their human followers); an entire library
of mythical books containing the "forbidden" truths about these
"gods"; and a fictionalized New England landscape analogous to
Hardy's Wessex or Faulkner's Yoknapatawpha County—are certainly found abundantly in Lovecraft's later tales and lend them a
kind of thematic unity not found in other work of their kind. But
if the "Cthulhu Mythos" has any significance, it is as an instanti-
ation of what David E. Schultz has termed an "anti-mythology":
whereas most of the religions and mythologies in human history
seek to reconcile human beings with the cosmos by depicting a
close, benign relationship between man and god, Lovecraft's
pseudomythology brutally shows that man is *not* the center of
the universe, that the "gods" care nothing for him, and that the
earth and all its inhabitants are but a momentary incident in the
unending cyclical chaos of the universe.

Lovecraft could hardly have imagined the radical evolution of
his work when he first began seriously writing fiction in 1917.
Bred from earliest childhood on the literature of the past, Lovecraft gained a poignant nostalgia for the eighteenth century.
What he later said of his poetry could apply in lesser degree to
his earlier stories as well:

In my metrical novitiate I was, alas, a chronic & inveterate mimic;
allowing my antiquarian tendencies to get the better of my abstract poetic feeling. As a result, the whole purpose of my writing
soon became distorted—till at length I wrote only as a means of
re-creating around me the atmosphere of my 18th century
favourites. (SL II.314)

What this meant, as far as his fiction was concerned, was that Lovecraft spent the bulk of his literary career attempting—if at times only subconsciously—to escape the overriding influence of his earliest mentor, Edgar Allan Poe. As Lovecraft's "God of Fiction" (SL I.20), Poe inevitably hangs heavy over such early works as "The Tomb" (1917) and "The Outsider" (1921).

In this sense, Lovecraft's discovery of the work of Lord Dunsany in 1919 was beneficial, if only because it resulted in a transference of influence from the American sphere to that of the great Irish fantasist. For two years Lovecraft produced a string of works imitative of his idol, who was then enjoying a tremendous vogue in America. While many of these tales of pure fantasy are undistinguished in themselves, they are of interest as representing the widest possible divergence in tone from the supernatural horror of his other work. Lovecraft was also aware of what he had gained from Dunsany, and as early as 1920 he observed: "The flight of imagination, and the delineation of pastoral or natural beauty, can be accomplished as well in prose as in verse—often better. It is this lesson which the inimitable Dunsany hath taught me" (SL I.110). This comment was made in a discussion of Lovecraft's verse writing; and it is no accident that his verse output declined dramatically after 1920. More to the point, Lovecraft learned from Dunsany how to enunciate his philosophical, aesthetic, and moral conceptions by means of fiction.

In 1923 the discovery of the Welsh writer Arthur Machen fired Lovecraft's imagination, although he did not produce any obvious imitations of Machen's work. This discovery coincided with Lovecraft's renewed interest in his New England heritage; he was at this time engaging in wide travels across his native region, absorbing both its rich history and its varied topography, and Machen's own evocations of Wales may have shown Lovecraft how to do the same for the land of his birth. The Marblehead of "The Festival" (1923), the Providence of "The Shunned House" (1924), and even the New York of "The Horror at Red Hook" and "He" owe something to Machen's example. Lovecraft was well on his way to becoming a significant local colorist, and "The Shadow Over Innsmouth" (1931) is perhaps the supreme example of this facet of his work.

Lovecraft's prose style has engendered widely divergent judgments, from the towering condemnation of Edmund Wilson to the adulation of his colleagues and disciples, who have sought to imitate (usually in vain) both his stylistic richness and his verbal witchery. Put very simply, Lovecraft's style is a melding of scientific realism and evocative prose-poetry. One is certainly free to dislike the style and to prefer the spareness of Hemingway or Sherwood Anderson; but it would be difficult to deny its appropriateness for Lovecraft's type of imaginative effect. At its best Lovecraft's work becomes a kind of incantation, seducing the mind into a momentary acceptance of the fantastic incidents being related. At its worst it becomes pompous and bombastic. But Lovecraft was almost always the master, rather than the slave, of his style—a point that can be emphasized by considering those two exquisite parodies of himself, "Herbert West—Reanimator" (1921–22) and "The Hound" (1922). And Lovecraft was capable of a far broader diversity of style than has commonly been granted—from the delicate prose-poetry of "Celephaïs" (1920) to the modernized Gothicism of "The Rats in the Walls" (1923) to the stupendous cosmicism of "The Call of Cthulhu" to the sober realism of "The Whisperer in Darkness" (1930) and "The Shadow Over Innsmouth."

I have not left myself much space for a discussion of Lovecraft's place in American literature. His work was once dismissed because it appeared in the cheap pulp magazines of the 1920s and 1930s; nowadays he has become an icon in popular culture in part *because* his work appeared there. But Lovecraft's involvement in the pulps was purely fortuitous and should not affect our evaluation of his status one way or the other: he was writing at a time when "genre" fiction in general, and weird fiction in particular, was slowly being banished from mainstream venues, and the pulps offered the only markets for those who wished to work in these literary realms. While most pulp fiction has rightly been condemned as being hackneyed, formulaic, and shoddily written, it should be acknowledged that a few writers rose above the mediocre average to produce outstanding works of their kind.

The publication of Lovecraft's letters, essays, and miscellany has provided us with the tools for a broader and more accurate gauge of his standing as a writer. This body of work reveals, firstly, that Lovecraft was a keen (if not especially original) thinker and an acute observer of his time, and, secondly, that he had the skill to embody his philosophical vision in tales that are meticulously crafted and endowed with a vitality of imagination rarely encountered in the entire range of literature. There may be those who banish all weird fiction into a kind of literary purgatory, but the achievements of Edgar Allan Poe, Ambrose Bierce, Lord Dunsany, Arthur Machen, Algernon Blackwood, H. P. Lovecraft, Shirley Jackson, and Ramsey Campbell are making this increasingly difficult to do. Lovecraft himself became one of the most articulate spokesmen for the dignity and worth of the weird tale as an art form; and an utterance made early in his career may be all the defense that his chosen literary mode requires:

> The imaginative writer devotes himself to art in its most essential sense. . . . He is a painter of moods and mind-pictures—a capturer and amplifier of elusive dreams and fancies—a voyager into those unheard-of lands which are glimpsed through the veil of actuality but rarely, and only by the most sensitive. . . . Pleasure to me is wonder—the unexplored, the unexpected, the thing that is hidden and the changeless thing that lurks behind superficial mutability. To trace the remote in the immediate; the eternal in the ephemeral; the past in the present; the infinite in the finite; these are to me the springs of delight and beauty. ("In Defence of Dagon" [1921]; MW 148, 155)

—S. T. JOSHI

ACKNOWLEDGMENTS

For assistance in the preparation of the text and notes I am grateful to Mike Ashley, Donald R. Burleson, Donovan K. Loucks, and especially David E. Schultz.

S. T. J.

SUGGESTIONS FOR FURTHER READING

PRIMARY

Lovecraft's tales, essays, poems, and letters have appeared in many editions, beginning with *The Outsider and Others* (1939). However, only certain recent editions can claim textual accuracy; other editions (including almost all current paperback editions in the United States and United Kingdom) contain numerous textual and typographical errors. Lovecraft's fiction and "revisions" can be found in four volumes published by Arkham House (Sauk City, WI) under my editorship:

The Dunwich Horror and Others (1984)
At the Mountains of Madness and Other Novels (1985)
Dagon and Other Macabre Tales (1986)
The Horror in the Museum and Other Revisions (1989)

Lovecraft's poetry has now been definitively gathered in my edition of *The Ancient Track: Complete Poetical Works* (West Warwick, RI: Necronomicon Press, 1999), superseding all previous editions.

A large selection of Lovecraft's essays can be found in my edition of *Miscellaneous Writings* (Arkham House, 1995). Among other volumes of essays are:

Commonplace Book, ed. David E. Schultz (Necronomicon Press, 1987)
The Conservative, ed. Marc A. Michaud (Necronomicon Press, 1976)
To Quebec and the Stars, ed. L. Sprague de Camp (West Kingston, RI: Donald M. Grant, 1976)

The major edition of Lovecraft's letters is *Selected Letters* (Arkham House, 1965–76; 5 vols.), edited by August Derleth, Donald Wandrei, and James Turner. This edition, however, is not annotated or indexed, contains numerous textual errors, and presents nearly all letters in various degrees of abridgement. More recent, annotated editions of letters, edited by David E. Schultz and myself and published by Necronomicon Press, include:

Letters to Henry Kuttner (1990)
Letters to Richard F. Searight (1992)
Letters to Robert Bloch (1993)
Letters to Samuel Loveman and Vincent Starrett (1994)

Schultz and I have also edited a volume largely culled from Lovecraft's letters: *Lord of a Visible World: An Autobiography in Letters* (Athens: Ohio University Press, 2000).

SECONDARY

Since about 1975, the literature on Lovecraft has been immense. Much biographical and critical work prior to that time is of little value, having been written largely by amateurs with little access to the full range of documentary evidence on Lovecraft (exceptions include the work of Fritz Leiber, Matthew H. Onderdonk, and George T. Wetzel). The following presents only a selection of the leading volumes on Lovecraft; see the notes for citations of additional articles.

The standard bibliography is my *H. P. Lovecraft and Lovecraft Criticism: An Annotated Bibliography* (Kent, OH: Kent State University Press, 1981). A supplement, co-compiled by L. D. Blackmore and myself, covering the years 1980–84, was issued by Necronomicon Press in 1985. The books in Lovecraft's library have been tallied in *Lovecraft's Library: A Catalogue* (Necronomicon Press, 1980), compiled by Marc A. Michaud and myself. An expanded edition can be found on the Necronomicon Press website (www.necropress.com).

My *H. P. Lovecraft: A Life* (Necronomicon Press, 1996) is the most exhaustive biographical treatment. L. Sprague de Camp's *Lovecraft: A Biography* (Garden City, NY: Doubleday, 1975) was the first full-length biography but was criticized for errors, omissions, and a lack of sympathy toward its subject. Many of Lovecraft's colleagues have written memoirs of varying value; these have now been collected by Peter Cannon in *Lovecraft Remembered* (Arkham House, 1998). Some further memoirs can be found in my slim collection, *Caverns Measureless to Man: 18 Memoirs of Lovecraft* (Necronomicon Press, 1996).

A selection of the best of the earlier criticism on Lovecraft can be found in my anthology, *H. P. Lovecraft: Four Decades of Criticism* (Ohio University Press, 1980). A substantial anthology of early and recent criticism is *Discovering H. P. Lovecraft*, ed. Darrell Schweitzer (Mercer Island, WA: Starmont House, 1987). Other recent critical treatments, on a wide variety of topics, can be found in *An Epicure in the Terrible: A Centennial Anthology of Essays in Honor of H. P. Lovecraft*, edited by David E. Schultz and myself (Rutherford, NJ: Fairleigh Dickinson University Press, 1991). Some of the better monographs and collections of essays on Lovecraft are:

Donald R. Burleson, *H. P. Lovecraft: A Critical Study* (Westport, CT: Greenwood Press, 1983), a sound general study.

Donald R. Burleson, *Lovecraft: Disturbing the Universe* (Lexington: University Press of Kentucky, 1990), a challenging deconstructionist approach to Lovecraft.

Peter Cannon, *H. P. Lovecraft* (New York: Twayne, 1989), another good general study with up-to-date references to the secondary literature.

S. T. Joshi, *H. P. Lovecraft: The Decline of the West* (Mercer Island, WA: Starmont House, 1990), a study of Lovecraft's philosophical thought.

S. T. Joshi, *A Subtler Magick: The Writings and Philosophy of H. P. Lovecraft* (San Bernadino, CA: Borgo Press, 1996), a general study.

Maurice Lévy, *Lovecraft: A Study in the Fantastic*, trans. S. T. Joshi (Detroit: Wayne State University Press, 1988), a revision of his Ph.D. dissertation for the Sorbonne and perhaps still the finest critical study of Lovecraft.

Steven J. Mariconda, *On the Emergence of "Cthulhu" and Other Observations* (Necronomicon Press, 1996), a collection of his penetrating articles on Lovecraft.

Dirk W. Mosig, *Mosig at Last: A Psychologist Looks at Love-*

craft (Necronomicon Press, 1997), a collection of articles by a pioneering scholar in Lovecraft studies.

Robert M. Price, *H. P. Lovecraft and the Cthulhu Mythos* (Mercer Island, WA: Starmont House, 1990), a collection of articles on the "Cthulhu Mythos" as developed by Lovecraft and other writers.

Barton L. St. Armand, *The Roots of Horror in the Fiction of H. P. Lovecraft* (Elizabethtown, NY: Dragon Press, 1977), a penetrating study of "The Rats in the Walls."

Barton L. St. Armand, *H. P. Lovecraft: New England Decadent* (Albuquerque, NM: Silver Scarab Press, 1979), an analysis of the melding of Puritanism and Decadence in Lovecraft's thought and work.

The semiannual journal *Lovecraft Studies* (Necronomicon Press) is the leading forum for scholarly treatments of Lovecraft.

A NOTE ON THE TEXT

The stories in this volume derive from my corrected editions of Lovecraft's stories: *The Dunwich Horror and Others* (1984), *At the Mountains of Madness and Other Novels* (1985), *Dagon and Other Macabre Tales* (1986), and *Miscellaneous Writings* (1995). These editions are based on consultations of Lovecraft's handwritten and typewritten manuscripts and early appearances in magazines. A few additional errors have been corrected.

THE CALL OF CTHULHU
AND OTHER
WEIRD STORIES

Dagon

I am writing this under an appreciable mental strain, since by tonight I shall be no more. Penniless, and at the end of my supply of the drug which alone makes life endurable, I can bear the torture no longer; and shall cast myself from this garret window into the squalid street below. Do not think from my slavery to morphine that I am a weakling or a degenerate. When you have read these hastily scrawled pages you may guess, though never fully realise, why it is that I must have forgetfulness or death.

It was in one of the most open and least frequented parts of the broad Pacific that the packet of which I was supercargo fell a victim to the German sea-raider. The great war was then at its very beginning, and the ocean forces of the Hun had not completely sunk to their later degradation;[1] so that our vessel was made a legitimate prize, whilst we of her crew were treated with all the fairness and consideration due us as naval prisoners. So liberal, indeed, was the discipline of our captors, that five days after we were taken I managed to escape alone in a small boat with water and provisions for a good length of time.

When I finally found myself adrift and free, I had but little idea of my surroundings. Never a competent navigator, I could only guess vaguely by the sun and stars that I was somewhat south of the equator. Of the longitude I knew nothing, and no island or coast-line was in sight. The weather kept fair, and for uncounted days I drifted aimlessly beneath the scorching sun; waiting either for some passing ship, or to be cast on the shores of some habitable land. But neither ship nor land appeared, and I began to despair in my solitude upon the heaving vastnesses of unbroken blue.

The change happened whilst I slept. Its details I shall never know; for my slumber, though troubled and dream-infested, was continuous. When at last I awaked, it was to discover myself half sucked into a slimy expanse of hellish black mire which extended

1

about me in monotonous undulations as far as I could see, and in which my boat lay grounded some distance away.

Though one might well imagine that my first sensation would be of wonder at so prodigious and unexpected a transformation of scenery, I was in reality more horrified than astonished; for there was in the air and in the rotting soil a sinister quality which chilled me to the very core. The region was putrid with the carcasses of decaying fish,[2] and of other less describable things which I saw protruding from the nasty mud of the unending plain. Perhaps I should not hope to convey in mere words the unutterable hideousness that can dwell in absolute silence and barren immensity. There was nothing within hearing, and nothing in sight save a vast reach of black slime; yet the very completeness of the stillness and the homogeneity of the landscape oppressed me with a nauseating fear.

The sun was blazing down from a sky which seemed to me almost black in its cloudless cruelty; as though reflecting the inky marsh beneath my feet. As I crawled into the stranded boat I realised that only one theory could explain my position.[3] Through some unprecedented volcanic upheaval, a portion of the ocean floor must have been thrown to the surface, exposing regions which for innumerable millions of years had lain hidden under unfathomable watery depths. So great was the extent of the new land which had risen beneath me, that I could not detect the faintest noise of the surging ocean, strain my ears as I might. Nor were there any sea-fowl to prey upon the dead things.

For several hours I sat thinking or brooding in the boat, which lay upon its side and afforded a slight shade as the sun moved across the heavens. As the day progressed, the ground lost some of its stickiness, and seemed likely to dry sufficiently for travelling purposes in a short time. That night I slept but little, and the next day I made for myself a pack containing food and water, preparatory to an overland journey in search of the vanished sea and possible rescue.

On the third morning I found the soil dry enough to walk upon with ease. The odour of the fish was maddening; but I was too much concerned with graver things to mind so slight an evil, and set out boldly for an unknown goal. All day I forged steadily westward, guided by a far-away hummock which rose higher than any other elevation on the rolling desert. That night I encamped, and on the following day still travelled toward the hummock, though that object seemed scarcely nearer than when I had first espied it. By the fourth evening I attained the base of the mound, which turned out to be much higher than it had appeared from a distance; an intervening valley setting it out in sharper relief from the general surface. Too weary to ascend, I slept in the shadow of the hill.

I know not why my dreams were so wild that night; but ere the waning and fantastically gibbous moon had risen far above the eastern plain, I was awake in a cold perspiration, determined to sleep no more. Such visions as I had experienced were too much for me to endure again. And in the glow of the moon I saw how unwise I had been to travel by day. Without the glare of the parching sun, my journey would have cost me less energy; indeed, I now felt quite able to perform the ascent which had deterred me at sunset. Picking up my pack, I started for the crest of the eminence.

I have said that the unbroken monotony of the rolling plain was a source of vague horror to me; but I think my horror was greater when I gained the summit of the mound and looked down the other side into an immeasurable pit or canyon, whose black recesses the moon had not yet soared high enough to illumine. I felt myself on the edge of the world; peering over the rim into a fathomless chaos of eternal night. Through my terror ran curious reminiscences of *Paradise Lost*, and of Satan's hideous climb through the unfashioned realms of darkness.[4]

As the moon climbed higher in the sky, I began to see that the slopes of the valley were not quite so perpendicular as I had imagined. Ledges and outcroppings of rock afforded fairly easy foot-holds for a descent, whilst after a drop of a few hundred feet, the declivity became very gradual. Urged on by an impulse which I cannot definitely analyse, I scrambled with difficulty down the rocks and stood on the gentler slope beneath, gazing into the Stygian deeps where no light had yet penetrated.

All at once my attention was captured by a vast and singular object on the opposite slope, which rose steeply about an hun-

dred yards ahead of me; an object that gleamed whitely in the
newly bestowed rays of the ascending moon. That it was merely
a gigantic piece of stone, I soon assured myself; but I was conscious of a distinct impression that its contour and position were
not altogether the work of Nature. A closer scrutiny filled me
with sensations I cannot express; for despite its enormous magnitude, and its position in an abyss which had yawned at the bottom of the sea since the world was young, I perceived beyond a
doubt that the strange object was a well-shaped monolith whose
massive bulk had known the workmanship and perhaps the worship of living and thinking creatures.

Dazed and frightened, yet not without a certain thrill of the
scientist's[5] or archaeologist's delight, I examined my surroundings more closely. The moon, now near the zenith, shone weirdly
and vividly above the towering steeps that hemmed in the chasm,
and revealed the fact that a far-flung body of water flowed at the
bottom, winding out of sight in both directions, and almost lapping my feet as I stood on the slope. Across the chasm, the
wavelets washed the base of the Cyclopean[6] monolith; on whose
surface I could now trace both inscriptions and crude sculptures.
The writing was in a system of hieroglyphics unknown to me,
and unlike anything I had ever seen in books; consisting for the
most part of conventionalised aquatic symbols such as fishes,
eels, octopi, crustaceans, molluscs, whales, and the like. Several
characters obviously represented marine things which are unknown to the modern world, but whose decomposing forms I
had observed on the ocean-risen plain.

It was the pictorial carving, however, that did most to hold me
spellbound. Plainly visible across the intervening water on account of their enormous size, were an array of bas-reliefs whose
subjects would have excited the envy of a Doré.[7] I think that
these things were supposed to depict men—at least, a certain sort
of men; though the creatures were shewn disporting like fishes in
the waters of some marine grotto, or paying homage at some
monolithic shrine which appeared to be under the waves as well.
Of their faces and forms I dare not speak in detail; for the mere
remembrance makes me grow faint. Grotesque beyond the imag-

ination of a Poe or a Bulwer,[8] they were damnably human in general outline despite webbed hands and feet, shockingly wide and flabby lips, glassy, bulging eyes, and other features less pleasant to recall. Curiously enough, they seemed to have been chiselled badly out of proportion with their scenic background; for one of the creatures was shewn in the act of killing a whale represented as but little larger than himself. I remarked, as I say, their grotesqueness and strange size; but in a moment decided that they were merely the imaginary gods of some primitive fishing or seafaring tribe; some tribe whose last descendant had perished eras before the first ancestor of the Piltdown[9] or Neanderthal Man was born. Awestruck at this unexpected glimpse into a past beyond the conception of the most daring anthropologist, I stood musing whilst the moon cast queer reflections on the silent channel before me.

Then suddenly I saw it. With only a slight churning to mark its rise to the surface, the thing slid into view above the dark waters. Vast, Polyphemus-like,[10] and loathsome, it darted like a stupendous monster of nightmares to the monolith, about which it flung its gigantic scaly arms, the while it bowed its hideous head and gave vent to certain measured sounds. I think I went mad then.

Of my frantic ascent of the slope and cliff, and of my delirious journey back to the stranded boat, I remember little. I believe I sang a great deal, and laughed oddly when I was unable to sing. I have indistinct recollections of a great storm some time after I reached the boat; at any rate, I know that I heard peals of thunder and other tones which Nature utters only in her wildest moods.

When I came out of the shadows I was in a San Francisco hospital; brought thither by the captain of the American ship which had picked up my boat in mid-ocean. In my delirium I had said much, but found that my words had been given scant attention. Of any land upheaval in the Pacific, my rescuers knew nothing; nor did I deem it necessary to insist upon a thing which I knew they could not believe. Once I sought out a celebrated ethnologist, and amused him with peculiar questions regarding the ancient Philistine legend of Dagon, the Fish-God;[11] but soon perceiving that he was hopelessly conventional, I did not press my inquiries.

It is at night, especially when the moon is gibbous and waning, that I see the thing. I tried morphine; but the drug has given only transient surcease, and has drawn me into its clutches as a hopeless slave. So now I am to end it all, having written a full account for the information or the contemptuous amusement of my fellow-men. Often I ask myself if it could not all have been a pure phantasm—a mere freak of fever as I lay sun-stricken and raving in the open boat after my escape from the German man-of-war. This I ask myself, but ever does there come before me a hideously vivid vision in reply. I cannot think of the deep sea without shuddering at the nameless things that may at this very moment be crawling and floundering on its slimy bed, worshipping their ancient stone idols and carving their own detestable likenesses on submarine obelisks of water-soaked granite. I dream of a day when they may rise above the billows to drag down in their reeking talons the remnants of puny, war-exhausted mankind—of a day when the land shall sink, and the dark ocean floor shall ascend amidst universal pandemonium.[12]

The end is near. I hear a noise at the door, as of some immense slippery body lumbering against it. It shall not find me. God, *that hand!* The window! The window!

The Statement of Randolph Carter

I repeat to you, gentlemen, that your inquisition is fruitless. Detain me here forever if you will; confine or execute me if you must have a victim to propitiate the illusion you call justice;[1] but I can say no more than I have said already. Everything that I can remember, I have told with perfect candour. Nothing has been distorted or concealed, and if anything remains vague, it is only because of the dark cloud which has come over my mind—that cloud and the nebulous nature of the horrors which brought it upon me.

Again I say, I do not know what has become of Harley Warren; though I think—almost hope—that he is in peaceful oblivion, if there be anywhere so blessed a thing.[2] It is true that I have for five years been his closest friend, and a partial sharer of his terrible researches into the unknown. I will not deny, though my memory is uncertain and indistinct, that this witness of yours may have seen us together as he says, on the Gainesville pike,[3] walking toward Big Cypress Swamp, at half past eleven on that awful night. That we bore electric lanterns, spades, and a curious coil of wire with attached instruments, I will even affirm; for these things all played a part in the single hideous scene which remains burned into my shaken recollection. But of what followed, and of the reason I was found alone and dazed on the edge of the swamp next morning, I must insist that I know nothing save what I have told you over and over again. You say to me that there is nothing in the swamp or near it which could form the setting of that frightful episode. I reply that I know nothing beyond what I saw. Vision or nightmare it may have been—vision or nightmare I fervently hope it was—yet it is all that my mind retains of what took place in those shocking hours after we left the sight of men. And why Harley Warren did not return, he or his shade—or some nameless *thing* I cannot describe—alone can tell.

As I have said before, the weird studies of Harley Warren were well known to me, and to some extent shared by me. Of his vast collection of strange, rare books on forbidden subjects I have read all that are written in the languages of which I am master; but these are few as compared with those in languages I cannot understand. Most, I believe, are in Arabic; and the fiend-inspired book which brought on the end—the book which he carried in his pocket out of the world—was written in characters whose like I never saw elsewhere.[4] Warren would never tell me just what was in that book. As to the nature of our studies—must I say again that I no longer retain full comprehension? It seems to me rather merciful that I do not, for they were terrible studies, which I pursued more through reluctant fascination than through actual inclination. Warren always dominated me, and sometimes I feared him. I remember how I shuddered at his facial expression on the night before the awful happening, when he talked so incessantly of his theory, *why certain corpses never decay, but rest firm and fat in their tombs for a thousand years.* But I do not fear him now, for I suspect that he has known horrors beyond my ken. Now I fear *for* him.

Once more I say that I have no clear idea of our object on that night. Certainly, it had much to do with something in the book which Warren carried with him—that ancient book in undecipherable characters which had come to him from India a month before—but I swear I do not know what it was that we expected to find. Your witness says he saw us at half past eleven on the Gainesville pike, headed for Big Cypress Swamp. This is probably true, but I have no distinct memory of it. The picture seared into my soul is of one scene only, and the hour must have been long after midnight; for a waning crescent moon was high in the vaporous heavens.

The place was an ancient cemetery; so ancient that I trembled at the manifold signs of immemorial years. It was in a deep, damp hollow, overgrown with rank grass, moss, and curious creeping weeds, and filled with a vague stench which my idle fancy associated absurdly with rotting stone. On every hand were the signs of neglect and decrepitude, and I seemed haunted by the notion that Warren and I were the first living creatures to invade a lethal silence of centuries. Over the valley's rim a wan, waning crescent moon peered through the noisome vapours that seemed to emanate from unheard-of catacombs, and by its feeble, wavering beams I could distinguish a repellent array of antique slabs, urns, cenotaphs, and mausolean facades; all crumbling, moss-grown, and moisture-stained, and partly concealed by the gross luxuriance of the unhealthy vegetation. My first vivid impression of my own presence in this terrible necropolis concerns the act of pausing with Warren before a certain half-obliterated sepulchre, and of throwing down some burdens which we seemed to have been carrying. I now observed that I had with me an electric lantern and two spades, whilst my companion was supplied with a similar lantern and a portable telephone outfit. No word was uttered, for the spot and the task seemed known to us; and without delay we seized our spades and commenced to clear away the grass, weeds, and drifted earth from the flat, archaic mortuary. After uncovering the entire surface, which consisted of three immense granite slabs, we stepped back some distance to survey the charnel scene; and Warren appeared to make some mental calculations. Then he returned to the sepulchre, and using his spade as a lever, sought to pry up the slab lying nearest to a stony ruin which may have been a monument in its day. He did not succeed, and motioned to me to come to his assistance. Finally our combined strength loosened the stone, which we raised and tipped to one side.

The removal of the slab revealed a black aperture, from which rushed an effluence of miasmal gases so nauseous that we started back in horror. After an interval, however, we approached the pit again, and found the exhalations less unbearable. Our lanterns disclosed the top of a flight of stone steps, dripping with some detestable ichor of the inner earth, and bordered by most walls encrusted with nitre. And now for the first time my memory records verbal discourse, Warren addressing me at length in his mellow tenor voice; a voice singularly unperturbed by our awesome surroundings.

"I'm sorry to have to ask you to stay on the surface," he said, "but it would be a crime to let anyone with your frail nerves go down there. You can't imagine, even from what you have read and from what I've told you, the things I shall have to see and do. It's fiendish work, Carter, and I doubt if any man without ironclad sensibilities could ever see it through and come up alive and sane.[5] I don't wish to offend you, and heaven knows I'd be glad enough to have you with me; but the responsibility is in a certain sense mine, and I couldn't drag a bundle of nerves like you down to probable death or madness. I tell you, you can't imagine what the thing is really like! But I promise to keep you informed over the telephone of every move—you see I've enough wire here to reach to the centre of the earth and back!"

I can still hear, in memory, those coolly spoken words; and I can still remember my remonstrances. I seemed desperately anxious to accompany my friend into those sepulchral depths, yet he proved inflexibly obdurate. At one time he threatened to abandon the expedition if I remained insistent; a threat which proved effective, since he alone held the key to the *thing*.[6] All this I can still remember, though I no longer know what manner of *thing* we sought. After he had secured my reluctant acquiescence in his design, Warren picked up the reel of wire and adjusted the instruments. At his nod I took one of the latter and seated myself upon an aged, discoloured gravestone close by the newly uncovered aperture. Then he shook my hand, shouldered the coil of wire, and disappeared within that indescribable ossuary. For a moment I kept sight of the glow of his lantern, and heard the rustle of the wire as he laid it down after him; but the glow soon disappeared abruptly, as if a turn in the stone staircase had been encountered, and the sound died away almost as quickly. I was alone, yet bound to the unknown depths by those magic strands whose insulated surface lay green beneath the struggling beams of that waning crescent moon.

In the lone silence of that hoary and deserted city of the dead, my mind conceived the most ghastly phantasies and illusions; and the grotesque shrines and monoliths seemed to assume a hideous personality—a half-sentience. Amorphous shadows seemed to lurk in the darker recesses of the weed-choked hollow and to flit as in some blasphemous ceremonial procession past the portals of the mouldering tombs in the hillside; shadows which could not have been cast by that pallid, peering crescent moon. I constantly consulted my watch by the light of my electric lantern, and listened with feverish anxiety at the receiver of the telephone; but for more than a quarter of an hour heard nothing. Then a faint clicking came from the instrument, and I called down to my friend in a tense voice. Apprehensive as I was, I was nevertheless unprepared for the words which came up from that uncanny vault in accents more alarmed and quivering than any I had heard before from Harley Warren. He who had so calmly left me a little while previously, now called from below in a shaky whisper more portentous than the loudest shriek:

"God! If you could see what I am seeing!"[7]

I could not answer. Speechless, I could only wait. Then came the frenzied tones again:

"Carter, it's terrible—monstrous—unbelievable!"

This time my voice did not fail me, and I poured into the transmitter a flood of excited questions. Terrified, I continued to repeat, "Warren, what is it? What is it?"

Once more came the voice of my friend, still hoarse with fear, and now apparently tinged with despair:

"I can't tell you, Carter! It's too utterly beyond thought —I dare not tell you—no man could know it and live—Great God! I never dreamed of THIS!"[8] Stillness again, save for my now incoherent torrent of shuddering inquiry. Then the voice of Warren in a pitch of wilder consternation:

"Carter! for the love of God, put back the slab and get out of this if you can! Quick!—leave everything else and make for the outside—it's your only chance! Do as I say, and don't ask me to explain!"

I heard, yet was able only to repeat my frantic questions. Around me were the tombs and the darkness and the shadows; below me, some peril beyond the radius of the human imagination. But my friend was in greater danger than I, and through my fear I felt a vague resentment that he should deem me capable of deserting him under such circumstances. More clicking, and after a pause a piteous cry from Warren:

"Beat it! For God's sake, put back the slab and beat it, Carter!"

Something in the boyish slang of my evidently stricken companion unleashed my faculties. I formed and shouted a resolution, "Warren, brace up! I'm coming down!" But at this offer the tone of my auditor changed to a scream of utter despair:

"Don't! You can't understand! It's too late—and my own fault. Put back the slab and run—there's nothing else you or anyone can do now!" The tone changed again, this time acquiring a softer quality, as of hopeless resignation. Yet it remained tense through anxiety for me.

"Quick—before it's too late!" I tried not to heed him; tried to break through the paralysis which held me, and to fulfil my vow to rush down to his aid. But his next whisper found me still held inert in the chains of stark horror.

"Carter—hurry! It's no use—you must go—better one than two—the slab—" A pause, more clicking, then the faint voice of Warren:

"Nearly over now—don't make it harder—cover up those damned steps and run for your life—you're losing time— So long, Carter—won't see you again." Here Warren's whisper swelled into a cry; a cry that gradually rose to a shriek fraught with all the horror of the ages—

"Curse these hellish things—legions— My God! Beat it! Beat it!"

After that was silence. I know not how many interminable aeons I sat stupefied; whispering, muttering, calling, screaming into that telephone. Over and over again through those aeons I whispered and muttered, called, shouted, and screamed, "Warren! Warren! Answer me—are you there?"

And then there came to me the crowning horror of all—the unbelievable, unthinkable, almost unmentionable thing. I have said that aeons seemed to elapse after Warren shrieked forth his last despairing warning, and that only my own cries now broke the hideous silence. But after a while there was a further clicking in the receiver, and I strained my ears to listen. Again I called down, "Warren, are you there?", and in answer heard the *thing* which has brought this cloud over my mind. I do not try, gentlemen, to account for that *thing*—that voice—nor can I venture to describe it in detail, since the first words took away my consciousness and created a mental blank which reaches to the time of my awakening in the hospital. Shall I say that the voice was deep; hollow; gelatinous; remote; unearthly; inhuman; disembodied? What shall I say? It was the end of my experience, and is the end of my story. I heard it, and knew no more. Heard it as I sat petrified in that unknown cemetery in the hollow, amidst the crumbling stones and the falling tombs, the rank vegetation and the miasmal vapours. Heard it well up from the innermost depths of that damnable open sepulchre as I watched amorphous, necrophagous shadows dance beneath an accursed waning moon. And this is what it said:

"YOU FOOL, WARREN IS DEAD!"

Facts Concerning the Late
Arthur Jermyn and His Family

Life is a hideous thing, and from the background behind what we know of it peer daemoniacal hints of truth which make it sometimes a thousandfold more hideous. Science, already oppressive with its shocking revelations, will perhaps be the ultimate exterminator of our human species—if separate species we be—for its reserve of unguessed horrors could never be borne by mortal brains if loosed upon the world.[1] If we knew what we are, we should do as Sir Arthur Jermyn[2] did; and Arthur Jermyn soaked himself in oil and set fire to his clothing one night. No one placed the charred fragments in an urn or set a memorial to him who had been; for certain papers and a certain boxed *object* were found, which made men wish to forget. Some who knew him do not admit that he ever existed.

Arthur Jerymn went out on the moor and burned himself after seeing the boxed *object* which had come from Africa. It was this *object*, and not his peculiar personal appearance, which made him end his life. Many would have disliked to live if possessed of the peculiar features of Arthur Jermyn, but he had been a poet and scholar and had not minded.[3] Learning was in his blood, for his great-grandfather, Sir Robert Jermyn, Bt., had been an anthropologist of note, whilst his great-great-great-grandfather, Sir Wade Jermyn, was one of the earliest explorers of the Congo region, and had written eruditely of its tribes, animals, and supposed antiquities. Indeed, old Sir Wade had possessed an intellectual zeal amounting almost to a mania; his bizarre conjectures on a prehistoric white Congolese civilisation earning him much ridicule when his book, *Observations on the Several Parts of Africa*, was published. In 1765 this fearless explorer had been placed in a madhouse at Huntingdon.[4]

Madness was in all the Jermyns, and people were glad there were not many of them. The line put forth no branches, and Arthur was the last of it. If he had not been, one cannot say what he would have done when the *object* came. The Jermyns never seemed to look quite right—something was amiss, though Arthur was the worst, and the old family portraits in Jermyn House shewed fine faces enough before Sir Wade's time. Certainly, the madness began with Sir Wade, whose wild stories of Africa were at once the delight and terror of his few friends. It shewed in his collection of trophies and specimens, which were not such as a normal man would accumulate and preserve, and appeared strikingly in the Oriental seclusion in which he kept his wife. The latter, he had said, was the daughter of a Portuguese trader whom he had met in Africa; and did not like English ways. She, with an infant son born in Africa, had accompanied him back for the second and longest of his trips, and had gone with him on the third and last, never returning. No one had ever seen her closely, not even the servants; for her disposition had been violent and singular. During her brief stay at Jermyn House she occupied a remote wing, and was waited on by her husband alone. Sir Wade was, indeed, most peculiar in his solicitude for his family; for when he returned to Africa he would permit no one to care for his young son save a loathsome black woman from Guinea. Upon coming back, after the death of Lady Jermyn, he himself assumed complete care of the boy.

But it was the talk of Sir Wade, especially when in his cups, which chiefly led his friends to deem him mad. In a rational age like the eighteenth century it was unwise for a man of learning to talk about wild sights and strange scenes under a Congo moon; of the gigantic walls and pillars of a forgotten city, crumbling and vine-grown, and of damp, silent, stone steps leading interminably down into the darkness of abysmal treasure-vaults and inconceivable catacombs. Especially was it unwise to rave of the living things that might haunt such a place; of creatures half of the jungle and half of the impiously aged city—fabulous creatures which even a Pliny[5] might describe with scepticism; things that might have sprung up after the great apes had overrun the dying city with the walls and the pillars, the vaults and the weird carvings. Yet after he came home for the last time Sir Wade would speak of such matters with a shudderingly uncanny zest, mostly after his third glass at the Knight's Head; boasting of what he had found in the jungle and of how he had dwelt among terrible ruins known only to him. And finally he had spoken of the living things in such a manner that he was taken to the mad-house. He had shewn little regret when shut into the barred room at Huntingdon, for his mind moved curiously. Ever since his son had commenced to grow out of infancy he had liked his home less and less, till at last he had seemed to dread it. The Knight's Head had been his headquarters, and when he was con-fined he expressed some vague gratitude as if for protection. Three years later he died.

Wade Jermyn's son Philip was a highly peculiar person. De-spite a strong physical resemblance to his father, his appearance and conduct were in many particulars so coarse that he was uni-versally shunned. Though he did not inherit the madness which was feared by some, he was densely stupid and given to brief pe-riods of uncontrollable violence. In frame he was small, but in-tensely powerful, and was of incredible agility. Twelve years after succeeding to his title he married the daughter of his gamekeeper, a person said to be of gypsy extraction, but before his son was born joined the navy as a common sailor, completing the general disgust which his habits and mesalliance had begun. After the close of the American war[6] he was heard of as a sailor on a mer-chantman in the African trade, having a kind of reputation for feats of strength and climbing, but finally disappearing one night as his ship lay off the Congo coast.

In the son of Sir Philip Jermyn the now accepted family pecu-liarity took a strange and fatal turn. Tall and fairly handsome, with a sort of weird Eastern grace despite certain slight oddities of proportion,[7] Robert Jermyn began life as a scholar and investi-gator. It was he who first studied scientifically the vast collection of relics which his mad grandfather had brought from Africa, and who made the family name as celebrated in ethnology as in exploration. In 1815 Sir Robert married a daughter of the sev-enth Viscount Brightholme and was subsequently blessed with three children, the eldest and youngest of whom were never pub-licly seen on account of deformities in mind and body. Saddened by these family misfortunes, the scientist sought relief in work, and made two long expeditions in the interior of Africa. In 1849 his second son, Nevil, a singularly repellent person who seemed to combine the surliness of Philip Jermyn with the hauteur of the Brightholmes, ran away with a vulgar dancer, but was pardoned upon his return in the following year. He came back to Jermyn House a widower with an infant son, Alfred, who was one day to be the father of Arthur Jermyn.

Friends said that it was this series of griefs which unhinged the mind of Sir Robert Jermyn, yet it was probably merely a bit of African folklore which caused the disaster. The elderly scholar had been collecting legends of the Onga tribes[8] near the field of his grandfather's and his own explorations, hoping in some way to account for Sir Wade's wild tales of a lost city peopled by strange hybrid creatures. A certain consistency in the strange papers of his ancestor suggested that the madman's imagination might have been stimulated by native myths. On October 19, 1852,[9] the explorer Samuel Seaton called at Jermyn House with a manuscript of notes collected among the Ongas, believing that certain legends of a grey city of white apes ruled by a white god might prove valuable to the ethnologist. In his conversation he probably supplied many additional details; the nature of which will never be known, since a hideous series of tragedies suddenly burst into being. When Sir Robert Jermyn emerged from his library he left behind the strangled corpse of the explorer, and before he could be restrained, had put an end to all three of his children; the two who were never seen, and the son who had run away. Nevil Jermyn died in the successful defence of his own two-year-old son, who had apparently been included in the old man's madly murderous scheme. Sir Robert himself, after repeated attempts at suicide and a stubborn refusal to utter any articulate sound, died of apoplexy in the second year of his confinement.[10]

Sir Alfred Jermyn was a baronet before his fourth birthday, but his tastes never matched his title. At twenty he had joined a band of music-hall performers, and at thirty-six had deserted his wife and child to travel with an itinerant American circus. His end was very revolting. Among the animals in the exhibition with which he travelled was a huge bull gorilla of lighter colour than the average; a surprisingly tractable beast of much popular-

ity with the performers. With this gorilla Alfred Jermyn was singularly fascinated, and on many occasions the two would eye
each other for long periods through the intervening bars. Eventually Jermyn asked and obtained permission to train the animal,
astonishing audiences and fellow-performers alike with his success. One morning in Chicago,[11] as the gorilla and Alfred Jermyn
were rehearsing an exceedingly clever boxing match, the former
delivered a blow of more than usual force, hurting both the body
and dignity of the amateur trainer. Of what followed, members
of "The Greatest Show on Earth"[12] do not like to speak. They
did not expect to hear Sir Alfred Jermyn emit a shrill, inhuman
scream, or to see him seize his clumsy antagonist with both
hands, dash it to the floor of the cage, and bite fiendishly at its
hairy throat. The gorilla was off its guard, but not for long, and
before anything could be done by the regular trainer the body
which had belonged to a baronet was past recognition.

II.

Arthur Jermyn was the son of Sir Alfred Jermyn and a music-
hall singer of unknown origin. When the husband and father deserted his family, the mother took the child to Jermyn House;
where there was none left to object to her presence.[13] She was not
without notions of what a nobleman's dignity should be, and
saw to it that her son received the best education which limited
money could provide. The family resources were now sadly
slender, and Jerymn House had fallen into woeful disrepair, but
young Arthur loved the old edifice and all its contents.[14] He was
not like any other Jermyn who had ever lived, for he was a poet
and a dreamer. Some of the neighbouring families who had heard
tales of old Sir Wade Jermyn's unseen Portuguese wife declared
that her Latin blood must be shewing itself; but most persons
merely sneered at his sensitiveness to beauty, attributing it to his
music-hall mother, who was socially unrecognised. The poetic
delicacy of Arthur Jermyn was the more remarkable because of
his uncouth personal appearance. Most of the Jermyns had possessed a subtly odd and repellent cast, but Arthur's case was very
striking. It is hard to say just what he resembled, but his expres-

sion, his facial angle, and the length of his arms gave a thrill of repulsion to those who met him for the first time.

It was the mind and character of Arthur Jermyn which atoned
for his aspect. Gifted and learned, he took highest honours at
Oxford and seemed likely to redeem the intellectual fame of his
family. Though of poetic rather than scientific temperament,
he planned to continue the work of his forefathers in African
ethnology and antiquities, utilising the truly wonderful though
strange collection of Sir Wade. With his fanciful mind he thought
often of the prehistoric civilisation in which the mad explorer
had so implicitly believed, and would weave tale after tale about
the silent jungle city mentioned in the latter's wilder notes and
paragraphs. For the nebulous utterances concerning a nameless,
unsuspected race of jungle hybrids he had a peculiar feeling of
mingled terror and attraction; speculation on the possible basis
of such a fancy, and seeking to obtain light among the more recent data gleaned by his great-grandfather and Samuel Seaton
amongst the Ongas.

In 1911, after the death of his mother, Sir Arthur Jermyn determined to pursue his investigations to the utmost extent. Selling a portion of his estate to obtain the requisite money, he
outfitted an expedition and sailed for the Congo. Arranging with
the Belgian authorities for a party of guides, he spent a year in
the Onga and Kaliri country,[15] finding data beyond the highest of
his expectations. Among the Kaliris was an aged chief called
Mwanu, who possessed not only a highly retentive memory, but
a singular degree of intelligence and interest in old legends. This
ancient confirmed every tale which Jermyn had heard, adding his
own account of the stone city and the white apes as it had been
told to him.

According to Mwanu, the grey city and the hybrid creatures
were no more, having been annihilated by the warlike N'bangus[16] many years ago. This tribe, after destroying most of the ed-
ifices and killing the live beings, had carried off the stuffed
goddess which had been the object of their quest; the white ape-
goddess which the strange beings worshipped, and which was
held by Congo tradition to be the form of one who had reigned
as a princess among those beings. Just what the white ape-like

creatures could have been, Mwanu had no idea, but he thought they were the builders of the ruined city. Jermyn could form no conjecture, but close questioning obtained a very picturesque legend of the stuffed goddess.

The ape-princess, it was said, became the consort of a great white god who had come out of the West. For a long time they had reigned over the city together, but when they had a son all three went away. Later the god and the princess had returned, and upon the death of the princess her divine husband had mummified the body and enshrined it in a vast house of stone, where it was worshipped. Then he had departed alone. The legend here seemed to present three variants. According to one story nothing further happened save that the stuffed goddess became a symbol of supremacy for whatever tribe might possess it. It was for this reason that the N'bangus carried it off. A second story told of the god's return and death at the feet of his enshrined wife. A third told of the return of the son, grown to manhood—or apehood or godhood, as the case might be—yet unconscious of his identity. Surely the imaginative blacks had made the most of whatever events might lie behind the extravagant legendry.

Of the reality of the jungle city described by old Sir Wade, Arthur Jermyn had no further doubt; and was hardly astonished when early in 1912 he came upon what was left of it. Its size must have been exaggerated, yet the stones lying about proved that it was no mere negro village. Unfortunately no carvings could be found, and the small size of the expedition prevented operations toward clearing the one visible passageway that seemed to lead down into the system of vaults which Sir Wade had mentioned. The white apes and the stuffed goddess were discussed with all the native chiefs of the region, but it remained for a European to improve on the data offered by old Mwanu. M. Verhaeren, Belgian agent[17] at a trading-post on the Congo, believed that he could not only locate but obtain the stuffed goddess, of which he had vaguely heard; since the once mighty N'bangus were now the submissive servants of King Albert's government,[18] and with but little persuasion could be induced to part with the gruesome deity they had carried off. When Jermyn sailed for England, therefore, it was with the exultant probability that he would within a few months receive a priceless ethnological relic confirming the wildest of his great-great-great-grandfather's narratives—that is, the wildest which he had ever heard. Countrymen near Jermyn House had perhaps heard wilder tales handed down from ancestors who had listened to Sir Wade around the tables of the Knight's Head.

Arthur Jermyn waited very patiently for the expected box from M. Verhaeren, meanwhile studying with increased diligence the manuscripts left by his mad ancestor. He began to feel closely akin to Sir Wade, and to seek relics of the latter's personal life in England as well as of his African exploits. Oral accounts of the mysterious and secluded wife had been numerous, but no tangible relic of her stay at Jermyn House remained. Jermyn wondered what circumstance had prompted or permitted such an effacement, and decided that the husband's insanity was the prime cause. His great-great-great-grandmother, he recalled, was said to have been the daughter of a Portuguese trader in Africa. No doubt her practical heritage and superficial knowledge of the Dark Continent had caused her to flout Sir Wade's talk of the interior, a thing which such a man would not be likely to forgive. She had died in Africa, perhaps dragged thither by a husband determined to prove what he had told. But as Jermyn indulged in these reflections he could not but smile at their futility, a century and a half after the death of both of his strange progenitors.

In June, 1913, a letter arrived from M. Verhaeren, telling of the finding of the stuffed goddess. It was, the Belgian averred, a most extraordinary object; an object quite beyond the power of a layman to classify. Whether it was human or simian only a scientist could determine, and the process of determination would be greatly hampered by its imperfect condition. Time and the Congo climate are not kind to mummies; especially when their preparation is as amateurish as seemed to be the case here. Around the creature's neck had been found a golden chain bearing an empty locket on which were armorial designs; no doubt some hapless traveller's keepsake, taken by the N'bangus and hung upon the goddess as a charm. In commenting on the contour of the mummy's face, M. Verhaeren suggested a whimsical comparison; or rather, expressed a humorous wonder just how it would strike his correspondent, but was too much interested scientifically to waste many words in levity. The stuffed goddess, he wrote, would arrive duly packed about a month after receipt of the letter.

The boxed object was delivered at Jermyn House on the afternoon of August 3, 1913, being conveyed immediately to the large chamber which housed the collection of African specimens as arranged by Sir Robert and Arthur. What ensued can best be gathered from the tales of servants and from things and papers later examined. Of the various tales that of aged Soames, the family butler, is most ample and coherent. According to this trustworthy man, Sir Arthur Jermyn dismissed everyone from the room before opening the box, though the distant sound of hammer and chisel shewed that he did not delay the operation. Nothing was heard for some time; just how long Soames cannot exactly estimate; but it was certainly less than a quarter of an hour later that the horrible scream, undoubtedly in Jermyn's voice, was heard. Immediately afterward Jermyn emerged from the room, rushing frantically toward the front of the house as if pursued by some hideous enemy. The expression on his face, a face ghastly enough in repose, was beyond description. When near the front door he seemed to think of something, and turned back in his flight, finally disappearing down the stairs to the cellar. The servants were utterly dumbfounded, and watched at the head of the stairs, but their master did not return. A smell of oil was all that came up from the regions below. After dark a rattling was heard at the door leading from the cellar into the courtyard; and a stable-boy saw Arthur Jermyn, glistening from head to foot with oil and redolent of that fluid, steal furtively out and vanish on the black moor surrounding the house. Then, in an exaltation of supreme horror, everyone saw the end. A spark appeared on the moor, a flame arose, and a pillar of human fire reached to the heavens. The house of Jermyn no longer existed.

The reason why Arthur Jermyn's charred fragments were not collected and buried lies in what was found afterward, principally the thing in the box. The stuffed goddess was a nauseous sight, withered and eaten away, but it was clearly a mummified white ape of some unknown species, less hairy than any recorded variety, and infinitely nearer mankind—quite shockingly so. Detailed description would be rather unpleasant, but two salient particulars must be told, for they fit in revoltingly with certain notes of Sir Wade Jermyn's African expeditions and with the Congolese legends of the white god and the ape-princess. The two particulars in question are these: the arms on the golden locket about the creature's neck were the Jermyn arms, and the jocose suggestion of M. Verhaeren about a certain resemblance as connected with the shrivelled face applied with vivid, ghastly, and unnatural horror to none other than the sensitive Arthur Jermyn, great-great-great-grandson of Sir Wade Jermyn and an unknown wife. Members of the Royal Anthropological Institute[19] burned the thing and threw the locket into a well, and some of them do not admit that Arthur Jermyn ever existed.

Celephaïs

In a dream Kuranes saw the city in the valley, and the sea-coast beyond, and the snowy peak overlooking the sea, and the gaily painted galleys that sail out of the harbour toward the distant regions where the sea meets the sky. In a dream it was also that he came by his name of Kuranes, for when awake he was called by another name. Perhaps it was natural for him to dream a new name; for he was the last of his family, and alone among the indifferent millions of London, so there were not many to speak to him and remind him who he had been. His money and lands were gone, and he did not care for the ways of people about him, but preferred to dream and write of his dreams. What he wrote was laughed at by those to whom he shewed it, so that after a time he kept his writings to himself, and finally ceased to write. The more he withdrew from the world about him, the more wonderful became his dreams; and it would have been quite futile to try to describe them on paper. Kuranes was not modern, and did not think like others who wrote. Whilst they strove to strip from life its embroidered robes of myth, and to shew in naked ugliness the foul thing that is reality, Kuranes sought for beauty alone.[1] When truth and experience failed to reveal it, he sought it in fancy and illusion, and found it on his very doorstep, amid the nebulous memories of childhood tales and dreams.[2]

There are not many persons who know what wonders are opened to them in the stories and visions of their youth; for when as children we listen and dream, we think but half-formed thoughts, and when as men we try to remember, we are dulled and prosaic with the poison of life. But some of us awake in the night with strange phantasms of enchanted hills and gardens, of fountains that sing in the sun, of golden cliffs overhanging murmuring seas, of plains that stretch down to sleeping cities of bronze and stone, and of shadowy companies of heroes that ride caparisoned white horses along the edges of thick forests; and then we know that we have looked back through the ivory gates into that world of wonder which was ours before we were wise and unhappy.

Kuranes came very suddenly upon his old world of child-hood. He had been dreaming of the house where he was born; the great stone house covered with ivy, where thirteen genera-tions of his ancestors had lived, and where he had hoped to die. It was moonlight, and he had stolen out into the fragrant sum-mer night, through the gardens, down the terraces, past the great oaks of the park, and along the long white road to the village. The village seemed very old, eaten away at the edge like the moon which had commenced to wane, and Kuranes wondered whether the peaked roofs of the small houses hid sleep or death. In the streets were spears of long grass, and the window-panes on either side were either broken or filmily staring. Kuranes had not lingered, but had plodded on as though summoned toward some goal. He dared not disobey the summons for fear it might prove an illusion like the urges and aspirations of waking life, which do not lead to any goal. Then he had been drawn down a lane that led off from the village street toward the channel cliffs, and had come to the end of things—to the precipice and the abyss where all the village and all the world fell abruptly into the unechoing emptiness of infinity, and where even the sky ahead was empty and unlit by the crumbling moon and the peering stars. Faith had urged him on, over the precipice and into the gulf, where he had floated down, down, down; past dark, shape-less, undreamed dreams, faintly glowing spheres that may have been partly dreamed dreams, and laughing winged things that seemed to mock the dreamers of all the worlds. Then a rift seemed to open in the darkness before him, and he saw the city of the valley, glistening radiantly far, far below, with a back-ground of sea and sky, and a snow-capped mountain near the shore.

Kuranes had awaked the very moment he beheld the city, yet he knew from his brief glance that it was none other than Cele-phaïs, in the Valley of Ooth-Nargai beyond the Tanarian Hills, where his spirit had dwelt all the eternity of an hour one summer afternoon very long ago, when he had slipt away from his nurse and let the warm sea-breeze lull him to sleep as he watched the clouds from the cliff near the village. He had protested then, when they had found him, waked him, and carried him home, for just as he was aroused he had been about to sail in a golden galley for those alluring regions where the sea meets the sky. And now he was equally resentful of awaking, for he had found his fabulous city after forty weary years.

But three nights afterward Kuranes came again to Celephaïs. As before, he dreamed first of the village that was asleep or dead, and of the abyss down which one must float silently; then the rift appeared again, and he beheld the glittering minarets of the city, and saw the graceful galleys riding at anchor in the blue harbour, and watched the gingko trees of Mount Aran[3] swaying in the sea-breeze. But this time he was not snatched away, and like a winged being settled gradually over a grassy hillside till finally his feet rested gently on the turf. He had indeed come back to the Valley of Ooth-Nargai and the splendid city of Celephaïs.

Down the hill amid scented grasses and brilliant flowers walked Kuranes, over the bubbling Naraxa on the small wooden bridge where he had carved his name so many years ago, and through the whispering grove to the great stone bridge by the city gate. All was as of old, nor were the marble walls discoloured, nor the polished bronze statues upon them tarnished. And Kuranes saw that he need not tremble lest the things he knew be vanished; for even the sentries on the ramparts were the same, and still as young as he remembered them. When he entered the city, past the bronze gates and over the onyx pavements, the merchants and camel-drivers greeted him as if he had never been away; and it was the same at the turquoise temple of Nath-Horthath, where the orchid-wreathed priests told him that there is no time in Ooth-Nargai, but only perpetual youth.[4] Then Kuranes walked through the Street of Pillars to the seaward wall, where gathered the traders and sailors, and strange men from the regions where the sea meets the sky. There he stayed long, gazing out over the bright harbour where the ripples sparked beneath an unknown sun, and where rode lightly the galleys from far places over the water. And he gazed also upon Mount Aran rising regally from the shore, its lower slopes green with swaying trees and its white summit touching the sky.

More than ever Kuranes wished to sail in a galley to the far places of which he had heard so many strange tales, and he sought again the captain who had agreed to carry him so long ago. He found the man, Athib, sitting on the same chest of spices he had sat upon before, and Athib seemed not to realise that any time had passed. Then the two rowed to a galley in the harbour, and giving orders to the oarsmen, commenced to sail out into the billowy Cerenerian Sea that leads to the sky. For several days they glided undulatingly over the water, till finally they came to the horizon, where the sea meets the sky. Here the galley paused not at all, but floated easily in the blue of the sky among fleecy clouds tinted with rose. And far beneath the keel Kuranes could see strange lands and rivers and cities of surpassing beauty, spread indolently in the sunshine which seemed never to lessen or disappear. At length Athib told him that their journey was near its end, and that they would soon enter the harbour of Serannian, the pink marble city of the clouds, which is built on that ethereal coast where the west wind flows into the sky; but as the highest of the city's carven towers came into sight there was a sound somewhere in space, and Kuranes awaked in his London garret.

For many months after that Kuranes sought the marvellous city of Celephaïs and its sky-bound galleys in vain; and though his dreams carried him to many gorgeous and unheard-of places, no one whom he met could tell him how to find Ooth-Nargai, beyond the Tanarian Hills. One night he went flying over dark mountains where there were faint, lone campfires at great distances apart, and strange, shaggy herds with tinkling bells on the leaders; and in the wildest part of this hilly country, so remote that few men could ever have seen it, he found a hideously ancient wall or causeway of stone zigzagging along the ridges and valleys; too gigantic ever to have risen by human hands, and of such a length that neither end of it could be seen. Beyond that wall in the grey dawn he came to a land of quaint gardens and cherry trees, and when the sun rose he beheld such a beauty of red and white flowers, green foliage and lawns, white paths, diamond brooks, blue lakelets, carven bridges, and red-roofed

pagodas, that he for a moment forgot Celephaïs in sheer delight.
But he remembered it again when he walked down a white path
toward a red-roofed pagoda, and would have questioned the
people of that land about it, had he not found that there were no
people there, but only birds and bees and butterflies. On another
night Kuranes walked up a damp stone spiral stairway endlessly,
and came to a tower window overlooking a mighty plain and
river lit by the full moon; and in the silent city that spread away
from the river-bank he thought he beheld some feature or
arrangement which he had known before. He would have descended and asked the way to Ooth-Nargai had not a fearsome
aurora sputtered up from some remote place beyond the horizon, shewing the ruin and antiquity of the city, and the stagna-
tion of the reedy river, and the death lying upon that land, as it
had lain since King Kynaratholis came home from his conquests
to find the vengeance of the gods.

So Kuranes sought fruitlessly for the marvellous city of Celephaïs and its galleys that sail to Serannian in the sky, meanwhile
seeing many wonders and once barely escaping from the high-
priest not to be described, which wears a yellow silken mask
over its face and dwells all alone in a prehistoric stone monastery
on the cold desert plateau of Leng.[5] In time he grew so impatient
of the bleak intervals of day that he began buying drugs in order
to increase his periods of sleep. Hasheesh helped a great deal, and
once sent him to a part of space where form does not exist, but
where glowing gases study the secrets of existence.[6] And a violet-
coloured gas told him that this part of space was outside what he
had called infinity. The gas had not heard of planets and organisms before, but identified Kuranes merely as one from the infinity where matter, energy, and gravitation exist. Kuranes was now
very anxious to return to minaret-studded Celephaïs, and increased his doses of drugs; but eventually he had no more money
left, and could buy no drugs. Then one summer day he was
turned out of his garret, and wandered aimlessly through the
streets, drifting over a bridge to a place where the houses grew
thinner and thinner. And it was there that fulfilment came, and
he met the cortege of knights come from Celephaïs to bear him
thither forever.

Handsome knights they were, astride roan horses and clad in shining armour with tabards of cloth-of-gold curiously emblazoned. So numerous were they, that Kuranes almost mistook them for an army, but their leader told him they were sent in his honour; since it was he who had created Ooth-Nargai in his dreams, on which account he was now to be appointed its chief god for evermore. Then they gave Kuranes a horse and placed him at the head of the cavalcade, and all rode majestically through the downs of Surrey and onward toward the region where Kuranes and his ancestors were born. It was very strange, but as the riders went on they seemed to gallop back through Time; for whenever they passed through a village in the twilight they saw only such houses and villages as Chaucer or men before him might have seen, and sometimes they saw knights on horseback with small companies of retainers. When it grew dark they travelled more softly, till soon they were flying uncannily as if in the air. In a dim dawn they came upon the village which Kuranes had seen alive in his childhood, and asleep or dead in his dreams. It was alive now, and early villagers courtesied as the horsemen clattered down the street and turned off into the lane that ends in the abyss of dream. Kuranes had previously entered that abyss only at night, and wondered what it would look like by day; so he watched anxiously as the column approached its brink. Just as they galloped up the rising ground to the precipice a golden glare came somewhere out of the east and hid all the landscape in its effulgent draperies. The abyss was now a seething chaos of roseate and cerulean splendour, and invisible voices sang exultantly as the knightly entourage plunged over the edge and floated gracefully down past glittering clouds and silvery coruscations. Endlessly down the horsemen floated, their chargers pawing the aether as if galloping over golden sands;[7] and then the luminous vapours spread apart to reveal a greater brightness, the brightness of the city of Celephaïs, and the sea-coast beyond, and the snowy peak overlooking the sea, and the gaily painted galleys that sail out of the harbour toward distant regions where the sea meets the sky.

And Kuranes reigned thereafter over Ooth-Nargai and all the neighbouring regions of dream, and held his court alternately in

Celephaïs and in the cloud-fashioned Serannian. He reigns there still, and will reign happily forever, though below the cliffs at Innsmouth[8] the channel tides played mockingly with the body of a tramp who had stumbled through the half-deserted village at dawn; played mockingly, and cast it upon the rocks by ivy-covered Trevor Towers, where a notably fat and especially offensive millionaire brewer enjoys the purchased atmosphere of extinct nobility.

Nyarlathotep

Nyarlathotep . . . the crawling chaos . . . I am the last . . . I will tell the audient void. . . .

I do not recall distinctly when it began, but it was months ago. The general tension was horrible. To a season of political and social upheaval was added a strange and brooding apprehension of hideous physical danger; a danger widespread and all-embracing, such a danger as may be imagined only in the most terrible phantasms of the night. I recall that the people went about with pale and worried faces, and whispered warnings and prophecies which no one dared consciously repeat or acknowledge to himself that he had heard. A sense of monstrous guilt was upon the land, and out of the abysses between the stars swept chill currents that made men shiver in dark and lonely places. There was a daemoniac alteration in the sequence of the seasons—the autumn heat lingered fearsomely, and everyone felt that the world and perhaps the universe had passed from the control of known gods or forces to that of gods or forces which were unknown.

And it was then that Nyarlathotep came out of Egypt. Who he was, none could tell, but he was of the old native blood and looked like a Pharaoh. The fellahin knelt when they saw him, yet could not say why. He said he had risen up out of the blackness of twenty-seven centuries,[1] and that he had heard messages from places not on this planet. Into the lands of civilisation came Nyarlathotep, swarthy, slender, and sinister, always buying strange instruments of glass and metal and combining them into instruments yet stranger. He spoke much of the sciences—of electricity and psychology—and gave exhibitions of power which sent his spectators away speechless, yet which swelled his fame to exceeding magnitude. Men advised one another to see Nyarlathotep, and shuddered. And where Nyarlathotep went, rest vanished; for the small hours were rent with the screams of nightmare. Never before had the screams of nightmare been such a public problem;

now the wise men almost wished they could forbid sleep in the
small hours, that the shrieks of cities might less horribly disturb
the pale, pitying moon as it glimmered on green waters gliding under bridges, and old steeples crumbling against a sickly sky.

I remember when Nyarlathotep came to my city—the great,
the old, the terrible city of unnumbered crimes. My friend had
told me of him, and of the impelling fascination and allurement
of his revelations, and I burned with eagerness to explore his uttermost mysteries.[2] My friend said they were horrible and impressive beyond my most fevered imaginings; that what was
thrown on a screen in the darkened room prophesied things
none but Nyarlathotep dared prophesy, and that in the sputter of
his sparks there was taken from men that which had never been
taken before yet which shewed only in the eyes. And I heard it
hinted abroad that those who knew Nyarlathotep looked on
sights which others saw not.

It was in the hot autumn that I went through the night with
the restless crowds to see Nyarlathotep; through the stifling
night and up the endless stairs into the choking room. And shadowed on a screen, I saw hooded forms amidst ruins, and yellow
evil faces peering from behind fallen monuments.[3] And I saw the
world battling against blackness; against the waves of destruction
from ultimate space; whirling, churning; struggling around the
dimming, cooling sun. Then the sparks played amazingly around
the heads of the spectators, and hair stood up on end whilst
shadows more grotesque than I can tell came out and squatted
on the heads. And when I, who was colder and more scientific
than the rest, mumbled a trembling protest about "imposture"
and "static electricity", Nyarlathotep drave us all out, down the
dizzy stairs into the damp, hot, deserted midnight streets. I
screamed aloud that I was *not* afraid; that I never could be afraid;
and others screamed with me for solace. We sware to one another that the city *was* exactly the same, and still alive; and when
the electric lights began to fade we cursed the company over and
over again, and laughed at the queer faces we made.

I believe we felt something coming down from the greenish
moon, for when we began to depend on its light we drifted into
curious involuntary formations and seemed to know our destina-

tions though we dared not think of them. Once we looked at the pavement and found the blocks loose and displaced by grass, with scarce a line of rusted metal to shew where the tramways had run. And again we saw a tram-car, lone, windowless, dilapidated, and almost on its side.⁴ When we gazed around the horizon, we could not find the third tower by the river, and noticed that the silhouette of the second tower was ragged at the top. Then we split up into narrow columns, each of which seemed drawn in a different direction. One disappeared in a narrow alley to the left, leaving only the echo of a shocking moan. Another filed down a weed-choked subway entrance, howling with a laughter that was mad. My own column was sucked toward the open country, and presently felt a chill which was not of the hot autumn; for as we stalked out on the dark moor, we beheld around us the hellish moon-glitter of evil snows. Trackless, inexplicable snows, swept asunder in one direction only, where lay a gulf all the blacker for its glittering walls. The column seemed very thin indeed as it plodded dreamily into the gulf. I lingered behind, for the black rift in the green-litten snow was frightful, and I thought I had heard the reverberations of a disquieting wail as my companions vanished; but my power to linger was slight. As if beckoned by those who had gone before, I half floated between the titanic snowdrifts, quivering and afraid, into the sightless vortex of the unimaginable.

Screamingly sentient, dumbly delirious, only the gods that were can tell. A sickened, sensitive shadow writhing in hands that are not hands, and whirled blindly past ghastly midnights of rotting creation, corpses of dead worlds with sores that were cities, charnel winds that brush the pallid stars and make them flicker low. Beyond the worlds vague ghosts of monstrous things; half-seen columns of unsanctified temples that rest on nameless rocks beneath space and reach up to dizzy vacua above the spheres of light and darkness. And through this revolting graveyard of the universe the muffled, maddening beating of drums, and thin, monotonous whine of blasphemous flutes from inconceivable, unlighted chambers beyond Time; the detestable pounding and piping whereunto dance slowly, awkwardly, and absurdly the gigantic, tenebrous ultimate gods—the blind, voiceless, mindless gargoyles whose soul is Nyarlathotep.

The Picture in the House

Searchers after horror haunt strange, far places. For them are the catacombs of Ptolemais,[1] and the carven mausolea of the nightmare countries. They climb to the moonlit towers of ruined Rhine castles, and falter down black cobwebbed steps beneath the scattered stones of forgotten cities in Asia. The haunted wood and the desolate mountain are their shrines, and they linger around the sinister monoliths on uninhabited islands. But the true epicure in the terrible, to whom a new thrill of unutterable ghastliness is the chief end and justification of existence, esteems most of all the ancient, lonely farmhouses of backwoods New England; for there the dark elements of strength, solitude, grotesqueness, and ignorance combine to form the perfection of the hideous.

Most horrible of all sights are the little unpainted wooden houses remote from travelled ways, usually squatted upon some damp, grassy slope or leaning against some gigantic outcropping of rock. Two hundred years and more they have leaned or squatted there, while the vines have crawled and the trees have swelled and spread. They are almost hidden now in lawless luxuriances of green and guardian shrouds of shadow; but the small-paned windows still stare shockingly, as if blinking through a lethal stupor which wards off madness by dulling the memory of unutterable things.

In such houses have dwelt generations of strange people, whose like the world has never seen.[2] Seized with a gloomy and fanatical belief which exiled them from their kind, their ancestors sought the wilderness for freedom. There the scions of a conquering race indeed flourished free from the restrictions of their fellows, but cowered in an appalling slavery to the dismal phantasms of their own minds. Divorced from the enlightenment of civilisation, the strength of these Puritans turned into singular channels; and in their isolation, morbid self-repression, and

34

struggle for life with relentless Nature, there came to them dark
furtive traits from the prehistoric depths of their cold Northern
heritage. By necessity practical and by philosophy stern, these
folk were not beautiful in their sins. Erring as all mortals must,
they were forced by their rigid code to seek concealment above
all else; so that they came to use less and less taste in what they
concealed.³ Only the silent, sleepy, staring houses in the backwoods can tell all that has lain hidden since the early days; and
they are not communicative, being loath to shake off the drowsiness which helps them forget. Sometimes one feels that it would
be merciful to tear down these houses, for they must often
dream.

It was to a time-battered edifice of this description that I was
driven one afternoon in November, 1896, by a rain of such chill-
ing copiousness that any shelter was preferable to exposure. I
had been travelling for some time amongst the people of the
Miskatonic Valley⁴ in quest of certain genealogical data; and from
the remote, devious, and problematical nature of my course, had
deemed it convenient to employ a bicycle despite the lateness of
the season.⁵ Now I found myself upon an apparently abandoned
road which I had chosen as the shortest cut to Arkham;⁶ over-
taken by the storm at a point far from any town, and confronted
with no refuge save the antique and repellent wooden building
which blinked with bleared windows from between two huge
leafless elms near the foot of a rocky hill. Distant though it was
from the remnant of a road, the house none the less impressed
me unfavourably the very moment I espied it. Honest, wholesome structures do not stare at travellers so slyly and hauntingly,
and in my genealogical researches I had encountered legends of a
century before which biassed me against places of this kind. Yet
the force of the elements was such as to overcome my scruples,
and I did not hesitate to wheel my machine up the weedy rise to
the closed door which seemed at once so suggestive and secretive.

I had somehow taken it for granted that the house was abandoned, yet as I approached it I was not so sure; for though the
walks were indeed overgrown with weeds, they seemed to retain
their nature a little too well to argue complete desertion. There-

fore instead of trying the door I knocked, feeling as I did so a trepidation I could scarcely explain. As I waited on the rough, mossy rock which served as a doorstep, I glanced at the neighbouring windows and the panes of the transom above me, and noticed that although old, rattling, and almost opaque with dirt, they were not broken. The building, then, must still be inhabited, despite its isolation and general neglect. However, my rapping evoked no response, so after repeating the summons I tried the rusty latch and found the door unfastened. Inside was a little vestibule with walls from which the plaster was falling, and through the doorway came a faint but peculiarly hateful odour. I entered, carrying my bicycle, and closed the door behind me. Ahead rose a narrow staircase, flanked by a small door probably leading to the cellar, while to the left and right were closed doors leading to rooms on the ground floor.

Leaning my cycle against the wall I opened the door at the left, and crossed into a small low-ceiled chamber but dimly lighted by its two dusty windows and furnished in the barest and most primitive possible way. It appeared to be a kind of sitting-room, for it had a table and several chairs, and an immense fireplace above which ticked an antique clock on a mantel. Books and papers were very few, and in the prevailing gloom I could not readily discern the titles. What interested me was the uniform air of archaism as displayed in every visible detail. Most of the houses in this region I had found rich in relics of the past, but here the antiquity was curiously complete; for in all the room I could not discover a single article of definitely post-revolutionary date. Had the furnishings been less humble, the place would have been a collector's paradise.

As I surveyed this quaint apartment, I felt an increase in that aversion first excited by the bleak exterior of the house. Just what it was that I feared or loathed, I could by no means define; but something in the whole atmosphere seemed redolent of unhallowed age, of unpleasant crudeness, and of secrets which should be forgotten. I felt disinclined to sit down, and wandered about examining the various articles which I had noticed. The first object of my curiosity was a book of medium size[7] lying upon the table and presenting such an antediluvian aspect that I marvelled at beholding it outside a museum or library. It was bound in leather with metal fittings, and was in an excellent state of preservation; being altogether an unusual sort of volume to encounter in an abode so lowly. When I opened it to the title page my wonder grew even greater, for it proved to be nothing less rare than Pigafetta's account of the Congo region, written in Latin from the notes of the sailor Lopez and printed at Frankfort in 1598.[8] I had often heard of this work, with its curious illustrations by the brothers De Bry,[9] hence for a moment forgot my uneasiness in my desire to turn the pages before me. The engravings were indeed interesting, drawn wholly from imagination and careless descriptions, and represented negroes with white skins and Caucasian features;[10] nor would I soon have closed the book had not an exceedingly trivial circumstance upset my tired nerves and revived my sensation of disquiet. What annoyed me was merely the persistent way in which the volume tended to fall open of itself at Plate XII, which represented in gruesome detail a butcher's shop of the cannibal Anziques. I experienced some shame at my susceptibility to so slight a thing, but the drawing nevertheless disturbed me, especially in connexion with some adjacent passages descriptive of Anzique gastronomy.

I had turned to a neighbouring shelf and was examining its meagre literary contents—an eighteenth-century Bible, a *Pilgrim's Progress* of like period, illustrated with grotesque woodcuts and printed by the almanack-maker Isaiah Thomas,[11] the rotting bulk of Cotton Mather's *Magnalia Christi Americana*,[12] and a few other books of evidently equal age—when my attention was aroused by the unmistakable sound of walking in the room overhead. At first astonished and startled, considering the lack of response to my recent knocking at the door, I immediately afterward concluded that the walker had just awakened from a sound sleep; and listened with less surprise as the footsteps sounded on the creaking stairs. The tread was heavy, yet seemed to contain a curious quality of cautiousness; a quality which I disliked the more because the tread was heavy. When I had entered the room I had shut the door behind me. Now, after

a moment of silence during which the walker may have been in-
specting my bicycle in the hall, I heard a fumbling at the latch
and saw the panelled portal swing open again.

In the doorway stood a person of such singular appearance
that I should have exclaimed aloud but for the restraints of good
breeding. Old, white-bearded, and ragged, my host possessed a
countenance and physique which inspired equal wonder and respect. His height could not have been less than six feet, and despite a general air of age and poverty he was stout and powerful
in proportion. His face, almost hidden by a long beard which
grew high on the cheeks, seemed abnormally ruddy and less
wrinkled than one might expect; while over a high forehead fell a
shock of white hair little thinned by the years. His blue eyes,
though a trifle bloodshot, seemed inexplicably keen and burning.
But for his horrible unkemptness the man would have been as
distinguished-looking as he was impressive. This unkemptness,
however, made him offensive despite his face and figure. Of what
his clothing consisted I could hardly tell, for it seemed to me no
more than a mass of tatters surmounting a pair of high, heavy
boots; and his lack of cleanliness surpassed description.[13]

The appearance of this man, and the instinctive fear he inspired, prepared me for something like enmity; so that I almost
shuddered through surprise and a sense of uncanny incongruity
when he motioned me to a chair and addressed me in a thin,
weak voice full of fawning respect and ingratiating hospitality.
His speech was very curious, an extreme form of Yankee dialect
I had thought long extinct; and I studied it closely as he sat down
opposite me for conversation.

"Ketched in the rain, be ye?" he greeted. "Glad ye was nigh
the haouse en' hed the sense ta come right in. I calc'late I was
asleep, else I'd a heerd ye—I ain't as young as I uster be, an' I
need a paowerful sight o' naps naowadays. Trav'lin' fur? I hain't
seed many folks 'long this rud sence they tuk off the Arkham
stage."[14]

I replied that I was going to Arkham, and apologised for my
rude entry into his domicile, whereupon he continued.

"Glad ta see ye, young Sir—new faces is scurce arount here,
an' I hain't got much ta cheer me up these days. Guess yew hail

from Bosting, don't ye? I never ben thar, but I kin tell a taown man when I see 'im—we hed one fer deestrick schoolmaster in 'eighty-four, but he quit suddent an' no one never heerd on 'im sence—" Here the old man lapsed into a kind of chuckle, and made no explanation when I questioned him. He seemed to be in an aboundingly good humour, yet to possess those eccentricities which one might guess from his grooming. For some time he rambled on with an almost feverish geniality, when it struck me to ask him how he came by so rare a book as Pigafetta's *Regnum Congo*. The effect of this volume had not left me, and I felt a certain hesitancy in speaking of it; but curiosity overmastered all the vague fears which had steadily accumulated since my first glimpse of the house. To my relief, the question did not seem an awkward one; for the old man answered freely and volubly.

"Oh, thet Afriky book? Cap'n Ebenezer Holt traded me thet in 'sixty-eight—him as was kilt in the war." Something about the name of Ebenezer Holt caused me to look up sharply. I had encountered it in my genealogical work, but not in any record since the Revolution. I wondered if my host could help me in the task at which I was labouring, and resolved to ask him about it later on. He continued.

"Ebenezer was on a Salem merchantman for years, an' picked up a sight o' queer stuff in every port. He got this in London, I guess—he uster like ter buy things at the shops. I was up ta his haouse onct, on the hill, tradin' hosses, when I see this book. I relished the picters, so he give it in on a swap. 'Tis a queer book—here, leave me git on my spectacles—" The old man fumbled among his rags, producing a pair of dirty and amazingly antique glasses with small octagonal lenses and steel bows. Donning these, he reached for the volume on the table and turned the pages lovingly.

"Ebenezer cud read a leetle o' this—'tis Latin—but I can't. I hed two er three schoolmasters read me a bit, and Passon Clark, him they say got draownded in the pond—kin yew make anything outen it?" I told him that I could, and translated for his benefit a paragraph near the beginning. If I erred, he was not scholar enough to correct me; for he seemed childishly pleased at my English version. His proximity was becoming obnoxious, yet

I saw no way to escape without offending him. I was amused at the childish fondness of this ignorant old man for the pictures in a book he could not read, and wondered how much better he could read the few books in English which adorned his room. This revelation of simplicity removed much of the ill-defined apprehension I had felt, and I smiled as my host rambled on:

"Queer haow picters kin set a body thinkin'. Take this un here near the front. Hev yew ever seed trees like thet, with big leaves a-floppin' over an' daown? And them men—them can't be niggers—they dew beat all. Kinder like Injuns, I guess, even ef they be in Afriky. Some o' these here critters looks like monkeys, or half monkeys an' half men, but I never heerd o' nothing like this un." Here he pointed to a fabulous creature of the artist, which one might describe as a sort of dragon with the head of an alligator.[15]

"But naow I'll shew ye the best un—over here nigh the middle—" The old man's speech grew a trifle thicker and his eyes assumed a brighter glow; but his fumbling hands, though seemingly clumsier than before, were entirely adequate to their mission. The book fell open, almost of its own accord and as if from frequent consultation at this place, to the repellent twelfth plate shewing a butcher's shop amongst the Anzique cannibals. My sense of restlessness returned, though I did not exhibit it. The especially bizarre thing was that the artist had made his Africans look like white men—the limbs and quarters hanging about the walls of the shop were ghastly, while the butcher with his axe was hideously incongruous. But my host seemed to relish the view as much as I disliked it.

"What d'ye think o' this—ain't never see the like hereabouts, eh? When I see this I telled Eb Holt, 'That's suthin' ta stir ye up an' make yer blood tickle!' When I read the Scripter about slayin'—like them Midianites was slew—I kinder think things, but I ain't got no picter of it. Here a body kin see all they is to it—I s'pose 'tis sinful, but ain't we all born an' livin' in sin?— Thet feller bein' chopped up gives me a tickle every time I look at 'im—I hev ta keep lookin' at 'im—see whar the butcher cut off his feet? Thar's his head on thet bench, with one arm side of it, an' t'other arm's on the graound side o' the meat block."

As the man mumbled on in his shocking ecstasy the expression on his hairy, spectacled face became indescribable, but his voice sank rather than mounted. My own sensations can scarcely be recorded. All the terror I had dimly felt before rushed upon me actively and vividly, and I knew that I loathed the ancient and abhorrent creature so near me with an infinite intensity. His madness, or at least his partial perversion, seemed beyond dispute. He was almost whispering now, with a huskiness more terrible than a scream, and I trembled as I listened.

"As I says, 'tis queer haow picters sets ye thinkin'. D'ye know, young Sir, I'm right sot on this un here. Arter I got the book off Eb I uster look at it a lot, especial when I'd heerd Passon Clark rant o' Sundays in his big wig. Onct I tried suthin' funny—here, young Sir, don't git skeert—all I done was ter look at the picter afore I kilt the sheep for market—killin' sheep was kinder more fun arter lookin' at it—" The tone of the old man now sank very low, sometimes becoming so faint that his words were hardly audible. I listened to the rain, and to the rattling of the bleared, small-paned windows, and marked a rumbling of approaching thunder quite unusual for the season. Once a terrific flash and peal shook the frail house to its foundations, but the whisperer seemed not to notice.

"Killin' sheep was kinder more fun—but d'ye know, 'twan't quite *satisfyin'*. Queer haow a *cravin'* gits a holt on ye—As ye love the Almighty, young man, don't tell nobody, but I swar ter Gawd thet picter begun ta make me *hungry fer victuals I couldn't raise nor buy*—here, set still, what's ailin' ye?—I didn't do nothin', only I wondered haow 'twud be ef I *did*—They say meat makes blood an' flesh, an' gives ye new life, so I wondered if 'twudn't make a man live longer an' longer ef 'twas *more the same*—" But the whisperer never continued. The interruption was not produced by my fright, nor by the rapidly increasing storm amidst whose fury I was presently to open my eyes on a smoky solitude of blackened ruins. It was produced by a very simple though somewhat unusual happening.

The open book lay flat between us, with the picture staring repulsively upward. As the old man whispered the words *"more the same"* a tiny spattering impact was heard, and something shewed on the yellowed paper of the upturned volume. I thought of the rain and of a leaky roof, but rain is not red. On the butcher's shop of the Anzique cannibals a small red spattering glistened picturesquely, lending vividness to the horror of the engraving. The old man saw it, and stopped whispering even before my expression of horror made it necessary; saw it and glanced quickly toward the floor of the room he had left an hour before. I followed his glance, and beheld just above us on the loose plaster of the ancient ceiling a large irregular spot of wet crimson which seemed to spread even as I viewed it. I did not shriek or move, but merely shut my eyes. A moment later came the titanic thunderbolt of thunderbolts; blasting that accursed house of unutterable secrets and bringing the oblivion which alone saved my mind.

The Outsider

That night the Baron dreamt of many a woe;
And all his warrior-guests, with shade and form
Of witch, and demon, and large coffin-worm,
Were long be-nightmared.

—*Keats.*[1]

Unhappy is he to whom the memories of childhood bring only fear and sadness. Wretched is he who looks back upon lone hours in vast and dismal chambers with brown hangings and maddening rows of antique books, or upon awed watches in twilight groves of grotesque, gigantic, and vine-encumbered trees that silently wave twisted branches far aloft. Such a lot the gods gave to me—to me, the dazed, the disappointed; the barren, the broken. And yet I am strangely content, and cling desperately to those sere memories, when my mind momentarily threatens to reach beyond to *the other*.

I know not where I was born, save that the castle was infinitely old and infinitely horrible; full of dark passages and having high ceilings where the eye could find only cobwebs and shadows. The stones in the crumbling corridors seemed always hideously damp, and there was an accursed smell everywhere, as of the piled-up corpses of dead generations. It was never light, so that I used sometimes to light candles and gaze steadily at them for relief; nor was there any sun outdoors, since the terrible trees grew high above the topmost accessible tower. There was one black tower which reached above the trees into the unknown outer sky, but that was partly ruined and could not be ascended save by a well-nigh impossible climb up the sheer wall, stone by stone.

I must have lived years in this place, but I cannot measure the time. Beings must have cared for my needs, yet I cannot recall any person except myself; or anything alive but the noiseless rats and bats and spiders. I think that whoever nursed me must have been shockingly aged, since my first conception of a living person was that of something mockingly like myself, yet distorted, shrivelled, and decaying like the castle. To me there was nothing grotesque in the bones and skeletons that strowed some of the stone crypts deep down among the foundations. I fantastically associated these things with every-day events, and thought them more natural than the coloured pictures of living beings which I found in many of the mouldy books. From such books I learned all that I know. No teacher urged or guided me, and I do not recall hearing any human voice in all those years—not even my own; for although I had read of speech, I had never thought to try to speak aloud. My aspect was a matter equally unthought of, for there were no mirrors in the castle, and I merely regarded myself by instinct as akin to the youthful figures I saw drawn and painted in the books. I felt conscious of youth because I remembered so little.

Outside, across the putrid moat and under the dark mute trees, I would often lie and dream for hours about what I read in the books; and would longingly picture myself amidst gay crowds in the sunny world beyond the endless forest. Once I tried to escape from the forest, but as I went farther from the castle the shade grew denser and the air more filled with brooding fear; so that I ran frantically back lest I lose my way in a labyrinth of nighted silence.

So through endless twilights I dreamed and waited, though I knew not what I waited for. Then in the shadowy solitude my longing for light grew so frantic that I could rest no more, and I lifted entreating hands to the single black ruined tower that reached above the forest into the unknown outer sky. And at last I resolved to scale that tower, fall though I might; since it were better to glimpse the sky and perish, than to live without ever beholding day.

In the dank twilight I climbed the worn and aged stone stairs till I reached the level where they ceased, and thereafter clung perilously to small footholds leading upward. Ghastly and terrible was that dead, stairless cylinder of rock; black, ruined, and deserted, and sinister with startled bats whose wings made no noise. But more ghastly and terrible still was the slowness of my progress; for climb as I might, the darkness overhead grew no thinner, and a new chill as of haunted and venerable mould assailed me. I shivered as I wondered why I did not reach the light, and would have looked down had I dared. I fancied that night had come suddenly upon me, and vainly groped with one free hand for a window embrasure, that I might peer out and above, and try to judge the height I had attained.

All at once, after an infinity of awesome, sightless crawling up that concave and desperate precipice, I felt my head touch a solid thing, and I knew that I must have gained the roof, or at least some kind of floor. In the darkness I raised my free hand and tested the barrier, finding it stone and immovable. Then came a deadly circuit of the tower, clinging to whatever holds the slimy wall could give; till finally my testing hand found the barrier yielding, and I turned upward again, pushing the slab or door with my head as I used both hands in my fearful ascent. There was no light revealed above, and as my hands went higher I knew that my climb was for the nonce ended; since the slab was the trap-door of an aperture leading to a level stone surface of greater circumference than the lower tower, no doubt the floor of some lofty and capacious observation chamber. I crawled through carefully, and tried to prevent the heavy slab from falling back into place; but failed in the latter attempt. As I lay exhausted on the stone floor I heard the eerie echoes of its fall, but hoped when necessary to pry it open again.

Believing I was now at a prodigious height, far above the accursed branches of the wood, I dragged myself up from the floor and fumbled about for windows, that I might look for the first time upon the sky, and the moon and stars of which I had read. But on every hand I was disappointed; since all that I found were vast shelves of marble, bearing odious oblong boxes of disturbing size. More and more I reflected, and wondered what hoary secrets might abide in this high apartment so many aeons cut off from the castle below. Then unexpectedly my hands came upon a doorway, where hung a portal of stone, rough with strange chiselling. Trying it, I found it locked; but with a supreme burst of strength I overcame all obstacles and dragged it open inward. As I did so there came to me the purest ecstasy I have ever known; for shining tranquilly through an ornate grating of iron, and down a short stone passageway of steps that ascended from the newly found doorway, was the radiant full moon, which I had never before seen save in dreams and in vague visions I dared not call memories.

Fancying now that I had attained the very pinnacle of the castle, I commenced to rush up the few steps beyond the door; but the sudden veiling of the moon by a cloud caused me to stumble, and I felt my way more slowly in the dark. It was still very dark when I reached the grating—which I tried carefully and found unlocked, but which I did not open for fear of falling from the amazing height to which I had climbed. Then the moon came out.

Most daemoniacal of all shocks is that of the abysmally unexpected and grotesquely unbelievable. Nothing I had before undergone could compare in terror with what I now saw; with the bizarre marvels that sight implied. The sight itself was as simple as it was stupefying, for it was merely this: instead of a dizzying prospect of treetops seen from a lofty eminence, there stretched around me on a level through the grating nothing less than *the solid ground,* decked and diversified by marble slabs and columns, and overshadowed by an ancient stone church, whose ruined spire gleamed spectrally in the moonlight.

Half unconscious, I opened the grating and staggered out upon the white gravel path that stretched away in two directions. My mind, stunned and chaotic as it was, still held the frantic craving for light; and not even the fantastic wonder which had happened could stay my course. I neither knew nor cared whether my experience was insanity, dreaming, or magic; but was determined to gaze on brilliance and gaiety at any cost. I knew not who I was or what I was, or what my surroundings might be; though as I continued to stumble along I became conscious of a kind of fearsome latent memory that made my progress not wholly fortuitous. I passed under an arch out of that region of slabs and columns, and wandered through the open country; sometimes following the visible road, but sometimes leaving it curiously to tread across meadows where only occasional ruins bespoke the ancient presence of a forgotten road. Once I swam across a swift river where crumbling, mossy masonry told of a bridge long vanished.

Over two hours must have passed before I reached what seemed to be my goal, a venerable ivied castle in a thickly wooded park; maddeningly familiar, yet full of perplexing strangeness to me. I saw that the moat was filled in, and that some of the well-known towers were demolished; whilst new wings existed to confuse the beholder. But what I observed with chief interest and delight were the open windows—gorgeously ablaze with light and sending forth sound of the gayest revelry. Advancing to one of these I looked in and saw an oddly dressed company, indeed; making merry, and speaking brightly to one another. I had never, seemingly, heard human speech before; and could guess only vaguely what was said. Some of the faces seemed to hold expressions that brought up incredibly remote recollections; others were utterly alien.

I now stepped through the low window into the brilliantly lighted room, stepping as I did so from my single bright moment of hope to my blackest convulsion of despair and realisation. The nightmare was quick to come; for as I entered, there occurred immediately one of the most terrifying demonstrations I had ever conceived. Scarcely had I crossed the sill when there descended upon the whole company a sudden and unheralded fear of hideous intensity, distorting every face and evoking the most horrible screams from nearly every throat. Flight was universal, and in the clamour and panic several fell in a swoon and were dragged away by their madly fleeing companions. Many covered their eyes with their hands, and plunged blindly and awkwardly in their race to escape; overturning furniture and stumbling against the walls before they managed to reach one of the many doors.

The cries were shocking; and as I stood in the brilliant apartment alone and dazed, listening to their vanishing echoes, I trembled at the thought of what might be lurking near me unseen. At a casual inspection the room seemed deserted, but when I moved toward one of the alcoves I thought I detected a presence there—

a hint of motion beyond the golden-arched doorway leading to another and somewhat similar room. As I approached the arch I began to perceive the presence more clearly; and then, with the first and last sound I ever uttered—a ghastly ululation that revolted me almost as poignantly as its noxious cause— I beheld in full, frightful vividness the inconceivable, inde- scribable, and unmentionable monstrosity which had by its simple appearance changed a merry company to a herd of deliri- ous fugitives.

I cannot even hint what it was like, for it was a compound of all that is unclean, uncanny, unwelcome, abnormal, and de- testable. It was the ghoulish shade of decay, antiquity, and deso- lation; the putrid, dripping eidolon of unwholesome revelation; the awful baring of that which the merciful earth should always hide. God knows it was not of this world—or no longer of this world—yet to my horror I saw in its eaten-away and bone- revealing outlines a leering, abhorrent travesty on the human shape; and in its mouldy, disintegrating apparel an unspeakable quality that chilled me even more.

I was almost paralysed, but not too much so to make a feeble effort toward flight; a backward stumble which failed to break the spell in which the nameless, voiceless monster held me. My eyes, bewitched by the glassy orbs which stared loathsomely into them, refused to close; though they were mercifully blurred, and shewed the terrible object but indistinctly after the first shock. I tried to raise my hand to shut out the sight, yet so stunned were my nerves that my arm could not fully obey my will. The attempt, however, was enough to disturb my balance; so that I had to stagger forward several steps to avoid falling. As I did so I became suddenly and agonisingly aware of the *nearness* of the carrion thing, whose hideous hollow breathing I half fan- cied I could hear. Nearly mad, I found myself yet able to throw out a hand to ward off the foetid apparition which pressed so close; when in one cataclysmic second of cosmic nightmarishness and hellish accident *my fingers touched the rotting outstretched paw of the monster beneath the golden arch.*

I did not shriek, but all the fiendish ghouls that ride the night-wind shrieked for me as in that same second there crashed down upon my mind a single and fleeting avalanche of soul-annihilating memory. I knew in that second all that had been; I remembered beyond the frightful castle and the trees, and recognised the altered edifice in which I now stood; I recognised, most terrible of all, the unholy abomination that stood leering before me as I withdrew my sullied fingers from its own.

But in the cosmos there is balm as well as bitterness, and that balm is nepenthe. In the supreme horror of that second I forgot what had horrified me, and the burst of black memory vanished in a chaos of echoing images. In a dream I fled from that haunted and accursed pile, and ran swiftly and silently in the moonlight. When I returned to the churchyard place of marble and went down the steps I found the stone trap-door immovable; but I was not sorry, for I had hated the antique castle and the trees. Now I ride with the mocking and friendly ghouls on the night-wind, and play by day amongst the catacombs of Nephren-Ka[2] in the sealed and unknown valley of Hadoth[3] by the Nile. I know that light is not for me, save that of the moon over the rock tombs of Neb,[4] nor any gaiety save the unnamed feasts of Nitokris beneath the Great Pyramid;[5] yet in my new wildness and freedom I almost welcome the bitterness of alienage.

For although nepenthe has calmed me, I know always that I am an outsider; a stranger in this century and among those who are still men. This I have known ever since I stretched out my fingers to the abomination within that great gilded frame; stretched out my fingers and touched *a cold and unyielding surface of polished glass.*

Herbert West—Reanimator

I. FROM THE DARK

Of Herbert West, who was my friend in college and in after life, I can speak only with extreme terror. This terror is not due altogether to the sinister manner of his recent disappearance, but was engendered by the whole nature of his life-work, and first gained its acute form more than seventeen years ago, when we were in the third year of our course at the Miskatonic University Medical School in Arkham.[1] While he was with me, the wonder and diabolism of his experiments fascinated me utterly, and I was his closest companion. Now that he is gone and the spell is broken, the actual fear is greater. Memories and possibilities are ever more hideous than realities.

The first horrible incident of our acquaintance was the greatest shock I ever experienced, and it is only with reluctance that I repeat it. As I have said, it happened when we were in the medical school, where West had already made himself notorious through his wild theories on the nature of death and the possibility of overcoming it artificially. His views, which were widely ridiculed by the faculty and his fellow-students, hinged on the essentially mechanistic nature of life; and concerned means for operating the organic machinery of mankind by calculated chemical action after the failure of natural processes. In his experiments with various animating solutions he had killed and treated immense numbers of rabbits, guinea-pigs, cats, dogs, and monkeys, till he had become the prime nuisance of the college. Several times he had actually obtained signs of life in animals supposedly dead; in many cases violent signs; but he soon saw that the perfection of this process, if indeed possible, would necessarily involve a lifetime of research. It likewise become clear that, since the same solution never worked alike on different organic species, he would require human subjects for further and more specialised progress. It was here that he first came into conflict with the college authorities, and was debarred from future experiments by no less a dignitary than the dean of the medical school himself—the learned and benevolent Dr. Allan Halsey,[2] whose work in behalf of the stricken is recalled by every old resident of Arkham.

I had always been exceptionally tolerant of West's pursuits, and we frequently discussed his theories, whose ramifications and corollaries were almost infinite. Holding with Haeckel[3] that all life is a chemical and physical process, and that the so-called "soul" is a myth,[4] my friend believed that artificial reanimation of the dead can depend only on the condition of the tissues; and that unless actual decomposition has set in, a corpse fully equipped with organs may with suitable measures be set going again in the peculiar fashion known as life. That the psychic or intellectual life might be impaired by the slight deterioration of sensitive brain-cells which even a short period of death would be apt to cause, West fully realised. It had at first been his hope to find a reagent which would restore vitality before the actual advent of death, and only repeated failures on animals had shewn him that the natural and artificial life-motions were incompatible. He then sought extreme freshness in his specimens, injecting his solutions into the blood immediately after the extinction of life. It was this circumstance which made the professors so carelessly sceptical, for they felt that true death had not occurred in any case. They did not stop to view the matter closely and reasoningly.

It was not long after the faculty had interdicted his work that West confided to me his resolution to get fresh human bodies in some manner, and continue in secret the experiments he could no longer perform openly. To hear him discussing ways and means was rather ghastly, for at the college we had never procured anatomical specimens ourselves. Whenever the morgue proved inadequate, two local negroes attended to this matter, and they were seldom questioned.[5] West was then a small, slender, spectacled youth with delicate features, yellow hair, pale blue eyes, and a soft voice, and it was uncanny to hear him dwelling on the relative merits of Christchurch Cemetery and the potter's field. We

finally decided on the potter's field, because practically every
body in Christchurch was embalmed; a thing of course ruinous
to West's researches.

I was by this time his active and enthralled assistant, and
helped him make all his decisions, not only concerning the
source of bodies but concerning a suitable place for our loathsome work. It was I who thought of the deserted Chapman
farmhouse beyond Meadow Hill,[6] where we fitted up on the
ground floor an operating room and a laboratory, each with dark
curtains to conceal our midnight doings. The place was far from
any road, and in sight of no other house, yet precautions were
none the less necessary; since rumours of strange lights, started
by chance nocturnal roamers, would soon bring disaster on our
enterprise. It was agreed to call the whole thing a chemical laboratory if discovery should occur. Gradually we equipped our sinister haunt of science with materials either purchased in Boston
or quietly borrowed from the college—materials carefully made
unrecognisable save to expert eyes—and provided spades and
picks for the many burials we should have to make in the cellar.
At the college we used an incinerator, but the apparatus was too
costly for our unauthorised laboratory. Bodies were always a
nuisance—even the small guinea-pig bodies from the slight clan-
destine experiments in West's room at the boarding-house.

We followed the local death-notices like ghouls, for our specimens demanded particular qualities. What we wanted were
corpses interred soon after death and without artificial preservation; preferably free from malforming disease, and certainly with
all organs present. Accident victims were our best hope. Not for
many weeks did we hear of anything suitable; though we talked
with morgue and hospital authorities, ostensibly in the college's
interest, as often as we could without exciting suspicion. We
found that the college had first choice in every case, so that it
might be necessary to remain in Arkham during the summer,
when only the limited summer-school classes were held. In the
end, though, luck favoured us; for one day we heard of an almost
ideal case in the potter's field; a brawny young workman
drowned only the morning before in Sumner's Pond, and buried
at the town's expense without delay or embalming. That after-

noon we found the new grave, and determined to begin work soon after midnight.

It was a repulsive task that we undertook in the black small hours, even though we lacked at that time the special horror of graveyards which later experiences brought to us. We carried spades and oil dark lanterns, for although electric torches were then manufactured, they were not as satisfactory as the tungsten contrivances of today. The process of unearthing was slow and sordid—it might have been gruesomely poetical if we had been artists instead of scientists[7]—and we were glad when our spades struck wood. When the pine box was fully uncovered West scrambled down and removed the lid, dragging out and propping up the contents. I reached down and hauled the contents out of the grave, and then both toiled hard to restore the spot to its former appearance. The affair made us rather nervous, especially the stiff form and vacant face of our first trophy, but we managed to remove all traces of our visit. When we had patted down the last shovelful of earth we put the specimen in a canvas sack and set out for the old Chapman place beyond Meadow Hill.

On an improvised dissecting-table in the old farmhouse, by the light of a powerful acetylene lamp, the specimen was not very spectral looking. It had been a sturdy and apparently unimaginative youth of wholesome plebeian type—large-framed, grey-eyed, and brown-haired—a sound animal without psychological subtleties, and probably having vital processes of the simplest and healthiest sort. Now, with the eyes closed, it looked more asleep than dead; though the expert test of my friend soon left no doubt on that score. We had at last what West had always longed for—a real dead man of the ideal kind, ready for the solution as prepared according to the most careful calculations and theories for human use. The tension on our part became very great. We knew that there was scarcely a chance for anything like complete success, and could not avoid hideous fears at possible grotesque results of partial animation. Especially were we apprehensive concerning the mind and impulses of the creature, since in the space following death some of the more delicate cerebral cells might well have suffered deterioration. I, myself, still held some curious notions about the traditional "soul" of man, and felt an awe at the secrets that might be told by one returning from the dead. I wondered what sights this placid youth might have seen in inaccessible spheres, and what he could relate if fully restored to life. But my wonder was not overwhelming, since for the most part I shared the materialism of my friend. He was calmer than I as he forced a large quantity of his fluid into a vein of the body's arm, immediately binding the incision securely.

The waiting was gruesome, but West never faltered. Every now and then he applied his stethoscope to the specimen, and bore the negative results philosophically. After about three-quarters of an hour without the least sign of life he disappoint-edly pronounced the solution inadequate, but determined to make the most of his opportunity and try one change in the for-mula before disposing of his ghastly prize. We had that afternoon dug a grave in the cellar, and would have to fill it by dawn—for although we had fixed a lock on the house we wished to shun even the remotest risk of a ghoulish discovery. Besides, the body would not be even approximately fresh the next night. So taking the solitary acetylene lamp into the adjacent laboratory, we left our silent guest on the slab in the dark, and bent every energy to the mixing of a new solution; the weighing and measuring super-vised by West with an almost fanatical care.

The awful event was very sudden, and wholly unexpected. I was pouring something from one test-tube to another, and West was busy over the alcohol blast-lamp which had to answer for a Bunsen burner in this gasless edifice, when from the pitch-black room we had left there burst the most appalling and daemoniac succession of cries that either of us had ever heard. Not more un-utterable could have been the chaos of hellish sound if the pit it-self had opened to release the agony of the damned, for in one inconceivable cacophony was centred all the supernal terror and unnatural despair of animate nature. Human it could not have been—it is not in man to make such sounds—and without a thought of our late employment or its possible discovery both West and I leaped to the nearest window like stricken animals; overturning tubes, lamp, and retorts, and vaulting madly into the starred abyss of the rural night. I think we screamed ourselves as we stumbled frantically toward the town, though as we reached the outskirts we put on a semblance of restraint—just enough to seem like belated revellers staggering home from a debauch.

We did not separate, but managed to get to West's room, where we whispered with the gas up until dawn. By then we had calmed ourselves a little with rational theories and plans for investigation, so that we could sleep through the day—classes being disregarded. But that evening two items in the paper, wholly unrelated, made it again impossible for us to sleep. The old deserted Chapman house had inexplicably burned to an amorphous heap of ashes; that we could understand because of the upset lamp.[8] Also, an attempt had been made to disturb a new grave in the potter's field, as if by futile and spadeless clawing at the earth. That we could not understand, for we had patted down the mould very carefully.

And for seventeen years after that West would look frequently over his shoulder, and complain of fancied footsteps behind him. Now he has disappeared.

II. THE PLAGUE-DAEMON

I shall never forget that hideous summer sixteen years ago, when like a noxious afrite from the halls of Eblis typhoid stalked leeringly through Arkham.[9] It is by that satanic scourge that most recall the year, for truly terror brooded with bat-wings over the piles of coffins in the tombs of Christchurch Cemetery; yet for me there is a greater horror in that time—a horror known to me alone now that Herbert West has disappeared.

West and I were doing post-graduate work in summer classes at the medical school of Miskatonic University, and my friend had attained a wide notoriety because of his experiments leading toward the revivification of the dead. After the scientific slaughter of uncounted small animals the freakish work had ostensibly stopped by order of our sceptical dean, Dr. Allan Halsey; though West had continued to perform certain secret tests in his dingy boarding-house room, and had on one terrible and unforgettable occasion taken a human body from its grave in the potter's field to a deserted farmhouse beyond Meadow Hill.

I was with him on that odious occasion, and saw him inject

into the still veins the elixir which he thought would to some extent restore life's chemical and physical processes. It had ended horribly—in a delirium of fear which we gradually came to attribute to our own overwrought nerves—and West had never afterward been able to shake off a maddening sensation of being haunted and hunted. The body had not been quite fresh enough; it is obvious that to restore normal mental attributes a body must be very fresh indeed; and a burning of the old house had prevented us from burying the thing. It would have been better if we could have known it was underground.

After that experience West had dropped his researches for some time; but as the zeal of the born scientist slowly returned, he again became importunate with the college faculty, pleading for the use of the dissecting-room and of fresh human specimens for the work he regarded as so overwhelmingly important. His pleas, however, were wholly in vain; for the decision of Dr. Halsey was inflexible, and the other professors all endorsed the verdict of their leader. In the radical theory of reanimation they saw nothing but the immature vagaries of a youthful enthusiast whose slight form, yellow hair, spectacled blue eyes, and soft voice gave no hint of the supernormal—almost diabolical—power of the cold brain within. I can see him now as he was then—and I shiver. He grew sterner of face, but never elderly.[10] And now Sefton Asylum has had the mishap and West has vanished.

West clashed disagreeably with Dr. Halsey near the end of our last undergraduate term in a wordy dispute that did less credit to him than to the kindly dean in point of courtesy. He felt that he was needlessly and irrationally retarded in a supremely great work; a work which he could of course conduct to suit himself in later years, but which he wished to begin while still possessed of the exceptional facilities of the university. That the tradition-bound elders should ignore his singular results on animals, and persist in their denial of the possibility of reanimation, was inexpressibly disgusting and almost incomprehensible to a youth of West's logical temperament. Only greater maturity could help him understand the chronic mental limitations of the "professor-doctor" type—the product of generations of pathetic Puritanism; kindly, conscientious, and sometimes gentle and amiable, yet always narrow, intolerant, custom-ridden, and lacking in perspective. Age has more charity for these incomplete yet high-souled characters, whose worst real vice is timidity, and who are ultimately punished by general ridicule for their intellectual sins—sins like Ptolemaism, Calvinism,[11] anti-Darwinism, anti-Nietzscheism, and every sort of Sabbatarianism and sumptuary legislation. West, young despite his marvellous scientific acquirements, had scant patience with good Dr. Halsey and his erudite colleagues; and nursed an increasing resentment, coupled with a desire to prove his theories to these obtuse worthies in some striking and dramatic fashion. Like most youths, he indulged in elaborate day-dreams of revenge, triumph, and final magnanimous forgiveness.

And then had come the scourge, grinning and lethal, from the nightmare caverns of Tartarus. West and I had graduated about the time of its beginning, but had remained for additional work at the summer school, so that we were in Arkham when it broke with full daemoniac fury upon the town. Though not as yet licenced physicians, we now had our degrees, and were pressed frantically into public service as the numbers of the stricken grew. The situation was almost past management, and deaths ensued too frequently for the local undertakers fully to handle. Burials without embalming were made in rapid succession, and even the Christchurch Cemetery receiving tomb was crammed with coffins of the unembalmed dead. This circumstance was not without effect on West, who thought often of the irony of the situation—so many fresh specimens, yet none for his persecuted researches! We were frightfully overworked, and the terrific mental and nervous strain made my friend brood morbidly.

But West's gentle enemies were no less harassed with prostrating duties. College had all but closed, and every doctor of the medical faculty was helping to fight the typhoid plague. Dr. Halsey in particular had distinguished himself in sacrificing service, applying his extreme skill with whole-hearted energy to cases which many others shunned because of danger or apparent hopelessness. Before a month was over the fearless dean had become a popular hero, though he seemed unconscious of his fame as he struggled to keep from collapsing with physical fatigue and

nervous exhaustion. West could not withhold admiration for the
fortitude of his foe, but because of this was even more determined to prove to him the truth of his amazing doctrines. Taking
advantage of the disorganisation of both college work and mu-
nicipal health regulations, he managed to get a recently deceased
body smuggled into the university dissecting-room one night,
and in my presence injected a new modification of his solution.
The thing actually opened its eyes, but only stared at the ceiling
with a look of soul-petrifying horror before collapsing into an
inertness from which nothing could rouse it. West said it was not
fresh enough—the hot summer air does not favour corpses. That
time we were almost caught before we incinerated the thing, and
West doubted the advisability of repeating his daring misuse of
the college laboratory.

The peak of the epidemic was reached in August. West and I
were almost dead, and Dr. Halsey did die on the 14th. The students all attended the hasty funeral on the 15th, and bought an
impressive wreath, though the latter was quite overshadowed by
the tributes sent by wealthy Arkham citizens and by the munici-
pality itself. It was almost a public affair, for the dean had surely
been a public benefactor. After the entombment we were all
somewhat depressed, and spent the afternoon at the bar of the
Commercial House; where West, though shaken by the death of
his chief opponent, chilled the rest of us with references to his
notorious theories. Most of the students went home, or to various duties, as the evening advanced; but West persuaded me to
aid him in "making a night of it". West's landlady saw us arrive at
his room about two in the morning, with a third man between
us; and told her husband that we had all evidently dined and
wined rather well.

Apparently this acidulous matron was right; for about 3 a.m.
the whole house was aroused by cries coming from West's room,
where when they broke down the door they found the two of us
unconscious on the blood-stained carpet, beaten, scratched, and
mauled, and with the broken remnants of West's bottles and instruments around us. Only an open window told what had become of our assailant, and many wondered how he himself had
fared after the terrific leap from the second story to the lawn

which he must have made. There were some strange garments in the room, but West upon regaining consciousness said they did not belong to the stranger, but were specimens collected for bacteriological analysis in the course of investigations on the transmission of germ diseases. He ordered them burnt as soon as possible in the capacious fireplace. To the police we both declared ignorance of our late companion's identity. He was, West nervously said, a congenial stranger whom we had met at some downtown bar of uncertain location. We had all been rather jovial, and West and I did not wish to have our pugnacious companion hunted down.

That same night saw the beginning of the second Arkham horror—the horror that to me eclipsed the plague itself. Christchurch Cemetery was the scene of a terrible killing; a watchman having been clawed to death in a manner not only too hideous for description, but raising a doubt as to the human agency of the deed. The victim had been seen alive considerably after midnight—the dawn revealed the unutterable thing. The manager of a circus at the neighbouring town of Bolton[12] was questioned, but he swore that no beast had at any time escaped from its cage. Those who found the body noted a trail of blood leading to the receiving tomb, here a small pool of red lay on the concrete just outside the gate. A fainter trail led away toward the woods, but it

evils danced on the roofs of Arkham, and unwled in the wind. Through the fevered town hich some said was greater than the plague, hispered was the embodied daemon-soul of ght houses were entered by a nameless thing death in its wake—in all, seventeen maimed nts of bodies were left behind by the voicer that crept abroad. A few persons had half and said it was white and like a malformed ape or anthropomorphic fiend. It had not left behind quite all that it had attacked, for sometimes it had been hungry. The number it had killed was fourteen; three of the bodies had been in stricken homes and had not been alive.

On the third night frantic bands of searchers, led by the police, captured it in a house on Crane Street[13] near the Miskatonic campus. They had organised the quest with care, keeping in touch by means of volunteer telephone stations, and when someone in the college district had reported hearing a scratching at a shuttered window, the net was quickly spread. On account of the general alarm and precautions, there were only two more victims, and the capture was effected without major casualties. The thing was finally stopped by a bullet, though not a fatal one, and was rushed to the local hospital amidst universal excitement and loathing.

For it had been a man.[14] This much was clear despite the nauseous eyes, the voiceless simianism, and the daemoniac savagery. They dressed its wound and carted it to the asylum at Sefton, where it beat its head against the wall of a padded cell for sixteen years— until the recent mishap, when it escaped under circumstances that few like to mention. What had most disgusted the researchers of Arkham was the thing they noticed when the monster's face was cleaned—the mocking, unbelievable resemblance to a learned and self-sacrificing martyr who had been entombed but three days before—the late Dr. Allan Halsey, public benefactor and dean of the medical school of Miskatonic University.

To the vanished Herbert West and to me the disgust and horror were supreme. I shudder tonight as I think of it; shudder even more than I did that morning when West muttered through his bandages,

"Damn it, it wasn't *quite* fresh enough!"

III. SIX SHOTS BY MIDNIGHT

It is uncommon to fire all six shots of a revolver with great suddenness when one would probably be sufficient, but many things in the life of Herbert West were uncommon. It is, for instance, not often that a young physician leaving college is obliged to conceal the principles which guide his selection of a home and office, yet that was the case with Herbert West. When he and I obtained our degrees at the medical school of Miskatonic University, and sought to relieve our poverty by setting up as general practitioners, we took great care not to say that we chose our house because it was fairly well isolated, and as near as possible to the potter's field.

Reticence such as this is seldom without a cause, nor indeed was ours; for our requirements were those resulting from a life-work distinctly unpopular. Outwardly we were doctors only, but beneath the surface were aims of far greater and more terrible moment—for the essence of Herbert West's existence was a quest amid black and forbidden realms of the unknown, in which he hoped to uncover the secret of life and restore to perpetual animation the graveyard's cold clay. Such a quest demands strange materials, among them fresh human bodies; and in order to keep supplied with these indispensable things one must live quietly and not far from a place of informal interment.

West and I had met in college, and I had been the only one to sympathise with his hideous experiments. Gradually I had come to be his inseparable assistant, and now that we were out of college we had to keep together. It was not easy to find a good opening for two doctors in company, but finally the influence of the university secured us a practice in Bolton—a factory town near Arkham, the seat of the college. The Bolton Worsted Mills are the largest in the Miskatonic Valley, and their polyglot employees are never popular as patients with the local physicians. We chose our house with the greatest care, seizing at last on a rather run-down cottage near the end of Pond Street; five numbers from the closest neighbour, and separated from the local potter's field by only a stretch of meadow land, bisected by a narrow neck of the rather dense forest which lies to the north. The distance was greater than we wished, but we could get no nearer house without going on the other side of the field, wholly out of the factory district. We were not much displeased, however, since there were no people between us and our sinister source of supplies. The walk was a trifle long, but we could haul our silent specimens undisturbed.

Our practice was surprisingly large from the very first—large enough to please most young doctors, and large enough to prove a bore and a burden to students whose real interest lay elsewhere. The mill-hands were of somewhat turbulent inclinations; and besides their many natural needs, their frequent clashes and

stabbing affrays gave us plenty to do. But what actually absorbed
our minds was the secret laboratory we had fitted up in the cellar—the laboratory with the long table under the electric lights,
where in the small hours of the morning we often injected West's
various solutions into the veins of the things we dragged from
the potter's field. West was experimenting madly to find something which would start man's vital motions anew after they had
been stopped by the thing we call death, but had encountered the
most ghastly obstacles. The solution had to be differently compounded for different types—what would serve for guinea-pigs
would not serve for human beings, and different human specimens required large modifications.

The bodies had to be exceedingly fresh, or the slight decomposition of brain tissue would render perfect reanimation
impossible. Indeed, the greatest problem was to get them fresh
enough—West had had horrible experiences during his secret
college researches with corpses of doubtful vintage. The results
of partial or imperfect animation were much more hideous than
were the total failures, and we both held fearsome recollections
of such things. Ever since our first daemoniac session in the deserted farmhouse on Meadow Hill in Arkham, we had felt a
brooding menace; and West, though a calm, blond, blue-eyed
scientific automaton in most respects, often confessed to a shuddering sensation of stealthy pursuit. He half felt that he was followed—a psychological delusion of shaken nerves, enhanced by
the undeniably disturbing fact that at least one of our reanimated
specimens was still alive—a frightful carnivorous thing in a padded cell at Sefton. Then there was another—our first—whose exact fate we had never learned.

We had fair luck with specimens in Bolton—much better than
in Arkham. We had not been settled a week before we got an accident victim on the very night of burial, and made it open its
eyes with an amazingly rational expression before the solution
failed. It had lost an arm—if it had been a perfect body we might
have succeeded better. Between then and the next January we secured three more; one total failure, one case of marked muscular
motion, and one rather shivery thing—it rose of itself and uttered a sound. Then came a period when luck was poor; inter-

ments fell off, and those that did occur were of specimens either too diseased or too maimed for use. We kept track of all the deaths and their circumstances with systematic care.

One March night, however, we unexpectedly obtained a specimen which did not come from the potter's field. In Bolton the prevailing spirit of Puritanism had outlawed the sport of boxing—with the usual result. Surreptitious and ill-conducted bouts among the mill-workers were common, and occasionally professional talent of low grade was imported. This late winter night there had been such a match; evidently with disastrous results, since two timorous Poles had come to us with incoherently whispered entreaties to attend to a very secret and desperate case. We followed them to an abandoned barn, where the remnants of a crowd of frightened foreigners were watching a silent black form on the floor.

The match had been between Kid O'Brien—a lubberly and now quaking youth with a most un-Hibernian hooked nose[15]—and Buck Robinson, "The Harlem Smoke". The negro had been knocked out, and a moment's examination shewed us that he would permanently remain so. He was a loathsome, gorilla-like thing, with abnormally long arms which I could not help calling fore legs, and a face that conjured up thoughts of unspeakable Congo secrets and tom-tom poundings under an eerie moon. The body must have looked even worse in life—but the world holds many ugly things. Fear was upon the whole pitiful crowd, for they did not know what the law would exact of them if the affair were not hushed up; and they were grateful when West, in spite of my involuntary shudders, offered to get rid of the thing quietly—for a purpose I knew too well.

There was bright moonlight over the snowless landscape, but we dressed the thing and carried it home between us through the deserted streets and meadows, as we had carried a similar thing one horrible night in Arkham. We approached the house from the field in the rear, took the specimen in the back door and down the cellar stairs, and prepared it for the usual experiment. Our fear of the police was absurdly great, though we had timed our trip to avoid the solitary patrolman of that section.

The result was wearily anticlimactic. Ghastly as our prize appeared, it was wholly unresponsive to every solution we injected in its black arm; solutions prepared from experience with white specimens only.[16] So as the hour grew dangerously near to dawn, we did as we had done with the others—dragged the thing across the meadows to the neck of the woods near the potter's field, and buried it there in the best sort of grave the frozen ground would furnish. The grave was not very deep, but fully as good as that of the previous specimen—the thing which had risen of itself and uttered a sound. In the light of our dark lanterns we carefully covered it with leaves and dead vines, fairly certain that the police would never find it in a forest so dim and dense.

The next day I was increasingly apprehensive about the police, for a patient brought rumours of a suspected fight and death. West had still another source of worry, for he had been called in the afternoon to a case which ended very threateningly. An Italian woman had become hysterical over her missing child—a lad of five who had strayed off early in the morning and failed to appear for dinner—and had developed symptoms highly alarming in view of an always weak heart.[17] It was a very foolish hysteria, for the boy had often run away before; but Italian peasants are exceedingly superstitious, and this woman seemed as much harassed by omens as by facts. About seven o'clock in the evening she had died, and her frantic husband had made a frightful scene in his efforts to kill West, whom he wildly blamed for not saving her life. Friends had held him when he drew a stiletto, but West departed amidst his inhuman shrieks, curses, and oaths of vengeance. In his latest affliction the fellow seemed to have forgotten his child, who was still missing as the night advanced. There was some talk of searching the woods, but most of the family's friends were busy with the dead woman and the screaming man. Altogether, the nervous strain upon West must have been tremendous. Thoughts of the police and of the mad Italian both weighed heavily.

We retired about eleven, but I did not sleep well. Bolton had a surprisingly good police force for so small a town, and I could not help fearing the mess which would ensue if the affair of the night before were ever tracked down. It might mean the end of all our local work—and perhaps prison for both West and me. I did not like those rumours of a fight which were floating about. After the clock had struck three the moon shone in my eyes, but I turned over without rising to pull down the shade. Then came the steady rattling at the back door.

I lay still and somewhat dazed, but before long heard West's rap on my door. He was clad in dressing-gown and slippers, and had in his hands a revolver and an electric flashlight. From the revolver I knew that he was thinking more of the crazed Italian than of the police.

"We'd better both go," he whispered. "It wouldn't do not to answer it anyway, and it may be a patient—it would be like one of those fools to try the back door."

So we both went down the stairs on tiptoe, with a fear partly justified and partly that which comes only from the soul of the weird small hours. The rattling continued, growing somewhat louder. When we reached the door I cautiously unbolted it and threw it open, and as the moon streamed revealingly down on the form silhouetted there, West did a peculiar thing. Despite the obvious danger of attracting notice and bringing down on our heads the dreaded police investigation—a thing which after all was mercifully averted by the relative isolation of our cottage— my friend suddenly, excitedly, and unnecessarily emptied all six chambers of his revolver into the nocturnal visitor.

For that visitor was neither Italian nor policeman. Looming hideously against the spectral moon was a gigantic misshapen thing not to be imagined save in nightmares—a glassy-eyed, ink-black apparition nearly on all fours, covered with bits of mould, leaves, and vines, foul with caked blood, and having between its glistening teeth a snow-white, terrible, cylindrical object terminating in a tiny hand.

IV. THE SCREAM OF THE DEAD

The scream of a dead man gave to me that acute and added horror of Dr. Herbert West which harassed the latter years of our companionship. It is natural that such a thing as a dead man's scream should give horror, for it is obviously not a pleasing or ordinary occurrence; but I was used to similar experiences, hence suffered on this occasion only because of a particular circumstance. And, as I have implied, it was not of the dead man himself that I became afraid.

Herbert West, whose associate and assistant I was, possessed scientific interests far beyond the usual routine of a village physician. That was why, when establishing his practice in Bolton, he had chosen an isolated house near the potter's field. Briefly and brutally stated, West's sole absorbing interest was a secret study of the phenomena of life and its cessation, leading toward the reanimation of the dead through injections of an excitant solution. For this ghastly experimenting it was necessary to have a constant supply of very fresh human bodies; very fresh because even the least decay hopelessly damaged the brain structure, and human because we found that the solution had to be compounded differently for different types of organisms. Scores of rabbits and guinea-pigs had been killed and treated, but their trail was a blind one. West head never fully succeeded because he had never been able to secure a corpse sufficiently fresh. What he wanted were bodies from which vitality had only just departed; bodies with every cell intact and capable of receiving again the impulse toward that mode of motion called life.[18] There was hope that this second and artificial life might be made perpetual by repetitions of the injection, but we had learned that an ordinary natural life would not respond to the action. To establish the artificial motion, natural life must be extinct—the specimens must be very fresh, but genuinely dead.

The awesome quest had begun when West and I were students at the Miskatonic University Medical School in Arkham, vividly conscious for the first time of the thoroughly mechanical nature of life. That was seven years before, but West looked scarcely a day older now—he was small, blond, clean-shaven, soft-voiced, and spectacled, with only an occasional flash of a cold blue eye to tell of the hardening and growing fanaticism of his character under the pressure of his terrible investigations. Our experiences had often been hideous in the extreme; the results of defective reanimation, when lumps of graveyard clay had been galvanised into morbid, unnatural, and brainless motion by various modifications of the vital solution.

One thing had uttered a nerve-shattering scream; another had risen violently, beaten us both to unconsciousness, and run amuck in a shocking way before it could be placed behind asylum bars; still another, a loathsome African monstrosity, had clawed out of its shallow grave and done a deed—West had had to shoot that object. We could not get bodies fresh enough to shew any trace of reason when reanimated, so had perforce created nameless horrors. It was disturbing to think that one, perhaps two, of our monsters still lived—that thought haunted us shadowingly, till finally West disappeared under frightful circumstances. But at the time of the scream in the cellar laboratory of the isolated Bolton cottage, our fears were subordinate to our anxiety for extremely fresh specimens. West was more avid than I, so that it almost seemed to me that he looked half-covetously at any very healthy living physique.

It was in July, 1910, that the bad luck regarding specimens began to turn. I had been on a long visit to my parents in Illinois,[19] and upon my return found West in a state of singular elation. He had, he told me excitedly, in all likelihood solved the problem of freshness through an approach from an entirely new angle—that of artificial preservation.[20] I had known that he was working on a new and highly unusual embalming compound, and was not surprised that it had turned out well; but until he explained the details I was rather puzzled as to how such a compound could help in our work, since the objectionable staleness of the specimens was largely due to delay occurring before we secured them. This, I now saw, West had clearly recognised; creating his embalming compound for future rather than immediate use, and trusting to fate to supply again some very recent and unburied corpse, as it had years before when we obtained the negro killed in the Bolton prize-fight. At last fate had been kind, so that on this occasion there lay in the secret cellar laboratory a corpse whose decay could not by any possibility have begun. What would happen on reanimation, and whether we could hope for a revival of mind and reason, West did not venture to predict. The experiment would be a landmark in our studies, and he had saved the new body for my return, so that both might share the spectacle in accustomed fashion.

West told me how he had obtained the specimen. It had been a vigorous man; a well-dressed stranger just off the train on his way to transact some business with the Bolton Worsted Mills.[21] The walk through the town had been long, and by the time the traveller paused at our cottage to ask the way to the factories his heart had become greatly overtaxed. He had refused a stimulant, and had suddenly dropped dead only a moment later. The body, as might be expected, seemed to West a heaven-sent gift. In his brief conversation the stranger had made it clear that he was unknown in Bolton, and a search of his pockets subsequently revealed him to be one Robert Leavitt of St. Louis, apparently without a family to make instant inquiries about his disappearance. If this man could not be restored to life, no one would know of our experiment. We buried our materials in a dense strip of woods between the house and the potter's field. If, on the other hand, he could be restored, our fame would be brilliantly and perpetually established. So without delay West had injected into the body's wrist the compound which would hold it fresh for use after my arrival. The matter of the presumably weak heart, which to my mind imperilled the success of our experiment, did not appear to trouble West extensively. He hoped at last to obtain what the had never obtained before—a rekindled spark of reason and perhaps a normal, living creature.

So on the night of July 18, 1910,[22] Herbert West and I stood in the cellar laboratory and gazed at a white, silent figure beneath the dazzling arc-light. The embalming compound had worked uncannily well, for as I stared fascinatedly at the sturdy frame which had lain two weeks without stiffening I was moved to seek West's assurance that the thing was really dead. This assurance he gave readily enough; reminding me that the reanimating solution was never used without careful tests as to life; since it could have no effect if any of the original vitality were present. As West proceeded to take preliminary steps, I was impressed by the vast intricacy of the new experiment; an intricacy so vast that he could trust no hand less delicate than his own. Forbidding me to touch the body, he first injected a drug in the wrist just beside the place his needle had punctured when injecting the embalming compound. This, he said, was to neutralise the compound and release the system to a normal relaxation so that the reanimating solution might freely work when injected. Slightly later, when a change and a gentle tremor seemed to affect the dead limbs, West stuffed a pillow-like object violently over the twitching face, not withdrawing it until the corpse appeared quiet and ready for our attempt at reanimation. The pale enthusiast now applied some last perfunctory tests for absolute lifelessness, withdrew satisfied, and finally injected into the left arm an accurately measured amount of the vital elixir, prepared during the afternoon with a greater care than we had used since college days, when our feats were new and groping. I cannot express the wild, breathless suspense with which we waited for results on this first really fresh specimen—the first we could reasonably expect to open its lips in rational speech, perhaps to tell of what it had seen beyond the unfathomable abyss.

West was a materialist, believing in no soul and attributing all the working of consciousness to bodily phenomena; consequently he looked for no revelation of hideous secrets from gulfs and caverns beyond death's barrier. I did not wholly disagree with him theoretically, yet held vague instinctive remnants of the primitive faith of my forefathers; so that I could not help eyeing the corpse with a certain amount of awe and terrible expectation. Besides—I could not extract from my memory that hideous, inhuman shriek we heard on the night we tried our first experiment in the deserted farmhouse at Arkham.

Very little time had elapsed before I saw the attempt was not to be a total failure. A touch of colour came to cheeks hitherto chalk-white, and spread out under the curiously ample stubble of sandy beard. West, who had his hand on the pulse of the left wrist, suddenly nodded significantly; and almost simultaneously a mist appeared on the mirror inclined above the body's mouth. There followed a few spasmodic muscular motions, and then an audible breathing and visible motion of the chest. I looked at the closed eyelids, and thought I detected a quivering. Then the lids opened, shewing eyes which were grey, calm, and alive, but still unintelligent and not even curious.

In a moment of fantastic whim I whispered questions to the reddening ears; questions of other worlds of which the memory might still be present. Subsequent terror drove them from my mind, but I think the last one, which I repeated, was: "Where have you been?" I do not yet know whether I was answered or not, for no sound came from the well-shaped mouth; but I do know that at that moment I firmly thought the thin lips moved silently, forming syllables I would have vocalised as "only now" if that phrase had possessed any sense or relevancy. At that moment, as I say, I was elated with the conviction that the one great goal had been attained; and that for the first time a reanimated corpse had uttered distinct words impelled by actual reason. In the next moment there was no doubt about the triumph; no doubt that the solution had truly accomplished, at least temporarily, its full mission of restoring rational and articulate life to the dead. But in that triumph there came to me the greatest of all horrors—not horror of the thing that spoke, but of the deed that I had witnessed and of the man with whom my professional fortunes were joined.

For that very fresh body, at last writhing into full and terrifying consciousness with eyes dilated at the memory of its last scene on earth, threw out its frantic hands in a life and death struggle with the air; and suddenly collapsing into a second and final dissolution from which there could be no return, screamed out the cry that will ring eternally in my aching brain:

"Help! Keep off, you cursed little tow-head fiend—keep that damned needle away from me!"

V. THE HORROR FROM THE SHADOWS

Many men have related hideous things, not mentioned in print, which happened on the battlefields of the Great War. Some of these things have made me faint, others have convulsed me with devastating nausea, while still others have made me tremble and look behind me in the dark; yet despite the worst of them I believe I can myself relate the most hideous thing of all—the shocking, the unnatural, the unbelievable horror from the shadows.

In 1915 I was a physician with the rank of First Lieutenant in a Canadian regiment in Flanders, one of many Americans to precede the government itself into the gigantic struggle.[23] I had not entered the army on my own initiative, but rather as a natural result of the enlistment of the man whose indispensable assistant I was—the celebrated Boston surgical specialist, Dr. Herbert West. Dr. West had been avid for a chance to serve as surgeon in a great war, and when the chance had come he carried me with him almost against my will. There were reasons why I would have been glad to let the war separate us; reasons why I found the practice of medicine and the companionship of West more and more irritating; but when he had gone to Ottawa and through a colleague's influence secured a medical commission as Major, I could not resist the imperious persuasion of one determined that I should accompany him in my usual capacity.

When I say that Dr. West was avid to serve in battle, I do not mean to imply that he was either naturally warlike or anxious for the safety of civilisation. Always an ice-cold intellectual machine; slight, blond, blue-eyed, and spectacled; I think he secretly sneered at my occasional martial enthusiasms and censures of supine neutrality.[24] There was, however, something he wanted in embattled Flanders; and in order to secure it he had to assume a military exterior. What he wanted was not a thing which many persons want, but something connected with the peculiar branch of medical science which he had chosen quite clandestinely to follow, and in which he had achieved amazing and occasionally hideous results. It was, in fact, nothing more or less than an abundant supply of freshly killed men in every stage of dismemberment.

Herbert West needed fresh bodies because his life-work was the reanimation of the dead. This work was not known to the fashionable clientele who had so swiftly built up his fame after his arrival in Boston; but was only too well known to me, who had been his closest friend and sole assistant since the old days in Miskatonic University Medical School at Arkham. It was in those college days that he had begun his terrible experiments, first on small animals and then on human bodies shockingly obtained. There was a solution which he injected into the veins of dead things, and if they were fresh enough they responded in strange ways. He had had much trouble in discovering the

proper formula, for each type of organism was found to need a
stimulus especially adapted to it. Terror stalked him when he
reflected on his partial failures; nameless things resulting from
imperfect solutions or from bodies insufficiently fresh. A certain number of these failures had remained alive—one was in an
asylum while others had vanished—and as he thought of conceivable yet virtually impossible eventualities he often shivered
beneath his usual stolidity.

West had soon learned that absolute freshness was the prime
requisite for useful specimens, and had accordingly resorted to
frightful and unnatural expedients in body-snatching. In college,
and during our early practice together in the factory town of
Bolton, my attitude toward him had been largely one of fascinated admiration; but as his boldness in methods grew, I began
to develop a gnawing fear. I did not like the way he looked at
healthy living bodies; and then there came a nightmarish session
in the cellar laboratory when I learned that a certain specimen
had been a living body when he secured it. That was the first
time he had ever been able to revive the quality of rational
thought in a corpse; and his success, obtained at such a loathsome cost, had completely hardened him.

Of his methods in the intervening five years I dare not speak.
I was held to him by sheer force of fear, and witnessed sights that
no human tongue could repeat. Gradually I came to find Herbert
West himself more horrible than anything he did—that was
when it dawned on me that his once normal scientific zeal for
prolonging life had subtly degenerated into a mere morbid and
ghoulish curiosity and secret sense of charnel picturesqueness.
His interest became a hellish and perverse addiction to the repel-
lently and fiendishly abnormal; he gloated calmly over artificial
monstrosities which would make most healthy men drop dead
from fright and disgust; he became, behind his pallid intellectual-
ity, a fastidious Baudelaire of physical experiment—a languid
Elagabalus of the tombs.[25]

Dangers he met unflinchingly; crimes he committed unmoved. I think the climax came when he had proved his point
that rational life can be restored, and had sought new worlds to
conquer by experimenting on the reanimation of detached parts

of bodies. He had wild and original ideas on the independent vital properties of organic cells and nerve-tissue separated from natural physiological systems; and achieved some hideous preliminary results in the form of never-dying, artificially nourished tissue obtained from the nearly hatched eggs of an indescribable tropical reptile. Two biological points he was exceedingly anxious to settle—first, whether any amount of consciousness and rational action be possible without the brain, proceeding from the spinal cord and various nerve-centres; and second, whether any kind of ethereal, intangible relation distinct from the material cells may exist to link the surgically separated parts of what has previously been a single living organism.[26] All this research work required a prodigious supply of freshly slaughtered human flesh—and that was why Herbert West had entered the Great War.

The phantasmal, unmentionable thing occurred one midnight late in March, 1915, in a field hospital behind the lines at St. Eloi.[27] I wonder even now if it could have been other than a daemoniac dream of delirium. West had a private laboratory in an east room of the barn-like temporary edifice, assigned him on his plea that he was devising new and radical methods for the treatment of hitherto hopeless cases of maiming. There he worked like a butcher in the midst of his gory wares—I could never get used to the levity with which he handled and classified certain things. At times he actually did perform marvels of surgery for the soldiers; but his chief delights were of a less public and philanthropic kind, requiring many explanations of sounds which seemed peculiar even amidst that babel of the damned. Among these sounds were frequent revolver-shots—surely not uncommon on a battlefield, but distinctly uncommon in an hospital. Dr. West's reanimated specimens were not meant for long existence or a large audience. Besides human tissue, West employed much of the reptile embryo tissue which he had cultivated with such singular results. It was better than human material for maintaining life in organless fragments, and that was now my friend's chief activity. In a dark corner of the laboratory, over a queerly incubating burner, he kept a large covered vat full of this reptilian cell-matter; which multiplied and grew puffily and hideously.

On the night of which I speak we had a splendid new specimen—a man at once physically powerful and of such high men-
tality that a sensitive nervous system was assured. It was rather
ironic, for he was the officer who had helped West to his commission, and who was now to have been our associate. Moreover,
he had in the past secretly studied the theory of reanimation to
some extent under West. Major Sir Eric Moreland Clapham-Lee,
D.S.O.,[28] was the greatest surgeon in our division, and had been
hastily assigned to the St. Eloi sector when news of the heavy
fighting reached headquarters. He had come in an aëroplane piloted by the intrepid Lieut. Ronald Hill, only to be shot down
when directly over his destination. The fall had been spectacular
and awful; Hill was unrecognisable afterward, but the wreck
yielded up the great surgeon in a nearly decapitated but otherwise intact condition. West had greedily seized the lifeless thing
which had once been his friend and fellow-scholar; and I shuddered when he finished severing the head, placed it in his hellish
vat of pulpy reptile-tissue to preserve it for future experiments,
and proceeded to treat the decapitated body on the operating
table. He injected new blood, joined certain veins, arteries, and
nerves at the headless neck, and closed the ghastly aperture with
engrafted skin from an unidentified specimen which had borne
an officer's uniform. I knew what he wanted—to see if this
highly organised body could exhibit, without its head, any of the
signs of mental life which had distinguished Sir Eric Moreland
Clapham-Lee. Once a student of reanimation, this silent trunk
was now gruesomely called upon to exemplify it.

I can still see Herbert West under the sinister electric light as
he injected his reanimating solution into the arm of the headless
body. The scene I cannot describe—I should faint if I tried it, for
there is madness in a room full of classified charnel t' ings, with
blood and lesser human debris almost ankle-deep on the slimy
floor, and with hideous reptilian abnormalities sprouting, bubbling, and baking over a winking bluish-green spectre of dim
flame in a far corner of black shadows.

The specimen, as West repeatedly observed, had a splendid
nervous system. Much was expected of it; and as a few twitching
motions began to appear, I could see the feverish interest on

West's face. He was ready, I think, to see proof of his increasingly strong opinion that consciousness, reason, and personality can exist independently of the brain—that man has no central connective spirit, but is merely a machine of nervous matter, each section more or less complete in itself. In one triumphant demonstration West was about to relegate the mystery of life to the category of myth. The body now twitched more vigorously, and beneath our avid eyes commenced to heave in a frightful way. The arms stirred disquietingly, the legs drew up, and various muscles contracted in a repulsive kind of writhing. Then the headless thing threw out its arms in a gesture which was unmistakably one of desperation—an intelligent desperation apparently sufficient to prove every theory of Herbert West. Certainly, the nerves were recalling the man's last act in life; the struggle to get free of the falling aëroplane.

What followed, I shall never positively know. It may have been wholly an hallucination from the shock caused at the instant by the sudden and complete destruction of the building in a cataclysm of German shell-fire—who can gainsay it, since West and I were the only proved survivors? West liked to think that before his recent disappearance, but there were times when he could not; for it was queer that we both had the same hallucination. The hideous occurrence itself was very simple, notable only for what it implied.

The body on the table had risen with a blind and terrible groping, and we had heard a sound. I should not call that sound a voice, for it was too awful. And yet its timbre was not the most awful thing about it. Neither was its message—it had merely screamed, "Jump, Ronald, for God's sake, jump!" The awful thing was its source.

For it had come from the large covered vat in that ghoulish corner of crawling black shadows.

VI. THE TOMB-LEGIONS

When Dr. Herbert West disappeared a year ago, the Boston police questioned me closely.[29] They suspected that I was holding something back, and perhaps suspected graver things; but I could not tell them the truth because they would not have believed it. They knew, indeed, that West had been connected with activities beyond the credence of ordinary men; for his hideous experiments in the reanimation of dead bodies had long been too extensive to admit of perfect secrecy; but the final soul-shattering catastrophe held elements of daemoniac phantasy which make even me doubt the reality of what I saw.

I was West's closest friend and only confidential assistant. We had met years before, in medical school, and from the first I had shared his terrible researches. He had slowly tried to perfect a solution which, injected into the veins of the newly deceased, would restore life; a labour demanding an abundance of fresh corpses and therefore involving the most unnatural actions. Still more shocking were the products of some of the experiments— grisly masses of flesh that had been dead, but that West waked to a blind, brainless, nauseous animation. These were the usual results, for in order to reawaken the mind it was necessary to have specimens so absolutely fresh that no decay could possibly affect the delicate brain-cells.

This need for very fresh corpses had been West's moral undoing. They were hard to get, and one awful day he had secured his specimen while it was still alive and vigorous. A struggle, a needle, and a powerful alkaloid had transformed it to a very fresh corpse, and the experiment had succeeded for a brief and memorable moment; but West had emerged with a soul calloused and seared, and a hardened eye which sometimes glanced with a kind of hideous and calculating appraisal at men of especially sensitive brain and especially vigorous physique. Toward the last I became acutely afraid of West, for he began to look at me that way. People did not seem to notice his glances, but they noticed my fear; and after his disappearance used that as a basis for some absurd suspicions.

West, in reality, was more afraid than I; for his abominable pursuits entailed a life of furtiveness and dread of every shadow. Partly it was the police he feared; but sometimes his nervousness was deeper and more nebulous, touching on certain indescribable things into which he had injected a morbid life, and from which he had not seen that life depart. He usually finished his experiments with a revolver, but a few times he had not been quick enough. There was that first specimen on whose rifled grave marks of clawing were later seen. There was also that Arkham professor's body which had done cannibal things before it had been captured and thrust unidentified into a madhouse cell at Sefton, where it beat the walls for sixteen years. Most of the other possibly surviving results were things less easy to speak of—for in later years West's scientific zeal had degenerated to an unhealthy and fantastic mania, and he had spent his chief skill in vitalising not entire human bodies but isolated parts of bodies, or parts joined to organic matter other than human. It had become fiendishly disgusting by the time he disappeared; many of the experiments could not even be hinted at in print. The Great War, through which both of us served as surgeons, had intensified this side of West.

In saying that West's fear of his specimens was nebulous, I have in mind particularly its complex nature. Part of it came merely from knowing of the existence of such nameless monsters, while another part arose from apprehension of the bodily harm they might under certain circumstances do him. Their disappearance added horror to the situation—of them all West knew the whereabouts of only one, the pitiful asylum thing. Then there was a more subtle fear—a very fantastic sensation resulting from a curious experiment in the Canadian army in 1915. West, in the midst of a severe battle, had reanimated Major Sir Eric Moreland Clapham-Lee, D.S.O., a fellow-physician who knew about his experiments and could have duplicated them. The head had been removed, so that the possibilities of quasi-intelligent life in the trunk might be investigated. Just as the building was wiped out by a German shell, there had been a success. The trunk had moved intelligently; and, unbelievable to relate, we were both sickeningly sure that articulate sounds had come from the detached head as it lay in a shadowy corner of the laboratory. The shell had been merciful, in a way—but West could never feel as certain as he wished, that we two were the only survivors. He used to make shuddering conjectures about the possible actions of a headless physician with the power of re-animating the dead.

West's last quarters were in a venerable house of much elegance, overlooking one of the oldest burying-grounds in Boston.[30] He had chosen the place for purely symbolic and fantastically aesthetic reasons, since most of the interments were of the colonial period and therefore of little use to a scientist seeking very fresh bodies. The laboratory was in a sub-cellar secretly constructed by imported workmen, and contained a huge incinerator for the quiet and complete disposal of such bodies, or fragments and synthetic mockeries of bodies, as might remain from the morbid experiments and unhallowed amusements of the owner. During the excavation of this cellar the workmen had struck some exceedingly ancient masonry; undoubtedly connected with the old burying-ground, yet far too deep to correspond with any known sepulchre therein. After a number of calculations West decided that it represented some secret chamber beneath the tomb of the Averills, where the last interment had been made in 1768. I was with him when he studied the nitrous, dripping walls laid bare by the spades and mattocks of the men, and was prepared for the gruesome thrill which would attend the uncovering of centuried grave-secrets; but for the first time West's new timidity conquered his natural curiosity, and he betrayed his degenerating fibre by ordering the masonry left intact and plastered over. Thus it remained till that final hellish night; part of the walls of the secret laboratory. I speak of West's decadence, but must add that it was a purely mental and intangible thing. Outwardly he was the same to the last—calm, cold, slight, and yellow-haired, with spectacled blue eyes and a general aspect of youth which years and fears seemed never to change. He seemed calm even when he thought of that clawed grave and looked over his shoulder; even when he thought of the carnivorous thing that gnawed and pawed at Sefton bars.

The end of Herbert West began one evening in our joint study when he was dividing his curious glance between the newspaper and me. A strange headline item had struck at him from the crumpled pages, and a nameless titan claw had seemed to reach down through sixteen years. Something fearsome and incredible had happened at Sefton Asylum fifty miles away, stunning the neighbourhood and baffling the police. In the small hours of the morning a body of silent men had entered the grounds and their leader had aroused the attendants. He was a menacing military figure who talked without moving his lips and whose voice seemed almost ventriloquially connected with an immense black case he carried. His expressionless face was handsome to the point of radiant beauty, but had shocked the superintendent when the hall light fell on it—for it was a wax face with eyes of painted glass. Some nameless accident had befallen this man. A larger man guided his steps; a repellent hulk whose bluish face seemed half eaten away by some unknown malady. The speaker had asked for the custody of the cannibal monster committed from Arkham sixteen years before; and upon being refused, gave a signal which precipitated a shocking riot. The fiends had beaten, trampled, and bitten every attendant who did not flee; killing four and finally succeeding in the liberation of the monster. Those victims who could recall the event without hysteria swore that the creatures had acted less like men than like unthinkable automata guided by the wax-faced leader. By the time help could be summoned, every trace of the men and of their mad charge had vanished.

From the hour of reading this item until midnight, West sat almost paralysed. At midnight the doorbell rang, startling him fearfully. All the servants were asleep in the attic, so I answered the bell. As I have told the police, there was no wagon in the street; but only a group of strange-looking figures bearing a large square box which they deposited in the hallway after one of them had grunted in a highly unnatural voice, "Express—prepaid." They filed out of the house with a jerky tread, and as I watched them go I had an odd idea that they were turning toward the ancient cemetery on which the back of the house abutted. When I slammed the door after them West came downstairs and looked at the box. It was about two feet square, and bore West's correct name and present address. It also bore the inscription, "From Eric Moreland Clapham-Lee, St. Eloi, Flanders". Six years before, in Flanders, a shelled hospital had fallen upon the headless reanimated trunk of Dr. Clapham-Lee, and upon the detached head which—perhaps—had uttered articulate sounds.

West was not even excited now. His condition was more

ghastly. Quickly he said, "It's the finish—but let's incinerate—this." We carried the thing down to the laboratory—listening. I do not remember many particulars—you can imagine my state of mind—but it is a vicious lie to say it was Herbert West's body which I put into the incinerator. We both inserted the whole unopened wooden box, closed the door, and started the electricity. Nor did any sound come from the box, after all.

It was West who first noticed the falling plaster on that part of the wall where the ancient tomb masonry had been covered up. I was going to run, but he stopped me. Then I saw a small black aperture, felt a ghoulish wind of ice, and smelled the charnel bowels of a putrescent earth. There was no sound, but just then the electric lights went out and I saw outlined against some phosphorescence of the nether world a horde of silent toiling things which only insanity—or worse—could create. Their outlines were human, semi-human, fractionally human, and not human at all—the horde was grotesquely heterogeneous. They were removing the stones quietly, one by one, from the centuried wall. And then, as the breach became large enough, they came out into the laboratory in single file; led by a stalking thing with a beautiful head made of wax. A sort of mad-eyed monstrosity behind the leader seized on Herbert West. West did not resist or utter a sound. Then they all sprang at him and tore him to pieces before my eyes, bearing the fragments away into that subterranean vault of fabulous abominations. West's head was carried off by the wax-headed leader, who wore a Canadian officer's uniform. As it disappeared I saw that the blue eyes behind the spectacles were hideously blazing with their first touch of frantic, visible emotion.

Servants found me unconscious in the morning. West was gone. The incinerator contained only unidentifiable ashes. Detectives have questioned me, but what can I say? The Sefton tragedy they will not connect with West; not that, nor the men with the box, whose existence they deny. I told them of the vault, and they pointed to the unbroken plaster wall and laughed. So I told them no more. They imply that I am a madman or a murderer—probably I am mad. But I might not be mad if those accursed tomb-legions had not been so silent.

The Hound

In my tortured ears there sounds unceasingly a nightmare whirring and flapping, and a faint, distant baying as of some gigantic hound.[1] It is not dream—it is not, I fear, even madness—for too much has already happened to give me these merciful doubts. St. John[2] is a mangled corpse; I alone know why, and such is my knowledge that I am about to blow out my brains for fear I shall be mangled in the same way. Down unlit and illimitable corridors of eldritch phantasy sweeps the black, shapeless Nemesis that drives me to self-annihilation.

May heaven forgive the folly and morbidity which led us both to so monstrous a fate! Wearied with the commonplaces of a prosaic world, where even the joys of romance and adventure soon grow stale, St. John and I had followed enthusiastically every aesthetic and intellectual movement which promised respite from our devastating ennui. The enigmas of the Symbolists and the ecstasies of the pre-Raphaelites all were ours in their time, but each new mood was drained too soon of its diverting novelty and appeal.[3] Only the sombre philosophy of the Decadents[4] could hold us, and this we found potent only by increasing gradually the depth and diabolism of our penetrations. Baudelaire and Huysmans[5] were soon exhausted of thrills, till finally there remained for us only the more direct stimuli of unnatural personal experiences and adventures. It was this frightful emotional need which led us eventually to that detestable course which even in my present fear I mention with shame and timidity—that hideous extremity of human outrage, the abhorred practice of grave-robbing.

I cannot reveal the details of our shocking expeditions, or catalogue even partly the worst of the trophies adorning the nameless museum we prepared in the great stone house where we jointly dwelt, alone and servantless. Our museum was a blasphemous, unthinkable place, where with the satanic taste of neurotic virtuosi we had assembled an universe of terror and decay to excite our jaded sensibilities. It was a secret room, far, far underground; where huge winged daemons carven of basalt and onyx vomited from wide grinning mouths weird green and orange light, and hidden pneumatic pipes ruffled into kaleidoscopic dances of death the lines of red charnel things hand in hand woven in voluminous black hangings. Through these pipes came at will the odours our moods most craved; sometimes the scent of pale funeral lilies, sometimes the narcotic incense of imagined Eastern shrines of the kingly dead, and sometimes—how I shudder to recall it!—the frightful, soul-upheaving stenches of the uncovered grave.

Around the walls of this repellent chamber were cases of antique mummies alternating with comely, life-like bodies perfectly stuffed and cured by the taxidermist's art, and with headstones snatched from the oldest churchyards of the world. Niches here and there contained skulls of all shapes, and heads preserved in various stages of dissolution. There one might find the rotting, bald pates of famous noblemen, and the fresh and radiantly golden heads of new-buried children. Statues and paintings there were, all of fiendish subjects and some executed by St. John and myself. A locked portfolio, bound in tanned human skin, held certain unknown and unnamable drawings which it was rumoured Goya had perpetrated but dared not acknowledge.[6] There were nauseous musical instruments, stringed, brass, and wood-wind, on which St. John and I sometimes produced dissonances of exquisite morbidity and cacodaemoniacal ghastliness; whilst in a multitude of inlaid ebony cabinets reposed the most incredible and unimaginable variety of tomb-loot ever assembled by human madness and perversity. It is of this loot in particular that I must not speak—thank God I had the courage to destroy it long before I thought of destroying myself.

The predatory excursions on which we collected our unmentionable treasures were always artistically memorable events. We were no vulgar ghouls, but worked only under certain conditions of mood, landscape, environment, weather, season, and moonlight. These pastimes were to us the most exquisite form of aesthetic expression, and we gave their details a fastidious technical care. An inappropriate hour, a jarring lighting effect, or a clumsy manipulation of the damp sod, would almost totally destroy for us that ecstatic titillation which followed the exhumation of some ominous, grinning secret of the earth. Our quest for novel scenes and piquant conditions was feverish and insatiate—St. John was always the leader, and he it was who led the way at last to that mocking, that accursed spot which brought us our hideous and inevitable doom.

By what malign fatality were we lured to that terrible Holland churchyard? I think it was the dark rumour and legendry, the tales of one buried for five centuries, who had himself been a ghoul in his time and had stolen a potent thing from a mighty sepulchre. I can recall the scene in these final moments—the pale autumnal moon over the graves, casting long horrible shadows; the grotesque trees, drooping sullenly to meet the neglected grass and the crumbling slabs; the vast legions of strangely colossal bats that flew against the moon; the antique ivied church pointing a huge spectral finger at the livid sky; the phosphorescent insects that danced like death-fires under the yews in a distant corner; the odours of mould, vegetation, and less explicable things that mingled feebly with the night-wind from over the far swamps and seas; and worst of all, the faint deep-toned baying of some gigantic hound which we could neither see nor definitely place. As we heard this suggestion of baying we shuddered, remembering the tales of the peasantry; for he whom we sought had centuries before been found in this selfsame spot, torn and mangled by the claws and teeth of some unspeakable beast.

I remembered how we delved in this ghoul's grave with our spades, and how we thrilled at the picture of ourselves, the grave, the pale watching moon, the horrible shadows, the grotesque trees, the titanic bats, the antique church, the dancing death-fires, the sickening odours, the gently moaning night-wind, and the strange, half-heard, directionless baying, of whose objective existence we could scarcely be sure. Then we struck a substance harder than the damp mould, and beheld a rotting oblong box crusted with mineral deposits from the long undisturbed ground. It was incredibly tough and thick, but so old that we finally pried it open and feasted our eyes on what it held.

Much—amazingly much—was left of the object despite the lapse of five hundred years. The skeleton, though crushed in places by the jaws of the thing that had killed it, held together with surprising firmness, and we gloated over the clean white skull and its long, firm teeth and its eyeless sockets that once had glowed with a charnel fever like our own. In the coffin lay an amulet of curious and exotic design, which had apparently been worn around the sleeper's neck. It was the oddly conventionalised figure of a crouching winged hound, or sphinx with a semi-canine face, and was exquisitely carved in antique Oriental fashion from a small piece of green jade. The expression on its features was repellent in the extreme, savouring at once of death, bestiality, and malevolence. Around the base was an inscription in characters which neither St. John nor I could identify; and on the bottom, like a maker's seal, was graven a grotesque and formidable skull.

Immediately upon beholding this amulet we knew that we must possess it; that this treasure alone was our logical pelf from the centuried grave. Even had its outlines been unfamiliar we would have desired it, but as we looked more closely we saw that it was not wholly unfamiliar. Alien it indeed was to all art and literature which sane and balanced readers know, but we recognised it as the thing hinted of in the forbidden *Necronomicon* of the mad Arab Abdul Alhazred;[7] the ghastly soul-symbol of the corpse-eating cult of inaccessible Leng, in Central Asia.[8] All too well did we trace the sinister lineaments described by the old Arab daemonologist; lineaments, he wrote, drawn from some obscure supernatural manifestation of the souls of those who vexed and gnawed at the dead.

Seizing the green jade object, we gave a last glance at the bleached and cavern-eyed face of its owner and closed up the grave as we found it. As we hastened from that abhorrent spot, the stolen amulet in St. John's pocket, we thought we saw the bats descend in a body to the earth we had so lately rifled, as if seeking for some cursed and unholy nourishment. But the autumn moon shone weak and pale, and we could not be sure. So, too, as we sailed the next day away from Holland to our home, we thought we heard the faint distant baying of some gigantic hound in the background. But the autumn wind moaned sad and wan, and we could not be sure.

II.

Less than a week after our return to England, strange things began to happen. We lived as recluses; devoid of friends, alone, and without servants in a few rooms of an ancient manor-house on a bleak and unfrequented moor; so that our doors were seldom disturbed by the knock of the visitor. Now, however, we were troubled by what seemed to be frequent fumblings in the night, not only around the doors but around the windows also, upper as well as lower. Once we fancied that a large, opaque body darkened the library window when the moon was shining against it, and another time we thought we heard a whirring or flapping sound not far off. On each occasion investigation revealed nothing, and we began to ascribe the occurrences to imagination alone—that same curiously disturbed imagination which still prolonged in our ears the faint far baying we thought we had heard in the Holland churchyard. The jade amulet now reposed in a niche in our museum, and sometimes we burned strangely scented candles before it. We read much in Alhazred's *Necronomicon* about its properties, and about the relation of ghouls' souls to the objects it symbolised; and were disturbed by what we read. Then terror came.

On the night of September 24, 19—, I heard a knock at my chamber door. Fancying it St. John's, I bade the knocker enter, but was answered only by a shrill laugh. There was no one in the corridor. When I aroused St. John from his sleep, he professed entire ignorance of the event, and became as worried as I. It was that night that the faint, distant baying over the moor became to us a certain and dreaded reality. Four days later, whilst we were both in the hidden museum, there came a low, cautious scratching at the single door which led to the secret library staircase. Our alarm was now divided, for besides our fear of the unknown,[9] we had always entertained a dread that our grisly collection might be discovered. Extinguishing all lights, we proceeded to the door and threw it suddenly open; whereupon we felt an unaccountable rush of air, and heard as if receding far away a queer combination of rustling, tittering, and articulate chatter. Whether we were mad, dreaming, or in our senses, we did not try to determine. We only realised, with the blackest of apprehensions, that the apparently disembodied chatter was beyond a doubt *in the Dutch language.*

After that we lived in growing horror and fascination. Mostly we held to the theory that we were jointly going mad from our life of unnatural excitements, but sometimes it pleased us more to dramatise ourselves as the victims of some creeping and appalling doom. Bizarre manifestations were now too frequent to count. Our lonely house was seemingly alive with the presence of some malign being whose nature we could not guess, and every night that daemoniac baying rolled over the windswept moor, always louder and louder. On October 29 we found in the soft earth underneath the library window a series of footprints utterly impossible to describe. They were as baffling as the hordes of great bats which haunted the old manor-house in unprecedented and increasing numbers.

The horror reached a culmination on November 18, when St. John, walking home after dark from the distant railway station, was seized by some frightful carnivorous thing and torn to ribbons. His screams had reached the house, and I had hastened to the terrible scene in time to hear a whir of wings and see a vague black cloudy thing silhouetted against the rising moon. My friend was dying when I spoke to him, and he could not answer coherently. All he could do was to whisper, "The amulet—that damned thing—."[10] Then he collapsed, an inert mass of mangled flesh.

I buried him the next midnight in one of our neglected gardens, and mumbled over his body one of the devilish rituals he had loved in life. And as I pronounced the last daemoniac sentence I heard afar on the moor the faint baying of some gigantic hound. The moon was up, but I dared not look at it. And when I saw on the dim-litten moor a wide nebulous shadow sweeping from mound to mound, I shut my eyes and threw myself face down upon the ground. When I arose trembling, I know not how much later, I staggered into the house and made shocking obeisances before the enshrined amulet of green jade.

Being now afraid to live alone in the ancient house on the moor, I departed on the following day for London, taking with me the amulet after destroying by fire and burial the rest of the impious collection in the museum. But after three nights I heard the baying again, and before a week was over felt strange eyes upon me whenever it was dark. One evening as I strolled on Victoria Embankment for some needed air, I saw a black shape obscure one of the reflections of the lamps in the water. A wind stronger than the night-wind rushed by, and I knew that what had befallen St. John must soon befall me.

The next day I carefully wrapped the green jade amulet and sailed for Holland. What mercy I might gain by returning the thing to its silent, sleeping owner I knew not; but I felt that I must at least try any step conceivably logical. What the hound was, and why it pursued me, were questions still vague; but I had first heard the baying in that ancient churchyard, and every subsequent event including St. John's dying whisper had served to connect the curse with the stealing of the amulet. Accordingly I sank into the nethermost abysses of despair when, at an inn in Rotterdam, I discovered that thieves had despoiled me of this sole means of salvation.

The baying was loud that evening, and in the morning I read of a nameless deed in the vilest quarter of the city. The rabble were in terror, for upon an evil tenement had fallen a red death[11] beyond the foulest previous crime of the neighbourhood. In a squalid thieves' den an entire family had been torn to shreds by an unknown thing which left no trace, and those around had heard all night above the usual clamour of drunken voices a faint, deep, insistent note as of a gigantic hound.

So at last I stood again in that unwholesome churchyard where a pale winter moon cast hideous shadows, and leafless trees drooped sullenly to meet the withered, frosty grass and cracking slabs, and the ivied church pointing a jeering finger at the unfriendly sky, and the night-wind howled maniacally from over frozen swamps and frigid seas. The baying was very faint

now, and it ceased altogether as I approached the ancient grave I
had once violated, and frightened away an abnormally large
horde of bats which had been hovering curiously around it.

I know not why I went thither unless to pray, or gibber out
insane pleas and apologies to the calm white thing that lay
within; but, whatever my reason, I attacked the half-frozen sod
with a desperation partly mine and partly that of a dominating
will outside myself. Excavation was much easier than I expected,
though at one point I encountered a queer interruption; when a
lean vulture darted down out of the cold sky and pecked frantically at the grave-earth until I killed him with a blow of my
spade.[12] Finally I reached the rotting oblong box and removed
the damp nitrous cover. This is the last rational act I ever performed.

For crouched within that centuried coffin, embraced by a
close-packed nightmare retinue of huge, sinewy, sleeping bats,
was the bony thing my friend and I had robbed; not clean and
placid as we had seen it then, but covered with caked blood and
shreds of alien flesh and hair, and leering sentiently at me with
phosphorescent sockets and sharp ensanguined fangs yawning
twistedly in mockery of my inevitable doom. And when it gave
from those grinning jaws a deep, sardonic bay as of some gigantic hound, and I saw that it held in its gory, filthy claw the lost
and fateful amulet of green jade, I merely screamed and ran away
idiotically, my screams soon dissolving into peals of hysterical
laughter.

Madness rides the star-wind . . . claws and teeth sharpened on
centuries of corpses . . . dripping death astride a Bacchanale of
bats from night-black ruins of buried temples of Belial.[13] . . .
Now, as the baying of that dead, fleshless monstrosity grows
louder and louder, and the stealthy whirring and flapping of
those accursed web-wings circles closer and closer, I shall seek
with my revolver the oblivion which is my only refuge from the
unnamed and unnamable.

The Rats in the Walls

On July 16, 1923, I moved into Exham Priory[1] after the last workman had finished his labours. The restoration had been a stupendous task, for little had remained of the deserted pile but a shell-like ruin; yet because it had been the seat of my ancestors I let no expense deter me. The place had not been inhabited since the reign of James the First, when a tragedy of intensely hideous, though largely unexplained, nature had struck down the master, five of his children, and several servants; and driven forth under a cloud of suspicion and terror the third son, my lineal progenitor and the only survivor of the abhorred line. With this sole heir denounced as a murderer, the estate had reverted to the crown, nor had the accused man made any attempt to exculpate himself or regain his property. Shaken by some horror greater that that of conscience or the law, and expressing only a frantic wish to exclude the ancient edifice from his sight and memory, Walter de la Poer,[2] eleventh Baron Exham, fled to Virginia and there founded the family which by the next century had become known as Delapore.

Exham Priory had remained untenanted, though later allotted to the estates of the Norrys family and much studied because of its peculiarly composite architecture; an architecture involving Gothic towers resting on a Saxon or Romanesque substructure, whose foundation in turn was of a still earlier order or blend of orders—Roman, and even Druidic or native Cymric,[3] if legends speak truly. This foundation was a very singular thing, being merged on one side with the solid limestone of the precipice from whose brink the priory overlooked a desolate valley three miles west of the village of Anchester.[4] Architects and antiquarians loved to examine this strange relic of forgotten centuries, but the country folk hated it. They had hated it hundreds of years before, when my ancestors lived there, and they hated it now, with the moss and mould of abandonment on it. I had not been a

day in Anchester before I knew I came of an accursed house.
And this week workmen have blown up Exham Priory, and are
busy obliterating the traces of its foundations.

The bare statistics of my ancestry I had always known, together with the fact that my first American forbear had come to
the colonies under a strange cloud. Of details, however, I had
been kept wholly ignorant through the policy of reticence
always maintained by the Delapores. Unlike our planter neighbors, we seldom boasted of crusading ancestors or other mediaeval and Renaissance heroes; nor was any kind of tradition
handed down except what may have been recorded in the sealed
envelope left before the Civil War by every squire to his eldest
son for posthumous opening. The glories we cherished were
those achieved since the migration; the glories of a proud and
honourable, if somewhat reserved and unsocial Virginia line.

During the war our fortunes were extinguished and our whole
existence changed by the burning of Carfax,[5] our home on the
banks of the James. My grandfather, advanced in years, had perished in that incendiary outrage, and with him the envelope that
bound us all to the past. I can recall that fire today as I saw it
then at the age of seven, with the Federal soldiers shouting, the
women screaming, and the negroes howling and praying. My father was in the army, defending Richmond, and after many for-
malities my mother and I were passed through the lines to join
him. When the war ended we all moved north, whence my
mother had come; and I grew to manhood, middle age, and ultimate wealth as a stolid Yankee. Neither my father nor I ever
knew what our hereditary envelope had contained, and as I
merged into the greyness of Massachusetts business life I lost all
interest in the mysteries which evidently lurked far back in my
family tree. Had I suspected their nature, how gladly I would
have left Exham Priory to its moss, bats, and cobwebs!

My father died in 1904, but without any message to leave me,
or to my only child, Alfred,[6] a motherless boy of ten. It was this
boy who reversed the order of family information; for although I
could give him only jesting conjectures about the past, he wrote
me of some very interesting ancestral legends when the late war
took him to England in 1917 as an aviation officer. Apparently

the Delapores had a colourful and perhaps sinister history, for a friend of my son's, Capt. Edward Norrys of the Royal Flying Corps, dwelt near the family seat at Anchester and related some peasant superstitions which few novelists could equal for wildness and incredibility. Norrys himself, of course, did not take them seriously; but they amused my son and made good material for his letters to me. It was this legendry which definitely turned my attention to my transatlantic heritage, and made me resolve to purchase and restore the family seat which Norrys shewed to Alfred in its picturesque desertion, and offered to get for him at a surprisingly reasonable figure, since his own uncle was the present owner.

I bought Exham Priory in 1918, but was almost immediately distracted from my plans of restoration by the return of my son as a maimed invalid. During the two years that he lived I thought of nothing but his care, having even placed my business under the direction of partners. In 1921, as I found myself bereaved and aimless, a retired manufacturer no longer young, I resolved to divert my remaining years with my new possession. Visiting Anchester in December, I was entertained by Capt. Norrys, a plump, amiable young man who had thought much of my son, and secured his assistance in gathering plans and anecdotes to guide in the coming restoration. Exham Priory itself I saw without emotion, a jumble of tottering mediaeval ruins covered with lichens and honeycombed with rooks' nests, perched perilously upon a precipice, and denuded of floors or other interior features save the stone walls of the separate towers.

As I gradually recovered the image of the edifice as it had been when my ancestor left it over three centuries before, I began to hire workmen for the reconstruction. In every case I was forced to go outside the immediate locality, for the Anchester villagers had an almost unbelievable fear and hatred of the place.[7] This sentiment was so great that it was sometimes communicated to the outside labourers, causing numerous desertions; whilst its scope appeared to include both the priory and its ancient family.

My son had told me that he was somewhat avoided during his visits because he was a de la Poer, and I now found myself subtly ostracised for a like reason until I convinced the peasants how little I knew of my heritage. Even then they sullenly disliked me, so that I had to collect most of the village traditions through the mediation of Norrys. What the people could not forgive, perhaps, was that I had come to restore a symbol so abhorrent to them; for, rationally or not, they viewed Exham Priory as nothing less than a haunt of fiends and werewolves.

Piecing together the tales which Norrys collected for me, and supplementing them with the accounts of several savants who had studied the ruins, I deduced that Exham Priory stood on the site of a prehistoric temple; a Druidical or ante-Druidical thing which must have been contemporary with Stonehenge.[8] That indescribable rites had been celebrated there, few doubted; and there were unpleasant tales of the transference of these rites into the Cybele-worship which the Romans had introduced.[9] Inscriptions still visible in the sub-cellar bore such unmistakable letters as "DIV . . . OPS . . . MAGNA. MAT . . ." sign of the Magna Mater[10] whose dark worship was once vainly forbidden to Roman citizens. Anchester had been the camp of the third Augustan legion,[11] as many remains attest, and it was said that the temple of Cybele was splendid and thronged with worshippers who performed nameless ceremonies at the bidding of a Phrygian priest. Tales added that the fall of the old religion did not end the orgies at the temple, but that the priests lived on in the new faith without real change. Likewise was it said that the rites did not vanish with the Roman power, and that certain among the Saxons added to what remained of the temple, and gave it the essential outline it subsequently preserved, making it the centre of a cult feared through half the heptarchy.[12] About 1000 A.D. the place is mentioned in a chronicle as being a substantial stone priory housing a strange and powerful monastic order and surrounded by extensive gardens which needed no walls to exclude a frightened populace. It was never destroyed by the Danes, though after the Norman Conquest it must have declined tremendously; since there was no impediment when Henry the Third granted the site to my ancestor, Gilbert de la Poer, First Baron Exham, in 1261.

Of my family before this date there is no evil report, but something strange must have happened then. In one chronicle there is a reference to a de la Poer as "cursed of God" in 1307, whilst village legendry had nothing but evil and frantic fear to tell of the castle that went up on the foundations of the old temple and priory. The fireside tales were of the most grisly description, all the ghastlier because of their frightened reticence and cloudly evasiveness. They represented my ancestors as a race of hereditary daemons beside whom Gilles de Retz and the Marquis de Sade[13] would seem the veriest tyros, and hinted whisperingly at their responsibility for the occasional disappearance of villagers through several generations.

The worst characters, apparently, were the barons and their direct heirs; at least, most was whispered about these. If of healthier inclinations, it was said, an heir would early and mysteriously die to make way for another more typical scion. There seemed to be an inner cult in the family, presided over by the head of the house, and sometimes closed except to a few members. Temperament rather than ancestry was evidently the basis of this cult, for it was entered by several who married into the family. Lady Margaret Trevor from Cornwall, wife of Godfrey, the second son of the fifth baron, became a favourite bane of children all over the countryside, and the daemon heroine of a particularly horrible old ballad not yet extinct near the Welsh border. Preserved in balladry, too, though not illustrating the same point, is the hideous tale of Lady Mary de la Poer, who shortly after her marraige to the Earl of Shrewsfield was killed by him and his mother, both of the slayers being absolved and blessed by the priest to whom they confessed what they dared not repeat to the world.

These myths and ballads, typical as they were of crude superstition, repelled me greatly. Their persistence, and their application to so long a line of my ancestors, were especially annoying; whilst the imputations of monstrous habits proved unpleasantly reminiscent of the one known scandal of my immediate forbears—the case of my cousin, young Randolph Delapore of Carfax, who went among the negroes and became a voodoo priest after he returned from the Mexican War.

I was much less disturbed by the vaguer tales of wails and howlings in the barren, windswept valley beneath the limestone cliff; of the graveyard stenches after the spring rains; of the floundering, squealing white thing on which Sir John Clave's horse had trod one night in a lonely field; and of the servant who had gone mad at what he saw in the priory in the full light of day. These things were hackneyed spectral lore, and I was at that time a pronounced sceptic.[14] The accounts of vanished peasants were less to be dismissed, though not especially significant in view of mediaeval custom. Prying curiosity meant death, and more than one severed head had been publicly shewn on the bastions—now effaced—around Exham Priory.

A few of the tales were exceedingly picturesque, and made me wish I had learnt more of comparative mythology in my youth.[15] There was, for instance, the belief that a legion of bat-winged devils kept Witches' Sabbath each night at the priory—a legion whose sustenance might explain the disproportionate abundance of coarse vegetables harvested in the vast gardens. And, most vivid of all, there was the dramatic epic of the rats—the scampering army of obscene vermin which had burst forth from the castle three months after the tragedy that doomed it to desertion—the lean, filthy, ravenous army which had swept all before it and devoured fowl, cats, dogs, hogs, sheep, and even two hapless human beings before its fury was spent. Around that unforgettable rodent army a whole separate cycle of myths revolves, for it scattered among the village homes and brought curses and horrors in its train.

Such was the lore that assailed me as I pushed to completion, with an elderly obstinacy, the work of restoring my ancestral home. It must not be imagined for a moment that these tales formed my principal psychological environment. On the other hand, I was constantly praised and encouraged by Capt. Norrys and the antiquarians who surrounded and aided me. When the task was done, over two years after its commencement, I viewed the great rooms, wainscotted walls, vaulted ceilings, mullioned windows, and broad staircases with a pride which fully compensated for the prodigious expense of the restoration. Every attribute of the Middle Ages was cunningly reproduced, and the new parts blended perfectly with the original walls and foundations. The seat of my fathers was complete, and I looked forward to redeeming at last the local fame of the line which ended in me. I would reside here permanently, and prove that a de la Poer (for I had adopted again the original spelling of the name) need not be a fiend. My comfort was perhaps augmented by the fact that, although Exham Priory was mediaevally fitted, its interior was in truth wholly new and free from old vermin and old ghosts alike.

As I have said, I moved in on July 16, 1923. My household consisted of seven servants and nine cats, of which latter species I am particularly fond. My eldest cat, "Nigger-Man",[16] was seven years old and had come with me from my home in Bolton, Massachusetts;[17] the others I had accumulated whilst living with Capt. Norrys' family during the restoration of the priory. For five days our routine proceeded with the utmost placidity, my time being spent mostly in the codification of old family data. I had now obtained some very circumstatial accounts of the final tragedy and flight of Walter de la Poer, which I conceived to be the probable contents of the hereditary paper lost in the fire at Carfax. It appeared that my ancestor was accused with much reason of having killed all the other members of his household, except four servant confederates, in their sleep, about two weeks after a shocking discovery which changed his whole demeanour, but which, except by implication, he disclosed to no one save perhaps the servants who assisted him and afterward fled beyond reach.[18]

This deliberate slaughter, which included a father, three brothers, and two sisters, was largely condoned by the villagers, and so slackly treated by the law that its perpetrator escaped honoured, unharmed, and undisguised to Virginia; the general whispered sentiment being that he had purged the land of an immemorial curse. What discovery had prompted an act so terrible, I could scarcely even conjecture. Walter de la Poer must have known for years the sinister tales about his family, so that this material could have given him no fresh impulse. Had he, then, witnessed some appalling ancient rite, or stumbled upon some frightful and revealing symbol in the priory or its vicinity? He was reputed to have been a shy, gentle youth in England. In Virginia he seemed not so much hard or bitter as harassed and apprehensive. He was spoken of in the diary of another gentleman-adventurer, Francis

Harley of Bellview, as a man of unexampled justice, honour, and delicacy.

On July 22 occurred the first incident which, though lightly dismissed at the time, takes on a preternatural significance in relation to later events. It was so simple as to be almost negligible, and could not possibly have been noticed under the circumstances; for it must be recalled that since I was in a building practically fresh and new except for the walls, and surrounded by a well-balanced staff of servitors, apprehension would have been absurd despite the locality. What I afterward remembered is merely this—that my old black cat, whose moods I know so well, was undoubtedly alert and anxious to an extent wholly out of keeping with his natural character. He roved from room to room, restless and disturbed, and sniffed constantly about the walls which formed part of the old Gothic structure. I realise how trite this sounds—like the inevitable dog in the ghost story, which always growls before his master sees the sheeted figure— yet I cannot consistently suppress it.

The following day a servant complained of restlessness among all the cats in the house. He came to me in my study, a lofty west room on the second story, with groined arches, black oak panelling, and a triple Gothic window overlooking the limestone cliff and desolate valley; and even as he spoke I saw the jetty form of Nigger-Man creeping along the west wall and scratching at the new panels which overlaid the ancient stone. I told the man that there must be some singular odour or emanation from the old stonework, imperceptible to human senses, but affecting the delicate organs of cats even through the new woodwork. This I truly believed, and when the fellow suggested the presence of mice or rats, I mentioned that there had been no rats there for three hundred years, and that even the field mice of the surrounding country could hardly be found in these high walls, where they had never been known to stray. That afternoon I called on Capt. Norrys, and he assured me that it would be quite incredible for field mice to infest the priory in such a sudden and unprecedented fashion.

That night, dispensing as usual with a valet, I retired in the west tower chamber which I had chosen as my own, reached from the study by a stone staircase and short gallery—the former partly ancient, the latter entirely restored. This room was circular, very high, and without wainscotting, being hung with arras which I had myself chosen in London. Seeing that Nigger-Man was with me, I shut the heavy Gothic door and retired by the light of the electric bulbs which so cleverly counterfeited candles, finally switching off the light and sinking on the carved and canopied four-poster, with the venerable cat in his accustomed place across my feet. I did not draw the curtains, but gazed out at the narrow north window which I faced. There was a suspicion of aurora in the sky, and the delicate traceries of the window were pleasantly silhouetted.

At some time I must have fallen quietly asleep, for I recall a distinct sense of leaving strange dreams, when the cat started violently from his placid position. I saw him in the faint auroral glow, head strained forward, fore feet on my ankles, and hind feet stretched behind. He was looking intensely at a point on the wall somewhat west of the window, a point which to my eye had nothing to mark it, but toward which all my attention was now directed. And as I watched, I knew that Nigger-Man was not vainly excited. Whether the arras actually moved I cannot say. I think it did, very slightly. But what I can swear to is that behind it I heard a low, distinct scurrying as of rats or mice. In a moment the cat had jumped bodily on the screening tapestry, bringing the affected section to the floor with his weight, and exposing a damp, ancient wall of stone; patched here and there by the restorers, and devoid of any trace of rodent prowlers. Nigger-Man raced up and down the floor by this part of the wall, clawing the fallen arras and seemingly trying at times to insert a paw between the wall and the oaken floor.[19] He found nothing, and after a time returned wearily to his place across my feet. I had not moved, but I did not sleep again that night.

In the morning I questioned all the servants, and found that none of them had noticed anything unusual, save that the cook remembered the actions of a cat which had rested on her windowsill. This cat had howled at some unknown hour of the night, awaking the cook in time for her to see him dart purposefully out of the open door down the stairs. I drowsed away the noontime, and in the afternoon called again on Capt. Norrys, who became exceedingly interested in what I told him. The odd incidents—so slight yet so curious—appealed to his sense of the picturesque, and elicited from him a number of reminiscences of local ghostly lore. We were genuinely perplexed at the presence of rats, and Norrys lent me some traps and Paris green,[20] which I had the servants place in strategic localities when I returned.

I retired early, being very sleepy, but was harassed by dreams of the most horrible sort. I seemed to be looking down from an immense height upon a twilit grotto, knee-deep with filth, where a white-bearded daemon swineherd drove about with his staff a flock of fungous, flabby beasts whose appearance filled me with unutterable loathing. Then, as the swineherd paused and nodded over his task, a mighty swarm of rats rained down on the stinking abyss and fell to devouring beasts and man alike.[21]

From this terrific vision I was abruptly awaked by the motions of Nigger-Man, who had been sleeping as usual across my feet. This time I did not have to question the source of his snarls and hisses, and of the fear which made him sink his claws into my ankle, unconcscious of their effect; for on every side of the chamber the walls were alive with nauseous sound—the verminous slithering of ravenous, gigantic rats. There was now no aurora to shew the state of the arras—the fallen section of which had been replaced—but I was not too frightened to switch on the light.

As the bulbs leapt into radiance I saw a hideous shaking all over the tapestry, causing the somewhat peculiar designs to execute a singular dance of death. This motion disappeared almost at once, and the sound with it. Springing out of bed, I poked at the arras with the long handle of a warming-pan that rested near, and lifted one section to see what lay beneath. There was nothing but the patched stone wall, and even the cat had lost his tense realisation of abnormal presences. When I examined the circular trap that had been placed in the room, I found all of the openings sprung, though no trace remained of what had been caught and had escaped.

Further sleep was out of the question, so, lighting a candle, I opened the door and went out in the gallery toward the stairs to my study, Nigger-Man following at my heels. Before we had reached the stone steps, however, the cat darted ahead of me and vanished down the ancient flight. As I descended the stairs myself, I became suddenly aware of sounds in the great room below; sounds of a nature which could not be mistaken. The oak-panelled walls were alive with rats, scampering and milling, whilst Nigger-Man was racing about with the fury of a baffled hunter. Reaching the bottom, I switched on the light, which did not this time cause the noise to subside. The rats continued their riot, stampeding with such force and distinctness that I could finally assign to their motions a definite direction. These creatures, in numbers apparently inexhaustible, were engaged in one stupendous migration from inconceivable heights to some depth conceivably, or inconceivably, below.

I now heard steps in the corridor, and in another moment two servants pushed open the massive door. They were searching the house for some unknown source of disturbance which had thrown all the cats into a snarling panic and caused them to plunge precipitately down several flights of stairs and squat, yowling, before the closed door to the sub-cellar. I asked them if they had heard the rats, but they replied in the negative. And when I turned to call their attention to the sounds in the panels, I realised that the noise had ceased. With the two men, I went down to the door of the sub-cellar, but found the cats already dispersed. Later I resolved to explore the crypt below, but for the present I merely made a round of the traps. All were sprung, yet all were tenantless. Satisfying myself that no one had heard the rats save the felines and me, I sat in my study till morning; thinking profoundly, and recalling every scrap of legend I had unearthed concerning the building I inhabited.

I slept some in the forenoon, leaning back in the one comfortable library chair which my mediaeval plan of furnishing could not banish. Later I telephoned to Capt. Norrys, who came over and helped me explore the sub-cellar. Absolutely nothing untoward was found, although we could not repress a thrill at the knowledge that this vault was built by Roman hands. Every low arch and massive pillar was Roman—not the debased Romanesque of the bungling Saxons, but the severe and harmonious classicism of the age of the Caesars; indeed, the walls abounded with inscriptions familiar to the antiquarians who had repeatedly explored the place—things like "P. GETAE. PROP . . . TEMP . . . DONA . . ." and "L. PRAEC . . . VS . . . PONTIFI . . . ATYS . . ."

The reference to Atys made me shiver, for I had read Catullus and knew something of the hideous rites of the Eastern god, whose worship was so mixed with that of Cybele.[22] Norrys and I, by the light of lanterns, tried to interpret the odd and nearly effaced designs on certain irregularly rectangular blocks of stone generally held to be altars, but could make nothing of them. We remembered that one pattern, a sort of rayed sun, was held by students to imply a non-Roman origin, suggesting that these altars had merely been adopted by the Roman priests from some older and perhaps aboriginal temple on the same site. On one of these blocks were some brown stains which made me wonder. The largest, in the centre of the room, had certain features on the upper surface which indicated its connexion with fire—probably burnt offerings.

Such were the sights in that crypt before whose door the cats had howled, and where Norrys and I now determined to pass the night. Couches were brought down by the servants, who were told not to mind any nocturnal actions of the cats, and Nigger-Man was admitted as much for help as for companionship. We decided to keep the great oak door—a modern replica with slits for ventilation—tightly closed; and, with this attended to, we retired with lanterns still burning to await whatever might occur.

The vault was very deep in the foundations of the priory, and undoubtedly far down on the face of the beetling limestone cliff overlooking the waste valley. That it had been the goal of the scuffling and unexplainable rats I could not doubt, though why, I could not tell. As we lay there expectantly, I found my vigil occasionally mixed with half-formed dreams from which the uneasy motions of the cat across my feet would rouse me. These dreams were not wholesome, but horribly like the one I had had the night before. I saw again the twilit grotto, and the swineherd with his unmentionable fungous beasts wallowing in filth, and as I looked at these things they seemed nearer and more distinct—so distinct that I could almost observe their features. Then I did observe the flabby features of one of them—and awaked with such a scream that Nigger-Man started up, whilst Capt. Norrys, who had not slept, laughed considerably. Norrys might have laughed more—or perhaps less—had he known what it was that made me scream. But I did not remember myself till later. Ultimate horror often paralyses memory in a merciful way.[23]

Norrys waked me when the phenomena began. Out of the same frightful dream I was called by his gentle shaking and his urging to listen to the cats. Indeed, there was much to listen to, for beyond the closed door at the head of the stone steps was a veritable nightmare of feline yelling and clawing, whilst Nigger-Man, unmindful of his kindred outside, was running excitedly around the bare stone walls, in which I heard the same babel of scurrying rats that had troubled me the night before.

An acute terror now rose within me, for here were anomalies which nothing normal could well explain. These rats, if not the creatures of a madness which I shared with the cats alone, must be burrowing and sliding in Roman walls I had thought to be of solid limestone blocks . . . unless perhaps the action of water through more than seventeen centuries had eaten winding tunnels which rodent bodies had worn clear and ample. . . . But even so, the spectral horror was no less; for if these were living vermin why did not Norrys hear their disgusting commotion? Why did he urge me to watch Nigger-Man and listen to the cats outside, and why did he guess wildly and vaguely at what could have aroused them?

By the time I had managed to tell him, as rationally as I could, what I thought I was hearing, my ears gave me the last fading impression of the scurrying; which had retreated *still downward,* far underneath this deepest of sub-cellars till it seemed as if the whole cliff below were riddled with questing rats. Norrys was not as sceptical as I had anticipated, but instead seemed profoundly moved. He motioned to me to notice that the cats at the door had ceased their clamour, as if giving up the rats for lost; whilst Nigger-Man had a burst of renewed restlessness, and was clawing frantically around the bottom of the large stone altar in the centre of the room, which was nearer Norrys' couch than mine.

My fear of the unknown was at this point very great.[24] Something astounding had occurred, and I saw that Capt. Norrys, a younger, stouter, and presumably more naturally materialistic man, was affected fully as much as myself—perhaps because of his lifelong and intimate familiarity with local legend. We could for the moment do nothing but watch the old black cat as he pawed with decreasing fervour at the base of the altar, occasionally looking up and mewing to me in that persuasive manner which he used when he wished me to perform some favour for him.

Norrys now took a lantern close to the altar and examined the place where Nigger-Man was pawing; silently kneeling and scraping away the lichens of centuries which joined the massive pre-Roman block to the tessellated floor. He did not find anything, and was about to abandon his efforts when I noticed a trivial circumstance which made me shudder, even though it implied nothing more than I had already imagined. I told him of it, and we both looked at its almost imperceptible manifestation with the fixedness of fascinated discovery and acknowledgment. It was only this—that the flame of the lantern set down near the altar was slightly but certainly flickering from a draught of air which it had not before received, and which came indubitably from the crevice between floor and altar where Norrys was scraping away the lichens.

We spent the rest of the night in the brilliantly lighted study, nervously discussing what we should do next. The discovery that some vault deeper than the deepest known masonry of the Romans underlay this accursed pile—some vault unsuspected by the curious antiquarians of three centuries—would have been sufficient to excite us without any background of the sinister. As it was, the fascination became twofold; and we paused in doubt whether to abandon our search and quit the priory forever in superstitious caution, or to gratify our sense of adventure and brave whatever horrors might await us in the unknown depths. By morning we had compromised, and decided to go to London to gather a group of archaeologists and scientific men fit to cope with the mystery. It should be mentioned that before leaving the sub-cellar we had vainly tried to move the central altar which we now recognised as the gate to a new pit of nameless fear. What secret would open the gate, wiser men than we would have to find.

During many days in London Capt. Norrys and I presented our facts, conjectures, and legendary anecdotes to five eminent authorities, all men who could be trusted to respect any family disclosures which future explorations might develop. We found most of them little disposed to scoff, but instead intensely interested and sincerely sympathetic. It is hardly necessary to name them all, but I may say that they included Sir William Brinton, whose excavations in the Troad excited most of the world in their day. As we all took the train for Anchester I felt myself poised on the brink of frightful revelations, a sensation symbolised by the air of mourning among the many Americans at the unexpected death of the President on the other side of the world.[25]

On the evening of August 7th we reached Exham Priory, where the servants assured me that nothing unusual had occurred. The cats, even old Nigger-Man, had been perfectly placid; and not a trap in the house had been sprung. We were to begin exploring on the following day, awaiting which I assigned well-appointed rooms to all my guests. I myself retired in my own tower chamber, with Nigger-Man across my feet. Sleep came quickly, but hideous dreams assailed me. There was a vision of a Roman feast like that of Trimalchio,[26] with a horror in a covered platter. Then came that damnable, recurrent thing about the swineherd and his filthy drove in the twilit grotto. Yet when I awoke it was full daylight, with normal sounds in the house below. The rats, living or spectral, had not troubled me; and Nigger-Man was quietly asleep. On going down, I found that the same tranquillity had prevailed elsewhere; a condition which one of the assembled savants—a fellow named Thornton, devoted to the psychic—rather absurdly laid to the fact that I had now been shewn the thing which certain forces had wished to shew me.

All was now ready, and at 11 a.m. our entire group of seven men, bearing powerful electric searchlights and implements of excavation, went down to the sub-cellar and bolted the door behind us. Nigger-Man was with us, for the investigators found no

occasion to despise his excitability, and were indeed anxious that
he be present in case of obscure rodent manifestations. We noted
the Roman inscriptions and unknown altar designs only briefly,
for three of the savants had already seen them, and all knew their
characteristics. Prime attention was paid to the momentous central altar, and within an hour Sir William Brinton had caused it to
tilt backward, balanced by some unknown species of counter-
weight.

There now lay revealed such a horror as would have overwhelmed us had we not been prepared. Through a nearly square
opening in the tiled floor, sprawling on a flight of stone steps so
prodigiously worn that it was little more than an inclined plane
at the centre, was a ghastly array of human or semi-human
bones. Those which retained their collocation as skeletons
shewed attitudes of panic fear, and over all were the marks of rodent gnawing. The skulls denoted nothing short of utter idiocy,
cretinism, or primitive semi-apedom. Above the hellishly littered
steps arched a descending passage seemingly chiselled from the
solid rock, and conducting a current of air. This current was not
a sudden and noxious rush as from a closed vault, but a cool
breeze with something of freshness in it. We did not pause long,
but shiveringly began to clear a passage down the steps. It was
then that Sir William, examining the hewn walls, made the odd
observation that the passage, according to the direction of the
strokes, must have been chiselled *from beneath*.

I must be very deliberate now, and choose my words.

After ploughing down a few steps amidst the gnawed bones
we saw that there was light ahead; not any mystic phosphorescence, but a filtered daylight which could not come except from
unknown fissures in the cliff that overlooked the waste valley.
That such fissures had escaped notice from outside was hardly
remarkable, for not only is the valley wholly uninhabited, but
the cliff is so high and beetling that only an aëronaut could study
its face in detail. A few steps more, and our breaths were literally
snatched from us by what we saw; so literally that Thornton, the
psychic investigator, actually fainted in the arms of the dazed
man who stood behind him. Norrys, his plump face utterly
white and flabby, simply cried out inarticulately; whilst I think

that what I did was to gasp or hiss, and cover my eyes. The man behind me—the only one of the party older than I—croaked the hackneyed "My God!" in the most cracked voice I ever heard. Of seven cultivated men, only Sir William Brinton retained his composure; a thing more to his credit because he led the party and must have seen the sight first.

It was a twilit grotto of enormous height, stretching away farther than any eye could see; a subterraneous world of limitless mystery and horrible suggestion. There were buildings and other architectural remains—in one terrified glance I saw a weird pattern of tumuli, a savage circle of monoliths, a low-domed Roman ruin, a sprawling Saxon pile, and an early English edifice of wood—but all these were dwarfed by the ghoulish spectacle presented by the general surface of the ground. For yards about the steps extended an insane tangle of human bones, or bones at least as human as those on the steps. Like a foamy sea they stretched, some fallen apart, but others wholly or partly articulated as skeletons; these latter invariably in postures of daemoniac frenzy, either fighting off some menace or clutching other forms with cannibal intent.

When Dr. Trask, the anthropologist, stooped to classify the skulls, he found a degraded mixture which utterly baffled him. They were mostly lower than the Piltdown man[27] in the scale of evolution, but in every case definitely human. Many were of higher grade, and a very few were the skulls of supremely and sensitively developed types. All the bones were gnawed, mostly by rats, but somewhat by others of the half-human drove. Mixed with them were many tiny bones of rats—fallen members of the lethal army which closed the ancient epic.

I wonder that any man among us lived and kept his sanity through that hideous day of discovery. Not Hoffmann or Huysmans[28] could conceive a scene more wildly incredible, more frenetically repellent, or more Gothically grotesque than the twilit grotto through which we seven staggered; each stumbling on revelation after revelation, and trying to keep for the nonce from thinking of the events which must have taken place there three hundred years, or a thousand, or two thousand, or ten thousand years ago. It was the antechamber of hell, and poor Thornton fainted again when Trask told him that some of the skeleton things must have descended as quadrupeds through the last twenty or more generations.

Horror piled on horror as we began to interpret the architectural remains. The quadruped things—with their occasional recruits from the biped class—had been kept in stone pens, out of which they must have broken in their last delirium of hunger or rat-fear. There had been great herds of them, evidently fattened on the coarse vegetables whose remains could be found as a sort of poisonous ensilage at the bottom of huge stone bins older than Rome. I knew now why my ancestors had had such excessive gardens—would to heaven I could forget! The purpose of the herds I did not have to ask.

Sir William, standing with his searchlight in the Roman ruin, translated aloud the most shocking ritual I have ever known;[29] and told of the diet of the antediluvian cult which the priests of Cybele found and mingled with their own. Norrys, used as he was to the trenches, could not walk straight when he came out of the English building. It was a butcher shop and kitchen—he had expected that—but it was too much to see familiar English implements in such a place, and to read familiar English *graffiti* there, some as recent as 1610. I could not go in that building— that building whose daemon activities were stopped only by the dagger of my ancestor Walter de la Poer.

What I did venture to enter was the low Saxon building, whose oaken door had fallen, and there I found a terrible row of ten stone cells with rusty bars. Three had tenants, all skeletons of high grade, and on the bony forefinger of one I found a seal ring with my own coat-of-arms. Sir William found a vault with far older cells below the Roman chapel, but these cells were empty. Below them was a low crypt with cases of formally arranged bones, some of them bearing terrible parallel inscriptions carved in Latin, Greek, and the tongue of Phrygia. Meanwhile, Dr. Trask had opened one of the prehistoric tumuli, and brought to light skulls which were slighty more human than a gorilla's, and which bore indescribable ideographic carvings. Through all this horror my cat stalked unperturbed. Once I saw him monstrously perched atop a mountain of bones, and wondered at the secrets that might lie behind his yellow eyes.

Having grasped to some slight degree the frightful revelations of this twilit area—an area so hideously foreshadowed by my recurrent dream—we turned to that apparently boundless depth of midnight cavern where no ray of light from the cliff could penetrate. We shall never know what sightless Stygian worlds yawn beyond the little distance we went, for it was decided that such secrets are not good for mankind. But there was plenty to engross us close at hand, for we had not gone far before the searchlights shewed that accursed infinity of pits in which the rats had feasted, and whose sudden lack of replenishment had driven the ravenous rodent army first to turn on the living herds of starving things, and then to burst forth from the priory in that historic orgy of devastation which the peasants will never forget.

God! those carrion black pits of sawed, picked bones and opened skulls! Those nightmare chasms choked with the pithecanthropoid,[30] Celtic, Roman, and English bones of countless unhallowed centuries! Some of them were full, and none can say how deep they had once been. Others were still bottomless to our searchlights, and peopled by unnamable fancies. What, I thought, of the hapless rats that stumbled into such traps amidst the blackness of their quests in this grisly Tartarus?

Once my foot slipped near a horribly yawning brink, and I had a moment of ecstatic fear. I must have been musing a long time, for I could not see any of the party but the plump Capt. Norrys. Then there came a sound from that inky, boundless, farther distance that I thought I knew; and I saw my old black cat dart past me like a winged Egyptian god,[31] straight into the illimitable gulf of the unknown. But I was not far behind, for there was no doubt after another second. It was the eldritch scurrying of those fiend-born rats, always questing for new horrors, and determined to lead me on even unto those grinning caverns of earth's centre where Nyarlathotep, the mad faceless god, howls blindly to the piping of two amorphous idiot flute-players.[32]

My searchlight expired, but still I ran. I heard voices, and yowls, and echoes, but above all there gently rose that impious, insidious scurrying; gently rising, rising, as a stiff bloated corpse gently rises above an oily river that flows under endless onyx bridges to a black, putrid sea. Something bumped into me— something soft and plump. It must have been the rats; the viscous, gelatinous, ravenous army that feast on the dead and the living. . . . Why shouldn't rats eat a de la Poer as a de la Poer eats forbidden things? . . . The war ate my boy, damn them all . . . and the Yanks ate Carfax with flames and burnt Grandsire Delapore and the secret . . . No, no, I tell you, I am *not* that daemon swineherd in the twilit grotto! It was *not* Edward Norrys' fat face on that flabby, fungous thing! Who says I am a de la Poer? He lived, but my boy died! . . . Shall a Norrys hold the lands of a de la Poer? . . . It's voodoo, I tell you . . . that spotted snake . . . Curse you, Thornton, I'll teach you to faint at what my family do! . . . 'Sblood, thou stinkard, I'll learn ye how to gust . . . wolde ye swynke me thilke wys? . . . *Magna Mater! Magna Mater! . . . Atys . . . Dia ad aghaidh 's ad aodann . . . agus bas dunach ort! Dhonas 's dholas ort, agus leat-sa! . . . Ungl . . . ungl . . . rrrlh . . . chchch . . .*[33]

That is what they say I said when they found me in the blackness after three hours; found me crouching in the blackness over the plump, half-eaten body of Capt. Norrys, with my own cat leaping and tearing at my throat. Now they have blown up Exham Priory, taken my Nigger-Man away from me, and shut me into this barred room at Hanwell[34] with fearful whispers about my heredity and experiences. Thornton is in the next room, but they prevent me from talking to him. They are trying, too, to suppress most of the facts concerning the priory. When I speak of poor Norrys they accuse me of a hideous thing, but they must know that I did not do it. They must know it was the rats; the slithering, scurrying rats whose scampering will never let me sleep; the daemon rats that race behind the padding in this room and beckon me down to greater horrors than I have ever known; the rats they can never hear; the rats, the rats in the walls.

The Festival

"Efficiunt Daemones, ut quae non sunt, sic tamen
quasi sint, conspicienda hominibus exhibeant."
—*Lactantius.*[1]

I was far from home, and the spell of the eastern sea was upon
me. In the twilight I heard it pounding on the rocks, and I knew
it lay just over the hill where the twisting willows writhed
against the clearing sky and the first stars of evening. And because my fathers had called me to the old town beyond, I pushed
on through the shallow, new-fallen snow along the road that
soared lonely up to where Aldebaran[2] twinkled among the trees;
on toward the very ancient town I had never seen but often
dreamed of.

It was the Yuletide, that men call Christmas though they
know in their heads it is older than Bethlehem and Babylon,
older than Memphis and mankind.[3] It was the Yuletide, and I had
come at last to the ancient sea town where my people had dwelt
and kept festival in the elder time when festival was forbidden;
where also they had commanded their sons to keep festival once
every century, that the memory of primal secrets might not be
forgotten. Mine were an old people, and were old even when this
land was settled three hundred years before. And they were
strange, because they had come as dark furtive folk from opiate
southern gardens of orchids, and spoken another tongue before
they learnt the tongue of the blue-eyed fishers. And now they
were scattered, and shared only the rituals of mysteries that none
living could understand. I was the only one who came back that
night to the old fishing town as legend bade, for only the poor
and the lonely remember.

Then beyond the hill's crest I saw Kingsport[4] outspread frost-
ily in the gloaming; snowy Kingsport with its ancient vanes

and steeples, ridgepoles and chimney-pots, wharves and small bridges, willow-trees and graveyards; endless labyrinths of steep, narrow, crooked streets, and dizzy church-crowned central peak that time durst not touch; ceaseless mazes of colonial houses piled and scattered at all angles and levels like a child's disordered blocks; antiquity hovering on grey wings over winter-whitened gables and gambrel roofs;[5] fanlights and small-paned windows one by one gleaming out in the cold dusk to join Orion[6] and the archaic stars. And against the rotting wharves the sea pounded; the secretive, immemorial sea out of which the people had come in the elder time.

Beside the road at its crest a still higher summit rose, bleak and windswept, and I saw that it was a burying-ground where black gravestones stuck ghoulishly through the snow like the decayed fingernails of a gigantic corpse.[7] The printless road was very lonely, and sometimes I thought I heard a distant horrible creaking as of a gibbet in the wind. They had hanged four kinsmen of mine for witchcraft in 1692, but I did not know just where.

As the road wound down the seaward slope I listened for the merry sounds of a village at evening, but did not hear them. Then I thought of the season, and felt that these old Puritan folk might well have Christmas customs strange to me,[8] and full of silent hearthside prayer. So after that I did not listen for merriment or look for wayfarers, but kept on down past the hushed lighted farmhouses and shadowy stone walls to where the signs of ancient shops and sea-taverns creaked in the salt breeze, and the grotesque knockers of pillared doorways glistened along deserted, unpaved lanes in the light of little, curtained windows.

I had seen maps of the town, and knew where to find the home of my people. It was told that I should be known and welcomed, for village legend lives long; so I hastened through Back Street to Circle Court, and across the fresh snow on the one full flagstone pavement in the town, to where Green Lane leads off behind the Market house.[9] The old maps still held good, and I had no trouble; though at Arkham they must have lied when they said the trolleys ran to this place, since I saw not a wire overhead.[10] Snow would have hid the rails in any case. I was glad

I had chosen to walk, for the white village had seemed very beautiful from the hill; and now I was eager to knock at the door of
my people, the seventh house on the left in Green Lane, with an
ancient peaked roof and jutting second story, all built before
1650.[11]

There were lights inside the house when I came upon it, and I
saw from the diamond window-panes that it must have been
kept very close to its antique state. The upper part overhung the
narrow grass-grown street and nearly met the overhanging part
of the house opposite, so that I was almost in a tunnel, with the
low stone doorstep wholly free from snow. There was no sidewalk, but many houses had high doors reached by double flights
of steps with iron railings. It was an odd scene, and because I was
strange to New England I had never known its like before.
Though it pleased me, I would have relished it better if there had
been footprints in the snow, and people in the streets, and a few
windows without drawn curtains.

When I sounded the archaic iron knocker I was half afraid.
Some fear had been gathering in me, perhaps because of the
strangeness of my heritage, and the bleakness of the evening, and
the queerness of the silence in that aged town of curious customs. And when my knock was answered I was fully afraid, because I had not heard any footsteps before the door creaked
open. But I was not afraid long, for the gowned, slippered old
man in the doorway had a bland face that reassured me; and
though he made signs that he was dumb, he wrote a quaint and
ancient welcome with the stylus and wax tablet he carried.

He beckoned me into a low, candle-lit room with massive exposed rafters and dark, stiff, sparse furniture of the seventeenth
century. The past was vivid there, for not an attribute was missing.[12] There was a cavernous fireplace and a spinning-wheel at
which a bent old woman in loose wrapper and deep poke-bonnet
sat back toward me, silently spinning despite the festive season.
An indefinite dampness seemed upon the place, and I marvelled
that no fire should be blazing. The high-backed settle faced the
row of curtained windows at the left, and seemed to be occupied,
though I was not sure. I did not like everything about what I saw,
and felt again the fear I had had. This fear grew stronger from

what had before lessened it, for the more I looked at the old man's bland face the more its very blandness terrified me. The eyes never moved, and the skin was too like wax. Finally I was sure it was not a face at all, but a fiendishly cunning mask.[13] But the flabby hands, curiously gloved, wrote genially on the tablet and told me I must wait a while before I could be led to the place of festival.

Pointing to a chair, table, and pile of books, the old man now left the room; and when I sat down to read I saw that the books were hoary and mouldy, and that they included old Morryster's wild *Marvells of Science*,[14] the terrible *Saducismus Triumphatus* of Joseph Glanvill, published in 1681,[15] the shocking *Daemonolatreia* of Remigius, printed in 1595 at Lyons,[16] and worst of all, the unmentionable *Necronomicon* of the mad Arab Abdul Alhazred,[17] in Olaus Wormius' forbidden Latin translation;[18] a book which I had never seen, but of which I had heard monstrous things whispered. No one spoke to me, but I could hear the creaking of signs in the wind outside, and the whir of the wheel as the bonneted old woman continued her silent spinning, spinning. I thought the room and the books and the people very morbid and disquieting, but because an old tradition of my fathers had summoned me to strange feastings, I resolved to expect queer things. So I tried to read, and soon became tremblingly absorbed by something I found in that accursed *Necronomicon*; a thought and a legend too hideous for sanity or consciousness. But I disliked it when I fancied I heard the closing of one of the windows that the settle faced, as if it had been stealthily opened. It had seemed to follow a whirring that was not of the old woman's spinning-wheel. This was not much, though, for the old woman was spinning very hard, and the aged clock had been striking. After that I lost the feeling that there were persons on the settle, and was reading intently and shudderingly when the old man came back booted and dressed in a loose antique costume, and sat down on that very bench, so that I could not see him. It was certainly nervous waiting, and the blasphemous book in my hands made it doubly so. When eleven struck, however, the old man stood up, glided to a massive carved chest in a corner, and got two hooded cloaks; one of which he donned, and the other of which he draped round the old woman, who was ceasing her monotonous spinning. Then they both started for the outer door; the woman lamely creeping, and the old man, after picking up the very book I had been reading, beckoning me as he drew his hood over that unmoving face or mask.

We went out into the moonless and tortuous network of that incredibly ancient town; went out as the lights in the curtained windows disappeared one by one, and the Dog Star[19] leered at the throng of cowled, cloaked figures that poured silently from every doorway and formed monstrous processions up this street and that, past the creaking signs and antediluvian gables, the thatched roofs and diamond-paned windows; threading precipitous lanes where decaying houses overlapped and crumbled together, gliding across open courts and churchyards where the bobbing lanthorns made eldritch drunken constellations.

Amid these hushed throngs I followed my voiceless guides; jostled by elbows that seemed preternaturally soft, and pressed by chests and stomachs that seemed abnormally pulpy; but seeing never a face and hearing never a word. Up, up, up the eerie columns slithered, and I saw that all the travellers were converging as they flowed near a sort of focus of crazy alleys at the top of a high hill in the centre of the town, where perched a great white church.[20] I had seen it from the road's crest when I looked at Kingsport in the new dusk, and it had made me shiver because Aldebaran had seemed to balance itself a moment on the ghostly spire.

There was an open space around the church; partly a churchyard with spectral shafts, and partly a half-paved square swept nearly bare of snow by the wind, and lined with unwholesomely archaic houses having peaked roofs and overhanging gables. Death-fires danced over the tombs, revealing gruesome vistas, though queerly failing to cast any shadows. Past the churchyard, where there were no houses, I could see over the hill's summit and watch the glimmer of stars on the harbour, though the town was invisible in the dark. Only once in a while a lanthorn bobbed horribly through serpentine alleys on its way to overtake the throng that was now slipping speechlessly into the church. I waited till the crowd had oozed into the black doorway, and till all the stragglers had followed. The old man was pulling at my sleeve, but I was determined to be the last. Then I finally went, the sinister man and the old spinning woman before me. Crossing the threshold into that swarming temple of unknown darkness, I turned once to look at the outside world as the churchyard phosphorescence cast a sickly glow on the hill-top pavement. And as I did so I shuddered. For though the wind had not left much snow, a few patches did remain on the path near the door; and in that fleeting backward look it seemed to my troubled eyes that they bore no mark of passing feet, not even mine.

The church was scarce lighted by all the lanthorns that had entered it, for most of the throng had already vanished. They had streamed up the aisle between the high white pews to the trapdoor of the vaults which yawned loathsomely open just before the pulpit, and were now squirming noiselessly in. I followed dumbly down the footworn steps and into the dank, suffocating crypt. The tail of that sinuous line of night-marchers seemed very horrible, and as I saw them wriggling into a venerable tomb they seemed more horrible still. Then I noticed that the tomb's floor had an aperture down which the throng was sliding, and in a moment we were all descending an ominous staircase of rough-hewn stone; a narrow spiral staircase damp and peculiarly odorous, that wound endlessly down into the bowels of the hill past monotonous walls of dripping stone blocks and crumbling mortar. It was a silent, shocking descent, and I observed after a horrible interval that the walls and steps were changing in nature, as if chiselled out of the solid rock. What mainly troubled me was that the myriad footfalls made no sound and set up no echoes. After more aeons of descent I saw some side passages or burrows leading from unknown recesses of blackness to this shaft of nighted mystery. Soon they became excessively numerous, like impious catacombs of nameless menace; and their pungent odour of decay grew quite unbearable. I knew we must have passed down through the mountain and beneath the earth of Kingsport itself, and I shivered that a town should be so aged and maggoty with subterraneous evil.

Then I saw the lurid shimmering of pale light, and heard the insidious lapping of sunless waters. Again I shivered, for I did not like the things the night had brought, and wished bitterly that no forefather had summoned me to this primal rite. As the steps and the passage grew broader, I heard another sound, the thin, whining mockery of a feeble flute; and suddenly there spread out before me the boundless vista of an inner world—a vast fungous shore litten by a belching column of sick greenish flame and washed by a wide oily river that flowed from abysses frightful and unsuspected to join the blackest gulfs of immemorial ocean.

Fainting and gasping, I looked at that unhallowed Erebus of titan toadstools, leprous fire, and slimy water, and saw the cloaked throngs forming a semicircle around the blazing pillar. It was the Yule-rite, older than man and fated to survive him; the primal rite of the solstice and of spring's promise beyond the snows; the rite of fire and evergreen, light and music. And in the Stygian grotto I saw them do the rite, and adore the sick pillar of flame, and throw into the water handfuls gouged out of the viscous vegetation which glittered green in the chlorotic glare. I saw this, and I saw something amorphously squatted far away from the light, piping noisomely on a flute; and as the thing piped I thought I heard noxious muffled flutterings in the foetid darkness where I could not see.[21] But what frightened me most was that flaming column; spouting volcanically from depths profound and inconceivable, casting no shadows as healthy flame should, and coating the nitrous stone above with a nasty, venomous verdigris. For in all that seething combustion no warmth lay, but only the clamminess of death and corruption.

The man who had brought me now squirmed to a point directly beside the hideous flame, and made stiff ceremonial motions to the semicircle he faced. At certain stages of the ritual they did grovelling obeisance, especially when he held above his head that abhorrent *Necronomicon* he had taken with him; and I shared all the obeisances because I had been summoned to this festival by the writings of my forefathers. Then the old man made a signal to the half-seen flute-player in the darkness, which player thereupon changed its feeble drone to a scarce louder drone in another key; precipitating as it did so a horror unthinkable and unexpected. At this horror I sank nearly to the lichened earth, transfixed with a dread not of this nor any world, but only of the mad spaces between the stars.

Out of the unimaginable blackness beyond the gangrenous glare of that cold flame, out of the Tartarean leagues through which that oily river rolled uncanny, unheard, and unsuspected, there flopped rhythmically a horde of tame, trained, hybrid winged things that no sound eye could ever wholly grasp, or sound brain ever wholly remember. They were not altogether crows, nor moles, nor buzzards, nor ants, nor vampire bats, nor decomposed human beings; but something I cannot and must not recall.[22] They flopped limply along, half with their webbed feet and half with their membraneous wings; and as they reached the throng of celebrants the cowled figures seized and mounted them, and rode off one by one along the reaches of that unlighted river, into pits and galleries of panic where poison springs feed frightful and undiscoverable cataracts.

The old spinning woman had gone with the throng, and the old man remained only because I had refused when he motioned me to seize an animal and ride like the rest. I saw when I staggered to my feet that the amorphous flute-player had rolled out of sight, but that two of the beasts were patiently standing by. As I hung back, the old man produced his stylus and tablet and wrote that he was the true deputy of my fathers who had founded the Yule worship in this ancient place; that it had been decreed I should come back, and that the most secret mysteries were yet to be performed. He wrote this in a very ancient hand, and when I still hesitated he pulled from his loose robe a seal ring and a watch, both with my family arms, to prove that he was what he said. But it was a hideous proof, because I knew from old papers that that watch had been buried with my great-great-great-great-grandfather in 1698.

Presently the old man drew back his hood and pointed to the family resemblance in his face, but I only shuddered, because I was sure that the face was merely a devilish waxen mask. The flopping animals were now scratching restlessly at the lichens, and I saw that the old man was nearly as restless himself. When one of the things began to waddle and edge away, he turned quickly to stop it; so that the suddenness of his motion dislodged the waxen mask from what should have been his head. And then, because that nightmare's position barred me from the stone staircase down which we had come, I flung myself into the oily underground river that bubbled somewhere to the caves of the sea; flung myself into that putrescent juice of earth's inner horrors before the madness of my screams could bring down upon me all the charnel legions these pest-gulfs might conceal.

At the hospital[23] they told me I had been found half frozen in Kingsport Harbour at dawn, clinging to the drifting spar that accident sent to save me. They told me I had taken the wrong fork of the hill road the night before,[24] and fallen over the cliffs at Orange Point;[25] a thing they deduced from prints found in the snow. There was nothing I could say, because everything was wrong. Everything was wrong, with the broad window shewing a sea of roofs in which only about one in five was ancient, and the sound of trolleys and motors in the streets below. They insisted that this was Kingsport, and I could not deny it. When I went delirious at hearing that the hospital stood near the old churchyard on Central Hill, they sent me to St. Mary's Hospital in Arkham, where I could have better care. I liked it there, for the doctors were broad-minded, and even lent me their influence in obtaining the carefully sheltered copy of Alhazred's objectionable *Necronomicon* from the library of Miskatonic University. They said something about a "psychosis", and agreed I had better get any harassing obsessions off my mind.

So I read again that hideous chapter, and shuddered doubly because it was indeed not new to me. I had seen it before, let footprints tell what they might; and where it was I had seen it were best forgotten. There was no one—in waking hours—who could remind me of it; but my dreams are filled with terror, because of phrases I dare not quote. I dare quote only one paragraph, put into such English as I can make from the awkward Low Latin.

"The nethermost caverns," wrote the mad Arab, "are not for the fathoming of eyes that see; for their marvels are strange and terrific. Cursed the ground where dead thoughts live new and oddly bodied, and evil the mind that is held by no head. Wisely did Ibn Schacabao[26] say, that happy is the tomb where no wizard hath lain, and happy the town at night whose wizards are all ashes. For it is of old rumour that the soul of the devil-bought hastes not from his charnel clay, but fats and instructs *the very worm that gnaws;* till out of corruption horrid life springs, and the dull scavengers of earth wax crafty to vex it and swell monstrous to plague it. Great holes secretly are digged where earth's pores ought to suffice, and things have learnt to walk that ought to crawl."

He

I saw him on a sleepless night when I was walking desperately to save my soul and my vision. My coming to New York had been a mistake; for whereas I had looked for poignant wonder and inspiration in the teeming labyrinths of ancient streets that twist endlessly from forgotten courts and squares and waterfronts to courts and squares and waterfronts equally forgotten, and in the Cyclopean[1] modern towers and pinnacles that rise blackly Babylonian under waning moons, I had found instead only a sense of horror and oppression which threatened to master, paralyse, and annihilate me.

The disillusion had been gradual. Coming for the first time upon the town, I had seen it in the sunset from a bridge, majestic above its waters, its incredible peaks and pyramids rising flower-like and delicate from pools of violet mist to play with the flaming golden clouds and the first stars of evening.[2] Then it had lighted up window by window above the shimmering tides where lanterns nodded and glided and deep horns bayed weird harmonies, and itself become a starry firmament of dream, redolent of faery music, and one with the marvels of Carcassonne and Samarcand and El Dorado[3] and all glorious and half-fabulous cities. Shortly afterward I was taken through those antique ways so dear to my fancy—narrow, curving alleys and passages where rows of red Georgian brick blinked with small-paned dormers above pillared doorways that had looked on gilded sedans and panelled coaches—and in the first flush of realisation of these long-wished things I thought I had indeed achieved such treasures as would make me in time a poet.

But success and happiness were not to be. Garish daylight shewed only squalor and alienage and the noxious elephantiasis of climbing, spreading stone where the moon had hinted of loveliness and elder magic; and the throngs of people that seethed through the flume-like streets were squat, swarthy strangers with hardened faces and narrow eyes, shrewd strangers without dreams and without kinship to the scenes about them, who could never mean aught to a blue-eyed man of the old folk, with the love of fair green lanes and white New England village steeples in his heart.

So instead of the poems I had hoped for, there came only a shuddering blankness and ineffable loneliness; and I saw at last a fearful truth which no one had ever dared to breathe before—the unwhisperable secret of secrets—the fact that this city of stone and stridor is not a sentient perpetuation of Old New York as London is of Old London and Paris of Old Paris, but that it is in fact quite dead, its sprawling body imperfectly embalmed and infested with queer animate things which have nothing to do with it as it was in life. Upon making this discovery I ceased to sleep comfortably; though something of resigned tranquillity came back as I gradually formed the habit of keeping off the streets by day and venturing abroad only at night, when darkness calls forth what little of the past still hovers wraith-like about, and old white doorways remember the stalwart forms that once passed through them. With this mode of relief I even wrote a few poems, and still refrained from going home to my people lest I seem to crawl back ignobly in defeat.[4]

Then, on a sleepless night's walk, I met the man. It was in a grotesque hidden courtyard of the Greenwich section, for there in my ignorance I had settled,[5] having heard of the place as the natural home of poets and artists. The archaic lanes and houses and unexpected bits of square and court[6] had indeed delighted me, and when I found the poets and artists to be loud-voiced pretenders whose quaintness is tinsel and whose lives are a denial of all that pure beauty which is poetry and art, I stayed on for love of these venerable things. I fancied them as they were in their prime, when Greenwich was a placid village not yet engulfed by the town; and in the hours before dawn, when all the revellers had slunk away, I used to wander alone among their cryptical windings and brood upon the curious arcana which generations must have deposited there. This kept my soul alive, and gave me a few of those dreams and visions for which the poet far within me cried out.

The man came upon me at about two one cloudy August morning, as I was threading a series of detached courtyards; now accessible only through the unlighted hallways of intervening buildings, but once forming parts of a continuous network of picturesque alleys. I had heard of them by vague rumour, and realised that they could not be upon any map of today; but the fact that they were forgotten only endeared them to me, so that I had sought them with twice my usual eagerness. Now that I had found them, my eagerness was again redoubled; for something in their arrangement dimly hinted that they might be only a few of many such, with dark, dumb counterparts wedged obscurely betwixt high blank walls and deserted rear tenements, or lurking lamplessly behind archways, unbetrayed by hordes of the foreign-speaking or guarded by furtive and uncommunicative artists whose practices do not invite publicity or the light of day.

He spoke to me without invitation, noting my mood and glances as I studied certain knockered doorways above iron-railed steps, the pallid glow of traceried transoms feebly lighting my face. His own face was in shadow, and he wore a wide-brimmed hat which somehow blended perfectly with the out-of-date cloak he affected; but I was subtly disquieted even before he addressed me. His form was very slight, thin almost to cadaverousness; and his voice proved phenomenally soft and hollow, through not particularly deep. He had, he said, noticed me several times at my wanderings; and inferred that I resembled him in loving the vestiges of former years. Would I not like the guidance of one long practiced in these explorations, and possessed of local information profoundly deeper than any which an obvious newcomer could possibly have gained?

As he spoke, I caught a glimpse of his face in the yellow beam from a solitary attic window. It was a noble, even a handsome, elderly countenance; and bore the marks of a lineage and refinement unusual for the age and place. Yet some quality about it disturbed me almost as much as its features pleased me—perhaps it was too white, or too expressionless, or too much out of keeping with the locality, to make me feel easy or comfortable. Nevertheless I followed him; for in those dreary days my quest for antique beauty and mystery was all that I had to keep my soul alive, and I reckoned it a rare favour of Fate to fall in with one whose kindred seekings seemed to have penetrated so much farther than mine.

Something in the night constrained the cloaked man to silence, and for a long hour he led me forward without needless words; making only the briefest of comments concerning ancient names and dates and changes, and directing my progress very largely by gestures as we squeezed through interstices, tiptoed through corridors, clambered over brick walls, and once crawled on hands and knees through a low, arched passage of stone whose immense length and tortuous twistings effaced at last every hint of geographical location I had managed to preserve. The things we saw were very old and marvellous, or at least they seemed so in the few straggling rays of light by which I viewed them, and I shall never forget the tottering Ionic columns and fluted pilasters and urn-headed iron fence-posts and flaring-lintelled windows and decorative fanlights that appeared to grow quainter and stranger the deeper we advanced into this inexhaustible maze of unknown antiquity.

We met no person, and as time passed the lighted windows became fewer and fewer. The street-lights we first encountered had been of oil, and of the ancient lozenge pattern. Later I noticed some with candles; and at last, after traversing a horrible unlighted court where my guide had to lead with his gloved hand through total blackness to a narrow wooden gate in a high wall, we came upon a fragment of alley lit only by lanterns in front of every seventh house—unbelievably colonial tin lanterns with conical tops and holes punched in the sides. This alley led steeply uphill—more steeply than I thought possible in this part of New York—and the upper end was blocked squarely by the ivy-clad wall of a private estate, beyond which I could see a pale cupola, and the tops of trees waving against a vague lightness in the sky. In this wall was a small, low-arched gate of nail-studded black oak, which the man proceeded to unlock with a ponderous key. Leading me within, he steered a course in utter blackness over what seemed to be a gravel path, and finally up a flight of stone steps to the door of the house, which he unlocked and opened for me.

We entered, and as we did so I grew faint from a reek of infinite mustiness which welled out to meet us, and which must have been the fruit of unwholesome centuries of decay. My host appeared not to notice this, and in courtesy I kept silent as he piloted me up a curving stairway, across a hall, and into a room whose door I heard him lock behind us. Then I saw him pull the curtains of the three small-paned windows that barely shewed themselves against the lightening sky; after which he crossed to the mantel, struck flint and steel, lighted two candles of a candelabrum of twelve sconces, and made a gesture enjoining soft-toned speech.

In this feeble radiance I saw that we were in a spacious, well-furnished, and panelled library dating from the first quarter of the eighteenth century, with splendid doorway pediments, a delightful Doric cornice, and a magnificently carved overmantel with scroll-and-urn top. Above the crowded bookshelves at intervals along the walls were well-wrought family portraits; all tarnished to an enigmatical dimness, and bearing an unmistakable likeness to the man who now motioned me to a chair beside the graceful Chippendale table.[7] Before seating himself across the table from me, my host paused for a moment as if in embarrassment; then, tardily removing his gloves, wide-brimmed hat, and cloak, stood theatrically revealed in full mid-Georgian costume from queued hair and neck ruffles to knee-breeches, silk hose, and the buckled shoes I had not previously noticed.[8] Now slowly sinking into a lyre-back chair, he commenced to eye me intently.

Without his hat he took on an aspect of extreme age which was scarcely visible before, and I wondered if this unperceived mark of singular longevity were not one of the sources of my original disquiet. When he spoke at length, his soft, hollow, and carefully muffled voice not infrequently quavered; and now and then I had great difficulty in following him as I listened with a thrill of amazement and half-disavowed alarm which grew each instant.

"You behold, Sir," my host began, "a man of very eccentrical habits, for whose costume no apology need be offered to one with your wit and inclinations. Reflecting upon better times, I have not scrupled to ascertain their ways and adopt their dress

...ers; an indulgence which offends none if practiced ...ostentation. It hath been my good-fortune to retain the ...at of my ancestors, swallowed though it was by two towns, first Greenwich, which built up hither after 1800, then New-York, which joined on near 1830. There were many reasons for the close keeping of this place in my family, and I have not been remiss in discharging such obligations. The squire who succeeded to it in 1768 studied sartain arts and made sartain discoveries, all connected with influences residing in this particular plot of ground, and eminently desarving of the strongest guarding. Some curious effects of these arts and discoveries I now purpose to shew you, under the strictest secrecy; and I believe I may rely on my judgment of men enough to have no distrust of either your interest or your fidelity."

He paused, but I could only nod my head. I have said that I was alarmed, yet to my soul nothing was more deadly than the material daylight world of New York, and whether this man were a harmless eccentric or a wielder of dangerous arts I had no choice save to follow him and slake my sense of wonder on whatever he might have to offer. So I listened.

"To—my ancestor—" he softly continued, "there appeared to reside some very remarkable qualities in the will of mankind; qualities having a little-suspected dominance not only over the acts of one's self and of others, but over every variety of force and substance in Nature, and over many elements and dimensions deemed more univarsal than Nature herself.[9] May I say that he flouted the sanctity of things as great as space and time, and that he put to strange uses the rites of sartain half-breed red Indians once encamped upon this hill? These Indians shewed choler when the place was built, and were plaguy pestilent in asking to visit the grounds at the full of the moon. For years they stole over the wall each month when they could, and by stealth performed sartain acts. Then, in '68, the new squire catched them at their doings, and stood still at what he saw. Thereafter he bargained with them and exchanged the free access of his grounds for the exact inwardness of what they did; larning that their grandfathers got part of their custom from red ancestors and part from an old Dutchman in the time of the States-General.[10] And pox on him, I'm afeared the squire must have sarved them monstrous bad rum—whether or not by intent—for a week after he larnt the secret he was the only man living that knew it. You, Sir, are the first outsider to be told there is a secret, and split me if I'd have risked tampering that much with—the powers—had ye not been so hot after bygone things."

I shuddered as the man grew colloquial—and with familiar speech of another day. He went on.

"But you must know, Sir, that what—the squire—got from those mongrel salvages[11] was but a small part of the larning he came to have. He had not been at Oxford for nothing, nor talked to no account with an ancient chymist[12] and astrologer in Paris. He was, in fine, made sensible that all the world is but the smoke of our intellects; past the bidding of the vulgar, but by the wise to be puffed out and drawn in like any cloud of prime Virginia tobacco.[13] What we want, we may make about us; and what we don't want, we may sweep away. I won't say that all this is wholly true in body, but 'tis sufficient true to furnish a very pretty spectacle now and then. You, I conceive, would be tickled by a better sight of sartain other years than your fancy affords you; so be pleased to hold back any fright at what I design to shew. Come to the window and be quiet."[14]

My host now took my hand to draw me to one of the two windows on the long side of the malodorous room, and at the first touch of his ungloved fingers I turned cold. His flesh, though dry and firm, was the quality of ice; and I almost shrank away from his pulling. But again I thought of the emptiness and horror of reality, and boldly prepared to follow whithersoever I might be led. Once at the window, the man drew apart the yellow silk curtains and directed my stare into the blackness outside. For a moment I saw nothing save a myriad of tiny dancing lights, far, far before me. Then, as if in response to an insidious motion of my host's hand, a flash of heat-lightning played over the scene, and I looked out upon a sea of luxuriant foliage—foliage unpolluted, and not the sea of roofs to be expected by any normal mind. On my right the Hudson glittered wickedly, and

in the distance ahead I saw the unhealthy shimmer of a vast salt
marsh constellated with nervous fireflies. The flash died, and an
evil smile illumined the waxy face of the aged necromancer.

"That was before my time—before the new squire's time.
Pray let us try again."

I was faint, even fainter than the hateful modernity of that accursed city had made me.

"Good God!" I whispered, "can you do that for *any time?*"
And as he nodded, and bared the black stumps of what had once
been yellow fangs, I clutched at the curtains to prevent myself
from falling. But he steadied me with that terrible, ice-cold claw,
and once more made his insidious gesture.

Again the lightning flashed—but this time upon a scene not
wholly strange. It was Greenwich, the Greenwich that used to
be, with here and there a roof or row of houses as we see it now,
yet with lovely green lanes and fields and bits of grassy common.
The marsh still glittered beyond, but in the farther distance I saw
the steeples of what was then all of New York; Trinity and St.
Paul's and the Brick Church dominating their sisters,[15] and a faint
haze of wood smoke hovering over the whole. I breathed hard,
but not so much from the sight itself as from the possibilities my
imagination terrifiedly conjured up.

"Can you—dare you—go *far?*" I spoke with awe, and I think
he shared it for a second, but the evil grin returned.

"*Far?* What I have seen would blast ye to a mad statue
of stone! Back, back—forward, *forward*—look, ye puling
lack-wit!"

And as he snarled the phrase under his breath he gestured
anew; bringing to the sky a flash more blinding than either which
had come before. For full three seconds I could glimpse that pan-
daemoniac sight, and in those seconds I saw a vista which will
ever afterward torment me in dreams. I saw the heavens verminous with strange flying things, and beneath them a hellish
black city of giant stone terraces with impious pyramids flung
savagely to the moon, and devil-lights burning from unnumbered windows. And swarming loathsomely on aërial galleries I
saw the yellow, squint-eyed people of that city,[16] robed horribly
in orange and red, and dancing insanely to the pounding of

fevered kettle-drums, and the clatter of obscene crotala, and the maniacal moaning of muted horns whose ceaseless dirges rose and fell undulantly like the waves of an unhallowed ocean of bitumen.

I saw this vista, I say, and heard as with the mind's ear the blasphemous domdaniel of cacophony which companioned it. It was the shrieking fulfilment of all the horror which that corpse-city had ever stirred in my soul, and forgetting every injunction to silence I screamed and screamed and screamed as my nerves gave way and the walls quivered about me.

Then, as the flash subsided, I saw that my host was trembling too; a look of shocking fear half blotting from his face the serpent distortion of rage which my screams had excited. He tottered, clutched at the curtains as I had done before, and wriggled his head wildly, like a hunted animal. God knows he had cause, for as the echoes of my screaming died away there came another sound so hellishly suggestive that only numbed emotion kept me sane and conscious. It was the steady, stealthy creaking of the stairs beyond the locked door, as with the ascent of a barefoot or skin-shod horde; and at the last the cautious, purposeful rattling of the brass latch that glowed in the feeble candlelight. The old man clawed and spat at me through the mouldy air, and barked things in his throat as he swayed with the yellow curtain he clutched.

"The full moon—damn ye—ye . . . ye yelping dog—ye called 'em, and they've come for me! Moccasined feet—dead men—Gad sink ye, ye red devils, but I poisoned no rum o' yours—han't I kept your pox-rotted magic safe?—ye swilled yourselves sick, curse ye, and ye must needs blame the squire—let go, you! Unhand that latch—I've naught for ye here—"

At this point three slow and very deliberate raps shook the panels of the door, and a white foam gathered at the mouth of the frantic magician. His fright, turning to steely despair, left room for a resurgence of his rage against me; and he staggered a step toward the table on whose edge I was steadying myself. The curtains, still clutched in his right hand as his left clawed out at me, grew taut and finally crashed down from their lofty fastenings; admitting to the room a flood of that full moonlight which the brightening of the sky had presaged. In those greenish beams the candles paled, and a new semblance of decay spread over the musk-reeking room with its wormy panelling, sagging floor, battered mantel, rickety furniture, and ragged draperies. It spread over the old man, too, whether from the same source or because of his fear and vehemence, and I saw him shrivel and blacken as he lurched near and strove to rend me with vulturine talons. Only his eyes stayed whole, and they glared with a propulsive, dilated incandescence which grew as the face around them charred and dwindled.

The rapping was now repeated with greater insistence, and this time bore a hint of metal. The black thing facing me had become only a head with eyes, impotently trying to wriggle across the sinking floor in my direction, and occasionally emitting feeble little spits of immortal malice. Now swift and splintering blows assailed the sickly panels, and I saw the gleam of a tomahawk as it cleft the rending wood. I did not move, for I could not; but watched dazedly as the door fell in pieces to admit a colossal, shapeless influx of inky substance starred with shining, malevolent eyes.[17] It poured thickly, like a flood of oil bursting a rotten bulkhead, overturned a chair as it spread, and finally flowed under the table and across the room to where the blackened head with the eyes still glared at me. Around that head it closed, totally swallowing it up, and in another moment it had begun to recede; bearing away its invisible burden without touching me, and flowing again out of that black doorway and down the unseen stairs, which creaked as before, though in reverse order.

Then the floor gave way at last, and I slid gaspingly down into the nighted chamber below, choking with cobwebs and half swooning with terror. The green moon, shining through broken windows, shewed me the hall door half open; and as I rose from the plaster-strown floor and twisted myself free from the sagged ceilings, I saw sweep past it an awful torrent of blackness, with scores of baleful eyes glowing in it. It was seeking the door to the cellar, and when it found it, it vanished therein. I now felt the floor of this lower room giving as that of the upper chamber had done, and once a crashing above had been followed by the fall past the west window of something which must have been the cupola. Now liberated for an instant from the wreckage, I rushed through the hall to the front door; and finding myself unable to open it, seized a chair and broke a window, climbing frenziedly out upon the unkempt lawn where moonlight danced over yard-high grass and weeds. The wall was high, and all the gates were locked; but moving a pile of boxes in a corner I managed to gain the top and cling to the great stone urn set there.

About me in my exhaustion I could see only strange walls and windows and old gambrel roofs. The steep street of my approach was nowhere visible, and the little I did see succumbed rapidly to a mist that rolled in from the river despite the glaring moonlight. Suddenly the urn to which I clung began to tremble, as if sharing my own lethal dizziness; and in another instant my body was plunging downward to I knew not what fate.

The man who found me said that I must have crawled a long way despite my broken bones, for a trail of blood stretched off as far as he dared look. The gathering rain soon effaced this link with the scene of my ordeal, and reports could state no more than that I had appeared from a place unknown, at the entrance of a little black court off Perry Street.

I never sought to return to those tenebrous labyrinths, nor would I direct any sane man thither if I could. Of who or what that ancient creature was, I have no idea; but I repeat that the city is dead and full of unsuspected horrors. Whither *he* has gone, I do not know; but I have gone home to the pure New England lanes up which fragrant sea-winds sweep at evening.[18]

Cool Air

You ask me to explain why I am afraid of a draught of cool air; why I shiver more than others upon entering a cold room, and seem nauseated and repelled when the chill of evening creeps through the heat of a mild autumn day. There are those who say I respond to cold as others do to a bad odour, and I am the last to deny the impression. What I will do is to relate the most horrible circumstance I ever encountered, and leave it to you to judge whether or not this forms a suitable explanation of my peculiarity.

It is a mistake to fancy that horror is associated inextricably with darkness, silence, and solitude. I found it in the glare of mid-afternoon, in the clangour of a metropolis, and in the teeming midst of a shabby and commonplace rooming-house with a prosaic landlady and two stalwart men by my side. In the spring of 1923 I had secured some dreary and unprofitable magazine work in the city of New York;[1] and being unable to pay any substantial rent, began drifting from one cheap boarding establishment to another in search of a room which might combine the qualities of decent cleanliness, endurable furnishings, and very reasonable price.[2] It soon developed that I had only a choice between different evils, but after a time I came upon a house in West Fourteenth Street which disgusted me much less than the others I had sampled.

The place was a four-story mansion of brownstone, dating apparently from the late forties, and fitted with woodwork and marble whose stained and sullied splendour argued a descent from high levels of tasteful opulence. In the rooms, large and lofty, and decorated with impossible paper and ridiculously ornate stucco cornices, there lingered a depressing mustiness and hint of obscure cookery; but the floors were clean, the linen tolerably regular, and the hot water not too often cold or turned off, so that I came to regard it as at least a bearable place to hibernate till one might really live again. The landlady, a slatternly, almost bearded Spanish woman named Herrero,[3] did not annoy me with gossip or with criticisms of the late-burning electric light in my third-floor front hall room; and my fellow-lodgers were as quiet and uncommunicative as one might desire, being mostly Spaniard a little above the coarsest and crudest grade.[4] Only the din of street cars in the thoroughfare below proved a serious annoyance.

I had been there about three weeks when the first odd incident occurred. One evening at about eight I heard a spattering on the floor and became suddenly aware that I had been smelling the pungent odour of ammonia for some time. Looking about, I saw that the ceiling was wet and dripping; the soaking apparently proceeding from a corner on the side toward the street. Anxious to stop the matter at its source, I hastened to the basement to tell the landlady; and was assured by her that the trouble would quickly be set right.

"Doctair Muñoz," she cried as she rushed upstairs ahead of me, "he have speel hees chemicals. He ees too seeck for doctair heemself—seecker and seecker all the time—but he weel not have no othair for help. He ees vairy queer in hees seeckness—all day he take funnee-smelling baths, and he cannot get excite or warm. All hees own housework he do—hees leetle room are full of bottles and machines, and he do not work as doctair. But he was great once—my fathair in Barcelona have hear of heem—and only joost now he feex a arm of the plumber that get hurt of sudden. He nevair go out, only on roof, and my boy Esteban, he breeng heem hees food and laundry and mediceens and chemicals. My Gawd, the sal-ammoniac that man use for keep heem cool!"

Mrs. Herrero disappeared up the staircase to the fourth floor, and I returned to my room. The ammonia ceased to drip, and as I cleaned up what had spilled and opened the window for air, I heard the landlady's heavy footsteps above me. Dr. Muñoz I had never heard, save for certain sounds as of some gasoline-driven mechanism; since his step was soft and gentle. I wondered for a moment what the strange affliction of this man might be, and whether his obstinate refusal of outside aid were not the result of a rather baseless eccentricity. There is, I reflected tritely, an infinite deal of pathos in the state of an eminent person who has come down in the world.

I might never have known Dr. Muñoz had it not been for the heart attack that suddenly seized me one forenoon as I sat writing in my room. Physicians had told me of the danger of those spells, and I knew there was no time to be lost; so remembering what the landlady had said about the invalid's help of the injured workman, I dragged myself upstairs and knocked feebly at the door above mine. My knock was answered in good English by a curious voice some distance to the right, asking my name and business; and these things being stated, there came an opening of the door next to the one I had sought.

A rush of cool air greeted me; and though the day was one of the hottest of late June, I shivered as I crossed the threshold into a large apartment whose rich and tasteful decoration surprised me in this nest of squalor and seediness. A folding couch now filled its diurnal role of sofa,[5] and the mahogany furniture, sumptuous hangings, old paintings, and mellow bookshelves all bespoke a gentleman's study rather than a boarding-house bedroom. I now saw that the hall room above mine—the "leetle room" of bottles and machines which Mrs. Herrero had mentioned—was merely the laboratory of the doctor; and that his main living quarters lay in the spacious adjoining room whose convenient alcoves and large contiguous bathroom permitted him to hide all dressers and obtrusive utilitarian devices. Dr. Muñoz, most certainly, was a man of birth, cultivation, and discrimination.

The figure before me was short but exquisitely proportioned, and clad in somewhat formal dress of perfect cut and fit. A highbred face of masterful though not arrogant expression was adorned by a short iron-grey full beard, and an old-fashioned pince-nez shielded the full, dark eyes and surmounted an aquiline nose which gave a Moorish touch to a physiognomy otherwise dominantly Celtiberian. Thick, well-trimmed hair that argued the punctual calls of a barber was parted gracefully above a high forehead; and the whole picture was one of striking intelligence and superior blood and breeding.

Nevertheless, as I saw Dr. Muñoz in that blast of cool air, I felt a repugnance which nothing in his aspect could justify. Only his lividly inclined complexion and coldness of touch could have afforded a physical basis for this feeling, and even these things should have been excusable considering the man's known invalidism. It might, too, have been the singular cold that alienated me; for such chilliness was abnormal on so hot a day, and the abnormal always excites aversion, distrust, and fear.

But repugnance was soon forgotten in admiration, for the strange physician's extreme skill at once became manifest despite the ice-coldness and shakiness of his bloodless-looking hands. He clearly understood my needs at a glance, and ministered to them with a master's deftness; the while reassuring me in finely modulated though oddly hollow and timbreless voice that he was the bitterest of sworn enemies to death, and had sunk his fortune and lost all his friends in a lifetime of bizarre experiment devoted to its bafflement and extirpation. Something of the benevolent fanatic seemed to reside in him, and he rambled on almost garrulously as he sounded my chest and mixed a suitable draught of drugs fetched from the smaller laboratory room. Evidently he found the society of a well-born man a rare novelty in this dingy environment, and was moved to unaccustomed speech as memories of better days surged over him.

His voice, if queer, was at least soothing; and I could not even perceive that he breathed as the fluent sentences rolled urbanely out. He sought to distract my mind from my own seizure by speaking of his theories and experiments; and I remember his tactfully consoling me about my weak heart by insisting that will and consciousness are stronger than organic life itself, so that if a bodily frame be but originally healthy and carefully preserved, it may through a scientific enhancement of these qualities retain a kind of nervous animation despite the most serious impairments, defects, or even absences in the battery of specific organs. He might, he half jestingly said, some day teach me to live—or at least to possess some kind of conscious existence—without any heart at all! For his part, he was afflicted with a complication of maladies requiring a very exact regimen which included constant cold. Any marked rise in temperature might, if prolonged, affect him fatally; and the frigidity of his habitation—some 55 or 56 degrees Fahrenheit—was maintained by an absorption system of ammonia cooling, the gasoline engine of whose pumps I had often heard in my own room below.

Relieved of my seizure in a marvellously short while, I left the shivery place a disciple and devotee of the gifted recluse. After that I paid him frequent overcoated calls; listening while he told of secret researches and almost ghastly results, and trembling a bit when I examined the unconventional and astonishingly ancient volumes on his shelves. I was eventually, I may add, almost cured of my disease for all time by his skilful ministrations. It seems that he did not scorn the incantations of the mediaevalists, since he believed these cryptic formulae to contain rare psychological stimuli which might conceivably have singular effects on the substance of a nervous system from which organic pulsations had fled. I was touched by his account of the aged Dr. Torres of Valencia, who had shared his earlier experiments with him through the great illness of eighteen years before, whence his present disorders proceeded. No sooner had the venerable practitioner saved his colleague than he himself succumbed to the grim enemy he had fought. Perhaps the strain had been too great; for Dr. Muñoz made it whisperingly clear—though not in detail—that the methods of healing had been most extraordinary, involving scenes and processes not welcomed by elderly and conservative Galens.

As the weeks passed, I observed with regret that my new friend was indeed slowly but unmistakably losing ground physically, as Mrs. Herrero had suggested. The livid aspect of his countenance was intensified, his voice became more hollow and indistinct, his muscular motions were less perfectly coördinated, and his mind and will displayed less resilience and initiative. Of this sad change he seemed by no means unaware, and little by little his expression and conversation both took on a gruesome irony which restored in me something of the subtle repulsion I had originally felt.

He developed strange caprices, acquiring a fondness for exotic spices and Egyptian incense till his room smelled like the vault of a sepulchred Pharaoh in the Valley of Kings. At the same time his demands for cold air increased, and with my aid he amplified the ammonia piping of his room and modified the pumps and feed of his refrigerating machine till he could keep the temperature as low as 34° or 40° and finally even 28°; the bathroom and laboratory, of course, being less chilled, in order that water might not freeze, and that chemical processes might not be impeded. The tenant adjoining him complained of the icy air from around the connecting door, so I helped him fit heavy hangings to obviate the difficulty. A kind of growing horror, of outré and morbid cast, seemed to possess him. He talked of death incessantly, but laughed hollowly when such things as burial or funeral arrangements were gently suggested.

All in all, he became a disconcerting and even gruesome companion; yet in my gratitude for his healing I could not well abandon him to the strangers around him, and was careful to dust his room and attend to his needs each day, muffled in a heavy ulster which I bought especially for the purpose. I likewise did much of his shopping, and gasped in bafflement at some of the chemicals he ordered from druggists and laboratory supply houses.

An increasing and unexplained atmosphere of panic seemed to rise around his apartment. The whole house, as I have said, had a musty odour; but the smell in his room was worse—and in spite of all the spices and incense, and the pungent chemicals of the now incessant baths which he insisted on taking unaided. I perceived that it must be connected with his ailment, and shuddered when I reflected on what that ailment might be. Mrs. Herrero crossed herself when she looked at him, and gave him up unreservedly to me; not even letting her son Esteban continue to run errands for him. When I suggested other physicians, the sufferer would fly into as much of a rage as he seemed to dare to entertain. He evidently feared the physical effect of violent emotion, yet his will and driving force waxed rather than waned, and he refused to be confined to his bed. The lassitude of his earlier ill days gave place to a return of his fiery purpose, so that he seemed about to hurl defiance at the death-daemon even as that ancient enemy seized him. The pretence of eating, always curiously like a formality with him, he virtually abandoned; and mental power alone appeared to keep him from total collapse.

He acquired a habit of writing long documents of some sort, which he carefully sealed and filled with injunctions that I transmit after his death to certain persons whom he named—for the most part lettered East Indians, but including a once celebrated French physician now generally thought dead, and about whom the most inconceivable things had been whispered. As it happened, I burned all these papers undelivered and unopened. His aspect and voice became utterly frightful, and his presence almost unbearable. One September day an unexpected glimpse of him induced an epileptic fit in a man who had come to repair his electric desk lamp; a fit for which he prescribed effectively whilst keeping himself well out of sight. That man, oddly enough, had been through the terrors of the Great War without having incurred any fright so thorough.[6]

Then, in the middle of October, the horror of horrors came with stupefying suddenness. One night about eleven the pump of the refrigerating machine broke down, so that within three hours the process of ammonia cooling became impossible. Dr. Muñoz summoned me by thumping on the floor, and I worked desperately to repair the injury while my host cursed in a tone whose lifeless, rattling hollowness surpassed description. My amateur efforts, however, proved of no use; and when I had brought in a mechanic from a neighbouring all-night garage we learned that nothing could be done till morning, when a new piston would have to be obtained. The moribund hermit's rage and fear, swelling to grotesque proportions, seemed likely to shatter what remained of his failing physique; and once a spasm caused him to clap his hands to his eyes and rush into the bathroom. He groped his way out with face tightly bandaged, and I never saw his eyes again.

The frigidity of the apartment was now sensibly diminishing, and at about 5 a.m. the doctor retired to the bathroom, commanding me to keep him supplied with all the ice I could obtain at all-night drug stores and cafeterias. As I would return from my sometimes discouraging trips and lay my spoils before the closed bathroom door, I could hear a restless splashing within, and a thick voice croaking out the order for "More—more!" At length a warm day broke, and the shops opened one by one. I asked Esteban either to help with the ice-fetching whilst I obtained the pump piston, or to order the piston while I continued with the ice; but instructed by his mother, he absolutely refused.

Finally I hired a seedy-looking loafer whom I encountered on the corner of Eighth Avenue to keep the patient supplied with ice from a little shop where I introduced him, and applied myself diligently to the task of finding a pump piston and engaging workmen competent to install it. The task seemed interminable, and I raged almost as violently as the hermit when I saw the hours slipping by in a breathless, foodless round of vain telephoning, and a hectic quest from place to place, hither and thither by subway and surface car. About noon I encountered a suitable supply house far downtown, and at approximately 1:30 p.m. arrived at my boarding-place with the necessary paraphernalia and two sturdy and intelligent mechanics. I had done all I could, and hoped I was in time.

Black terror, however, had preceded me. The house was in utter turmoil, and above the chatter of awed voices I heard a man praying in a deep basso. Fiendish things were in the air, and lodgers told over the beads of their rosaries as they caught the odour from beneath the doctor's closed door. The lounger I had hired, it seems, had fled screaming and mad-eyed not long after his second delivery of ice; perhaps as a result of excessive curiosity. He could not, of course, have locked the door behind him; yet it was now fastened, presumably from the inside. There was no sound within save a nameless sort of slow, thick dripping.

Briefly consulting with Mrs. Herrero and the workmen despite a fear that gnawed my inmost soul, I advised the breaking down of the door; but the landlady found a way to turn the key from the outside with some wire device. We had previously opened the doors of all the other rooms on that hall, and flung all the windows to the very top. Now, noses protected by handkerchiefs, we tremblingly invaded the accursed south room which blazed with the warm sun of early afternoon.

A kind of dark, slimy trail led from the open bathroom door

to the hall door, and thence to the desk, where a terrible little pool had accumulated. Something was scrawled there in pencil in an awful, blind hand on a piece of paper hideously smeared as though by the very claws that traced the hurried last words. Then the trail led to the couch and ended unutterably.

What was, or had been, on the couch I cannot and dare not say here. But this is what I shiveringly puzzled out on the stickily smeared paper before I drew a match and burned it to a crisp; what I puzzled out in terror as the landlady and two mechanics rushed frantically from that hellish place to babble their incoherent stories at the nearest police station. The nauseous words seemed well-nigh incredible in that yellow sunlight, with the clatter of cars and motor trucks ascending clamorously from crowded Fourteenth Street, yet I confess that I believed them then. Whether I believe them now I honestly do not know. There are things about which it is better not to speculate, and all that I can say is that I hate the smell of ammonia, and grow faint at a draught of unusually cool air.

"The end," ran the noisome scrawl, "is here. No more ice— the man looked and ran away. Warmer every minute, and the tissues can't last. I fancy you know—what I said about the will and the nerves and the preserved body after the organs ceased to work. It was good theory, but couldn't keep up indefinitely. There was a gradual deterioration I had not foreseen. Dr. Torres knew, but the shock killed him. He couldn't stand what he had to do—he had to get me in a strange, dark place when he minded my letter and nursed me back. And the organs never would work again. It had to be done my way—artificial preservation—*for you see I died that time eighteen years ago.*"

The Call of Cthulhu

*(Found Among the Papers of the Late
Francis Wayland Thurston,*[1] *of Boston)*

"Of such great powers or beings there may be conceivably a survival . . . a survival of a hugely remote
period when . . . consciousness was manifested, perhaps, in shapes and forms long since withdrawn before the tide of advancing humanity . . . forms of
which poetry and legend alone have caught a flying
memory and called them gods, monsters, mythical
beings of all sorts and kinds. . . ."

—*Algernon Blackwood.*[2]

I.
THE HORROR IN CLAY.

The most merciful thing in the world, I think, is the inability of
the human mind to correlate all its contents. We live on a placid
island of ignorance in the midst of black seas of infinity, and it
was not meant that we should voyage far. The sciences, each
straining in its own direction, have hitherto harmed us little; but
some day the piecing together of dissociated knowledge will
open up such terrifying vistas of reality, and of our frightful position therein, that we shall either go mad from the revelation
or flee from the deadly light into the peace and safety of a new
dark age.[3]

Theosophists[4] have guessed at the awesome grandeur of the
cosmic cycle wherein our world and human race form transient
incidents. They have hinted at strange survivals in terms which
would freeze the blood if not masked by a bland optimism. But
it is not from them that there came the single glimpse of forbidden aeons which chills me when I think of it and maddens me

when I dream of it. That glimpse, like all dread glimpses of truth, flashed out from an accidental piecing together of separated things—in this case an old newspaper item and the notes of a dead professor. I hope that no one else will accomplish this piecing out; certainly, if I live, I shall never knowingly supply a link in so hideous a chain. I think that the professor, too, intended to keep silent regarding the part he knew, and that he would have destroyed his notes had not sudden death seized him.

My knowledge of the thing began in the winter of 1926–27 with the death of my grand-uncle George Gammell Angell,[5] Professor Emeritus of Semitic Languages in Brown University, Providence, Rhode Island. Professor Angell was widely known as an authority on ancient inscriptions, and had frequently been resorted to by the heads of prominent museums; so that his passing at the age of ninety-two may be recalled by many. Locally, interest was intensified by the obscurity of the cause of death. The professor had been stricken whilst returning from the Newport boat; falling suddenly, as witnesses said, after having been jostled by a nautical-looking negro who had come from one of the queer dark courts on the precipitous hillside[6] which formed a short cut from the waterfront to the deceased's home in Williams Street. Physicians were unable to find any visible disorder, but concluded after perplexed debate that some obscure lesion of the heart, induced by the brisk ascent of so steep a hill by so elderly a man, was responsible for the end. At the time I saw no reason to dissent from this dictum, but latterly I am inclined to wonder—and more than wonder.

As my grand-uncle's heir and executor, for he died a childless widower, I was expected to go over his papers with some thoroughness; and for that purpose moved his entire set of files and boxes to my quarters in Boston. Much of the material which I correlated will be later published by the American Archaeological Society,[7] but there was one box which I found exceedingly puzzling, and which I felt much averse from shewing to other eyes. It had been locked, and I did not find the key till it occurred to me to examine the personal ring which the professor carried always in his pocket. Then indeed I succeeded in opening it, but when I did so seemed only to be confronted by a greater and more closely locked barrier. For what could be the meaning of the queer clay bas-relief and the disjointed jottings, ramblings, and cuttings which I found? Had my uncle, in his latter years, become credulous of the most superficial impostures? I resolved to search out the eccentric sculptor responsible for this apparent disturbance of an old man's peace of mind.

The bas-relief was a rough rectangle less than an inch thick and about five by six inches in area; obviously of modern origin. Its designs, however, were far from modern in atmosphere and suggestion; for although the vagaries of cubism and futurism[8] are many and wild, they do not often reproduce that cryptic regularity which lurks in prehistoric writing. And writing of some kind the bulk of these designs seemed certainly to be; though my memory, despite much familiarity with the papers and collections of my uncle, failed in any way to identify this particular species, or even to hint at its remotest affiliations.

Above these apparent hieroglyphics was a figure of evidently pictorial intent, though its impressionistic execution forbade a very clear idea of its nature. It seemed to be a sort of monster, or symbol representing a monster, of a form which only a diseased fancy could conceive. If I say that my somewhat extravagant imagination yielded simultaneous pictures of an octopus, a dragon, and a human caricature, I shall not be unfaithful to the spirit of the thing. A pulpy, tentacled head surmounted a grotesque and scaly body with rudimentary wings; but it was the *general outline* of the whole which made it most shockingly frightful. Behind the figure was a vague suggestion of a Cyclopean architectural background.

The writing accompanying this oddity was, aside from a stack of press cuttings, in Professor Angell's most recent hand; and made no pretence to literary style. What seemed to be the main document was headed "CTHULHU CULT" in characters painstakingly printed to avoid the erroneous reading of a word so unheard-of.[9] The manuscript was divided into two sections, the first of which was headed "1925—Dream and Dream Work of H. A. Wilcox, 7 Thomas St., Providence, R.I.", and the second, "Narrative of Inspector John R. Legrasse, 121 Bienville St., New Orleans, La., at 1908 A. A. S. Mtg.—Notes on Same, &

Prof. Webb's Acct." The other manuscript papers were all brief notes, some of them accounts of the queer dreams of different persons, some of them citations from theosophical books and magazines (notably W. Scott-Elliot's *Atlantis and the Lost Lemuria*),[10] and the rest comments on long-surviving secret societies and hidden cults, with references to passages in such mythological and anthropological source-books as Frazer's *Golden Bough* and Miss Murray's *Witch-Cult in Western Europe*.[11] The cuttings largely alluded to outré mental illnesses and outbreaks of group folly or mania in the spring of 1925.

The first half of the principal manuscript told a very peculiar tale. It appears that on March 1st, 1925, a thin, dark young man of neurotic and excited aspect had called upon Professor Angell bearing the singular clay bas-relief, which was then exceedingly damp and fresh. His card bore the name of Henry Anthony Wilcox,[12] and my uncle had recognised him as the youngest son of an excellent family slightly known to him, who had latterly been studying sculpture at the Rhode Island School of Design and living alone at the Fleur-de-Lys Building near that institution.[13] Wilcox was a precocious youth of known genius but great eccentricity, and had from childhood excited attention through the strange stories and odd dreams he was in the habit of relating. He called himself "psychically hypersensitive", but the staid folk of the ancient commercial city dismissed him as merely "queer". Never mingling much with his kind, he had dropped gradually from social visibility, and was now known only to a small group of aesthetes from other towns. Even the Providence Art Club,[14] anxious to preserve its conservatism, had found him quite hopeless.

On the occasion of the visit, ran the professor's manuscript, the sculptor abruptly asked for the benefit of his host's archaeological knowledge in identifying the hieroglyphics on the bas-relief. He spoke in a dreamy, stilted manner which suggested pose and alienated sympathy; and my uncle shewed some sharpness in replying, for the conspicuous freshness of the tablet implied kinship with anything but archaeology. Young Wilcox's rejoinder, which impressed my uncle enough to make him recall and record it verbatim, was of a fantastically poetic cast which must have typified his whole conversation, and which I have since found highly characteristic of him. He said, "It is new, indeed, for I made it last night in a dream of strange cities; and dreams are older then brooding Tyre, or the contemplative Sphinx, or garden-girdled Babylon."[15]

It was then that he began that rambling tale which suddenly played upon a sleeping memory and won the fevered interest of my uncle. There had been a slight earthquake tremor the night before, the most considerable felt in New England for some years;[16] and Wilcox's imagination had been keenly affected. Upon retiring, he had had an unprecedented dream of great Cyclopean cities of titan blocks and sky-flung monoliths, all dripping with green ooze and sinister with latent horror. Hieroglyphics had covered the walls and pillars, and from some undetermined point below had come a voice that was not a voice; a chaotic sensation which only fancy would transmute into sound, but which he attempted to render by the almost unpronounceable jumble of letters, "*Cthulhu fhtagn*".[17]

This verbal jumble was the key to the recollection which excited and disturbed Professor Angell. He questioned the sculptor with scientific minuteness; and studied with almost frantic intensity the bas-relief on which the youth had found himself working, chilled and clad only in his night-clothes, when waking had stolen bewilderingly over him. My uncle blamed his old age, Wilcox afterward said, for his slowness in recognising both hieroglyphics and pictorial design. Many of his questions seemed highly out-of-place to his visitor, especially those which tried to connect the latter with strange cults or societies; and Wilcox could not understand the repeated promises of silence which he was offered in exchange for an admission of membership in some widespread mystical or paganly religious body. When Professor Angell became convinced that the sculptor was indeed ignorant of any cult or system of cryptic lore, he besieged his visitor with demands for future reports of dreams. This bore regular fruit, for after the first interview the manuscript records daily calls of the young man, during which he related startling fragments of nocturnal imagery whose burden was always some terrible Cyclopean vista of dark and dripping stone, with a subterrene voice or intelligence shouting monotonously in enigmatical sense-impacts uninscribable save as gibberish. The two sounds most frequently repeated are those rendered by the letters "*Cthulhu*" and "*R'lyeh*".

On March 23d, the manuscript continued, Wilcox failed to appear; and inquiries at his quarters revealed that he had been stricken with an obscure sort of fever and taken to the home of his family in Waterman Street.[18] He had cried out in the night, arousing several other artists in the building, and had manifested since then only alternations of unconsciousness and delirium. My uncle at once telephoned the family, and from that time forward kept close watch of the case; calling often at the Thayer Street[19] office of Dr. Tobey, whom he learned to be in charge. The youth's febrile mind, apparently, was dwelling on strange things; and the doctor shuddered now and then as he spoke of them. They included not only a repetition of what he had formerly dreamed, but touched wildly on a gigantic thing "miles high" which walked or lumbered about. He at no time fully described this object, but occasional frantic words, as repeated by Dr. Tobey, convinced the professor that it must be identical with the nameless monstrosity he had sought to depict in his dream-sculpture. Reference to this object, the doctor added, was invariably a prelude to the young man's subsidence into lethargy. His temperature, oddly enough, was not greatly above normal; but his whole condition was otherwise such as to suggest true fever rather than mental disorder.

On April 2nd at about 3 p.m. every trace of Wilcox's malady suddenly ceased. He sat upright in bed, astonished to find himself at home and completely ignorant of what had happened in dream or reality since the night of March 22nd. Pronounced well by his physician, he returned to his quarters in three days; but to Professor Angell he was of no further assistance. All traces of strange dreaming had vanished with his recovery, and my uncle kept no record of his night-thoughts after a week of pointless and irrelevant accounts of thoroughly usual visions.

Here the first part of the manuscript ended, but references to certain of the scattered notes gave me much material for thought—so much, in fact, that only the ingrained scepticism then forming my philosophy can account for my continued distrust of the artist. The notes in question were those descriptive of the dreams of various persons covering the same period as that in which young Wilcox had had his strange visitations. My uncle, it seems, had quickly instituted a prodigiously far-flung body of inquiries amongst nearly all the friends whom he could question without impertinence, asking for nightly reports of their dreams, and the dates of any notable visions for some time past. The reception of his request seems to have been varied; but he must, at the very least, have received more responses than any ordinary man could have handled without a secretary. This original correspondence was not preserved, but his notes formed a thorough and really significant digest. Average people in society and business—New England's traditional "salt of the earth"—gave an almost completely negative result, though scattered cases of uneasy but formless nocturnal impressions appear here and there, always between March 23d and April 2nd —the period of young Wilcox's delirium. Scientific men were little more affected, though four cases of vague description suggest fugitive glimpses of strange landscapes, and in one case there is mentioned a dread of something abnormal.

It was from the artists and poets that the pertinent answers came, and I know that panic would have broken loose had they been able to compare notes. As it was, lacking their original letters, I half suspected the compiler of having asked leading questions, or of having edited the correspondence in corroboration of what he had latently resolved to see. That is why I continued to feel that Wilcox, somehow cognisant of the old data which my uncle had possessed, had been imposing on the veteran scientist. These responses from aesthetes told a disturbing tale. From February 28th to April 2nd a large proportion of them had dreamed very bizarre things, the intensity of the dreams being immeasurably the stronger during the period of the sculptor's delirium. Over a fourth of those who reported anything, reported scenes and half-sounds not unlike those which Wilcox had described; and some of the dreamers confessed acute fear of the gigantic nameless thing visible toward the last. One case, which the note describes with emphasis, was very sad. The subject, a widely known architect with leanings toward theosophy and occultism, went violently insane on the date of young Wilcox's seizure, and expired several months later after incessant screamings to be saved from some escaped denizen of hell. Had my uncle referred to these cases by name instead of merely by number, I should have attempted some corroboration and personal investigation; but as it was, I succeeded in tracing down only a few. All of these, however, bore out the notes in full. I have often wondered if all the objects of the professor's questioning felt as puzzled as did this fraction. It is well that no explanation shall ever reach them.

The press cuttings, as I have intimated, touched on cases of panic, mania, and eccentricity during the given period. Professor Angell must have employed a cutting bureau, for the number of extracts was tremendous and the sources scattered throughout the globe. Here was a nocturnal suicide in London, where a lone sleeper had leaped from a window after a shocking cry. Here likewise a rambling letter to the editor of a paper in South America, where a fanatic deduces a dire future from visions he has seen. A despatch from California describes a theosophist colony as donning white robes en masse for some "glorious fulfilment" which never arrives, whilst items from India speak guardedly of serious native unrest toward the end of March. Voodoo orgies multiply in Hayti, and African outposts report ominous mutterings. American officers in the Philippines find certain tribes bothersome about this time, and New York policemen are mobbed by hysterical Levantines on the night of March 22–23. The west of Ireland, too, is full of wild rumour and legendry, and a fantastic painter named Ardois-Bonnot hangs a blasphemous "Dream Landscape" in the Paris spring salon of 1926. And so numerous are the recorded troubles in insane asylums, that only a miracle can have stopped the medical fraternity from noting strange parallelisms and drawing mystified conclusions. A weird bunch of cuttings, all told; and I can at this date scarcely envisage the callous rationalism with which I set them aside. But I was then convinced that young Wilcox had known of the older matters mentioned by the professor.

II.
THE TALE OF INSPECTOR LEGRASSE.

The older matters which had made the sculptor's dream and bas-relief so significant to my uncle formed the subject of the second half of his long manuscript. Once before, it appears, Professor Angell had seen the hellish outlines of the nameless monstrosity, puzzled over the unknown hieroglyphics, and heard the ominous syllables which can be rendered only as "*Cthulhu*"; and all this in so stirring and horrible a connexion that it is small wonder he pursued young Wilcox with queries and demands for data.

The earlier experience had come in 1908, seventeen years before, when the American Archaeological Society held its annual meeting in St. Louis. Professor Angell, as befitted one of his authority and attainments, had had a prominent part in all the deliberations; and was one of the first to be approached by the several outsiders who took advantage of the convocation to offer questions for correct answering and problems for expert solution.

The chief of these outsiders, and in a short time the focus of interest for the entire meeting, was a commonplace-looking middle-aged man who had travelled all the way from New Orleans for certain special information unobtainable from any local source. His name was John Raymond Legrasse, and he was by profession an Inspector of Police. With him he bore the subject of his visit, a grotesque, repulsive, and apparently very ancient stone statuette whose origin he was at a loss to determine. It must not be fancied that Inspector Legrasse had the least interest in archaeology. On the contrary, his wish for enlightenment was prompted by purely professional considerations. The statuette, idol, fetish, or whatever it was, had been captured some months before in the wooded swamps south of New Orleans during a raid on a supposed voodoo meeting; and so singular and hideous were the rites connected with it, that the police could not but realise that they had stumbled on a dark cult totally unknown to them, and infinitely more diabolic than even the blackest of the African voodoo circles. Of its origin, apart from the erratic and unbelievable tales extorted from the captured members, absolutely nothing was to be discovered; hence the anxiety of the police for any antiquarian lore which might help them to place the frightful symbol, and through it track down the cult to its fountain-head.

Inspector Legrasse was scarcely prepared for the sensation which his offering created. One sight of the thing had been enough to throw the assembled men of science into a state of tense excitement, and they lost no time in crowding around him to gaze at the diminutive figure whose utter strangeness and air of genuinely abysmal antiquity hinted so potently at unopened and archaic vistas. No recognised school of sculpture had animated this terrible object, yet centuries and even thousands of years seemed recorded in its dim and greenish surface of unplaceable stone.

The figure, which was finally passed slowly from man to man for close and careful study, was between seven and eight inches in height, and of exquisitely artistic workmanship. It represented a monster of vaguely anthropoid outline, but with an octopus-like head whose face was a mass of feelers, a scaly, rubbery-looking body, prodigious claws on hind and fore feet, and long, narrow wings behind. This thing, which seemed instinct with a fearsome and unnatural malignancy, was of a somewhat bloated corpulence, and squatted evilly on a rectangular block or pedestal covered with undecipherable characters. The tips of the wings touched the back edge of the block, the seat occupied the centre, whilst the long, curved claws of the doubled-up, crouching hind legs gripped the front edge and extended a quarter of the way down toward the bottom of the pedestal. The cephalopod head was bent forward, so that the ends of the facial feelers brushed the backs of huge fore paws which clasped the croucher's elevated knees. The aspect of the whole was abnormally life-like, and the more subtly fearful because its source was so totally unknown. Its vast, awesome, and incalculable age was unmistakable; yet not one link did it shew with any known type of art belonging to civilisation's youth—or indeed to any other time. Totally separate and apart, its very material was a mystery; for the soapy, greenish-black stone with its golden or iridescent

flecks and striations resembled nothing familiar to geology or
mineralogy. The characters along the base were equally baffling;
and no member present, despite a representation of half the
world's expert learning in this field, could form the least notion
of even the remotest linguistic kinship. They, like the subject and
material, belonged to something horribly remote and distinct
from mankind as we know it; something frightfully suggestive of
old and unhallowed cycles of life in which our world and our
conceptions have no part.[20]

And yet, as the members severally shook their heads and confessed defeat at the Inspector's problem, there was one man in
that gathering who suspected a touch of bizarre familiarity in the
monstrous shape and writing, and who presently told with some
diffidence of the odd trifle he knew. This person was the late
William Channing Webb, Professor of Anthropology in Prince-
ton University, and an explorer of no slight note. Professor
Webb had been engaged, forty-eight years before, in a tour of
Greenland and Iceland in search of some Runic inscriptions
which he failed to unearth; and whilst high up on the West
Greenland coast had encountered a singular tribe or cult of degenerate Esquimaux[21] whose religion, a curious form of devil-
worship, chilled him with its deliberate bloodthirstiness and
repulsiveness. It was a faith of which other Esquimaux knew little, and which they mentioned only with shudders, saying that it
had come down from horribly ancient aeons before ever the
world was made. Besides nameless rites and human sacrifices
there were certain queer hereditary rituals addressed to a
supreme elder devil or *tornasuk;* and of this Professor Webb had
taken a careful phonetic copy from an aged *angekok* or wizard-
priest, expressing the sounds in Roman letters as best he knew
how.[22] But just now of prime significance was the fetish which
this cult had cherished, and around which they danced when the
aurora leaped high over the ice cliffs. It was, the professor stated,
a very crude bas-relief of stone, comprising a hideous picture and
some cryptic writing. And so far as he could tell, it was a rough
parallel in all essential features of the bestial thing now lying before the meeting.

This data,[23] received with suspense and astonishment by the assembled members, proved doubly exciting to Inspector Legrasse; and he began at once to ply his informant with questions. Having noted and copied an oral ritual among the swamp cult-worshippers his men had arrested, he besought the professor to remember as best he might the syllables taken down amongst the diabolist Esquimaux. There then followed an exhaustive comparison of details, and a moment of really awed silence when both detective and scientist agreed on the virtual identity of the phrase common to two hellish rituals so many worlds of distance apart. What, in substance, both the Esquimau wizards and the Louisiana swamp-priests had chanted to their kindred idols was something very like this—the word-divisions being guessed at from traditional breaks in the phrase as chanted aloud:

"Ph'nglui mglw'nafh Cthulhu R'lyeh wgah'nagl fhtagn."

Legrasse had one point in advance of Professor Webb, for several among his mongrel prisoners had repeated to him what older celebrants had told them the words meant. This text, as given, ran something like this:

"In his house at R'lyeh dead Cthulhu waits dreaming."

And now, in response to a general and urgent demand, Inspector Legrasse related as fully as possible his experience with the swamp worshippers; telling a story to which I could see my uncle attached profound significance. It savoured of the wildest dreams of myth-maker and theosophist, and disclosed an astonishing degree of cosmic imagination among such half-castes and pariahs as might be expected to possess it.

On November 1st, 1907, there had come to the New Orleans police a frantic summons from the swamp and lagoon country to the south. The squatters there, mostly primitive but good-natured descendants of Lafitte's men,[24] were in the grip of stark terror from an unknown thing which had stolen upon them in the night. It was voodoo, apparently, but voodoo of a more terrible sort than they had ever known; and some of their women and children had disappeared since the malevolent tom-tom had begun its incessant beating far within the black haunted woods where no dweller ventured. There were insane shouts and harrowing screams, soul-chilling chants and dancing devil-flames;

and, the frightened messenger added, the people could stand it no more.

So a body of twenty police, filling two carriages and an automobile, had set out in the late afternoon with the shivering squatter as a guide. At the end of the passable road they alighted, and for miles splashed on in silence through the terrible cypress woods where day never came. Ugly roots and malignant hanging nooses of Spanish moss beset them, and now and then a pile of dank stones or fragment of a rotting wall intensified by its hint of morbid habitation a depression which every malformed tree and every fungous islet combined to create. At length the squatter settlement, a miserable huddle of huts, hove in sight; and hysterical dwellers ran out to cluster around the group of bobbing lanterns. The muffled beat of tom-toms was now faintly audible far, far ahead; and a curdling shriek came at infrequent intervals when the wind shifted. A reddish glare, too, seemed to filter through the pale undergrowth beyond endless avenues of forest night. Reluctant even to be left alone again, each one of the cowed squatters refused point-blank to advance another inch toward the scene of unholy worship, so Inspector Legrasse and his nineteen colleagues plunged on unguided into black arcades of horror that none of them had ever trod before.

The region now entered by the police was one of traditionally evil repute, substantially unknown and untraversed by white men. There were legends of a hidden lake unglimpsed by mortal sight, in which dwelt a huge, formless white polypous thing with luminous eyes; and squatters whispered that bat-winged devils flew up out of caverns in inner earth to worship it at midnight. They said it had been there before D'Iberville, before La Salle,[25] before the Indians, and before even the wholesome beasts and birds of the woods. It was nightmare itself, and to see it was to die. But it made men dream, and so they knew enough to keep away. The present voodoo orgy was, indeed, on the merest fringe of this abhorred area, but that location was bad enough; hence perhaps the very place of the worship had terrified the squatters more than the shocking sounds and incidents.

Only poetry or madness could do justice to the noises heard by Legrasse's men as they ploughed on through the black morass toward the red glare and the muffled tom-toms. There are vocal qualities peculiar to men, and vocal qualities peculiar to beasts; and it is terrible to hear the one when the source should yield the other. Animal fury and orgiastic licence here whipped themselves to daemoniac heights by howls and squawking ecstasies that tore and reverberated through those nighted woods like pestilential tempests from the gulfs of hell. Now and then the less organised ululation would cease, and from what seemed a well-drilled chorus of hoarse voices would rise in sing-song chant that hideous phrase or ritual:

"*Ph'nglui mglw'nafh Cthulhu R'lyeh wgah'nagl fhtagn.*"

Then the men, having reached a spot where the trees were thinner, came suddenly in sight of the spectacle itself. Four of them reeled, one fainted, and two were shaken into a frantic cry which the mad cacophony of the orgy fortunately deadened. Legrasse dashed swamp water on the face of the fainting man, and all stood trembling and nearly hypnotised with horror.

In a natural glade of the swamp stood a grassy island of perhaps an acre's extent, clear of trees and tolerably dry. On this now leaped and twisted a more indescribable horde of human abnormality than any but a Sime or an Angarola could paint.[26] Void of clothing, this hybrid spawn were braying, bellowing, and writhing about a monstrous ring-shaped bonfire; in the centre of which, revealed by occasional rifts in the curtain of flame, stood a great granite monolith some eight feet in height; on top of which, incongruous with its diminutiveness, rested the noxious carven statuette. From a wide circle of ten scaffolds set up at regular intervals with the flame-girt monolith as a centre hung, head downward, the oddly marred bodies of the helpless squatters who had disappeared. It was inside this circle that the ring of worshippers jumped and roared, the general direction of the mass motion being from left to right in endless Bacchanal between the ring of bodies and the ring of fire.

It may have been only imagination and it may have been only echoes which induced one of the men, an excitable Spaniard, to fancy he heard antiphonal responses to the ritual from some far and unillumined spot deeper within the wood of ancient legendry and horror. This man, Joseph D. Galvez, I later met and questioned; and he proved distractingly imaginative. He indeed went so far as to hint of the faint beating of great wings, and of a glimpse of shining eyes and a mountainous white bulk beyond the remotest trees—but I suppose he had been hearing too much native superstition.

Actually, the horrified pause of the men was of comparatively brief duration. Duty came first; and although there must have been nearly a hundred mongrel celebrants in the throng, the police relied on their firearms and plunged determinedly into the nauseous rout. For five minutes the resultant din and chaos were beyond description. Wild blows were struck, shots were fired, and escapes were made; but in the end Legrasse was able to count some forty-seven sullen prisoners, whom he forced to dress in haste and fall into line between two rows of policemen. Five of the worshippers lay dead, and two severely wounded ones were carried away on improvised stretchers by their fellow-prisoners. The image on the monolith, of course, was carefully removed and carried back by Legrasse.

Examined at headquarters after a trip of intense strain and weariness, the prisoners all proved to be men of a very low, mixed-blooded, and mentally aberrant type. Most were seamen, and a sprinkling of negroes and mulattoes, largely West Indians or Brava Portuguese from the Cape Verde Islands,[27] gave a colouring of voodooism to the heterogeneous cult. But before many questions were asked, it became manifest that something far deeper and older than negro fetichism[28] was involved. Degraded and ignorant as they were, the creatures held with surprising consistency to the central idea of their loathsome faith.

They worshipped, so they said, the Great Old Ones who lived ages before there were any men, and who came to the young world out of the sky. Those Old Ones were gone now, inside the earth and under the sea; but their dead bodies had told their secrets in dreams to the first men, who formed a cult which had never died. This was that cult, and the prisoners said it had always existed and always would exist, hidden in distant wastes and dark places all over the world until the time when the great priest Cthulhu, from his dark house in the mighty city of R'lyeh[29] under the waters, should rise and bring the earth again beneath his sway. Some day he would call, when the stars were ready, and the secret cult would always be waiting to liberate him.

Meanwhile no more must be told. There was a secret which even torture could not extract. Mankind was not absolutely alone among the conscious things of earth, for shapes came out of the dark to visit the faithful few. But these were not the Great Old Ones. No man had ever seen the Old Ones. The carven idol was great Cthulhu, but none might say whether or not the others were precisely like him. No one could read the old writing now, but things were told by word of mouth. The chanted ritual was not the secret—that was never spoken aloud, only whispered. The chant meant only this: "In his house at R'lyeh dead Cthulhu waits dreaming."

Only two of the prisoners were found sane enough to be hanged, and the rest were committed to various institutions. All denied a part in the ritual murders, and averred that the killing had been done by Black Winged Ones which had come to them from their immemorial meeting-place in the haunted wood. But of those mysterious allies no coherent account could ever be gained. What the police did extract, came mainly from an immensely aged mestizo named Castro,[30] who claimed to have sailed to strange ports and talked with undying leaders of the cult in the mountains of China.[31]

Old Castro remembered bits of hideous legend that paled the speculations of theosophists and made man and the world seem recent and transient indeed. There had been aeons when other Things ruled on the earth, and They had had great cities. Remains of Them, he said the deathless Chinamen had told him, were still to be found as Cyclopean stones on islands in the Pacific. They all died vast epochs of time before men came, but there were arts which could revive Them when the stars had come round again to the right positions in the cycle of eternity. They had, indeed, come themselves from the stars, and brought Their images with Them.

These Great Old Ones, Castro continued, were not composed altogether of flesh and blood. They had shape—for did not this star-fashioned image prove it?—but that shape was not made of

matter. When the stars were right, They could plunge
to world through the sky; but when the stars were w
could not live. But although They no longer lived, The
never really die. They all lay in stone houses in Their great
R'lyeh, preserved by the spells of mighty Cthulhu for a glo us
resurrection when the stars and the earth might once more be
ready for Them. But at that time some force from outside must
serve to liberate Their bodies. The spells that preserved Them intact likewise prevented Them from making an initial move, and
They could only lie awake in the dark and think whilst uncounted millions of years rolled by. They knew all that was occurring in the universe, but Their mode of speech was transmitted
thought. Even now They talked in Their tombs. When, after infinities of chaos, the first men came, the Great Old Ones spoke to
the sensitive among them by moulding their dreams; for only
thus could Their language reach the fleshly minds of mammals.

Then, whispered Castro, those first men formed the cult
around small idols which the Great Ones shewed them; idols
brought in dim aeras from dark stars. That cult would never die
till the stars came right again, and the secret priests would take
great Cthulhu from His tomb to revive His subjects and resume
His rule of earth. The time would be easy to know, for then
mankind would have become as the Great Old Ones; free and
wild and beyond good and evil,[32] with laws and morals thrown
aside and all men shouting and killing and revelling in joy. Then
the liberated Old Ones would teach them new ways to shout and
kill and revel and enjoy themselves, and all the earth would flame
with a holocaust of ecstasy and freedom. Meanwhile the cult, by
appropriate rites, must keep alive the memory of those ancient
ways and shadow forth the prophecy of their return.

In the elder time chosen men had talked with the entombed
Old Ones in dreams, but then something had happened. The
great stone city R'lyeh, with its monoliths and sepulchres, had
sunk beneath the waves; and the deep waters, full of the one primal mystery through which not even thought can pass, had cut
off the spectral intercourse. But memory never died, and high-
priests said that the city would rise again when the stars were
right. Then came out of the earth the black spirits of earth,

mouldy and shadowy, and full of dim rumours picked up in caverns beneath forgotten sea-bottoms. But of them old Castro dared not speak much. He cut himself off hurriedly, and no amount of persuasion or subtlety could elicit more in this direction. The *size* of the Old Ones, too, he curiously declined to mention. Of the cult, he said that he thought the centre lay amid the pathless deserts of Arabia, where Irem, the City of Pillars,[33] dreams hidden and untouched. It was not allied to the European witch-cult, and was virtually unknown beyond its members. No book had ever really hinted of it, though the deathless Chinamen said that there were double meanings in the *Necronomicon* of the mad Arab Abdul Alhazred which the initiated might read as they chose, especially the much-discussed couplet:

> *"That is not dead which can eternal lie,*
> *And with strange aeons even death may die."*[34]

Legrasse, deeply impressed and not a little bewildered, had inquired in vain concerning the historic affiliations of the cult. Castro, apparently, had told the truth when he said that it was wholly secret. The authorities at Tulane University could shed no light upon either cult or image, and now the detective had come to the highest authorities in the country and met with no more than the Greenland tale of Professor Webb.

The feverish interest aroused at the meeting by Legrasse's tale, corroborated as it was by the statuette, is echoed in the subsequent correspondence of those who attended; although scant mention occurs in the formal publications of the society. Caution is the first care of those accustomed to face occasional charlatanry and imposture. Legrasse for some time lent the image to Professor Webb, but at the latter's death it was returned to him and remains in his possession, where I viewed it not long ago. It is truly a terrible thing, and unmistakably akin to the dream-sculpture of young Wilcox.

That my uncle was excited by the tale of the sculptor I did not wonder, for what thoughts must arise upon hearing, after a knowledge of what Legrasse had learned of the cult, of a sensitive young man who had *dreamed* not only the figure and exact hieroglyphics of the swamp-found image and the Greenland devil tablet, but had come *in his dreams* upon at least three of the precise words of the formula uttered alike by Esquimau diabolists and mongrel Louisianans? Professor Angell's instant start on an investigation of the utmost thoroughness was eminently natural; though privately I suspected young Wilcox of having heard of the cult in some indirect way, and of having invented a series of dreams to heighten and continue the mystery at my uncle's expense. The dream-narratives and cuttings collected by the professor were, of course, strong corroboration; but the rationalism of my mind and the extravagance of the whole subject led me to adopt what I thought the most sensible conclusions. So, after thoroughly studying the manuscript again and correlating the theosophical and anthropological notes with the cult narrative of Legrasse, I made a trip to Providence to see the sculptor and give him the rebuke I thought proper for so boldly imposing upon a learned and aged man.

Wilcox still lived alone in the Fleur-de-Lys Building in Thomas Street, a hideous Victorian imitation of seventeenth-century Breton architecture which flaunts its stuccoed front amidst the lovely colonial houses on the ancient hill, and under the very shadow of the finest Georgian steeple in America.[35] I found him at work in his rooms, and at once conceded from the specimens scattered about that his genius is indeed profound and authentic. He will, I believe, some time be heard from as one of the great decadents; for he has crystallised in clay and will one day mirror in marble those nightmares and phantasies which Arthur Machen evokes in prose, and Clark Ashton Smith makes visible in verse and in painting.[36]

Dark, frail, and somewhat unkempt in aspect, he turned languidly at my knock and asked me my business without rising. When I told him who I was, he displayed some interest; for my uncle had excited his curiosity in probing his strange dreams, yet had never explained the reason for the study. I did not enlarge his knowledge in this regard, but sought with some subtlety to draw him out. In a short time I became convinced of his absolute sincerity, for he spoke of the dreams in a manner none could mistake. They and their subconscious residuum had influenced his art profoundly, and he shewed me a morbid statue whose contours almost made me shake with the potency of its black suggestion. He could not recall having seen the original of this thing except in his own dream bas-relief, but the outlines had formed themselves insensibly under his hands. It was, no doubt, the giant shape he had raved of in delirium. That he really knew nothing of the hidden cult, save from what my uncle's relentless catechism had let fall, he soon made clear; and again I strove to think of some way in which he could possibly have received the weird impressions.

He talked of his dreams in a strangely poetic fashion; making me see with terrible vividness the damp Cyclopean city of slimy green stone—whose *geometry*, he oddly said, was *all wrong*—and hear with frightened expectancy the ceaseless, half-mental calling from underground: "*Cthulhu fhtagn*", "*Cthulhu fhtagn*". These words had formed part of that dread ritual which told of dead Cthulhu's dream-vigil in his stone vault at R'lyeh, and I felt deeply moved despite my rational beliefs. Wilcox, I was sure, had heard of the cult in some casual way, and had soon forgotten it amidst the mass of his equally weird reading and imagining. Later, by virtue of its sheer impressiveness, it had found subconscious expression in dreams, in the bas-relief, and in the terrible statue I now beheld; so that his imposture upon my uncle had been a very innocent one. The youth was of a type, at once slightly affected and slightly ill-mannered, which I could never like; but I was willing enough now to admit both his genius and his honesty. I took leave of him amicably, and wish him all the success his talent promises.

The matter of the cult still remained to fascinate me, and at times I had visions of personal fame from researches into its origin and connexions. I visited New Orleans, talked with Legrasse and others of that old-time raiding-party, saw the frightful image, and even questioned such of the mongrel prisoners as still survived. Old Castro, unfortunately, had been dead for some years. What I now heard so graphically at first-hand, though it was really no more than a detailed confirmation of what my uncle had written, excited me afresh; for I felt sure that I was on the track of a very real, very secret, and very ancient religion whose discovery would make me an anthropologist of note. My attitude was still one of absolute materialism, *as I wish it still were*, and I discounted with almost inexplicable perversity the coincidence of the dream notes and odd cuttings collected by Professor Angell.

One thing I began to suspect, and which I now fear I *know*, is that my uncle's death was far from natural. He fell on a narrow hill street leading up from an ancient waterfront swarming with foreign mongrels, after a careless push from a negro sailor. I did not forget the mixed blood and marine pursuits of the cult-members in Louisiana, and would not be surprised to learn of secret methods and poison needles as ruthless and as anciently known as the cryptic rites and beliefs. Legrasse and his men, it is true, have been let alone; but in Norway a certain seaman who saw things is dead. Might not the deeper inquiries of my uncle after encountering the sculptor's data have come to sinister ears? I think Professor Angell died because he knew too much, or because he was likely to learn too much. Whether I shall go as he did remains to be seen, for I have learned much now.

III.
THE MADNESS FROM THE SEA.

If heaven ever wishes to grant me a boon, it will be a total effacing of the results of a mere chance which fixed my eye on a certain stray piece of shelf-paper. It was nothing on which I would naturally have stumbled in the course of my daily round, for it was an old number of an Australian journal, the *Sydney Bulletin* for April 18, 1925.[37] It had escaped even the cutting bureau which had at the time of its issuance been avidly collecting material for my uncle's research.

I had largely given over my inquiries into what Professor Angell called the "Cthulhu Cult", and was visiting a learned friend in Paterson, New Jersey; the curator of a local museum and a mineralogist of note.[38] Examining one day the reserve specimens roughly set on the storage shelves in a rear room of the museum, my eye was caught by an odd picture in one of the old papers spread beneath the stones. It was the *Sydney Bulletin* I have mentioned, for my friend has wide affiliations in all conceivable foreign parts; and the picture was a half-tone cut of a hideous stone image almost identical with that which Legrasse had found in the swamp.

Eagerly clearing the sheet of its precious contents, I scanned the item in detail; and was disappointed to find it of only moderate length. What it suggested, however, was of portentous significance to my flagging quest; and I carefully tore it out for immediate action. It read as follows:

MYSTERY DERELICT FOUND AT SEA

*Vigilant Arrives With Helpless Armed New Zealand Yacht in Tow.
One Survivor and Dead Man Found Aboard. Tale of
Desperate Battle and Deaths at Sea.
Rescued Seaman Refuses
Particulars of Strange Experience.
Odd Idol Found in His Possession. Inquiry
to Follow.*

The Morrison Co.'s freighter *Vigilant*, bound from Valparaiso, arrived this morning at its wharf in Darling Harbour, having in tow the battled and disabled but heavily armed steam yacht *Alert* of Dunedin, N. Z., which was sighted April 12th in S. Latitude 34° 21´, W. Longitude 152° 17´[39] with one living and one dead man aboard.

The *Vigilant* left Valparaiso March 25th, and on April 2nd was driven considerably south of her course by exceptionally heavy storms and monster waves. On April 12th the derelict was sighted; and though apparently deserted, was found upon boarding to contain one survivor in a half-delirious condition and one man who had evidently been dead for more than a week. The living man was clutching a horrible stone idol of unknown origin, about a foot in height, regarding whose nature authorities at Sydney University, the Royal Society, and the Museum in College Street[40] all profess complete bafflement, and which the survivor says he found in the cabin of the yacht, in a small carved shrine of common pattern.

This man, after recovering his senses, told an exceedingly strange story of piracy and slaughter. He is Gustaf Johansen, a Norwegian of some intelligence, and had been second mate of the two-masted schooner *Emma* of Auckland, which sailed for

Callao February 20th with a complement of eleven men. The *Emma*, he says, was delayed and thrown widely south of her course by the great storm of March 1st, and on March 22nd, in S. Latitude 49° 51´, W. Longitude 128° 34´,[41] encountered the *Alert*, manned by a queer and evil-looking crew of Kanakas[42] and half-castes. Being ordered peremptorily to turn back, Capt. Collins refused; whereupon the strange crew began to fire savagely and without warning upon the schooner with a peculiarly heavy battery of brass cannon forming part of the yacht's equipment. The *Emma*'s men shewed fight, says the survivor, and though the schooner began to sink from shots beneath the waterline they managed to heave alongside their enemy and board her, grappling with the savage crew on the yacht's deck, and being forced to kill them all, the number being slightly superior, because of their particularly abhorrent and desperate though rather clumsy mode of fighting.

Three of the *Emma*'s men, including Capt. Collins and First Mate Green, were killed; and the remaining eight under Second Mate Johansen proceeded to navigate the captured yacht, going ahead in their original direction to see if any reason for their ordering back had existed. The next day, it appears, they raised and landed on a small island, although none is known to exist in that part of the ocean; and six of the men somehow died ashore, though Johansen is queerly reticent about this part of his story, and speaks only of their falling into a rock chasm. Later, it seems, he and one companion boarded the yacht and tried to manage her, but were beaten about by the storm of April 2nd. From that time till his rescue on the 12th the man remembers little, and he does not even recall when William Briden, his companion, died. Briden's death reveals no apparent cause, and was probably due to excitement or exposure. Cable advices from Dunedin report that the *Alert* was well known there as an island trader, and bore an evil reputation along the waterfront. It was owned by a curious group of half-castes whose frequent meetings and night trips to the woods attracted no little curiosity; and it had set sail in great haste just after the storm and earth tremors of March 1st. Our Auckland correspondent gives the *Emma* and her crew an excellent reputation, and Johansen is described as a sober and worthy man. The admiralty will institute an inquiry on the whole matter beginning tomorrow, at which every effort will be made to induce Johansen to speak more freely than he has done hitherto.

This was all, together with the picture of the hellish image; but what a train of ideas it started in my mind! Here were new treasuries of data on the Cthulhu Cult, and evidence that it had strange interests at sea as well as on land. What motive prompted the hybrid crew to order back the *Emma* as they sailed about with their hideous idol? What was the unknown island on which six of the *Emma*'s crew had died, and about which the mate Johansen was so secretive? What had the vice-admiralty's investigation brought out, and what was known of the noxious cult in Dunedin? And most marvellous of all, what deep and more than natural linkage of dates was this which gave a malign and now undeniable significance to the various turns of events so carefully noted by my uncle?

March 1st—our February 28th according to the International Date Line—the earthquake and storm had come. From Dunedin the *Alert* and her noisome crew had darted eagerly forth as if imperiously summoned, and on the other side of the earth poets and artists had begun to dream of a strange, dank Cyclopean city whilst a young sculptor had moulded in his sleep the form of the dreaded Cthulhu. March 23d the crew of the *Emma* landed on an unknown island and left six men dead; and on that date the dreams of sensitive men assumed a heightened vividness and darkened with dread of a giant monster's malign pursuit, whilst an architect had gone mad and a sculptor had lapsed suddenly into delirium! And what of this storm of April 2nd—the date on which all dreams of the dank city ceased, and Wilcox emerged unharmed from the bondage of strange fever? What of all this—and of those hints of old Castro about the sunken, star-born Old Ones and their coming reign; their faithful cult *and their mastery of dreams?* Was I tottering on the brink of cosmic horrors beyond man's power to bear? If so, they must be horrors of the mind alone, for in some way the second of April had put a stop to whatever monstrous menace had begun its siege of mankind's soul.

That evening, after a day of hurried cabling and arranging, I bade my host adieu and took a train for San Francisco. In less than a month I was in Dunedin; where, however, I found that little was known of the strange cult-members who had lingered in the old sea-taverns. Waterfront scum was far too common for special mention; though there was vague talk about one inland trip these mongrels had made, during which faint drumming and red flame were noted on the distant hills. In Auckland I learned that Johansen had returned *with yellow hair turned white* after a perfunctory and inconclusive questioning at Sydney, and had thereafter sold his cottage in West Street and sailed with his wife to his old home in Oslo. Of his stirring experience he would tell his friends no more than he had told the admiralty officials, and all they could do was to give me his Oslo address.

After that I went to Sydney and talked profitlessly with sea-men and members of the vice-admiralty court. I saw the *Alert,* now sold and in commercial use, at Circular Quay in Sydney Cove, but gained nothing from its non-committal bulk. The crouching image with its cuttlefish head, dragon body, scaly wings, and hieroglyphed pedestal, was preserved in the Museum at Hyde Park; and I studied it long and well, finding it a thing of balefully exquisite workmanship, and with the same utter mys-tery, terrible antiquity, and unearthly strangeness of material which I had noted in Legrasse's smaller specimen. Geologists, the curator told me, had found it a monstrous puzzle; for they vowed that the world held no rock like it. Then I thought with a shudder of what old Castro had told Legrasse about the primal Great Ones: "They had come from the stars, and had brought Their images with Them."

Shaken with such a mental revolution as I had never before known, I now resolved to visit Mate Johansen in Oslo. Sailing for London, I reëmbarked at once for the Norwegian capital; and one autumn day landed at the trim wharves in the shadow of the Egeberg.[43] Johansen's address, I discovered, lay in the Old Town of King Harold Haardrada, which kept alive the name of Oslo during all the centuries that the greater city masqueraded as "Christiana".[44] I made the brief trip by taxicab, and knocked with palpitant heart at the door of a neat and ancient building with plastered front. A sad-faced woman in black answered my summons, and I was stung with disappointment when she told me in halting English that Gustaf Johansen was no more.

He had not survived his return, said his wife, for the doings at sea in 1925 had broken him. He had told her no more than he had told the public, but had left a long manuscript—of "technical matters" as he said—written in English, evidently in order to safeguard her from the peril of casual perusal. During a walk through a narrow lane near the Gothenburg dock,[45] a bundle of papers falling from an attic window had knocked him down. Two Lascar sailors[46] at once helped him to his feet, but before the ambulance could reach him he was dead. Physicians found no adequate cause for the end, and laid it to heart trouble and a weakened constitution.

I now felt gnawing at my vitals that dark terror which will never leave me till I, too, am at rest; "accidentally" or otherwise. Persuading the widow that my connexion with her husband's "technical matters" was sufficient to entitle me to his manuscript, I bore the document away and began to read it on the London boat. It was a simple, rambling thing—a naive sailor's effort at a post-facto diary—and strove to recall day by day that last awful voyage. I cannot attempt to transcribe it verbatim in all its cloudiness and redundance, but I will tell its gist enough to shew why the sound of the water against the vessel's sides became so unendurable to me that I stopped my ears with cotton.

Johansen, thank God, did not know quite all, even though he saw the city and the Thing, but I shall never sleep calmly again when I think of the horrors that lurk ceaselessly behind life in time and in space, and of those unhallowed blasphemies from elder stars which dream beneath the sea, known and favoured by a nightmare cult ready and eager to loose them on the world whenever another earthquake shall heave their monstrous stone city again to the sun and air.

Johansen's voyage had begun just as he told it to the vice-admiralty. The *Emma*, in ballast, had cleared Auckland on February 20th, and had felt the full force of that earthquake-born tempest which must have heaved up from the sea-bottom the horrors that filled men's dreams. Once more under control, the ship was making good progress when held up by the *Alert* on March 22nd, and I could feel the mate's regret as he wrote of her bombardment and sinking. Of the swarthy cult-fiends on the *Alert* he speaks with significant horror. There was some pecu-

liarly abominable quality about them which made th
tion seem almost a duty, and Johansen shews ingenud
at the charge of ruthlessness brought against his party
proceedings of the court of inquiry. Then, driven ahea... ...cu-
riosity in their captured yacht under Johansen's command,
the men sight a great stone pillar sticking out of the sea, and in
S. Latitude 47° 9′, W. Longitude 126° 43′[47] come upon a coast-
line of mingled mud, ooze, and weedy Cyclopean masonry
which can be nothing less than the tangible substance of earth's
supreme terror—the nightmare corpse-city of R'lyeh, that was
built in measureless aeons behind history by the vast, loathsome
shapes that seeped down from the dark stars. There lay great
Cthulhu and his hordes, hidden in green slimy vaults and sending out at last, after cycles incalculable, the thoughts that spread
fear to the dreams of the sensitive and called imperiously to the
faithful to come on a pilgrimage of liberation and restoration. All
this Johansen did not suspect, but God knows he soon saw
enough!

I suppose that only a single mountain-top, the hideous
monolith-crowned citadel whereon great Cthulhu was buried,
actually emerged from the waters. When I think of the *extent* of
all that may be brooding down there I almost wish to kill myself
forthwith. Johansen and his men were awed by the cosmic
majesty of this dripping Babylon of elder daemons, and must
have guessed without guidance that it was nothing of this or of
any sane planet. Awe at the unbelievable size of the greenish
stone blocks, at the dizzying height of the great carven monolith,
and at the stupefying identity of the colossal statues and bas-
reliefs with the queer image found in the shrine on the *Alert*, is
poignantly visible in every line of the mate's frightened description.

Without knowing what futurism is like, Johansen achieved
something very close to it when he spoke of the city; for instead
of describing any definite structure or building, he dwells only
on broad impressions of vast angles and stone surfaces—surfaces
too great to belong to any thing right or proper for this earth,
and impious with horrible images and hieroglyphs. I mention his
talk about *angles* because it suggests something Wilcox had told

me of his awful dreams. He has said that the *geometry* of the dream-place he saw was abnormal, non-Euclidean,[48] and loathsomely redolent of spheres and dimensions apart from ours. Now an unlettered seaman felt the same thing whilst gazing at the terrible reality.

Johansen and his men landed at a sloping mud-bank on this monstrous Acropolis, and clambered slipperily up over titan oozy blocks which could have been no mortal staircase. The very sun of heaven seemed distorted when viewed through the polarising miasma welling out from this sea-soaked perversion, and twisted menace and suspense lurked leeringly in those crazily elusive angles of carven rock where a second glance shewed concavity after the first shewed convexity.

Something very like fright had come over all the explorers before anything more definite than rock and ooze and weed was seen. Each would have fled had he not feared the scorn of the others, and it was only half-heartedly that they searched—vainly, as it proved—for some portable souvenir to bear away.

It was Rodriguez the Portuguese who climbed up the foot of the monolith and shouted of what he had found. The rest followed him, and looked curiously at the immense carved door with the now familiar squid-dragon bas-relief. It was, Johansen said, like a great barn-door; and they all felt that it was a door because of the ornate lintel, threshold, and jambs around it, though they could not decide whether it lay flat like a trap-door or slantwise like an outside cellar-door. As Wilcox would have said, the geometry of the place was all wrong. One could not be sure that the sea and the ground were horizontal, hence the relative position of everything else seemed phantasmally variable.

Briden pushed at the stone in several places without result. Then Donovan felt over it delicately around the edge, pressing each point separately as he went. He climbed interminably along the grotesque stone moulding—that is, one would call it climbing if the thing was not after all horizontal—and the men wondered how any door in the universe could be so vast. Then, very softly and slowly, the acre-great panel began to give inward at the top; and they saw that it was balanced. Donovan slid or somehow propelled himself down or along the jamb and re-

joined his fellows, and everyone watched the
the monstrously carven portal. In this phantasy
tortion it moved anomalously in a diagonal way,
rules of matter and perspective seemed upset.

The aperture was black with a darkness almost ma
tenebrousness was indeed a *positive quality*;[49] for it
such parts of the inner walls as ought to have been revealed, and
actually burst forth like smoke from its aeon-long imprisonment,
visibly darkening the sun as it slunk away into the shrunken and
gibbous sky on flapping membraneous wings. The odour arising
from the newly opened depths was intolerable, and at length the
quick-eared Hawkins thought he heard a nasty, slopping sound
down there. Everyone listened, and everyone was listening
still when It lumbered slobberingly into sight and gropingly
squeezed Its gelatinous green immensity through the black doorway into the tainted outside air of that poison city of madness.

Poor Johansen's handwriting almost gave out when he wrote
of this. Of the six men who never reached the ship, he thinks two
perished of pure fright in that accursed instant. The Thing cannot be described—there is no language for such abysms of
shrieking and immemorial lunacy, such eldritch contradictions of
all matter, force, and cosmic order. A mountain walked or stumbled. God! What wonder that across the earth a great architect
went mad, and poor Wilcox raved with fever in that telepathic
instant? The Thing of the idols, the green, sticky spawn of the
stars, had awaked to claim his own. The stars were right again,
and what an age-old cult had failed to do by design, a band of innocent sailors had done by accident. After vigintillions of years
great Cthulhu was loose again, and ravening for delight.

Three men were swept up by the flabby claws before anybody
turned. God rest them, if there be any rest in the universe. They
were Donovan, Guerrera, and Ångstrom. Parker slipped as the
other three were plunging frenziedly over endless vistas of
green-crusted rock to the boat, and Johansen swears he was
swallowed up by an angle of masonry which shouldn't have been
there; an angle which was acute, but behaved as if it were obtuse.
So only Briden and Johansen reached the boat, and pulled desperately for the *Alert* as the mountainous monstrosity flopped

down the slimy stones and hesitated floundering at the edge of the water.

Steam had not been suffered to go down entirely, despite the departure of all hands for the shore; and it was the work of only a few moments of feverish rushing up and down between wheel and engines to get the *Alert* under way. Slowly, amidst the distorted horrors of that indescribable scene, she began to churn the lethal waters; whilst on the masonry of that charnel shore that was not of earth the titan Thing from the stars slavered and gibbered like Polypheme cursing the fleeing ship of Odysseus. Then, bolder than the storied Cyclops, great Cthulhu slid greasily into the water and began to pursue with vast waveraising strokes of cosmic potency. Briden looked back and went mad,[50] laughing shrilly as he kept on laughing at intervals till death found him one night in the cabin whilst Johansen was wandering deliriously.

But Johansen had not given out yet. Knowing that the Thing could surely overtake the *Alert* until steam was fully up, he resolved on a desperate chance; and, setting the engine for full speed, ran lightning-like on deck and reversed the wheel. There was a mighty eddying and foaming in the noisome brine, and as the steam mounted higher and higher the brave Norwegian drove his vessel head on against the pursuing jelly which rose above the unclean froth like the stern of a daemon galleon. The awful squid-head with writhing feelers came nearly up to the bowsprit of the sturdy yacht, but Johansen drove on relentlessly. There was a bursting as of an exploding bladder, a slushy nastiness as of a cloven sunfish, a stench as of a thousand opened graves, and a sound that the chronicler would not put on paper. For an instant the ship was befouled by an acrid and blinding green cloud, and then there was only a venomous seething astern; where—God in heaven!—the scattered plasticity of that nameless sky-spawn was nebulously *recombining* in its hateful original form, whilst its distance widened every second as the *Alert* gained impetus from its mounting steam.

That was all. After that Johansen only brooded over the idol in the cabin and attended to a few matters of food for himself and the laughing maniac by his side. He did not try to navigate after the first bold flight, for the reaction had taken something out of his soul. Then came the storm of April 2nd, and a gathering of the clouds about his consciousness. There is a sense of spectral whirling through liquid gulfs of infinity, of dizzying rides through reeling universes on a comet's tail, and of hysterical plunges from the pit to the moon and from the moon back again to the pit, all livened by a cachinnating chorus of the distorted, hilarious elder gods and the green, bat-winged mocking imps of Tartarus.

Out of that dream came rescue—the *Vigilant,* the vice-admiralty court, the streets of Dunedin, and the long voyage back home to the old house by the Egeberg. He could not tell—they would think him mad. He would write of what he knew before death came, but his wife must not guess. Death would be a boon if only it could blot out the memories.

That was the document I read, and now I have placed it in the tin box beside the bas-relief and the papers of Professor Angell. With it shall go this record of mine—this test of my own sanity, wherein is pieced together that which I hope may never be pieced together again. I have looked upon all that the universe has to hold of horror, and even the skies of spring and the flowers of summer must ever afterward be poison to me. But I do not think my life will be long. As my uncle went, as poor Johansen went, so I shall go. I know too much, and the cult still lives.

Cthulhu still lives, too, I suppose, again in that chasm of stone which has shielded him since the sun was young. His accursed city is sunken once more, for the *Vigilant* sailed over the spot after the April storm; but his ministers on earth still bellow and prance and slay around idol-capped monoliths in lonely places. He must have been trapped by the sinking whilst within his black abyss, or the world would by now be screaming with fright and frenzy. Who knows the end? What has risen may sink, and what has sunk may rise. Loathsomeness waits and dreams in the deep, and decay spreads over the tottering cities of men. A time will come—but I must not and cannot think! Let me pray that, if I do not survive this manuscript, my executors may put caution before audacity and see that it meets no other eye.

The Colour Out of Space

West of Arkham the hills rise wild, and there are valleys with deep woods that no axe has ever cut. There are dark narrow glens where the trees slope fantastically, and where thin brooklets trickle without ever having caught the glint of sunlight. On the gentler slopes there are farms, ancient and rocky, with squat, moss-coated cottages brooding eternally over old New England secrets in the lee of great ledges; but these are all vacant now, the wide chimneys crumbling and the shingled sides bulging perilously beneath low gambrel roofs.

The old folk have gone away, and foreigners do not like to live there. French-Canadians have tried it, Italians have tried it, and the Poles have come and departed. It is not because of anything that can be seen or heard or handled, but because of something that is imagined. The place is not good for the imagination, and does not bring restful dreams at night. It must be this which keeps the foreigners away, for old Ammi Pierce has never told them of anything he recalls from the strange days. Ammi, whose head has been a little queer for years, is the only one who still remains, or who ever talks of the strange days; and he dares to do this because his house is so near the open fields and the travelled roads around Arkham.

There was once a road over the hills and through the valleys, that ran straight where the blasted heath is now; but people ceased to use it and a new road was laid curving far toward the south. Traces of the old one can still be found amidst the weeds of a returning wilderness, and some of them will doubtless linger even when half the hollows are flooded for the new reservoir. Then the dark woods will be cut down and the blasted heath will slumber far below blue waters whose surface will mirror the sky and ripple in the sun. And the secrets of the strange days will be one with the deep's secrets; one with the hidden lore of old ocean, and all the mystery of primal earth.

When I went into the hills and vales to survey for the new reservoir they told me the place was evil. They told me this in Arkham, and because that is a very old town full of witch legends I thought the evil must be something which grandams had whispered to children through centuries. The name "blasted heath" seemed to me very odd and theatrical, and I wondered how it had come into the folklore of a Puritan people. Then I saw that dark westward tangle of glens and slopes for myself, and ceased to wonder at anything besides its own elder mystery. It was morning when I saw it, but shadow lurked always there. The trees grew too thickly, and their trunks were too big for any healthy New England wood. There was too much silence in the dim alleys between them, and the floor was too soft with the dank moss and mattings of infinite years of decay.

In the open spaces, mostly along the line of the old road, there were little hillside farms; sometimes with all the buildings standing, sometimes with only one or two, and sometimes with only a lone chimney or fast-filling cellar. Weeds and briers reigned, and furtive wild things rustled in the undergrowth. Upon everything was a haze of restlessness and oppression; a touch of the unreal and the grotesque, as if some vital element of perspective or chiaroscuro were awry. I did not wonder that the foreigners would not stay, for this was no region to sleep in. It was too much like a landscape of Salvator Rosa; too much like some forbidden woodcut in a tale of terror.[1]

But even all this was not so bad as the blasted heath. I knew it the moment I came upon it at the bottom of a spacious valley; for no other name could fit such a thing, or any other thing fit such a name. It was as if the poet had coined the phrase from having seen this one particular region.[2] It must, I thought as I viewed it, be the outcome of a fire; but why had nothing new ever grown over those five acres of grey desolation that sprawled open to the sky like a great spot eaten by acid in the woods and fields? It lay largely to the north of the ancient road line, but encroached a little on the other side. I felt an odd reluctance about approaching, and did so at last only because my business took me through and past it. There was no vegetation of any kind on that broad expanse, but only a fine grey dust or ash which no wind seemed ever to blow about. The trees near it were sickly and stunted, and many dead trunks stood or lay rotting at the rim. As I walked hurriedly by I saw the tumbled bricks and stones of an old chimney and cellar on my right, and the yawning black maw of an abandoned well whose stagnant vapours played strange tricks with the hues of the sunlight. Even the long, dark woodland climb beyond seemed welcome in contrast, and I marvelled no more at the frightened whispers of Arkham people. There had been no house or ruin near; even in the old days the place must have been lonely and remote. And at twilight, dreading to repass that ominous spot, I walked circuitously back to the town by the curving road on the south. I vaguely wished some clouds would gather, for an odd timidity about the deep skyey voids above had crept into my soul.

In the evening I asked old people in Arkham about the blasted heath, and what was meant by that phrase "strange days" which so many evasively muttered. I could not, however, get any good answers, except that all the mystery was much more recent than I had dreamed. It was not a matter of old legendry at all, but something within the lifetime of those who spoke. It had happened in the 'eighties, and a family had disappeared or was killed. Speakers would not be exact; and because they all told me to pay no attention to old Ammi Pierce's crazy tales, I sought him out the next morning, having heard that he lived alone in the ancient tottering cottage where the trees first begin to get thick. It was a fearsomely archaic place, and had begun to exude the faint miasmal odour which clings about houses that have stood too long. Only with persistent knocking could I rouse the aged man, and when he shuffled timidly to the door I could tell he was not glad to see me. He was not so feeble as I had expected; but his eyes drooped in a curious way, and his unkempt clothing and white beard made him seem very worn and dismal. Not knowing just how he could best be launched on his tales, I feigned a matter of business; told him of my surveying, and asked vague questions about the district. He was far brighter and more educated than I had been led to think, and before I knew it had grasped quite as much of the subject as any man I had talked with in Arkham. He was not like other rustics I had known in the sections where reservoirs were to be. From him there were no protests at the miles of old wood and farmland to be blotted out, though perhaps there would have been had not his home lain outside the bounds of the future lake. Relief was all that he shewed; relief at the doom of the dark ancient valleys through which he had roamed all his life. They were better under water now—better under water since the strange days. And with this opening his husky voice sank low, while his body leaned forward and his right forefinger began to point shakily and impressively.

It was then that I heard the story, and as the rambling voice scraped and whispered on I shivered again and again despite the summer day. Often I had to recall the speaker from ramblings, piece out scientific points which he knew only by a fading parrot memory of professors' talk, or bridge over gaps where his sense of logic and continuity broke down. When he was done I did not wonder that his mind had snapped a trifle, or that the folk of Arkham would not speak much of the blasted heath. I hurried back before sunset to my hotel, unwilling to have the stars come out above me in the open; and the next day returned to Boston to give up my position. I could not go into that dim chaos of old forest and slope again, or face another time that grey blasted heath where the black well yawned deep beside the tumbled bricks and stones. The reservoir will soon be built now, and all those elder secrets will be safe forever under watery fathoms. But even then I do not believe I would like to visit that country by night—at least, not when the sinister stars are out; and nothing could bribe me to drink the new city water of Arkham.

It all began, old Ammi said, with the meteorite. Before that time there had been no wild legends at all since the witch trials, and even then these western woods were not feared half so much as the small island in the Miskatonic where the devil held court beside a curious stone altar older than the Indians.[3] These were not haunted woods, and their fantastic dusk was never terrible till the strange days. Then there had come that white noontide cloud, that string of explosions in the air, and that pillar of smoke from the valley far in the wood. And by night all Arkham had heard of the great rock that fell out of the sky and bedded itself in the ground beside the well at the Nahum Gardner place.[4] That

was the house which had stood where the blasted heath was to
come—the trim white Nahum Gardner house amidst its fertile
gardens and orchards.

Nahum had come to town to tell people about the stone, and
had dropped in at Ammi Pierce's on the way. Ammi was forty
then, and all the queer things were fixed very strongly in his
mind. He and his wife had gone with the three professors from
Miskatonic University who hastened out the next morning to see
the weird visitor from unknown stellar space, and had wondered
why Nahum had called it so large the day before. It had shrunk,
Nahum said as he pointed out the big brownish mound above
the ripped earth and charred grass near the archaic well-sweep in
his front yard; but the wise men answered that stones do not
shrink. Its heat lingered persistently, and Nahum declared it had
glowed faintly in the night. The professors tried it with a geolo-
gist's hammer and found it was oddly soft. It was, in truth, so
soft as to be almost plastic; and they gouged rather than chipped
a specimen to take back to the college for testing. They took it in
an old pail borrowed from Nahum's kitchen, for even the small
piece refused to grow cool. On the trip back they stopped at
Ammi's to rest, and seemed thoughtful when Mrs. Pierce remarked that the fragment was growing smaller and burning the
bottom of the pail. Truly, it was not large, but perhaps they had
taken less than they thought.

The day after that—all this was in June of '82—the professors
had trooped out again in a great excitement. As they passed
Ammi's they told him what queer things the specimen had done,
and how it had faded wholly away when they put it in a glass
beaker. The beaker had gone, too, and the wise men talked of the
strange stone's affinity for silicon. It had acted quite unbelievably
in that well-ordered laboratory; doing nothing at all and shewing
no occluded gases when heated on charcoal, being wholly negative in the borax bead, and soon proving itself absolutely non-
volatile at any producible temperature, including that of the
oxy-hydrogen blowpipe.[5] On an anvil it appeared highly mal-
leable, and in the dark its luminosity was very marked. Stub-
bornly refusing to grow cool, it soon had the college in a state of
real excitement; and when upon heating before the spectroscope[6]

it displayed shining bands unlike any known colours of the normal spectrum there was much breathless talk of new elements, bizarre optical properties, and other things which puzzled men of science are wont to say when faced by the unknown.

Hot as it was, they tested it in a crucible with all the proper reagents. Water did nothing. Hydrochloric acid was the same. Nitric acid and even aqua regia merely hissed and spattered against its torrid invulnerability.[7] Ammi had difficulty in recalling all these things, but recognised some solvents as I mentioned them in the usual order of use. There were ammonia and caustic soda, alcohol and ether, nauseous carbon disulphide and a dozen others;[8] but although the weight grew steadily less as time passed, and the fragment seemed to be slightly cooling, there was no change in the solvents to shew that they had attacked the substance at all. It was a metal, though, beyond a doubt. It was magnetic, for one thing; and after its immersion in the acid solvents there seemed to be faint traces of the Widmannstätten figures found on meteoric iron.[9] When the cooling had grown very considerable, the testing was carried on in glass; and it was in a glass beaker that they left all the chips made of the original fragment during the work. The next morning both chips and beaker were gone without trace, and only a charred spot marked the place on the wooden shelf where they had been.

All this the professors told Ammi as they paused at his door, and once more he went with them to see the stony messenger from the stars, though this time his wife did not accompany him. It had now most certainly shrunk, and even the sober professors could not doubt the truth of what they saw. All around the dwindling brown lump near the well was a vacant space, except where the earth had caved in; and whereas it had been a good seven feet across the day before, it was now scarcely five. It was still hot, and the sages studied its surface curiously as they detached another and larger piece with hammer and chisel. They gouged deeply this time, and as they pried away the smaller mass they saw that the core of the thing was not quite homogeneous.

They had uncovered what seemed to be the side of a large coloured globule imbedded in the substance. The colour, which resembled some of the bands in the meteor's strange spectrum, was almost impossible to describe; and it was only by analogy that they called it colour at all.[10] Its texture was glossy, and upon tapping it appeared to promise both brittleness and hollowness. One of the professors gave it a smart blow with a hammer, and it burst with a nervous little pop. Nothing was emitted, and all trace of the thing vanished with the puncturing. If left behind a hollow spherical space about three inches across, and all thought it probable that others would be discovered as the enclosing substance wasted away.

Conjecture was vain; so after a futile attempt to find additional globules by drilling, the seekers left again with their new specimen—which proved, however, as baffling in the laboratory as its predecessor had been. Aside from being almost plastic, having heat, magnetism, and slight luminosity, cooling slightly in powerful acids, possessing an unknown spectrum, wasting away in air, and attacking silicon compounds with mutual destruction as a result, it presented no identifying features whatsoever; and at the end of the tests the college scientists were forced to own that they could not place it. It was nothing of this earth, but a piece of the great outside; and as such dowered with outside properties and obedient to outside laws.

That night there was a thunderstorm, and when the professors went out to Nahum's the next day they met with a bitter disappointment. The stone, magnetic as it had been, must have had some peculiar electrical property; for it had "drawn the lightning", as Nahum said, with a singular persistence. Six times within an hour the farmer saw the lightning strike the furrow in the front yard, and when the storm was over nothing remained but a ragged pit by the ancient well-sweep, half-choked with caved-in earth. Digging had borne no fruit, and the scientists verified the fact of the utter vanishment. The failure was total; so that nothing was left to do but go back to the laboratory and test again the disappearing fragment left carefully cased in lead. That fragment lasted a week, at the end of which nothing of value had been learned of it. When it had gone, no residue was left behind, and in time the professors felt scarcely sure they had indeed seen with waking eyes that cryptic vestige of the fathomless gulfs outside; that lone, weird message from other universes and other realms of matter, force, and entity.

As was natural, the Arkham papers made much of the incident with its collegiate sponsoring, and sent reporters to talk with Nahum Gardner and his family. At least one Boston daily also sent a scribe, and Nahum quickly became a kind of local celebrity. He was a lean, genial person of about fifty, living with his wife and three sons on the pleasant farmstead in the valley. He and Ammi exchanged visits frequently, as did their wives; and Ammi had nothing but praise for him after all these years. He seemed slightly proud of the notice his place had attracted, and talked often of the meteorite in the succeeding weeks. That July and August were hot, and Nahum worked hard at his haying in the ten-acre pasture across Chapman's Brook;[11] his rattling wain wearing deep ruts in the shadowy lanes between. The labour tired him more than it had in other years, and he felt that age was beginning to tell on him.

Then fell the time of fruit and harvest. The pears and apples slowly ripened, and Nahum vowed that his orchards were prospering as never before. The fruit was growing to phenomenal size and unwonted gloss, and in such abundance that extra barrels were ordered to handle the future crop. But with the ripening came sore disappointment; for of all that gorgeous array of specious lusciousness not one single jot was fit to eat. Into the fine flavour of the pears and apples had crept a stealthy bitterness and sickishness, so that even the smallest of bites induced a lasting disgust. It was the same with the melons and tomatoes, and Nahum sadly saw that his entire crop was lost. Quick to connect events, he declared that the meteorite had poisoned the soil, and thanked heaven that most of the other crops were in the upland lot along the road.

Winter came early, and was very cold. Ammi saw Nahum less often than usual, and observed that he had begun to look worried. The rest of his family, too, seemed to have grown taciturn; and were far from steady in their chuchgoing or their attendance at the various social events of the countryside. For this reserve or melancholy no cause could be found, though all the household

confessed now and then to poorer health and a feeling of vague
disquiet. Nahum himself gave the most definite statement of
anyone when he said he was disturbed about certain footprints in
the snow. They were the usual winter prints of red squirrels,
white rabbits, and foxes, but the brooding farmer professed to
see something not quite right about their nature and arrangement. He was never specific, but appeared to think that they
were not as characteristic of the anatomy and habit of squirrels
and rabbits and foxes as they ought to be. Ammi listened without interest to this talk until one night when he drove past
Nahum's house in his sleigh on the way back from Clark's Corners.[12] There had been a moon, and a rabbit had run across the
road, and the leaps of the rabbit were longer than either Ammi or
his horse liked. The latter, indeed, had almost run away when
brought up by a firm rein. Thereafter Ammi gave Nahum's tales
more respect, and wondered why the Gardner dogs seemed so
cowed and quivering every morning. They had, it developed,
nearly lost the spirit to bark.

In February the McGregor boys from Meadow Hill were out
shooting woodchucks, and not far from the Gardner place
bagged a very peculiar specimen. The proportions of its body
seemed slightly altered in a queer way impossible to describe,
while its face had taken on an expression which no one ever saw
in a woodchuck before. The boys were genuinely frightened, and
threw the thing away at once, so that only their grotesque tales
of it ever reached the people of the countryside. But the shying
of the horses near Nahum's house had now become an acknowledged thing, and all the basis for a cycle of whispered legend was
fast taking form.

People vowed that the snow melted faster around Nahum's
than it did anywhere else, and early in March there was an awed
discussion in Potter's general store in Clark's Corners. Stephen
Rice[13] had driven past Gardner's in the morning, and had noticed
the skunk-cabbages coming up through the mud by the woods
across the road. Never were things of such size seen before, and
they had held strange colours that could not be put into any
words. Their shapes were monstrous, and the horse had snorted
at an odour which struck Stephen as wholly unprecedented. That

afternoon several persons drove past to see the abnormal growth, and all agreed that plants of that kind ought never to sprout in a healthy world. The bad fruit of the fall before was freely mentioned, and it went from mouth to mouth that there was poison in Nahum's ground. Of course it was the meteorite; and remembering how strange the men from the college had found that stone to be, several farmers spoke about the matter to them.

One day they paid Nahum a visit; but having no love of wild tales and folklore were very conservative in what they inferred. The plants were certainly odd, but all skunk-cabbages are more or less odd in shape and odour and hue. Perhaps some mineral element from the stone had entered the soil, but it would soon be washed away. And as for the footprints and frightened horses—of course this was mere country talk which such a phenomenon as the aërolite would be certain to start. There was really nothing for serious men to do in cases of wild gossip, for superstitious rustics will say and believe anything. And so all through the strange days the professors stayed away in contempt. Only one of them, when given two phials of dust for analysis in a police job over a year and a half later, recalled that the queer colour of that skunk-cabbage had been very like one of the anomalous bands of light shewn by the meteor fragment in the college spectroscope, and like the brittle globule found imbedded in the stone from the abyss. The samples in this analysis case gave the same odd bands at first, though later they lost the property.

The trees budded prematurely around Nahum's, and at night they swayed ominously in the wind. Nahum's second son Thaddeus, a lad of fifteen, swore that they swayed also when there was no wind; but even the gossips would not credit this. Certainly, however, restlessness was in the air. The entire Gardner family developed the habit of stealthy listening, though not for any sound which they could consciously name. The listening was, indeed, rather a product of moments when consciousness seemed half to slip away. Unfortunately such moments increased week by week, till it became common speech that "something was wrong with all Nahum's folks". When the early saxifrage came out it had another strange colour; not quite like that of the skunk-cabbage, but plainly related and equally unknown to anyone who saw it. Nahum took some blossoms to Arkham and shewed them to the editor of the *Gazette*,[14] but that dignitary did no more than write a humorous article about them, in which the dark fears of rustics were held up to polite ridicule. It was a mistake of Nahum's to tell a stolid city man about the way the great, overgrown mourning-cloak butterflies behaved in connexion with these saxifrages.

April brought a kind of madness to the country folk, and began that disuse of the road past Nahum's which led to its ultimate abandonment. It was the vegetation. All the orchard trees blossomed forth in strange colours, and through the stony soil of the yard and adjacent pasturage there sprang up a bizarre growth which only a botanist could connect with the proper flora of the region. No sane wholesome colours were anywhere to be seen except in the green grass and leafage; but everywhere those hectic and prismatic variants of some diseased, underlying primary tone without a place among the known tints of earth. The Dutchman's breeches became a thing of sinister menace, and the bloodroots grew insolent in their chromatic perversion. Ammi and the Gardners thought that most of the colours had a sort of haunting familiarity, and decided that they reminded one of the brittle globule in the meteor. Nahum ploughed and sowed the ten-acre pasture and the upland lot, but did nothing with the land around the house. He knew it would be of no use, and hoped that the summer's strange growths would draw all the poison from the soil. He was prepared for almost anything now, and had grown used to the sense of something near him waiting to be heard. The shunning of his house by neighbours told on him, of course; but it told on his wife more. The boys were better off, being at school each day; but they could not help being frightened by the gossip. Thaddeus, an especially sensitive youth, suffered the most.

In May the insects came, and Nahum's place became a nightmare of buzzing and crawling. Most of the creatures seemed not quite usual in their aspects and motions, and their nocturnal habits contradicted all former experience. The Gardners took to watching at night—watching in all directions at random for something . . . they could not tell what. It was then that they all owned that Thaddeus had been right about the trees. Mrs. Gardner was the next to see it from the window as she watched the swollen boughs of a maple against a moonlit sky. The boughs surely moved, and there was no wind. It must be the sap. Strangeness had come into everything growing now. Yet it was none of Nahum's family at all who made the next discovery. Familiarity had dulled them, and what they could not see was glimpsed by a timid woodmill salesman from Bolton[15] who drove by one night in ignorance of the country legends. What he told in Arkham was given a short paragraph in the *Gazette*; and it was there that all the farmers, Nahum included, saw it first. The night had been dark and the buggy-lamps faint, but around a farm in the valley which everyone knew from the account must be Nahum's the darkness had been less thick. A dim though distinct luminosity seemed to inhere in all the vegetation, grass, leaves, and blossoms alike, while at one moment a detached piece of the phosphorescence appeared to stir furtively in the yard near the barn.

The grass had so far seemed untouched, and the cows were freely pastured in the lot near the house, but toward the end of May the milk began to be bad. Then Nahum had the cows driven to the uplands, after which the trouble ceased. Not long after this the change in grass and leaves became apparent to the eye. All the verdure was going grey, and was developing a highly singular quality of brittleness. Ammi was now the only person who ever visited the place, and his visits were becoming fewer and fewer. When school closed the Gardners were virtually cut off from the world, and sometimes let Ammi do their errands in town. They were failing curiously both physically and mentally, and no one was surprised when the news of Mrs. Gardner's madness stole around.

It happened in June, about the anniversary of the meteor's fall, and the poor woman screamed about things in the air which she could not describe. In her raving there was not a single specific noun, but only verbs and pronouns.[16] Things moved and changed and fluttered, and ears tingled to impulses which were not wholly sounds. Something was taken away—she was being drained of something—something was fastening itself on her that ought not to be—someone must make it keep off—nothing was ever still in the night—the walls and windows shifted. Nahum did not send her to the county asylum, but let her wander about the house as long as she was harmless to herself and others. Even when her expression changed he did nothing. But when the boys grew afraid of her, and Thaddeus nearly fainted at the way she made faces at him, he decided to keep her locked up in the attic.[17] By July she had ceased to speak and crawled on all fours, and before that month was over Nahum got the mad notion that she was slightly luminous in the dark, as he now clearly saw was the case with the nearby vegetation.

It was a little before this that the horses had stampeded. Something had aroused them in the night, and their neighing and kicking in the stalls had been terrible. There seemed virtually nothing to do to calm them, and when Nahum opened the stable door they all bolted out like frightened woodland deer. It took a week to track all four, and when found they were seen to be quite useless and unmanageable. Something had snapped in their brains, and each one had to be shot for its own good. Nahum borrowed a horse from Ammi for his haying, but found it would not approach the barn. It shied, balked, and whinnied, and in the end he could do nothing but drive it into the yard while the men used their own strength to get the heavy wagon near enough the hayloft for convenient pitching. And all the while the vegetation was turning grey and brittle. Even the flowers whose hues had been so strange were greying now, and the fruit was coming out grey and dwarfed and tasteless. The asters and goldenrod bloomed grey and distorted, and the roses and zinneas and hollyhocks in the front yard were such blasphemous-looking things that Nahum's oldest boy Zenas cut them down. The strangely puffed insects died about that time, even the bees that had left their hives and taken to the woods.

By September all the vegetation was fast crumbling to a greyish powder, and Nahum feared that the trees would die before the poison was out of the soil. His wife now had spells of terrific screaming, and he and the boys were in a constant state of nervous tension. They shunned people now, and when school opened the boys did not go. But it was Ammi, on one of his rare visits, who first realised that the well water was no longer good. It had an evil taste that was not exactly foetid nor exactly salty, and Ammi advised his friend to dig another well on higher ground to use till the soil was good again. Nahum, however, ignored the warning, for he had by that time become calloused to strange and unpleasant things. He and the boys continued to use the tainted supply, drinking it as listlessly and mechanically as they ate their meagre and ill-cooked meals and did their thankless and monotonous chores through the aimless days. There was something of stolid resignation about them all, as if they walked half in another world between lines of nameless guards to a certain and familiar doom.

Thaddeus went mad in September after a visit to the well. He had gone with a pail and had come back empty-handed, shrieking and waving his arms, and sometimes lapsing into an inane titter or a whisper about "the moving colours down there". Two in one family was pretty bad, but Nahum was very brave about it. He let the boy run about for a week until he began stumbling and hurting himself, and then he shut him in an attic room across the hall from his mother's. The way they screamed at each other from behind their locked doors was very terrible, especially to little Merwin, who fancied they talked in some terrible language that was not of earth. Merwin was getting frightfully imaginative, and his restlessness was worse after the shutting away of the brother who had been his greatest playmate.

Almost at the same time the mortality among the livestock commenced. Poultry turned greyish and died very quickly, their meat being found dry and noisome upon cutting. Hogs grew inordinately fat, then suddenly began to undergo loathsome changes which no one could explain. Their meat was of course useless, and Nahum was at his wit's end. No rural veterinary would approach his place, and the city veterinary from Arkham was openly baffled. The swine began growing grey and brittle and falling to pieces before they died, and their eyes and muzzles developed singular alterations. It was very inexplicable, for they had never been fed from the tainted vegetation. Then something struck the cows. Certain areas or sometimes the whole body would be uncannily shrivelled or compressed, and atrocious collapses or disintegrations were common. In the last stages—and death was always the result—there would be a greying and turning brittle like that which beset the hogs. There could be no question of poison, for all the cases occurred in a locked and undisturbed barn. No bites of prowling things could have brought the virus, for what live beast of earth can pass through solid obstacles? It must only be natural disease—yet what disease could wreak such results was beyond any mind's guessing. When the harvest came there was not an animal surviving on the place, for the stock and poultry were dead and the dogs had run away. These dogs, three in number, had all vanished one night and were never heard of again. The five cats had left some time before, but their going was scarcely noticed since there now seemed to be no mice, and only Mrs. Gardner had made pets of the graceful felines.

On the nineteenth of October Nahum staggered into Ammi's house with hideous news. The death had come to poor Thaddeus in his attic room, and it had come in a way which could not be told. Nahum had dug a grave in the railed family plot behind the farm, and had put therein what he found. There could have been nothing from outside, for the small barred window and locked door were intact; but it was much as it had been in the barn. Ammi and his wife consoled the stricken man as best they could, but shuddered as they did so. Stark terror seemed to cling around the Gardners and all they touched, and the very presence of one in the house was a breath from regions unnamed and unnamable. Ammi accompanied Nahum home with the greatest reluctance, and did what he might to calm the hysterical sobbing of little Merwin. Zenas needed no calming. He had come of late to do nothing but stare into space and obey what his father told him; and Ammi thought that his fate was very merciful. Now and then Merwin's screams were answered faintly from the attic, and in response to an inquiring look Nahum said that his wife was getting very feeble. When night approached, Ammi managed to get away; for not even friendship could make him stay in that spot when the faint glow of the vegetation began and the trees may or may not have swayed without wind. It was really lucky for Ammi that he was not more imaginative. Even as things were, his mind was bent ever so slightly; but had he been able to connect and reflect upon all the portents around him he must inevitably have turned a total maniac. In the twilight he hastened home, the screams of the mad woman and the nervous child ringing horribly in his ears.

Three days later Nahum lurched into Ammi's kitchen in the early morning, and in the absence of his host stammered out a desperate tale once more, while Mrs. Pierce listened in a clutching fright. It was little Merwin this time. He was gone. He had gone out late at night with a lantern and pail for water, and had never come back. He'd been going to pieces for days, and hardly knew what he was about. Screamed at everything. There had been a frantic shriek from the yard then, but before the father could get to the door, the boy was gone. There was no glow from the lantern he had taken, and of the child himself no trace. At the time Nahum thought the lantern and pail were gone too; but when dawn came, and the man had plodded back from his all-night search of the woods and fields, he had found some very curious things near the well. There was a crushed and apparently somewhat melted mass of iron which had certainly been the lantern; while a bent bail and twisted iron hoops beside it, both half-fused, seemed to hint at the remnants of the pail. That was all. Nahum was past imagining, Mrs. Pierce was blank, and Ammi, when he had reached home and heard the tale, could give no guess. Merwin was gone, and there would be no use in telling the people around, who shunned all Gardners now. No use, either, in telling the city people at Arkham who laughed at everything. Thad had gone, and now Mernie was gone. Something was creeping and creeping and waiting to be seen and felt and heard. Nahum would go soon, and he wanted Ammi to look after his wife and Zenas if they survived him. It must all be a judgment of some sort; though he could not fancy what for, since he had always walked uprightly in the Lord's ways so far as he knew.[18]

For over two weeks Ammi saw nothing of Nahum; and then, worried about what might have happened, he overcame his fears and paid the Gardner place a visit. There was no smoke from the great chimney, and for a moment the visitor was apprehensive of the worst. The aspect of the whole farm was shocking—greyish

withered grass and leaves on the ground, vines falling in brittle
wreckage from archaic walls and gables, and great bare trees
clawing up at the grey November sky with a studied malevolence
which Ammi could not but feel had come from some subtle
change in the tilt of the branches. But Nahum was alive, after all.
He was weak, and lying on a couch in the low-ceiled kitchen, but
perfectly conscious and able to give simple orders to Zenas. The
room was deadly cold; and as Ammi visibly shivered, the host
shouted huskily to Zenas for more wood. Wood, indeed, was
sorely needed; since the cavernous fireplace was unlit and empty,
with a cloud of soot blowing about in the chill wind that came
down the chimney. Presently Nahum asked him if the extra
wood had made him any more comfortable, and then Ammi saw
what had happened. The stoutest cord had broken at last, and the
hapless farmer's mind was proof against more sorrow.

Questioning tactfully, Ammi could get no clear data at all
about the missing Zenas. "In the well—he lives in the well—"
was all that the clouded father would say. Then there flashed
across the visitor's mind a sudden thought of the mad wife, and
he changed his line of inquiry. "Nabby? Why, here she is!" was
the surprised response of poor Nahum, and Ammi soon saw that
he must search for himself. Leaving the harmless babbler on the
couch, he took the keys from their nail beside the door and
climbed the creaking stairs to the attic. It was very close and noisome up there, and no sound could be heard from any direction.
Of the four doors in sight, only one was locked, and on this he
tried various keys on the ring he had taken. The third key proved
the right one, and after some fumbling Ammi threw open the
low white door.

It was quite dark inside, for the window was small and half-
obscured by the crude wooden bars; and Ammi could see nothing at all on the wide-planked floor. The stench was beyond
enduring, and before proceeding further he had to retreat to another room and return with his lungs filled with breathable air.
When he did enter he saw something dark in the corner, and
upon seeing it more clearly he screamed outright. While he
screamed he thought a momentary cloud eclipsed the window,
and a second later he felt himself brushed as if by some hateful

current of vapour. Strange colours danced before his eyes; and had not a present horror numbed him he would have thought of the globule in the meteor that the geologists hammer had shattered, and of the morbid vegetation that had sprouted in the spring. As it was he thought only of the blasphemous monstrosity which confronted him, and which all too clearly had shared the nameless fate of young Thaddeus and the livestock. But the terrible thing about this horror was that it very slowly and perceptibly moved as it continued to crumble.

Ammi would give me no added particulars to this scene, but the shape in the corner does not reappear in his tale as a moving object. There are things which cannot be mentioned, and what is done in common humanity is sometimes cruelly judged by the law. I gathered that no moving thing was left in that attic room, and that to leave anything capable of motion there would have been a deed so monstrous as to damn any accountable being to eternal torment. Anyone but a stolid farmer would have fainted or gone mad, but Ammi walked conscious through that low doorway and locked the accursed secret behind him. There would be Nahum to deal with now; he must be fed and tended, and removed to some place where he could be cared for.

Commencing his descent of the dark stairs, Ammi heard a thud below him. He even thought a scream had been suddenly choked off, and recalled nervously the clammy vapour which had brushed by him in that frightful room above. What presence had his cry and entry started up? Halted by some vague fear, he heard still further sounds below. Indubitably there was a sort of heavy dragging, and a most detestably sticky noise as of some fiendish and unclean species of suction. With an associative sense goaded to feverish heights, he thought unaccountably of what he had seen upstairs. Good God! What eldritch dream-world was this into which he had blundered? He dared move neither backward nor forward, but stood there trembling at the black curve of the boxed-in staircase. Every trifle of the scene burned itself into his brain. The sounds, the sense of dread expectancy, the darkness, the steepness of the narrow steps—and merciful heaven! . . . the faint but unmistakable luminosity of all the woodwork in sight; steps, sides, exposed laths, and beams alike!

Then there burst forth a frantic whinny from Ammi's horse outside, followed at once by a clatter which told of a frenzied runaway. In another moment horse and buggy had gone beyond earshot, leaving the frightened man on the dark stairs to guess what had sent them. But that was not all. There had been another sound out there. A sort of liquid splash—water—it must have been the well. He had left Hero untied near it, and a buggy-wheel must have brushed the coping and knocked in a stone. And still the pale phosphorescence glowed in that detestably ancient woodwork. God! how old the house was! Most of it built before 1670, and the gambrel roof not later than 1730.

A feeble scratching on the floor downstairs now sounded distinctly, and Ammi's grip tightened on a heavy stick he had picked up in the attic for some purpose. Slowly nerving himself, he finished his descent and walked boldly toward the kitchen. But he did not complete the walk, because what he sought was no longer there. It had come to meet him, and it was still alive after a fashion. Whether it had crawled or whether it had been dragged by any external force, Ammi could not say; but the death had been at it. Everything had happened in the last half-hour, but collapse, greying, and disintegration were already far advanced. There was a horrible brittleness, and dry fragments were scaling off. Ammi could not touch it, but looked horrifiedly into the distorted parody that had been a face. "What was it, Nahum—what was it?" He whispered, and the cleft, bulging lips were just able to crackle out a final answer.

"Nothin' . . . nothin' . . . the colour . . . it burns . . . cold an' wet . . . but it burns . . . it lived in the well . . . I seen it . . . a kind o' smoke . . . jest like the flowers last spring . . . the well shone at night . . . Thad an' Mernie an' Zenas . . . everything alive . . . suckin' the life out of everthing . . . in that stone . . . it must a' come in that stone . . . pizened the whole place . . . dun't know what it wants . . . that round thing them men from the college dug outen the stone . . . they smashed it . . . it was that same colour . . . jest the same, like the flowers an' plants . . . must a' ben more of 'em . . . seeds . . . seeds . . . they growed . . . I seen it the fust time this week . . . must a' got strong on Zenas . . . he was a big boy, full o' life . . . it beats down your mind an' then gits ye

. . . burns ye up . . . in the well water . . . you was right about that . . . evil water . . . Zenas never come back from the well . . . can't git away . . . draws ye . . . ye know summ'at's comin', but 'tain't no use . . . I seen it time an' agin senct Zenas was took . . . whar's Nabby, Ammi? . . . my head's no good . . . dun't know how long senct I fed her . . . it'll git her ef we ain't keerful . . . jest a colour . . . her face is gettin' to hev that colour sometimes towards night . . . an' it burns an' sucks . . . it come from some place whar things ain't as they is here . . . one o' them professors said so . . . he was right . . . look out, Ammi, it'll do suthin' more . . . sucks the life out. . . ."

But that was all. That which spoke could speak no more because it had completely caved in. Ammi laid a red checked tablecloth over what was left and reeled out the back door into the fields. He climbed the slope to the ten-acre pasture and stumbled home by the north road and the woods. He could not pass that well from which his horse had run away. He had looked at it through the window, and had seen that no stone was missing from the rim. Then the lurching buggy had not dislodged anything after all—the splash had been something else—something which went into the well after it had done with poor Nahum. . . .

When Ammi reached his house the horse and buggy had arrived before him and thrown his wife into fits of anxiety. Reassuring her without explanations, he set out at once for Arkham and notified the authorities that the Gardner family was no more. He indulged in no details, but merely told of the deaths of Nahum and Nabby, that of Thaddeus already being known, and mentioned that the cause seemed to be the same strange ailment which had killed the livestock. He also stated that Merwin and Zenas had disappeared. There was considerable questioning at the police station, and in the end Ammi was compelled to take three officers to the Gardner farm, together with the coroner, the medical examiner, and the veterinary who had treated the diseased animals. He went much against his will, for the afternoon was advancing and he feared the fall of night over that accursed place, but it was some comfort to have so many people with him.

The six men drove out in a democrat-wagon, following

Ammi's buggy, and arrived at the pest-ridden farmhouse about four o'clock. Used as the officers were to gruesome experiences, not one remained unmoved at what was found in the attic and under the red checked tablecloth on the floor below. The whole aspect of the farm with its grey desolation was terrible enough, but those two crumbling objects were beyond all bounds. No one could look long at them, and even the medical examiner admitted that there was very little to examine. Specimens could be analysed, of course, so he busied himself in obtaining them—and here it develops that a very puzzling aftermath occurred at the college laboratory where the two phials of dust were finally taken. Under the spectroscope both samples gave off an unknown spectrum, in which many of the baffling bands were precisely like those which the strange meteor had yielded in the previous year. The property of emitting this spectrum vanished in a month, the dust thereafter consisting mainly of alkaline phosphates and carbonates.

Ammi would not have told the men about the well if he had thought they meant to do anything then and there. It was getting toward sunset, and he was anxious to be away. But he could not help glancing nervously at the stony curb by the great sweep, and when a detective questioned him he admitted that Nahum had feared something down there—so much so that he had never even thought of searching it for Merwin or Zenas. After that nothing would do but that they empty and explore the well immediately, so Ammi had to wait trembling while pail after pail of rank water was hauled up and splashed on the soaking ground outside. The men sniffed in disgust at the fluid, and toward the last held their noses against the foetor they were uncovering. It was not so long a job as they had feared it would be, since the water was phenomenally low. There is no need to speak too exactly of what they found. Merwin and Zenas were both there, in part, though the vestiges were mainly skeletal. There were also a small deer and a large dog in about the same state, and a number of bones of smaller animals. The ooze and slime at the bottom seemed inexplicably porous and bubbling, and a man who descended on hand-holds with a long pole found that he could sink the wooden shaft to any depth in the mud of the floor without meeting any solid obstruction.

Twilight had now fallen, and lanterns were brought from the house. Then, when it was seen that nothing further could be gained from the well, everyone went indoors and conferred in the ancient sitting-room while the intermittent light of a spectral half-moon played wanly on the grey desolation outside. The men were frankly nonplussed by the entire case, and could find no convincing common element to link the strange vegetable conditions, the unknown disease of livestock and humans, and the unaccountable deaths of Merwin and Zenas in the tainted well. They had heard the common country talk, it is true; but could not believe that anything contrary to natural law had occurred.[19] No doubt the meteor had poisoned the soil, but the illness of persons and animals who had eaten nothing grown in that soil was another matter. Was it the well water? Very possibly. It might be a good idea to analyse it. But what peculiar madness could have made both boys jump into the well? Their deeds were so similar—and the fragments shewed that they had both suffered from the grey brittle death. Why was everything so grey and brittle?

It was the coroner, seated near a window overlooking the yard, who first noticed the glow about the well. Night had fully set in, and all the abhorrent grounds seemed faintly luminous with more than the fitful moonbeams; but this new glow was something definite and distinct, and appeared to shoot up from the black pit like a softened ray from a searchlight, giving dull reflections in the little ground pools where the water had been emptied. It had a very queer colour, and as all the men clustered round the window Ammi gave a violent start. For this strange beam of ghastly miasma was to him of no unfamiliar hue. He had seen that colour before, and feared to think what it might mean. He had seen it in the nasty brittle globule in the aërolite two summers ago, had seen it in the crazy vegetation of the springtime, and had thought he had seen it for an instant that very morning against the small barred window of that terrible attic room where nameless things had happened. It had flashed there a second, and a clammy and hateful current of vapour had brushed past him—and then poor Nahum had been taken by something of that colour. He had said so at the last—said it was like the globule and the plants. After that had come the runaway in the yard and the splash in the well—and now that well was belching forth to the night a pale insidious beam of the same daemoniac tint.

It does credit to the alertness of Ammi's mind that he puzzled even at that tense moment over a point which was essentially scientific. He could not but wonder at his gleaning of the same impression from a vapour glimpsed in the daytime, against a window opening on the morning sky, and from a nocturnal exhalation seen as a phosphorescent mist against the black and blasted landscape. It wasn't right—it was against Nature—and he thought of those terrible last words of his stricken friend, "It come from some place whar things ain't as they is here . . . one o' them professors said so. . . ."

All three horses outside, tied to a pair of shrivelled saplings by the road, were now neighing and pawing frantically. The wagon driver started for the door to do something, but Ammi laid a shaky hand on his shoulder. "Dun't go out thar," he whispered. "They's more to this nor what we know. Nahum said somethin' lived in the well that sucks your life out. He said it must be some'at growed from a round ball like one we all seen in the meteor stone that fell a year ago June. Sucks an' burns, he said, an' is jest a cloud of colour like that light out thar now, that ye can hardly see an' can't tell what it is. Nahum thought it feeds on everything livin' an' gits stronger all the time. He said he seen it this last week. It must be somethin' from away off in the sky like the men from the college last year says the meteor stone was. The way it's made an' the way it works ain't like no way o' God's world. It's some'at from beyond."

So the men paused indecisively as the light from the well grew stronger and the hitched horses pawed and whinnied in increasing frenzy. It was truly an awful moment; with terror in that ancient and accursed house itself, four monstrous sets of fragments—two from the house and two from the well—in the woodshed behind, and that shaft of unknown and unholy iridescence from the slimy depths in front. Ammi had restrained the driver on impulse, forgetting how uninjured he himself was after the clammy brushing of that coloured vapour in the attic room, but perhaps it is just as well that he acted as he did. No one will ever know what was abroad that night; and though the blasphemy from beyond had not so far hurt any human of unweakened mind, there is no telling what it might not have done at that last moment, and with its seemingly increased strength and the special signs of purpose it was soon to display beneath the half-clouded moonlit sky.

All at once one of the detectives at the window gave a short, sharp gasp. The others looked at him, and then quickly followed his own gaze upward to the point at which its idle straying had been suddenly arrested. There was no need for words. What had been disputed in country gossip was disputable no longer, and it is because of the thing which every man of that party agreed in whispering later on that the strange days are never talked about in Arkham. It is necessary to premise that there was no wind at that hour of the evening. One did arise not long afterward, but there was absolutely none then. Even the dry tips of the lingering hedge-mustard, grey and blighted, and the fringe on the roof of the standing democrat-wagon were unstirred. And yet amid that tense, godless calm the high bare boughs of all the trees in the yard were moving. They were twitching morbidly and spasmodically, clawing in convulsive and epileptic madness at the moonlit clouds; scratching impotently in the noxious air as if jerked by some alien and bodiless line of linkage with subterrene horrors writhing and struggling below the black roots.

Not a man breathed for several seconds. Then a cloud of darker depth passed over the moon, and the silhouette of clutching branches faded out momentarily. At this there was a general cry; muffled with awe, but husky and almost identical from every throat. For the terror had not faded with the silhouette, and in a fearsome instant of deeper darkness the watchers saw wriggling at that treetop height a thousand tiny points of faint and unhallowed radiance, tipping each bough like the fire of St. Elmo or the flames that came down on the apostles' heads at Pentecost.[20] It was a monstrous constellation of unnatural light,

like a glutted swarm of corpse-fed fireflies dancing hellish sara-
bands over an accursed marsh; and its colour was that same
nameless intrusion which Ammi had come to recognise and
dread. All the while the shaft of phosphorescence from the well
was getting brighter and brighter, bringing to the minds of the
huddled men a sense of doom and abnormality which far out-
raced any image their conscious minds could form. It was no
longer *shining* out, it was *pouring* out; and as the shapeless
stream of unplaceable colour left the well it seemed to flow directly into the sky.

The veterinary shivered, and walked to the front door to drop
the heavy extra bar across it. Ammi shook no less, and had to tug
and point for lack of a controllable voice when he wished to
draw notice to the growing luminosity of the trees. The neighing
and stamping of the horses had become utterly frightful, but not
a soul of that group in the old house would have ventured forth
for any earthly reward. With the moments the shining of the
trees increased, while their restless branches seemed to strain
more and more toward verticality. The wood of the well-sweep
was shining now, and presently a policeman dumbly pointed to
some wooden sheds and bee-hives near the stone wall on the
west. They were commencing to shine, too, though the tethered
vehicles of the visitors seemed so far unaffected. Then there was
a wild commotion and clopping in the road, and as Ammi
quenched the lamp for better seeing they realised that the span of
frantic greys had broke their sapling and run off with the democrat-
wagon.

The shock served to loosen several tongues, and embarrassed
whispers were exchanged. "It spreads on everything organic
that's been around here," muttered the medical examiner. No one
replied, but the man who had been in the well gave a hint that his
long pole must have stirred up something intangible. "It was awful," he added. "There was no bottom at all. Just ooze and bubbles and the feeling of something lurking under there." Ammi's
horse still pawed and screamed deafeningly in the road outside,
and nearly drowned its owner's faint quaver as he mumbled his
formless reflections. "It come from that stone . . . it growed
down thar . . . it got everything livin' . . . it fed itself on 'em, mind

and body . . . Thad an' Mernie, Zenas an' Nabby . . . Nahum was the last . . . they all drunk the water . . . it got strong on 'em . . . it come from beyond, whar things ain't like they be here . . . now it's goin' home. . . ."

At this point, as the column of unknown colour flared suddenly stronger and began to weave itself into fantastic suggestions of shape which each spectator later described differently, there came from poor Hero such a sound as no man before or since ever heard from a horse. Every person in that low-pitched sitting room stopped his ears, and Ammi turned away from the window in horror and nausea. Words could not convey it—when Ammi looked out again the hapless beast lay huddled inert on the moonlit ground between the splintered shafts of the buggy. That was the last of Hero till they buried him next day. But the present was no time to mourn, for almost at this instant a detective silently called attention to something terrible in the very room with them. In the absence of the lamplight it was clear that a faint phosphorescence had begun to pervade the entire apartment. It glowed on the broad-planked floor and the fragment of rag carpet, and shimmered over the sashes of the small-paned windows. It ran up and down the exposed corner-posts, coruscated about the shelf and mantel, and infected the very doors and furniture. Each minute saw it strengthen, and at last it was very plain that healthy living things must leave that house.

Ammi shewed them the back door and the path up through the fields to the ten-acre pasture. They walked and stumbled as in a dream, and did not dare look back till they were far away on the high ground. They were glad of the path, for they could not have gone the front way, by that well. It was bad enough passing the glowing barn and sheds, and those shining orchard trees with the gnarled, fiendish contours; but thank heaven the branches did their worst twisting high up. The moon went under some very black clouds as they crossed the rustic bridge over Chapman's Brook, and it was blind groping from there to the open meadows.

When they looked back toward the valley and the distant Gardner place at the bottom they saw a fearsome sight. All the farm was shining with the hideous unknown blend of colour;

trees, buildings, and even such grass and herbage as had not been wholly changed to lethal grey brittleness. The boughs were all straining skyward, tipped with tongues of foul flame, and lambent tricklings of the same monstrous fire were creeping about the ridgepoles of the house, barn, and sheds. It was a scene from a vision of Fuseli,[21] and over all the rest reigned that riot of luminous amorphousness, that alien and undimensioned rainbow of cryptic poison from the well—seething, feeling, lapping, reaching, scintillating, straining, and malignly bubbling in its cosmic and unrecognisable chromaticism.

Then without warning the hideous thing shot vertically up toward the sky like a rocket or meteor, leaving behind no trail and disappearing though a round and curiously regular hole in the clouds before any man could gasp or cry out. No watcher can ever forget that sight, and Ammi stared blankly at the stars of Cygnus, Deneb twinkling above the others, where the unknown colour had melted into the Milky Way. But his gaze was the next moment called swiftly to earth by the crackling in the valley. It was just that. Only a wooden ripping and crackling, not an explosion, as so many others of the party vowed. Yet the outcome was the same, for in one feverish, kaleidoscopic instant there burst up from that doomed and accursed farm a gleamingly eruptive cataclysm of unnatural sparks and substance; blurring the glance of the few who saw it, and sending forth to the zenith a bombarding cloudburst of such coloured and fantastic fragments as our universe must needs disown. Through quickly reclosing vapours they followed the great morbidity that had vanished, and in another second they had vanished too. Behind and below was only a darkness to which the men dared not return, and all about was a mounting wind which seemed to sweep down in black, frore gusts from interstellar space. It shrieked and howled, and lashed the fields and distorted woods in a mad cosmic frenzy, till soon the trembling party realised it would be no use waiting for the moon to shew what was left down there at Nahum's.

Too awed even to hint theories, the seven shaking men trudged back toward Arkham by the north road. Ammi was worse than his fellows, and begged them to see him inside his own kitchen, instead of keeping straight on to town. He did not wish to cross the nighted, wind-whipped woods alone to his home on the main road. For he had had an added shock that the others were spared, and was crushed forever with a brooding fear he dared not even mention for many years to come. As the rest of the watchers on that tempestuous hill had stolidly set their faces toward the road, Ammi had looked back an instant at the shadowed valley of desolation so lately sheltering his ill-starred friend. And from that stricken, far-away spot he had seen something feebly rise, only to sink down again upon the place from which the great shapeless horror had shot into the sky. It was just a colour—but not any colour of our earth or heavens. And because Ammi recognised that colour, and knew that this last faint remnant must still lurk down there in the well, he has never been quite right since.

Ammi would never go near the place again. It is over half a century now since the horror happened, but he has never been there, and will be glad when the new reservoir blots it out. I shall be glad, too, for I do not like the way the sunlight changed colour around the mouth of that abandoned well I passed. I hope the water will always be very deep—but even so, I shall never drink it. I do not think I shall visit the Arkham country hereafter. Three of the men who had been with Ammi returned the next morning to see the ruins by daylight, but there were not any real ruins. Only the bricks of the chimney, the stones of the cellar, some mineral and metallic litter here and there, and the rim of that nefandous well. Save for Ammi's dead horse, which they towed away and buried, and the buggy which they shortly returned to him, everything that had ever been living had gone. Five eldritch acres of dusty grey desert remained, nor has anything ever grown there since. To this day it sprawls open to the sky like a great spot eaten by acid in the woods and fields, and the few who have ever dared glimpse it in spite of the rural tales have named it "the blasted heath".

The rural tales are queer. They might be even queerer if city men and college chemists could be interested enough to analyse the water from that disused well, or the grey dust that no wind seems ever to disperse. Botanists, too, ought to study the stunted flora on the borders of that spot, for they might shed light on the country notion that the blight is spreading—little by little, perhaps an inch a year. People say the colour of the neighbouring herbage is not quite right in the spring, and that wild things leave queer prints in the light winter snow. Snow never seems quite so heavy on the blasted heath as it is elsewhere. Horses—the few that are left in this motor age—grow skittish in the silent valley; and hunters cannot depend on their dogs too near the splotch of greyish dust.

They say the mental influences are very bad, too. Numbers went queer in the years after Nahum's taking, and always they lacked the power to get away. Then the stronger-minded folk all left the region, and only the foreigners tried to live in the crumbling old homesteads. They could not stay, though; and one sometimes wonders what insight beyond ours their wild, weird stores of whispered magic have given them. Their dreams at night, they protest, are very horrible in that grotesque country; and surely the very look of the dark realm is enough to stir a morbid fancy. No traveller has ever escaped a sense of strangeness in those deep ravines, and artists shiver as they paint thick woods whose mystery is as much of the spirit as of the eye. I myself am curious about the sensation I derived from my one lone walk before Ammi told me his tale. When twilight came I had vaguely wished some clouds would gather, for an odd timidity about the deep skyey voids above had crept into my soul.

Do not ask me for my opinion. I do not know—that is all. There was no one but Ammi to question; for Arkham people will not talk about the strange days, and all three professors who saw the aërolite and its coloured globule are dead. There were other globules—depend upon that. One must have fed itself and escaped, and probably there was another which was too late. No doubt it is still down the well—I know there was something wrong with the sunlight I saw above that miasmal brink. The rustics say the blight creeps an inch a year, so perhaps there is a kind of growth or nourishment even now. But whatever daemon hatchling is there, it must be tethered to something or else it would quickly spread. Is it fastened to the roots of those trees that claw the air? One of the current Arkham tales is about fat oaks that shine and move as they ought not to do at night.

What it is, only God knows. In terms of matter I suppose the thing Ammi described would be called a gas, but this gas obeyed laws that are not of our cosmos.[22] This was no fruit of such worlds and suns as shine on the telescopes and photographic plates of our observatories. This was no breath from the skies whose motions and dimensions our astronomers measure or deem too vast to measure. It was just a colour out of space—a frightful messenger from unformed realms of infinity beyond all Nature as we know it; from realms whose mere existence stuns the brain and numbs us with the black extra-cosmic gulfs it throws open before our frenzied eyes.

I doubt very much if Ammi consciously lied to me, and I do not think his tale was all a freak of madness as the townfolk had forewarned. Something terrible came to the hills and valleys on that meteor, and something terrible—though I know not in what proportion—still remains. I shall be glad to see the water come. Meanwhile I hope nothing will happen to Ammi. He saw so much of the thing—and its influence was so insidious. Why has he never been able to move away? How clearly he recalled those dying words of Nahum's—"can't git away . . . draws ye . . . ye know summ'at's comin', but 'tain't no use. . . ." Ammi is such a good old man—when the reservoir gang gets to work I must write the chief engineer to keep a sharp watch on him. I would hate to think of him as the grey, twisted, brittle monstrosity which persists more and more in troubling my sleep.

The Whisperer in Darkness

I.

Bear in mind closely that I did not see any actual visual horror at the end. To say that a mental shock was the cause of what I inferred—that last straw which sent me racing out of the lonely Akeley farmhouse and through the wild domed hills[1] of Vermont in a commandeered motor at night—is to ignore the plainest facts of my final experience. Notwithstanding the deep extent to which I shared the information and speculations of Henry Akeley, the things I saw and heard, and the admitted vividness of the impression produced on me by these things, I cannot prove even now whether I was right or wrong in my hideous inference. For after all, Akeley's disappearance establishes nothing. People found nothing amiss in his house despite the bullet-marks on the outside and inside. It was just as though he had walked out casually for a ramble in the hills and failed to return. There was not even a sign that a guest had been there, or that those horrible cylinders and machines had been stored in the study. That he had mortally feared the crowded green hills and endless trickle of brooks among which he had been born and reared, means nothing at all, either; for thousands are subject to just such morbid fears. Eccentricity, moreover, could easily account for his strange acts and apprehensions toward the last.

The whole matter began, so far as I am concerned, with the historic and unprecedented Vermont floods of November 3, 1927.[2] I was then, as now, an instructor of literature at Miskatonic University in Arkham, Massachusetts, and an enthusiastic amateur student of New England folklore. Shortly after the flood, amidst the varied reports of hardship, suffering, and organised relief which filled the press, there appeared certain odd stories of things found floating in some of the swollen rivers; so that many of my friends embarked on curious discussions and appealed to me to shed what light I could on the subject. I felt flattered at having my folklore study taken so seriously, and did what I could to belittle the wild, vague tales which seemed so clearly an outgrowth of old rustic superstitions. It amused me to find several persons of education who insisted that some stratum of obscure, distorted fact might underlie the rumours.

The tales thus brought to my notice came mostly through newspaper cuttings; though one yarn had an oral source and was repeated to a friend of mine in a letter from his mother in Hardwick, Vermont. The type of thing described was essentially the same in all cases, though there seemed to be three separate instances involved—one connected with the Winooski River near Montpelier, another attached to the West River in Windham County beyond Newfane, and a third centring in the Passumpsic in Caledonia County above Lyndonville.[3] Of course many of the stray items mentioned other instances, but on analysis they all seemed to boil down to these three. In each case country folk reported seeing one or more very bizarre and disturbing objects in the surging waters that poured down from the unfrequented hills, and there was a widespread tendency to connect these sights with a primitive, half-forgotten cycle of whispered legend which old people resurrected for the occasion.

What people thought they saw were organic shapes not quite like any they had ever seen before. Naturally, there were many human bodies washed along by the streams in that tragic period; but those who described these strange shapes felt quite sure that they were not human, despite some superficial resemblances in size and general outline. Nor, said the witnesses, could they have been any kind of animal known to Vermont. They were pinkish things about five feet long; with crustaceous bodies bearing vast pairs of dorsal fins or membraneous wings and several sets of articulated limbs, and with a sort of convoluted ellipsoid, covered with multitudes of very short antennae, where a head would ordinarily be. It was really remarkable how closely the reports from different sources tended to coincide; though the wonder was lessened by the fact that the old legends, shared at one time throughout the hill country, furnished a morbidly vivid picture which might well have coloured the imaginations of all the witnesses concerned. It was my conclusion that such witnesses—in every case naive and simple backwoods folk—had glimpsed the battered and bloated bodies of human beings or farm animals in the whirling currents; and had allowed the half-remembered folklore to invest these pitiful objects with fantastic attributes.

The ancient folklore, while cloudy, evasive, and largely forgotten by the present generation, was of a highly singular character, and obviously reflected the influence of still earlier Indian tales. I knew it well, though I had never been in Vermont, through the exceedingly rare monograph of Eli Davenport,[4] which embraces material orally obtained prior to 1839 among the oldest people of the state. This material, moreover, closely coincided with tales which I had personally heard from elderly rustics in the mountains of New Hampshire. Briefly summarised, it hinted at a hidden race of monstrous beings which lurked somewhere among the remoter hills—in the deep woods of the highest peaks, and the dark valleys where streams trickle from unknown sources. These beings were seldom glimpsed, but evidences of their presence were reported by those who had ventured farther than usual up the slopes of certain mountains or into certain deep, steep-sided gorges that even the wolves shunned.

There were queer footprints or claw-prints in the mud of brook-margins and barren patches, and curious circles of stones, with the grass around them worn away, which did not seem to have been placed or entirely shaped by Nature. There were, too, certain caves of problematical depth in the sides of the hills; with mouths closed by boulders in a manner scarcely accidental, and with more than an average quota of the queer prints leading both toward and away from them—if indeed the direction of these prints could be justly estimated. And worst of all, there were the things which adventurous people had seen very rarely in the twilight of the remotest valleys and the dense perpendicular woods above the limits of normal hill-climbing.

It would have been less uncomfortable if the stray accounts of these things had not agreed so well. As it was, nearly all the rumours had several points in common; averring that the creatures were a sort of huge, light-red crab with many pairs of legs and with two great bat-like wings in the middle of the back. They sometimes walked on all their legs, and sometimes on the hindmost pair only, using the others to convey large objects of indeterminate nature. On one occasion they were spied in considerable numbers, a detachment of them wading along a shallow woodland watercourse three abreast in evidently disciplined formation. Once a specimen was seen flying—launching itself from the top of a bald, lonely hill at night and vanishing in the sky after its great flapping wings had been silhouetted an instant against the full moon.

These things seemed content, on the whole, to let mankind alone; though they were at times held responsible for the disappearance of venturesome individuals—especially persons who built houses too close to certain valleys or too high up on certain mountains. Many localities came to be known as inadvisable to settle in, the feeling persisting long after the cause was forgotten. People would look up at some of the neighbouring mountain-precipices with a shudder, even when not recalling how many settlers had been lost, and how many farmhouses burnt to ashes, on the lower slopes of those grim, green sentinels.

But while according to the earliest legends the creatures would appear to have harmed only those trespassing on their privacy; there were later accounts of their curiosity respecting men, and of their attempts to establish secret outposts in the human world. There were tales of the queer claw-prints seen around farmhouse windows in the morning, and of occasional disappearances in regions outside the obviously haunted areas. Tales, besides, of buzzing voices in imitation of human speech which made surprising offers to lone travellers on roads and cart-paths in the deep woods, and of children frightened out of their wits by things seen or heard where the primal forest pressed close upon their dooryards. In the final layer of legends—the layer just preceding the decline of superstition and the abandonment of close contact with the dreaded places—there are shocked references to hermits and remote farmers who at some period of life appeared to have undergone a repellent mental change, and who were shunned and whispered about as mortals who had sold themselves to the strange beings. In one of the northeastern counties it seemed to be a fashion about 1800 to accuse eccentric and unpopular recluses of being allies or representatives of the abhorred things.

As to what the things were—explanations naturally varied. The common name applied to them was "those ones", or "the old ones",[5] though other terms had a local and transient use. Perhaps the bulk of the Puritan settlers set them down bluntly as familiars of the devil, and made them a basis of awed theological speculation. Those with Celtic legendry in their heritage— mainly the Scotch-Irish element of New Hampshire, and their kindred who had settled in Vermont on Governor Wentworth's colonial grants[6]—linked them vaguely with the malign fairies and "little people" of the bogs and raths,[7] and protected themselves with scraps of incantation handed down through many generations. But the Indians had the most fantastic theories of all. While different tribal legends differed, there was a marked consensus of belief in certain vital particulars; it being unanimously agreed that the creatures were not native to this earth.

The Pennacook[8] myths, which were the most consistent and picturesque, taught that the Winged Ones came from the Great Bear in the sky, and had mines in our earthly hills whence they took a kind of stone they could not get on any other world. They did not live here, said the myths, but merely maintained outposts and flew back with vast cargoes of stone to their own stars in the north. They harmed only those earth-people who got too near them or spied upon them. Animals shunned them through instinctive hatred, not because of being hunted. They could not eat the things and animals of earth, but brought their own food from the stars. It was bad to get near them, and sometimes young hunters who went into their hills never came back. It was not good, either, to listen to what they whispered at night in the forest with voices like a bee's that tried to be like the voices of men. They knew the speech of all kinds of men—Pennacooks, Hurons, men of the Five Nations—but did not seem to have or need any speech of their own. They talked with their heads, which changed colour in different ways to mean different things.

All the legendry, of course, white and Indian alike, died down during the nineteenth century, except for occasional atavistical flareups. The ways of the Vermonters became settled; and once their habitual paths and dwellings were established according to a certain fixed plan, they remembered less and less what fears and avoidances had determined that plan, and even that there had been any fears or avoidances. Most people simply knew that certain hilly regions were considered as highly unhealthy, unprofitable, and generally unlucky to live in, and that the farther one kept from them the better off one usually was. In time the ruts of custom and economic interest became so deeply cut in approved places that there was no longer any reason for going outside them, and the haunted hills were left deserted by accident rather than by design. Save during infrequent local scares, only wonder-loving grandmothers and retrospective nonagenarians ever whispered of beings dwelling in those hills; and even such whisperers admitted that there was not much to fear from those things now that they were used to the presence of houses and settlements, and now that human beings let their chosen territory severely alone.

All this I had known from my reading, and from certain folk-tales picked up in New Hampshire; hence when the flood-time rumours began to appear, I could easily guess what imaginative background had evolved them. I took great pains to explain this to my friends, and was correspondingly amused when several contentious souls continued to insist on a possible element of truth in the reports. Such persons tried to point out that the early legends had a significant persistence and uniformity, and that the virtually unexplored nature of the Vermont hills made it unwise to be dogmatic about what might or might not dwell among them; nor could they be silenced by my assurance that all the myths were of a well-known pattern common to most of mankind and determined by early phases of imaginative experience which always produced the same type of delusion.

It was of no use to demonstrate to such opponents that the Vermont myths differed but little in essence from those universal legends of natural personification which filled the ancient world with fauns and dryads and satyrs, suggested the *kallikanzari*[9] of modern Greece, and gave to wild Wales and Ireland their dark hints of strange, small, and terrible hidden races of troglodytes and burrowers. No use, either, to point out the even more startlingly similar belief of the Nepalese hill tribes in the dreaded *Mi-Go* or "Abominable Snow-Men" who lurk hideously amidst the ice and rock pinnacles of the Himalayan summits.[10] When I brought up this evidence, my opponents turned it against me by claiming that it must imply some actual historicity for the ancient tales; that it must argue the real existence of some queer elder earth-race, driven to hiding after the advent and dominance of mankind, which might very conceivably have survived in reduced numbers to relatively recent times—or even to the present.

The more I laughed at such theories, the more these stubborn friends asseverated them; adding that even without the heritage of legend the recent reports were too clear, consistent, detailed, and sanely prosaic in manner of telling, to be completely ignored. Two or three fanatical extremists went so far as to hint at possible meanings in the ancient Indian tales which gave the hidden beings a non-terrestrial origin; citing the extravagant books of Charles Fort[11] with their claims that voyagers from other worlds and outer space have often visited the earth. Most of my foes, however, were merely romanticists who insisted on trying to transfer to real life the fantastic lore of lurking "little people" made popular by the magnificent horror-fiction of Arthur Machen.

II.

As was only natural under the circumstances, this piquant debating finally got into print in the form of letters to the *Arkham Advertiser*;[12] some of which were copied in the press of those Vermont regions whence the flood-stories came. The *Rutland Herald*[13] gave half a page of extracts from the letters on both sides, while the *Brattleboro Reformer*[14] reprinted one of my long historical and mythological summaries in full, with some accompanying comments in "The Pendrifter's" thoughtful column which supported and applauded my sceptical conclusions. By the spring of 1928 I was almost a well-known figure in Vermont, notwithstanding the fact that I had never set foot in the state.

Then came the challenging letters from Henry Akeley[15] which impressed me so profoundly, and which took me for the first and last time to that fascinating realm of crowded green precipices and muttering forest streams.

Most of what I now know of Henry Wentworth Akeley was gathered by correspondence with his neighbours, and with his only son in California, after my experience in his lonely farmhouse. He was, I discovered, the last representative on his home soil of a long, locally distinguished line of jurists, administrators, and gentlemen-agriculturists. In him, however, the family mentally had veered away from practical affairs to pure scholarship; so that he had been a notable student of mathematics, astronomy, biology, anthropology, and folklore at the University of Vermont. I had never previously heard of him, and he did not give many autobiographical details in his communications; but from the first I saw he was a man of character, education, and intelligence, albeit a recluse with very little worldly sophistication.

Despite the incredible nature of what he claimed, I could not help at once taking Akeley more seriously than I had taken any of the other challengers of my views. For one thing, he was really close to the actual phenomena—visible and tangible—that he speculated so grotesquely about; and for another thing, he was amazingly willing to leave his conclusions in a tentative state like a true man of science. He had no personal preferences to advance, and was always guided by what he took to be solid evidence. Of course I began by considering him mistaken, but gave him credit for being intelligently mistaken; and at no time did I emulate some of his friends in attributing his ideas, and his fear of the lonely green hills, to insanity. I could see that there was a great deal to the man, and knew that what he reported must surely come from strange circumstances deserving investigation, however little it might have to do with the fantastic causes he assigned. Later on I received from him certain material proofs which placed the matter on a somewhat different and bewilderingly bizarre basis.

I cannot do better than transcribe in full, so far as is possible, the long letter in which Akeley introduced himself, and which formed such an important landmark in my own intellectual history. It is no longer in my possession, but my memory holds almost every word of its portentous message; and again I affirm my confidence in the sanity of the man who wrote it. Here is the text—a text which reached me in the cramped, archaic-looking scrawl of one who had obviously not mingled much with the world during his sedate, scholarly life.

> R.F.D. #2,
> Townshend, Windham Co.,
> Vermont.
> May 5, 1928.

Albert N. Wilmarth, Esq.,[16]
118 Saltonstall St.,[17]
Arkham, Mass.,

My dear Sir:—

I have read with great interest the *Brattleboro Reformer's* reprint (Apr. 23, '28) of your letter on the recent stories of strange bodies seen floating in our flooded streams last fall, and on the curious folklore they so well agree with. It is easy to see why an outlander would take the position you take, and even why "Pendrifter" agrees with you. That is the attitude generally taken by educated persons both in and out of Vermont, and was my own attitude as a young man (I am now 57) before my studies, both general and in Davenport's book, led me to do some exploring in parts of the hills hereabouts not usually visited.

I was directed toward such studies by the queer old tales I used to hear from elderly farmers of the more ignorant sort, but now I wish I had let the whole matter alone. I might say, with all proper modesty, that the subject of anthropology and folklore is by no means strange to me. I took a good deal of it at college, and am familiar with most of the standard authorities such as Tylor, Lubbock, Frazer, Quatrefages, Murray, Osborn, Keith, Boule, G. Elliot Smith, and so on.[18] It is no news to me that tales of hidden races are as old as all mankind. I have seen the reprints of letters from you, and those arguing with you, in the *Rutland Herald*, and guess I know about where your controversy stands at the present time.

What I desire to say now is, that I am afraid your adversaries are nearer right than yourself, even though all reason seems to be on your side. They are nearer right than they realise themselves—for of course they go only by theory, and cannot know what I know. If I knew as little of the matter as they, I would not feel justified in believing as they do. I would be wholly on your side.

You can see that I am having a hard time getting to the point, probably because I really dread getting to the point; but the upshot of the matter is that *I have certain evidence that monstrous things do indeed live in the woods on the high hills which nobody visits.* I have not seen any of the things floating in the rivers, as reported, *but I have seen things like them* under circumstances I dread to repeat. I have seen footprints, and of late have seen them nearer my own home (I live in the old Akeley place south of Townshend Village, on the side of Dark Mountain) than I dare tell you now. And I have overhead voices in the woods at certain points that I will not even begin to describe on paper.

At one place I heard them so much that I took a phonograph there—with a dictaphone attachment and wax blank—and I shall try to arrange to have you hear the record I got.[19] I have run it on the machine for some of the old people up here, and one of the voices had nearly scared them paralysed by reason of its likeness to a certain voice (that buzzing voice in the woods which Davenport mentions) that their grandmothers have told about and mimicked for them. I know what most people think of a man who tells about "hearing voices"—but before you draw conclusions just listen to this record and ask some of the older backwoods people what they think of it. If you can account for it normally, very well; but there must be something behind it. *Ex nihilo nihil fit,* you know.[20]

Now my object in writing you is not to start an argument, but to give you information which I think a man of your tastes will find deeply interesting. *This is private. Publicly I am on your side,* for certain things shew me that it does not do for people to know too much about these matters. My own studies are now wholly private, and I would not think of saying anything to attract people's attention and cause them to visit the places I have explored. It is true—terribly true—*that there are non-human creatures watching us all the time;* with spies among us gathering information. It is from a wretched man who, if he was sane (as I think he was), *was one of those spies,* that I got a large part of my clues to the matter. He later killed himself, but I have reason to think there are others now.

The things come from another planet, being able to live in interstellar space and fly through it on clumsy, powerful wings which have a way of resisting the ether[21] but which are too poor at steering to be of much use in helping them about on earth. I will tell you about this later if you do not dismiss me at once as a madman. They come here to get metals from mines that go deep under the hills, *and I think I know where they come from.* They will not hurt us if we let them alone, but no one can say what will happen if we get too curious about them. Of course a good army of men could wipe out their mining colony. That is what they are afraid of. But if that happened, more would come from *outside*—any number of them. They could easily conquer the earth, but have not tried so far because they have not needed to. They would rather leave things as they are to save bother.[22]

I think they mean to get rid of me because of what I have discovered. There is a great black stone with unknown hieroglyphics half worn away which I found in the woods on Round Hill, east of here; and after I took it home everything became different. If they think I suspect too much they will either kill me *or take me off the earth to where they come from.* They like to take away men of learning once in a while, to keep informed on the state of things in the human world.[23]

This leads me to my secondary purpose in addressing you— namely, to urge you to hush up the present debate rather than give it more publicity. *People must be kept away from these hills,* and in order to effect this, their curiosity ought not to be aroused any further. Heaven knows there is peril enough anyway, with promoters and real estate men flooding Vermont with herds of summer people to overrun the wild places and cover the hills with cheap bungalows.

I shall welcome further communication with you, and shall try to send you that phonograph record and black stone (which is so worn that photographs don't shew much) by express if you are willing. I say "try" because I think those creatures have a way of tampering with things around here. There is a sullen, furtive fellow named Brown, on a farm near the village, who I think is their spy. Little by little they are trying to cut me off from our world because I know too much about their world.

They have the most amazing way of finding out what I do.

You may not even get this letter. I think I shall have to leave this part of the country and go to live with my son in San Diego, Cal., if things get any worse, but it is not easy to give up the place you were born in, and where your family has lived for six generations. Also, I would hardly dare sell this house to anybody now that the *creatures* have taken notice of it. They seem to be trying to get the black stone back and destroy the phonograph record, but I shall not let them if I can help it. My great police dogs always hold them back, for there are very few here as yet, and they are clumsy in getting about. As I have said, their wings are not much use for short flights on earth. I am on the very brink of deciphering that stone—in a very terrible way—and with your knowledge of folk-lore you may be able to supply missing links enough to help me. I suppose you know all about the fearful myths antedating the coming of man to the earth—the Yog-Sothoth and Cthulhu cycles[24]—which are hinted at in the *Necronomicon.* I had access to a copy of that once, and hear that you have one in your college library under lock and key.

To conclude, Mr. Wilmarth, I think that with our respective studies we can be very useful to each other. I don't wish to put you in any peril, and suppose I ought to warn you that possession of the stone and the record won't be very safe; but I think you will find any risks worth running for the sake of knowledge.[25] I will drive down to Newfane or Brattleboro to send whatever you authorise me to send, for the express offices there are more to be trusted. I might say that I live quite alone now, since I can't keep hired help any more. They won't stay because of the things that try to get near the house at night, and that keep the dogs barking continually. I am glad I didn't get as deep as this into the business while my wife was alive, for it would have driven her mad.

Hoping that I am not bothering you unduly, and that you will decide to get in touch with me rather than throw this letter into the waste basket as a madman's raving, I am

Yrs. very truly,

HENRY W. AKELEY

P.S. I am making some extra prints of certain photographs taken by me, which I think will help to prove a number of the points I have touched on.[26] The old people think they are monstrously true. I shall send you these very soon if you are interested. H.W.A.

It would be difficult to describe my sentiments upon reading this strange document for the first time. By all ordinary rules, I ought to have laughed more loudly at these extravagances than at the far milder theories which had previously moved me to mirth; yet something in the tone of the letter made me take it with paradoxical seriousness. Not that I believed for a moment in the hidden race from the stars which my correspondent spoke of; but that, after some grave preliminary doubts, I grew to feel oddly sure of his sanity and sincerity, and of his confrontation by some genuine though singular and abnormal phenomenon which he could not explain except in this imaginative way. It could not be as he thought it, I reflected, yet on the other hand it could not be otherwise than worthy of investigation. The man seemed unduly excited and alarmed about something, but it was hard to think that all cause was lacking. He was so specific and logical in certain ways—and after all, his yarn did fit in so perplexingly well with some of the old myths—even the wildest Indian legends.

That he had really overheard disturbing voices in the hills, and had really found the black stone he spoke about, was wholly possible despite the crazy inferences he had made—inferences probably suggested by the man who had claimed to be a spy of the outer beings and had later killed himself. It was easy to deduce that this man must have been wholly insane, but that he probably had a streak of perverse outward logic which made the naive Akeley—already prepared for such things by his folklore studies—believe his tale. As for the latest developments—it appeared from his inability to keep hired help that Akeley's humbler rustic neighbours were as convinced as he that his house was besieged by uncanny things at night. The dogs really barked, too.

And then the matter of that phonograph record, which I could not but believe he had obtained in the way he said. It must mean something; whether animal noises deceptively like human speech, or the speech of some hidden, night-haunting human being decayed to a state not much above that of lower animals. From this my thoughts went back to the black hieroglyphed stone, and to speculations upon what it might mean. Then, too, what of the photographs which Akeley said he was about to send, and which the old people had found so convincingly terrible?

As I re-read the cramped handwriting I felt as never before that my credulous opponents might have more on their side than I had conceded. After all, there might be some queer and perhaps hereditarily misshapen outcasts in those shunned hills, even though no such race of star-born monsters as folklore claimed. And if there were, then the presence of strange bodies in the flooded streams would not be wholly beyond belief. Was it too presumptuous to suppose that both the old legends and the recent reports had this much of reality behind them? But even as I harboured these doubts I felt ashamed that so fantastic a piece of bizarrerie as Henry Akeley's wild letter had brought them up.

In the end I answered Akeley's letter, adopting a tone of friendly interest and soliciting further particulars. His reply came almost by return mail; and contained, true to promise, a number of kodak views of scenes and objects illustrating what he had to tell. Glancing at these pictures as I took them from the envelope, I felt a curious sense of fright and nearness to forbidden things; for in spite of the vagueness of most of them, they had a damnably suggestive power which was intensified by the fact of their being genuine photographs—actual optical links with what they portrayed, and the product of an impersonal transmitting process without prejudice, fallibility, or mendacity.

The more I looked at them, the more I saw that my serious estimate of Akeley and his story had not been unjustified. Certainly, these pictures carried conclusive evidence of something in the Vermont hills which was at least vastly outside the radius of our common knowledge and belief. The worst thing of all was the footprint—a view taken where the sun shone on a mud patch somewhere in a deserted upland. This was no cheaply counterfeited thing, I could see at a glance; for the sharply defined pebbles and grass-blades in the field of vision gave a clear index of scale and left no possibility of a tricky double exposure. I have called the thing a "footprint", but "claw-print" would be a better term. Even now I can scarcely describe it save to say that it was hideously crab-like, and that there seemed to be some ambiguity about its direction. It was not a very deep or fresh print, but seemed to be about the size of an average man's foot. From a central pad, pairs of saw-toothed nippers projected in opposite directions—quite baffling as to function, if indeed the whole object were exclusively an organ of locomotion.

Another photograph—evidently a time-exposure taken in deep shadow—was of the mouth of a woodland cave, with a boulder of rounded regularity choking the aperture. On the bare ground in front of it one could just discern a dense network of curious tracks, and when I studied the picture with a magnifier I felt uneasily sure that the tracks were like the one in the other view. A third picture shewed a druid-like circle of standing stones on the summit of a wild hill.[27] Around the cryptic circle the grass was very much beaten down and worn away, though I could not detect any footprints even with the glass. The extreme remoteness of the place was apparent from the veritable sea of tenantless mountains which formed the background and stretched away toward a misty horizon.

But if the most disturbing of all the views was that of the footprint, the most curiously suggestive was that of the great black stone found in the Round Hill woods.[28] Akeley had photographed it on what was evidently his study table, for I could see rows of books and a bust of Milton in the background.[29] The thing, as nearly as one might guess, had faced the camera vertically with a somewhat irregularly curved surface of one by two feet; but to say anything definite about that surface, or about the general shape of the whole mass, almost defies the power of language. What outlandish geometrical principles had guided its cutting—for artificially cut it surely was—I could not even begin to guess; and never before had I seen anything which struck me as so strangely and unmistakably alien to this world. Of the hieroglyphics on the surface I could discern very few, but one or two that I did see gave me rather a shock. Of course they might be fraudulent, for others besides myself had read the monstrous and abhorred *Necronomicon* of the mad Arab Abdul Alhazred; but it nevertheless made me shiver to recognise certain ideographs which study had taught me to link with the most bloodcurdling and blasphemous whispers of things that had had a kind of mad half-existence before the earth and the other inner worlds of the solar system were made.

Of the five remaining pictures, three were of swamp and hill scenes which seemed to bear traces of hidden and unwholesome tenancy. Another was of a queer mark in the ground very near Akeley's house, which he said he had photographed the morning after a night on which the dogs had barked more violently than usual. It was very blurred, and one could really draw no certain conclusions from it; but it did seem fiendishly like that other mark or claw-print photographed on the deserted upland. The final picture was of the Akeley place itself; a trim white house of two stories and attic, about a century and a quarter old, and with a well-kept lawn and stone-bordered path leading up to a tastefully carved Georgian doorway. There were several huge police dogs on the lawn, squatting near a pleasant-faced man with a close-cropped grey beard whom I took to be Akeley himself—his own photographer, one might infer from the tube-connected bulb in his right hand.

From the pictures I turned to the bulky, closely written letter itself; and for the next three hours was immersed in a gulf of unutterable horror. Where Akeley had given only outlines before, he now entered into minute details; presenting long transcripts of words overheard in the woods at night, long accounts of monstrous pinkish forms spied in thickets at twilight on the hills, and a terrible cosmic narrative derived from the application of profound and varied scholarship to the endless bygone discourses of the mad self-styled spy who had killed himself. I found myself faced by names and terms that I had heard elsewhere in the most hideous of connexions—Yuggoth, Great Cthulhu, Tsathoggua, Yog-Sothoth, R'lyeh, Nyarlathotep, Azathoth, Hastur, Yian, Leng, the Lake of Hali, Bethmoora, the Yellow Sign, L'mur-Kathulos, Bran, and the Magnum Innominandum[30]—and was drawn back through nameless aeons and inconceivable dimensions to worlds of elder, outer entity at which the crazed author of the *Necronomicon* had only guessed in the vaguest way. I was told of the pits of primal life, and of the streams that had trickled down therefrom; and finally, of the tiny rivulet from one of those streams which had become entangled with the destinies of our own earth.

My brain whirled; and where before I had attempted to explain things away, I now began to believe in the most abnormal and incredible wonders. The array of vital evidence was damnably vast and overwhelming; and the cool, scientific attitude of Akeley—an attitude removed as far as imaginable from the demented, the fanatical, the hysterical, or even the extravagantly speculative—had a tremendous effect on my thought and judgment. By the time I laid the frightful letter aside I could understand the fears he had come to entertain, and was ready to do anything in my power to keep people away from those wild, haunted hills. Even now, when time has dulled the impression and made me half question my own experience and horrible doubts, there are things in that letter of Akeley's which I would not quote, or even form into words on paper. I am almost glad that the letter and record and photographs are gone now—and I wish, for reasons I shall soon make clear, that the new planet beyond Neptune had not been discovered.

With the reading of that letter my public debating about the Vermont horror permanently ended. Arguments from opponents remained unanswered or put off with promises, and eventually the controversy petered out into oblivion. During late May and June I was in constant correspondence with Akeley; though once in a while a letter would be lost, so that we would have to retrace our ground and perform considerable laborious copying. What we were trying to do, as a whole, was to compare notes in matters of obscure mythological scholarship and arrive at a clearer correlation of the Vermont horrors with the general body of primitive world legend.

For one thing, we virtually decided that these morbidities and the hellish Himalayan *Mi-Go* were one and the same order of incarnated nightmare. There were also absorbing zoölogical conjectures, which I would have referred to Professor Dexter[31] in my own college but for Akeley's imperative command to tell no one of the matter before us. If I seem to disobey that command now, it is only because I think that at this stage a warning about those farther Vermont hills—and about those Himalayan peaks which bold explorers are more and more determined to ascend—is more conducive to public safety than silence would be. One specific thing we were leading up to was a deciphering of the hieroglyphics on that infamous black stone—a deciphering which might well place us in possession of secrets deeper and more dizzying than any formerly known to man.

III.

Toward the end of June the phonograph record came—shipped from Brattleboro, since Akeley was unwilling to trust conditions on the branch line north of there. He had begun to feel an increased sense of espionage, aggravated by the loss of some of our letters; and said much about the insidious deeds of certain men whom he considered tools and agents of the hidden beings. Most of all he suspected the surly farmer Walter Brown, who lived alone on a run-down hillside place near the deep woods, and who was often seen loafing around corners in Brattleboro, Bellows Falls, Newfane, and South Londonderry in the most inexplicable and seemingly unmotivated way. Brown's voice, he felt convinced, was one of those he had overheard on a certain occasion in a very terrible conversation; and he had once found a footprint or claw-print near Brown's house which might possess the most ominous significance. It had been curiously near some of Brown's own footprints—footprints that faced toward it.

So the record was shipped from Brattleboro, whither Akeley drove in his Ford car along the lonely Vermont back roads. He confessed in an accompanying note that he was beginning to be afraid of those roads, and that he would not even go into Townshend for supplies now except in broad daylight. It did not pay, he repeated again and again, to know too much unless one were very remote from those silent and problematical hills. He would be going to California pretty soon to live with his son, though it was hard to leave a place where all one's memories and ancestral feelings centred.

Before trying the record on the commercial machine which I borrowed from the college administration building I carefully went over all the explanatory matter in Akeley's various letters. This record, he had said, was obtained about 1 a.m. on the first of May, 1915, near the closed mouth of a cave where the wooded west slope of Dark Mountain rises out of Lee's Swamp.[32] The place had always been unusually plagued with strange voices, this being the reason he had brought the phonograph, dictaphone, and blank in expectation of results. Former experience had told him that May-Eve—the hideous Sabbat-night of underground European legend—would probably be more fruitful than any other date, and he was not disappointed. It was noteworthy, though, that he never again heard voices at that particular spot.

Unlike most of the overheard forest voices, the substance of the record was quasi-ritualistic, and included one palpably human voice which Akeley had never been able to place. It was not Brown's, but seemed to be that of a man of greater cultivation. The second voice, however, was the real crux of the thing—for this was the accursed *buzzing* which had no likeness to humanity despite the human words which it uttered in good English grammar and a scholarly accent.

The recording phonograph and dictaphone had not worked uniformly well, and had of course been at a great disadvantage because of the remote and muffled nature of the overheard ritual; so that the actual speech secured was very fragmentary. Akeley had given me a transcript of what he believed the spoken words to be, and I glanced through this again as I prepared the machine for action. The text was darkly mysterious rather than openly horrible, though a knowledge of its origin and manner of gathering gave it all the associative horror which any words could well possess. I will present it here in full as I remember it—and I am fairly confident that I know it correctly by heart, not only from reading the transcript, but from playing the record itself over and over again. It is not a thing which one might readily forget!

(INDISTINGUISHABLE SOUNDS)

(A CULTIVATED MALE HUMAN VOICE)

. . . is the Lord of the Woods, even to . . . and the gifts of the men of Leng . . . so from the wells of night to the gulfs of space, and from the gulfs of space to the wells of night, ever the praises of Great Cthulhu, of Tsathoggua, and of Him Who is not to be

Named. Ever Their praises, and abundance to the Black Goat of the Woods. Iä! Shub-Niggurath! The Goat with a Thousand Young![33]

(A BUZZING IMITATION OF HUMAN SPEECH)

Iä! Shub-Niggurath! The Black Goat of the Woods with a Thousand Young!

(HUMAN VOICE)

And it has come to pass that the Lord of the Woods, being . . . seven and nine, down the onyx steps . . . (tri)butes to Him in the Gulf, Azathoth, He of Whom Thou hast taught us marv(els) . . . on the wings of night out beyond space, out beyond th . . . to That whereof Yuggoth is the youngest child, rolling alone in black aether at the rim. . . .

(BUZZING VOICE)

. . . go out among men and find the ways thereof, that He in the Gulf may know. To Nyarlathotep, Mighty Messenger, must all things be told. And He shall put on the semblance of men, the waxen mask and the robe that hides, and come down from the world of Seven Suns to mock. . . .

(HUMAN VOICE)

. . . (Nyarl)athotep, Great Messenger, bringer of strange joy to Yuggoth through the void, Father of the Million Favoured Ones, Stalker among. . . .

(SPEECH CUT OFF BY END OF RECORD)

Such were the words for which I was to listen when I started the phonograph. It was with a trace of genuine dread and reluctance that I pressed the lever and heard the preliminary scratching of the sapphire point, and I was glad that the first faint, fragmentary words were in a human voice—a mellow, educated voice which seemed vaguely Bostonian in accent, and which

was certainly not that of any native of the Vermont hills. As I
listened to the tantalisingly feeble rendering, I seemed to find
the speech identical with Akeley's carefully prepared transcript.
On it chanted, in that mellow Bostonian voice . . . "Iä! Shub-
Niggurath! The Goat with a Thousand Young! . . ."

And then I heard *the other voice.* To this hour I shudder ret-
rospectively when I think of how it struck me, prepared though
I was by Akeley's accounts. Those to whom I have since described the record profess to find nothing but cheap imposture
or madness in it; but *could they have heard the accursed thing itself,* or read the bulk of Akeley's correspondence (especially that
terrible and encyclopaedic second letter), I know they would
think differently. It is, after all, a tremendous pity that I did not
disobey Akeley and play the record for others—a tremendous
pity, too, that all of his letters were lost. To me, with my first-
hand impression of the actual sounds, and with my knowledge of
the background and surrounding circumstances, the voice was a
monstrous thing. It swiftly followed the human voice in ritualis-
tic response, but in my imagination it was a morbid echo winging its way across unimaginable abysses from unimaginable
outer hells. It is more than two years now since I last ran off that
blasphemous waxen cylinder; but at this moment, and at all other
moments, I can still hear that feeble, fiendish buzzing as it
reached me for the first time.

"*Iä! Shub-Niggurath! The Black Goat of the Woods with a
Thousand Young!*"

But though that voice is always in my ears, I have not even yet
been able to analyse it well enough for a graphic description. It
was like the drone of some loathsome, gigantic insect ponder-
ously shaped into the articulate speech of an alien species, and I
am perfectly certain that the organs producing it can have no resemblance to the vocal organs of man, or indeed to those of any
of the mammalia. There were singularities of timbre, range, and
overtones which placed this phenomenon wholly outside the
sphere of humanity and earth-life. Its sudden advent that first
time almost stunned me, and I heard the rest of the record
through in a sort of abstracted daze. When the longer passage of
buzzing came, there was a sharp intensification of that feeling of

blasphemous infinity which had struck me during the shorter and earlier passage. At last the record ended abruptly, during an unusually clear speech of the human and Bostonian voice; but I sat stupidly staring long after the machine had automatically stopped.

I hardly need say that I gave that shocking record many another playing, and that I made exhaustive attempts at analysis and comment in comparing notes with Akeley. It would be both useless and disturbing to repeat here all that we concluded; but I may hint that we agreed in believing we had secured a clue to the source of some of the most repulsive primordial customs in the cryptic elder religions of mankind. It seemed plain to us, also, that there were ancient and elaborate alliances between the hidden outer creatures and certain members of the human race. How extensive these alliances were, and how their state today might compare with their state in earlier ages, we had no means of guessing; yet at best there was room for a limitless amount of horrified speculation. There seemed to be an awful, immemorial linkage in several definite stages betwixt man and nameless infinity. The blasphemies which appeared on earth, it was hinted, came from the dark planet Yuggoth, at the rim of the solar system; but this was itself merely the populous outpost of a frightful interstellar race whose ultimate source must lie far outside even the Einsteinian space-time continuum or greatest known cosmos.[34]

Meanwhile we continued to discuss the black stone and the best way of getting it to Arkham—Akeley deeming it inadvisable to have me visit him at the scene of his nightmare studies. For some reason or other, Akeley was afraid to trust the thing to any ordinary or expected transportation route. His final idea was to take it across county to Bellows Falls and ship it on the Boston and Maine system through Keene and Winchendon and Fitchburg, even though this would necessitate his driving along somewhat lonelier and more forest-traversing hill roads than the main highway to Brattleboro. He said he had noticed a man around the express office at Brattleboro when he had sent the phonograph record, whose actions and expression had been far from reassuring. This man had seemed too anxious to talk with the clerks, and had taken the train on which the record was shipped. Akeley confessed that he had not felt strictly at ease about that record until he heard from me of its safe receipt.

About this time—the second week in July—another letter of mine went astray, as I learned through an anxious communication from Akeley. After that he told me to address him no more at Townshend, but to send all mail in care of the General Delivery at Brattleboro; whither he would make frequent trips either in his car or on the motor-coach line which had lately replaced passenger service on the lagging branch railway. I could see that he was getting more and more anxious, for he went into much detail about the increased barking of the dogs on moonless nights, and about the fresh claw-prints he sometimes found in the road and in the mud at the back of his farmyard when morning came. Once he told about a veritable army of prints drawn up in a line facing an equally thick and resolute line of dog-tracks, and sent a loathsomely disturbing kodak picture to prove it. That was after a night on which the dogs had outdone themselves in barking and howling.

On the morning of Wednesday, July 18, I received a telegram from Bellows Falls, in which Akeley said he was expressing the black stone over the B. & M. on Train No. 5508, leaving Bellows Falls at 12:15 p.m., standard time, and due at the North Station in Boston at 4:12 p.m. It ought, I calculated, to get up to Arkham at least by the next noon; and accordingly I stayed in all Thursday morning to receive it. But noon came and went without its advent, and when I telephoned down to the express office I was informed that no shipment for me had arrived. My next act, performed amidst a growing alarm, was to give a long-distance phone call to the express agent at the Boston North Station; and I was scarcely surprised to learn that my consignment had not appeared. Train No. 5508 had pulled in only 35 minutes late on the day before, but had contained no box addressed to me. The agent promised, however, to institute a searching inquiry; and I ended the day by sending Akeley a night-letter outlining the situation.

With commendable promptness a report came from the Boston office on the following afternoon, the agent telephoning as soon as he learned the facts. It seemed that the railway express clerk on No. 5508 had been able to recall an incident which might have much bearing on my loss—an argument with a very curious-voiced man, lean, sandy, and rustic-looking, when the train was waiting at Keene, N.H., shortly after one o'clock standard time.

The man, he said, was greatly excited about a heavy box which he claimed to expect, but which was neither on the train nor entered on the company's books. He had given the name of Stanley Adams, and had had such a queerly thick droning voice, that it made the clerk abnormally dizzy and sleepy to listen to him. The clerk could not remember quite how the conversation had ended, but recalled starting into a fuller awakeness when the train began to move. The Boston agent added that this clerk was a young man of wholly unquestioned veracity and reliability, of known antecedents and long with the company.

That evening I went to Boston to interview the clerk in person, having obtained his name and address from the office. He was a frank, prepossessing fellow, but I saw that he could add nothing to his original account. Oddly, he was scarcely sure that he could even recognise the strange inquirer again. Realising that he had no more to tell, I returned to Arkham and sat up till morning writing letters to Akeley, to the express company, and to the police department and station agent in Keene. I felt that the strange-voiced man who had so queerly affected the clerk must have a pivotal place in the ominous business, and hoped that Keene station employees and telegraph-office records might tell something about him and about how he happened to make his inquiry when and where he did.

I must admit, however, that all my investigations came to nothing. The queer-voiced man had indeed been noticed around the Keene station in the early afternoon of July 18, and one lounger seemed to couple him vaguely with a heavy box; but he was altogether unknown, and had not been seen before or since. He had not visited the telegraph office or received any message so far as could be learned, nor had any message which might justly be considered a notice of the black stone's presence on No. 5508 come through the office for anyone. Naturally Akeley joined with me in conducting these inquiries, and even made a personal trip to Keene to question the people around the station; but his attitude toward the matter was more fatalistic than mine. He seemed to find the loss of the box a portentous and menacing fulfilment of inevitable tendencies, and had no real hope at all of its recovery. He spoke of the undoubted telepathic and hypnotic powers of the hill creatures and their agents, and in one letter hinted that he did not believe the stone was on this earth any longer. For my part, I was duly enraged, for I had felt there was at least a chance of learning profound and astonishing things from the old, blurred hieroglyphs. The matter would have rankled bitterly in my mind had not Akeley's immediate subsequent letters brought up a new phase of the whole horrible hill problem which at once seized all my attention.

IV.

The unknown things, Akeley wrote in a script grown pitifully tremulous, had begun to close in on him with a wholly new degree of determination. The nocturnal barking of the dogs whenever the moon was dim or absent was hideous now, and there had been attempts to molest him on the lonely roads he had to traverse by day. On the second of August, while bound for the village in his car, he had found a tree-trunk laid in his path at a point where the highway ran through a deep patch of woods; while the savage barking of the two great dogs he had with him told all too well of the things which must have been lurking near. What would have happened had the dogs not been there, he did not dare guess—but he never went out now without at least two of his faithful and powerful pack. Other road experiences had occurred on August 5th and 6th; a shot grazing his car on one occasion, and the barking of the dogs telling of unholy woodland presences on the other.

On August 15th I received a frantic letter which disturbed me greatly, and which made me wish Akeley could put aside his lonely reticence and call in the aid of the law. There had been frightful happenings on the night of the 12–13th, bullets flying outside the farmhouse, and three of the twelve great dogs being found shot dead in the morning. There were myriads of claw-prints in the road, with the human prints of Walter Brown among them. Akeley had started to telephone to Brattleboro for more dogs, but the wire had gone dead before he had a chance to say much. Later he went to Brattleboro in his car, and learned there that linemen had found the main telephone cable neatly cut at a point where it ran through the deserted hills north of New-fane. But he was about to start home with four fine new dogs, and several cases of ammunition for his big-game repeating rifle. The letter was written at the post office in Brattleboro, and came through to me without delay.

My attitude toward the matter was by this time quickly slip-ping from a scientific to an alarmedly personal one. I was afraid for Akeley in his remote, lonely farmhouse, and half afraid for myself because of my now definite connexion with the strange hill problem. The thing was *reaching out* so. Would it suck me in and engulf me? In replying to his letter I urged him to seek help, and hinted that I might take action myself if he did not. I spoke of visiting Vermont in person in spite of his wishes, and of help-ing him explain the situation to the proper authorities. In return, however, I received only a telegram from Bellows Falls which read thus:

APPRECIATE YOUR POSITION BUT CAN DO NOTH-ING. TAKE NO ACTION YOURSELF FOR IT COULD ONLY HARM BOTH. WAIT FOR EXPLANATION.
                                        HENRY AKELY[35]

But the affair was steadily deepening. Upon my replying to the telegram I received a shaky note from Akeley with the aston-ishing news that he had not only never sent the wire, but had not received the letter from me to which it was an obvious reply. Hasty inquiries by him at Bellows Falls had brought out that the message was deposited by a strange sandy-haired man with a cu-riously thick, droning voice, though more than this he could not learn. The clerk shewed him the original text as scrawled in pen-cil by the sender, but the handwriting was wholly unfamiliar. It was noticeable that the signature was misspelled—A-K-E-L-Y, without the second "E". Certain conjectures were inevitable, but amidst the obvious crisis he did not stop to elaborate upon them.

He spoke of the death of more dogs and the purchase of still others, and of the exchange of gunfire which had become a settled feature each moonless night. Brown's prints, and the prints of at least one or two more shod human figures, were now found regularly among the claw-prints in the road, and at the back of the farmyard. It was, Akeley admitted, a pretty bad business; and before long he would probably have to go to live with his California son whether or not he could sell the old place. But it was not easy to leave the only spot one could really think of as home. He must try to hang on a little longer; perhaps he could scare off the intruders—especially if he openly gave up all further attempts to penetrate their secrets.

Writing Akeley at once, I renewed my offers of aid, and spoke again of visiting him and helping him convince the authorities of his dire peril. In his reply he seemed less set against that plan than his past attitude would have led one to predict, but said he would like to hold off a little while longer—long enough to get his things in order and reconcile himself to the idea of leaving an almost morbidly cherished birthplace. People looked askance at his studies and speculations, and it would be better to get quietly off without setting the countryside in a turmoil and creating widespread doubts of his own sanity. He had had enough, he admitted, but he wanted to make a dignified exit if he could.

This letter reached me on the twenty-eighth of August, and I prepared and mailed as encouraging a reply as I could. Apparently the encouragement had effect, for Akeley had fewer terrors to report when he acknowledged my note. He was not very optimistic, though, and expressed the belief that it was only the full moon season which was holding the creatures off. He hoped there would not be many densely cloudy nights, and talked vaguely of boarding in Brattleboro when the moon waned. Again I wrote him encouragingly, but on September 5th there came a fresh communication which had obviously crossed my letter in the mails; and to this I could not give any such hopeful response. In view of its importance I believe I had better give it in full—as best I can do from memory of the shaky script. It ran substantially as follows:

Monday.

Dear Wilmarth—

A rather discouraging P.S. to my last. Last night was thickly cloudy—though no rain—and not a bit of moonlight got through. Things were pretty bad, and I think the end is getting near, in spite of all we have hoped. After midnight something landed on the roof of the house, and the dogs all rushed up to see what it was. I could hear them snapping and tearing around, and then one managed to get on the roof by jumping from the low ell. There was a terrible fight up there, and I heard a frightful *buzzing* which I'll never forget. And then there was a shocking smell. About the same time bullets came through the window and nearly grazed me. I think the main line of the hill creatures had got close to the house when the dogs divided because of the roof business. What was up there I don't know yet, but I'm afraid the creatures are learning to steer better with their space wings. I put out the light and used the windows for loopholes, and raked all around the house with rifle fire aimed just high enough not to hit the dogs. That seemed to end the business, but in the morning I found great pools of blood in the yard, beside pools of a green sticky stuff that had the worst odour I have ever smelled. I climbed up on the roof and found more of the sticky stuff there. Five of the dogs were killed—I'm afraid I hit one by aiming too low, for he was shot in the back. Now I am setting the panes the shots broke, and am going to Brattleboro for more dogs. I guess the men at the kennels think I am crazy. Will drop another note later. Suppose I'll be ready for moving in a week or two, though it nearly kills me to think of it.

Hastily—
AKELEY

But this was not the only letter from Akeley to cross mine. On the next morning—September 6th—still another came; this time a frantic scrawl which utterly unnerved me and put me at a loss what to say or do next. Again I cannot do better than quote the text as faithfully as memory will let me.

Tuesday.

Clouds didn't break, so no moon again—and going into the wane anyhow. I'd have the house wired for electricity and put in a searchlight if I didn't know they'd cut the cables as fast as they could be mended.

I think I am going crazy. It may be that all I have ever written you is a dream or madness. It was bad enough before, but this time it is too much. *They talked to me last night*—talked in that cursed buzzing voice and told me things *that I dare not repeat to you.* I heard them plainly over the barking of the dogs, and once when they were drowned out *a human voice helped them.* Keep out of this, Wilmarth—it is worse than either you or I ever suspected. *They don't mean to let me get to California now—they want to take me off alive, or what theoretically and mentally amounts to alive*—not only to Yuggoth, but beyond that—away outside the galaxy *and possibly beyond the last curved rim of space.* I told them I wouldn't go where they wish, *or in the terrible way they propose to take me,* but I'm afraid it will be no use. My place is so far out that they may come by day as well as by night before long. Six more dogs killed, and I felt presences all along the wooded parts of the road when I drove to Brattleboro today.

It was a mistake for me to try to send you that phonograph record and black stone. Better smash the record before it's too late. Will drop you another line tomorrow if I'm still here. Wish I could arrange to get my books and things to Brattleboro and board there. I would run off without anything if I could, but something inside my mind holds me back. I can slip out to Brattleboro, where I ought to be safe, but I feel just as much a prisoner there as at the house. And I seem to know that I couldn't get much farther even if I dropped everything and tried. It is horrible—don't get mixed up in this.

Yrs—AKELEY

I did not sleep at all the night after receiving this terrible thing, and was utterly baffled as to Akeley's remaining degree of sanity. The substance of the note was wholly insane, yet the manner of expression—in view of all that had gone before—had a grimly potent quality of convincingness. I made no attempt to answer it, thinking it better to wait until Akeley might have time to reply to my latest communication. Such a reply indeed came on the following day, though the fresh material in it quite overshadowed any of the points brought up by the letter it nominally answered. Here is what I recall of the text, scrawled and blotted as it was in the course of a plainly frantic and hurried composition.

Wednesday.

W—

Yr letter came, but it's no use to discuss anything any more. I am fully resigned. Wonder that I have even enough will power left to fight them off. Can't escape even if I were willing to give up everything and run. They'll get me.

Had a letter from them yesterday[36]—R.F.D. man brought it while I was at Brattleboro. Typed and postmarked Bellows Falls. Tells what they want to do with me—I can't repeat it. Look out for yourself, too! Smash that record. Cloudy nights keep up, and moon waning all the time. Wish I dared to get help—it might brace up my will power—but everyone who would dare to come at all would call me crazy unless there happened to be some proof. Couldn't ask people to come for no reason at all—am all out of touch with everybody and have been for years.

But I haven't told you the worst, Wilmarth. Brace up to read this, for it will give you a shock. I am telling the truth, though. It is this—*I have seen and touched one of the things, or part of one of the things.* God, man, but it's awful! It was dead, of course. One of the dogs had it, and I found it near the kennel this morning. I tried to save it in the woodshed to convince people of the whole thing, but it all evaporated in a few hours. Nothing left. You know, all those things in the rivers were seen only on the first morning after the flood. And here's the worst. I tried to photograph it for you, but when I developed the film *there wasn't anything visible except the woodshed.* What can the thing have been made of? I saw it and felt it, and they all leave footprints. It was surely made of matter—but what kind of matter? The shape can't be described. It was a great crab with a lot of pyramided fleshy rings or knots of thick, ropy stuff covered with feelers where a man's head would be. That sticky green stuff is its blood or juice. And there are more of them due on earth any minute.

Walter Brown is missing—hasn't been seen loafing around any

of his usual corners in the villages hereabouts. I must have got him with one of my shots, though the creatures always seem to try to take their dead and wounded away.

Got into town this afternoon without any trouble, but am afraid they're beginning to hold off because they're sure of me. Am writing this in Brattleboro P.O. This may be goodbye—if it is, write my son George Goodenough Akeley,[37] 176 Pleasant St., San Diego, Cal., *but don't come up here.* Write the boy if you don't hear from me in a week, and watch the papers for news.

I'm going to play my last two cards now—if I have the will power left. First to try poison gas on the things (I've got the right chemicals and have fixed up masks for myself and the dogs) and then if that doesn't work, tell the sheriff. They can lock me in a madhouse if they want to—it'll be better than what the *other creatures* would do. Perhaps I can get them to pay attention to the prints around the house—they are faint, but I can find them every morning. Suppose, though, police would say I faked them somehow; for they all think I'm a queer character.

Must try to have a state policeman spend a night here and see for himself—though it would be just like the creatures to learn about it and hold off that night. They cut my wires whenever I try to telephone in the night—the linemen think it is very queer, and may testify for me if they don't go and imagine I cut them myself. I haven't tried to keep them repaired for over a week now.

I could get some of the ignorant people to testify for me about the reality of the horrors, but everybody laughs at what they say, and anyway, they have shunned my place for so long that they don't know any of the new events. You couldn't get one of those run-down farmers to come within a mile of my house for love or money. The mail-carrier hears what they say and jokes me about it—God! If I only dared tell him how real it is! I think I'll try to get him to notice the prints, but he comes in the afternoon and they're usually about gone by that time. If I kept one by setting a box or pan over it, he'd think surely it was a fake or joke.

Wish I hadn't gotten to be such a hermit, so folks don't drop around as they used to. I've never dared shew the black stone or the kodak pictures, or play that record, to anybody but the ignorant people. The others would say I faked the whole business and do nothing but laugh. But I may yet try shewing the pictures. They give those claw-prints clearly, even if the things that made them can't be photographed. What a shame nobody else saw that *thing* this morning before it went to nothing!

But I don't know as I care. After what I've been through, a madhouse is as good a place as any. The doctors can help me make up my mind to get away from this house, and that is all that will save me.

Write my son George if you don't hear soon. Goodbye, smash that record, and don't mix up in this.

Yrs—AKELEY

The letter frankly plunged me into the blackest of terror. I did not know what to say in answer, but scratched off some incoherent words of advice and encouragement and sent them by registered mail. I recall urging Akeley to move to Brattleboro at once, and place himself under the protection of the authorities; adding that I would come to that town with the phonograph record and help convince the courts of his sanity. It was time, too, I think I wrote, to alarm the people generally against this thing in their midst. It will be observed that at this moment of stress my own belief in all Akeley had told and claimed was virtually complete, though I did think his failure to get a picture of the dead monster was due not to any freak of Nature but to some excited slip of his own.

V.

Then, apparently crossing my incoherent note and reaching me Saturday afternoon, September 8th, came that curiously different and calming letter neatly typed on a new machine; that strange letter of reassurance and invitation which must have marked so prodigious a transition in the whole nightmare drama of the lonely hills. Again I will quote from memory—seeking for special reasons to preserve as much of the flavour of the style as I can. It was postmarked Bellows Falls, and the signature as well as the body of the letter was typed—as is frequent with beginners in typing. The text, though, was marvellously accurate for a tyro's work; and I concluded that Akeley must have used a ma-

chine at some previous period—perhaps in college. To say that
the letter relieved me would be only fair, yet beneath my relief
lay a substratum of uneasiness. If Akeley had been sane in his
terror, was he now sane in his deliverance? And the sort of "improved rapport" mentioned . . . what was it? The entire thing implied such a diametrical reversal of Akeley's previous attitude!
But here is the substance of the text, carefully transcribed from a
memory in which I take some pride.

> Townshend, Vermont,
> Thursday, Sept. 6, 1928.

My dear Wilmarth:—

It gives me great pleasure to be able to set you at rest regarding
all the silly things I've been writing you. I say "silly", although by
that I mean my frightened attitude rather than my descriptions of
certain phenomena. Those phenomena are real and important
enough; my mistake had been in establishing an anomalous attitude toward them.

I think I mentioned that my strange visitors were beginning to
communicate with me, and to attempt such communication. Last
night this exchange of speech became actual. In response to certain signals I admitted to the house a messenger from those
outside—a fellow-human, let me hasten to say. He told me much
that neither you nor I had even begun to guess, and shewed
clearly how totally we had misjudged and misinterpreted the purpose of the Outer Ones in maintaining their secret colony on this
planet.

It seems that the evil legends about what they have offered to
men, and what they wish in connexion with the earth, are wholly
the result of an ignorant misconception of allegorical speech—
speech, of course, moulded by cultural backgrounds and thought-
habits vastly different from anything we dream of. My own
conjectures, I freely own, shot as widely past the mark as any of
the guesses of illiterate farmers and savage Indians. What I had
thought morbid and shameful and ignominious is in reality awesome and mind-expanding and even *glorious*—my previous estimate being merely a phase of man's eternal tendency to hate and
fear and shrink from the *utterly different*.

Now I regret the harm I have inflicted upon these alien and incredible beings in the course of our nightly skirmishes. If only I had consented to talk peacefully and reasonably with them in the first place! But they bear me no grudge, their emotions being organised very differently from ours. It is their misfortune to have had as their human agents in Vermont some very inferior specimens—the late Walter Brown, for example. He prejudiced me vastly against them. Actually, they have never knowingly harmed men, but have often been cruelly wronged and spied upon by our species. There is a whole secret cult of evil men (a man of your mystical erudition will understand me when I link them with Hastur and the Yellow Sign) devoted to the purpose of tracking them down and injuring them on behalf of monstrous powers from other dimensions. It is against these aggressors—not against normal humanity—that the drastic precautions of the Outer Ones are directed. Incidentally, I learned that many of our lost letters were stolen not by the Outer Ones but by the emissaries of this malign cult.

All that the Outer Ones wish of man is peace and non-molestation and an increasing intellectual rapport. This latter is absolutely necessary now that our inventions and devices are expanding our knowledge and motions, and making it more and more impossible for the Outer Ones' necessary outposts to exist *secretly* on this planet. The alien beings desire to know mankind more fully, and to have a few of mankind's philosophic and scientific leaders know more about them. With such an exchange of knowledge all perils will pass, and a satisfactory *modus vivendi* be established. The very idea of any attempt to *enslave* or *degrade* mankind is ridiculous.

As a beginning of this improved rapport, the Outer Ones have naturally chosen me—whose knowledge of them is already so considerable—as their primary interpreter on earth. Much was told me last night—facts of the most stupendous and vista-opening nature—and more will be subsequently communicated to me both orally and in writing. I shall not be called upon to make any trip *outside* just yet, though I shall probably *wish* to do so later on—employing special means and transcending everything which we have hitherto been accustomed to regard as human experience. My house will be besieged no longer. Everything has reverted to normal, and the dogs will have no further occupation. In place of terror I have been given a rich boon of knowledge and intellectual adventure which few other mortals have ever shared.

The Outer Beings are perhaps the most marvellous organic things in or beyond all space and time—members of a cosmos-wide race of which all other life-forms are merely degenerate variants. They are more vegetable than animal,[38] if these terms can be applied to the sort of matter composing them, and have a somewhat fungoid structure; though the presence of a chlorophyll-like substance and a very singular nutritive system differentiate them altogether from true cormophytic fungi. Indeed, the type is composed of a form of matter totally alien to our part of space—with electrons having a wholly different vibration-rate. That is why the beings cannot be photographed on the *ordinary* camera films and plates of our known universe, even though our eyes can see them. With proper knowledge, however, any good chemist could make a photographic emulsion which would record their images.

The genus is unique in its ability to traverse the heatless and airless interstellar void in full corporeal form, and some of its variants cannot do this without mechanical aid or curious surgical transpositions. Only a few species have the ether-resisting wings characteristic of the Vermont variety. Those inhabiting certain remote peaks in the Old World were brought in other ways. Their external resemblance to animal life, and to the sort of structure we understand as material, is a matter of parallel evolution rather than of close kinship. Their brain-capacity exceeds that of any other surviving life-form, although the winged types of our hill country are by no means the most highly developed. Telepathy is their usual means of discourse, though they have rudimentary vocal organs which, after a slight operation (for surgery is an incredibly expert and every-day thing among them), can roughly duplicate the speech of such types of organism as still use speech.

Their main *immediate* abode is a still undiscovered and almost lightless planet at the very edge of our solar system—beyond Neptune, and the ninth in distance from the sun. It is, as we have inferred, the object mystically hinted at as "Yuggoth" in certain ancient and forbidden writings; and it will soon be the scene of a strange focussing of thought upon our world in an effort to facilitate mental rapport. I would not be surprised if astronomers became sufficiently sensitive to these thought-currents to discover Yuggoth when the Outer Ones wish them to do so. But Yuggoth, of course, is only the stepping-stone. The main body of the beings inhabits strangely organised abysses wholly beyond the utmost reach of any human imagination. The space-time globule which we recognise as the totality of all cosmic entity is only an atom in the genuine infinity which is theirs. *And as much of this infinity as any human brain can hold is eventually to be opened up to me, as it has been to not more than fifty other men since the human race has existed.*

You will probably call this raving at first, Wilmarth, but in time you will appreciate the titanic opportunity I have stumbled upon. I want you to share as much of it as is possible, and to that end must tell you thousands of things that won't go on paper. In the past I have warned you not to come to see me. Now that all is safe, I take pleasure in rescinding that warning and inviting you.

Can't you make a trip up here before your college term opens? It would be marvellously delightful if you could. Bring along the phonograph record and all my letters to you as consultative data—we shall need them in piecing together the whole tremendous story. You might bring the kodak prints, too, since I seem to have mislaid the negatives and my own prints in all this recent excitement. But what a wealth of facts I have to add to all this groping and tentative material—*and what a stupendous device I have to supplement my additions!*

Don't hesitate—I am free from espionage now, and you will not meet anything unnatural or disturbing. Just come along and let my car meet you at the Brattleboro station—prepare to stay as long as you can, and expect many an evening of discussion of things beyond all human conjecture. Don't tell anyone about it, of course—for this matter must not get to the promiscuous public.

The train service to Brattleboro is not bad—you can get a time-table in Boston. Take the B. & M. to Greenfield, and then change for the brief remainder of the way. I suggest your taking the convenient 4:10 p.m.—standard—from Boston. This gets you into Greenfield at 7:35, and at 9:19 a train leaves there which reaches Brattleboro at 10:01. That is week-days. Let me know the date and I'll have my car on hand at the station.

Pardon this typed letter, but my handwriting has grown shaky of late, as you know, and I don't feel equal to long stretches of script. I got this new Corona in Brattleboro yesterday—it seems to work very well.

Awaiting word, and hoping to see you shortly with the phonograph record and all my letters—and the kodak prints—

I am
Yours in anticipation,
HENRY W. AKELEY.

To Albert N. Wilmarth, Esq.,
    Miskatonic University,
        Arkham, Mass.

The complexity of my emotions upon reading, re-reading, and pondering over this strange and unlooked-for letter is past adequate description. I have said that I was at once relieved and made uneasy, but this expresses only crudely the overtones of diverse and largely subconscious feelings which comprised both the relief and the uneasiness. To begin with, the thing was so antipodally at variance with the whole chain of horrors preceding it—the change of mood from stark terror to cool complacency and even exultation was so unheralded, lightning-like, and complete! I could scarcely believe that a single day could so alter the psychological perspective of one who had written that final frenzied bulletin of Wednesday, no matter what relieving disclosures that day might have brought. At certain moments a sense of conflicting unrealities made me wonder whether this whole distantly reported drama of fantastic forces were not a kind of half-illusory dream created largely within my own mind. Then I thought of the phonograph record and gave way to still greater bewilderment.

The letter seemed so unlike anything which could have been expected! As I analysed my impression, I saw that it consisted of two distinct phases. First, granting that Akeley had been sane before and was still sane, the indicated change in the situation itself was so swift and unthinkable. And secondly, the change in Akeley's own manner, attitude, and language was so vastly beyond the normal or the predictable. The man's whole personality seemed to have undergone an insidious mutation—a mutation so deep that one could scarcely reconcile his two aspects with the supposition that both represented equal sanity. Word-choice, spelling—all were subtly different. And with my academic sensitiveness to prose style, I could trace profound divergences in his commonest reactions and rhythm-responses. Certainly, the emotional cataclysm or revelation which could produce so radical an overturn must be an extreme one indeed! Yet in another way the letter seemed quite characteristic of Akeley. The same old passion for infinity—the same old scholarly inquisitiveness. I could not a moment—or more than a moment—credit the idea of spuriousness or malign substitution. Did not the invitation—the willingness to have me test the truth of the letter in person—prove its genuineness?

I did not retire Saturday night, but sat up thinking of the shadows and marvels behind the letter I had received. My mind, aching from the quick succession of monstrous conceptions it had been forced to confront during the last four months, worked upon this startling new material in a cycle of doubt and acceptance which repeated most of the steps experienced in facing the earlier wonders; till long before dawn a burning interest and curiosity had begun to replace the original storm of perplexity and uneasiness. Mad or sane, metamorphosed or merely relieved, the chances were that Akeley had actually encountered some stupendous change of perspective in his hazardous research; some change at once diminishing his danger—real or fancied—and opening dizzy new vistas of cosmic and superhuman knowledge. My own zeal for the unknown flared up to meet his, and I felt myself touched by the contagion of the morbid barrier-breaking. To shake off the maddening and wearying limitations of time and space and natural law—to be linked with the vast *outside*—to come close to the nighted and abysmal secrets of the infinite and the ultimate—surely such a thing was worth the risk of one's life, soul, and sanity![39] And Akeley had said there was no longer any peril—he had invited me to visit him instead of warning me away as before. I tingled at the thought of what he might now have to tell me—there was an almost paralysing fascination in the thought of sitting in that lonely and lately beleaguered farmhouse with a man who had talked with actual emissaries from outer space; sitting there with the terrible record and the pile of letters in which Akeley had summarised his earlier conclusions.

So late Sunday morning I telegraphed Akeley that I would

meet him in Brattleboro on the following Wednesday—September 12th—if that date were convenient for him. In only one respect did I depart from his suggestions, and that concerned the choice of a train. Frankly, I did not feel like arriving in that haunted Vermont region late at night; so instead of accepting the train he chose I telephoned the station and devised another arrangement. By rising early and taking the 8:07 a.m. (standard) into Boston, I could catch the 9:25 for Greenfield; arriving there at 12:22 noon. This connected exactly with a train reaching Brattleboro at 1:08 p.m.—a much more comfortable hour than 10:01 for meeting Akeley and riding with him into the close-packed, secret-guarding hills.

I mentioned this choice in my telegram, and was glad to learn in the reply which came toward evening that it had met with my prospective host's endorsement. His wire ran thus:

ARRANGEMENT SATISFACTORY. WILL MEET 1:08 TRAIN WEDNESDAY. DON'T FORGET RECORD AND LETTERS AND PRINTS. KEEP DESTINATION QUIET. EXPECT GREAT REVELATIONS.
                                        AKELEY.

Receipt of this message in direct response to one sent to Akeley—and necessarily delivered to his house from the Townshend station either by official messenger or by a restored telephone service—removed any lingering subconscious doubts I may have had about the authorship of the perplexing letter. My relief was marked—indeed, it was greater than I could account for at that time; since all such doubts had been rather deeply buried. But I slept soundly and long that night, and was eagerly busy with preparations during the ensuing two days.

VI.

On Wednesday I started as agreed, taking with me a valise full of simple necessities and scientific data, including the hideous phonograph record, the kodak prints, and the entire file of Akeley's correspondence. As requested, I had told no one where I

was going; for I could see that the matter demanded utmost privacy, even allowing for its most favourable turns. The thought of
actual mental contact with alien, outside entities was stupefying
enough to my trained and somewhat prepared mind; and this being so, what might one think of its effect on the vast masses of
uninformed laymen? I do not know whether dread or adventurous expectancy was uppermost in me as I changed trains in
Boston and began the long westward run out of familiar regions
into those I knew less thoroughly. Waltham—Concord—Ayer—
Fitchburg—Gardner—Athol—

My train reached Greenfield seven minutes late, but the
northbound connecting express had been held. Transferring in
haste, I felt a curious breathlessness as the cars rumbled on
through the early afternoon sunlight into territories I had always
read of but had never before visited. I knew I was entering an altogether older-fashioned and more primitive New England than
the mechanised, urbanised coastal and southern areas where all
my life had been spent; an unspoiled, ancestral New England
without the foreigners and factory-smoke, billboards and concrete roads, of the sections which modernity has touched. There
would be odd survivals of that continuous native life whose deep
roots make it the one authentic outgrowth of the landscape—the
continuous native life which keeps alive strange ancient memories, and fertilises the soil for shadowy, marvellous, and seldom-
mentioned beliefs.[40]

Now and then I saw the blue Connecticut River gleaming in
the sun, and after leaving Northfield we crossed it. Ahead
loomed green and cryptical hills, and when the conductor came
around I learned that I was at last in Vermont. He told me to set
my watch back an hour, since the northern hill country will have
no dealings with new-fangled daylight time schemes.[41] As I did
so it seemed to me that I was likewise turning the calendar back
a century.

The train kept close to the river, and across in New Hampshire I could see the approaching slope of steep Wantastiquet,[42]
about which singular old legends cluster. Then streets appeared
on my left, and a green island shewed in the stream on my right.
People rose and filed to the door, and I followed them. The car

stopped, and I alighted beneath the long train-shed of the Brattleboro station.

Looking over the line of waiting motors I hesitated a moment to see which one might turn out to be the Akeley Ford, but my identity was divined before I could take the initiative. And yet it was clearly not Akeley himself who advanced to meet me with an outstretched hand and a mellowly phrased query as to whether I was indeed Mr. Albert N. Wilmarth of Arkham. This man bore no resemblance to the bearded, grizzled Akeley of the snapshot; but was a younger and more urban person, fashionably dressed, and wearing only a small, dark moustache. His cultivated voice held an odd and almost disturbing hint of vague familiarity, though I could not definitely place it in my memory.

As I surveyed him I heard him explaining that he was a friend of my prospective host's who had come down from Townshend in his stead. Akeley, he declared, had suffered a sudden attack of some asthmatic trouble, and did not feel equal to making a trip in the outdoor air. It was not serious, however, and there was to be no change in plans regarding my visit. I could not make out just how much this Mr. Noyes—as he announced himself—knew of Akeley's researches and discoveries, though it seemed to me that his casual manner stamped him as a comparative outsider. Remembering what a hermit Akeley had been, I was a trifle surprised at the ready availability of such a friend; but did not let my puzzlement deter me from entering the motor to which he gestured me. It was not the small ancient car I had expected from Akeley's descriptions, but a large and immaculate specimen of recent pattern—apparently Noyes's own, and bearing Massachusetts licence plates with the amusing "sacred codfish" device of that year. My guide, I concluded, must be a summer transient in the Townshend region.

Noyes climbed into the car beside me and started it at once. I was glad that he did not overflow with conversation, for some peculiar atmospheric tensity made me feel disinclined to talk. The town seemed very attractive in the afternoon sunlight as we swept up an incline and turned to the right into the main street. It drowsed like the older New England cities which one remembers from boyhood, and something in the collocation of roofs and steeples and chimneys and brick walls formed contours touching deep viol-strings of ancestral emotion. I could tell that I was at the gateway of a region half-bewitched through the piling-up of unbroken time-accumulations; a region where old, strange things have had a chance to grow and linger because they have never been stirred up.[43]

As we passed out of Brattleboro my sense of constraint and foreboding increased, for a vague quality in the hill-crowded countryside with its towering, threatening, close-pressing green and granite slopes hinted at obscure secrets and immemorial survivals which might or might not be hostile to mankind. For a time our course followed a broad, shallow river which flowed down from unknown hills in the north, and I shivered when my companion told me it was the West River. It was in this stream, I recalled from newspaper items, that one of the morbid crab-like beings had been seen floating after the floods.

Gradually the country around us grew wilder and more deserted. Archaic covered bridges lingered fearsomely out of the past in pockets of the hills, and the half-abandoned railway track paralleling the river seemed to exhale a nebulously visible air of desolation. There were awesome sweeps of vivid valley where great cliffs rose, New England's virgin granite shewing grey and austere through the verdure that scaled the crests. There were gorges where untamed streams leaped, bearing down toward the river the unimagined secrets of a thousand pathless peaks. Branching away now and then were narrow, half-concealed roads that bored their way through solid, luxuriant masses of forest among whose primal trees whole armies of elemental spirits might well lurk. As I saw these I thought of how Akeley had been molested by unseen agencies on his drives along this very route, and did not wonder that such things could be.

The quaint, sightly village of Newfane, reached in less than an hour, was our last link with that world which man can definitely call his own by virtue of conquest and complete occupancy. After that we cast off all allegiance to immediate, tangible, and time-touched things, and entered a fantastic world of hushed unreality in which the narrow, ribbon-like road rose and fell and curved with an almost sentient and purposeful caprice amidst the tenantless green peaks and half-deserted valleys. Except for the sound of the motor, and the faint stir of the few lonely farms we passed at infrequent intervals, the only thing that reached my ears was the gurgling, insidious trickle of strange waters from numberless hidden fountains in the shadowy woods.

The nearness and intimacy of the dwarfed, domed hills now became veritably breath-taking. Their steepness and abruptness were even greater than I had imagined from hearsay, and suggested nothing in common with the prosaic objective world we know. The dense, unvisited woods on those inaccessible slopes seemed to harbour alien and incredible things, and I felt that the very outline of the hills themselves held some strange and aeon-forgotten meaning, as if they were vast hieroglyphs left by a rumoured titan race whose glories live only in rare, deep dreams. All the legends of the past, and all the stupefying imputations of Henry Akeley's letters and exhibits, welled up in my memory to heighten the atmosphere of tension and growing menace. The purpose of my visit, and the frightful abnormalities it postulated, struck me all at once with a chill sensation that nearly overbalanced my ardour for strange delvings.[44]

My guide must have noticed my disturbed attitude; for as the road grew wilder and more irregular, and our motion slower and more jolting, his occasional pleasant comments expanded into a steadier flow of discourse. He spoke of the beauty and weirdness of the country, and revealed some acquaintance with the folklore studies of my prospective host. From his polite questions it was obvious that he knew I had come for a scientific purpose, and that I was bringing data of some importance; but he gave no sign of appreciating the depth and awfulness of the knowledge which Akeley had finally reached.

His manner was so cheerful, normal, and urbane that his remarks ought to have calmed and reassured me; but oddly enough, I felt only the more disturbed as we bumped and veered onward into the unknown wilderness of hills and woods. At times it seemed as if he were pumping me to see what I knew of the monstrous secrets of the place, and with every fresh utterance that vague, teasing, baffling *familiarity* in his voice increased. It was not an ordinary or healthy familiarity despite the thoroughly wholesome and cultivated nature of the voice. I somehow linked it with forgotten nightmares, and felt that I might go mad if I recognised it. If any good excuse had existed, I think I would have turned back from my visit. As it was, I could not well do so—and it occurred to me that a cool, scientific conversation with Akeley himself after my arrival would help greatly to pull me together.

Besides, there was a strangely calming element of cosmic beauty in the hypnotic landscape through which we climbed and plunged fantastically. Time had lost itself in the labyrinths behind, and around us stretched only the flowering waves of faery and the recaptured loveliness of vanished centuries—the hoary groves, the untainted pastures edged with gay autumnal blossoms, and at vast intervals the small brown farmsteads nestling amidst huge trees beneath vertical precipices of fragrant brier and meadow-grass. Even the sunlight assumed a supernal glamour, as if some special atmosphere or exhalation mantled the whole region. I had seen nothing like it before save in the magic vistas that sometimes form the backgrounds of Italian primitives. Sodoma and Leonardo conceived such expanses, but only in the distance, and through the vaultings of Renaissance arcades.[45] We were now burrowing bodily through the midst of the picture, and I seemed to find in its necromancy a thing I had innately known or inherited, and for which I had always been vainly searching.[46]

Suddenly, after rounding an obtuse angle at the top of a sharp ascent, the car came to a standstill. On my left, across a well-kept lawn which stretched to the road and flaunted a border of whitewashed stones, rose a white, two-and-a-half-story house of unusual size and elegance for the region, with a congeries of continuous or arcade-linked barns, sheds, and windmill behind and to the right. I recognised it at once from the snapshot I had received, and was not surprised to see the name of Henry Akeley on the galvanised-iron mail-box near the road. For some distance back of the house a level stretch of marshy and sparsely wooded land extended, beyond which soared a steep, thickly forested hillside ending in a jagged leafy crest. This latter, I knew, was the summit of Dark Mountain, half way up which we must have climbed already.

Alighting from the car and taking my valise, Noyes asked me to wait while he went in and notified Akeley of my advent. He himself, he added, had important business elsewhere, and could not stop for more than a moment. As he briskly walked up the path to the house I climbed out of the car myself, wishing to stretch my legs a little before settling down to a sedentary conversation. My feeling of nervousness and tension had risen to a maximum again now that I was on the actual scene of the morbid beleaguering described so hauntingly in Akeley's letters, and I honestly dreaded the coming discussions which were to link me with such alien and forbidden worlds.

Close contact with the utterly bizarre is often more terrifying than inspiring, and it did not cheer me to think that this very bit of dusty road was the place where those monstrous tracks and that foetid green ichor had been found after moonless nights of fear and death. Idly I noticed that none of Akeley's dogs seemed to be about. Had he sold them all as soon as the Outer Ones made peace with him? Try as I might, I could not have the same confidence in the depth and sincerity of that peace which appeared in Akeley's final and queerly different letter. After all, he was a man of much simplicity and with little worldly experience. Was there not, perhaps, some deep and sinister undercurrent beneath the surface of the new alliance?

Led by my thoughts, my eyes turned downward to the powdery road surface which had held such hideous testimonies. The last few days had been dry, and tracks of all sorts cluttered the rutted, irregular highway despite the unfrequented nature of the district. With a vague curiosity I began to trace the outline of some of the heterogeneous impressions, trying meanwhile to curb the flights of macabre fancy which the place and its memories suggested. There was something menacing and uncomfortable in the funereal stillness, in the muffled, subtle trickle of distant brooks, and in the crowding green peaks and black-wooded precipices that choked the narrow horizon.

And then an image shot into my consciousness which made those vague menaces and flights of fancy seem mild and insignificant indeed. I have said that I was scanning the miscellaneous prints in the road with a kind of idle curiosity—but all at once that curiosity was shockingly snuffed out by a sudden and paralysing gust of active terror. For though the dust tracks were in general confused and overlapping, and unlikely to arrest any casual gaze, my restless vision had caught certain details near the spot where the path to the house joined the highway; and had recognised beyond doubt or hope the frightful significance of those details. It was not for nothing, alas, that I had pored for hours over the kodak views of the Outer Ones' claw-prints which Akeley had sent. Too well did I know the marks of those loathsome nippers, and that hint of ambiguous direction which stamped the horrors as no creatures of this planet. No chance had been left me for merciful mistake. Here, indeed, in objective form before my own eyes, and surely made not many hours ago, were at least three marks which stood out blasphemously among the surprising plethora of blurred footprints leading to and from the Akeley farmhouse. *They were the hellish tracks of the living fungi from Yuggoth.*

I pulled myself together in time to stifle a scream. After all, what more was there than I might have expected, assuming that I had really believed Akeley's letters? He had spoken of making peace with the things. Why, then, was it strange that some of them had visited his house? But the terror was stronger than the reassurance. Could any man be expected to look unmoved for the first time upon the claw-marks of animate beings from outer depths of space? Just then I saw Noyes emerge from the door and approach with a brisk step. I must, I reflected, keep command of myself, for the chances were this genial friend knew nothing of Akeley's profoundest and most stupendous probings into the forbidden.

Akeley, Noyes hastened to inform me, was glad and ready to see me; although his sudden attack of asthma would prevent him from being a very competent host for a day or two. These spells hit him hard when they came, and were always accompanied by a debilitating fever and general weakness. He never was good for much while they lasted—had to talk in a whisper, and was very clumsy and feeble in getting about. His feet and ankles swelled, too, so that he had to bandage them like a gouty old beef-eater. Today he was in rather bad shape, so that I would have to attend very largely to my own needs; but he was none the less eager for conversation. I would find him in the study at the left of the front hall—the room where the blinds were shut. He had to keep the sunlight out when he was ill, for his eyes were very sensitive.

As Noyes bade me adieu and rode off northward in his car I began to walk slowly toward the house. The door had been left ajar for me; but before approaching and entering I cast a searching glance around the whole place, trying to decide what had struck me as so intangibly queer about it. The barns and sheds looked trimly prosaic enough, and I noticed Akeley's battered Ford in its capacious, unguarded shelter. Then the secret of the queerness reached me. It was the total silence. Ordinarily a farm is at least moderately murmurous from its various kinds of livestock, but here all signs of life were missing. What of the hens and the hogs? The cows, of which Akeley had said he possessed several, might conceivably be out to pasture, and the dogs might possibly have been sold; but the absence of any trace of cackling or grunting was truly singular.

I did not pause long on the path, but resolutely entered the open house door and closed it behind me. It had cost me a distinct psychological effort to do so, and now that I was shut inside I had a momentary longing for precipitate retreat. Not that the place was in the least sinister in visual suggestion; on the contrary, I thought the graceful late-colonial hallway very tasteful and wholesome, and admired the evident breeding of the man who had furnished it. What made me wish to flee was something very attenuated and indefinable. Perhaps it was a certain odd odour which I thought I noticed—though I well know how common musty odours are in even the best of ancient farmhouses.

VII.

Refusing to let these cloudy qualms overmaster me, I recalled Noyes's instructions and pushed open the six-panelled, brass-latched white door on my left. The room beyond was darkened, as I had known before; and as I entered it I noticed that the queer odour was stronger there. There likewise appeared to be some faint, half-imaginary rhythm or vibration in the air. For a moment the closed blinds allowed me to see very little, but then a kind of apologetic hacking or whispering sound drew my attention to a great easy-chair in the farther, darker corner of the room. Within its shadowy depths I saw the white blur of a man's face and hands; and in a moment I had crossed to greet the figure who had tried to speak. Dim though the light was, I perceived that this was indeed my host. I had studied the kodak picture repeatedly, and there could be no mistake about this firm, weather-beaten face with the cropped, grizzled beard.

But as I looked again my recognition was mixed with sadness and anxiety; for certainly, this face was that of a very sick man. I felt that there must be something more than asthma behind that strained, rigid, immobile expression and unwinking glassy stare; and realised how terribly the strain of his frightful experiences must have told on him. Was it not enough to break any human being—even a younger man than this intrepid delver into the forbidden? The strange and sudden relief, I feared, had come too late to save him from something like a general breakdown. There was a touch of the pitiful in the limp, lifeless way his lean hands rested in his lap. He had on a loose dressing-gown, and was swathed around the head and high around the neck with a vivid yellow scarf or hood.

And then I saw that he was trying to talk in the same hacking whisper with which he had greeted me. It was a hard whisper to catch at first, since the grey moustache concealed all movements of the lips, and something in its timbre disturbed me greatly; but by concentrating my attention I could soon make out its purport surprisingly well. The accent was by no means a rustic one, and the language was even more polished than correspondence had led me to expect.

"Mr. Wilmarth, I presume? You must pardon my not rising. I am quite ill, as Mr. Noyes must have told you; but I could not resist having you come just the same. You know what I wrote in my last letter—there is so much to tell you tomorrow when I shall feel better. I can't say how glad I am to see you in person after all our many letters. You have the file with you, of course? And the kodak prints and record? Noyes put your valise in the hall—I suppose you saw it. For tonight I fear you'll have to wait on yourself to a great extent. Your room is upstairs—the one over this—and you'll see the bathroom door open at the head of the staircase. There's a meal spread for you in the dining-room— right through this door at your right—which you can take whenever you feel like it. I'll be a better host tomorrow—but just now weakness leaves me helpless.

"Make yourself at home—you might take out the letters and pictures and record and put them on the table here before you go upstairs with your bag. It is here that we shall discuss them—you can see my phonograph on that corner stand.

"No, thanks—there's nothing you can do for me. I know these spells of old. Just come back for a little quiet visiting before night, and then go to bed when you please. I'll rest right here— perhaps sleep here all night as I often do. In the morning I'll be far better able to go into the things we must go into. You realise, of course, the utterly stupendous nature of the matter before us. To us, as to only a few men on this earth, there will be opened up gulfs of time and space and knowledge beyond anything within the conception of human science and philosophy.

"Do you know that Einstein is wrong, and that certain objects and forces *can* move with a velocity greater than that of light? With proper aid I expect to go backward and forward in time, and actually *see* and *feel* the earth of remote past and future epochs.[47] You can't imagine the degree to which those beings have carried science. There is nothing they can't do with the mind and body of living organisms. I expect to visit other planets, and even other stars and galaxies. The first trip will be to Yuggoth, the nearest world fully peopled by the beings. It is a strange dark orb at the very rim of our solar system—unknown to earthly astronomers as yet. But I must have written you about this. At the proper time, you know, the beings there will direct thought-currents toward us and cause it to be discovered—or perhaps let one of their human allies give the scientists a hint.

"There are mighty cities on Yuggoth—great tiers of terraced towers built of black stone like the specimen I tried to send you.

That came from Yuggoth. The sun shines there no brighter than a star, but the beings need no light. They have other, subtler senses, and put no windows in their great houses and temples. Light even hurts and hampers and confuses them, for it does not exist at all in the black cosmos outside time and space where they came from originally. To visit Yuggoth would drive any weak man mad—yet I am going there. The black rivers of pitch that flow under those mysterious Cyclopean bridges—things built by some elder race extinct and forgotten before the things came to Yuggoth from the ultimate voids—ought to be enough to make any man a Dante or Poe if he can keep sane long enough to tell what he has seen.

"But remember—that dark world of fungoid gardens and windowless cities isn't really terrible. It is only to us that it would seem so. Probably this world seemed just as terrible to the beings when they first explored it in the primal age. You know they were here long before the fabulous epoch of Cthulhu was over, and remember all about sunken R'lyeh when it was above the waters.[48] They've been inside the earth, too—there are openings which human beings know nothing of—some of them in these very Vermont hills—and great worlds of unknown life down there; blue-litten K'n-yan, red-litten Yoth, and black, lightless N'kai.[49] It's from N'kai that frightful Tsathoggua came—you know, the amorphous, toad-like god-creature mentioned in the Pnakotic Manuscripts and the *Necronomicon* and the Commoriom myth-cycle preserved by the Atlantean high-priest Klarkash-Ton.[50]

"But we will talk of all this later on. It must be four or five o'clock by this time. Better bring the stuff from your bag, take a bite, and then come back for a comfortable chat."

Very slowly I turned and began to obey my host; fetching my valise, extracting and despositing the desired articles, and finally ascending to the room designated as mine. With the memory of that roadside claw-print fresh in my mind, Akeley's whispered paragraphs had affected me queerly; and the hints of familiarity with this unknown world of fungous life—forbidden Yuggoth—made my flesh creep more than I cared to own. I was tremendously sorry about Akeley's illness, but had to confess that his

hoarse whisper had a hateful as well as pitiful quality. If only he
wouldn't *gloat* so about Yuggoth and its black secrets!

My room proved a very pleasant and well-furnished one, devoid alike of the musty odour and disturbing sense of vibration;
and after leaving my valise there I descended again to greet
Akeley and take the lunch he had set out for me. The dining-
room was just beyond the study, and I saw that a kitchen ell extended still farther in the same direction. On the dining-table an
ample array of sandwiches, cake, and cheese awaited me, and a
Thermos-bottle beside a cup and saucer testified that hot coffee
had not been forgotten.[51] After a well-relished meal I poured myself a liberal cup of coffee, but found that the culinary standard
had suffered a lapse in this one detail. My first spoonful revealed
a faintly unpleasant acrid taste, so that I did not take more.
Throughout the lunch I thought of Akeley sitting silently in the
great chair in the darkened next room. Once I went in to beg him
to share the repast, but he whispered that he could eat nothing as
yet. Later on, just before he slept, he would take some malted
milk—all he ought to have that day.

After lunch I insisted on clearing the dishes away and washing
them in the kitchen sink—incidentally emptying the coffee
which I had not been able to appreciate. Then returning to the
darkened study I drew up a chair near my host's corner and prepared for such conversation as he might feel inclined to conduct.
The letters, pictures, and record were still on the large centre-
table, but for the nonce we did not have to draw upon them. Before long I forgot even the bizarre odour and curious suggestions
of vibration.

I have said that there were things in some of Akeley's letters—
especially the second and most voluminous one—which I would
not dare to quote or even form into words on paper. This hesitancy applies with still greater force to the things I heard whispered that evening in the darkened room among the lonely
haunted hills. Of the extent of the cosmic horrors unfolded by
that raucous voice I cannot even hint. He had known hideous
things before, but what he had learned since making his pact
with the Outside Things was almost too much for sanity to bear.
Even now I absolutely refuse to believe what he implied about

the constitution of ultimate infinity, the juxtaposition of dimensions, and the frightful position of our known cosmos of space and time in the unending chain of linked cosmos-atoms which makes up the immediate super-cosmos of curves, angles, and material and semi-material electronic organisation.

Never was a sane man more dangerously close to the arcana of basic entity—never was an organic brain nearer to utter annihilation in the chaos that transcends form and force and symmetry. I learned whence Cthulhu *first* came, and why half the great temporary stars of history had flared forth.[52] I guessed—from hints which made even my informant pause timidly—the secret behind the Magellanic Clouds and globular nebulae, and the black truth veiled by the immemorial allegory of Tao.[53] The nature of the Doels[54] was plainly revealed, and I was told the essence (though not the source) of the Hounds of Tindalos. The legend of Yig, Father of Serpents,[55] remained figurative no longer, and I started with loathing when told of the monstrous nuclear chaos beyond angled space which the *Necronomicon* had mercifully cloaked under the name of Azathoth. It was shocking to have the foulest nightmares of secret myth cleared up in concrete terms whose stark, morbid hatefulness exceeded the boldest hints of ancient and mediaeval mystics. Ineluctably I was led to believe that the first whisperers of these accursed tales must have had discourse with Akeley's Outer Ones, and perhaps have visited outer cosmic realms as Akeley now proposed visiting them.

I was told of the Black Stone and what it implied, and was glad that it had not reached me. My guesses about those hieroglyphics had been all too correct! And yet Akeley now seemed reconciled to the whole fiendish system he had stumbled upon; reconciled and eager to probe farther into the monstrous abyss. I wondered what beings he had talked with since his last letter to me, and whether many of them had been as human as that first emissary he had mentioned. The tension in my head grew insufferable, and I built up all sorts of wild theories about the queer, persistent odour and those insidious hints of vibration in the darkened room.

Night was falling now, and as I recalled what Akeley had written me about those earlier nights I shuddered to think there would be no moon. Nor did I like the way the farmhouse nestled in the lee of that colossal forested slope leading up to Dark Mountain's unvisited crest. With Akeley's permission I lighted a small oil lamp, turned it low, and set it on a distant bookcase beside the ghostly bust of Milton; but afterward I was sorry I had done so, for it made my host's strained, immobile face and listless hands look damnably abnormal and corpse-like. He seemed half-incapable of motion, though I saw him nod stiffly once in a while.

After what he had told, I could scarcely imagine what profounder secrets he was saving for the morrow; but at last it developed that his trip to Yuggoth and beyond—*and my own possible participation in it*—was to be the next day's topic. He must have been amused by the start of horror I gave at hearing a cosmic voyage on my part proposed, for his head wabbled violently when I shewed my fear. Subsequently he spoke very gently of how human beings might accomplish—and several times had accomplished—the seemingly impossible flight across the interstellar void. It seemed *that complete human bodies did not indeed make the trip*, but that the prodigious surgical, biological, chemical, and mechanical skill of the Outer Ones had found a way to convey human brains without their concomitant physical structure.

There was a harmless way to extract a brain, and a way to keep the organic residue alive during its absence. The bare, compact cerebral matter was then immersed in an occasionally replenished fluid with an ether-tight cylinder of a metal mined in Yuggoth, certain electrodes reaching through and connecting at will with elaborate instruments capable of duplicating the three vital faculties of sight, hearing, and speech. For the winged fungus-beings to carry the brain-cylinders intact through space was an easy matter. Then, on every planet covered by their civilisation, they would find plenty of adjustable faculty-instruments capable of being connected with the encased brains; so that after a little fitting these travelling intelligences could be given a full sensory and articulate life—albeit a bodiless and mechanical one—at each stage of their journeying through and beyond the space-time continuum. It was as simple as carrying a phonograph record about and playing it wherever a phonograph of the corresponding make exists. Of its success there could be no question. Akeley was not afraid. Had it not been brilliantly accomplished again and again?

For the first time one of the inert, wasted hands raised itself and pointed to a high shelf on the farther side of the room. There, in a neat row, stood more than a dozen cylinders of a metal I had never seen before—cylinders about a foot high and somewhat less in diameter, with three curious sockets set in an isosceles triangle over the front convex surface of each. One of them was linked at two of the sockets to a pair of singular-looking machines that stood in the background. Of their purport I did not need to be told, and I shivered as with ague. Then I saw the hand point to a much nearer corner where some intricate instruments with attached cords and plugs, several of them much like the two devices on the shelf behind the cylinders, were huddled together.

"There are four kinds of instruments here, Wilmarth," whispered the voice. "Four kinds—three faculties each—makes twelve pieces in all. You see there are four different sorts of beings presented in those cylinders up there. Three humans, six fungoid beings who can't navigate space corporeally, two beings from Neptune (God! if you could see the body this type has on its own planet!), and the rest entities from the central caverns of an especially interesting dark star beyond the galaxy. In the principal outpost inside Round Hill you'll now and then find more cylinders and machines—cylinders of extra-cosmic brains with different senses from any we know—allies and explorers from the uttermost Outside—and special machines for giving them impressions and expression in the several ways suited at once to them and to the comprehensions of different types of listeners. Round Hill, like most of the beings' main outposts all through the various universes, is a very cosmopolitan place! Of course, only the more common types have been lent to me for experiment.

"Here—take the three machines I point to and set them on the table. That tall one with the two glass lenses in front—then the box with the vacuum tubes and sounding-board—and now the one with the metal disc on top. Now for the cylinder with the label 'B-67' pasted on it. Just stand in that Windsor chair to reach the shelf. Heavy? Never mind! Be sure of the number—B-67. Don't bother that fresh, shiny cylinder joined to the two testing instruments—the one with my name on it. Set B-67 on the table near where you've put the machines—and see that the dial switch on all three machines is jammed over to the extreme left.

"Now connect the cord of the lens machine with the upper socket on the cylinder—there! Join the tube machine to the lower left-hand socket, and the disc apparatus to the outer socket. Now move all the dial switches on the machines over to the extreme right—first the lens one, then the disc one, and then the tube one. That's right. I might as well tell you that this is a human being—just like any of us. I'll give you a taste of some of the others tomorrow."

To this day I do not know why I obeyed those whispers so slavishly, or whether I thought Akeley was mad or sane. After what had gone before, I ought to have been prepared for anything; but this mechanical mummery seemed so like the typical vagaries of crazed inventors and scientists that it struck a chord of doubt which even the preceding discourse had not excited. What the whisperer implied was beyond all human belief—yet were not the other things still farther beyond, and less preposterous only because of their remoteness from tangible concrete proof?

As my mind reeled amidst this chaos, I became conscious of a mixed grating and whirring from all three machines lately linked to the cylinder—a grating and whirring which soon subsided into a virtual noiselessness. What was about to happen? Was I to hear a voice? And if so, what proof would I have that it was not some cleverly concocted radio device talked into by a concealed but closely watching speaker? Even now I am unwilling to swear just what I heard, or just what phenomenon really took place before me. But something certainly seemed to take place.

To be brief and plain, the machine with the tubes and sound-box began to speak, and with a point and intelligence which left no doubt that the speaker was actually present and observing us.

The voice was loud, metallic, lifeless, and plainly mechanical in every detail of its production. It was incapable of inflection or expressiveness, but scraped and rattled on with a deadly precision and deliberation.

"Mr. Wilmarth," it said, "I hope I do not startle you. I am a human being like yourself, though my body is now resting safely under proper vitalising treatment inside Round Hill, about a mile and a half east of here. I myself am here with you—my brain is in that cylinder and I see, hear, and speak through these electronic vibrators. In a week I am going across the void as I have been many times before, and I expect to have the pleasure of Mr. Akeley's company. I wish I might have yours as well; for I know you by sight and reputation, and have kept close track of your correspondence with our friend. I am, of course, one of the men who have become allied with the outside beings visiting our planet. I met them first in the Himalayas, and have helped them in various ways. In return they have given me experiences such as few men have ever had.

"Do you realise what it means when I say I have been on thirty-seven different celestial bodies—planets, dark stars, and less definable objects—including eight outside our galaxy and two outside the curved cosmos of space and time? All this has not harmed me in the least. My brain has been removed from my body by fissions so adroit that it would be crude to call the operation surgery. The visiting beings have methods which make these extractions easy and almost normal—and one's body never ages when the brain is out of it. The brain, I may add, is virtually immortal with its mechanical faculties and a limited nourishment supplied by occasional changes of the preserving fluid.

"Altogether, I hope most heartily that you will decide to come with Mr. Akeley and me. The visitors are eager to know men of knowledge like yourself, and to shew them the great abysses that most of us have had to dream about in fanciful ignorance. It may seem strange at first to meet them, but I know you will be above minding that. I think Mr. Noyes will go along, too—the man who doubtless brought you up here in his car. He has been one of us for years—I suppose you recognised his voice as one of those on the record Mr. Akeley sent you."

At my violent start the speaker paused a moment before concluding.

"So, Mr. Wilmarth, I will leave the matter to you; merely adding that a man with your love of strangeness and folklore ought never to miss such a chance as this. There is nothing to fear. All transitions are painless, and there is much to enjoy in a wholly mechanised state of sensation. When the electrodes are disconnected, one merely drops off into a sleep of especially vivid and fantastic dreams.

"And now, if you don't mind, we might adjourn our session till tomorrow. Good night—just turn all the switches back to the left; never mind the exact order, though you might let the lens machine be last. Good night, Mr. Akeley—treat our guest well! Ready now with those switches?"

That was all. I obeyed mechanically and shut off all three switches, though dazed with doubt of everything that had occurred. My head was still reeling as I heard Akeley's whispering voice telling me that I might leave all the apparatus on the table just as it was. He did not essay any comment on what had happened, and indeed no comment could have conveyed much to my burdened faculties. I heard him telling me I could take the lamp to use in my room, and deduced that he wished to rest alone in the dark. It was surely time he rested, for his discourse of the afternoon and evening had been such as to exhaust even a vigorous man. Still dazed, I bade my host good night and went upstairs with the lamp, although I had an excellent pocket flashlight with me.

I was glad to be out of that downstairs study with the queer odour and vague suggestions of vibration, yet could not of course escape a hideous sense of dread and peril and cosmic abnormality as I thought of the place I was in and the forces I was meeting. The wild, lonely region, the black, mysteriously forested slope towering so close behind the house, the footprints in the road, the sick, motionless whisperer in the dark, the hellish cylinders and machines, and above all the invitations to strange surgery and stranger voyagings—these things, all so new and in such sudden succession, rushed in on me with a cumulative force which sapped my will and almost undermined my physical strength.

To discover that my guide Noyes was the human celebrant in that monstrous bygone Sabbat-ritual on the phonograph record was a particular shock, though I had previously sensed a dim, re-pellent familiarity in his voice. Another special shock came from my own attitude toward my host whenever I paused to analyse it; for much as I had instinctively liked Akeley as revealed in his cor-respondence, I now found that he filled me with a distinct repul-sion. His illness ought to have excited my pity; but instead, it gave me a kind of shudder. He was so rigid and inert and corpse-like—and that incessant whispering was so hateful and unhuman!

It occurred to me that this whispering was different from any-thing else of the kind I had ever heard; that, despite the curious motionlessness of the speaker's moustache-screened lips, it had a latent strength and carrying-power remarkable for the wheez-ings of an asthmatic. I had been able to understand the speaker when wholly across the room, and once or twice it had seemed to me that the faint but penetrant sounds represented not so much weakness as deliberate repression—for what reason I could not guess. From the first I had felt a disturbing quality in their timbre. Now, when I tried to weigh the matter, I thought I could trace this impression to a kind of subconscious familiarity like that which had made Noyes's voice so hazily ominous. But when or where I had encountered the thing it hinted at, was more than I could tell.

One thing was certain—I would not spend another night here. My scientific zeal had vanished amidst fear and loathing, and I felt nothing now but a wish to escape from this net of morbidity and unnatural revelation. I knew enough now. It must indeed be true that cosmic linkages do exist—but such things are surely not meant for normal human beings to meddle with.

Blasphemous influences seemed to surround me and press chokingly upon my senses. Sleep, I decided, would be out of the question; so I merely extinguished the lamp and threw myself on the bed fully dressed.[56] No doubt it was absurd, but I kept ready for some unknown emergency; gripping in my right hand the re-volver I had brought along, and holding the pocket flashlight in my left. Not a sound came from below, and I could imagine how my host was sitting there with cadaverous stiffness in the dark.

Somewhere I heard a clock ticking, and was vaguely grateful for the normality of the sound. It reminded me, though, of another thing about the region which disturbed me—the total absence of animal life. There were certainly no farm beasts about, and now I realised that even the accustomed night-noises of wild living things were absent. Except for the sinister trickle of distant unseen waters, that stillness was anomalous—interplanetary— and I wondered what star-spawned, intangible blight could be hanging over the region. I recalled from old legends that dogs and other beasts had always hated the Outer Ones, and thought of what those tracks in the road might mean.

VIII.

Do not ask me how long my unexpected lapse into slumber lasted, or how much of what ensued was sheer dream. If I tell you that I awaked at a certain time, and heard and saw certain things, you will merely answer that I did not wake then; and that everything was a dream until the moment when I rushed out of the house, stumbled to the shed where I had seen the old Ford, and seized that ancient vehicle for a mad, aimless race over the haunted hills which at last landed me—after hours of jolting and winding through forest-threatened labyrinths—in a village which turned out to be Townshend.

You will also, of course, discount everything else in my report; and declare that all the pictures, record-sounds, cylinder-and-machine sounds, and kindred evidences were bits of pure deception practiced on me by the missing Henry Akeley. You will even hint that he conspired with other eccentrics to carry out a silly and elaborate hoax—that he had the express shipment removed at Keene, and that he had Noyes make that terrifying wax record. It is odd, though, that Noyes has not even yet been identified; that he was unknown at any of the villages near Akeley's place, though he must have been frequently in the region. I wish I had stopped to memorise the licence-number of his car— or perhaps it is better after all that I did not. For I, despite all you can say, and despite all I sometimes try to say to myself, know that loathsome outside influences must be lurking there in the

half-unknown hills—and that those influences have spies and
emissaries in the world of men. To keep as far as possible from
such influences and such emissaries is all that I ask of life in
future.

When my frantic story sent a sheriff's posse out to the farmhouse, Akeley was gone without leaving a trace. His loose
dressing-gown, yellow scarf, and foot-bandages lay on the study
floor near his corner easy-chair, and it could not be decided
whether any of his other apparel had vanished with him. The
dogs and livestock were indeed missing, and there were some curious bullet-holes both on the house's exterior and on some of
the walls within; but beyond this nothing unusual could be detected. No cylinders or machines, none of the evidences I had
brought in my valise, no queer odour or vibration-sense, no
footprints in the road, and none of the problematical things I
glimpsed at the very last.

I stayed a week in Brattleboro after my escape, making inquiries among people of every kind who had known Akeley; and
the results convince me that the matter is no figment of dream or
delusion. Akeley's queer purchases of dogs and ammunition and
chemicals, and the cutting of his telephone wires, are matters of
record; while all who knew him—including his son in California—concede that his occasional remarks on strange studies had
a certain consistency. Solid citizens believe he was mad, and un-
hesitatingly pronounce all reported evidences mere hoaxes devised with insane cunning and perhaps abetted by eccentric
associates; but the lowlier country folk sustain his statements in
every detail. He had shewed some of these rustics his photographs and black stone, and had played the hideous record for
them; and they all said the footprints and buzzing voice were like
those described in ancestral legends.

They said, too, that suspicious sights and sounds had been noticed increasingly around Akeley's house after he found the
black stone, and that the place was now avoided by everybody
except the mail man and other casual, tough-minded people.
Dark Mountain and Round Hill were both notoriously haunted
spots, and I could find no one who had ever closely explored either. Occasional disappearances of natives throughout the dis-

trict's history were well attested, and these now included the semi-vagabond Walter Brown, whom Akeley's letters had mentioned. I even came upon one farmer who thought he had personally glimpsed one of the queer bodies at flood-time in the swollen West River, but his tale was too confused to be really valuable.

When I left Brattleboro I resolved never to go back to Vermont, and I feel quite certain I shall keep my resolution. Those wild hills are surely the outpost of a frightful cosmic race—as I doubt all the less since reading that a new ninth planet has been glimpsed beyond Neptune, just as those influences had said it would be glimpsed. Astronomers, with a hideous appropriateness they little suspect, have named this thing "Pluto".[57] I feel, beyond question, that it is nothing less than nighted Yuggoth—and I shiver when I try to figure out the real reason *why* its monstrous denizens wish it to be known in this way at this especial time. I vainly try to assure myself that these daemoniac creatures are not gradually leading up to some new policy hurtful to the earth and its normal inhabitants.

But I have still to tell of the ending of that terrible night in the farmhouse. As I have said, I did finally drop into a troubled doze; a doze filled with bits of dream which involved monstrous landscape-glimpses. Just what awaked me I cannot yet say, but that I did indeed awake at this given point I feel very certain. My first confused impression was of stealthily creaking floor-boards in the hall outside my door, and of a clumsy, muffled fumbling at the latch. This, however, ceased almost at once; so that my really clear impressions began with the voices heard from the study below. There seemed to be several speakers, and I judged that they were controversially engaged.

By the time I had listened a few seconds I was broad awake, for the nature of the voices was such as to make all thought of sleep ridiculous. The tones were curiously varied, and no one who had listened to that accursed phonograph record could harbour any doubts about the nature of at least two of them. Hideous though the idea was, I knew that I was under the same roof with nameless things from abysmal space; for those two voices were unmistakably the blasphemous buzzings which the Outside Beings used in their communication with men. The two were individually different—different in pitch, accent, and tempo—but they were both of the same damnable general kind.

A third voice was indubitably that of a mechanical utterance-machine connected with one of the detached brains in the cylinders. There was as little doubt about that as about the buzzings; for the loud, metallic, lifeless voice of the previous evening, with its inflectionless, expressionless scraping and rattling, and its impersonal precision and deliberation, had been utterly unforgettable. For a time I did not pause to question whether the intelligence behind the scraping was the identical one which had formerly talked to me; but shortly afterward I reflected that *any* brain would emit vocal sounds of the same quality if linked to the same mechanical speech-producer; the only possible differences being in language, rhythm, speed, and pronunciation. To complete the eldritch colloquy there were two actually human voices—one the crude speech of an unknown and evidently rustic man, and the other the suave Bostonian tones of my erstwhile guide Noyes.

As I tried to catch the words which the stoutly fashioned floor so bafflingly intercepted, I was also conscious of a great deal of stirring and scratching and shuffling in the room below; so that I could not escape the impression that it was full of living beings—many more than the few whose speech I could single out. The exact nature of this stirring is extremely hard to describe, for very few good bases of comparison exist. Objects seemed now and then to move across the room like conscious entities; the sound of their footfalls having something about it like a loose, hard-surfaced clattering—as of the contact of ill-coördinated surfaces of horn or hard rubber. It was, to use a more concrete but less accurate comparison, as if people with loose, splintery wooden shoes were shambling and rattling about on the polished board floor. On the nature and appearance of those responsible for the sounds, I did not care to speculate.

Before long I saw that it would be impossible to distinguish any connected discourse. Isolated words—including the names of Akeley and myself—now and then floated up, especially when

uttered by the mechanical speech-producer; but their true significance was lost for want of continuous context. Today I refuse to
form any definite deductions from them, and even their frightful
effect on me was one of *suggestion* rather than of *revelation*. A
terrible and abnormal conclave, I felt certain, was assembled below me; but for what shocking deliberations I could not tell. It
was curious how this unquestioned sense of the malign and the
blasphemous pervaded me despite Akeley's assurances of the
Outsiders' friendliness.

With patient listening I began to distinguish clearly between
voices, even though I could not grasp much of what any of the
voices said. I seemed to catch certain typical emotions behind
some of the speakers. One of the buzzing voices, for example,
held an unmistakable note of authority; whilst the mechanical
voice, notwithstanding its artificial loudness and regularity,
seemed to be in a position of subordination and pleading.
Noyes's tones exuded a kind of conciliatory atmosphere. The
others I could make no attempt to interpret. I did not hear the
familiar whisper of Akeley, but well knew that such a sound
could never penetrate the solid flooring of my room.

I will try to set down some of the few disjointed words and
other sounds I caught, labelling the speakers of the words as best
I know how. It was from the speech-machine that I first picked
up a few recognisable phrases.[58]

(THE SPEECH-MACHINE)

". . . brought it on myself . . . sent back the letters and the
record . . . end on it . . . taken in . . . seeing and hearing . . . damn
you . . . impersonal force, after all . . . fresh, shiny cylinder . . .
great God. . . ."

(FIRST BUZZING VOICE)

". . . time we stopped . . . small and human . . . Akeley . . . brain
. . . saying. . . ."

(SECOND BUZZING VOICE)

". . . Nyarlathotep . . . Wilmarth . . . records and letters . . .
cheap imposture. . . ."

(NOYES)

". . . (an unpronounceable word or name, possibly *N'gah-Kthun*) . . . harmless . . . peace . . . couple of weeks . . . theatrical . . . told you that before. . . ."

(FIRST BUZZING VOICE)

". . . no reason . . . original plan . . . effects . . . Noyes can watch . . . Round Hill . . . fresh cylinder . . . Noyes's car. . . ."

(NOYES)

". . . well . . . all yours . . . down here . . . rest . . . place. . . ."

(SEVERAL VOICES AT ONCE IN
INDISTINGUISHABLE SPEECH)

(MANY FOOTSTEPS, INCLUDING THE PECULIAR
LOOSE STIRRING OR CLATTERING)

(A CURIOUS SORT OF FLAPPING SOUND)

(THE SOUND OF AN AUTOMOBILE
STARTING AND RECEDING)

(SILENCE)

That is the substance of what my ears brought me as I lay rigid upon that strange upstairs bed in the haunted farmhouse among the daemonic hills—lay there fully dressed, with a revolver clenched in my right hand and a pocket flashlight gripped in my left. I became, as I have said, broad awake; but a kind of obscure paralysis nevertheless kept me inert till long after the last echoes of the sounds had died away. I heard the wooden, deliberate ticking of the ancient Connecticut clock somewhere far below, and at last made out the irregular snoring of a sleeper. Akeley must have dozed off after the strange session, and I could well believe that he needed to do so.

Just what to think or what to do was more than I could decide. After all, what *had* I heard beyond things which previous information might have led me to expect? Had I not known that the nameless Outsiders were now freely admitted to the farm-house? No doubt Akeley had been surprised by an unexpected visit from them. Yet something in that fragmentary discourse had chilled me immeasurably, raised the most grotesque and horrible doubts, and made me wish fervently that I might wake up and prove everything a dream. I think my subconscious mind must have caught something which my consciousness has not yet recognised. But what of Akeley? Was he not my friend, and would he not have protested if any harm were meant me? The peaceful snoring below seemed to cast ridicule on all my suddenly intensified fears.

Was it possible that Akeley had been imposed upon and used as a lure to draw me into the hills with the letters and pictures and phonograph record? Did those beings mean to engulf us both in a common destruction because we had come to know too much? Again I thought of the abruptness and unnaturalness of that change in the situation which must have occurred between Akeley's penultimate and final letters. Something, my instinct told me, was terribly wrong. All was not as it seemed. That acrid coffee which I refused—had there not been an attempt by some hidden, unknown entity to drug it? I must talk to Akeley at once, and restore his sense of proportion. They had hypnotised him with their promises of cosmic revelations, but now he must listen to reason. We must get out of this before it would be too late. If he lacked the will power to make the break for liberty, I would supply it. Or if I could not persuade him to go, I could at least go myself. Surely he would let me take his Ford and leave it in a garage at Brattleboro. I had noticed it in the shed—the door being left unlocked and open now that peril was deemed past—and I believed there was a good chance of its being ready for instant use. That momentary dislike of Akeley which I had felt during and after the evening's conversation was all gone now. He was in a position much like my own, and we must stick together. Knowing his indisposed condition, I hated to wake him at this juncture, but I knew that I must. I could not stay in this place till morning as matters stood.

At last I felt able to act, and stretched myself vigorously to regain command of my muscles. Arising with a caution more impulsive than deliberate, I found and donned my hat, took my valise, and started downstairs with the flashlight's aid. In my nervousness I kept the revolver clutched in my right hand, being able to take care of both valise and flashlight with my left. Why I exerted these precautions I do not really know, since I was even then on my way to awaken the only other occupant of the house.

As I half tiptoed down the creaking stairs to the lower hall I could hear the sleeper more plainly, and noticed that he must be in the room on my left—the living-room I had not entered. On my right was the gaping blackness of the study in which I had heard the voices. Pushing open the unlatched door of the living-room I traced a path with the flashlight toward the source of the snoring, and finally turned the beams on the sleeper's face. But in the next second I hastily turned them away and commenced a cat-like retreat to the hall, my caution this time springing from reason as well as from instinct. For the sleeper on the couch was not Akeley at all, but my quondam guide Noyes.

Just what the real situation was, I could not guess; but common sense told me that the safest thing was to find out as much as possible before arousing anybody. Regaining the hall, I silently closed and latched the living-room door after me; thereby lessening the chances of awaking Noyes. I now cautiously entered the dark study, where I expected to find Akeley, whether asleep or awake, in the great corner chair which was evidently his favourite resting-place. As I advanced, the beams of my flashlight caught the great centre-table, revealing one of the hellish cylinders with sight and hearing machines attached, and with a speech-machine standing close by, ready to be connected at any moment. This, I reflected, must be the encased brain I had heard talking during the frightful conference; and for a second I had a perverse impulse to attach the speech-machine and see what it would say.

It must, I thought, be conscious of my presence even now; since the sight and hearing attachments could not fail to disclose the rays of my flashlight and the faint creaking of the floor beneath my feet. But in the end I did not dare meddle with the thing. I idly saw that it was the fresh, shiny cylinder with Akeley's name on it, which I had noticed on the shelf earlier in the evening and which my host had told me not to bother. Looking back at that moment, I can only regret my timidity and wish that I had boldly caused the apparatus to speak. God knows what mysteries and horrible doubts and questions of identity it might have cleared up! But then, it may be merciful that I let it alone.

From the table I turned my flashlight to the corner where I thought Akeley was, but found to my perplexity that the great easy-chair was empty of any human occupant asleep or awake. From the seat to the floor there trailed voluminously the familiar old dressing-gown, and near it on the floor lay the yellow scarf and the huge foot-bandages I had thought so odd. As I hesitated, striving to conjecture where Akeley might be, and why he had so suddenly discarded his necessary sick-room garments, I observed that the queer odour and sense of vibration were no longer in the room. What had been their cause? Curiously it occurred to me that I had noticed them only in Akeley's vicinity. They had been strongest where he sat, and wholly absent except in the room with him or just outside the doors of that room. I paused, letting the flashlight wander about the dark study and racking my brain for explanations of the turn affairs had taken.

Would to heaven I had quietly left the place before allowing that light to rest again on the vacant chair. As it turned out, I did not leave quietly; but with a muffled shriek which must have disturbed, though it did not quite awake, the sleeping sentinel across the hall. That shriek, and Noyes's still-unbroken snore, are the last sounds I ever heard in that morbidity-choked farmhouse beneath the black-wooded crest of a haunted mountain— that focus of trans-cosmic horror amidst the lonely green hills and curse-muttering brooks of a spectral rustic land.

It is a wonder that I did not drop flashlight, valise, and revolver in my wild scramble, but somehow I failed to lose any of these. I actually managed to get out of that room and that house without making any further noise, to drag myself and my belongings safely into the old Ford in the shed, and to set that archaic vehicle in motion toward some unknown point of safety in the black, moonless night. The ride that followed was a piece of delirium out of Poe or Rimbaud[59] or the drawings of Doré, but finally I reached Townshend. That is all. If my sanity is still unshaken, I am lucky. Sometimes I fear what the years will bring, especially since that new planet Pluto has been so curiously discovered.

As I have implied, I let my flashlight return to the vacant easy-chair after its circuit of the room; then noticing for the first time the presence of certain objects in the seat, made inconspicuous by the adjacent loose folds of the empty dressing-gown. These are the objects, three in number, which the investigators did not find when they came later on. As I said at the outset, there was nothing of actual visual horror about them. The trouble was in what they led one to infer. Even now I have my moments of half-doubt—moments in which I half accept the scepticism of those who attribute my whole experience to dream and nerves and delusion.

The three things were damnably clever constructions of their kind, and were furnished with ingenious metallic clamps to attach them to organic developments of which I dare not form any conjecture. I hope—devoutly hope—that they were the waxen products of a master artist, despite what my inmost fears tell me. Great God! That whisperer in darkness with its morbid odour and vibrations! Sorcerer, emissary, changeling, outsider . . . that hideous repressed buzzing . . . and all the time in that fresh, shiny cylinder on the shelf . . . poor devil . . . "prodigious surgical, biological, chemical, and mechanical skill". . .

For the things in the chair, perfect to the last, subtle detail of microscopic resemblance—or identity—were the face and hands of Henry Wentworth Akeley.

The Shadow Over Innsmouth

I.

During the winter of 1927–28 officials of the Federal government made a strange and secret investigation of certain conditions in the ancient Massachusetts seaport of Innsmouth.[1] The public first learned of it in February, when a vast series of raids and arrests occurred, followed by the deliberate burning and dynamiting—under suitable precautions—of an enormous number of crumbling, worm-eaten, and supposedly empty houses along the abandoned waterfront. Uninquiring souls let this occurrence pass as one of the major clashes in a spasmodic war on liquor.

Keener news-followers, however, wondered at the prodigious number of arrests, the abnormally large force of men used in making them, and the secrecy surrounding the disposal of the prisoners. No trials, or even definite charges, were reported; nor were any of the captives seen thereafter in the regular gaols of the nation. There were vague statements about disease and concentration camps,[2] and later about dispersal in various naval and military prisons, but nothing positive ever developed. Innsmouth itself was left almost depopulated, and is even now only beginning to shew signs of a sluggishly revived existence.

Complaints from many liberal organisations were met with long confidential discussions, and representatives were taken on trips to certain camps and prisons. As a result, these societies became surprisingly passive and reticent. Newspaper men were harder to manage, but seemed largely to coöperate with the government in the end. Only one paper—a tabloid always discounted because of its wild policy—mentioned the deep-diving submarine that discharged torpedoes downward in the marine abyss just beyond Devil Reef. That item, gathered by chance in a haunt of sailors, seemed indeed rather far-fetched; since the low, black reef lies a full mile and a half out from Innsmouth Harbour.

People around the country and in the nearby towns muttered a great deal among themselves, but said very little to the outer world. They had talked about dying and half-deserted Innsmouth for nearly a century, and nothing new could be wilder or more hideous than what they had whispered and hinted years before. Many things had taught them secretiveness, and there was now no need to exert pressure on them. Besides, they really knew very little; for wide salt marshes, desolate and unpeopled, keep neighbours off from Innsmouth on the landward side.

But at last I am going to defy the ban on speech about this thing. Results, I am certain, are so thorough that no public harm save a shock of repulsion could ever accrue from a hinting of what was found by those horrified raiders at Innsmouth. Besides, what was found might possibly have more than one explanation. I do not know just how much of the whole tale has been told even to me, and I have many reasons for not wishing to probe deeper. For my contact with this affair has been closer than that of any other layman, and I have carried away impressions which are yet to drive me to drastic measures.

It was I who fled frantically out of Innsmouth in the early morning hours of July 16, 1927, and whose frightened appeals for government inquiry and action brought on the whole reported episode. I was willing enough to stay mute while the affair was fresh and uncertain; but now that it is an old story, with public interest and curiosity gone, I have an odd craving to whisper about those few frightful hours in that ill-rumoured and evilly shadowed seaport of death and blasphemous abnormality. The mere telling helps me to restore confidence in my own faculties; to reassure myself that I was not simply the first to succumb to a contagious nightmare hallucination. It helps me, too, in making up my mind regarding a certain terrible step which lies ahead of me.

I never heard of Innsmouth till the day before I saw it for the first and—so far—last time. I was celebrating my coming of age by a tour of New England—sightseeing, antiquarian, and ge-

nealogical[3]—and had planned to go directly from ancient Newburyport[4] to Arkham, whence my mother's family was derived. I
had no car, but was travelling by train, trolley, and motor-coach,
always seeking the cheapest possible route. In Newburyport
they told me that the steam train was the thing to take to
Arkham; and it was only at the station ticket-office, when I de-
murred at the high fare, that I learned about Innsmouth. The
stout, shrewd-faced agent, whose speech shewed him to be no
local man, seemed sympathetic toward my efforts at economy,
and made a suggestion that none of my other informants had
offered.

"You *could* take that old bus, I suppose," he said with a certain hesitation, "but it ain't thought much of hereabouts. It goes
through Innsmouth—you may have heard about that—and so
the people don't like it. Run by an Innsmouth fellow—Joe Sargent—but never gets any custom from here, or Arkham either, I
guess. Wonder it keeps running at all. I s'pose it's cheap enough,
but I never see more'n two or three people in it—nobody but
those Innsmouth folks. Leaves the Square—front of Hammond's
Drug Store—at 10 a.m. and 7 p.m. unless they've changed lately.
Looks like a terrible rattletrap—I've never ben on it."

That was the first I ever heard of shadowed Innsmouth. Any
reference to a town not shewn on common maps or listed in recent guide-books would have interested me, and the agent's odd
manner of allusion roused something like real curiosity. A town
able to inspire such dislike in its neighbours, I thought, must be
at least rather unusual, and worthy of a tourist's attention. If it
came before Arkham I would stop off there—and so I asked the
agent to tell me something about it. He was very deliberate, and
spoke with an air of feeling slightly superior to what he said.

"Innsmouth? Well, it's a queer kind of a town down at
the mouth of the Manuxet.[5] Used to be almost a city—quite a
port before the War of 1812—but all gone to pieces in the
last hundred years or so. No railroad now—B. & M.[6] never
went through, and the branch line from Rowley was given up
years ago.

"More empty houses than there are people, I guess, and no
business to speak of except fishing and lobstering. Everybody

trades mostly here or in Arkham or Ipswich. Once they had quite a few mills, but nothing's left now except one gold refinery running on the leanest kind of part time.

"That refinery, though, used to be a big thing, and Old Man Marsh, who owns it, must be richer'n Croesus.[7] Queer old duck, though, and sticks mighty close in his home. He's supposed to have developed some skin disease or deformity late in life that makes him keep out of sight. Grandson of Captain Obed Marsh, who founded the business. His mother seems to've ben some kind of foreigner[8]—they say a South Sea islander—so everybody raised Cain when he married an Ipswich girl fifty years ago. They always do that about Innsmouth people, and folks here and hereabouts always try to cover up any Innsmouth blood they have in 'em. But Marsh's children and grandchildren look just like anyone else so far's I can see. I've had 'em pointed out to me here—though, come to think of it, the elder children don't seem to be around lately. Never saw the old man.

"And why is everybody so down on Innsmouth? Well, young fellow, you mustn't take too much stock in what people around here say. They're hard to get started, but once they do get started they never let up. They've ben telling things about Innsmouth—whispering 'em, mostly—for the last hundred years, I guess, and I gather they're more scared than anything else. Some of the stories would make you laugh—about old Captain Marsh driving bargains with the devil and bringing imps out of hell to live in Innsmouth, or about some kind of devil-worship and awful sacrifices in some place near the wharves that people stumbled on around 1845 or thereabouts—but I come from Panton, Vermont,[9] and that kind of story don't go down with me.

"You ought to hear, though, what some of the old-timers tell about the black reef off the coast—Devil Reef, they call it. It's well above water a good part of the time, and never much below it, but at that you could hardly call it an island. The story is that there's a whole legion of devils seen sometimes on that reef—sprawled about, or darting in and out of some kind of caves near the top.[10] It's a rugged, uneven thing, a good bit over a mile out, and toward the end of shipping days sailors used to make big detours just to avoid it.

"That is, sailors that didn't hail from Innsmouth. One of the things they had against old Captain Marsh was that he was supposed to land on it sometimes at night when the tide was right. Maybe he did, for I dare say the rock formation was interesting, and it's just barely possible he was looking for pirate loot and maybe finding it; but there was talk of his dealing with daemons there. Fact is, I guess on the whole it was really the Captain that gave the bad reputation to the reef.

"That was before the big epidemic of 1846, when over half the folks in Innsmouth was carried off. They never did quite figure out what the trouble was, but it was probably some foreign kind of disease brought from China or somewhere by the shipping. It surely was bad enough—there was riots over it, and all sorts of ghastly doings that I don't believe ever got outside of town—and it left the place in awful shape. Never came back—there can't be more'n 300 or 400 people living there now.

"But the real thing behind the way folks feel is simply race prejudice—and I don't say I'm blaming those that hold it. I hate those Innsmouth folks myself, and I wouldn't care to go to their town. I s'pose you know—though I can see you're a Westerner by your talk—what a lot our New England ships used to have to do with queer ports in Africa, Asia, the South Seas, and everywhere else, and what queer kinds of people they sometimes brought back with 'em. You've probably heard about the Salem man that came home with a Chinese wife, and maybe you know there's still a bunch of Fiji Islanders somewhere around Cape Cod.[11]

"Well, there must be something like that back of the Innsmouth people. The place always was badly cut off from the rest of the country by marshes and creeks, and we can't be sure about the ins and outs of the matter; but it's pretty clear that old Captain Marsh must have brought home some odd specimens when he had all three of his ships in commission back in the twenties and thirties. There certainly is a strange kind of streak in the Innsmouth folk today—I don't know how to explain it, but it sort of makes you crawl. You'll notice a little in Sargent if you take his bus. Some of 'em have queer narrow heads with flat noses and bulgy, stary eyes that never seem to shut, and their skin ain't quite right. Rough and scabby, and the sides of their necks are all shrivelled or creased up. Get bald, too, very young. The older fellows look the worst—fact is, I don't believe I've ever seen a very old chap of that kind. Guess they must die of looking in the glass![12] Animals hate 'em—they used to have lots of horse trouble before autos came in.

"Nobody around here or in Arkham or Ipswich will have anything to do with 'em, and they act kind of offish themselves when they come to town or when anyone tries to fish on their grounds. Queer how fish are always thick off Innsmouth Harbour when there ain't any anywhere else around—but just try to fish there yourself and see how the folks chase you off! Those people used to come here on the railroad—walking and taking the train at Rowley after the branch was dropped—but now they use that bus.

"Yes, there's a hotel in Innsmouth—called the Gilman House[13]—but I don't believe it can amount to much. I wouldn't advise you to try it. Better stay over here and take the ten o'clock bus tomorrow morning; then you can get an evening bus there for Arkham at eight o'clock. There was a factory inspector who stopped at the Gilman a couple of years ago, and he had a lot of unpleasant hints about the place. Seems they get a queer crowd there, for this fellow heard voices in the other rooms—though most of 'em was empty—that gave him the shivers. It was foreign talk, he thought, but he said the bad thing about it was the kind of voice that sometimes spoke. It sounded so unnatural—slopping-like, he said—that he didn't dare undress and go to sleep. Just waited up and lit out the first thing in the morning. The talk went on most all night.

"This fellow—Casey,[14] his name was—had a lot to say about how the Innsmouth folks watched him and seemed kind of on guard. He found the Marsh refinery a queer place—it's in an old mill on the lower falls of the Manuxet. What he said tallied up with what I'd heard. Books in bad shape, and no clear account of any kind of dealings. You know it's always ben a kind of mystery where the Marshes get the gold they refine. They've never seemed to do much buying in that line, but years ago they shipped out an enormous lot of ingots.

"Used to be talk of a queer foreign kind of jewellery that the sailors and refinery men sometimes sold on the sly, or that was seen once or twice on some of the Marsh womenfolks. People allowed maybe old Captain Obed traded for it in some heathen port, especially since he was always ordering stacks of glass beads and trinkets such as seafaring men used to get for native trade. Others thought and still think he'd found an old pirate cache out on Devil Reef. But here's a funny thing. The old Captain's ben dead these sixty years, and there ain't ben a good-sized ship out of the place since the Civil War; but just the same the Marshes still keep on buying a few of those native trade things—mostly glass and rubber gewgaws, they tell me. Maybe the Innsmouth folk like 'em to look at themselves—Gawd knows they've gotten to be about as bad as South Sea cannibals and Guinea savages.

"That plague of '46 must have taken off the best blood in the place. Anyway, they're a doubtful lot now, and the Marshes and the other rich folks are as bad as any. As I told you, there probably ain't more'n 400 people in the whole town in spite of all the streets they say there are. I guess they're what they call 'white trash' down South—lawless and sly, and full of secret doings.[15] They get a lot of fish and lobsters and do exporting by truck. Queer how the fish swarm right there and nowhere else.

"Nobody can ever keep track of these people, and state school officials and census men have a devil of a time. You can bet that prying strangers ain't welcome around Innsmouth. I've heard personally of more'n one business or government man that's disappeared there, and there's loose talk of one who went crazy and is out at Danvers now.[16] They must have fixed up some awful scare for that fellow.

"That's why I wouldn't go at night if I was you. I've never ben there and have no wish to go, but I guess a daytime trip couldn't hurt you—even though the people hereabouts will advise you not to make it. If you're just sightseeing, and looking for old-time stuff, Innsmouth ought to be quite a place for you."

And so I spent part of that evening at the Newburyport Public Library[17] looking up data about Innsmouth. When I had tried to question the natives in the shops, the lunch room, the garages, and the fire station, I had found them even harder to get started than the ticket-agent had predicted; and realised that I could not spare the time to overcome their first instinctive reticences. They had a kind of obscure suspiciousness, as if there were something amiss with anyone too much interested in Innsmouth. At the Y.M.C.A., where I was stopping,[18] the clerk merely discouraged my going to such a dismal, decadent place; and the people at the library shewed much the same attitude. Clearly, in the eyes of the educated, Innsmouth was merely an exaggerated case of civic degeneration.

The Essex County histories on the library shelves had very little to say, except that the town was founded in 1643, noted for shipbuilding before the Revolution, a seat of great marine prosperity in the early nineteenth century, and later a minor factory centre using the Manuxet as power. The epidemic and riots of 1846 were very sparsely treated, as if they formed a discredit to the county.

References to decline were few, though the significance of the later record was unmistakable. After the Civil War all industrial life was confined to the Marsh Refining Company, and the marketing of gold ingots formed the only remaining bit of major commerce aside from the eternal fishing. That fishing paid less and less as the price of the commodity fell and large-scale corporations offered competition, but there was never a dearth of fish around Innsmouth Harbour. Foreigners seldom settled there, and there was some discreetly veiled evidence that a number of Poles and Portuguese who had tried it had been scattered in a peculiarly drastic fashion.[19]

Most interesting of all was a glancing refererence to the strange jewellery vaguely associated with Innsmouth. It had evidently impressed the whole countryside more than a little, for mention was made of specimens in the museum of Miskatonic University at Arkham, and in the display room of the Newburyport Historical Society.[20] The fragmentary descriptions of these things were bald and prosaic, but they hinted to me an undercurrent of persistent strangeness. Something about them seemed so odd and provocative that I could not put them out of my mind, and despite the relative lateness of the hour I resolved to see the local sample—said to be a large, queerly proportioned thing evidently meant for a tiara—if it could possibly be arranged.

The librarian gave me a note of introduction to the curator of the Society, a Miss Anna Tilton, who lived nearby, and after a brief explanation that ancient gentlewoman was kind enough to pilot me into the closed building, since the hour was not outrageously late. The collection was a notable one indeed, but in my present mood I had eyes for nothing but the bizarre object which glistened in a corner cupboard under the electric lights.

It took no excessive sensitiveness to beauty to make me literally gasp at the strange, unearthly splendour of the alien, opulent phantasy that rested there on a purple velvet cushion. Even now I can hardly describe what I saw, though it was clearly enough a sort of tiara, as the description had said. It was tall in front, and with a very large and curiously irregular periphery, as if designed for a head of almost freakishly elliptical outline. The material seemed to be predominantly gold, though a weird lighter lustrousness hinted at some strange alloy with an equally beautiful and scarcely identifiable metal. Its condition was almost perfect, and one could have spent hours in studying the striking and puzzlingly untraditional designs—some simply geometrical, and some plainly marine—chased or moulded in high relief on its surface with a craftsmanship of incredible skill and grace.

The longer I looked, the more the thing fascinated me; and in this fascination there was a curiously disturbing element hardly to be classified or accounted for. At first I decided that it was the queer other-worldly quality of the art which made me uneasy. All other art objects I had ever seen either belonged to some known racial or national stream, or else were consciously modernistic defiances of every recognised stream. This tiara was neither. It clearly belonged to some settled technique of infinite maturity and perfection, yet that technique was utterly remote from any—Eastern or Western, ancient or modern—which I had ever heard of or seen exemplified. It was as if the workmanship were that of another planet.[21]

However, I soon saw that my uneasiness had a second and perhaps equally potent source residing in the pictorial and mathematical suggestions of the strange designs. The patterns all hinted of remote secrets and unimaginable abysses in time and space, and the monotonously aquatic nature of the reliefs became almost sinister. Among these reliefs were fabulous monsters of abhorrent grotesqueness and malignity—half ichthyic and half batrachian in suggestion—which one could not dissociate from a certain haunting and uncomfortable sense of pseudo-memory, as if they called up some image from deep cells and tissues whose retentive functions are wholly primal and awesomely ancestral. At times I fancied that every contour of these blasphemous fish-frogs was overflowing with the ultimate quintessence of un-known and inhuman evil.

In odd contrast to the tiara's aspect was its brief and prosy history as related by Miss Tilton. It had been pawned for a ridiculous sum at a shop in State Street in 1873, by a drunken Innsmouth man shortly afterward killed in a brawl. The Society had acquired it directly from the pawnbroker, at once giving it a display worthy of its quality. It was labelled as of probable East-Indian or Indo-Chinese provenance, though the attribution was frankly tentative.

Miss Tilton, comparing all possible hypotheses regarding its origin and its presence in New England, was inclined to believe that it formed part of some exotic pirate hoard discovered by old Captain Obed Marsh. This view was surely not weakened by the insistent offers of purchase at a high price which the Marshes be-gan to make as soon as they knew of its presence, and which they repeated to this day despite the Society's unvarying determina-tion not to sell.

As the good lady shewed me out of the building she made it clear that the pirate theory of the Marsh fortune was a popular one among the intelligent people of the region. Her own attitude toward shadowed Innsmouth—which she had never seen—was one of disgust at a community slipping far down the cultural scale, and she assured me that the rumours of devil-worship were partly justified by a peculiar secret cult which had gained force there and engulfed all the orthodox churches.

It was called, she said, "The Esoteric Order of Dagon", and was undoubtedly a debased, quasi-pagan thing imported from the East a century before, at a time when the Innsmouth fisheries seemed to be going barren. Its persistence among a simple people was quite natural in view of the sudden and permanent return of abundantly fine fishing, and it soon came to be the greatest influence on the town, replacing Freemasonry[22] altogether and taking up headquarters in the old Masonic Hall on New Church Green.

All this, to the pious Miss Tilton, formed an excellent reason for shunning the ancient town of decay and desolation; but to me it was merely a fresh incentive. To my architectural and historical anticipations was now added an acute anthropological zeal, and I could scarcely sleep in my small room at the "Y" as the night wore away.

II.

Shortly before ten the next morning I stood with one small valise in front of Hammond's Drug Store in old Market Square waiting for the Innsmouth bus. As the hour for its arrival drew near I noticed a general drift of the loungers to other places up the street, or to the Ideal Lunch across the square. Evidently the ticket-agent had not exaggerated the dislike which local people bore toward Innsmouth and its denizens. In a few moments a small motor-coach of extreme decrepitude and dirty grey colour rattled down State Street, made a turn, and drew up at the curb beside me. I felt immediately that it was the right one; a guess which the half-illegible sign on the windshield—"*Arkham-Innsmouth-Newb'port*"—soon verified.

There were only three passengers—dark, unkempt men of sullen visage and somewhat youthful cast—and when the vehicle stopped they clumsily shambled out and began walking up State Street in a silent, almost furtive fashion. The driver also alighted, and I watched him as he went into the drug store to make some purchase. This, I reflected, must be the Joe Sargent mentioned by the ticket-agent; and even before I noticed any details there spread over me a wave of spontaneous aversion which could be neither checked nor explained. It suddenly struck me as very natural that the local people should not wish to ride on a bus owned and driven by this man, or to visit any oftener than possible the habitat of such a man and his kinsfolk.

When the driver came out of the store I looked at him more carefully and tried to determine the source of my evil impression. He was a thin, stoop-shouldered man not much under six feet tall, dressed in shabby blue civilian clothes and wearing a frayed grey golf cap. His age was perhaps thirty-five, but the odd, deep creases in the side of his neck made him seem older when one did not study his dull, expressionless face. He had a narrow head, bulging, watery blue eyes that seemed never to wink, a flat nose, a receding forehead and chin, and singularly undeveloped ears. His long, thick lip and coarse-pored, greyish cheeks seemed almost beardless except for some sparse yellow hairs that straggled and curled in irregular patches; and in places the surface seemed queerly irregular, as if peeling from some cutaneous disease. His hands were large and heavily veined, and had a very unusual greyish-blue tinge. The fingers were strikingly short in proportion to the rest of the structure, and seemed to have a tendency to curl closely into the huge palm. As he walked toward the bus I observed his peculiarly shambling gait and saw that his feet were inordinately immense. The more I studied them the more I wondered how he could buy any shoes to fit them.

A certain greasiness about the fellow increased my dislike. He was evidently given to working or lounging around the fish docks, and carried with him much of their characteristic smell. Just what foreign blood was in him I could not even guess. His oddities certainly did not look Asiatic, Polynesian, Levantine,[23] or negroid, yet I could see why the people found him alien. I myself would have thought of biological degeneration rather than alienage.

I was sorry when I saw that there would be no other passengers on the bus. Somehow I did not like the idea of riding alone with this driver. But as leaving time obviously approached I conquered my qualms and followed the man aboard, extending him a dollar bill and murmuring the single word, "Innsmouth". He looked curiously at me for a second as he returned forty cents change without speaking. I took a seat far behind him, but on the same side of the bus, since I wished to watch the shore during the journey.

At length the decrepit vehicle started with a jerk, and rattled noisily past the old brick buildings of State Street amidst a cloud of vapour from the exhaust. Glancing at the people on the sidewalks, I thought I detected in them a curious wish to avoid looking at the bus—or at least a wish to avoid seeming to look at it. Then we turned to the left into High Street, where the going was smoother; flying by stately old mansions of the early republic and still older colonial farmhouses, passing the Lower Green and Parker River, and finally emerging into a long, monotonous stretch of open shore country.

The day was warm and sunny, but the landscape of sand, sedge-grass, and stunted shrubbery became more and more desolate as we proceeded. Out the window I could see the blue water and the sandy line of Plum Island,[24] and we presently drew very near the beach as our narrow road veered off from the main highway to Rowley and Ipswich. There were no visible houses, and I could tell by the state of the road that traffic was very light hereabouts. The small, weather-worn telephone poles carried only two wires. Now and then we crossed crude wooden bridges over tidal creeks that wound far inland and promoted the general isolation of the region.

Once in a while I noticed dead stumps and crumbling foundation-walls above the drifting sand, and recalled the old tradition quoted in one of the histories I had read, that this was once a fertile and thickly settled countryside. The change, it was said, came simultaneously with the Innsmouth epidemic of 1846, and was thought by simple folk to have a dark connexion with hidden forces of evil. Actually, it was caused by the unwise cutting of woodlands near the shore, which robbed the soil of its best protection and opened the way for waves of wind-blown sand.

At last we lost sight of Plum Island and saw the vast expanse of the open Atlantic on our left. Our narrow course began to climb steeply, and I felt a singular sense of disquiet in looking at the lonely crest ahead where the rutted roadway met the sky. It was as if the bus were about to keep on in its ascent, leaving the sane earth altogether and merging with the unknown arcana of upper air and cryptical sky. The smell of the sea took on ominous implications, and the silent driver's bent, rigid back and narrow head became more and more hateful. As I looked at him I saw that the back of his head was almost as hairless as his face, having only a few straggling yellow strands upon a grey scabrous surface.

Then we reached the crest and beheld the outspread valley beyond, where the Manuxet joins the sea just north of the long line of cliffs that culminate in Kingsport Head[25] and veer off toward Cape Ann. On the far, misty horizon I could just make out the dizzy profile of the Head, topped by the queer ancient house of which so many legends are told;[26] but for the moment all my attention was captured by the nearer panorama just below me. I had, I realised, come face to face with rumour-shadowed Innsmouth.

It was a town of wide extent and dense construction, yet one with a portentous dearth of visible life. From the tangle of chimney-pots scarcely a wisp of smoke came, and the three tall steeples loomed stark and unpainted against the seaward horizon. One of them was crumbling down at the top, and in that and another there were only black gaping holes where clock-dials should have been. The vast huddle of sagging gambrel roofs and peaked gables conveyed with offensive clearness the idea of wormy decay, and as we approached along the now descending road I could see that many roofs had wholly caved in. There were some large square Georgian houses, too, with hipped roofs, cupolas, and railed "widow's walks". These were mostly well back from the water, and one or two seemed to be in moderately sound condition. Stretching inland from among them I saw the rusted, grass-grown line of the abandoned railway, with leaning telegraph-poles now devoid of wires, and the half-obscured lines of the old carriage roads to Rowley and Ipswich.

The decay was worst close to the waterfront, though in its very midst I could spy the white belfry of a fairly well-preserved brick structure which looked like a small factory. The harbour, long clogged with sand, was enclosed by an ancient stone breakwater; on which I could begin to discern the minute forms of a few seated fishermen, and at whose end were what looked like the foundations of a bygone lighthouse. A sandy tongue had formed inside this barrier, and upon it I saw a few decrepit cabins, moored dories, and scattered lobster-pots. The only deep water seemed to be where the river poured out past the belfried structure and turned southward to join the ocean at the breakwater's end.

Here and there the ruins of wharves jutted out from the shore to end in indeterminate rottenness, those farthest south seeming the most decayed. And far out at sea, despite a high tide, I glimpsed a long, black line scarcely rising above the water yet carrying a suggestion of odd latent malignancy. This, I knew, must be Devil Reef. As I looked, a subtle, curious sense of beckoning seemed superadded to the grim repulsion; and oddly enough, I found this overtone more disturbing than the primary impression.

We met no one on the road, but presently began to pass deserted farms in varying stages of ruin. Then I noticed a few inhabited houses with rags stuffed in the broken windows and shells and dead fish lying about the littered yards. Once or twice I saw listless-looking people working in barren gardens or digging clams on the fishy-smelling beach below, and groups of dirty, simian-visaged children playing around weed-grown doorsteps. Somehow these people seemed more disquieting than the dismal buildings, for almost every one had certain peculiarities of face and motions which I instinctively disliked without being able to define or comprehend them. For a second I thought this typical physique suggested some picture I had seen, perhaps in a book, under circumstances of particular horror or melancholy; but this pseudo-recollection passed very quickly.

As the bus reached a lower level I began to catch the steady note of a waterfall through the unnatural stillness. The leaning, unpainted houses grew thicker, lined both sides of the road, and displayed more urban tendencies than did those we were leaving behind. The panorama ahead had contracted to a street scene, and in spots I could see where a cobblestone pavement and stretches of brick sidewalk had formerly existed. All the houses were apparently deserted, and there were occasional gaps where tumbledown chimneys and cellar walls told of buildings that had collapsed. Pervading everything was the most nauseous fishy odour imaginable.

Soon cross streets and junctions began to appear; those on the left leading to shoreward realms of unpaved squalor and decay, while those on the right shewed vistas of departed grandeur. So far I had seen no people in the town, but there now came signs of a sparse habitation—curtained windows here and there, and an occasional battered motor-car at the curb. Pavement and sidewalks were increasingly well defined, and though most of the houses were quite old—wood and brick structures of the early nineteenth century—they were obviously kept fit for habitation. As an amateur antiquarian I almost lost my olfactory disgust and my feeling of menace and repulsion amidst this rich, unaltered survival from the past.

But I was not to reach my destination without one very strong impression of poignantly disagreeable quality. The bus had come to a sort of open concourse or radial point with churches on two sides and the bedraggled remains of a circular green in the centre, and I was looking at a large pillared hall on the right-hand junction ahead. The structure's once white paint was now grey and peeling, and the black and gold sign on the pediment was so faded that I could only with difficulty make out the words "Esoteric Order of Dagon". This, then, was the former Masonic Hall now given over to a degraded cult. As I strained to decipher this inscription my notice was distracted by the raucous tones of a cracked bell across the street, and I quickly turned to look out the window on my side of the coach.[27]

The sound came from a squat-towered stone church of manifestly later date than most of the houses, built in a clumsy Gothic[28] fashion and having a disproportionately high basement with shuttered windows. Though the hands of its clock were missing on the side I glimpsed, I knew that those hoarse strokes were telling the hour of eleven. Then suddenly all thoughts of time were blotted out by an onrushing image of sharp intensity and unaccountable horror which had seized me before I knew what it really was. The door of the church basement was open, revealing a rectangle of blackness inside. And as I looked, a certain object crossed or seemed to cross that dark rectangle; burning into my brain a momentary conception of nightmare which was all the more maddening because analysis could not shew a single nightmarish quality in it.

It was a living object—the first except the driver that I had seen since entering the compact part of the town—and had I been in a steadier mood I would have found nothing whatever of terror in it. Clearly, as I realised a moment later, it was the pastor; clad in some peculiar vestments doubtless introduced since the Order of Dagon had modified the ritual of the local churches. The thing which had probably caught my first subconscious glance and supplied the touch of bizarre horror was the tall tiara he wore; an almost exact duplicate of the one Miss Tilton had shewn me the previous evening. This, acting on my imagination, had supplied namelessly sinister qualities to the indeterminate face and robed, shambling form beneath it. There was not, I soon decided, any reason why I should have felt that shuddering touch of evil pseudo-memory. Was it not natural that a local mystery cult should adopt among its regimentals an unique type of head-dress made familiar to the community in some strange way—perhaps as treasure-trove?

A very thin sprinkling of repellent-looking youngish people now became visible on the sidewalks—lone individuals, and silent knots of two or three.[29] The lower floors of the crumbling houses sometimes harboured small shops with dingy signs, and I noticed a parked truck or two as we rattled along. The sound of waterfalls became more and more distinct, and presently I saw a fairly deep river-gorge ahead, spanned by a wide, iron-railed highway bridge beyond which a large square opened out. As we clanked over the bridge I looked out on both sides and observed some factory buildings on the edge of the grassy bluff or part way down. The water far below was very abundant, and I could see two vigorous sets of falls upstream on my right and at least one downstream on my left. From this point the noise was quite deafening. Then we rolled into the large semicircular square across the river and drew up on the right-hand side in front of a tall, cupola-crowned building with remnants of yellow paint and with a half-effaced sign proclaiming it to be the Gilman House.

I was glad to get out of that bus, and at once proceeded to check my valise in the shabby hotel lobby. There was only one person in sight—an elderly man without what I had come to call the "Innsmouth look"—and I decided not to ask him any of the questions which bothered me; remembering that odd things had been noticed in this hotel. Instead, I strolled out on the square, from which the bus had already gone, and studied the scene minutely and appraisingly.

One side of the cobblestoned open space was the straight line of the river; the other was a semicircle of slant-roofed brick buildings of about the 1800 period, from which several streets radiated away to the southeast, south, and southwest. Lamps were depressingly few and small—all low-powered incandescents—and I was glad that my plans called for departure before dark, even though I knew the moon would be bright. The buildings were all in fair condition, and included perhaps a dozen shops in current operation; of which one was a grocery of the First National chain,[30] others a dismal restaurant, a drug store, and a wholesale fish-dealer's office, and still another, at the eastern extremity of the square near the river, an office of the town's only industry—the Marsh Refining Company. There were perhaps ten people visible, and four or five automobiles and motor trucks stood scattered about. I did not need to be told that this was the civic centre of Innsmouth. Eastward I could catch blue glimpses of the harbour, against which rose the decaying remains of three once beautiful Georgian steeples. And toward the shore on the opposite bank of the river I saw the white belfry surmounting what I took to be the Marsh refinery.

For some reason or other I chose to make my first inquiries at the chain grocery, whose personnel was not likely to be native to Innsmouth. I found a solitary boy of about seventeen in charge, and was pleased to note the brightness and affability which promised cheerful information. He seemed exceptionally eager to talk, and I soon gathered that he did not like the place, its fishy smell, or its furtive people. A word with any outsider was a relief to him. He hailed from Arkham, boarded with a family who came from Ipswich, and went back home whenever he got a moment off. His family did not like him to work in Innsmouth, but the chain had transferred him there and he did not wish to give up his job.

There was, he said, no public library or chamber of commerce in Innsmouth, but I could probably find my way about. The street I had come down was Federal. West of that were the fine old residence streets—Broad, Washington, Lafayette, and Adams—and east of it were the shoreward slums. It was in these slums—along Main Street—that I would find the old Georgian churches, but they were all long abandoned. It would be well not to make oneself too conspicuous in such neighbourhoods—especially north of the river—since the people were sullen and hostile. Some strangers had even disappeared.

Certain spots were almost forbidden territory, as he had learned at considerable cost. One must not, for example, linger much around the Marsh refinery, or around any of the still used churches, or around the pillared Order of Dagon Hall at New Church Green. Those churches were very odd—all violently disavowed by their respective denominations elsewhere, and apparently using the queerest kind of ceremonials and clerical vestments. Their creeds were heterodox and mysterious, involving hints of certain marvellous transformations leading to bodily immortality—of a sort—on this earth. The youth's own pastor—Dr. Wallace of Asbury M. E. Church in Arkham—had gravely urged him not to join any church in Innsmouth.

As for the Innsmouth people—the youth hardly knew what to make of them. They were as furtive and seldom seen as animals that live in burrows, and one could hardly imagine how they passed the time apart from their desultory fishing. Perhaps—judging from the quantities of bootleg liquor they consumed—they lay for most of the daylight hours in an alcoholic stupor. They seemed sullenly banded together in some sort of fellowship and understanding—despising the world as if they had access to other and preferable spheres of entity. Their appearance—especially those staring, unwinking eyes which one never saw shut—was certainly shocking enough; and their voices were disgusting. It was awful to hear them chanting in their churches at night, and especially during their main festivals or revivals, which fell twice a year on April 30th and October 31st.[31]

They were very fond of the water, and swam a great deal in

both river and harbour. Swimming races out to Devil Reef were very common, and everyone in sight seemed well able to share in this arduous sport. When one came to think of it, it was generally only rather young people who were seen about in public, and of these the oldest were apt to be the most tainted-looking. When exceptions did occur, they were mostly persons with no trace of aberrancy, like the old clerk at the hotel. One wondered what became of the bulk of the older folk, and whether the "Innsmouth look" were not a strange and insidious disease-phenomenon which increased its hold as years advanced.

Only a very rare affliction, of course, could bring about such vast and radical anatomical changes in a single individual after maturity—changes involving osseous factors as basic as the shape of the skull—but then, even this aspect was no more baffling and unheard-of than the visible features of the malady as a whole. It would be hard, the youth implied, to form any real conclusions regarding such a matter; since one never came to know the natives personally no matter how long one might live in Innsmouth.

The youth was certain that many specimens even worse than the worst visible ones were kept locked indoors in some places. People sometimes heard the queerest kind of sounds. The tottering waterfront hovels north of the river were reputedly connected by hidden tunnels, being thus a veritable warren of unseen abnormalities. What kind of foreign blood—if any—these beings had, it was impossible to tell. They sometimes kept certain especially repulsive characters out of sight when government agents and others from the outside world came to town.

It would be of no use, my informant said, to ask the natives anything about the place. The only one who would talk was a very aged but normal-looking man who lived at the poorhouse on the north rim of the town and spent his time walking about or lounging around the fire station. This hoary character, Zadok Allen,[32] was ninety-six years old and somewhat touched in the head, besides being the town drunkard. He was a strange, furtive creature who constantly looked over his shoulder as if afraid of something, and when sober could not be persuaded to talk at all with strangers. He was, however, unable to resist any offer of his favourite poison; and once drunk would furnish the most astonishing fragments of whispered reminiscence.

After all, though, little useful data could be gained from him; since his stories were all insane, incomplete hints of impossible marvels and horrors which could have no source save in his own disordered fancy. Nobody believed him, but the natives did not like him to drink and talk with strangers; and it was not always safe to be seen questioning him. It was probably from him that some of the wildest popular whispers and delusions were derived.

Several non-native residents had reported monstrous glimpses from time to time, but between old Zadok's tales and the malformed denizens it was no wonder such illusions were current. None of the non-natives ever stayed out late at night, there being a widespread impression that it was not wise to do so. Besides, the streets were loathsomely dark.

As for business—the abundance of fish was certainly almost uncanny, but the natives were taking less and less advantage of it. Moreover, prices were falling and competition was growing. Of course the town's real business was the refinery, whose commercial office was on the square only a few doors east of where we stood. Old Man Marsh was never seen, but sometimes went to the works in a closed, curtained car.

There were all sorts of rumours about how Marsh had come to look. He had once been a great dandy,[33] and people said he still wore the frock-coated finery of the Edwardian age, curiously adapted to certain deformities. His sons had formerly conducted the office in the square, but latterly they had been keeping out of sight a good deal and leaving the brunt of affairs to the younger generation. The sons and their sisters had come to look very queer, especially the elder ones; and it was said that their health was failing.

One of the Marsh daughters was a repellent, reptilian-looking woman who wore an excess of weird jewellery clearly of the same exotic tradition as that to which the strange tiara belonged. My informant had noticed it many times, and had heard it spoken of as coming from some secret hoard, either of pirates or of daemons. The clergymen—or priests, or whatever they were called nowadays—also wore this kind of ornament as a head-dress; but one seldom caught glimpses of them. Other specimens the youth had not seen, though many were rumoured to exist around Innsmouth.

The Marshes, together with the other three gently bred fami-lies of the town—the Waites, the Gilmans, and the Eliots—were all very retiring. They lived in immense houses along Washing-ton Street, and several were reputed to harbour in concealment certain living kinsfolk whose personal aspect forbade public view, and whose deaths had been reported and recorded.

Warning me that many of the street signs were down, the youth drew for my benefit a rough but ample and painstaking sketch map of the town's salient features. After a moment's study I felt sure that it would be of great help, and pocketed it with profuse thanks. Disliking the dinginess of the single restaurant I had seen, I bought a fair supply of cheese crackers and ginger wafers[34] to serve as a lunch later on. My programme, I decided, would be to thread the principal streets, talk with any non-natives I might encounter, and catch the eight o'clock coach for Arkham. The town, I could see, formed a significant and exag-gerated example of communal decay; but being no sociologist I would limit my serious observations to the field of architecture.

Thus I began my systematic though half-bewildered tour of Innsmouth's narrow, shadow-blighted ways. Crossing the bridge and turning toward the roar of the lower falls, I passed close to the Marsh refinery, which seemed oddly free from the noise of industry. This building stood on the steep river bluff near a bridge and an open confluence of streets which I took to be the earliest civic centre, displaced after the Revolution by the present Town Square.

Re-crossing the gorge on the Main Street bridge, I struck a re-gion of utter desertion which somehow made me shudder. Col-lapsing huddles of gambrel roofs formed a jagged and fantastic skyline, above which rose the ghoulish, decapitated steeple of an ancient church. Some houses along Main Street were tenanted, but most were tightly boarded up. Down unpaved side streets I saw the black, gaping windows of deserted hovels, many of which leaned at perilous and incredible angles through the sinking of part of the foundations. Those windows stared so spectrally that it took courage to turn eastward toward the waterfront. Certainly, the terror of a deserted house swells in geometrical rather than arithmetical progression as houses multiply to form a city of stark desolation. The sight of such endless avenues of fishy-eyed vacancy and death, and the thought of such linked infinities of black, brooding compartments given over to cobwebs and memories and the conqueror worm,[35] start up vestigial fears and aversions that not even the stoutest philosophy can disperse.

Fish Street was as deserted as Main, though it differed in having many brick and stone warehouses still in excellent shape. Water Street was almost its duplicate, save that there were great seaward gaps where wharves had been. Not a living thing did I see, except for the scattered fishermen on the distant breakwater, and not a sound did I hear save the lapping of the harbour tides and the roar of the falls in the Manuxet. The town was getting more and more on my nerves, and I looked behind me furtively as I picked my way back over the tottering Water Street bridge. The Fish Street bridge, according to the sketch, was in ruins.

North of the city there were traces of squalid life—active fish-packing houses in Water Street, smoking chimneys and patched roofs here and there, occasional sounds from indeterminate sources, and infrequent shambling forms in the dismal streets and unpaved lanes—but I seemed to find this even more oppressive than the southerly desertion. For one thing, the people were more hideous and abnormal than those near the centre of the town; so that I was several times evilly reminded of something utterly fantastic which I could not quite place. Undoubtedly the alien strain in the Innsmouth folk was stronger here than farther inland—unless, indeed, the "Innsmouth look" were a disease rather than a blood strain, in which case this district might be held to harbour the more advanced cases.

One detail that annoyed me was the *distribution* of the few faint sounds I heard. They ought naturally to have come wholly from the visibly inhabited houses, yet in reality were often strongest inside the most rigidly boarded-up facades. There were creakings, scurryings, and hoarse doubtful noises; and I thought uncomfortably about the hidden tunnels suggested by the grocery boy. Suddenly I found myself wondering what the voices of those denizens would be like. I had heard no speech so far in this quarter, and was unaccountably anxious not to do so.

Pausing only long enough to look at two fine but ruinous old churches at Main and Church Streets, I hastened out of that vile waterfront slum. My next logical goal was New Church Green, but somehow or other I could not bear to repass the church in whose basement I had glimpsed the inexplicably frightening form of that strangely diademed priest or pastor. Besides, the grocery youth had told me that the churches, as well as the Order of Dagon Hall, were not advisable neighbourhoods for strangers.

Accordingly I kept north along Main to Martin, then turning inland, crossing Federal Street safely north of the Green, and entering the decayed patrician neighbourhood of northern Broad, Washington, Lafayette, and Adams Streets. Though these stately old avenues were ill-surfaced and unkempt, their elm-shaded dignity had not entirely departed. Mansion after mansion claimed my gaze, most of them decrepit and boarded up amidst neglected grounds, but one or two in each street shewing signs of occupancy. In Washington Street there was a row of four or five in excellent repair and with finely tended lawns and gardens. The most sumptuous of these—with wide terraced parterres extending back the whole way to Lafayette Street—I took to be the home of Old Man Marsh, the afflicted refinery owner.

In all these streets no living thing was visible, and I wondered at the complete absense of cats and dogs from Innsmouth. Another thing which puzzled and disturbed me, even in some of the best-preserved mansions, was the tightly shuttered condition of many third-story and attic windows. Furtiveness and secretiveness seemed universal in this hushed city of alienage and death, and I could not escape the sensation of being watched from ambush on every hand by sly, staring eyes that never shut.

I shivered as the cracked stroke of three sounded from a belfry on my left. Too well did I recall the squat church from which those notes came. Following Washington Street toward the river,

I now faced a new zone of former industry and commerce; noting the ruins of a factory ahead, and seeing others, with the traces of an old railway station and covered railway bridge beyond, up the gorge on my right.

The uncertain bridge now before me was posted with a warning sign, but I took the risk and crossed again to the south bank where traces of life reappeared. Furtive, shambling creatures stared cryptically in my direction, and more normal faces eyed me coldly and curiously. Innsmouth was rapidly becoming intolerable, and I turned down Paine Street toward the Square in the hope of getting some vehicle to take me to Arkham before the still-distant starting-time of that sinister bus.

It was then that I saw the tumbledown fire station on my left, and noticed the red-faced, bushy-bearded, watery-eyed old man in nondescript rags who sat on a bench in front of it talking with a pair of unkempt but not abnormal-looking firemen. This, of course, must be Zadok Allen, the half-crazed, liquorish nonagenarian whose tales of old Innsmouth and its shadow were so hideous and incredible.

III.

It must have been some imp of the perverse[36]—or some sardonic pull from dark, hidden sources—which made me change my plans as I did. I had long before resolved to limit my observations to architecture alone, and I was even then hurrying toward the Square in an effort to get quick transportation out of this festering city of death and decay; but the sight of old Zadok Allen set up new currents in my mind and made me slacken my pace uncertainly.

I had been assured that the old man could do nothing but hint at wild, disjointed, and incredible legends, and I had been warned that the natives made it unsafe to be seen talking with him; yet the thought of this aged witness to the town's decay, with memories going back to the early days of ships and factories, was a lure that no amount of reason could make me resist. After all, the strangest and maddest of myths are often merely symbols or allegories based upon truth—and old Zadok must have seen everything which went on around Innsmouth for the last ninety years. Curiosity flared up beyond sense and caution, and in my youthful egotism I fancied I might be able to sift a nucleus of real history from the confused, extravagant outpouring I would probably extract with the aid of raw whiskey.

I knew that I could not accost him then and there, for the firemen would surely notice and object. Instead, I reflected, I would prepare by getting some bootleg liquor at a place where the grocery boy had told me it was plentiful. Then I would loaf near the fire station in apparent casualness, and fall in with Old Zadok after he had started on one of his frequent rambles. The youth said that he was very restless, seldom sitting around the station for more than an hour or two at a time.

A quart bottle of whiskey was easily, though not cheaply, obtained in the rear of a dingy variety-store just off the Square in Eliot Street. The dirty-looking fellow who waited on me had a touch of the staring "Innsmouth look", but was quite civil in his way; being perhaps used to the custom of such convivial strangers—truckmen, gold-buyers, and the like—as were occasionally in town.

Reëntering the Square I saw that luck was with me; for—shuffling out of Paine Street around the corner of the Gilman House—I glimpsed nothing less than the tall, lean, tattered form of old Zadok Allen himself. In accordance with my plan, I attracted his attention by brandishing my newly purchased bottle; and soon realised that he had begun to shuffle wistfully after me as I turned into Waite Street on my way to the most deserted region I could think of.

I was steering my course by the map the grocery boy had prepared, and was aiming for the wholly abandoned stretch of southern waterfront which I had previously visited. The only people in sight there had been the fishermen on the distant breakwater; and by going a few squares south I could get beyond the range of these, finding a pair of seats on some abandoned wharf and being free to question old Zadok unobserved for an indefinite time. Before I reached Main Street I could hear a faint

and wheezy "Hey, Mister!" behind me, and I presently allowed
the old man to catch up and take copious pulls from the quart
bottle.

I began putting out feelers as we walked along to Water Street
and turned southward amidst the omnipresent desolation and
crazily tilted ruins, but found that the aged tongue did not
loosen as quickly as I had expected. At length I saw a grass-
grown opening toward the sea between crumbling brick walls,
with the weedy length of an earth-and-masonry wharf projecting
beyond. Piles of moss-covered stones near the water promised
tolerable seats, and the scene was sheltered from all possible view
by a ruined warehouse on the north. Here, I thought, was the
ideal place for a long secret colloquy; so I guided my companion
down the lane and picked out spots to sit in among the mossy
stones. The air of death and desertion was ghoulish, and the
smell of fish almost insufferable; but I was resolved to let nothing deter me.

About four hours remained for conversation if I were to catch
the eight o'clock coach for Arkham, and I began to dole out
more liquor to the ancient tippler; meanwhile eating my own
frugal lunch. In my donations I was careful not to overshoot the
mark, for I did not wish Zadok's vinous garrulousness to pass
into a stupor. After an hour his furtive taciturnity shewed signs
of disappearing, but much to my disappointment he still side-
tracked my questions about Innsmouth and its shadow-haunted
past. He would babble of current topics, revealing a wide acquaintance with newspapers and a great tendency to philoso-
phise in a sententious village fashion.

Toward the end of the second hour I feared my quart of
whiskey would not be enough to produce results, and was wondering whether I had better leave old Zadok and go back for
more. Just then, however, chance made the opening which my
questions had been unable to make; and the wheezing ancient's
ramblings took a turn that caused me to lean forward and listen
alertly. My back was toward the fishy-smelling sea, but he was
facing it, and something or other had caused his wandering gaze
to light on the low, distant line of Devil Reef, then shewing
plainly and almost fascinatingly above the waves. The sight

seemed to displease him, for he began a series of weak curses which ended in a confidential whisper and a knowing leer. He bent toward me, took hold of my coat lapel, and hissed out some hints that could not be mistaken.

"Thar's whar it all begun—that cursed place of all wickedness whar the deep water starts. Gate o' hell—sheer drop daown to a bottom no saoundin'-line kin tech.[37] Ol' Cap'n Obed done it— him that faound aout more'n was good fer him in the Saouth Sea islands.

"Everybody was in a bad way them days. Trade fallin' off, mills losin' business—even the new ones—an' the best of our menfolks kilt a-privateerin' in the War of 1812 or lost with the *Elizy* brig an' the *Ranger* snow[38]—both of 'em Gilman venters. Obed Marsh he had three ships afloat—brigantine *Columby*, brig *Hetty*, an' barque *Sumatry Queen*. He was the only one as kep' on with the East-Injy an' Pacific trade, though Esdras Martin's barkentine *Malay Pride* made a venter as late as 'twenty-eight.

"Never was nobody like Cap'n Obed—old limb o' Satan! Heh, heh! I kin mind him a-tellin' abaout furren parts, an' callin' all the folks stupid fer goin' to Christian meetin' an' bearin' their burdens meek an' lowly. Says they'd orter git better gods like some o' the folks in the Injies—gods as ud bring 'em good fishin' in return for their sacrifices, an' ud reely answer folks's prayers.

"Matt Eliot, his fust mate, talked a lot, too, only he was agin' folks's doin' any heathen things. Told abaout an island east of Otaheité[39] whar they was a lot o' stone ruins older'n anybody knew anything abaout, kind o' like them on Ponape, in the Carolines,[40] but with carvin's of faces that looked like the big statues on Easter Island. They was a little volcanic island near thar, too, whar they was other ruins with diff'rent carvin's—ruins all wore away like they'd ben under the sea onct, an' with picters of awful monsters all over 'em.

"Wal, Sir, Matt he says the natives araound thar had all the fish they cud ketch, an' sported bracelets an' armlets an' head rigs made aout of a queer kind o' gold an' covered with picters o' monsters jest like the ones carved over the ruins on the little island—sorter fish-like frogs or frog-like fishes that was drawed in all kinds o' positions like they was human bein's. Nobody cud git aout o' them whar they got all the stuff, an' all the other natives wondered haow they managed to find fish in plenty even when the very next islands had lean pickin's. Matt he got to wonderin' too, an' so did Cap'n Obed. Obed he notices, besides, that lots of the han'some young folks ud drop aout o' sight fer good from year to year, an' that they wa'n't many old folks araound. Also, he thinks some of the folks looks durned queer even fer Kanakys.[41]

"It took Obed to git the truth aout o' them heathen. I dun't know haow he done it, but he begun by tradin' fer the gold-like things they wore. Ast 'em whar they come from, an' ef they cud git more, an' finally wormed the story aout o' the old chief—Walakea, they called him. Nobody but Obed ud ever a believed the old yeller devil, but the Cap'n cud read folks like they was books. Heh, hch! Nobody never believes me naow when I tell 'em, an' I dun't s'pose you will, young feller—though come to look at ye, ye hev kind o' got them sharp-readin' eyes like Obed had."

The old man's whisper grew fainter, and I found myself shuddering at the terrible and sincere portentousness of his intonation, even though I knew his tale could be nothing but drunken phantasy.

"Wal, Sir, Obed he larnt that they's things on this arth as most folks never heerd abaout—an' wouldn't believe ef they did hear. It seems these Kanakys was sacrificin' heaps o' their young men an' maidens to some kind o' god-things that lived under the sea, an' gittin' all kinds o' favour in return.[42] They met the things on the little islet with the queer ruins, an' it seems them awful picters o' frog-fish monsters was supposed to be picters o' these things. Mebbe they was the kind o' critters as got all the mermaid stories an' sech started. They had all kinds o' cities on the sea-bottom, an' this island was heaved up from thar.[43] Seems they was some of the things alive in the stone buildin's when the island come up sudden to the surface. That's haow the Kanakys got wind they was daown thar. Made sign-talk as soon as they got over bein' skeert, an' pieced up a bargain afore long.

"Them things liked human sacrifices. Had had 'em ages afore, but lost track o' the upper world arter a time. What they done to the victims it ain't fer me to say, an' I guess Obed wa'n't none too sharp abaout askin'. But it was all right with the heathens, because they'd ben havin' a hard time an' was desp'rate abaout everything. They give a sarten number o' young folks to the sea-things twict every year—May-Eve an' Hallowe'en—reg'lar as cud be. Also give some o' the carved knick-knacks they made. What the things agreed to give in return was plenty o' fish—they druv 'em in from all over the sea—an' a few gold-like things naow an' then.

"Wal, as I says, the natives met the things on the little volcanic islet—goin' thar in canoes with the sacrifices et cet'ry, and bringin' back any of the gold-like jools as was comin' to 'em. At fust the things didn't never go onto the main island, but arter a time they come to want to. Seems they hankered arter mixin' with the folks, an' havin' j'int ceremonies on the big days—May-Eve an' Hallowe'en. Ye see, they was able to live both in an' aout o' water—what they call amphibians, I guess. The Kanakys told 'em as haow folks from the other islands might wanta wipe 'em aout ef they got wind o' their bein' thar, but says they dun't keer much, because they cud wipe aout the hull brood o' humans ef they was willin' to bother—that is, any as didn't heve sarten signs sech as was used onct by the lost Old Ones,[44] whoever they was. But not wantin' to bother, they'd lay low when anybody visited the island.

"When it come to matin' with them toad-lookin' fishes, the Kanakys kind o' balked, but finally they larnt something as put a new face on the matter. Seems that human folks has got a kind o' relation to sech water-beasts—that everything alive come aout o' the water onct, an' only needs a little change to go back agin. Them things told the Kanakys that ef they mixed bloods there'd be children as ud look human at fust, but later turn more'n more like the things, till finally they'd take to the water an' jine the main lot o' things daown thar. An' this is the important part, young feller—them as turned into fish things an' went into the water *wouldn't never die*. Them things never died excep' they was kilt violent.

"Wal, Sir, it seems by the time Obed knowed them islanders

they was all full o' fish blood from them deep-water things.
When they got old an' begun to shew it, they was kep' hid until
they felt like takin' to the water an' quittin' the place. Some was
more teched than others, an' some never did change quite
enough to take to the water; but mostly they turned aout jest the
way them things said. Them as was born more like the things
changed arly, but them as was nearly human sometimes stayed
on the island till they was past seventy, though they'd usually go
daown under fer trial trips afore that. Folks as had took to the
water gen'rally come back a good deal to visit, so's a man ud often be a-talkin' to his own five-times-great-grandfather, who'd
left the dry land a couple o' hundred years or so afore.

"Everybody got aout o' the idee o' dyin'—excep' in canoe
wars with the other islanders, or as sacrifices to the sea-gods
daown below, or from snake-bite or plague or sharp gallopin'
ailments or somethin' afore they cud take to the water—but simply looked forrad to a kind o' change that wa'n't a bit horrible
arter a while. They thought what they'd got was well wuth all
they'd had to give up—an' I guess Obed kind o' come to think
the same hisself when he'd chewed over old Walakea's story a bit.
Walakea, though, was one of the few as hadn't got none of the
fish blood—bein' of a royal line that intermarried with royal
lines on other islands.

"Walakea he shewed Obed a lot o' rites an' incantations as had
to do with the sea-things, an' let him see some o' the folks in the
village as had changed a lot from human shape. Somehaow or
other, though, he never would let him see one of the reg'lar
things from right aout o' the water. In the end he give him a
funny kind o' thingumajig made aout o' lead or something, that
he said ud bring up the fish things from any place in the water
whar they might be a nest of 'em. The idee was to drop it daown
with the right kind o' prayers an' sech. Walakea allaowed as the
things was scattered all over the world, so's anybody that looked
abaout cud find a nest an' bring 'em up ef they was wanted.

"Matt he didn't like this business at all, an' wanted Obed shud
keep away from the island; but the Cap'n was sharp fer gain, an'
faound he cud git them gold-like things so cheap it ud pay him to
make a specialty of 'em. Things went on that way fer years, an'

Obed got enough o' that gold-like stuff to make him start the re-finery in Waite's old run-daown fullin' mill. He didn't dass sell the pieces like they was, fer folks ud be all the time askin' ques-tions. All the same his crews ud git a piece an' dispose of it naow and then, even though they was swore to keep quiet; an' he let his women-folks wear some o' the pieces as was more human-like than most.

"Wal, come abaout 'thutty-eight—when I was seven year' old[45]—Obed he faound the island people all wiped aout between v'yages. Seems the other islanders had got wind o' what was goin' on, an' had took matters into their own hands. S'pose they musta had, arter all, them old magic signs as the sea-things says was the only things they was afeard of. No tellin' what any o' them Kanakys will chance to git a holt of when the sea-bottom throws up some island with ruins older'n the deluge. Pious cusses, these was—they didn't leave nothin' standin' on either the main island or the little volcanic islet excep' what parts of the ruins was too big to knock daown. In some places they was little stones strewed abaout—like charms—with somethin' on 'em like what ye call a swastika naowadays.[46] Prob'ly them was the Old Ones' signs. Folks all wiped aout, no trace o' no gold-like things, an' none o' the nearby Kanakys ud breathe a word abaout the matter. Wouldn't even admit they'd ever ben people on that island.

"That naturally hit Obed pretty hard, seein' as his normal trade was doin' very poor. It hit the whole of Innsmouth, too, because in seafarin' days what profited the master of a ship gen'lly profited the crew proportionate. Most o' the folks araound the taown took the hard times kind o' sheep-like an' re-signed, but they was in bad shape because the fishin' was peterin' aout an' the mills wa'n't doin' none too well.

"Then's the time Obed he begun a-cursin' at the folks fer bein' dull sheep an' prayin' to a Christian heaven as didn't help 'em none. He told 'em he'd knowed of folks as prayed to gods that give somethin' ye reely need, an' says ef a good bunch o' men ud stand by him, he cud mebbe git a holt o' sarten paowers as ud bring plenty o' fish an' quite a bit o' gold. O' course them as sarved on the *Sumatry Queen* an' seed the island knowed

what he meant, an' wan'n't none too anxious to git clost to sea-
things like they'd heerd tell on, but them as didn't know what
'twas all abaout got kind o' swayed by what Obed had to say, an'
begun to ast him what he cud do to set 'em on the way to the
faith as ud bring 'em results."

Here the old man faltered, mumbled, and lapsed into a moody
and apprehensive silence; glancing nervously over his shoulder
and then turning back to stare fascinatedly at the distant black
reef. When I spoke to him he did not answer, so I knew I would
have to let him finish the bottle. The insane yarn I was hearing interested me profoundly, for I fancied there was contained
within it a sort of crude allegory based upon the strangenesses of
Innsmouth and elaborated by an imagination at once creative
and full of scraps of exotic legend. Not for a moment did I believe that the tale had any really substantial foundation; but none
the less the account held a hint of genuine terror, if only because
it brought in references to strange jewels clearly akin to the malign tiara I had seen at Newburyport. Perhaps the ornaments
had, after all, come from some strange island; and possibly the
wild stories were lies of the bygone Obed himself rather than of
this antique toper.

I handed Zadok the bottle, and he drained it to the last drop.
It was curious how he could stand so much whiskey, for not
even a trace of thickness had come into his high, wheezy voice.
He licked the nose of the bottle and slipped it into his pocket,
then beginning to nod and whisper softly to himself. I bent close
to catch any articulate words he might utter, and thought I saw a
sardonic smile behind the stained, bushy whiskers. Yes—he was
really forming words, and I could grasp a fair proportion of
them.

"Poor Matt—Matt he allus was agin' it—tried to line up the
folks on his side, an' had long talks with the preachers—no use—
they run the Congregational parson aout o' taown, an' the
Methodist feller quit—never did see Resolved Babcock, the Baptist parson, agin—Wrath o' Jehovy—I was a mighty little critter,
but I heerd what I heerd an' seen what I seen—Dagon an' Ashtoreth—Belial an' Beëlzebub—Golden Caff an' the idols o'

Canaan an' the Philistines—Babylonish abominations—*Mene, mene, tekel, upharsin*—"⁴⁷

He stopped again, and from the look in his watery blue eyes I feared he was close to a stupor after all. But when I gently shook his shoulder he turned on me with astonishing alertness and snapped out some more obscure phrases.

"Dun't believe me, hey? Heh, heh, heh—then jest tell me, young feller, why Cap'n Obed an' twenty odd other folks used to row aout to Devil Reef in the dead o' night an' chant things so laoud ye cud hear 'em all over taown when the wind was right? Tell me that, hey? An' tell me why Obed was allus droppin' heavy things daown into the deep water t'other side o' the reef whar the bottom shoots daown like a cliff lower'n ye kin saound? Tell me what he done with that funny-shaped lead thingumajig as Walakea give him? Hey, boy? An' what did they all haowl on May-Eve, an' agin the next Hallowe'en? An' why'd the new church parsons—fellers as used to be sailors—wear them queer robes an' cover theirselves with them gold-like things Obed brung? Hey?"

The watery blue eyes were almost savage and maniacal now, and the dirty white beard bristled electrically. Old Zadok probably saw me shrink back, for he had begun to cackle evilly.

"Heh, heh, heh, heh! Beginnin' to see, hey? Mebbe ye'd like to a ben me in them days, when I seed things at night aout to sea from the cupalo top o' my haouse. Oh, I kin tell ye, little pitchers hev big ears, an' I wa'n't missin' nothin' o' what was gossiped abaout Cap'n Obed an' the folks aout to the reef! Heh, heh, heh! Haow abaout the night I took my pa's ship's glass up to the cupalo an' seed the reef a-bristlin' thick with shapes that dove off quick soon's the moon riz? Obed an' the folks was in a dory, but them shapes dove off the far side into the deep water an' never come up. . . . Haow'd ye like to be a little shaver alone up in a cupalo a-watchin' shapes *as wa'n't human shapes?* . . . Hey? . . . Heh, heh, heh, heh. . . ."

The old man was getting hysterical, and I began to shiver with a nameless alarm. He laid a gnarled claw on my shoulder, and it seemed to me that its shaking was not altogether that of mirth.

"S'pose one night ye seed somethin' heavy heaved offen Obed's dory beyond the reef, an' then larned nex' day a young feller was missin' from home? Hey? Did anybody ever see hide or hair o' Hiram Gilman agin? Did they? An' Nick Pierce, an' Luelly Waite, an' Adoniram Saouthwick, an' Henry Garrison? Hey? Heh, heh, heh, heh. . . . Shapes talkin' sign language with their hands . . . them as had reel hands. . . .

"Wal, Sir, that was the time Obed begun to git on his feet agin. Folks see his three darters a-wearin' gold-like things as nobody'd never see on 'em afore, an' smoke started comin' aout o' the refin'ry chimbly. Other folks were prosp'rin', too—fish begun to swarm into the harbour fit to kill, an' heaven knows what sized cargoes we begun to ship aout to Newb'ryport, Arkham, an' Boston. 'Twas then Obed got the ol' branch railrud put through. Some Kingsport fishermen heerd abaout the ketch an' come up in sloops, but they was all lost. Nobody never see 'em agin. An' jest then our folks organised the Esoteric Order o' Dagon, an' bought Masonic Hall offen Calvary Commandery[48] for it . . . heh, heh, heh! Matt Eliot was a Mason an' agin' the sellin', but he dropped aout o' sight jest then.

"Remember, I ain't sayin' Obed was set on hevin' things jest like they was on that Kanaky isle. I dun't think he aimed at fust to do no mixin', nor raise no younguns to take to the water an' turn into fishes with eternal life. He wanted them gold things, an' was willin' to pay heavy, an' I guess the *others* was satisfied fer a while. . . .

"Come in 'forty-six the taown done some lookin' an' thinkin' fer itself. Too many folks missin'—too much wild preachin' at meetin' of a Sunday—too much talk abaout that reef. I guess I done a bit by tellin' Selectman[49] Mowry what I see from the cupalo. They was a party one night as follered Obed's craowd aout to the reef, an' I heered shots betwixt the dories. Nex' day Obed an' thutty-two others was in gaol, with everbody a-wonderin' jest what was afoot an' jest what charge agin' 'em cud be got to holt. God, ef anybody'd look'd ahead . . . a couple o' weeks later, when nothin' had ben throwed into the sea fer that long. . . ."

Zadok was shewing signs of fright and exhaustion, and I let him keep silence for a while, though glancing apprehensively at my watch. The tide had turned and was coming in now, and the sound of the waves seemed to arouse him. I was glad of that tide, for at high water the fishy smell might not be so bad. Again I strained to catch his whispers.

"That awful night . . . I seed 'em . . . I was up in the cupalo . . . hordes of 'em . . . swarms of 'em . . . all over the reef an' swimmin' up the harbour into the Manuxet. . . . God, what happened in the streets of Innsmouth that night . . . they rattled our door, but pa wouldn't open . . . then he clumb aout the kitchen winder with his musket to find Selectman Mowry an' see what he cud do. . . . Maounds o' the dead an' the dyin' . . . shots an' screams . . . shaoutin' in Ol' Squar an' Taown Squar an' New Church Green . . . gaol throwed open . . . proclamation . . . treason . . . called it the plague when folks come in an' faound haff our people missin' . . . nobody left but them as ud jine in with Obed an' them things or else keep quiet . . . never heerd o' my pa no more. . . ."

The old man was panting, and perspiring profusely. His grip on my shoulder tightened.

"Everything cleaned up in the mornin'—but they was *traces*. . . . Obed he kinder takes charge an' says things is goin' to be changed . . . *others'll* worship with us at meetin'-time, an' sarten haouses hez got to entertain *guests* . . . *they* wanted to mix like they done with the Kanakys, an' he fer one didn't feel baound to stop 'em. Far gone, was Obed . . . jest like a crazy man on the subjeck. He says they brung us fish an' treasure, an' shud hev what they hankered arter. . . .

"Nothin' was to be diff'runt on the aoutside, only we was to keep shy o' strangers ef we knowed what was good fer us. We all hed to take the Oath o' Dagon, an' later on they was secon' an' third Oaths that some on us took. Them as ud help special, ud git special rewards—gold an' sech—No use balkin', fer they was millions of 'em daown thar. They'd ruther not start risin' an' wipin' aout humankind, but ef they was gave away an' forced to, they cud do a lot toward jest that. We didn't hev them old charms to cut 'em off like folks in the Saouth Sea did, an' them Kanakys wudn't never give away their secrets.

"Yield up enough sacrifices an' savage knick-knacks an' harbourage in the taown when they wanted it, an' they'd let well enough alone. Wudn't bother no strangers as might bear tales aoutside—that is, withaout they got pryin'. All in the band of the faithful—Order o' Dagon—an' the children shud never die, but go back to the Mother Hydra an' Father Dagon what we all come from onct—*Iä! Iä! Cthulhu fhtagn! Ph'nglui mglw'nafh Cthulhu R'lyeh wgah-nagl fhtagn*—"[50]

Old Zadok was fast lapsing into stark raving, and I held my breath. Poor old soul—to what pitiful depths of hallucination had his liquor, plus his hatred of the decay, alienage, and disease around him, brought that fertile, imaginative brain! He began to moan now, and tears were coursing down his channelled cheeks into the depths of his beard.

"God, what I seen senct I was fifteen year' old—*Mene, mene, tekel, upharsin!*—the folks as was missin', an' them as kilt theirselves—them as told things in Arkham or Ipswich or sech places was all called crazy, like you're a-callin' me right naow—but God, what I seen—They'd a kilt me long ago fer what I know, only I'd took the fust an' secon' Oaths o' Dagon offen Obed, so was pertected unlessen a jury of 'em proved I told things knowin' an' delib'rit . . . but I wudn't take the third Oath—I'd a died ruther'n take that—

"It got wuss araound Civil War time, *when children born senct 'forty-six begun to grow up*—some of 'em, that is. I was afeard—never did no pryin' arter that awful night, an' never see one of—*them*—clost to in all my life. That is, never no fullblooded one. I went to the war, an' ef I'd a had any guts or sense I'd a never come back, but settled away from here. But folks wrote me things wa'n't so bad. That, I s'pose, was because gov'munt draft men was in taown arter 'sixty-three. Arter the war it was jest as bad agin. People begun to fall off—mills an' shops shet daown—shippin' stopped an' the harbour choked up—railrud give up—but *they* . . . they never stopped swimmin' in an' aout o' the river from that cursed reef o' Satan—an' more an' more attic winders got a-boarded up, an' more an' more noises was heerd in haouses as wa'n't s'posed to hev nobody in 'em. . . .

"Folks aoutside hev their stories abaout us—s'pose you've heerd a plenty on 'em, seein' what questions ye ast—stories abaout things they've seed naow an' then, an' abaout that queer joolry as still comes in from somewhars an' ain't quite all melted up—but nothin' never gits def'nite. Nobody'll believe nothin'. They call them gold-like things pirate loot, an' allaow the Innsmouth folks hez furren blood or is distempered or somethin'. Besides, them that lives here shoo off as many strangers as they kin, an' encourage the rest nòt to git very cur'ous, specially raound night time. Beasts balk at the critters—hosses wuss'n mules—but when they got autos that was all right.

"In 'forty-six Cap'n Obed took a second wife *that nobody in the taown never see*[51]—some says he didn't want to, but was made to by them as he'd called in—had three children by her—two as disappeared young, but one gal as looked like anybody else an' was eddicated in Europe. Obed finally got her married off by a trick to an Arkham feller as didn't suspect nothin'. But nobody aoutside'll hev nothin' to do with Innsmouth folks naow. Barnabas Marsh that runs the refin'ry naow is Obed's grandson by his fust wife—son of Onesiphorus, his eldest son, *but his mother was another o' them as wa'n't never seed aoutdoors.*

"Right naow Barnabas is abaout changed. Can't shet his eyes no more, an' is all aout o' shape. They say he still wears clothes, but he'll take to the water soon. Mebbe he's tried it already—they do sometimes go daown fer little spells afore they go fer good. Ain't ben seed abaout in public fer nigh on ten year'. Dun't know haow his poor wife kin feel—she come from Ipswich, an' they nigh lynched Barnabas when he courted her fifty odd year' ago. Obed he died in 'seventy-eight, an' all the next gen'ration is gone naow—the fust wife's children dead, an' the rest . . . God knows. . . ."

The sound of the incoming tide was now very insistent, and little by little it seemed to change the old man's mood from maudlin tearfulness to watchful fear. He would pause now and then to renew those nervous glances over his shoulder or out toward the reef, and despite the wild absurdity of his tale, I could not help beginning to share his vague apprehensiveness. Zadok now grew shriller, and seemed to be trying to whip up his courage with louder speech.

"Hey, yew, why dun't ye say somethin'? Haow'd ye like to be livin' in a taown like this, with everything a-rottin' an' a-dyin', an' boarded-up monsters crawlin' an' bleatin' an' barkin' an' hoppin' araoun' black cellars an' attics every way ye turn? Hey? Haow'd ye like to hear the haowlin' night arter night from the churches an' Order o' Dagon Hall, *an' know what's doin' part o' the haowlin'*? Haow'd ye like to hear what comes from that awful reef every May-Eve an' Hallowmass? Hey? Think the old man's crazy, eh? Wal, Sir, *let me tell ye that ain't the wust!*"

Zadok was really screaming now, and the mad frenzy of his voice disturbed me more than I care to own.

"Curse ye, dun't set thar a-starin' at me with them eyes—I tell Obed Marsh he's in hell, an' hez got to stay thar! Heh, heh . . . in hell, I says! Can't git me—I hain't done nothin' nor told nobody nothin'—

"Oh, you, young feller? Wal, even ef I hain't told nobody nothin' yet, I'm a-goin' to naow! You jest set still an' listen to me, boy—this is what I ain't never told nobody. . . . I says I didn't do no pryin' arter that night—*but I faound things aout jest the same!*

"Yew want to know what the reel horror is, hey? Wal, it's this—it ain't what them fish devils *hez done, but what they're a-goin' to do!* They're a-bringin' things up aout o' whar they come from into the taown—ben doin' it fer years, an' slackenin' up lately. Them haouses north o' the river betwixt Water an' Main Streets is full of 'em—them devils *an' what they brung*—an' when they git ready. . . . I say, *when they git ready* . . . ever hear tell of a *shoggoth?* . . .[52]

"Hey, d'ye hear me? I tell ye *I know what them things be—I seen 'em one night when* . . . EH—AHHHH—AH! E'YAA-HHHH. . . ."

The hideous suddeness and inhuman frightfulness of the old man's shriek almost made me faint. His eyes, looking past me toward the malodorous sea, were positively starting from his head; while his face was a mask of fear worthy of Greek tragedy. His bony claw dug monstrously into my shoulder, and he made no motion as I turned my head to look at whatever he had glimpsed.

There was nothing that I could see. Only the incoming tide,

with perhaps one set of ripples more local than the long-flung line of breakers. But now Zadok was shaking me, and I turned back to watch the melting of that fear-frozen face into a chaos of twitching eyelids and mumbling gums. Presently his voice came back—albeit as a trembling whisper.

"*Git aout o' here!* Git aout o' here! *They seen us*—git aout fer your life! Dun't wait fer nothin'—*they know naow*— Run fer it—quick—*aout o' this taown*—"

Another heavy wave dashed against the loosening masonry of the bygone wharf, and changed the mad ancient's whisper to another inhuman and blood-curdling scream.

"E—YAAHHHH! . . . YHAAAAAAA! . . ."

Before I could recover my scattered wits he had relaxed his clutch on my shoulder and dashed wildly inland toward the street, reeling northward around the ruined warehouse wall.

I glanced back at the sea, but there was nothing there. And when I reached Water Street and looked along it toward the north there was no remaining trace of Zadok Allen.

IV.

I can hardly describe the mood in which I was left by this harrowing episode—an episode at once mad and pitiful, grotesque and terrifying. The grocery boy had prepared me for it, yet the reality left me none the less bewildered and disturbed. Puerile though the story was, old Zadok's insane earnestness and horror had communicated to me a mounting unrest which joined with my earlier sense of loathing for the town and its blight of intangible shadow.

Later I might sift the tale and extract some nucleus of historic allegory; just now I wished to put it out of my head. The hour had grown perilously late—my watch said 7:15, and the Arkham bus left Town Square at eight—so I tried to give my thoughts as neutral and practical a cast as possible, meanwhile walking rapidly through the deserted streets of gaping roofs and leaning houses toward the hotel where I had checked my valise and would find my bus.

Though the golden light of late afternoon gave the ancient

roofs and decrepit chimneys an air of mystic loveliness and peace, I could not help glancing over my shoulder now and then. I would surely be very glad to get out of malodorous and fear-shadowed Innsmouth, and wished there were some other vehicle than the bus driven by that sinister-looking fellow Sargent. Yet I did not hurry too precipitately, for there were architectural details worth viewing at every silent corner; and I could easily, I calculated, cover the necessary distance in a half-hour.

Studying the grocery youth's map and seeking a route I had not traversed before, I chose Marsh Street instead of State for my approach to Town Square. Near the corner of Fall Street I began to see scattered groups of furtive whisperers, and when I finally reached the Square I saw that almost all the loiterers were congregated around the door of the Gilman House. It seemed as if many bulging, watery, unwinking eyes looked oddly at me as I claimed my valise in the lobby, and I hoped that none of these unpleasant creatures would be my fellow-passengers on the coach.

The bus, rather early, rattled in with three passengers somewhat before eight, and an evil-looking fellow on the sidewalk muttered a few indistinguishable words to the driver. Sargent threw out a mail-bag and a roll of newspapers, and entered the hotel; while the passengers—the same men whom I had seen arriving in Newburyport that morning—shambled to the sidewalk and exchanged some faint guttural words with a loafer in a language I could have sworn was not English. I boarded the empty coach and took the same seat I had taken before, but was hardly settled before Sargent reappeared and began mumbling in a throaty voice of peculiar repulsiveness.

I was, it appeared, in very bad luck. There had been something wrong with the engine, despite the excellent time made from Newburyport, and the bus could not complete the journey to Arkham. No, it could not possibly be repaired that night, nor was there any other way of getting transportation out of Innsmouth, either to Arkham or elsewhere. Sargent was sorry, but I would have to stop over at the Gilman. Probably the clerk would make the price easy for me, but there was nothing else to do. Almost dazed by this sudden obstacle, and violently dreading the fall of night in this decaying and half-unlighted town, I left the bus and reëntered the hotel lobby; where the sullen, queer-looking night clerk told me I could have Room 428 on next the top floor—large, but without running water—for a dollar.[53]

Despite what I had heard of this hotel in Newburyport, I signed the register, paid my dollar, let the clerk take my valise, and followed that sour, solitary attendant up three creaking flights of stairs past dusty corridors which seemed wholly devoid of life. My room, a dismal rear one with two windows and bare, cheap furnishings, overlooked a dingy courtyard otherwise hemmed in by low, deserted brick blocks, and commanded a view of decrepit westward-stretching roofs with a marshy countryside beyond. At the end of the corridor was a bathroom—a discouraging relique with ancient marble bowl, tin tub, faint electric light, and musty wooden panelling around all the plumbing fixtures.

It being still daylight, I descended to the Square and looked around for a dinner of some sort; noticing as I did so the strange glances I received from the unwholesome loafers. Since the grocery was closed, I was forced to patronise the restaurant I had shunned before; a stooped, narrow-headed man with staring, unwinking eyes, and a flat-nosed wench with unbelievably thick, clumsy hands being in attendance. The service was of the counter type, and it relieved me to find that much was evidently served from cans and packages. A bowl of vegetable soup with crackers was enough for me,[54] and I soon headed back for my cheerless room at the Gilman; getting an evening paper and a flyspecked magazine from the evil-visaged clerk at the rickety stand beside his desk.

As twilight deepened I turned on the one feeble electric bulb over the cheap, iron-framed bed, and tried as best I could to continue the reading I had begun. I felt it advisable to keep my mind wholesomely occupied, for it would not do to brood over the abnormalities of this ancient, blight-shadowed town while I was still within its borders. The insane yarn I had heard from the aged drunkard did not promise very pleasant dreams, and I felt I must keep the image of his wild, watery eyes as far as possible from my imagination.

Also, I must not dwell on what that factory inspector had told the Newburyport ticket-agent about the Gilman House and the voices of its nocturnal tenants—not on that, nor on the face beneath the tiara in the black church doorway; the face for whose horror my conscious mind could not account. It would perhaps have been easier to keep my thoughts from disturbing topics had the room not been so gruesomely musty. As it was, the lethal mustiness blended hideously with the town's general fishy odour and persistently focussed one's fancy on death and decay.

Another thing that disturbed me was the absence of a bolt on the door of my room. One had been there, as marks clearly shewed, but there were signs of recent removal. No doubt it had become out of order, like so many other things in this decrepit edifice. In my nervousness I looked around and discovered a bolt on the clothes-press which seemed to be of the same size, judging from the marks, as the one formerly on the door. To gain a partial relief from the general tension I busied myself by transferring this hardware to the vacant place with the aid of a handy three-in-one device including a screw-driver which I kept on my key-ring. The bolt fitted perfectly, and I was somewhat relieved when I knew that I could shoot it firmly upon retiring. Not that I had any real apprehension of its need, but that any symbol of security was welcome in an environment of this kind. There were adequate bolts on the two lateral doors to connecting rooms, and these I proceeded to fasten.

I did not undress, but decided to read till I was sleepy and then lie down with only my coat, collar, and shoes off. Taking a pocket flashlight from my valise, I placed it in my trousers, so that I could read my watch if I woke up later in the dark. Drowsiness, however, did not come; and when I stopped to analyse my thoughts I found to my disquiet that I was really unconsciously listening for something—listening for something which I dreaded but could not name. That inspector's story must have worked on my imagination more deeply than I had suspected. Again I tried to read, but found that I made no progess.

After a time I seemed to hear the stairs and corridors creak at intervals as if with footsteps, and wondered if the other rooms were beginning to fill up. There were no voices, however, and it struck me that there was something subtly furtive about the creaking. I did not like it, and debated whether I had better try to sleep at all. This town had some queer people, and there had undoubtedly been several disappearances. Was this one of those inns where travellers were slain for their money? Surely I had no look of excessive prosperity. Or were the townsfolk really so resentful about curious visitors? Had my obvious sightseeing, with its frequent map-consultations, aroused unfavourable notice? It occurred to me that I must be in a highly nervous state to let a few random creakings set me off speculating in this fashion—but I regretted none the less that I was unarmed.

At length, feeling a fatigue which had nothing of drowsiness in it, I bolted the newly outfitted hall door, turned off the light, and threw myself down on the hard, uneven bed—coat, collar, shoes, and all. In the darkness every faint noise of the night seemed magnified, and a flood of doubly unpleasant thoughts swept over me. I was sorry I had put out the light, yet was too tired to rise and turn it on again. Then, after a long, dreary interval, and prefaced by a fresh creaking of stairs and corridor, there came that soft, damnably unmistakable sound which seemed like a malign fulfilment of all my apprehensions. Without the least shadow of a doubt, the lock on my hall door was being tried—cautiously, furtively, tentatively—with a key.

My sensations upon recognising this sign of actual peril were perhaps less rather than more tumultuous because of my previous vague fears. I had been, albeit without definite reason, instinctively on my guard—and that was to my advantage in the new and real crisis, whatever it might turn out to be. Nevertheless the change in the menace from vague premonition to immediate reality was a profound shock, and fell upon me with the force of a genuine blow. It never once occurred to me that the fumbling might be a mere mistake. Malign purpose was all I could think of, and I kept deathly quiet, awaiting the would-be intruder's next move.

After a time the cautious rattling ceased, and I heard the room to the north entered with a pass-key. Then the lock of the connecting door to my room was softly tried. The bolt held, of course, and I heard the floor creak as the prowler left the room.

After a moment there came another soft rattling, and I knew that the room to the south of me was being entered. Again a furtive trying of a bolted connecting door, and again a receding creaking. This time the creaking went along the hall and down the stairs, so I knew that the prowler had realised the bolted condition of my doors and was giving up his attempt for a greater or lesser time, as the future would shew.

The readiness with which I fell into a plan of action proves that I must have been subconsciously fearing some menace and considering possible avenues of escape for hours. From the first I felt that the unseen fumbler meant a danger not to be met or dealt with, but only to be fled from as precipitately as possible. The one thing to do was to get out of that hotel alive as quickly as I could, and through some channel other than the front stairs and lobby.

Rising softly and throwing my flashlight on the switch, I sought to light the bulb over my bed in order to choose and pocket some belongings for a swift, valiseless flight. Nothing, however, happened; and I saw that the power had been cut off. Clearly, some cryptic, evil movement was afoot on a large scale—just what, I could not say. As I stood pondering with my hand on the now useless switch I heard a muffled creaking on the floor below, and thought I could barely distinguish voices in conversation. A moment later I felt less sure that the deeper sounds were voices, since the apparent hoarse barkings and loose-syllabled croakings bore so little resemblance to recognised human speech. Then I thought with renewed force of what the factory inspector had heard in the night in this mouldering and pestilential building.

Having filled my pockets with the flashlight's aid, I put on my hat and tiptoed to the windows to consider chances of descent. Despite the state's safety regulations there was no fire escape on this side of the hotel, and I saw that my windows commanded only a sheer three-story drop to the cobbled courtyard. On the right and left, however, some ancient brick business blocks abutted on the hotel; their slant roofs coming up to a reasonable jumping distance from my fourth-story level. To reach either of these lines of buildings I would have to be in a room two doors from my own—in one case on the north and in the other case on the south—and my mind instantly set to work calculating what chances I had of making the transfer.

I could not, I decided, risk an emergence into the corridor; where my footsteps would surely be heard, and where the difficulties of entering the desired room would be insuperable. My progress, if it was to be made at all, would have to be through the less solidly built connecting doors of the rooms; the locks and bolts of which I would have to force violently, using my shoulder as a battering-ram whenever they were set against me. This, I thought, would be possible owing to the rickety nature of the house and its fixtures; but I realised I could not do it noiselessly. I would have to count on sheer speed, and the chance of getting to a window before any hostile forces became coördinated enough to open the right door toward me with a pass-key. My own outer door I reinforced by pushing the bureau against it— little by little, in order to make a minimum of sound.

I perceived that my chances were very slender, and was fully prepared for any calamity. Even getting to another roof would not solve the problem, for there would then remain the task of reaching the ground and escaping from the town. One thing in my favour was the deserted and ruinous state of the abutting buildings, and the number of skylights gaping blackly open in each row.

Gathering from the grocery boy's map that the best route out of town was southward, I glanced first at the connecting door on the south side of the room. It was designed to open in my direction, hence I saw—after drawing the bolt and finding other fastenings in place—it was not a favourable one for forcing. Accordingly abandoning it as a route, I cautiously moved the bedstead against it to hamper any attack which might be made on it later from the next room. The door on the north was hung to open away from me, and this—though a test proved it to be locked or bolted from the other side—I knew must be my route. If I could gain the roofs of the buildings in Paine Street and descend successfully to the ground level, I might perhaps dart through the courtyard and the adjacent or opposite buildings to Washington or Bates—or else emerge in Paine and edge around southward into Washington. In any case, I would aim to strike Washington somehow and get quickly out of the Town Square region. My preference would be to avoid Paine, since the fire station there might be open all night.

As I thought of these things I looked out over the squalid sea of decaying roofs below me, now brightened by the beams of a moon not much past full. On the right the black gash of the river-gorge clove the panorama; abandoned factories and railway station clinging barnacle-like to its sides. Beyond it the rusted railway and the Rowley road led off through a flat, marshy terrain dotted with islets of higher and dryer scrub-grown land. On the left the creek-threaded countryside was nearer, the narrow road to Ipswich gleaming white in the moonlight. I could not see from my side of the hotel the southward route toward Arkham which I had determined to take.

I was irresolutely speculating on when I had better attack the northward door, and on how I could least audibly manage it, when I noticed that the vague noises underfoot had given place to a fresh and heavier creaking of the stairs. A wavering flicker of light shewed through my transom, and the boards of the corridor began to groan with a ponderous load. Muffled sounds of possible vocal origin approached, and at length a firm knock came at my outer door.

For a moment I simply held my breath and waited. Eternities seemed to elapse, and the nauseous fishy odour of my environment seemed to mount suddenly and spectacularly. Then the knocking was repeated—continuously, and with growing insistence. I knew that the time for action had come, and forthwith drew the bolt of the northward connecting door, bracing myself for the task of battering it open. The knocking waxed louder, and I hoped that its volume would cover the sound of my efforts. At last beginning my attempt, I lunged again and again at the thin panelling with my left shoulder, heedless of shock or pain. The door resisted even more than I had expected, but I did not give in. And all the while the clamour at the door increased.

Finally the connecting door gave, but with such a crash that I knew those outside must have heard. Instantly the outside knocking became a violent battering, while keys sounded ominously in the hall doors of the rooms on both sides of me. Rushing through the newly opened connexion, I succeeded in bolting the northerly hall door before the lock could be turned; but even as I did so I heard the hall door of the third room—the one from whose window I had hoped to reach the roof below—being tried with a pass-key.

For an instant I felt absolute despair, since my trapping in a chamber with no window egress seemed complete. A wave of almost abnormal horror swept over me, and invested with a terrible but unexplainable singularity the flashlight-glimpsed dust prints made by the intruder who had lately tried my door from this room. Then, with a dazed automatism which persisted despite hopelessness, I made for the next connecting door and performed the blind motion of pushing at it in an effort to get through and—granting that fastenings might be as providentially intact as in this second room—bolt the hall door beyond before the lock could be turned from outside.

Sheer fortunate chance gave me my reprieve—for the connecting door before me was not only unlocked but actually ajar. In a second I was through, and had my right knee and shoulder against a hall door which was visibly opening inward. My pressure took the opener off guard, for the thing shut as I pushed, so that I could slip the well-conditioned bolt as I had done with the other door. As I gained this respite I heard the battering at the two other doors abate, while a confused clatter came from the connecting door I had shielded with the bedstead. Evidently the bulk of my assailants had entered the southerly room and were massing in a lateral attack. But at the same moment a pass-key sounded in the next door to the north, and I knew that a nearer peril was at hand.

The northward connecting door was wide open, but there was no time to think about checking the already turning lock in the hall. All I could do was to shut and bolt the open connecting door, as well as its mate on the opposite side—pushing a bedstead against the one and a bureau against the other, and moving a washstand in front of the hall door. I must, I saw, trust to such makeshift barriers to shield me till I could get out the window and on the roof of the Paine Street block. But even in this acute

moment my chief horror was something apart from the immediate weakness of my defences. I was shuddering because not one
of my pursuers, despite some hideous pantings, gruntings, and
subdued barkings at odd intervals, was uttering an unmuffled or
intelligible vocal sound.

As I moved the furniture and rushed toward the windows I
heard a frightful scurrying along the corridor toward the room
north of me, and perceived that the southward battering had
ceased. Plainly, most of my opponents were about to concentrate
against the feeble connecting door which they knew must open
directly on me. Outside, the moon played on the ridgepole of the
block below, and I saw that the jump would be desperately hazardous because of the steep surface on which I must land.

Surveying the conditions, I chose the more southerly of the
two windows as my avenue of escape; planning to land on the inner slope of the roof and make for the nearest skylight. Once inside one of the decrepit brick structures I would have to reckon
with pursuit; but I hoped to descend and dodge in and out of
yawning doorways along the shadowed courtyard, eventually
getting to Washington Street and slipping out of town toward
the south.

The clatter at the northerly connecting door was now terrific,
and I saw that the weak panelling was beginning to splinter. Obviously, the besiegers had brought some ponderous object into
play as a battering-ram. The bedstead, however, still held firm; so
that I had at least a faint chance of making good my escape. As I
opened the window I noticed that it was flanked by heavy velour
draperies suspended from a pole by brass rings, and also that
there was a large projecting catch for the shutters on the exterior.
Seeing a possible means of avoiding the dangerous jump, I
yanked at the hangings and brought them down, pole and all;
then quickly hooking two of the rings in the shutter catch and
flinging the drapery outside. The heavy folds reached fully to the
abutting roof, and I saw that the rings and catch would be likely
to bear my weight. So, climbing out of the window and down
the improvised rope ladder, I left behind me forever the morbid
and horror-infested fabric of the Gilman House.

I landed safely on the loose slates of the steep roof, and succeeded in gaining the gaping black skylight without a slip. Glancing up at the window I had left, I observed it was still dark, though far across the crumbling chimneys to the north I could see lights ominously blazing in the Order of Dagon Hall, the Baptist church, and the Congregational church which I recalled so shiveringly. There had seemed to be no one in the courtyard below, and I hoped there would be a chance to get away before the spreading of a general alarm. Flashing my pocket lamp into the skylight, I saw that there were no steps down. The distance was slight, however, so I clambered over the brink and dropped; striking a dusty floor littered with crumbling boxes and barrels.

The place was ghoulish-looking, but I was past minding such impressions and made at once for the staircase revealed by my flashlight—after a hasty glance at my watch, which shewed the hour to be 2 a.m. The steps creaked, but seemed tolerably sound; and I raced down past a barn-like second story to the ground floor. The desolation was complete, and only echoes answered my footfalls. At length I reached the lower hall, at one end of which I saw a faint luminous rectangle marking the ruined Paine Street doorway. Heading the other way, I found the back door also open; and darted out and down five stone steps to the grass-grown cobblestones of the courtyard.

The moonbeams did not reach down here, but I could just see my way about without using the flashlight. Some of the windows on the Gilman House side were faintly glowing, and I thought I heard confused sounds within. Walking softly over to the Washington Street side I perceived several open doorways, and chose the nearest as my route out. The hallway inside was black, and when I reached the opposite end I saw that the street door was wedged immovably shut. Resolved to try another building, I groped my way back toward the courtyard, but stopped short when close to the doorway.

For out of an opened door in the Gilman House a large crowd of doubtful shapes was pouring—lanterns bobbing in the darkness, and horrible croaking voices exchanging low cries in what was certainly not English. The figures moved uncertainly, and I realised to my relief that they did not know where I had gone; but for all that they sent a shiver of horror through my frame.

Their features were indistinguishable, but their crouching, shambling gait was abominably repellent. And worst of all, I perceived that one figure was strangely robed, and unmistakably surmounted by a tall tiara of a design altogether too familiar. As the figures spread throughout the courtyard, I felt my fears increase. Suppose I could find no egress from this building on the street side? The fishy odour was detestable, and I wondered I could stand it without fainting. Again groping toward the street, I opened a door off the hall and came upon an empty room with closely shuttered but sashless windows. Fumbling in the rays of my flashlight, I found I could open the shutters; and in another moment had climbed outside and was carefully closing the aperture in its original manner.

I was now in Washington Street, and for the moment saw no living thing nor any light save that of the moon. From several directions in the distance, however, I could hear the sound of hoarse voices, of footsteps, and of a curious kind of pattering which did not sound quite like footsteps. Plainly I had no time to lose. The points of the compass were clear to me, and I was glad that all the street-lights were turned off, as is often the custom on strongly moonlit nights in unprosperous rural regions. Some of the sounds came from the south, yet I retained my design of escaping in that direction. There would, I knew, be plenty of deserted doorways to shelter me in case I met any person or group who looked like pursuers.

I walked rapidly, softly, and close to the ruined houses. While hatless and dishevelled after my arduous climb, I did not look especially noticeable; and stood a good chance of passing unheeded if forced to encounter any casual wayfarer. At Bates Street I drew into a yawning vestibule while two shambling figures crossed in front of me, but was soon on my way again and approaching the open space where Eliot Street obliquely crosses Washington at the intersection of South. Though I had never seen this space, it had looked dangerous to me on the grocery youth's map; since the moonlight would have free play there. There was no use trying to evade it, for any alternative course would involve detours of possibly disastrous visibility and delaying effect. The only thing to do was to cross it boldly and openly; imitating the typical shamble of the Innsmouth folk as best I could, and trusting that no one—or at least no pursuer of mine—would be there.

Just how fully the pursuit was organised—and indeed, just what its purpose might be—I could form no idea. There seemed to be unusual activity in the town, but I judged that the news of my escape from the Gilman had not yet spread. I would, of course, soon have to shift from Washington to some other south-ward street; for that party from the hotel would doubtless be af-ter me. I must have left dust prints in that last old building, revealing how I had gained the street.

The open space was, as I had expected, strongly moonlit; and I saw the remains of a park-like, iron-railed green in its centre. Fortunately no one was about, though a curious sort of buzz or roar seemed to be increasing in the direction of Town Square. South Street was very wide, leading directly down a slight decliv-ity to the waterfront and commanding a long view out at sea; and I hoped that no one would be glancing up it from afar as I crossed in the bright moonlight.

My progress was unimpeded, and no fresh sound arose to hint that I had been spied. Glancing about me, I involuntarily let my pace slacken for a second to take in the sight of the sea, gorgeous in the burning moonlight at the street's end. Far out beyond the breakwater was the dim, dark line of Devil Reef, and as I glimpsed it I could not help thinking of all the hideous legends I had heard in the last thirty-four hours—legends which portrayed this ragged rock as a veritable gateway to realms of unfathomed horror and inconceivable abnormality.

Then, without warning, I saw the intermittent flashes of light on the distant reef. They were definite and unmistakable, and awaked in my mind a blind horror beyond all rational propor-tion. My muscles tightened for panic flight, held in only by a cer-tain unconscious caution and half-hypnotic fascination. And to make matters worse, there now flashed forth from the lofty cupola of the Gilman House, which loomed up to the northeast behind me, a series of analogous though differently spaced gleams which could be nothing less than an answering signal.

Controlling my muscles, and realising afresh how plainly visi-ble I was, I resumed my brisker and feignedly shambling pace;

though keeping my eyes on that hellish and ominous reef as long as the opening of South Street gave me a seaward view. What the whole proceeding meant, I could not imagine; unless it involved some strange rite connected with Devil Reef, or unless some party had landed from a ship on that sinister rock. I now bent to the left around the ruinous green; still gazing toward the ocean as it blazed in the spectral summer moonlight, and watching the cryptical flashing of those nameless, unexplainable beacons.

It was then that the most horrible impression of all was borne in upon me—the impression which destroyed my last vestige of self-control and set me running frantically southward past the yawning black doorways and fishily staring windows of that deserted nightmare street. For at a closer glance I saw that the moonlit waters between the reef and the shore were far from empty. They were alive with a teeming horde of shapes swimming inward toward the town; and even at my vast distance and in my single moment of perception I could tell that the bobbing heads and flailing arms were alien and aberrant in a way scarcely to be expressed or consciously formulated.

My frantic running ceased before I had covered a block, for at my left I began to hear something like the hue and cry of organised pursuit. There were footsteps and guttural sounds, and a rattling motor wheezed south along Federal Street. In a second all my plans were utterly changed—for if the southward highway were blocked ahead of me, I must clearly find another egress from Innsmouth. I paused and drew into a gaping doorway, reflecting how lucky I was to have left the moonlit open space before these pursuers came down the parallel street.

A second reflection was less comforting. Since the pursuit was down another street, it was plain that the party was not following me directly. It had not seen me, but was simply obeying a general plan of cutting off my escape. This, however, implied that all roads leading out of Innsmouth were similarly patrolled; for the denizens could not have known what route I intended to take. If this were so, I would have to make my retreat across country away from any road; but how could I do that in view of the marshy and creek-riddled nature of all the surrounding region?

For a moment my brain reeled—both from sheer hopelessness and from a rapid increase in the omnipresent fishy odour.

Then I thought of the abandoned railway to Rowley, whose solid line of ballasted, weed-grown earth still stretched off to the northwest from the crumbling station on the edge of the river-gorge. There was just a chance that the townsfolk would not think of that; since its brier-choked desertion made it half-impassable, and the unlikeliest of all avenues for a fugitive to choose. I had seen it clearly from my hotel window, and knew about how it lay. Most of its earlier length was uncomfortably visible from the Rowley road, and from high places in the town itself; but one could perhaps crawl inconspicuously through the undergrowth. At any rate, it would form my only chance of de-liverance, and there was nothing to do but try it.

Drawing inside the hall of my deserted shelter, I once more consulted the grocery boy's map with the aid of the flashlight. The immediate problem was how to reach the ancient railway; and I now saw that the safest course was ahead to Babson Street,[55] then west to Lafayette—there edging around but not crossing an open space homologous to the one I had traversed—and subsequently back northward and westward in a zigzagging line through Lafayette, Bates, Adams, and Bank Streets—the lat-ter skirting the river-gorge—to the abandoned and dilapidated station I had seen from my window. My reason for going ahead to Babson was that I wished neither to re-cross the eariler open space nor to begin my westward course along a cross street as broad as South.

Starting once more, I crossed the street to the right-hand side in order to edge around into Babson as inconspicuously as possi-ble. Noises still continued in Federal Street, and as I glanced behind me I thought I saw a gleam of light near the building through which I had escaped. Anxious to leave Washington Street, I broke into a quiet dog-trot, trusting to luck not to en-counter any observing eye. Next the corner of Babson Street I saw to my alarm that one of the houses was still inhabited, as at-tested by curtains at the window; but there were no lights within, and I passed it without disaster.

In Babson Street, which crossed Federal and might thus reveal
me to the searchers, I clung as closely as possible to the sagging,
uneven buildings; twice pausing in a doorway as the noises behind me momentarily increased. The open space ahead shone
wide and desolate under the moon, but my route would not
force me to cross it. During my second pause I began to detect a
fresh distribution of the vague sounds; and upon looking cautiously out from cover beheld a motor-car darting across the
open space, bound outward along Eliot Street, which there inter-
sects both Babson and Lafayette.

As I watched—choked by a sudden rise in the fishy odour
after a short abatement—I saw a band of uncouth, crouching
shapes loping and shambling in the same direction; and knew
that this must be the party guarding the Ipswich road, since that
highway forms an extension of Eliot Street. Two of the figures I
glimpsed were in voluminous robes, and one wore a peaked dia-
dem which glistened whitely in the moonlight. The gait of this
figure was so odd that it sent a chill through me—for it seemed
to me the creature was almost *hopping*.

When the last of the band was out of sight I resumed my
progress; darting around the corner into Lafayette Street,
and crossing Eliot very hurriedly lest stragglers of the party be
still advancing along that thoroughfare. I did hear some croaking
and clattering sounds far off toward Town Square, but accomplished the passage without disaster. My greatest dread was in re-
crossing broad and moonlit South Street—with its seaward
view—and I had to nerve myself for the ordeal. Someone might
easily be looking, and possible Eliot Street stragglers could not
fail to glimpse me from either of two points. At the last moment
I decided I had better slacken my trot and make the crossing as
before in the shambling gait of an average Innsmouth native.

When the view of the water again opened out—this time on
my right—I was half-determined not to look at it at all. I could
not, however, resist; but cast a sidelong glance as I carefully and
imitatively shambled toward the protecting shadows ahead.
There was no ship visible, as I had half expected there would be.
Instead, the first thing which caught my eye was a small rowboat
pulling in toward the abandoned wharves and laden with some

bulky, tarpaulin-covered object. Its rowers, though distantly and indistinctly seen, were of an especially repellent aspect. Several swimmers were still discernible; while on the far black reef I could see a faint, steady glow unlike the winking beacon visible before, and of a curious colour which I could not precisely identify. Above the slant roofs ahead and to the right there loomed the tall cupola of the Gilman House, but it was completely dark. The fishy odour, dispelled for a moment by some merciful breeze, now closed in again with maddening intensity.

I had not quite crossed the street when I heard a muttering band advancing along Washington from the north. As they reached the broad open space where I had had my first disquieting glimpse of the moonlit water I could see them plainly only a block away—and was horrified by the bestial abnormality of their faces and the dog-like sub-humanness of their crouching gait. One man moved in a positively simian way, with long arms freqently touching the ground; while another figure—robed and tiaraed—seemed to progress in an almost hopping fashion. I judged this party to be the one I had seen in the Gilman's courtyard—the one, therefore, most closely on my trail. As some of the figures turned to look in my direction I was transfixed with fright, yet managed to preserve the casual, shambling gait I had assumed. To this day I do not know whether they saw me or not. If they did, my stratagem must have deceived them, for they passed on across the moonlit space without varying their course—meanwhile croaking and jabbering in some hateful guttural patois I could not identify.

Once more in shadow, I resumed my former dog-trot past the leaning and decrepit houses that stared blankly into the night. Having crossed to the western sidewalk I rounded the nearest corner into Bates Street, where I kept close to the buildings on the southern side. I passed two houses shewing signs of habitation, one of which had faint lights in upper rooms, yet met with no obstacle. As I turned into Adams Street I felt measurably safer, but received a shock when a man reeled out of a black doorway directly in front of me. He proved, however, too hopelessly drunk to be a menace; so that I reached the dismal ruins of the Bank Street warehouses in safety.

No one was stirring in that dead street beside the river-gorge, and the roar of the waterfalls quite drowned my footsteps. It was a long dog-trot to the ruined station, and the great brick warehouse walls around me seemed somehow more terrifying than the fronts of private houses. At last I saw the ancient arcaded station—or what was left of it—and made directly for the tracks that started from its farther end.

The rails were rusty but mainly intact, and not more than half the ties had rotted away. Walking or running on such a surface was very difficult; but I did my best, and on the whole made very fair time. For some distance the line kept on along the gorge's brink, but at length I reached the long covered bridge where it crossed the chasm at a dizzy height. The condition of this bridge would determine my next step. If humanly possible, I would use it; if not, I would have to risk more street wandering and take the nearest intact highway bridge.

The vast, barn-like length of the old bridge gleamed spectrally in the moonlight, and I saw that the ties were safe for at least a few feet within. Entering, I began to use my flashlight, and was almost knocked down by the cloud of bats that flapped past me. About half way across there was a perilous gap in the ties which I feared for a moment would halt me; but in the end I risked a desperate jump which fortunately succeeded.

I was glad to see the moonlight again when I emerged from that macabre tunnel. The old tracks crossed River Street at grade,[56] and at once veered off into a region increasingly rural and with less and less of Innsmouth's abhorrent fishy odour. Here the dense growth of weeds and briers hindered me and cruelly tore my clothes, but I was none the less glad that they were there to give me concealment in case of peril. I knew that much of my route must be visible from the Rowley road.

The marshy region began very shortly, with the single track on a low, grassy embankment where the weedy growth was somewhat thinner. Then came a sort of island of higher ground, where the line passed through a shallow open cut choked with bushes and brambles. I was very glad of this partial shelter, since at this point the Rowley road was uncomfortably near according to my window view. At the end of the cut it would cross the track and swerve off to a safer distance; but meanwhile I must be exceedingly careful. I was by this time thankfully certain that the railway itself was not patrolled.

Just before entering the cut I glanced behind me, but saw no pursuer. The ancient spires and roofs of decaying Innsmouth gleamed lovely and ethereal in the magic yellow moonlight, and I thought of how they must have looked in the old days before the shadow fell. Then, as my gaze circled inland from the town, something less tranquil arrested my notice and held me immobile for a second.

What I saw—or fancied I saw—was a disturbing suggestion of undulant motion far to the south; a suggestion which made me conclude that a very large horde must be pouring out of the city along the level Ipswich road. The distance was great, and I could distinguish nothing in detail; but I did not at all like the look of that moving column. It undulated too much, and glistened too brightly in the rays of the now westering moon. There was a suggestion of sound, too, though the wind was blowing the other way—a suggestion of bestial scraping and bellowing even worse than the muttering of the parties I had lately overheard.

All sorts of unpleasant conjectures crossed my mind. I thought of those very extreme Innsmouth types said to be hidden in crumbling, centuried warrens near the waterfront. I thought, too, of those nameless swimmers I had seen. Counting the parties so far glimpsed, as well as those presumably covering other roads, the number of my pursuers must be strangely large for a town as depopulated as Innsmouth.

Whence could come the dense personnel of such a column as I now beheld? Did those ancient, unplumbed warrens teem with a twisted, uncatalogued, and unsuspected life? Or had some unseen ship indeed landed a legion of unknown outsiders on that hellish reef? Who were they? Why were they there? And if such a column of them was scouring the Ipswich road, would the patrols on the other roads be likewise augmented?

I had entered the brush-grown cut and was struggling along at a very slow pace when that damnable fishy odour again waxed dominant. Had the wind suddenly changed eastward, so that it blew in from the sea and over the town? It must have, I concluded, since I now began to hear shocking guttural murmurs from that hitherto silent direction. There was another sound, too—a kind of wholesale, colossal flopping or pattering which somehow called up images of the most detestable sort. It made me think illogically of that unpleasantly undulating column on the far-off Ipswich road.

And then both stench and sounds grew stronger, so that I paused shivering and grateful for the cut's protection. It was here, I recalled, that the Rowley road drew so close to the old railway before crossing westward and diverging. Something was coming along that road, and I must lie low till its passage and vanishment in the distance. Thank heaven these creatures employed no dogs for tracking—though perhaps that would have been impossible amidst the omnipresent regional odour. Crouched in the bushes of that sandy cleft I felt reasonably safe, even though I knew the searchers would have to cross the track in front of me not much more than a hundred yards away. I would be able to see them, but they could not, except by a malign miracle, see me.

All at once I began dreading to look at them as they passed. I saw the close moonlit space where they would surge by, and had curious thoughts about the irredeemable pollution of that space. They would perhaps be the worst of all Innsmouth types—something one would not care to remember.

The stench waxed overpowering, and the noises swelled to a bestial babel of croaking, baying, and barking without the least suggestion of human speech. Were these indeed the voices of my pursuers? Did they have dogs after all? So far I had seen none of the lower animals in Innsmouth. That flopping or pattering was monstrous—I could not look upon the degenerate creatures responsible for it. I would keep my eyes shut till the sounds receded toward the west. The horde was very close now—the air foul with their hoarse snarlings, and the ground almost shaking with their alien-rhythmed footfalls. My breath nearly ceased to come, and I put every ounce of will power into the task of holding my eyelids down.

I am not even yet willing to say whether what followed was a hideous actuality or only a nightmare hallucination. The later action of the government, after my frantic appeals, would tend to confirm it as a monstrous truth; but could not an hallucination have been repeated under the quasi-hypnotic spell of that ancient, haunted, and shadowed town? Such places have strange properties, and the legacy of insane legend might well have acted on more than one human imagination amidst those dead, stench-cursed streets and huddles of rotting roofs and crumbling steeples. Is it not possible that the germ of an actual contagious madness lurks in the depths of that shadow over Innsmouth? Who can be sure of reality after hearing things like the tale of old Zadok Allen? The government men never found poor Zadok, and have no conjectures to make as to what became of him. Where does madness leave off and reality begin? Is it possible that even my latest fear is sheer delusion?

But I must try to tell what I thought I saw that night under the mocking yellow moon—saw surging and hopping down the Rowley road in plain sight in front of me as I crouched among the wild brambles of that desolate railway cut. Of course my resolution to keep my eyes shut had failed. It was foredoomed to failure—for who could crouch blindly while a legion of croaking, baying entities of unknown source flopped noisomely past, scarcely more than a hundred yards away?

I thought I was prepared for the worst, and I really ought to have been prepared considering what I had seen before. My other pursuers had been accursedly abnormal—so should I not have been ready to face a *strengthening* of that abnormal element; to look upon forms in which there was no mixture of the normal at all?[57] I did not open my eyes until the raucous clamour came loudly from a point obviously straight ahead. Then I knew that a long section of them must be plainly in sight where the sides of the cut flattened out and the road crossed the track—and I could no longer keep myself from sampling whatever horror that leering yellow moon might have to shew.

It was the end, for whatever remains to me of life on the surface of this earth, of every vestige of mental peace and confidence in the integrity of Nature and of the human mind. Nothing that

I could have imagined—nothing, even, that I could have gathered
had I credited old Zadok's crazy tale in the most literal way—
would be in any way comparable to the daemoniac, blasphemous
reality that I saw—or believe I saw. I have tried to hint what it
was in order to postpone the horror of writing it down baldly.
Can it be possible that this planet has actually spawned such
things; that human eyes have truly seen, as objective flesh, what
man has hitherto known only in febrile phantasy and tenuous
legend?

And yet I saw them in a limitless stream—flopping, hopping,
croaking, bleating—surging inhumanly through the spectral
moonlight in a grotesque, malignant saraband of fantastic nightmare. And some of them had tall tiaras of that nameless whitish-
gold metal . . . and some were strangely robed . . . and one, who
led the way, was clad in a ghoulishly humped black coat and
striped trousers, and had a man's felt hat perched on the shapeless thing that answered for a head. . . .[58]

I think their predominant colour was a greyish-green, though
they had white bellies. They were mostly shiny and slippery, but
the ridges of their backs were scaly. Their forms vaguely suggested the anthropoid, while their heads were the heads of fish,
with prodigious bulging eyes that never closed. At the sides of
their necks were palpitating gills, and their long paws were
webbed. They hopped irregularly, sometimes on two legs and
sometimes on four. I was somehow glad that they had no more
than four limbs. Their croaking, baying voices, clearly used for
articulate speech, held all the dark shades of expression which
their staring faces lacked.

But for all of their monstrousness they were not unfamiliar to
me. I knew too well what they must be—for was not the memory of that evil tiara at Newburyport still fresh? They were the
blasphemous fish-frogs of the nameless design—living and horrible—and as I saw them I knew also of what that humped, tiaraed
priest in the black church basement had so fearsomely reminded
me. Their number was past guessing. It seemed to me that there
were limitless swarms of them—and certainly my momentary
glimpse could have shewn only the least fraction. In another in-

stant everything was blotted out by a merciful fit of fainting; the first I had ever had.

V.

It was a gentle daylight rain that awaked me from my stupor in the brush-grown railway cut, and when I staggered out to the roadway ahead I saw no trace of any prints in the fresh mud. The fishy odour, too, was gone. Innsmouth's ruined roofs and toppling steeples loomed up greyly toward the southeast, but not a living creature did I spy in all the desolate salt marshes around. My watch was still going, and told me that the hour was past noon.

The reality of what I had been through was highly uncertain in my mind, but I felt that something hideous lay in the background. I must get away from evil-shadowed Innsmouth—and accordingly I began to test my cramped, wearied powers of locomotion. Despite weakness, hunger, horror, and bewilderment I found myself after a long time able to walk; so started slowly along the muddy road to Rowley. Before evening I was in the village, getting a meal and providing myself with presentable clothes. I caught the night train to Arkham, and the next day talked long and earnestly with government officials there; a process I later repeated in Boston. With the main result of these colloquies the public is now familiar—and I wish, for normality's sake, there were nothing more to tell. Perhaps it is madness that is overtaking me—yet perhaps a greater horror—or a greater marvel—is reaching out.

As may well be imagined, I gave up most of the foreplanned features of the rest of my tour—the scenic, architectural, and antiquarian diversions on which I had counted so heavily. Nor did I dare look for that piece of strange jewellery said to be in the Miskatonic University Museum. I did, however, improve my stay in Arkham by collecting some genealogical notes I had long wished to possess; very rough and hasty data, it is true, but capable of good use later on when I might have time to collate and codify them. The curator of the historical society there—Mr. E.

Lapham Peabody[59]—was very courteous about assisting me, and expressed unusual interest when I told him I was a grandson of Eliza Orne of Arkham, who was born in 1867 and had married James Williamson of Ohio at the age of seventeen.

It seemed that a maternal uncle of mine had been there many years before on a quest much like my own; and that my grandmother's family was a topic of some local curiosity. There had, Mr. Peabody said, been considerable discussion about the marriage of her father, Benjamin Orne,[60] just after the Civil War; since the ancestry of the bride was peculiarly puzzling. That bride was understood to have been an orphaned Marsh of New Hampshire—a cousin of the Essex County Marshes—but her education had been in France and she knew very little of her family. A guardian had deposited funds in a Boston bank to maintain her and her French governess; but that guardian's name was unfamiliar to Arkham people, and in time he dropped out of sight, so that the governess assumed his role by court appointment. The Frenchwoman—now long dead—was very taciturn, and there were those who said she could have told more than she did.

But the most baffling thing was the inability of anyone to place the recorded parents of the young woman—Enoch and Lydia (Meserve) Marsh—among the known families of New Hampshire. Possibly, many suggested, she was the natural daughter of some Marsh of prominence—she certainly had the true Marsh eyes. Most of the puzzling was done after her early death, which took place at the birth of my grandmother—her only child. Having formed some disagreeable impressions connected with the name of Marsh, I did not welcome the news that it belonged on my own ancestral tree; nor was I pleased by Mr. Peabody's suggestion that I had the true Marsh eyes myself. However, I was grateful for data which I knew would prove valuable; and took copious notes and lists of book references regarding the well-documented Orne family.

I went directly home to Toledo from Boston, and later spent a month at Maumee recuperating from my ordeal. In September I entered Oberlin for my final year, and from then till the next June was busy with studies and other wholesome activities—reminded of the bygone terror only by occasional official visits from government men in connexion with the campaign which my pleas and evidence had started. Around the middle of July— just a year after the Innsmouth experience—I spent a week with my late mother's family in Cleveland;[61] checking some of my new genealogical data with the various notes, traditions, and bits of heirloom material in existence there, and seeing what kind of connected chart I could construct.

I did not exactly relish the task, for the atmosphere of the Williamson home had always depressed me. There was a strain of morbidity there, and my mother had never encouraged my visiting her parents as a child, although she always welcomed her father when he came to Toledo. My Arkham-born grandmother had seemed strange and terrifying to me, and I do not think I grieved when she disappeared. I was eight years old then, and it was said that she had wandered off in grief after the suicide of my uncle Douglas, her eldest son. He had shot himself after a trip to New England—the same trip, no doubt, which had caused him to be recalled at the Arkham Historical Society.

This uncle had resembled her, and I had never liked him either. Something about the staring, unwinking expression of both of them had given me a vague, unaccountable uneasiness. My mother and uncle Walter had not looked like that. They were like their father, though poor little cousin Lawrence—Walter's son—had been an almost perfect duplicate of his grandmother before his condition took him to the permanent seclusion of a sanitarium at Canton.[62] I had not seen him in four years, but my uncle once implied that his state, both mental and physical, was very bad. This worry had probably been a major cause of his mother's death two years before.

My grandfather and his widowed son Walter now comprised the Cleveland household, but the memory of older times hung thickly over it. I still disliked the place, and tried to get my researches done as quickly as possible. Williamson records and traditions were supplied in abundance by my grandfather; though for Orne material I had to depend on my uncle Walter, who put at my disposal the contents of all his files, including notes, letters, cuttings, heirlooms, photographs, and miniatures.

It was in going over the letters and pictures on the Orne side that I began to acquire a sort of terror of my own ancestry. As I have said, my grandmother and uncle Douglas had always disturbed me. Now, years after their passing, I gazed at their pictured faces with a measurably heightened feeling of repulsion and alienation. I could not at first understand the change, but gradually a horrible sort of *comparison* began to obtrude itself on my unconscious mind despite the steady refusal of my consciousness to admit even the least suspicion of it. It was clear that the typical expression of these faces now suggested something it had not suggested before—something which would bring stark panic if too openly thought of.

But the worst shock came when my uncle shewed me the Orne jewellery in a downtown safe-deposit vault. Some of the items were delicate and inspiring enough, but there was one box of strange old pieces descended from my mysterious great-grandmother which my uncle was almost reluctant to produce. They were, he said, of very grotesque and almost repulsive design, and had never to his knowledge been publicly worn; though my grandmother used to enjoy looking at them. Vague legends of bad luck clustered around them, and my great-grandmother's French governess had said they ought not to be worn in New England, though it would be quite safe to wear them in Europe.

As my uncle began slowly and grudgingly to unwrap the things he urged me not to be shocked by the strangeness and frequent hideousness of the designs. Artists and archaeologists who had seen them pronounced the workmanship superlatively and exotically exquisite, though no one seemed able to define their exact material or assign them to any specific art tradition. There were two armlets, a tiara, and a kind of pectoral; the latter having in high relief certain figures of almost unbearable extravagance.

During this description I had kept a tight rein on my emotions, but my face must have betrayed my mounting fears. My uncle looked concerned, and paused in his unwrapping to study my countenance. I motioned to him to continue, which he did with renewed signs of reluctance. He seemed to expect some demonstration when the first piece—the tiara—became visible, but I doubt if he expected quite what actually happened. I did not expect it, either, for I thought I was thoroughly forewarned regarding what the jewellery would turn out to be. What I did was to faint silently away, just as I had done in that brier-choked railway cut a year before.

From that day on my life has been a nightmare of brooding and apprehension, nor do I know how much is hideous truth and how much madness. My great-grandmother had been a Marsh of unknown source whose husband lived in Arkham—and did not Zadok say that the daughter of Obed Marsh by a monstrous mother was married to an Arkham man through a trick? What was it the ancient toper had muttered about the likeness of my eyes to Captain Obed's? In Arkham, too, the curator had told me I had the true Marsh eyes. Was Obed Marsh my own great-great-grandfather? Who—or *what*—then, was my great-great-grandmother? But perhaps this was all madness. Those whitish-gold ornaments might easily have been bought from some Innsmouth sailor by the father of my great-grandmother, whoever he was. And that look in the staring-eyed faces of my grandmother and self-slain uncle might be sheer fancy on my part—sheer fancy, bolstered up by the Innsmouth shadow which had so darkly coloured my imagination. But why had my uncle killed himself after an ancestral quest in New England?

For more than two years I fought off these reflections with partial success. My father secured me a place in an insurance office, and I buried myself in routine as deeply as possible. In the winter of 1930–31, however, the dreams began. They were very sparse and insidious at first, but increased in frequency and vividness as the weeks went by. Great watery spaces opened out before me, and I seemed to wander through titanic sunken porticos and labyrinths of weedy Cyclopean walls with grotesque fishes as my companions. Then the *other shapes* began to appear, filling me with nameless horror the moment I awoke. But during the dreams they did not horrify me at all—I was one with them; wearing their unhuman trappings, treading their aqueous ways, and praying monstrously at their evil sea-bottom temples.

There was much more than I could remember, but even what I did remember each morning would be enough to stamp me as a madman or a genius if ever I dared write it down. Some frightful influence, I felt, was seeking gradually to drag me out of the sane world of wholesome life into unnamable abysses of blackness and alienage; and the process told heavily on me. My health and appearance grew steadily worse, till finally I was forced to give up my position and adopt the static, secluded life of an invalid. Some odd nervous affliction had me in its grip, and I found myself at times almost unable to shut my eyes.

It was then that I began to study the mirror with mounting alarm. The slow ravages of disease are not pleasant to watch, but in my case there was something subtler and more puzzling in the background. My father seemed to notice it, too, for he began looking at me curiously and almost affrightedly. What was taking place in me? Could it be that I was coming to resemble my grandmother and uncle Douglas?

One night I had a frightful dream in which I met my grandmother under the sea. She lived in a phosphorescent palace of many terraces, with gardens of strange leprous corals and grotesque brachiate efflorescences, and welcomed me with a warmth that may have been sardonic. She had changed—as those who take to the water change—and told me she had never died. Instead, she had gone to a spot her dead son had learned about, and had leaped to a realm whose wonders—destined for him as well—he had spurned with a smoking pistol. This was to be my realm, too—I could not escape it. I would never die, but would live with those who had lived since before man ever walked the earth.

I met also that which had been her grandmother. For eighty thousand years Pth'thya-l'yi had lived in Y'ha-nthlei, and thither she had gone back after Obed Marsh was dead. Y'ha-nthlei was not destroyed when the upper-earth men shot death into the sea. It was hurt, but not destroyed. The Deep Ones could never be destroyed, even though the palaeogean magic of the forgotten Old Ones might sometimes check them. For the present they would rest; but some day, if they remembered, they would rise again for the tribute Great Cthulhu craved. It would be a city greater than Innsmouth next time. They had planned to spread, and had brought up that which would help them, but now they must wait once more. For bringing the upper-earth men's death I must do a penance, but that would not be heavy. This was the dream in which I saw a *shoggoth* for the first time, and the sight set me awake in a frenzy of screaming. That morning the mirror definitely told me I had acquired *the Innsmouth look*.

So far I have not shot myself as my uncle Douglas did. I bought an automatic and almost took the step, but certain dreams deterred me. The tense extremes of horror are lessening, and I feel queerly drawn toward the unknown sea-deeps instead of fearing them. I hear and do strange things in sleep, and awake with a kind of exaltation instead of terror. I do not believe I need to wait for the full change as most have waited. If I did, my father would probably shut me up in a sanitarium as my poor little cousin is shut up. Stupendous and unheard-of splendours await me below, and I shall seek them soon. *Iä-R'lyeh! Cthulhu fhtagn! Iä! Iä!* No, I shall not shoot myself—I cannot be made to shoot myself!

I shall plan my cousin's escape from that Canton madhouse, and together we shall go to marvel-shadowed Innsmouth. We shall swim out to that brooding reef in the sea and dive down through black abysses to Cyclopean and many-columned Y'hanthlei, and in that lair of the Deep Ones we shall dwell amidst wonder and glory for ever.[63]

The Haunter of the Dark

(Dedicated to Robert Bloch)

I have seen the dark universe yawning
  Where the black planets roll without aim—
Where they roll in their horror unheeded,
  Without knowledge or lustre or name.
                                    —*Nemesis*.[1]

Cautious investigators will hesitate to challenge the common belief that Robert Blake was killed by lightning, or by some profound nervous shock derived from an electrical discharge. It is true that the window he faced was unbroken, but Nature has shewn herself capable of many freakish performances. The expression on his face may easily have arisen from some obscure muscular source unrelated to anything he saw, while the entries in his diary are clearly the result of a fantastic imagination aroused by certain local superstitions and by certain old matters he had uncovered. As for the anomalous conditions at the deserted church on Federal Hill[2]—the shrewd analyst is not slow in attributing them to some charlatanry, conscious or unconscious, with at least some of which Blake was secretly connected.

For after all, the victim was a writer and painter wholly devoted to the field of myth, dream, terror, and superstition, and avid in his quest for scenes and effects of a bizarre, spectral sort. His earlier stay in the city—a visit to a strange old man as deeply given to occult and forbidden lore as he—had ended amidst death and flame, and it must have been some morbid instinct which drew him back from his home in Milwaukee. He may have known of the old stories despite his statements to the contrary in the diary, and his death may have nipped in the bud some stupendous hoax destined to have a literary reflection.

Among those, however, who have examined and correlated all this evidence, there remain several who cling to less rational and commonplace theories. They are inclined to take much of Blake's diary at its face value, and point significantly to certain facts such as the undoubted genuineness of the old church record, the verified existence of the disliked and unorthodox Starry Wisdom sect prior to 1877, the recorded disappearance of an inquisitive reporter named Edwin M. Lillibridge in 1893, and—above all—the look of monstrous, transfiguring fear on the face of the young writer when he died. It was one of these believers who, moved to fanatical extremes, threw into the bay the curiously angled stone and its strangely adorned metal box found in the old church steeple—the black windowless steeple, and not the tower where Blake's diary said those things originally were.³ Though widely censured both officially and unofficially, this man—a reputable physician with a taste for odd folklore—averred that he had rid the earth of something too dangerous to rest upon it.

Between these two schools of opinion the reader must judge for himself. The papers have given the tangible details from a sceptical angle, leaving for others the drawing of the picture as Robert Blake saw it—or thought he saw it—or pretended to see it. Now, studying the diary closely, dispassionately, and at leisure, let us summarise the dark chain of events from the expressed point of view of their chief actor.

Young Blake returned to Providence in the winter of 1934–5, taking the upper floor of a venerable dwelling in a grassy court off College Street—on the crest of the great eastward hill near the Brown University campus and behind the marble John Hay Library.⁴ It was a cosy and fascinating place, in a little garden oasis of village-like antiquity where huge, friendly cats sunned themselves atop a convenient shed. The square Georgian house had a monitor roof, classic doorway with fan carving, small-paned windows, and all the other earmarks of early nineteenth-century workmanship.⁵ Inside were six-panelled doors, wide floor-boards, a curving colonial staircase, white Adam-period mantels, and a rear set of rooms three steps below the general level.

Blake's study, a large southwest chamber, overlooked the

front garden on one side, while its west windows—before one of
which he had his desk—faced off from the brow of the hill and
commanded a splendid view of the lower town's outspread roofs
and of the mystical sunsets that flamed behind them. On the
far horizon were the open countryside's purple slopes. Against
these, some two miles away, rose the spectral hump of Federal
Hill, bristling with huddled roofs and steeples whose remote
outlines wavered mysteriously, taking fantastic forms as the
smoke of the city swirled up and enmeshed them. Blake had a
curious sense that he was looking upon some unknown, ethereal
world which might or might not vanish in dream if ever he tried
to seek it out and enter it in person.

Having sent home for most of his books, Blake bought some
antique furniture suitable to his quarters and settled down to
write and paint—living alone, and attending to the simple housework himself. His studio was in a north attic room, where the
panes of the monitor roof furnished admirable lighting. During
that first winter he produced five of his best-known short
stories—"The Burrower Beneath", "The Stairs in the Crypt",
"Shaggai", "In the Vale of Pnath", and "The Feaster from the
Stars"[6]—and painted seven canvases; studies of nameless, unhuman monsters, and profoundly alien, non-terrestrial landscapes.

At sunset he would often sit at his desk and gaze dreamily off
at the outspread west—the dark towers of Memorial Hall[7] just
below, the Georgian court-house belfry, the lofty pinnacles of
the downtown section, and that shimmering, spire-crowned
mound in the distance whose unknown streets and labyrinthine
gables so potently provoked his fancy. From his few local ac-
quaintances he learned that the far-off slope was a vast Italian
quarter, though most of the houses were remnants of older Yankee and Irish days. Now and then he would train his field-glasses
on that spectral, unreachable world beyond the curling smoke;
picking out individual roofs and chimneys and steeples, and
speculating upon the bizarre and curious mysteries they might
house. Even with optical aid Federal Hill seemed somehow alien,
half fabulous, and linked to the unreal, intangible marvels of
Blake's own tales and pictures. The feeling would persist long af-

ter the hill had faded into the violet, lamp-starred twilight, and the court-house floodlights and the red Industrial Trust beacon[8] had blazed up to make the night grotesque.

Of all the distant objects on Federal Hill, a certain huge, dark church most fascinated Blake. It stood out with especial distinctness at certain hours of the day, and at sunset the great tower and tapering steeple loomed blackly against the flaming sky. It seemed to rest on especially high ground; for the grimy facade, and the obliquely seen north side with sloping roof and the tops of great pointed windows, rose boldly above the tangle of surrounding ridgepoles and chimney-pots. Peculiarly grim and austere, it appeared to be built of stone, stained and weathered with the smoke and storms of a century and more. The style, so far as the glass could shew, was that earliest experimental form of Gothic revival which preceded the stately Upjohn period and held over some of the outlines and proportions of the Georgian age. Perhaps it was reared around 1810 or 1815.

As months passed, Blake watched the far-off, forbidding structure with an oddly mounting interest. Since the vast windows were never lighted, he knew that it must be vacant. The longer he watched, the more his imagination worked, till at length he began to fancy curious things. He believed that a vague, singular aura of desolation hovered over the place, so that even the pigeons and swallows shunned its smoky eaves. Around other towers and belfries his glass would reveal great flocks of birds, but here they never rested. At least, that is what he thought and set down in his diary. He pointed the place out to several friends, but none of them had even been on Federal Hill or possessed the faintest notion of what the church was or had been.

In the spring a deep restlessness gripped Blake. He had begun his long-planned novel—based on a supposed survival of the witch-cult in Maine—but was strangely unable to make progress with it. More and more he would sit at his westward window and gaze at the distant hill and the black, frowning steeple shunned by the birds. When the delicate leaves came out on the garden boughs the world was filled with a new beauty, but

Blake's restlessness was merely increased. It was then that he first thought of crossing the city and climbing bodily up that fabulous slope into the smoke-wreathed world of dream.

Late in April, just before the aeon-shadowed Walpurgis time,[9] Blake make his first trip into the unknown. Plodding through the endless downtown streets and the bleak, decayed squares beyond, he came finally upon the ascending avenue of century-worn steps, sagging Doric porches, and blear-paned cupolas which he felt must lead up to the long-known, unreachable world beyond the mists. There were dingy blue-and-white street signs which meant nothing to him, and presently he noted the strange, dark faces of the drifting crowds, and the foreign signs over curious shops in brown, decade-weathered buildings. Nowhere could he find any of the objects he had seen from afar; so that once more he half fancied that the Federal Hill of that distant view was a dream-world never to be trod by living human feet.[10]

Now and then a battered church facade or crumbling spire came in sight, but never the blackened pile that he sought. When he asked a shopkeeper about a great stone church the man smiled and shook his head, though he spoke English freely. As Blake climbed higher, the region seemed stranger and stranger, with bewildering mazes of brooding brown alleys leading eternally off to the south. He crossed two or three broad avenues, and once thought he glimpsed a familiar tower. Again he asked a merchant about the massive church of stone, and this time he could have sworn that the plea of ignorance was feigned. The dark man's face had a look of fear which he tried to hide, and Blake saw him make a curious sign with his right hand.[11]

Then suddenly a black spire stood out against the cloudy sky on his left, above the tiers of brown roofs lining the tangled southerly alleys.[12] Blake knew at once what it was, and plunged toward it through the squalid, unpaved lanes that climbed from the avenue. Twice he lost his way, but he somehow dared not ask any of the patriarchs or housewives who sat on their doorsteps, or any of the children who shouted and played in the mud of the shadowy lanes.

At last he saw the tower plain against the southwest, and a

huge stone bulk rose darkly at the end of an alley. Presently he stood in a windswept open square, quaintly cobblestoned, with a high bank wall on the farther side. This was the end of his quest; for upon the wide, iron-railed, weed-grown plateau which the wall supported—a separate, lesser world raised fully six feet above the surrounding streets—there stood a grim, titan bulk whose identity, despite Blake's new perspective, was beyond dispute.

The vacant church was in a state of great decrepitude. Some of the high stone buttresses had fallen, and several delicate finials lay half lost among the brown, neglected weeds and grasses. The sooty Gothic windows were largely unbroken, though many of the stone mullions were missing. Blake wondered how the obscurely painted panes could have survived so well, in view of the known habits of small boys the world over. The massive doors were intact and tightly closed. Around the top of the bank wall, fully enclosing the grounds, was a rusty iron fence whose gate— at the head of a flight of steps from the square—was visibly padlocked. The path from the gate to the building was completely overgrown. Desolation and decay hung like a pall above the place, and in the birdless eaves and black, ivyless walls Blake felt a touch of the dimly sinister beyond his power to define.

There were very few people in the square, but Blake saw a policeman at the northerly end and approached him with questions about the church. He was a great wholesome Irishman, and it seemed odd that he would do little more than make the sign of the cross and mutter that people never spoke of that building. When Blake pressed him he said very hurriedly that the Italian priests warned everybody against it, vowing that a monstrous evil had once dwelt there and left its mark. He himself had heard dark whispers of it from his father, who recalled certain sounds and rumours from his boyhood.[13]

There had been a bad sect there in the ould days—an outlaw sect that called up awful things from some unknown gulf of night. It had taken a good priest to exorcise what had come, though there did be those who said that merely the light could do it. If Father O'Malley were alive there would be many the thing he could tell. But now there was nothing to do but let it alone. It hurt nobody now, and those that owned it were dead or far away. They had run away like rats after the threatening talk in '77, when people began to mind the way folks vanished now and then in the neighbourhood. Some day the city would step in and take the property for lack of heirs, but little good would come of anybody's touching it. Better it be left alone for the years to topple, lest things be stirred that ought to rest forever in their black abyss.

After the policeman had gone Blake stood staring at the sullen steepled pile. It excited him to find that the structure seemed as sinister to others as to him, and he wondered what grain of truth might lie behind the old tales the bluecoat had repeated. Probably they were mere legends evoked by the evil look of the place, but even so, they were like a strange coming to life of one of his own stories.

The afternoon sun came out from behind dispersing clouds, but seemed unable to light up the stained, sooty walls of the old temple that towered on its high plateau. It was odd that the green of spring had not touched the brown, withered growths in the raised, iron-fenced yard. Blake found himself edging nearer the raised area and examining the bank wall and rusted fence for possible avenues of ingress. There was a terrible lure about the blackened fane which was not to be resisted. The fence had no opening near the steps, but around on the north side were some missing bars. He could go up the steps and walk around on the narrow coping outside the fence till he came to the gap. If the people feared the place so wildly, he would encounter no interference.

He was on the embankment and almost inside the fence before anyone noticed him. Then, looking down, he saw the few people in the square edging away and making the same sign with their right hands that the shopkeeper in the avenue had made. Several windows were slammed down, and a fat woman darted into the street and pulled some small children inside a rickety, unpainted house. The gap in the fence was very easy to pass through, and before long Blake found himself wading amidst the rotting, tangled growths of the deserted yard. Here and there the worn stump of a headstone told him that there had once been burials in this field; but that, he saw, must have been very long ago. The sheer bulk of the church was oppressive now that he was close to it, but he conquered his mood and approached to try the three great doors in the facade. All were securely locked, so he began a circuit of the Cyclopean building in quest of some minor and more penetrable opening. Even then he could not be sure that he wished to enter that haunt of desertion and shadow, yet the pull of its strangeness dragged him on automatically.

A yawning and unprotected cellar window in the rear furnished the needed aperture. Peering in, Blake saw a subterrene gulf of cobwebs and dust faintly litten by the western sun's filtered rays. Debris, old barrels, and ruined boxes and furniture of numerous sorts met his eye, though over everything lay a shroud of dust which softened all sharp outlines. The rusted remains of a hot-air furnace shewed that the building had been used and kept in shape as late as mid-Victorian times.

Acting almost without conscious initiative, Blake crawled through the window and let himself down to the dust-carpeted and debris-strown concrete floor. The vaulted cellar was a vast one, without partitions; and in a corner far to the right, amid dense shadows, he saw a black archway evidently leading upstairs. He felt a peculiar sense of oppression at being actually within the great spectral building, but kept it in check as he cautiously scouted about—finding a still-intact barrel amid the dust, and rolling it over to the open window to provide for his exit. Then, bracing himself, he crossed the wide, cobweb-festooned space toward the arch. Half choked with the omnipresent dust, and covered with ghostly gossamer fibres, he reached and began to climb the worn stone steps which rose into the darkness. He had no light, but groped carefully with his hands. After a sharp turn he felt a closed door ahead, and a little fumbling revealed its ancient latch. It opened inward, and beyond it he saw a dimly illumined corridor lined with worm-eaten panelling.

Once on the ground floor, Blake began exploring in a rapid fashion. All the inner doors were unlocked, so that he freely passed from room to room. The colossal nave was an almost eldritch place with its drifts and mountains of dust over box pews, altar, hourglass pulpit, and sounding-board, and its titanic ropes of cobweb stretching among the pointed arches of the gallery and entwining the clustered Gothic columns. Over all this hushed desolation played a hideous leaden light as the declining afternoon sun sent its rays through the strange, half-blackened panes of the great apsidal windows.

The paintings on those windows were so obscured by soot that Blake could scarcely decipher what they had represented, but from the little he could make out he did not like them. The designs were largely conventional, and his knowledge of obscure symbolism told him much concerning some of the ancient patterns. The few saints depicted bore expressions distinctly open to criticism, while one of the windows seemed to shew merely a dark space with spirals of curious luminosity scattered about in it. Turning away from the windows, Blake noticed that the cobwebbed cross above the altar was not of the ordinary kind, but resembled the primordial ankh or crux ansata of shadowy Egypt.[14]

In a rear vestry room beside the apse Blake found a rotting desk and ceiling-high shelves of mildewed, disintegrating books. Here for the first time he received a positive shock of objective horror, for the titles of those books told him much. They were the black, forbidden things which most sane people have never even heard of, or have heard of only in furtive, timorous whispers; the banned and dreaded repositories of equivocal secrets and immemorial formulae which have trickled down the stream of time from the days of man's youth, and the dim, fabulous days before man was. He had himself read many of them—a Latin version of the abhorred *Necronomicon*, the sinister *Liber Ivonis*, the infamous *Cultes des Goules* of Comte d'Erlette, the *Unaussprechlichen Kulten* of von Junzt, and old Ludvig Prinn's hellish *De Vermis Mysteriis*. But there were others he had known merely by reputation or not at all—the Pnakotic Manuscripts, the *Book of Dzyan*, and a crumbling volume in wholly unidentifiable characters yet with certain symbols and diagrams shudderingly recognisable to the occult student.[15] Clearly, the lingering local rumours had not lied. This place had once been the seat of an evil older than mankind and wider than the known universe.

In the ruined desk was a small leather-bound record-book

filled with entries in some odd cryptographic medium. The manuscript writing consisted of the common traditional symbols used today in astronomy and anciently in alchemy, astrology, and other dubious arts—the devices of the sun, moon, planets, aspects, and zodiacal signs—here massed in solid pages of text, with divisions and paragraphings suggesting that each symbol answered to some alphabetical letter.

In the hope of later solving the cryptogram, Blake bore off this volume in his coat pocket. Many of the great tomes on the shelves fascinated him unutterably, and he felt tempted to borrow them at some later time. He wondered how they could have remained undisturbed so long. Was he the first to conquer the clutching, pervasive fear which had for nearly sixty years protected this deserted place from visitors?

Having now thoroughly explored the ground floor, Blake ploughed again through the dust of the spectral nave to the front vestibule, where he had seen a door and staircase presumably leading up to the blackened tower and steeple—objects so long familiar to him at a distance. The ascent was a choking experience, for dust lay thick, while the spiders had done their worst in this constricted place. The staircase was a spiral with high, narrow wooden treads, and now and then Blake passed a clouded window looking dizzily out over the city. Though he had seen no ropes below, he expected to find a bell or peal of bells in the tower whose narrow, louver-boarded lancet windows his field-glass had studied so often. Here he was doomed to disappointment; for when he attained the top of the stairs he found the tower chamber vacant of chimes, and clearly devoted to vastly different purposes.

The room, about fifteen feet square, was faintly lighted by four lancet windows, one on each side, which were glazed within their screening of decayed louver-boards. These had been further fitted with tight, opaque screens, but the latter were now largely rotted away. In the centre of the dust-laden floor rose a curiously angled stone pillar some four feet in height and two in average diameter, covered on each side with bizarre, crudely incised, and wholly unrecognisable hieroglyphs. On this pillar rested a metal box of peculiarly asymmetrical form; its hinged lid thrown back, and its interior holding what looked beneath the decade-deep dust to be an egg-shaped or irregularly spherical object some four inches through. Around the pillar in a rough circle were seven high-backed Gothic chairs still largely intact, while behind them, ranging along the dark-panelled walls, were seven colossal images of crumbling, black-painted plaster, resembling more than anything else the cryptic carven megaliths of mysterious Easter Island.[16] In one corner of the cobwebbed chamber a ladder was built into the wall, leading up to the closed trap-door of the windowless steeple above.

As Blake grew accustomed to the feeble light he noticed odd bas-reliefs on the strange open box of yellowish metal.[17] Approaching, he tried to clear the dust away with his hands and handkerchief, and saw that the figurings were of a monstrous and utterly alien kind; depicting entities which, though seemingly alive, resembled no known life-form ever evolved on this planet. The four-inch seeming sphere turned out to be a nearly black, red-striated polyhedron with many irregular flat surfaces; either a very remarkable crystal of some sort, or an artificial object of carved and highly polished mineral matter. It did not touch the bottom of the box, but was held suspended by means of a metal band around its centre, with seven queerly designed supports extending horizontally to angles of the box's inner wall near the top. This stone, once exposed, exerted upon Blake an almost alarming fascination. He could scarcely tear his eyes from it, and as he looked at its glistening surfaces he almost fancied it was transparent, with half-formed worlds of wonder within. Into his mind floated pictures of alien orbs with great stone towers, and other orbs with titan mountains and no mark of life, and still remoter spaces where only a stirring in vague blacknesses told of the presence of consciousness and will.

When he did look away, it was to notice a somewhat singular mound of dust in the far corner near the ladder to the steeple. Just why it took his attention he could not tell, but something in its contours carried a message to his unconscious mind. Ploughing toward it, and brushing aside the hanging cobwebs as he went, he began to discern something grim about it. Hand and handkerchief soon revealed the truth, and Blake gasped with a baffling mixture of emotions. It was a human skeleton, and it must have been there for a very long time. The clothing was in shreds, but some buttons and fragments of cloth bespoke a man's grey suit. There were other bits of evidence—shoes, metal clasps, huge buttons for round cuffs, a stickpin of bygone pattern, a reporter's badge with the name of the old *Providence Telegram*,[18] and a crumbling leather pocketbook. Blake examined the latter with care, finding within it several bills of antiquated issue, a celluloid advertising calendar for 1893, some cards with the name "Edwin M. Lillibridge", and a paper covered with pencilled memoranda.

This paper held much of a puzzling nature, and Blake read it carefully at the dim westward window. Its disjointed text included such phrases as the following:

"Prof. Enoch Bowen home from Egypt May 1844—buys old Free-Will Church in July—his archaeological work & studies in occult well known."

"Dr. Drowne of 4th Baptist warns against Starry Wisdom in sermon Dec. 29, 1844."

"Congregation 97 by end of '45."

"1846—3 disappearances—first mention of Shining Trapezohedron."

"7 disappearances 1848—stories of blood sacrifice begin."

"Investigation 1853 comes to nothing—stories of sounds."

"Fr. O'Malley tells of devil-worship with box found in great Egyptian ruins—says they call up something that can't exist in light. Flees a little light, and banished by strong light. Then has to be summoned again. Probably got this from deathbed confession of Francis X. Feeney,[19] who had joined Starry Wisdom in '49. These people say the Shining Trapezohedron shews them heaven & other worlds, & that the Haunter of the Dark tells them secrets in some way."

"Story of Orrin B. Eddy[20] 1857. They call it up by gazing at the crystal, & have a secret language of their own."

"200 or more in cong. 1863, exclusive of men at front."

"Irish boys mob church in 1869 after Patrick Regan's disappearance."

"Veiled article in J. March 14, '72, but people don't talk about it."

"6 disappearances 1876—secret committee calls on Mayor Doyle."[21]

"Action promised Feb. 1877—church closes in April."

"Gang—Federal Hill Boys—threaten Dr. —— and vestrymen in May."

"181 persons leave city before end of '77—mention no names."

"Ghost stories begin around 1880—try to ascertain truth of report that no human being has entered church since 1877."

"Ask Lanigan for photograph of place taken 1851." . . .

Restoring the paper to the pocketbook and placing the latter in his coat, Blake turned to look down at the skeleton in the dust. The implications of the notes were clear, and there could be no doubt but that this man had come to the deserted edifice forty-two years before in quest of a newspaper sensation which no one else had been bold enough to attempt. Perhaps no one else had known of his plan—who could tell? But he had never returned to his paper. Had some bravely suppressed fear risen to overcome him and bring on sudden heart-failure? Blake stooped over the gleaming bones and noted their peculiar state. Some of them were badly scattered, and a few seemed oddly *dissolved* at the ends. Others were strangely yellowed, with vague suggestions of charring. This charring extended to some of the fragments of clothing. The skull was in a very peculiar state—stained yellow, and with a charred aperture in the top as if some powerful acid had eaten through the solid bone. What had happened to the skeleton during its four decades of silent entombment here Blake could not imagine.

Before he realised it, he was looking at the stone again, and letting its curious influence call up a nebulous pageantry in his mind. He saw processions of robed, hooded figures whose outlines were not human, and looked on endless leagues of desert lined with carved, sky-reaching monoliths. He saw towers and walls in nighted depths under the sea, and vortices of space where wisps of black mist floated before thin shimmerings of cold purple haze. And beyond all else he glimpsed an infinite gulf of darkness, where solid and semi-solid forms were known only by their windy stirrings, and cloudy patterns of force seemed to superimpose order on chaos and hold forth a key to all the paradoxes and arcana of the worlds we know.

Then all at once the spell was broken by an access of gnawing, indeterminate panic fear. Blake choked and turned away from the stone, conscious of some formless alien presence close to him and watching him with horrible intentness. He felt entangled with something—something which was not in the stone, but which had looked through it at him—something which would ceaselessly follow him with a cognition that was not physical sight. Plainly, the place was getting on his nerves—as well it might in view of his gruesome find. The light was waning, too, and since he had no illuminant with him he knew he would have to be leaving soon.

It was then, in the gathering twilight, that he thought he saw a faint trace of luminosity in the crazily angled stone. He had tried to look away from it, but some obscure compulsion drew his eyes back. Was there a subtle phosphorescence of radio-activity about the thing? What was it that the dead man's notes had said concerning a *Shining Trapezohedron?* What, anyway, was this abandoned lair of cosmic evil? What had been done here, and what might still be lurking in the bird-shunned shadows? It seemed now as if an elusive touch of foetor had arisen somewhere close by, though its source was not apparent. Blake seized the cover of the long-open box and snapped it down. It moved easily on its alien hinges, and closed completely over the unmistakably glowing stone.

At the sharp click of that closing a soft stirring sound seemed to come from the steeple's eternal blackness overhead, beyond the trap-door. Rats, without question—the only living things to reveal their presence in this accursed pile since he had entered it. And yet that stirring in the steeple frightened him horribly, so that he plunged almost wildly down the spiral stairs, across the ghoulish nave, into the vaulted basement, out amidst the gathering dusk of the deserted square, and down through the teeming, fear-haunted alleys and avenues of Federal Hill toward the sane central streets and the home-like brick sidewalks of the college district.

During the days which followed, Blake told no one of his expedition. Instead, he read much in certain books, examined long years of newspaper files downtown, and worked feverishly at the cryptogram in that leather volume from the cobwebbed vestry room. The cipher, he soon saw, was no simple one; and after a long period of endeavour he felt sure that its language could not be English, Latin, Greek, French, Spanish, Italian, or German. Evidently he would have to draw upon the deepest wells of his strange erudition.

Every evening the old impulse to gaze westward returned, and he saw the black steeple as of yore amongst the bristling roofs of a distant and half-fabulous world. But now it held a fresh note of terror for him. He knew the heritage of evil lore it masked, and with the knowledge his vision ran riot in queer new ways. The birds of spring were returning, and as he watched their sunset flights he fancied they avoided the gaunt, lone spire as never before. When a flock of them approached it, he thought, they would wheel and scatter in panic confusion—and he could guess at the wild twitterings which failed to reach him across the intervening miles.

It was in June that Blake's diary told of his victory over the cryptogram. The text was, he found, in the dark Aklo language[22] used by certain cults of evil antiquity, and known to him in a halting way through previous researches. The diary is strangely reticent about what Blake deciphered, but he was patently awed and disconcerted by his results. There are references to a Haunter of the Dark awaked by gazing into the Shining Trapezohedron, and insane conjectures about the black gulfs of chaos from which it was called. The being is spoken of as holding all knowledge, and demanding monstrous sacrifices. Some of Blake's entries shew fear lest the thing, which he seemed to regard as summoned, stalk abroad; though he adds that the street-lights form a bulwark which cannot be crossed.

Of the Shining Trapezohedron he speaks often, calling it a window on all time and space, and tracing its history from the days it was fashioned on dark Yuggoth, before ever the Old Ones brought it to earth. It was treasured and placed in its curious box by the crinoid things of Antarctica, salvaged from their ruins by the serpent-men of Valusia,[23] and peered at aeons later in

Lemuria by the first human beings. It crossed strange lands and stranger seas, and sank with Atlantis before a Minoan fisher meshed it in his net and sold it to swarthy merchants from nighted Khem.[24] The Pharaoh Nephren-Ka[25] built around it a temple with a windowless crypt, and did that which caused his name to be stricken from all monuments and records. Then it slept in the ruins of that evil fane which the priests and the new Pharaoh destroyed, till the delver's spade once more brought it forth to curse mankind.

Early in July the newspapers oddly supplement Blake's entries, though in so brief and casual a way that only the diary has called general attention to their contribution. It appears that a new fear has been growing on Federal Hill since a stranger had entered the dreaded church. The Italians whispered of unaccustomed stirrings and bumpings and scrapings in the dark windowless steeple, and called on their priests to banish an entity which haunted their dreams. Something, they said, was constantly watching at a door to see if it were dark enough to venture forth. Press items mentioned the long-standing local superstitions, but failed to shed much light on the earlier background of the horror. It was obvious that the young reporters of today are no antiquarians. In writing of these things in his diary, Blake expresses a curious kind of remorse, and talks of the duty of burying the Shining Trapezohedron and of banishing what he had evoked by letting daylight into the hideous spire. At the same time, however, he displays the dangerous extent of his fascination, and admits a morbid longing—pervading even his dreams—to visit the accursed tower and gaze again into the cosmic secrets of the glowing stone.

Then something in the *Journal*[26] on the morning of July 17 threw the diarist into a veritable fever of horror. It was only a variant of the other half-humorous items about the Federal Hill restlessness, but to Blake it was somehow very terrible indeed. In the night a thunderstorm had put the city's lighting-system out of commission for a full hour, and in that black interval the Italians had nearly gone mad with fright.[27] Those living near the dreaded church had sworn that the thing in the steeple had taken advantage of the street-lamps' absence and gone down into the body of the church, flopping and bumping around in a viscous, altogether dreadful way. Toward the last it had bumped up to the tower, where there were sounds of the shattering of glass. It could go wherever the darkness reached, but light would always send it fleeing.

When the current blazed on again there had been a shocking commotion in the tower, for even the feeble light trickling through the grime-blackened, louver-boarded windows was too much for the thing. It had bumped and slithered up into its tene-brous steeple just in time—for a long dose of light would have sent it back into the abyss whence the crazy stranger had called it. During the dark hour praying crowds had clustered round the church in the rain with lighted candles and lamps somehow shielded with folded paper and umbrellas—a guard of light to save the city from the nightmare that stalks in darkness. Once, those nearest the church declared, the outer door had rattled hideously.

But even this was not the worst. That evening in the *Bulletin*[28] Blake read of what the reporters had found. Aroused at last to the whimsical news value of the scare, a pair of them had defied the frantic crowds of Italians and crawled into the church through the cellar window after trying the doors in vain. They found the dust of the vestibule and of the spectral nave ploughed up in a singular way, with pits of rotted cushions and satin pew-linings scattered curiously around. There was a bad odour every-where, and here and there were bits of yellow stain and patches of what looked like charring. Opening the door to the tower, and pausing a moment at the suspicion of a scraping sound above, they found the narrow spiral stairs wiped roughly clean.

In the tower itself a similarly half-swept condition existed. They spoke of the heptagonal stone pillar, the overturned Gothic chairs, and the bizarre plaster images; though strangely enough the metal box and the old mutilated skeleton were not mentioned. What disturbed Blake the most—except for the hints of stains and charring and bad odours—was the final detail that explained the crashing glass. Every one of the tower's lancet windows was bro-ken, and two of them had been darkened in a crude and hurried way by the stuffing of satin pew-linings and cushion-horsehair into the spaces between the slanting exterior louver-boards. More satin fragments and bunches of horsehair lay scattered around the newly swept floor, as if someone had been interrupted in the act of restoring the tower to the absolute blackness of its tightly curtained days.

Yellowish stains and charred patches were found on the ladder to the windowless spire, but when a reporter climbed up, opened the horizontally sliding trap-door, and shot a feeble flashlight beam into the black and strangely foetid space, he saw nothing but darkness, and an heterogeneous litter of shapeless fragments near the aperture. The verdict, of course, was charlatanry. Somebody had played a joke on the superstitious hill-dwellers, or else some fanatic had striven to bolster up their fears for their own supposed good. Or perhaps some of the younger and more sophisticated dwellers had staged an elaborate hoax on the outside world. There was an amusing aftermath when the police sent an officer to verify the reports. Three men in succession found ways of evading the assignment, and the fourth went very reluctantly and returned very soon without adding to the account given by the reporters.

From this point onward Blake's diary shews a mounting tide of insidious horror and nervous apprehension. He upbraids himself for not doing something, and speculates wildly on the consequences of another electrical breakdown. It has been verified that on three occasions—during thunderstorms—he telephoned the electric light company in a frantic vein and asked that desperate precautions against a lapse of power be taken. Now and then his entries shew concern over the failure of the reporters to find the metal box and stone, and the strangely marred old skeleton, when they explored the shadowy tower room. He assumed that these things had been removed—whither, and by whom or what, he could only guess. But his worst fears concerned himself, and the kind of unholy rapport he felt to exist between his mind and that lurking horror in the distant steeple—that monstrous thing of night which his rashness had called out of the ultimate black spaces. He seemed to feel a constant tugging at his will, and callers of that period remember how he would sit abstractedly at his desk and stare out of the west window at that far-off, spire-

bristling mound beyond the swirling smoke of the city. His entries dwell monotonously on certain terrible dreams, and of a
strengthening of the unholy rapport in his sleep. There is mention of a night when he awaked to find himself fully dressed, outdoors, and headed automatically down College Hill toward the
west. Again and again he dwells on the fact that the thing in the
steeple knows where to find him.

The week following July 30 is recalled as the time of Blake's
partial breakdown. He did not dress, and ordered all his food by
telephone. Visitors remarked the cords he kept near his bed, and
he said that sleep-walking had forced him to bind his ankles
every night with knots which would probably hold or else
waken him with the labour of untying.

In his diary he told of the hideous experience which had
brought the collapse. After retiring on the night of the 30th he
had suddenly found himself groping about in an almost black
space. All he could see were short, faint, horizontal streaks of
bluish light, but he could smell an overpowering foetor and hear
a curious jumble of soft, furtive sounds above him. Whenever he
moved he stumbled over something, and at each noise there
would come a sort of answering sound from above—a vague stirring, mixed with the cautious sliding of wood on wood.

Once his groping hands encountered a pillar of stone with a
vacant top, whilst later he found himself clutching the rungs of a
ladder built into the wall, and fumbling his uncertain way upward toward some region of intenser stench where a hot, searing
blast beat down against him. Before his eyes a kaleidoscopic
range of phantasmal images played, all of them dissolving at intervals into the picture of a vast, unplumbed abyss of night
wherein whirled suns and worlds of an even profounder blackness. He thought of the ancient legends of Ultimate Chaos, at
whose centre sprawls the blind idiot god Azathoth, Lord of All
Things, encircled by his flopping horde of mindless and amorphous dancers, and lulled by the thin monotonous piping of a
daemoniac flute held in nameless paws.[29]

Then a sharp report from the outer world broke through his
stupor and roused him to the unutterable horror of his position. What it was, he never knew—perhaps it was some belated

peal from the fireworks heard all summer on Federal Hill as the dwellers hail their various patron saints, or the saints of their native villages in Italy. In any event he shrieked aloud, dropped frantically from the ladder, and stumbled blindly across the obstructed floor of the almost lightless chamber that encompassed him.

He knew instantly where he was, and plunged recklessly down the narrow spiral staircase, tripping and bruising himself at every turn. There was a nightmare flight through a vast cobwebbed nave whose ghostly arches reached up to realms of leering shadow, a sightless scramble through a littered basement, a climb to regions of air and street-lights outside, and a mad racing down a spectral hill of gibbering gables, across a grim, silent city of tall black towers, and up the steep eastward precipice to his own ancient door.

On regaining consciousness in the morning he found himself lying on his study floor fully dressed. Dirt and cobwebs covered him, and every inch of his body seemed sore and bruised. When he faced the mirror he saw that his hair was badly scorched, while a trace of strange, evil odour seemed to cling to his upper outer clothing. It was then that his nerves broke down. Thereafter, lounging exhaustedly about in a dressing-gown, he did little but stare from his west window, shiver at the threat of thunder, and make wild entries in his diary.

The great storm broke just before midnight on August 8th. Lightning struck repeatedly in all parts of the city, and two remarkable fireballs were reported. The rain was torrential, while a constant fusillade of thunder brought sleeplessness to thousands. Blake was utterly frantic in his fear for the lighting system, and tried to telephone the company around 1 a.m., though by that time service had been temporarily cut off in the interest of safety. He recorded everything in his diary—the large, nervous, and often undecipherable hieroglyphs telling their own story of growing frenzy and despair, and of entries scrawled blindly in the dark.

He had to keep the house dark in order to see out the window, and it appears that most of his time was spent at his desk, peering anxiously through the rain across the glistening miles of downtown roofs at the constellation of distant lights marking Federal Hill. Now and then he would fumblingly make an entry in his diary, so that detached phrases such as "The lights must not go"; "It knows where I am"; "I must destroy it"; and "It is calling to me, but perhaps it means no injury this time"; are found scattered down two of the pages.

Then the lights went out all over the city. It happened at 2:12 a.m., according to power-house records, but Blake's diary gives no indication of the time. The entry is merely, "Lights out—God help me." On Federal Hill there were watchers as anxious as he, and rain-soaked knots of men paraded the square and alleys around the evil church with umbrella-shaded candles, electric flashlights, oil lanterns, crucifixes, and obscure charms of the many sorts common in southern Italy. They blessed each flash of lightning, and made cryptical signs of fear with their right hands when a turn in the storm caused the flashes to lessen and finally to cease altogether. A rising wind blew out most of the candles, so that the scene grew threateningly dark. Someone roused Father Merluzzo of Spirito Santo Church,[30] and he hastened to the dismal square to pronounce whatever helpful syllables he could. Of the restless and curious sounds in the blackened tower, there could be no doubt whatever.

For what happened at 2:35 we have the testimony of the priest, a young, intelligent, and well-educated person; of Patrolman William J. Monahan of the Central Station, an officer of the highest reliability who had paused at that part of his beat to inspect the crowd; and of most of the seventy-eight men who had gathered around the church's high bank wall—especially those in the square where the eastward facade was visible. Of course there was nothing which can be proved as being outside the order of Nature. The possible causes of such an event are many. No one can speak with certainty of the obscure chemical processes arising in a vast, ancient, ill-aired, and long-deserted building of heterogeneous contents. Mephitic vapours—spontaneous combustion—pressure of gases born of long decay—any one of numberless phenomena might be responsible. And then, of course, the factor of conscious charlatanry can by no means be excluded. The thing was really quite simple in itself, and covered less than three minutes of actual time. Father Merluzzo, always a precise man, looked at his watch repeatedly.

It started with a definite swelling of the dull fumbling sounds inside the black tower. There had for some time been a vague ex- halation of strange, evil odours from the church, and this had now become emphatic and offensive. Then at last there was a sound of splintering wood, and a large, heavy object crashed down in the yard beneath the frowning easterly facade. The tower was invisible now that the candles would not burn, but as the object neared the ground the people knew that it was the smoke-grimed louver-boarding of the tower's east window.

Immediately afterward an utterly unbearable foetor welled forth from the unseen heights, choking and sickening the trem- bling watchers, and almost prostrating those in the square. At the same time the air trembled with a vibration as of flapping wings, and a sudden east-blowing wind more violent than any previous blast snatched off the hats and wrenched the dripping umbrellas of the crowd. Nothing definite could be seen in the candleless night, though some upward-looking spectators thought they glimpsed a great spreading blur of denser blackness against the inky sky—something like a formless cloud of smoke that shot with meteor-like speed toward the east.

That was all. The watchers were half numbed with fright, awe, and discomfort, and scarcely knew what to do, or whether to do anything at all. Not knowing what had happened, they did not relax their vigil; and a moment later they sent up a prayer as a sharp flash of belated lightning, followed by an earsplitting crash of sound, rent the flooded heavens. Half an hour later the rain stopped, and in fifteen minutes more the street-lights sprang on again, sending the weary, bedraggled watchers relievedly back to their homes.

The next day's papers gave these matters minor mention in connexion with the general storm reports. It seems that the great lightning flash and deafening explosion which followed the Fed- eral Hill occurrence were even more tremendous farther east, where a burst of the singular foetor was likewise noticed. The phenomenon was most marked over College Hill, where the crash awaked all the sleeping inhabitants and led to a bewildered round of speculations. Of those who were already awake only a few saw the anomalous blaze of light near the top of the hill, or noticed the inexplicable upward rush of air which almost stripped the leaves from the tees and blasted the plants in the gardens. It was agreed that the lone, sudden lightning-bolt must have struck somewhere in this neighbourhood, though no trace of its striking could afterward be found. A youth in the Tau Omega fraternity house thought he saw a grotesque and hideous mass of smoke in the air just as the preliminary flash burst, but his observation has not been verified. All of the few observers, however, agree as to the violent gust from the west and the flood of intolerable stench which preceded the belated stroke; whilst evidence concerning the momentary burned odour after the stroke is equally general.

These points were discussed very carefully because of their probable connexion with the death of Robert Blake. Students in the Psi Delta house, whose upper rear windows looked into Blake's study,[31] noticed the blurred white face at the westward window on the morning of the 9th, and wondered what was wrong with the expression. When they saw the same face in the same position that evening, they felt worried, and watched for the lights to come up in his apartment. Later they rang the bell of the darkened flat, and finally had a policeman force the door.

The rigid body sat bolt upright at the desk by the window, and when the intruders saw the glassy, bulging eyes, and the marks of stark, convulsive fright on the twisted features, they turned away in sickened dismay. Shortly afterward the coroner's physician made an examination, and despite the unbroken window reported electrical shock, or nervous tension induced by electrical discharge, as the cause of death. The hideous expression he ignored altogether, deeming it a not improbable result of the profound shock as experienced by a person of such abnormal imagination and unbalanced emotions. He deduced these latter qualities from books, paintings, and manuscripts found in the apartment, and from the blindly scrawled entries in the diary on the desk. Blake had prolonged his frenzied jottings to the last, and the broken-pointed pencil was found clutched in his spasmodically contracted right hand.

The entries after the failure of the lights were highly disjointed, and legible only in part. From them certain investigators have drawn conclusions differing greatly from the materialistic official verdict, but such speculations have little chance for belief among the conservative. The case of these imaginative theorists has not been helped by the action of superstitious Dr. Dexter, who threw the curious box and angled stone—an object certainly self-luminous as seen in the black windowless steeple where it was found—into the deepest channel of Narragansett Bay. Excessive imagination and neurotic unbalance on Blake's part, aggravated by knowledge of the evil bygone cult whose startling traces he had uncovered, form the dominant interpretation given those final frenzied jottings. These are the entries—or all that can be made of them.

"Lights still out—must be five minutes now. Everything depends on lightning. Yaddith[32] grant it will keep up! . . . Some influence seems beating through it. . . . Rain and thunder and wind deafen. . . . The thing is taking hold of my mind. . . .

"Trouble with memory. I see things I never knew before. Other worlds and other galaxies . . . Dark. . . . The lightning seems dark and the darkness seems light. . . .

"It cannot be the real hill and church that I see in the pitch-darkness. Must be retinal impression left by flashes. Heaven grant the Italians are out with their candles if the lightning stops!

"What am I afraid of? Is it not an avatar of Nyarlathotep, who in antique and shadowy Khem even took the form of man? I remember Yuggoth, and more distant Shaggai, and the ultimate void of the black planets. . . .

"The long, winging flight through the void . . . cannot cross the universe of light . . . re-created by the thoughts caught in the Shining Trapezohedron . . . send it through the horrible abysses of radiance. . . .

"My name is Blake—Robert Harrison Blake of 620 East Knapp Street, Milwaukee, Wisconsin. . . . I am on this planet. . . .

"Azathoth have mercy!—the lightning no longer flashes—horrible—I can see everything with a monstrous sense that is not sight—light is dark and dark is light . . . those people on the hill . . . guard . . . candles and charms . . . their priests. . . .

"Sense of distance gone—far is near and near is far. No light—

no glass—see that steeple—that tower—window—can hear—
Roderick Usher[33]—am mad or going mad—the thing is stirring
and fumbling in the tower—I am it and it is I—I want to get out
. . . must get out and unify the forces. . . . It knows where I am. . . .

   "I am Robert Blake, but I see the tower in the dark. There is a
monstrous odour . . . senses transfigured . . . boarding at that tower
window cracking and giving way. . . . Iä . . . . ngai . . . ygg. . . .

   "I see it—coming here—hell-wind—titan blur—black wings—
Yog-Sothoth save me—the three-lobed burning eye. . . ."

EXPLANATORY NOTES

ABBREVIATIONS:

AT = *The Ancient Track: Complete Poetical Works* (Necronomicon Press, 1999)

D = *Dagon and Other Macabre Tales* (Arkham House, 1986)

DH = *The Dunwich Horror and Others* (Arkham House, 1984)

HM = *The Horror in the Museum and Other Revisions* (Arkham House, 1989)

JHL = John Hay Library, Brown University (Providence, RI)

Life = S. T. Joshi, *H. P. Lovecraft: A Life* (Necronomicon Press, 1996)

MM = *At the Mountains of Madness and Other Novels* (Arkham House, 1985)

MW = *Miscellaneous Writings* (Arkham House, 1995)

OED = *Oxford English Dictionary* (1933 ed.)

SL = *Selected Letters* (Arkham House, 1965–76; 5 vols.)

INTRODUCTION

1. W. Paul Cook, *In Memoriam: Howard Phillips Lovecraft* (North Montpelier, VT: Driftwind Press, 1941), p. 15; quoted in *Life* 397.

DAGON

"Dagon" was written in the summer of 1917, shortly after the writing of "The Tomb"; these two stories constituted the first fiction Lovecraft had written since his abandonment of story writing in 1908. The tale was first published in W. Paul Cook's amateur journal, the *Vagrant*, for November 1919. Its publication in *Weird Tales* for October 1923 constituted Lovecraft's first appearance in that legendary pulp magazine.

Lovecraft notes that "Dagon" was at least in part inspired by a dream. John Ravenor Bullen, a member of the Transatlantic Circulator (an Anglo-American group of amateur journalists who exchanged and criticized one another's manuscripts), noted: "We are told that [the narrator] crawled into the stranded boat (which lay grounded some distance away). Could he, half-sucked into mire, crawl to his boat?" Lovecraft responded: ". . . the hero-victim is half-sucked into the mire, yet he *does* crawl! He pulls himself along in the detestable ooze, tenaciously though it cling to him. I know, for I dreamed that whole hideous crawl, and can yet feel the ooze sucking me down!" ("In Defence of Dagon" [1921]; MW 150).

There may also be contemporary literary influences on the story. William Fulwiler is probably correct in sensing the general influence of Irvin S. Cobb's "Fishhead"—a tale of a loathsome fishlike human being who haunts an isolated lake, and a tale that Lovecraft praised in a letter to the editor when it appeared in the *Argosy* on January 11, 1913—although that story's influence on a later work, "The Shadow over Innsmouth," is still more evident.

Further Reading
William Fulwiler, "'The Tomb' and 'Dagon': A Double Dissection,"
Crypt of Cthulhu No. 38 (Eastertide 1986): 8–14.

1. A reference to such incidents as the sinking of the *Lusitania* by a German submarine on May 7, 1915; 1,200 people, including 128 Americans, died. Lovecraft condemned the act in the poem "The Crime of Crimes" (*Interesting Items*, July 1915).

2. This detail would have been particularly sensitive to Lovecraft, who throughout his life exhibited a violent dislike of seafood. Cf. a passage later in the story: "The odour of the fish was maddening . . ."

3. This incident was evidently the kernel of the dream on which the story was based (see introductory note).

4. The reference is to John Milton's *Paradise Lost* (1667), 2:871–1055, when Satan determines to leave Hell and ascend to the newly fashioned Earth.

5. John Ravenor Bullen of the Transatlantic Circulator had expressed doubt as to the propriety of the word "scientist," regarding it as a neologism. Although Lovecraft did not change the text here, he later used the more standard term "man of science" in other stories. Cf. *At the Mountains of Madness* (1931): "I am forced into speech because men of science have refused to follow my advice without knowing why" (MM 3).

6. *Cyclopean*: An ancient style of masonry in which stones of immense size were used. The term is derived from the Greeks' belief that such structures were the work of a race of giants called the Cyclopes.

7. Gustave Doré (1832–1883), French painter and illustrator. Lovecraft saw his illustrations to *Paradise Lost* (1866), *The Divine Comedy* (1861–68), and Coleridge's *Rime of the Ancient Mariner* (1876) as a boy; they had much to do with his early interest in weird fiction. Cf. "Pickman's Model" (1926), in reference to the masters of fantastic art: "There's something those fellows catch—beyond life—that they're able to make us catch for a second. Doré had it. . . . And Pickman had it as no man ever had it before or—I hope to heaven—ever will again" (DH 13).

8. American short story writer Edgar Allan Poe (1809–1849) was the chief literary influence upon Lovecraft, who discovered him at the age of eight. British novelist Edward Bulwer-Lytton (1803–1873) is most noted for *The Last Days of Pompeii* (1834), but he also wrote the classic haunted house tale "The Haunted and the Haunters; or, The House and the Brain" (1859) as well as the weird novels *Zanoni* (1842) and *A Strange Story* (1862).

9. Lovecraft mentions the Piltdown man in several tales. This hoax was perpetrated in 1912, when a human brain case very similar to that of a modern human being, juxtaposed to a jawbone resembling an ape's, was found near the town of Piltdown, in the south of England. The hoax was exploded only in 1953. There is still debate as to its originator.

10. The name of the Cyclops in Homer's *Odyssey* is Polyphemus. Cf. the description of Cthulhu in "The Call of Cthulhu" (1926): ". . . on the masonry of that charnel shore that was not of earth the titan Thing from the stars slavered and gibbered like Polypheme cursing the fleeing ship of

Odysseus. Then, bolder than the storied Cyclops, great Cthulhu slid greasily into the water . . ." (p. 170).

11. Dagon or Dagan was the chief god of the Philistines, borrowed by them from the Canaanites. It was not a fish god, but more likely a weather god or vegetation deity. Early biblical scholars wrongly assumed that the name coincided with the Semitic *dag on* ("fish of sadness"). In Judges 16:23–31 Samson overthrows the Temple of Dagon at Gaza.

12. Cf. "The Call of Cthulhu": "Loathsomeness waits and dreams in the deep, and decay spreads over the tottering cities of men" (p. 171).

THE STATEMENT OF RANDOLPH CARTER

"The Statement of Randolph Carter" was written in late December 1919 and first published in W. Paul Cook's *Vagrant* for May 1920. Its first professional magazine appearance was in *Weird Tales* for February 1925.

It is well known that this story is—or was claimed by Lovecraft to be—an almost literal transcript of a dream Lovecraft had, probably in early December 1919, in which he and Samuel Loveman (1887–1976) make a fateful trip to an ancient cemetery and Loveman suffers some horrible but mysterious fate after he descends alone into a crypt. The story purports to be a kind of affidavit given to the police by Randolph Carter (Lovecraft) concerning the disappearance of Harley Warren (Loveman).

The tale is manifestly based upon a letter to the Gallomo (a correspondence cycle among Alfred Galpin, Lovecraft, and Maurice W. Moe) of December 11, 1919, in which Lovecraft recounts the dream; it is evident that Lovecraft in the letter has already begun to fashion the dream creatively so that it results in an effective and suspenseful narrative.

Aside from the obvious change of character names, there appears to be another significant change between the letter and the story—the locale. Both the letter and the story are vague as to the actual location of the events of the narrative. In the letter Lovecraft suggests, but does not explicitly declare, that the dream occurred in some old New England cemetery: writing to two Midwesterners, Lovecraft states, "I suppose no Wisconsinite can picture such a thing—but we have them in New-England; horrible old places where the slate stones are graven with odd letters and grotesque designs such as a skull and crossbones" (SL I.94). In the story mention is made of the "Gainsville [*sic*] pike" and "Big Cypress Swamp"; these are the only topographical sites mentioned in the story. It appears that Lovecraft has misspelled the name of the well-known city of Gainesville, Florida; moreover, cypress swamps are certainly more common in the South than in New England. If we may draw upon evidence of later stories, we can note that in "The Silver Key" (1926) Harley Warren is referred to as "a man in the South," while in "Through the Gates of the Silver Key" (1932–33) he is mentioned as a "South Carolina mystic." Loveman had for part of the war been stationed at Camp Gordon, Georgia, so perhaps he described certain features of the local terrain to Lovecraft in letters.

1. *the illusion you call justice*: A reflection of Lovecraft's adoption of Nietzsche's cynical view of abstract ethical precepts. "As the savage progresses, he acquires experience and formulates codes of 'right' and 'wrong' from his memories of those courses which have helped or hurt him. . . . Then out of the principle of barter comes the illusion of 'justice' . . . " ("In Defence of Dagon"; MW 165). The view is derived from Nietzsche's *On the Genealogy of Morals* (1887).

2. "Personally I should not care for immortality in the least. There is nothing better than oblivion, since in oblivion there is no wish unfulfilled" ("In Defence of Dagon"; MW 166). This is the burden of the prose-poem "Ex Oblivione" (1921).

3. The reading in Lovecraft's typescript is "Gainsville"; but this is apparently an error, as he is presumably referring to the city in Florida (see introductory note).

4. This is one of the first instances of the "mythical book" topos in Lovecraft. The book in question is clearly not the *Necronomicon* (for which see n. 7 to "The Hound"), since that book exists in Arabic, Greek, Latin, and English, and the narrator is clearly familiar with these languages.

   In the present instance, the conception (in the dream, at any rate) was apparently inspired by Samuel Loveman's extensive collection of rare and obscure volumes: "All that I recall is that we were following up some idea which Loveman had gained as the result of extensive reading in some rare old books, of which he possessed the only existing copies. (Loveman, you may know, has a vast library of rare first editions and other treasures precious to the bibliophile's heart.)" (SL I.95).

5. At this point in the dream, Loveman says to Lovecraft: "At any rate, this is no place for anybody who can't pass an army physical examination" (SL I.95)—a telling reference to Lovecraft's rejection on physical grounds of his attempt to enlist in the Rhode Island National Guard (and, later, the U.S. Army) upon the United States' declaration of war against Germany in May 1917 (see SL I.45–49).

6. In the dream Loveman threatened to "call the thing off and get another fellow-explorer—he mentioned a 'Dr. Burke,' a name altogether unfamiliar to me" (SL I.96).

7. In the dream Loveman utters a prefatory remark: "Lovecraft—I think I'm finding it—" (SL I.96).

8. In the dream Loveman says: "I can't tell you—I don't dare—I never dreamed of *this*—I can't tell— It's enough to unseat any mind—wait— What's this?" (SL I.96).

FACTS CONCERNING THE LATE ARTHUR JERMYN AND HIS FAMILY

This story first appeared in the amateur journal, the *Wolverine* (edited by Horace L. Lawson), for March and June 1921; this was the only time until recent corrected editions that the full title of the story was printed. When it appeared in *Weird Tales* for April 1924 the editor, Edwin Baird, gave it the title "The White Ape," much to Lovecraft's disgust; in the *Weird Tales* reprint of May 1935 it was titled simply "Arthur Jermyn."

This seemingly straightforward story of an explorer, Sir Wade Jermyn, who marries an ape-goddess, and whose offspring bear the physical and mental stigmata of the unnatural union, appears more complicated than it seems. The resounding opening utterance, one of the most celebrated passages in Lovecraft's fiction, contains one curious phrase: "Science . . . will perhaps be the ultimate exterminator of our human species—if separate species we be . . ." That last clause is critical: this *generalized* statement concerning the possibility that human beings may not be entirely "human" is not logically deducible from a *single* case of miscegenation. What Lovecraft appears to be suggesting is that the inhabitants of the primeval African city of "white apes" are not only the "missing link" between ape and human but also *the ultimate source for all white civilization*. The entire white race is derived from this primal race in Africa, a race that had corrupted itself by intermingling with apes. This is the only explanation for the narrator's opening statement, "If we knew what we are, we should do as Sir Arthur Jermyn did [i.e., commit suicide]": we may not have a white ape in our immediate ancestry, but we are all the products of an ultimate miscegenation.

Lovecraft makes a suggestive remark on the literary inspiration for this tale, in a letter to Edwin Baird published in *Weird Tales* for March 1924:

> [The] origin [of "Arthur Jermyn"] is rather curious—and far removed from the atmosphere it suggests. Somebody had been harassing me into reading some work of the iconoclastic moderns—these young chaps why pry behind exteriors and unveil nasty hidden motives and secret stigmata—and I had nearly fallen asleep over the tame backstairs gossip of Anderson's *Winesburg, Ohio*. The sainted Sherwood, as you know, laid bare the dark area which many whited village lives concealed, and it occurred to me that I, in my weirder medium, could probably devise some secret behind a man's ancestry which would make the worst of Anderson's disclosures sound like the annual report of a Sabbath school. Hence Arthur Jermyn. (MW 508)

It is one in which the few instances in which a contemporary work of mainstream literature had even an indirect influence on Lovecraft's fiction.

Several provocative details in the story make it evident that Lovecraft was portraying himself and his family situation in his characterization of Arthur Jermyn.

Further Reading
S. T. Joshi, "What Happens in 'Arthur Jermyn,'" *Crypt of Cthulhu* No. 75 (Michaelmas 1990): 27–28.

1. Compare the more refined expression of these same conceptions in the opening paragraph of "The Call of Cthulhu" (p. 141). Cf. also a com-

ment in a letter of 1916: "To the scientist there is the joy in pursuing truth which nearly counteracts the depressing revelations of truth" (SL I.27).

2. Jermyn is an actual aristocratic family in England. Henry Jermyn's allegiance to the monarchy caused him to be named the first Baron Jermyn in 1643; in 1660 he became the first Earl of St. Albans.

3. For the possible autobiographical significance of this description see Clara Hess's memoir of Lovecraft and his mother, in which she remarks that "Mrs. Lovecraft talked continuously of her unfortunate son who was so hideous that he hid from everyone and did not like to walk upon the streets where people could gaze at him" (cited in *Life* 85).

4. There was no insane asylum in the town of Huntingdon (the county seat of the former county of Huntingdonshire, now merged with Cambridgeshire) at this time.

5. The reference is the the *Naturalis Historia* of Pliny the Elder (23–79 CE), an immense compilation of scientific information and misinformation.

6. I.e., American War of Independence (1775–83).

7. The description is somewhat reminiscent of Lovecraft's later conception of the god Nyarlathotep: "Then down the wide lane betwixt the two columns a lone figure strode; a tall, slim figure with the young face of an antique Pharaoh, gay with prismatic robes and crowned with a golden pshent that glowed with inherent light" (*The Dream-Quest of Unknown Kadath* [1926–27]; MM 398).

8. *Onga tribes*: mythical.

9. Lovecraft's mother was born on October 17, 1857.

10. As Kenneth W. Faig has pointed out, this description corresponds with Lovecraft's conception of the confinement of his father Winfield in Butler Hospital in 1893–98: "In April, 1893, my father was stricken with a complete paralysis resulting from a brain overtaxed with study & business cares. He lived for five years at a hospital, but was never again able to move hand or foot, or to utter a sound" (SL I.33). In fact, Winfield had paresis (i.e., syphilis), and was not paralyzed at all; and there are frequent reports of his loud shoutings (see *Life* 14–15). But since Lovecraft evidently never saw his father in the hospital, he was perhaps told that Winfield had "paralysis" and therefore could not be seen.

11. Note that it was in Chicago where Lovecraft's father had the nervous breakdown that led to his confinement at Butler Hospital.

12. In 1881 P. T. Barnum (1810–1891), who had operated a succession of circuses and freak shows since 1835, teamed up with J. A. Bailey (1847–1906) to establish the Barnum & Bailey Circus, calling it "The Greatest Show on Earth."

13. This series of events is roughly paralleled by the return of Lovecraft and his mother to the family home in Providence in 1893 after his father's breakdown.

14. Lovecraft himself was greatly attached to his birthplace, 454 Angell Street in Providence: "I can yet see the great glass chandeliers, & the ornate newel-post cluster with blue porcelain trimmings, which adorned

the spacious rooms & hallways of [the] house where I was born & lived the first fourteen years of my life" (Lovecraft to Donald Wandrei, 21 April 1927; ms., JHL). He claimed that he seriously contemplated suicide when his family was forced by economic necessity to move out of the house and into smaller quarters in 1904 (see SL IV.357–60).

15. *Kaliri country*: mythical.
16. *N'bangus*: mythical.
17. The agent is Belgian because Leopold II of Belgium had established the Congo Free State in 1885, chiefly as a financial venture. International criticism over the exploitation of the region led to its becoming a Belgian colony in 1908. Its independence was achieved in 1960, and it is now called Zaire.
18. Albert I (1875–1934), King of Belgium from 1909 to 1934. He visited the Congo in 1909.
19. Properly, the Royal Anthropological Institute of Great Britain and Ireland, founded in 1871.

CELEPHAÏS

"Celephaïs" was written in early November 1920, but it did not appear in print until Sonia H. Greene published it in her amateur journal, the *Rainbow*, for May 1922. It then appeared in the semi-pro magazine *Marvel Tales* (edited by William L. Crawford) for May 1934 and posthumously in *Weird Tales* for June–July 1939.

Lovecraft indicates that the story was ultimately based upon an entry in his commonplace book reading simply: "Dream of flying over city" (MW 87). Another entry in the commonplace book was perhaps also an inspiration: "Man journeys into the past—or imaginative realm—leaving bodily shell behind" (MW 88).

But if we are to seek a literary inspiration for "Celephaïs," we need not look far; for the tale is surprisingly similar in conception to Lord Dunsany's "The Coronation of Mr. Thomas Shap," in *The Book of Wonder* (1912). In this story a businessman imagines himself the King of Larkar, and as he continues to dwell obsessively on (and in) this imaginary realm his work in the real world suffers, until finally he is placed in a madhouse.

"Celephaïs" gains added importance for the contrast it provides to a much later work that is only superficially in the Dunsanian vein, *The Dream-Quest of Unknown Kadath*. This novel, written after Lovecraft's New York "exile" of 1924–26, exhibits a marked, almost antipodal, alteration in his aesthetic of beauty, and when Kuranes reappears in it he and his imagined realm take on a very different cast. We are now told that Kuranes "could no more find content in those places [of his imagination], but had formed a mighty longing for the English cliffs and downlands of his boyhood" (MM 354). Just as Lovecraft felt the need to return to his New England roots after two years in New York, so too does Randolph Carter in the novel find that the "sunset city" of his dreams is nothing more than the memories of his boyhood in Boston. Both Lovecraft and his imagination had come home.

1. Two years after writing this story, Lovecraft first enunciated a theory of aesthetics that took cognizance of the artistic changes being wrought by the radical increase of knowledge in his time: "Art has been wrecked by a complete consciousness of the universe which shews that the world is to each man only a rubbish-heap limned by his individual perception. It will be saved, if at all, by the next and last step of disillusion; the realisation that complete consciousness and truth are themselves valueless, and that to acquire any genuine artistic titillation we must artificially invent limitations of consciousness and feign a pattern of life common to all mankind—most naturally the simple old pattern which ancient and groping tradition first gave us" ("Lord Dunsany and His Work" [1922]; MW 110). Throughout his life Lovecraft scorned mundane realism and adhered to Oscar Wilde's dictum: "The artist is the creator of beautiful things."

2. Recall Nyarlathotep's words to Randolph Carter, who had been seeking a magical "sunset city" of his dreams: "For know you, that your gold and marble city of wonder is only the sum of what you have seen and loved in youth" (The Dream-Quest of Unknown Kadath; MM 400).

3. Lovecraft evidently believed "Aran" to be his own coinage and was unaware of the Aran Islands off the western coast of Ireland (the setting of J. M. Synge's play Riders to the Sea [1904]).

4. A frequent notion in Lovecraft. Cf. "The White Ship" (1919): "In the land of Sona-Nyl there is neither time nor space, neither suffering nor death; and there I dwelt for many aeons" (D 39). In "The Dreams in the Witch House" (1932) the idea is given a pseudo-scientific basis: "Time could not exist in certain belts of space, and by entering and remaining in such a belt one might preserve one's life and age infinitely; never suffering organic metabolism or deterioration except for slight amounts incurred during visits to one's own or similar planes" (MM 285–86). The conception is probably derived from Lord Dunsany; cf. a comment of an inhabitant of Astahahn, in "Idle Days on the Yann": "Here we have fettered and manacled Time, who would otherwise slay the gods." A Dreamer's Tales and Other Stories (New York: Modern Library, 1918), p. 40.

5. Leng, first mentioned here, reappears in many of Lovecraft's tales. In "The Hound" (1922) it is transferred to the real world, in "Central Asia" (see p. 86); in The Dream-Quest of Unknown Kadath it returns to dreamland; and in At the Mountains of Madness (1931) it is identified with the immense mountain range in Antarctica: "Of all existing lands it was infinitely the most ancient; and the conviction grew upon us that this hideous upland must indeed be the fabled nightmare plateau of Leng which even the mad author of the Necronomicon was reluctant to discuss" (MM 70).

6. Cf. a philosophical comment in 1916: "How do we know that that form of atomic and molecular motion called 'life' is the highest of all forms? Perhaps the dominant creature—the most rational and God-like of all beings—is an invisible gas!" (SL I.24).

7. The image is probably borrowed from the climactic scene in Ambrose Bierce's "A Horseman in the Sky" (in *Tales of Soldiers and Civilians* [1891]): "Lifting his eyes to the dizzy altitude of [the cliff's] summit the officer saw an astonishing sight—a man on horseback riding down into the valley through the air! Straight upright sat the rider, in military fashion, with a firm seat in the saddle, a strong clutch upon the reign to hold his charger from too impetuous a plunge. From his bare head his long hair streamed upward, waving like a plume." Lovecraft had first read Bierce only a year before writing "Celephaïs."

8. Later transferred to New England; see n. 1 to "The Shadow over Innsmouth."

NYARLATHOTEP

"Nyarlathotep" is another story based upon a dream: Lovecraft dramatically remarks that he wrote the first paragraph (meaning, presumably, the lengthy second paragraph, following the fragmentary utterances in the first paragraph) *"before I fully awaked"* (SL I.160). (The letter to Rheinhart Kleiner of December 14, 1920, containing this remark has been misdated in *Selected Letters* to December 14, 1921.) It was first published in the *United Amateur* for November 1920; but that amateur journal (then being edited by Lovecraft) was at this time habitually late and probably appeared only in early 1921. The story was never professionally published in Lovecraft's lifetime.

The dream inspiring the tale again involved Samuel Loveman. Lovecraft notes that the peculiar name Nyarlathotep came to him in the dream, but one can conjecture at least a partial influence in two names found in Lord Dunsany's work: the minor god Mynarthitep (mentioned in "The Sorrow of Search," in *Time and the Gods* [1906]) and the prophet Alhireth-Hotep (mentioned in *The Gods of Pegana* [1905]). *Hotep* is, of course, an Egyptian root, and Nyarlathotep is said in the prose-poem to have come "out of Egypt."

Can there be a real source for Nyarlathotep? Will Murray has conjectured that this "itinerant showman" was based upon Nicola Tesla (1856–1943), the eccentric scientist and inventor who created a sensation at the turn of the century for his strange electrical experiments. Physically, Tesla looked nothing like Nyarlathotep; but there are enough suggestive similarities between Tesla's and Nyarlathotep's lecture performances—and the shock and disturbance they inspired—to make a connection likely.

Nyarlathotep recurs throughout Lovecraft's later fiction and becomes one of the chief "gods" in his invented pantheon. But he appears in such widely divergent forms that it may not be possible to establish a single or coherent symbolism for him; to say merely, as some critics have done, that he is a "shapeshifter" (something Lovecraft never genuinely suggests) is only to admit that even his physical form is not consistent from story to story, much less his thematic significance. For further appearances of Nyarlathotep, see "The Whisperer in Darkness" and "The Haunter of the Dark."

Further Reading
Will Murray, "Behind the Mask of Nyarlathotep," *Lovecraft Studies*
No. 25 (Fall 1991): 25–29.

1. This would place Nyarlathotep's emergence in the 22nd Dynasty of
   Egypt (940–730 BCE).
2. This sentence is a direct reflection of the dream that inspired the tale. In
   the dream Samuel Loveman writes a note to Lovecraft: "Don't fail to see
   Nyarlathotep if he comes to Providence. He is horrible—horrible beyond anything you can imagine—but wonderful. He haunts one for
   hours afterward. I am still shuddering at what he showed" (SL I.161).
3. The suggestion is that the "yellow races" have overwhelmed Caucasian
   civilization. Cf. a similar glimpse of the future in "He" (pp. 128–129).
4. Lovecraft's boyhood fascination with trolleys is evident in some of his
   juvenile prose and poetry. A dream of 1927 reflects the same imagery:
   "After walking for some distance, I encounter'd the rusty tracks of a
   street-railway, & the worm-eaten poles which still held the limp and sagging trolley wire. Following this line, I soon came upon a yellow,
   vestibuled car numbered 1852—of a plain, double-trucked type common
   from 1900 to 1910" (SL II.199).

THE PICTURE IN THE HOUSE

"The Picture in the House" was written on December 12, 1920. It first
appeared in the *National Amateur* dated July 1919, but that issue actually appeared in the summer of 1921. Its first professional appearance
was in *Weird Tales* for January 1924.

This is the first of Lovecraft's tales not merely to utilize an authentic
New England setting but to draw upon what Lovecraft himself clearly
felt to be the weird heritage of New England history, specifically the history of Massachusetts. As a Rhode Islander, Lovecraft could look upon
the "Puritan theocracy" of Massachusetts with suitably abstract horror
and even a certain condescension; in the story he somewhat flamboyantly
portrays the lurking hideousness of the repressed colonial tradition.

The use of the backwoods New England dialect by the old man calls
for some comment. The fact that the narrator believes it to have been
"long extinct" not merely is a hint that the man is preternaturally aged as
a result of his cannibalism, but may perhaps be a clue to its literary inspiration. Jason C. Eckhardt has plausibly suggested that the dialect derives from James Russell Lowell's *Biglow Papers* (1848–62). Lowell
presents a similar version of this dialect, stating that it was itself no
longer current in his time.

Lovecraft's citation of Pigafetta's *Regnum Congo* has excited the attention of many readers. This is an actual volume, but Lovecraft has
made a number of errors in describing it, because he derived all his information about it from an essay in Thomas Henry Huxley's *Man's
Place in Nature and Other Anthropological Essays* (1894). Lovecraft
once chided Poe for his "second-hand erudition" (SL IV.162), but has
here fallen into the same error himself.

Further Reading
Jason C. Eckhardt, "The Cosmic Yankee," in *An Epicure in the Terrible: A Centennial Anthology of Essays in Honor of H. P. Lovecraft*, ed. David E. Schultz and S. T. Joshi (Rutherford, NJ: Fairleigh Dickinson University Press, 1991), pp. 78–100.

S. T. Joshi, "Lovecraft and the *Regnum Congo*," *Crypt of Cthulhu* No. 28 (Yuletide 1984): 13–17.

Robert H. Waugh, "'The Picture in the House': Images of Complicity," *Lovecraft Studies* No. 32 (Spring 1995): 2–8.

1. Ptolemais was a coastal city in Cyrenaica (now Libya) and was given its name by Ptolemy III (Euergetes) of Egypt (r. 247–222 BCE), who united Cyrenaica with Egypt. There do not appear to be any catacombs there; but a modern traveler makes note of "the huge Hellenistic tower-tomb, placed high on a cube of solid rock jutting up in isolation above the city's largest ancient quarry: the building stone has been hacked away to leave it free on its pinnacle. The tomb stands over forty feet high, a pink monolith, and was constructed for multiple burial; but no one is clear for whom." Anthony Thwaite, *The Deserts of Hesperides: An Experience of Libya* (London: Secker & Warburg, 1969), p. 73.
2. The reference, of course, is to the Puritans, whom Lovecraft always scorned as benighted and lacking the refined culture of his beloved eighteenth century. "It is the night-black Massachusetts legendry which packs the really macabre 'kick'. Here is material for a really profound study in group-neuroticism; for certainly, no one can deny the existence of a profoundly morbid streak in the Puritan imagination" (SL III.174–75).
3. In less hyperbolic language, Lovecraft repeats many of these points in his discussion of the historical background of Nathaniel Hawthorne's weird tales in "Supernatural Horror in Literature" (1927): " . . . the free rein given under the influence of Puritan theocracy to all manner of notions respecting man's relation to the stern and vengeful God of the Calvinists, and to the sulphureous Adversary of that God, about whom so much was thundered in the pulpits each Sunday; and the morbid introspection developed by an isolated backwoods life devoid of normal amusements and of the recreational mood, harassed by commands for theological self-examination, keyed to unnatural emotional repression, and forming above all a mere grim struggle for survival—all these things conspired to produce an environment in which the black whisperings of sinister grandams were heard far beyond the chimney corner, and in which tales of witchcraft and unbelievable secret monstrosities lingered long after the dread days of the Salem nightmare" (D 401).
4. The first mention of this locale in Lovecraft. Its exact location in this story is unclear. The term probably is an adaptation of Housatonic (a river in western Massachusetts and Connecticut) and other Indian names.
5. Lovecraft reports that in his youth he was a "veritable bike-centaur" (SL V.104), but he reluctantly gave up bicycle riding because it was not considered appropriate for adults.

6. The first mention of this celebrated city in Lovecraft. Will Murray has conjectured that the name was derived from the central Massachusetts town of Oakham, but Robert Marten has presented strong evidence that it may have been coined from a town in Rhode Island (now assimilated into the community of Fiskville) named Arkwright. See Robert D. Marten, "Arkham Country: In Rescue of the Lost Searchers," *Lovecraft Studies* No. 39 (Summer 1998): 14–15.

7. Actually the book (Pigafetta's *Regnum Congo*, for which see the following note) is only 60 pages in the Latin edition of 1598.

8. Lovecraft, who derived his knowledge of Pigafetta exclusively from an appendix to Thomas Henry Huxley's "On the Methods and Results of Ethnology" (in *Man's Place in Nature and Other Anthropological Essays* [1894]), has committed several errors here in his account of the book. Filippo Pigafetta (1533–1604) wrote a work in Italian entitled *Relatione del reame di Congo et delle cironvicine contrade* (1591), an account of the travels in the Congo of a sailor, Duarte Lopes. It was translated into Dutch in 1596, into English and German in 1597, and into Latin (by A. C. Reinius) as *Regnum Congo* in 1598.

9. The plates by the brothers De Bry first appeared in the German edition of 1597.

10. If Lovecraft had consulted the actual plates of *Regnum Congo*, he would not have made this remark, for there the Africans appear properly negroid. The "Caucasian" features Lovecraft detects were the result of an inaccurate redrawing of the De Bry plates by W. H. Wesley, who illustrated Huxley's *Man's Place in Nature*.

11. John Bunyan (1628–1688), *The Pilgrim's Progress* (Worcester, MA: Isaiah Thomas, 1791). Thomas (1749–1831) was a noted New England printer who issued an *Almanack* beginning in 1802. Lovecraft was an ardent collector of New England almanacs.

12. Lovecraft owned an ancestral copy of the first edition of Cotton Mather's *Magnalia Christi Americana* (1702).

13. In the first printing of this story (*National Amateur*, "July 1919") Lovecraft disastrously telegraphs the climax by adding here: "On a beard which might have been patriarchal were unsightly stains, some of them disgustingly suggestive of blood." He removed the sentence in subsequent appearances.

14. Lovecraft uses this New England dialect in a number of other stories, notably "The Dunwich Horror" (1928) and "The Shadow Over Innsmouth" (1931). See the introductory note for the possibility that it was derived from James Russell Lowell's *Biglow Papers*. (Lovecraft had read the *Biglow Papers* as early as August 1916.) When, however, Lovecraft visited Vermont in the summer of 1928, he made an interesting discovery: "Whether you believe it or not, the rustics hereabouts *actually* say 'caow', 'daown', 'araound', &c.—& employ in daily speech a thousand colourful country-idioms which we know only in literature" (Lovecraft to Lillian D. Clark, 19 June 1928; ms., JHL).

15. This account is derived entirely from Huxley's verbal description of the De Bry plate ("It may be that these apes are as much figments of

the imagination of the ingenious brothers as the winged, two-legged, crocodile-headed dragon which adorns the same plate"), since this part of the plate was not copied by Huxley's illustrator, W. H. Wesley.

THE OUTSIDER

"The Outsider" was probably written in the summer of 1921. It was one of the few stories of this period not to appear in an amateur journal, its first publication being in *Weird Tales* for April 1926.

On the level of plot, "The Outsider" makes little sense. What exactly is the nature of the "castle" in which the Outsider dwells? If it is truly underground, how is it that the creature spends time in the "endless forest" surrounding it? Taking these and other implausibilities—if the story is to be held to rigid standards of realism—into account, and noting the epigraph from Keats's *Eve of St. Agnes*, William Fulwiler has suggested that "The Outsider" is merely the account of a dream. There is something to be said for this, and this explanation would certainly account for the seemingly "irrational" elements in the tale; but the story does offer some further complexities of plot. The Outsider's puzzlement at the present shape of the ivied castle, as he sees it from a distance, makes it evident that he is a long-dead ancestor of the current occupants. His emergence in the topmost tower of his underground castle places him in a room containing "vast shelves of marble, bearing odious oblong boxes of disturbing size"— clearly the mausoleum of the castle on the surface. Of course, even if the Outsider is some centuried ancestor, there is no explanation for how he has managed to survive—or rise from the dead—after all this time.

Many commentators have speculated on a literary influence for the story, especially its concluding image of the Outsider looking at himself in a mirror. Colin Wilson has suggested both Poe's classic story of a double, "William Wilson," and Wilde's fairy tale "The Birthday of the Infanta," in which a twelve-year-old princess is initially described as "the most graceful of all and the most tastefully attired" but proves to be "a monster, the most grotesque monster he had ever beheld." George T. Wetzel has put forth Hawthorne's curious sketch, "Fragments from the Journal of a Solitary Man," in which a man dreams that he is walking down Broadway in his shroud, coming to this realization only when he "threw [his] eyes on a looking-glass which stood deep within the nearest shop." There is also the celebrated passage in Mary Shelley's *Frankenstein* in which the monster first sees himself in a pool. This influence seems more likely in view of the fact that an earlier scene in the story, where the Outsider disturbs the party by stepping through the window, may also have been derived from *Frankenstein*: "'One of the best of [the cottages] I entered, but I had hardly placed my foot within the door before the children shrieked, and one of the women fainted.'"

Stylistically, of course, the story is a homage to Poe. Lovecraft admits as much in a 1931 letter:

To my mind this tale . . . is too glibly *mechanical* in its climactic effect, & almost comic in the bombastic pomposity of its language. As I re-read it, I can hardly understand how I could have let myself be tangled up in such baroque & windy rhetoric as recently as ten years ago. It represents my literal though unconscious imitation of Poe at its very height. (SL III.379)

Aside from the Poe-esque diction, the story might be considered an indirect echo of "The Masque of the Red Death," where the figure of the Red Death (the plague) stalks through a mansion where Prince Prospero is giving a lavish masked ball.

This endlessly interpretable story has inspired much commentary in recent years. Robert H. Waugh in particular has written several thought-provoking papers using the story as the springboard for wide-ranging discussions of Lovecraft's philosophical and aesthetic thought. Donald R. Burleson sees the final image of the tale as emblematic of Lovecraft's work as a whole.

Further Reading

Carl Buchanan, "'The Outsider' as an Homage to Poe," *Lovecraft Studies* No. 31 (Fall 1994): 12–17.

Donald R. Burleson, "On Lovecraft's Themes: Touching the Glass," in *An Epicure in the Terrible: A Centennial Anthology of Essays in Honor of H. P. Lovecraft*, ed. David E. Schultz and S. T. Joshi (Rutherford, NJ: Fairleigh Dickinson University Press, 1991), pp. 135–47.

William Fulwiler, "Reflections on 'The Outsider,'" *Lovecraft Studies* No. 2 (Spring 1980): 3–4.

Paul Montelone, "The Inner Significance of 'The Outsider,'" *Lovecraft Studies* No. 35 (Fall 1996): 9–21.

Robert H. Waugh, "The Outsider, the Autodidact, and Other Professions," *Lovecraft Studies* No. 27 (Fall 1992): 4–15; No. 28 (Spring 1993): 18–33.

———, "'The Outsider,' the Terminal Climax, and Other Conclusions," *Lovecraft Studies* No. 34 (Spring 1996): 13–24.

1. From *The Eve of St. Agnes* (1820), ll. 372–75, by John Keats (1795–1821).
2. Lovecraft's coinage. He reappears in several later stories, including *The Case of Charles Dexter Ward* (1927; MM 197) and "The Haunter of the Dark" (see p. 353). See also a Ka-Nefer cited in Lovecraft's revision of Duane W. Rimel's "The Tree on the Hill" (1934; HM 405).
3. Lovecraft's coinage; cited also in *The Case of Charles Dexter Ward* ("Nephren-Ka nai Hadoth": MM 197).
4. *Neb*: mythical.
5. Nitokris was a queen of Egypt in the 6th Dynasty (c. 2180 BCE). Lovecraft also cites her in his Egyptian horror tale, "Under the Pyramids" (1924), ghostwritten for Harry Houdini: " . . . was it not in this [pyramid] that they had buried Queen Nitokris alive in the Sixth Dynasty; subtle Queen Nitokris, who once invited all her enemies to a feast in a temple below the Nile, and drowned them by opening the water-gates?"

(D 226). This anecdote (first found in Herodotus, *Histories* 2.100) was the basis of Lord Dunsany's play *The Queen's Enemies* (1916), which Lovecraft heard Dunsany read aloud in Boston in 1919 (SL I.91).

HERBERT WEST—REANIMATOR

"Herbert West—Reanimator" was written from September 1921 to June 1922 for George Julian Houtain's crude and flamboyant humor magazine, *Home Brew*, where it appeared serially from February to July 1922 under the title "Grewsome Tales." It constituted Lovecraft's first professional publication of fiction, as he was paid $5.00 for each episode.

Lovecraft takes a certain masochistic pleasure in complaining at being reduced to the level of a Grub Street hack. Over and over during this period he emits whines like the following:

> Now this is manifestly inartistic. To write to order, to drag one figure through a series of artificial episodes, involves the violation of all that spontaneity and singleness of impression which should characterise short story work. It reduces the unhappy author from art to the commonplace level of mechanical and unimaginative hack-work. Nevertheless, when one needs the money one is not scrupulous—so I have accepted the job! (SL I.158)

One gets the impression that Lovecraft actually got a kick out of this literary slumming.

Although the six episodes of "Herbert West—Reanimator" were written over a long period, the tale does maintain unity of a sort, and Lovecraft seems to have conceived it in its totality from the beginning: in the final episode all the imperfectly resurrected corpses raised by Herbert West come back to dispatch him hideously. In other ways the story builds up a certain cumulative power and suspense, and it is by no means Lovecraft's poorest fictional work. The structural weaknesses necessitated by the serial format are obvious—the need to recapitulate the plot of the preceding episodes at the beginning of each new one, the need for a horrific climax at the end of each episode. But one wonders whether the plot summaries were necessary: why did Lovecraft not have Houtain supply synopses as headnotes to each successive story? There are in fact headnotes to each segment, but they are wholly fatuous puffs or teasers written by Houtain to spur reader interest. Lovecraft learned better in his second *Home Brew* serial, "The Lurking Fear," where he must have instructed Houtain to provide just such synopses to free him from the burden of doing so.

It has been taken for granted that the obvious literary influence upon the story is *Frankenstein*; but I wonder whether this is the case. The method of West's reanimation of the dead (whole bodies that have died only recently) is very different from that of Victor Frankenstein (the assembling of a composite body from disparate parts of bodies), and only the most general influence can perhaps be detected. The core of the story is so elementary a weird conception that no literary source need be postulated.

1. The first mention of this imaginary institution of higher learning, although the Miskatonic Valley had been cited in "The Picture in the House" (p 36 and n. 4).
2. Halsey is an old family name in Providence. The so-called "Halsey Mansion" at 140 Prospect Street is the home of Charles Dexter Ward in *The Case of Charles Dexter Ward*.
3. Ernst Haeckel (1834–1919) was a German biologist and philosopher who, with Thomas Henry Huxley, became a leading proponent of Darwin's theory of evolution. Lovecraft was much influenced by Haeckel's *Die Welträthsel* (1899; translated in 1900 as *The Riddle of the Universe*) and its advocacy of materialism.
4. Lovecraft was convinced that the distinction between "living" and "dead" matter was merely chemical: "The first appearance of life on any planet need be nothing more than a *change of motion* among certain molecules, atoms, and electrons. There is nothing new or occult. Since 1828 organic compounds have been synthesised, and he is indeed a bold speculator who will deny the possibility of actual abiogenesis as a future achievement of chemistry" ("In Defence of Dagon"; MW 158–59).
5. Lovecraft may be thinking of Ambrose Bierce's brief excursion into graveyard humor, "One Summer Night" (1906; included in the revised edition of *Can Such Things Be?* [1910]), in which two medical students and an African American named Jess dig up a corpse.
6. Cited also in "The Unnamable" (1923), "The Colour Out of Space" (p. 180), and "The Dreams in the Witch House" (1932).
7. Lovecraft would later elaborate upon this theme in "The Hound" (see esp. pp. 84–85).
8. Possibly an allusion to a real event in Providence in 1920: "But the event of the season was the burning of the large Chapman house last Wednesday night—the yellow house across two lawns to the north of #598 Angell. . . . Where that evening had stood the unoccupied Chapman house, recently sold and undergoing repairs, was now a titanic pillar of roaring, living flame amidst the deserted night—reaching into the illimitable heavens and lighting the country for miles around" (SL I.108).
9. The imagery is derived from the Arabian novel *Vathek* (1786) by William Beckford (for which see introductory note to "The Hound"). An afrite is, in Islam, an evil demon or monster. Eblis is the Islamic devil.
10. Cf. the description of Joseph Curwen in *The Case of Charles Dexter Ward*, who extends his life by the practice of alchemy: "Now the first odd thing about Joseph Curwen was that he did not seem to grow much older than he had been on his arrival. . . . always did he retain the nondescript aspect of a man not greatly over thirty or thirty-five" (MM 117–18).
11. Ptolemaism is a denial of the Copernican theory that the earth revolves around the sun. Calvinism is a strict adherence to the doctrines of John Calvin (1509–1564), especially the notion that souls are predestined to achieve salvation or damnation regardless of any actions performed in life.
12. Bolton is an actual town in east-central Massachusetts, but its description

later in the story as a "factory town" is quite wide of the mark, as it is a tiny agricultural community. Robert D. Marten (see n. 6 to "The Picture in the House") has recently conjectured that Lovecraft invented the name without awareness that it was an existing town.

13. Nathaniel Wingate Peaslee in "The Shadow out of Time" (1934–35) lives at 27 Crane Street in Arkham.

14. Cf. Lovecraft's juvenile story "The Beast in the Cave" (1905), in which the protagonist finally learns the identity of the apelike thing he encounters in Mammoth Cave: "The creature I had killed, the strange beast of the unfathomed cave was, or had at one time been, a **MAN!!!**" (D 328).

15. The remark suggests that O'Brien is not in fact Irish, but perhaps Jewish, and is attempting to capitalize on the fame of the great Irish-American boxer of the 1880s, John L. Sullivan.

16. The suggestion of biological racism here is countered by the later revelation that the solution does in fact work on the African American Robinson.

17. In "The Dreams in the Witch House" "the two-year-old child of a clod-like laundry worker named Anastasia Wolejko" (MM 288) is kidnapped, and is later discovered to be the victim of the witch Keziah Mason.

18. Cf. Lovecraft's essay "The Materialist Today" (1926): "To the materialist, mind seems very clearly not a *thing*, but a *mode of motion or form of energy*" (MW 177).

19. Although most of Lovecraft's maternal ancestors were from Rhode Island, he did have a connection with Illinois. James Phillips (1794–1878), uncle of Lovecraft's grandfather Whipple Phillips, became one of the original settlers of the temperance town of Delavan, Illinois (about twenty miles south of Peoria) in 1843.

20. This is the solution adopted by Dr. Muñoz in "Cool Air": "It had to be done my way—artificial preservation . . . " (p. 140).

21. There is here perhaps a faint allusion to Lovecraft's father, Winfield Scott Lovecraft (1853–1898), who was listed as a "Commercial Traveller" in his medical records. However, this apparently meant that he traveled to offer his wares (jewelry from Gorham & Co., Silversmiths, of Providence) to the trade, and did not sell door-to-door.

22. Lovecraft's father died on July 19, 1898.

23. Recall Lovecraft's own attempt to enlist in the R.I. National Guard in 1917 (see n. 5 to "The Statement of Randolph Carter").

24. Lovecraft frequently fulminated in 1914–17 against American neutrality during the early stages of World War I, writing such essays as "The Renaissance of Manhood" (1917) and such patriotic poems as "An American to Mother England" (1916).

25. For Baudelaire see n. 5 to "The Hound." Elagabalus (or Heliogabalus) is the nickname of M. Aurelius Antoninus, Emperor of Rome (218–222), derived from his worship of the sun-god (Elah-Gabal) of Emesa. He achieved notoriety as a voluptuary and was murdered by his own troops.

26. This second point is so contrary to conventional materialist thought that it constitutes a tip of the hat that the story has now descended into self-parody.

27. *St. Eloi*: A hamlet about three miles southeast of Ypres in Belgium, where the Germans and the British fought a major battle on March 14, 1915.
28. *D.S.O.*: Distinguished Service Order, an order of military merit established by Queen Victoria in 1886.
29. Cf. the questioning of the narrator in "The Statement of Randolph Carter" (p. 7).
30. Several burying-grounds in Boston date to the seventeenth century. The central incidents in "Pickman's Model" (1926) take place in Copp's Hill Burying Ground in the North End, where interments date to 1660.

THE HOUND

"The Hound" was written in October 1922 and first published in *Weird Tales* for February 1924 (reprinted in *Weird Tales* for September 1929).

On the evening of September 16, 1922, Lovecraft and Rheinhart Kleiner explored the exquisite Dutch Reformed Church (1796) on Flatbush Avenue in Brooklyn, quite near to Sonia Greene's apartment at 259 Parkside Avenue. This magnificent structure contains a sinister old churchyard at its rear, full of crumbling slabs in Dutch. What did Lovecraft do?

> From one of the crumbling gravestones—dated 1747—I chipped a small piece to carry away. It lies before me as I write—& ought to suggest some sort of a horror-story. I must some night place it beneath my pillow as I sleep . . . who can say what *thing* might not come out of the centuried earth to exact vengeance for his desecrated tomb? (Lovecraft to Lillian D. Clark, 29 September 1922; ms., JHL.)

True enough, the incident led directly to the writing of "The Hound."

"The Hound" has been roundly abused for being overwritten; but it has somehow managed to escape most critics' attention that the story is an obvious self-parody. This becomes increasingly evident from many literary allusions and also from such grotesque utterances as "Bizarre manifestations were now too frequent to count." And yet, the story is undeniably successful as an experiment in sheer flamboyance and excess, so long as one keeps in mind that Lovecraft was aiming for such an effect and was doing so at least partially with tongue in cheek.

Some autobiographical touches in the story are worth commenting upon. While St. John is clearly meant to be Kleiner, the connection rests only in the name (see n. 2), as his character is not described in any detail. One wonders whether the museum of tomb-loot collected by the two protagonists is a playful reference to Samuel Loveman's impressive collection of *objets d'art* (not taken from tombs, one must hasten to add). Lovecraft first saw this collection in September 1922 and was much impressed by it.

As Steven J. Mariconda has demonstrated, a central literary influence on the story is Joris-Karl Huysmans' *A Rebours*. The narrators' "devasting ennui" is a reflection of the boredom that leads Huysmans' protagonist, Des Esseintes, to seek more and more peculiar means to retain his interest in life.

William Beckford's Arabian tale *Vathek* (1786)—which Lovecraft first read in late July 1921—is another literary influence worth noting. Specifically, Lovecraft was taken with one of Samuel Henley's notes to the novel, relating to ghouls:

> Goul or *ghul*, in Arabic, signifies any terrifying object which deprives people of the use of their senses; hence it became the appellative of that species of monster which was supposed to haunt forests, cemeteries, and other lonely places, and believed not only to tear in pieces the living, but to dig up and devour the dead.

Lovecraft used ghouls in many later tales, notably *The Dream-Quest of Unknown Kadath*.

Further Reading

Steven J. Mariconda, "'The Hound'—A Dead Dog?" in Mariconda's *On the Emergence of "Cthulhu" and Other Observations* (West Warwick, RI: Necronomicon Press, 1995), pp. 45–49.

Barton L. St. Armand, *H. P. Lovecraft: New England Decadent* (Albuquerque, NM: Silver Scarab Press, 1979).

1. A clear nod to Sir Arthur Conan Doyle's *The Hound of the Baskervilles* (1902). At the end of chapter 2 of that novel a character cries: "Mr. Holmes, they were the footprints of a gigantic hound!"
2. Lovecraft frequently referred to Rheinhart Kleiner as Randolph St. John, as if he were a relative of the British author and political figure Henry St. John, Viscount Bolingbroke (1678–1751). See SL I.113.
3. The Symbolists were a French literary and artistic school of the later nineteenth century that reacted to the prevailing realism of the period by stressing suggestion and implication over plain statement; its chief proponents were Stéphane Mallarmé, Paul Verlaine, and Arthur Rimbaud. The Pre-Raphaelite Brotherhood was a group of artists and poets of the later nineteenth century—including William Morris, Dante Gabriel Rossetti, and Edward Burne-Jones—who sought to evoke the style and atmosphere of Italian art prior to the dominance of Raphael (1483–1520).
4. The Decadents were a group of French writers in the 1880s and 1890s who emphasized futility, ennui, and scorn of conventional morality. Insofar as they had a leader, it was Jules Laforgue. Symbolism in part grew out of the Decadent movement.
5. Charles Pierre Baudelaire (1821–1867), French poet and translator of Edgar Allan Poe. Lovecraft owned a volume called *Baudelaire: His Prose and Poetry*, ed. T. R. Smith (New York: Boni & Liveright/Modern Library, 1919), from which he derived the epigraph to "Hypnos" (1923). His friend Clark Ashton Smith, with whom he had just come into epis-

tolary contact at the time he wrote "The Hound," would later translate much of Baudelaire's poem cycle, *Les Fleurs du mal*.

Joris-Karl Huysmans (1848–1907) was a French novelist associated with the Symbolists. Lovecraft owned *Against the Grain (A Rebours)*, tr. John Howard (New York: A. & C. Boni, 1930), and also read Huysmans' great novel of Satanism, *Là-Bas*.

6. The surviving typescript of the story reads at this point: " . . . held the unknown and unnamable drawings of Clark Ashton Smith." Lovecraft was persuaded by his colleague C. M. Eddy to remove the reference, on the belief that "the editor [of *Weird Tales*] would object to such exploitation of an artist-poet whose work I am trying to push" (SL I.292).

As for the Spanish painter Francisco José de Goya y Lucientes (1746–1828), Lovecraft initially felt that the horror in his paintings was too *"thickly laid on"* (SL 1.228), but later ranked him as a master of pictorial weirdness along with Aubrey Beardsley, Gustave Doré, John Martin, Felicien Rops, and Henry Fuseli (see SL IV.378–79).

7. This is the first citation of the *Necronomicon* in Lovecraft's fiction, and the first time that it is attributed to Abdul Alhazred (although Alhazred had been named as the author of an "inexplicable couplet" in "The Nameless City" [1921]). The title *Necronomicon* is, as George T. Wetzel has pointed out, probably derived from the *Astronomica*, a work on astronomy by the Latin poet Manilius (he and his work are frequently cited in Lovecraft's astronomy columns in the Providence *Evening News* of 1914–18). Lovecraft's knowledge of Greek and Greek etymology, however, was very rudimentary, and the derivation he gives for the word—*"necros, corpse; nomos, law; eikon, image* = An Image [or Picture] of the Law of the Dead" (SL V.418)—is almost entirely wrong. By the rules of Greek etymology (*necros*, corpse; *nemo*, to study or classify; *-ikon*, neuter singular adjectival suffix) the word simply means "A Study or Classification of the Dead."

In "History of the *Necronomicon*" (1927; MW 52–53) Lovecraft devised an Arabic title for the work—*Al Azif* (derived from Samuel Henley's notes on William Beckford's *Vathek* and referring to the nocturnal buzzing of insects)—and an entire history of its writing and publication, from its composition c. 730 by Alhazred, a Greek translation in 950 by Theodorus Philetas (where the title *Necronomicon* was bestowed upon it), its burning by the Patriarch Michael in 1050, a Latin translation by Olaus Wormius in 1228 (although Wormius in fact was a Danish scholar of the seventeenth century [see n. 18 to "The Festival"]), a German black-letter edition in the fifteenth century, an Italian edition of the Greek text in the sixteenth century, and a Spanish reprint of the Latin text in the seventeenth century.

Lovecraft coined the name Abdul Alhazred as early as the age of five, bestowing it upon himself when he was in his *Arabian Nights* phase. Years later he wrote: "I can't quite recall where I did get *Abdul Alhazred*. There is a dim recollection which associates it with a certain elder—the family lawyer [Albert A. Baker], as it happens, but I can't remember whether I asked him to make up an Arabic name for me, or

whether I merely asked him to criticise a choice I had otherwise made"
(Lovecraft to Robert E. Howard, 16 January 1932; cited in *Life* 19).

 8. See n. 5 to "Celephaïs."

 9. Cf. Lovecraft's celebrated formulation at the beginning of "Supernatural
Horror in Literature": "The oldest and strongest emotion of mankind is
fear, and the oldest and strongest kind of fear is fear of the unknown"
(D 365).

10. A nod to Ambrose Bierce's "The Damned Thing" (1893), first collected
in the revised edition of *In the Midst of Life* (Putnam's, 1898) and later
transferred to the revised edition of Bierce's collection of weird tales,
Can Such Things Be? (Collected Works, Vol. III [1910]).

11. An allusion to Poe's "The Masque of the Red Death" (1842), where the
phrase refers to the plague. For the story's influence on "The Outsider"
see above (p. 376).

12. Lovecraft reports that this detail had a real parallel during his excursion
to the cemetery of the Dutch Reformed Church in Brooklyn: "A flock
of birds descended from the sky and pecked queerly at the ancient turf,
as if seeking some strange kind of nourishment in that hoary and sepulchral place" (Lovecraft to Maurice W. Moe, [c. August 1922]; ms., private collection).

13. Belial is mentioned in the Dead Sea Scrolls as the leader of the children
of darkness against the children of light. He is referred to several times in
the Old Testament as symbolizing the powers of chaos, sickness, and
death, and once in the New Testament (II Cor. 6:15) as synonymous
with Satan.

THE RATS IN THE WALLS

"The Rats in the Walls" was written in late August or early September
1923: Lovecraft announces its completion in a letter of September 4 (SL
I.250). It first appeared in *Weird Tales* for March 1924 after being rejected by Robert H. Davis of the *Argosy All-Story Weekly* for being (in
Lovecraft's words) "too horrible for the tender sensibilities of a delicately nurtured publick" (SL I.259).

   Certain surface features of the tale—and perhaps one essential kernel
of the plot—were taken from other works. As Steven J. Mariconda has
pointed out, Lovecraft's account of the "epic of the rats" appears to be
derived from a chapter in S. Baring-Gould's *Curious Myths of the Middle Ages* (1869), of which Lovecraft speaks highly in "Supernatural Horror in Literature" and which he had probably read by this time. The
Gaelic portions of de la Poer's concluding cries were lifted directly from
Fiona Macleod's "The Sin-Eater," which Lovecraft read in Joseph Lewis
French's anthology, *Best Psychic Stories* (1920).

   More significantly, the very idea of atavism or reversion to type
seems to have been taken from a story by Irvin S. Cobb, "The Unbroken
Chain," published in *Cosmopolitan* for September 1923 (the issue, as is
still customary with many magazines, was probably on the stands at
least a month before its cover date) and later collected in Cobb's collection *On an Island That Cost $24.00* (1926). Lovecraft admits that Frank

Belknap Long gave him the magazine appearance of this story in 1923, and he alludes to it without title in "Supernatural Horror in Literature." This tale deals with a Frenchman who has a small proportion of negroid blood from a slave brought to America in 1819. When he is run down by a train, he cries out in an African language—"*Niama tumba!*"—the words that his black ancestor shouted when he was attacked by a rhinoceros in Africa.

In a late letter Lovecraft states that "The Rats in the Walls" was "suggested by a very commonplace incident—the cracking of wallpaper late at night, and the chain of imaginings resulting from it" (SL V.181). This is curious because this specific image does not actually occur in the story. Lovecraft has recorded the kernel of the idea in his commonplace book: "Wall paper cracks off in sinister shape—man dies of fright" (MW 93). And yet, an earlier entry is also suggestive: "Horrible secret in crypt of ancient castle—discovered by dweller" (MW 91). The story may then be a fusion of images and conceptions that had been percolating in his mind for years.

Further Reading

Steven J. Mariconda, "*Curious Myths of the Middle Ages* and 'The Rats in the Walls,'" in Mariconda's *On the Emergence of "Cthulhu" and Other Observations* (West Warwick, RI: Necronomicon Press, 1995), pp. 53–56.

Paul Montelone, "'The Rats in the Walls': A Study in Pessimism," *Lovecraft Studies* No. 32 (Spring 1995): 18–26.

Barton L. St. Armand, *The Roots of Horror in the Fiction of H. P. Lovecraft* (Elizabethtown, NY: Dragon Press, 1977).

1. The name is probably derived from Hexham in Northumberland, cited also in *The Case of Charles Dexter Ward* (MM 220). Lovecraft knew that his paternal grandmother Helen Allgood was "of the line of Nunwick, near Hexham" (SL II.179).
2. Commentators have noted that the name E. A. Poe is concealed in the name de la Poer. In fact, Poe's erstwhile fiancée, the Providence poet Sarah Helen (Power) Whitman, traced a relationship between herself and Poe through an ancient kinsman named Poer or De Le Poer. The matter is discussed in Caroline Ticknor's *Poe's Helen* (1916), which Lovecraft owned.
3. *Cymric:* Formerly applied to what was believed to be the second wave of Celtic immigrants to England, who drove the first group, the Gaels, farther north. The theory is no longer accepted.
4. *Anchester:* Either imaginary or an error for Ancaster in Lincolnshire or Alchester in Oxfordshire.
5. Cf. Carfax Abbey, Dracula's home near London in Bram Stoker's *Dracula* (1897).
6. The name is perhaps an allusion to Lovecraft's friend Alfred Galpin (1901–1983), whom Lovecraft actually called "my son Alfredus" (SL I.191) when he first met him in 1922.

7. In "The Moon-Bog" (1921) Denys Barry wishes to drain a bog on his property in Ireland, but the local residents refuse to help him: "in their place he sent for labourers from the north . . . " (D 119). Cf. also the comment of an Australian miner in "The Shadow out of Time": "I can get together a dozen miners for the heavy digging—the blacks would be of no use, for I've found that they have an almost maniacal fear of this particular spot" (DH 405).

8. The Druids were the priestly caste among the Celts; they were ruthlessly suppressed by the Romans in the first century CE. The earliest portions of Stonehenge probably date to c. 1900–1400 BCE, and may have been used for druidic rites at some point.

9. The worship of Cybele, a goddess from Anatolia and Phrygia, was introduced to Rome in 204 BCE.

10. Magna Mater ("Great Mother") is an attribute of Cybele.

11. In fact, it was the Second Augustan Legion that was stationed in Britain, and its base was Isca Silurum (Caerleon-on-Usk) in Wales.

12. *heptarchy:* The seven kingdoms of Anglo-Saxon England: Northumbria, Mercia, East Anglia, Wessex, Kent, Essex, and Sussex.

13. Gilles de Retz (or Rais) (1396–1440) was a French nobleman accused (falsely, it appears) of murder, necromancy, and the kidnapping of children. Donatien Alphonse François, marquis de Sade (1740–1814) became renowned for sexual perversions carried out on prostitutes and servants and for many works featuring lengthy and explicit descriptions of sexual activity. His name is the source of the word *sadism.*

14. Cf. the narrator of "The Call of Cthulhu": ". . . references to certain of the scattered notes gave me much material for thought—so much, in fact, that only the ingrained scepticism then forming my philosophy can account for my continued distrust . . . " (pp. 146–147).

15. The comparative study of mythology, especially the tracing of similarities or links between widely differing myth-cycles, was coming into its own at the turn of the century, chiefly under the influence of Sir James George Frazer's *The Golden Bough* (see n. 11 to "The Call of Cthulhu").

16. Lovecraft owned a cat of this name as a boy; it ran away in 1904, when his family moved from 454 Angell Street to 598 Angell Street.

17. See n. 12 to "Herbert West—Reanimator."

18. Cf. Sir Robert Jermyn's attempt, in "Facts Concerning the Late Arthur Jermyn and His Family" (p. 17), to kill his entire family in an effort to put an end to his tainted line.

19. A nod to Edgar Allan Poe, who uses an arras or tapestry in several tales to great effect, notably "Metzengerstein," "Ligeia," and "The Fall of the House of Usher."

20. *Paris green:* A type of poison or insecticide.

21. Cf. Lovecraft's account of a dream in 1920: "I was alone in black space, when suddenly, ahead of me, there arose out of some hidden pit a huge, white-robed man with a bald head and snowy beard. Across his shoulders was slung the corpse of a younger man—cleanshaven, and grizzled of hair, and clad in a similar robe" (SL I.102).

22. The reference is to Catullus 63 (the "Attis" poem), in which Attis tells of

his mad love for Cybele and his subsequent self-castration. *Atys* is a variant spelling found in the ninth edition of the *Encyclopaedia Britannica*, which Lovecraft owned.

23. Cf. "The Outsider" (p. 50): "For in the cosmos there is balm as well as bitterness, and that balm is nepenthe" (i.e., loss of memory).

24. See n. 9 to "The Hound."

25. Warren Gamaliel Harding (1865–1923), died on August 2, 1923, of coronary thrombosis after two and a half years as the twenty-ninth president of the United States.

26. A character in the lengthiest surviving segment of the *Satyricon*, a novel by T. Petronius Arbiter (first c. CE). Trimalchio is a spectacularly wealthy freedman who gives a vulgarly lavish dinner for his many guests.

27. See n. 9 to "Dagon."

28. Ernst Theodor Amadeus Hoffmann (1776–1822) was a German writer of tales of horror and the grotesque; they exercised a considerable influence on Poe, but Lovecraft did not care greatly for them. For Huysmans see n. 5 to "The Hound."

29. In "The Horror at Red Hook" (1925) investigators come upon an incantation scribbled in an underground vault in Brooklyn: "One frequently repeated motto was in a sort of Hebraised Hellenistic Greek, and suggested the most terrible daemon-evocations of the Alexandrian decadence" (D 256).

30. *Pithecanthrope* was a neo-Greek coinage (from *pithekos*, ape, and *anthropos*, man) devised by Ernst Haeckel (see n. 7 to "Herbert West—Reanimator") to denote the hypothetical link between man and ape.

31. The description is perhaps meant to evoke the Egyptian cat goddess Bast, although Bast did not have wings.

32. See the prose-poem "Nyarlathotep" (p. 33).

33. The succession of languages—archaic English ("'Sblood, thou stinkard . . . "), Middle English ("wolde ye swynke . . . "), Latin ("Magna Mater! . . . "), Gaelic ("Dia ad aghaidh . . . "), and primitive grunts—is intended to convey the narrator's sudden descent upon the evolutionary scale. The Gaelic is copied directly from "The Sin-Eater" (1895) by Fiona Macleod (pseudonym of William Sharp, 1856–1905), which Lovecraft read in Joseph Lewis French's *The Best Psychic Stories* (New York: Boni & Liveright/Modern Library, 1920), where it is presented as a curse. In a footnote Macleod translates the text as follows: "God against thee and in thy face . . . and may a death of woe be yours . . . Evil and sorrow to thee and thine!"

34. An actual madhouse in England, although Lovecraft probably learned of it from its citation in Lord Dunsany's "The Coronation of Mr. Shap," in The *Book of Wonder* (1912).

THE FESTIVAL

"The Festival," written probably in October 1923, was first published in *Weird Tales* for January 1925.

The ultimate inspiration for the story was Lovecraft's ecstatic discovery, in December 1922, of the remarkably well-preserved colonial town of Marblehead, Massachusetts. In a letter of 1930 he announces that the first moment he beheld Marblehead was:

> the most powerful single emotional climax experienced during my nearly forty years of existence. In a flash all the past of New England—all the past of Old England—all the past of Anglo-Saxonom and the Western World—swept over me and identified me with the stupendous totality of all things in such a way as it never did before and never will again. That was the high tide of my life. (SL III.126–27)

Many features in the story are exact echoes of the topography of Marblehead. It seems odd that Lovecraft required almost a year and at least four or five further trips to Marblehead to write the tale; but he frequently needed lengthy periods of reflection before topographical or other impressions settled sufficiently in his mind to emerge in the form of weird fiction.

There is a literary (or scientific) influence on the tale as well. In 1933 Lovecraft stated in reference to the tale: "In intimating an alien race I had in mind the survival of some clan of pre-Aryan sorcerers who preserved primitive rites like those of the witch-cult—I had just been reading Miss Murray's *The Witch-Cult in Western Europe*" (SL IV.297). This landmark work of anthropology by Margaret A. Murray, published in 1921, made the claim (now regarded by modern scholars as highly unlikely) that the witch-cult in both Europe and America had its origin in a pre-Aryan race that was driven underground but continued to lurk in the hidden corners of the earth. Lovecraft—having just read a very similar fictional exposition of the idea in Machen's stories of the "Little People"—was much taken with this conception and would allude to it in many subsequent references to the Salem witches in his tales; it would also enter his tales not set in New England (see the mention of Murray in "The Call of Cthulhu" [p. 44]). Murray's theory so perfectly meshed with some of Lovecraft's own *literary* tropes that he found it compelling as fact: he had conceived the notion of "alien" (i.e., non-human or not entirely human) races lurking on the underside of civilization as early as "Dagon" and "The Temple"; then he found it in an author (Machen) whose work he perhaps saw as a striking anticipation of his own; so that when a respected scholar actually propounded a theory that echoed this trope, he naturally embraced it.

1. The epigraph is from the *Divinae Institutiones* (2.15) of the ancient theologian L. Caelius Firmianus Lactantius (c. 240–c. 320); but Lovecraft derived it from Cotton Mather's *Magnalia Christi Americana* (1702), where it is cited in the Appendix ("Pietas in Patriam") to Book II. It translates to: "Devils so work that things which are not appear to men as if they were real" (tr. Kenneth B. Murdock).
2. *Aldebaran:* A giant star in the constellation Taurus, hence sometimes referred to as Alpha Tauri.

3. Cf. the description of the "nameless city" in Arabia in "The Nameless City" (1921): "It must have been thus before the first stones of Memphis were laid, and while the bricks of Babylon were yet unbaked" (D 98).

4. The mythical seaport in Massachusetts had first been invented in "The Terrible Old Man" (1920), but that story was written more than two years before Lovecraft visited Marblehead; it was only here that the town was definitively identified with Marblehead.

5. This distinctively New England architectural feature was for Lovecraft always an intimation of antiquity, as few houses with the gambrel roof were built after 1750. Cf. *The Case of Charles Dexter Ward*: ". . . before him was a wooden antique with an Ionic-pilastered pair of doorways, and beside him a prehistoric gambrel-roofer with a bit of primeval farmyard remaining" (MM 114).

6. *Orion:* A constellation containing such stars as Betelgeuse and Rigel; its "sword" contains the Orion nebula.

7. The image is taken directly from Lovecraft's first view of Old Burying Hill in Marblehead, "where the dark headstones clawed up thro' the virgin snow like the decay'd fingernails of some gigantick corpse" (SL I.205).

8. The original Puritans did not celebrate Christmas or Easter becuase they placed little emphasis on the symbolism of Christ's nativity or resurrection.

9. The route taken by the narrator probably led, in the actual town of Marblehead, along Elm Street to its junction at Green Street (Lovecraft's probable "Circle Court"), down Mugford Street (the extension of Green) to Washington Street and the heart of the old part of town. The Market House presumably refers to the Old Town House (1727) on Washington Street.

10. Cf. Lovecraft's first impression of Marblehead: "Wires are few and inconspicuous. Tramway rails look like deep ruts" (SL I.205).

11. The house probably corresponds to an actual house in Marblehead at 1 Mugford Street (across the street from the Old Town House), which has an overhanging second story.

12. Cf. Lovecraft's description in 1923 of the Rebekah Nurse house (1636) on the outskirts of Salem: "I travers'd two immense rooms on the ground floor—sombre, barren, panell'd apartments with colossal fireplaces in the vast central chimney, and with occasional pieces of the plain, heavy furniture and primitive farm and domestick utensils of the ancient yeomanry. In these wide, low-pitch'd rooms a spectral menace broods—for to my imagination the seventeenth century is as full of macabre mystery, repression, and ghoulish adumbrations as the eighteenth century is full of taste, gayety, grace, and beauty. This was a typical Puritan abode; where amidst the bare, ugly necessities of life, and without learning, beauty, culture, freedom, or ornament, terrible sternfac'd folk in conical hats or poke-bonnets dwelt two hundred and fifty and more years ago . . . " (SL I.222).

13. The mask motif is one repeatedly used by Lovecraft, most notably in "The Whisperer in Darkness" (p. 221).

14. A mythical book invented by Ambrose Bierce in "The Man and the Snake" (1890), in *Tales of Soldiers and Civilians* (1891).

15. An actual work by the theologian and philosopher Joseph Glanvill (1636–1680). Glanvill himself is cited in epigraphs to Poe's "Ligeia" and "A Descent into the Maelström" (although the former citation may be Poe's invention), but his work (*Saducism Defeated*) is not. Its full title— *Saducismus Triumphatus; or, Full and Plain Evidence Concerning Witches and Apparitions* (1689)—shows that it is a defense of belief in witchcraft.

16. Another real book (1595), by Nicholas Remi (1530–1612). Montague Summers translated it as *Demonolatry* (London: J. Rodker, 1930; rpt. New York: Barnes & Noble, 1970).

17. See n. 7 to "The Hound."

18. Olaus Wormius (Ole Wurm, 1588–1654) was a Danish philologist and historian. Lovecraft erred in dating him to the thirteenth century, probably because he misread a passage in Hugh Blair's *Lectures on Rhetoric and Belles Lettres* (1783) in which Wormius was mentioned. See my article, "Lovecraft, Regner Lodbrog, and Olaus Wormius," *Crypt of Cthulhu* No. 89 (Eastertide 1995): 3–7.

19. *Dog Star:* Informal name for Sirius, alluding to its reemergence in the southeastern sky in late July after a long absence. The nickname derives from its position in the constellation Canis Major (The Greater Dog).

20. It has been widely assumed that the actual church Lovecraft had in mind is St. Michael's Episcopal Church in Frog Lane, but there is now reason to doubt this attribution. As Donovan K. Loucks has pointed out to me, a later passage in this story (see p. 119) makes clear that the church and its churchyard are on Central Hill; and in several other stories it is remarked at this church is Congregational (cf. "The Silver Key"; MM 416). If Lovecraft had a specific Congregational church in Marblehead in mind, he may have been referring either to the First Meeting House (built in 1648 on Old Burial Hill) or the Second Congregational Church (built in 1715 at 28 Mugford Street), or a fusion of the two.

21. For this recurring image in Lovecraft's work see "Nyarlathotep" (p 33). In later stories Lovecraft makes frequent mention of "the boundless daemon-sultan Azathoth, . . . who gnaws hungrily in inconceivable, unlighted chambers beyond time amidst the muffled, maddening beating of vile drums and the thin, monotonous whine of accursed flutes" (*The Dream-Quest of Unknown Kadath;* MM 308). The imagery was probably derived in part from Lord Dunsany's *The Gods of Pegāna* (1905), where the creator-god Mana-Yood-Sushai is lulled to sleep by the repeated drumming of Skarl; were Skarl to cease from drumming, Mana-Yood-Sushai would awaken "and there will be worlds nor gods no more."

22. Cthulhu, as depicted in the bas-relief of the artist Henry Anthony Wilcox, is similarly hybrid in appearance: "If I say that my somewhat extravagant imagination yielded simultaneous pictures of an octopus, a dragon, and a human caricature, I shall not be unfaithful to the spirit of the thing" (p. 143).

23. Possibly an allusion to the Mary A. Alley Hospital at 6 Franklin Street in Marblehead, established in 1920 after Alley willed her home to the city to serve as an emergency hospital.
24. Cf. the opening of "The Dunwich Horror" (1928): "When a traveller in north central Massachusetts takes the wrong fork at the junction of the Aylesbury pike just beyond Dean's Corners he comes upon a lonely and curious country" (DH 156).
25. *Orange Point*: An in-joke, as there is a Peach Point in Marblehead.
26. Mythical; mentioned again in *The Case of Charles Dexter Ward* (MM 151).

HE

"He" was written during the night of August 10–11, 1925, as Lovecraft went on a solitary all-night expedition through various parts of the New York metropolitan area that led him finally to Scott Park in Elizabeth, New Jersey. The story was published in *Weird Tales* for September 1926.

The fact that at the end of the tale the narrator finds himself "at the entrance of a little black court off Perry Street" indicates that this segment of the tale was inspired by a very similar expedition Lovecraft took on August 29, 1924—a "lone tour of colonial exploration" that led to Perry Street in Greenwich Village, "in an effort to ferret out the nameless hidden court which the *Evening Post* had written up that day" (Lovecraft to Lillian D. Clark, 29–30 September 1924; ms., JHL). Lovecraft is referring to an article in the *New York Evening Post* for August 29, in a regular column entitled "Little Sketches About Town." This column contained both a line drawing of the "lost lane" in Perry Street and a brief writeup. The actual location is 93 Perry Street, an apartment building that contains an archway leading to a lane between three buildings. According to an historical monograph on Perry Street, this general area was heavily settled by Indians (they had named it Sapohanican); moreover, a sumptuous mansion was built in the block bounded by Perry, Charles, Bleecker, and West Fourth Streets sometime between 1726 and 1744, being the residence of a succession of wealthy citizens until it was razed in 1865. Lovecraft almost certainly knew the history of the area, and he has deftly incorporated it into his tale.

Further Reading

Kenneth W. Faig, Jr., "Lovecraft's 'He,'" *Lovecraft Studies* No. 37 (Fall 1997): 17–25.

S. T. Joshi, "Lovecraft and Dunsany's *Chronicles of Rodriguez*," *Crypt of Cthulhu* No. 82 (Hallowmass 1992): 3–6.

Elaine Schechter, *Perry Street—Then and Now* (New York: Privately printed, 1972).

1. See n. 6 to "Dagon."
2. This is an accurate reflection of Lovecraft's first view of Manhattan in April 1922: "Out of the waters it rose at twilight; cold, proud, and beautiful; an Eastern city of wonder whose brothers the mountains are. It

was not like any city of earth, for above purple mists rose towers, spires, and pyramids which one may only dream of in opiate lands beyond the Oxus; towers, spires and pyramids that no man could fashion, but that bloomed flower-like and delicate; bridges up which fairies walk to the sky; the visions of giants that play with the clouds" (SL I.179).

3. Carcassonne is an actual city in southwestern France. It was founded in the fifth century CE by the Iberians and still contains fine remains of medieval fortifications. Lovecraft was probably thinking specifically of Lord Dunsany's tale "Carcassonne," in *A Dreamer's Tales* (1910). Samarcand is a city now in Uzbekistan, founded in the fourth century BCE (under the name Maracanda) as the capital of Sogdiana. It was captured in 329 BCE by Alexander the Great, and was later ruled successively by the Turks, the Arabs, and the Mongols. Lovecraft's mythical city Sarkomand (cited in *The Dream-Quest of Unknown Kadath*) is probably an adaptation of the name. El Dorado ("The Gilded Man") originally referred to rumors of a legendary ruler of an Indian town near Bogotá, Colombia, who was thought to cover his body with gold dust for festivals; later it was believed that the town possessed immense quantities of gold, leading many explorers (including Gonzalo Pizarro and Sir Walter Raleigh) to seek it.

4. During Lovecraft's two-year stay in New York, he wrote only the stories "The Shunned House" (1924), "The Horror at Red Hook" (1925), "He" (1925), "In the Vault" (1925), and "Cool Air" (1926), and about twenty poems, including "Providence," "Solstice" (both 1924), "My Favourite Character," "The Cats," "Primavera," "A Year Off," "To an Infant," "October" (all 1925), and "Hallowe'en in a Suburb" (1926). He also wrote the bulk of his critical treatise, "Supernatural Horror in Literature."

5. In fact, Lovecraft resided in Brooklyn for the entirety of his stay in the New York area, living at his wife Sonia's apartment at 259 Parkside Avenue in 1924 and in a single-room apartment at 169 Clinton Street in 1925–26.

6. Lovecraft is probably referring specifically to the still existing courtyards at Milligan Place and Patchin Place, which he discovered during a pedestrian tour of exploration in the fall of 1924. "If these ancient spots were fascinating in the busy hours of twilight, fancy their utter and poignant charm in the sinister hours before dawn, when only cats, criminals, astronomers, and poetic antiquarians roam the waking world! . . . Truly, we had cast the modern and visible world aside, and were sporting through the centuries with the spirit of timeless antiquity!" (Lovecraft to Lillian D. Clark, 29–30 September 1924; ms., JHL).

7. The British cabinetmaker Thomas Chippendale (1718–1779) began work in the 1750s; his products became a byword for Rococo elegance.

8. Cf. Lovecraft's comment in 1914 in attestation of his devotion to the eighteenth century: "Verily, I ought to be wearing a powdered wig and knee-breeches" (SL I.4).

9. A common motif in Lovecraft, especially as applied to his "Faustian" characters. Its first expression occurs somewhat flamboyantly in "From

Beyond" (1920), when Crawford Tillinghast cries: "I have harnessed the shadows that stride from world to world to sow death and madness. . . . Space belongs to me, do you hear?" (D 96). Cf. also "Hypnos" (1923): "I will hint—only hint—that he had designs which involved the rulership of the visible universe and more; designs whereby the earth and the stars would move at his command, and the destinies of all living things be his" (D 166).

10. The reference is to the period during which New York was ruled by the Dutch (1624–64). The States-General is the Parliament of Holland.

11. Archaic spelling of *savages*.

12. As Lovecraft remarks in *The Case of Charles Dexter Ward*, the term *chymist* is a synonym for *alchemist* (see MM 119).

13. Cf. "Hypnos": "The cosmos of our waking knowledge, born from such an universe as a bubble is born from the pipe of a jester, touches it only as such a bubble may touch its sardonic source when sucked back by the jester's whim" (D 165).

14. The following scene, where the protagonist shows the narrator visions of past and future New York, appears to have been inspired by a similar episode in Lord Dunsany's novel *The Chronicles of Rodriguez* (1922), in which a wizard shows the protagonists visions of past and future wars (including the horrors of World War I) through a magic window. See my article cited above.

15. Three exquisite churches in lower Manhattan, two of them still standing. Trinity (Episcopal) Church, at Broadway and Wall Street, was built in 1839–46 in the Gothic Revival style. St. Paul's (Episcopal) Chapel at Broadway and Fulton Street was built in 1764–68. Lovecraft married Sonia H. Greene in this church on March 3, 1924. The Brick Presbyterian Church, built in 1766–67, was formerly at Park Row and Nassau Street; it was torn down in 1857.

16. As early as 1919 Lovecraft had stated: "Orientals must be kept in their native East till the fall of the white race. Sooner or later a great Japanese war will take place . . . The more numerous Chinese are a menace of the still more distant future. They will probably be the exterminators of Caucasian civilisation" (SL I.90). See also n. 3 to "Nyarlathotep."

17. This entity might have been an early conception of the shoggoth as described in *At the Mountains of Madness* (1931): "It was a terrible, indescribable thing . . . a shapeless congeries of protoplasmic bubbles, faintly self-luminous, and with myriads of temporary eyes forming and unforming as pustules of greenish light all over the tunnel-filling front that bore down upon us" (MM 101).

18. In fact Lovecraft did not return to Providence until April 17, 1926, eight months after writing "He."

COOL AIR

"Cool Air" was written in late February 1926. Rejected by *Weird Tales*, it first appeared in the obscure pulp magazine *Tales of Magic and Mystery* for March 1928.

The setting of the tale is the brownstone occupied by Lovecraft's friend George Kirk both as a residence and as the site of his Chelsea Book Shop at 317 West 14th Street (between Eighth and Ninth Avenues) in Manhattan. Kirk moved into the place in late summer of 1925, but by October he had moved to 365 West 15th Street. Lovecraft therefore had access to the 14th Street residence only for about two months, but it was ample time for him to become familiar with it. Very shortly after Kirk moved in, Lovecraft describes the place:

> Kirk has hired a pair of immense Victorian rooms as combined office & residence. . . . It is a typical Victorian home of New York's "Age of Innocence," with tiled hall, carved marble mantels, vast pier glasses & mantel mirrors with massive gilt frames, incredibly high ceilings covered with stucco ornamentation, round arched doorways with elaborate rococo pediments, & all the other earmarks of New York's age of vast wealth & impossible taste. Kirk's rooms are the great ground-floor parlours, connected by an open arch, & having windows only in the front room. These two windows open to the south on 14th St., & have the disadvantage of admitting all the babel & clangour of that great crosstown thoroughfare with its teeming traffick & ceaseless street-cars. (Lovecraft to Lillian D. Clark, 19–23 August 1925; ms., JHL.)

Even the ammonia cooling system used in the story has an autobiographical source. In August 1925 Lillian Clark had told Lovecraft of a visit to a theatre in Providence, to which he replied: "Glad you have kept up with the Albee Co., though surprised to hear that the theatre is *hot*. They have a fine ammonia cooling system installed, & if they do not use it it can only be through a niggardly sense of economy" (Lovecraft to Lillian D. Clark, 7 August 1925; ms., JHL).

Interestingly, Lovecraft later admitted that the chief literary inspiration for the tale was not (as many readers have believed) Poe's "Facts in the Case of M. Valdemar" but Machen's "The Novel of the White Powder," where a hapless student unwittingly takes a drug that reduces him to "a dark and putrid mass, seething with corruption and hideous rottenness, neither liquid nor solid, but melting and changing before our eyes, and bubbling with unctuous oily bubbles like boiling pitch." And yet, one can hardly deny that M. Valdemar, the man who, after his presumed death, is kept alive after a fashion for months by hypnosis and who at the end collapses "in a nearly liquid mass of loathsome—of detestable putridity," was somewhere in the back of Lovecraft's mind in the writing of "Cool Air." This story, much more than the mediocre "The Horror at Red Hook," is Lovecraft's most successful evocation of the horror to be found in the teeming clangor of America's only true megalopolis.

1. Lovecraft had come to New York in March 1924. Aside from writing random stories for *Weird Tales*, he was intermittently engaged in some poorly paying work on what appears to have been a humor

magazine conceived by *Weird Tales'* former owner, J. C. Henneberger. Lovecraft also attempted to find work on the staffs of New York book and magazine publishers, but his efforts led to nothing and he remained virtually without an income of his own during his entire New York stay.

2. The apartment at 169 Clinton Street rented for $40 a month (later changed to the slightly higher rate of $10 per week). Of the building Lovecraft later wrote: "Naturally I would have shunned a lodging which seemed to savour of coarseness, but here again unusual conditions conspired to deceive me. I still think that none but a seer and prophet could have escaped error, and that the house *had* until almost that precise time been of the quality I thought I had found" (SL II.114).

3. Lovecraft's landlady at 169 Clinton Street was an Irishwoman, Mrs. Burns.

4. Lovecraft complained not of "Spaniards" (Hispanics) but of a Syrian who had the room next to his "and played eldritch and whining monotones on a strange bagpipe which made me dream ghoulish and incredible things of crypts under Bagdad and limitless corridors of Eblis beneath the moon-cursed ruins of Istakhar" (SL II.116).

5. Lovecraft himself had such a folding couch both at 169 Clinton Street and, upon his return to Providence, at 10 Barnes Street. In planning for that return he writes: "Only one thing I must have *now*, & that is a *couch*. I *will not* have a *bed* in my room, for it must be primarily a pleasant study as now" (Lovecraft to Lillian D. Clark, 27 March 1926; ms., JHL).

6. Cf. the narrator's comment upon seeing Richard Upton Pickman's terrifying canvases in "Pickman's Model" (1926): "I want to assure you again . . . that I'm no mollycoddle to scream at anything which shews a bit of departure from the usual. I'm middle-aged and decently sophisticated, and I guess you saw enough of me in France to know I'm not easily knocked out" (DH 20).

7. A recurring motif in Lovecraft. Cf. "The Tomb" (1917): "But in that instant of curiosity was born . . . madly unreasoning desire" (D 5); "The Nameless City" (1921): "curiosity [was] stronger than fear" (D 101); "The Shadow Over Innsmouth": "Curiosity flared up beyond sense and caution . . ." (p. 294).

THE CALL OF CTHULHU

"The Call of Cthulhu" was written probably in August or September 1926, some months after Lovecraft's return to Providence from New York; but it had been plotted a full year earlier, as recorded in an entry in his 1925 diary, under the date August 12–13, 1925: "Write out story plot— 'The Call of Cthulhu' " (ms., JHL). After being initially rejected by *Weird Tales*, it was resubmitted in July 1927 and accepted, appearing in the issue for February 1928.

The origin of the tale goes back even beyond the evidently detailed plot-synopsis of 1925. Its kernel is recorded in an entry in his commonplace book that must date to 1920:

Man visits museum of antiquities—asks that it accept a bas-relief *he has* just made—*old* & learned curator laughs & says he cannot accept anything so modern. Man says that 'dreams are older than brooding Egypt or the contemplative Sphinx or garden-girdled Babylonia' & that he had fashioned the sculpture in his dreams. Curator bids him shew his product, & when he does so curator shews horror, asks who the man may be. He tells modern name. "No—*before that*" says curator. Man does not remember except in dreams. Then curator offers high price, but man fears he means to destroy sculpture. Asks fabulous price—curator will consult directors.

Add good development & describe nature of bas-relief. (MW 88)

This is a literal encapsulation of a dream Lovecraft had in early 1920, which he describes at length in two letters of the period (cf. SL I.114–15). The entry has been quoted at length to give some idea of how tangential are the inspirational foci of some of Lovecraft's tales. Only a small portion of this plot-kernel has made its way into the finished story; indeed, nothing is left except the mere fashioning of a strange bas-relief by a modern sculptor under the influence of dreams.

The fact that the extraterrestrial entity Cthulhu can influence the dreams of especially sensitive individuals is a tip of the hat to the dominant literary influence on the tale, Guy de Maupassant's "The Horla." In "Supernatural Horror in Literature" Lovecraft writes that the story "relat[es] the advent to France of an invisible being who lives on water and milk, sways the minds of others, and seems to be the vanguard of a horde of extra-terrestrial organisms arrived on earth to subjugate and overwhelm mankind . . ." (D 392–93). Cthulhu is not, of course, invisible, but the rest of the description tallies with the events of the story.

Robert M. Price points to another significant influence on the tale—theosophy. The theosophical movement originated with Helena Petrovna Blavatsky, whose *Isis Unveiled* (1877) and *The Secret Doctrine* (1888–97) introduced this peculiar mélange of science, mysticism, and religion into the West. Lovecraft of course did not believe in theosophy, but found many of its cosmic speculations imaginatively stimulating.

"The Call of Cthulhu" is manifestly an exhaustive rewriting of "Dagon," and could be said to begin a tendency found frequently in Lovecraft's later tales whereby he reworks (usually to much better advantage) themes and conceptions utilized in earlier stories.

Further Reading

Peter Cannon, "The Late Francis Wayland Thurston, of Boston: Lovecraft's Last Dilettante," *Lovecraft Studies* Nos. 19/20 (Fall 1989): 32, 39.

Stefan Dziemianowicz, "On 'The Call of Cthulhu,' " *Lovecraft Studies* No. 33 (Fall 1995): 30–35.

Steven J. Mariconda, "On the Emergence of 'Cthulhu,' " in Mariconda's *On the Emergence of "Cthulhu" and Other Observations* (West Warwick, RI: Necronomicon Press, 1995), pp. 63–66.

Robert M. Price, "Lovecraft's Use of Theosophy," in Price's *H. P. Lovecraft and the Cthulhu Mythos* (Mercer Island, WA: Starmont House, 1990), pp. 12–19.

1. The name is largely derived from an old and distinguished Providence family. Francis Wayland (1796–1865) was president of Brown University from 1827 to 1855.
2. From *The Centaur* (1911), ch. 10. The passage is part of a statement by the protagonist of the novel, Terence O'Malley; the first and third sets of ellipses are Blackwood's, the second omits the word "her" (i.e., Earth's). The British writer Algernon Blackwood (1869–1951) was a significant influence on Lovecraft, who encountered his work in 1924. Lovecraft found Blackwood's cosmic vision especially stimulating; its finest expression perhaps comes in the celebrated novelette "The Willows," which Lovecraft ranked as the finest weird tale in literature. *The Centaur* is the centerpiece of Blackwood's mystical philosophy, which sought an "expansion of consciousness" so that the unity of all Nature could be perceived.
3. Compare an earlier expression of this idea in the opening paragraph of "Facts Concerning the Late Arthur Jermyn and His Family" (p. 14).
4. Blavatsky claimed to base theosophy on an ancient work called *The Book of Dzyan,* but this work is a fabrication of her own. Lovecraft later encountered *The Book of Dzyan* (SL IV.155; see also "The Haunter of the Dark" [p. 346]) but did not realize its relation to theosophy.
5. The professor's name is significant. Angell is among the oldest families in Providence; one of the city's principal thoroughfares, Angell Street (on which Lovecraft lived from 1890 to 1924), is named for Thomas Angel or Angell, one of Roger Williams's original companions in settling Providence in 1636. Gammell is a legitimate variant of Gamwell; Lovecraft's maternal aunt was Annie E. Phillips Gamwell (1866–1941). Lovecraft would have attended Brown University had he not suffered the nervous breakdown in 1908 that forced him to abandon high school without a diploma.
6. Lovecraft refers to College Hill, east of the Providence River, upon which Brown University resides. In *The Case of Charles Dexter Ward* he refers to one of the streets leading up the hill as "vertical Jenkes Street" (MM 113).
7. *American Archaeological Society*: mythical.
8. Cubism was the artistic movement initiated in 1907 by George Bracques (1882–1963) and Pablo Picasso (1881–1973). Lovecraft probably alludes to its extensive use of geometrical elements. Futurism was a short-lived revolutionary artistic movement begun in 1909 by the Italian poet Filippo Marinetti (1875–1944). It emphasized dynamic motion over stasis, and also sought to give artistic expression to such modern developments as mechanization and speed. Although Futurism faded as a coherent movement before World War I, it was a significant influence upon

Dadaism and Surrealism. Cf. *At the Mountains of Madness* in regard to the art of the Old Ones in their Antarctic city: "Those who see our photographs will probably find its closest analogue in certain grotesque conceptions of the most daring futurists" (MM 57).

9. On the pronunciation of *Cthulhu* Lovecraft has left several accounts, all slightly differing; his associates have also supplied contradictory testimonies. The most definitive statement by Lovecraft occurs in a letter of 1934: ". . . the word is supposed to represent a fumbling human attempt to catch the phonetics of an *absolutely non-human* word. The name of the hellish entity was invented by beings whose vocal organs were not like man's, hence it has no relation to the human speech equipment. The syllables were determined by a physiological equipment wholly unlike ours, *hence could never be uttered perfectly by human throats.* . . . The actual sound—as nearly as human organs could imitate it or human letters record it—may be taken as something like *Khlûl'-hloo,* with the first syllable pronounced gutturally and very thickly. The *u* is about like that in *full*; and the first syllable is not unlike *klul* in sound, hence the *h* represents the guttural thickness" (SL V.10–11).

10. *The Story of Atlantis and the Lost Lemuria* (1925) by W. Scott-Elliot is a reprint of two separate works issued by the Theosophical Publishing Company, *The Story of Atlantis* (1896) and *The Lost Lemuria* (1904). Lovecraft read the work no later than June 1926 (SL II.58).

11. *The Golden Bough* (1890–1915) by Sir James George Frazer (1854–1941) is a landmark anthropological work that presented a comparative study of ancient and modern religious rituals. It exercised considerable fascination upon a variety of creative writers; see John B. Vickery, *The Literary Impact of* The Golden Bough (1973), and Robert Fraser, ed., *Sir James Frazer and the Literary Imagination* (1990). For Murray's *The Witch-Cult in Western Europe*, see the introductory note to "The Festival" (p. 387).

12. Wilcox is a name from Lovecraft's ancestry: Lovecraft's great-great-great-grandmother was Hannah Wilcox.

13. The Fleur-de-Lys Building at 7 Thomas Street—designed by Edmund R. Willson and erected in 1886 by Sidney R. Burleigh—stands near the foot of College Hill, just south of Benefit Street.

14. The Providence Art Club at 11 Thomas Street is half a block north of the Fleur-de-Lys Building.

15. A nearly exact duplication of the words spoken by Lovecraft himself in the dream of 1920 that inspired this facet of the story: " 'This,' I said, 'was fashioned in my dreams; and the dreams of man are older than brooding Egypt or the contemplative Sphinx or garden-girdled Babylon' " (SL I.114).

16. Lovecraft was in New York when an earthquake that affected the entire Northeast occurred on February 28, 1925. His only contemporaneous account of it is found in a laconic diary entry for that day: "house shakes 9:30 p m" (ms., JHL).

17. Cf. the cries of Wilbur Whateley's unearthly twin in "The Dunwich Horror" (1928): "It is almost erroneous to call them *sounds* at all, since so much of their ghastly, infra-bass timbre spoke to dim seats of con-

sciousness and terror far subtler than the ear; yet one must do so, since their form was indisputably though vaguely that of half-articulate *words*" (DH 195).

18. Waterman Street is another major thoroughfare in Providence, running west to east one block south of Angell Street.

19. Thayer Street is a thoroughfare at the eastern end of College Hill, running perpendicular to Angell and Waterman Streets.

20. Cf. the narrator's view of a tiara made by the Innsmouth denizens in "The Shadow over Innsmouth": "It clearly belonged to some settled technique of infinite maturity and perfection, yet that technique was utterly remote from any—Eastern or Western, ancient or modern—which I had ever heard of or seen exemplified. It was as if the workmanship were that of another planet" (p. 278).

21. A now archaic spelling of *Eskimo*, derived from the French.

22. Lovecraft has cribbed this information from the article on "Eskimo" in the ninth edition of the *Encyclopaedia Britannica*, making some spelling errors in the process. In a discussion of the Eskimos' religion the author of the article writes: "The mediums between the *inua* [supernatural powers] and mankind are the *angakoks* (Esk. plur., *angakut*) or wizards, who possess the peculiar gift of *angakoonek*—the state of 'being angakok'— which they have acquired with the aid of guardian spirits called *tornat* (plural of *tôrnak*), who again are ruled by *tornarsuk*, the supreme deity or devil of all."

23. Surprisingly for one well versed in Latin, Lovecraft repeatedly and erroneously used the word *data* in the singular.

24. Jean Lafitte (1780?–1825?) was a privateer who had established himself in New Orleans by 1809 and fought valiantly for the United States in the War of 1812.

25. Pierre Le Moyne d'Iberville (1661–1706) was a French-Canadian who explored the northern coast of the Gulf of Mexico and the mouth of the Mississippi River beginning in 1699, building several forts in the area. René-Robert Cavelier, sieur de La Salle (1643–1687) was a French explorer who canvassed the entire Mississippi River in the 1680s, reaching the Gulf of Mexico on April 9, 1682.

26. Sidney H. Sime (1867–1941), British artist and illustrator, gained greatest fame for illustrating many of the early volumes of Lord Dunsany. Anthony Angarola (1893–1929) was an American book illustrator. Cf. "Pickman's Model": "There's something those fellows catch—that they're able to make us catch for a second. Doré had it. Sime has it. Angarola of Chicago has it" (DH 13).

27. *Brava Portuguese:* A term formerly used to designate the Portuguese colonists of the Cape Verde Islands off the western coast of Africa; the name derives from Brava, the most southerly of the islands. Portugal had settled the islands beginning in the late fifteenth century.

28. Now archaic variant spelling of *fetishism*.

29. Lovecraft's initial rendering of this name, when he first fashioned the plot of the story in 1925, was *L'yeh* (see Lovecraft to Lillian D. Clark, 14–19 November 1925; ms., JHL).

30. The name is not a reference to Lovecraft's colleague and revision-client Adolphe de Castro (1859–1959), since de Castro did not get in touch with Lovecraft until 1927.

31. A nod to theosophy, since Blavatsky and her followers adopted the Tibetan belief that the "holy city of Shamballah" was the spiritual center of the world and the home of certain "Masters" who sent out telepathic messages to the faithful.

32. An obvious reference to the radical morality propounded by Nietzsche in *Beyond Good and Evil* (1886). During Lovecraft's initial absorption of Nietzsche, however, in 1919–21, he wrote: "Lest you fancy that I am making an idol of Nietzsche . . . , let me state clearly that I do not swallow him whole. His ethical system is a joke—or a poet's dream, which amounts to the same thing" (SL I.134).

33. An actual location in Arabia. Lovecraft derived his knowledge of it from the ninth edition of the *Encyclopaedia Britannica* (entry on "Arabia"): "Very gorgeous are the descriptions given of 'Irem,' the 'city of pillars,' as the Koran styles it, supposed to have been erected by Shedad, the latest despot of 'Ad, in the regions of Hadramaut; and which yet, after the annihilation of its tenants, remains entire, so Arabs say, invisible to ordinary eyes, but occasionally, and at rare intervals, revealed to some heaven-favoured traveller." Lovecraft based his early story "The Nameless City" (1921) upon this passage.

34. The couplet was first cited in "The Nameless City" (D 99).

35. That is, the First Baptist Church, founded in 1638 by Roger Williams. The present building dates to 1775. Lovecraft remarks after visiting it in 1923: "This is my maternal ancestral church, but I had not been in the main auditorium since 1895, or in the building at all since 1907, when I gave an illustrated astronomical lecture in the vestry to the Boys' Club" (SL I.277). On this occasion Lovecraft tried to play "Yes, We Have No Bananas" on the church's organ, but was "balk'd by lack of power, since the machine is not a self-starter."

36. Arthur Machen (1863–1947), Welsh author and significant influence on Lovecraft. Clark Ashton Smith (1893–1961) first came into epistolary contact with Lovecraft in 1922 and remained one of his closest colleagues, even though they never met. Smith was a poet, fiction writer, painter, and sculptor.

37. The Sydney *Bulletin* was founded in 1880.

38. An exact description of Lovecraft's friend James Ferdinand Morton (1870–1941), who became curator of the Paterson (NJ) Museum in 1925. Lovecraft, who first met Morton in 1922, visited him frequently at the museum and also assisted him in rock-gathering expeditions in New England.

39. This would be in the Pacific Ocean about 50 miles southeast of Sydney.

40. Sydney University, the first university in Australia, was founded in 1850. *Royal Society* refers to the Royal Society of New South Wales. The "Museum in College Street" is the Australian Museum (formerly the Colonial Museum), founded in 1827. It is one of the ten leading natural history museums in the world.

41. This would be about 1300 miles southwest of Tasmania, in the region of the Pacific Ocean called the Southeast Indian Ridge.
42. *Kanakas:* More properly Kanaks, the native Melanesians on the island of New Caledonia. Cf. Zadok Allen's frequent references to "Kanakys" in "The Shadow over Innsmouth" (pp. 298f.).
43. *Egeberg:* More properly Ekeberg, a steep hill to the east of Oslo, at the base of which the ancient town was built.
44. Harold III (1015–1066), King of Norway from 1046 to 1066, was the reputed founder of Oslo in 1050. King Christian IV renamed the city Christiania after its destruction by fire in 1624; it did not resume the name Oslo until 1924.
45. *Gothenburg dock:* More properly Göteborg, the principal seaport of Norway, about 80 miles southeast of Oslo.
46. *Lascar sailors:* Former designation for sailors from the East Indies.
47. This would be about 300 miles northwest of the previous location (see n. 41).
48. A recurring motif in Lovecraft. Cf. *At the Mountains of Madness*: "There were geometrical forms for which an Euclid could scarcely find a name—cones of all degrees of irregularity and truncation; terraces of every sort of provocative disproportion; shafts with odd bulbous enlargements; broken columns in curious groups; and five-pointed or five-ridged arrangements of mad grotesqueness" (MM 51).
49. A direct borrowing from Poe's "The Fall of the House of Usher": ". . . the more bitterly did I perceive the futility of all attempt at cheering a mind from which darkness, as if an inherent positive quality, poured forth upon all objects of the moral and physical universe . . ."
50. Cf. the narrator's comment upon seeing the monster in "Dagon": "I think I went mad then" (p. 5). For another ominous glance backward see the conclusion of *At the Mountains of Madness*, when the protagonists simultaneously turn their heads back while fleeing the shoggoth.

THE COLOUR OUT OF SPACE

The last tale of Lovecraft's great spate of fiction-writing of 1926–27 (during which he wrote two short novels, two novelettes, and several short stories), "The Colour Out of Space," was written in March 1927. It was first published in *Amazing Stories* (the first science fiction magazine, founded in 1926) for September 1927; but Lovecraft was incensed that its editor, Hugo Gernsback, paid him only $25 (1/5¢ a word) for the story, and he never submitted anything to Gernsback again. Despite the claims of Sam Moskowitz and others that the story may have been submitted first to *Weird Tales* or the *Argosy*, the documentary evidence suggests that it was submitted only to *Amazing*.

Lovecraft was correct in calling this tale an "atmospheric study" (SL II.114), for he has rarely captured the atmosphere of inexplicable horror better than here. First let us consider the setting. The reservoir mentioned in the tale is a very real one: the Quabbin Reservoir, plans for which were announced in 1926, although it was not completed until 1939. And yet, Lovecraft declares in a late letter that it was not this reservoir but the Scituate Reservoir in Rhode Island (built in 1926) that caused him to use the reservoir element in the story (Lovecraft to Richard Ely Morse, 13 October 1935; ms., JHL). He saw this reservoir when he passed through the west-central part of the state in late October 1926. It is hard to imagine, however, that Lovecraft was not also thinking of the Quabbin, which is located exactly in the area of central Massachusetts where the tale takes place, and which involved the abandonment and submersion of entire towns in the region.

"The Colour Out of Space" is the first of Lovecraft's major tales to effect that union of horror and science fiction which would become the hallmark of his later work. It continues the pattern already established in "The Call of Cthulhu" of transferring "the focus of supernatural dread from man and his little world and his gods, to the stars and the black and unplumbed gulfs of intergalactic space," as Fritz Leiber ably stated in "A Literary Copernicus" (1949). In a sense, of course, Lovecraft was taking the easy way out: by simply having his entities come from some remote corner of the universe, he could attribute nearly any physical properties to them and not be required to give a plausible explanation for them. But the abundance of chemical and biological verisimilitude Lovecraft provides makes these unknown properties very convincing, as does the gradually enveloping atmosphere of the tale.

Further Reading

Steven J. Mariconda, "The Subversion of Sense in 'The Colour Out of Space,'" in Mariconda's On the Emergence of "Cthulhu" and Other Observations (West Warwick, RI: Necronomicon Press, 1995), pp. 63–66.

Robert M. Price, "A Biblical Antecedent for 'The Colour Out of Space,'" Lovecraft Studies No. 25 (Fall 1991): 23–25.

1. The paintings of Salvator Rosa (1615–1673) are known for their wild, desolate landscapes. Lovecraft would have seen several of his paintings at the Metropolitan Museum of Art in New York. The expression "tale of terror" brings to mind the Gothic novels of the late eighteenth and early nineteenth centuries. Cf. Edith Birkhead's pioneering study, The Tale of Terror (1921), which Lovecraft read.
2. Actually, two poets used the phrase "blasted heath." In Shakespeare's Macbeth, Macbeth says to the witches: "Say from whence / You owe this strange intelligence, or why / Upon this blasted heath you stop our way / With such prophetic greeting" (1.3.75–78). In Milton's Paradise Lost we find the following: " . . . as, when Heaven's fire / Hath scathed the forest oaks or mountain pines, / With singed top their stately growth, though bare, / Stands on the blasted heath" (1.612–15). Lovecraft was probably thinking of the latter passage.
3. For this "small island" cf. "The Dreams in the Witch House" (1932): " . . . there was a clearly visible living figure on that desolate island, and a second glance told him it was certainly the strange old woman whose sinister aspect had worked itself so disastrously into his dreams" (MM 274).
4. While Gardner is a common name throughout New England (it is, e.g., a

city in north-central Massachusetts, and as such is mentioned in "The Whisperer in Darkness" [p 240]), the name perhaps also has a punning signification (i.e., a *gardener* of very strange crops).

5. *Occluded gases* are gases retained within certain substances, chiefly metals, and customarily released when the metal is heated to a sufficient temperature. *Borax beads* are "Beads made of borax [$Na_2B_4O_7$], used in blowpipe analysis to distinguish the metallic oxides, and test minerals by the characteristic colours which they give in the oxidizing and the reducing flame" (OED). The *oxy-hydrogen blowpipe* is an instrument used for a variety of purposes including chemical analysis, with a flame comprised of a mixture of oxygen and hydrogen.

6. The spectroscope is an instrument that separates light into its constituent wavelengths so as to form a spectrum. In his youth Lovecraft performed much spectroscopic analysis as part of his enthusiasm for chemistry: "One phase of chemistry in which I dabbled was spectrum-analysis, & I still have my spectroscope—a rather low-priced diffraction instrument costing $15.00. I have also a still cheaper pocket spectroscope, which was the delight of my fellow students at H[ope] S[treet] H[igh] S[chool]" (Lovecraft to Alfred Galpin, 29 August 1918; ms., JHL).

7. *Hydrochloric acid:* HCl, a mixture of hydrogen and chlorine. *Nitric acid:* HNO_3, a mixture of hydrogen, nitrogen, and oxygen; formerly called *aqua fortis. Aqua regia:* A mixture of nitric and hydrochloric acid.

8. *Ammonia:* NH_3, a compound of nitrogen and hydrogen. *Caustic soda:* Sodium hydroxide (NaOH). *Alcohol:* Probably ethyl alcohol (C_2H_5OH). *Ether:* $C_4H_{10}O$. *Carbon disulphide:* CS_2, a compound of carbon and sulphur. Lovecraft deems it "nauseous" because it has a foul odor, like that of rotten eggs.

9. Widmannstätten figures, named after Aloys von Widmannstätten (1754–1849), who discovered them, are patterns of intersecting bands that are exhibited when polished surfaces of most iron meteorites are etched in nitric acid.

10. Cf. Ambrose Bierce's "The Damned Thing" (1893): " 'At each end of the solar spectrum the chemist can detect the presence of what are known as "actinic" rays. They represent colors—integral colors in the composition of light—which we are unable to discern. The human eye is an imperfect instrument; its range is but a few octaves of the real "chromatic scale." I am not mad; there are colors that we cannot see. And, God help me! the Damned Thing is of such a color!' "

11. *Chapman's Brook:* Cf. the Chapman farmhouse cited in "Herbert West—Reanimator" (p. 53).

12. Cf. the imaginary Dean's Corners mentioned in "The Dunwich Horror" (DH 155–56).

13. A Professor Warren Rice is a minor character in "The Dunwich Horror."

14. The Arkham *Gazette* is perhaps modelled upon the Salem *Gazette,* a paper that published from 1790 to 1908. The *Arkham Advertiser* is presumably its successor; see n. 12 to "The Whisperer in Darkness."

15. For Bolton see n. 12 to "Herbert West—Reanimator."

16. Lovecraft may be referring to the kind of utterances expressed by a mad

character in his earlier story, "The Temple" (1920): "*He* is calling! *He* is calling! I hear him! We must go!" (D 65).

17. Consider Lovecraft's comment in a letter a few months after writing this story: "Living things—usually insane or idiotic members of the family—concealed in the garrets or secret rooms of old houses are or at least have been literal realities in rural New England—I was told by someone of how he stopped at a lone farmhouse on some errand years ago, and was nearly frightened out of his wits by the opening of a sliding panel in the kitchen wall, and the appearance at the aperture of the most horrible, dirt-caked, and matted-bearded face he had ever conceived possible to exist!" (SL II.139). Charlotte Perkins Gilman's celebrated horror tale, "The Yellow Wall Paper" (1892), is based upon such a conception.

18. The phrase "walk uprightly" is found in several passages of the Bible. Cf. Psalms 15:11: "For the Lord God is a sun and shield: the Lord will give grace and glory: no good thing will be withheld from them that walk uprightly."

19. See n. 39 to "The Whisperer in Darkness."

20. St. Elmo's fire, named after a fourth-century saint, Erasmus (a patron of sailors), is a bluish light sometimes seen on the tips of tall objects during a thunderstorm. It is caused by an accumulation of a positive charge resulting from the negative charge in storm clouds. Pentecost (from the Greek *pentekoste,* "fiftieth") was originally a Hebrew agricultural festival (the fiftieth day after Passover). On the first Pentecost after the death and resurrection of Jesus, the apostles gathered in Jerusalem; there was a sudden sound from heaven as of rushing wind and "there appeared unto them cloven tongues like as of fire, and it sat upon each of them" (Acts 2:3).

21. Henry Fuseli (Heinrich Füssli, 1741–1825) was a Swiss-born painter who resided in England. Cf. "Pickman's Model" (1926): "I don't have to tell you why a Fuseli really brings a shiver while a cheap ghost-story frontispiece really brings a laugh" (DH 13).

22. Cf. n. 6 to "Celephaïs."

THE WHISPERER IN DARKNESS

"The Whisperer in Darkness" was begun in February 1930 and completed in September. It was first published in *Weird Tales* for August 1931, earning Lovecraft a check for $350, the largest sum he would ever earn for a single story.

The genesis of the tale is nearly as interesting as the tale itself; Steven J. Mariconda has studied the matter in detail, and in large part I am echoing his conclusions. The very real Vermont floods of 1927 no doubt stimulated Lovecraft's imagination, although the general Vermont background of the tale is derived from Lovecraft's visits to that state in 1927 and 1928, where he stayed with his friend Vrest Orton. Whole passages of the essay "Vermont—A First Impression" (*Driftwind,* March 1928; MW 293–96) have been bodily inserted into the text, but they have been altered in such a way as to emphasize both the terror and the fascination of the rustic landscape.

The character Henry Wentworth Akeley is based in part on the rustic Bert G. Akley whom Lovecraft met on his 1928 trip. Akeley's secluded farmhouse seems to be a commingling of the Orton residence in Brattleboro and the home of the poet Arthur Goodenough farther to the north. Several other citations of real events or persons augment the verisimilitude of the tale.

The actual writing of the tale was very difficult and unusually prolonged. Lovecraft "provisionally finished" the story in Charleston, South Carolina, in May 1930; but it underwent significant revisions after Lovecraft read parts of it to both Frank Belknap Long in New York and to Bernard Austin Dwyer in Kingston, N.Y. The nature of these revisions is not entirely clear, but it appears that at least one point on which Dwyer suggested alteration is a warning that Akeley's brain (now enclosed in the brain-canisters in his farmhouse) gives to Wilmarth to flee the place—a warning that is so obvious that it would dilute the purported "surprise" ending of the story (if indeed the story in this version ended as it did). It also appears that Dwyer recommended that Wilmarth be made a rather less gullible figure, but on this point Lovecraft did not make much headway: although random details were apparently inserted to heighten Wilmarth's skepticism, especially in regard to the obviously forged final letter by "Akeley," he still seems very naive in proceeding blithely up to Vermont with all the documentary evidence he has received from Akeley.

Lovecraft has ingeniously woven into the story the contemporaneous discovery of the planet Pluto, which he whimsically identified with Yuggoth, invented a year previously in his sonnet cycle *Fungi from Yuggoth* (1929–30).

One point of controversy in the story is the possibility that the false Akeley who greets Wilmarth at the end is not merely one of the fungi from Yuggoth but Nyarlathotep himself, whom the aliens worship. The evidence comes chiefly from the phonograph recording of the ritual in the woods made by Akeley, in which one of the fungi declares, "To Nyarlathotep, Mighty Messenger, must all things be told. And He shall put on the semblance of men, the waxen mask and the robe that hides, and come down from the world of Seven Suns to mock . . ." This seems a clear allusion to Nyarlathotep disguised with Akeley's face and hands; but if so, it means that at this time Nyarlathotep actually *is*, in bodily form, one of the fungi—especially if, as seems likely, Nyarlathotep is one of the two buzzing voices Wilmarth overhears at the end (the one who "held an unmistakable note of authority"). And yet, there are problems with this identification. If Nyarlathotep is (as critics have termed it) a "shapeshifter," why would he have to don the face and hands of Akeley instead of merely reshaping himself as Akeley? It does not appear as if Lovecraft has entirely thought through the role of Nyarlathotep in this story; and, to my mind, Nyarlathotep never gains a coherent personality in the whole of Lovecraft's work.

Further Reading

Donald R. Burleson, "Humour Beneath Horror: Some Sources for 'The Dunwich Horror' and 'The Whisperer in Darkness,' " *Lovecraft Studies* No. 2 (Spring 1980): 5–15.

Steven J. Mariconda, "Tightening the Coil: The Revision of 'The Whisperer in Darkness,' " *Lovecraft Studies* No. 32 (Spring 1995): 12–17.

1. *wild domed hills:* A phrase Lovecraft frequently uses to characterize Arthur Machen's descriptions of the Welsh countryside. The actual phrase does not, however, seem to be found in Machen's work. Lovecraft makes the connection explicit in a letter: "The scenery [of Vermont]—endless wild domed hills & hanging woods & mysterious brooklets that tumble & gurgle through forest ravines—is worthy of Machen's Gwent country . . . " (Lovecraft to Donald Wandrei, 26 June 1928; ms., JHL).

2. An actual event that was widely reported in newspapers. See Lovecraft to Arthur Harris, 12 January 1928: "Last November there were some unprecedentedly severe floods in New England—not affecting Providence, but ravaging much of the territory covered by my summer pilgrimage" (ms., JHL). Lovecraft had visited Vermont, as well as portions of New Hampshire and Massachusetts, in the summer of 1927.

3. The areas mentioned are all in the northwest portion of the state, beyond Montpelier.

4. *Eli Davenport:* mythical.

5. Cf. the Great Old Ones in "The Call of Cthulhu" (p. 155). Lovecraft uses this term frequently in his tales, in reference to several clearly different species of alien entities: "The Old Ones were, the Old Ones are, and the Old Ones shall be" ("The Dunwich Horror"; DH 170); "Of the life of the Old Ones . . . volumes could be written" (*At the Mountains of Madness*; MM 63).

6. Benning Wentworth (1696–1770), provincial governor of New Hampshire (1741–66), made large grants of land between 1749 and 1764 west of the Connecticut River, in what is now Vermont. Vermont was never a provincial colony; it became a state only after the Revolution.

7. Machen made great use of the "little people" throughout his fiction. See p. 208 below.

8. The Pennacooks are an Indian tribe originally inhabiting New Hampshire, Vermont, northeastern Massachusetts, and southwestern Maine. By 1700 they had fled the encroachments of the British colonists and joined the Abnakis in Canada. Burleson notes: "Although there is virtually no written material on Pennacook myth, the Pennacooks having been nearly obliterated in the early 1600s by a plague, it is known that as Western Abenakis (or Abnakis) they shared with the Eastern Abenakis a myth concerning 'a dread flying creature named *bmola*' [*Handbook of North American Indians*, gen. ed. William C. Sturtevant (Washington: Smithsonian Institution, 1978), XV, 159]."

9. A *kallikantzaros* is a Christmastide sprite.

10. The Abominable Snowman or *yeti* is a monster said to inhabit the Himalayas at or above the snow line. Mi-Gö ("wild man") is the Tibetan term; *yeti* is used by the Newari-speaking peoples of Nepal.

11. American writer Charles Fort (1874–1932) collected accounts (generally from newspaper reports) of bizarre happenings and incorporated them into several volumes—*The Book of the Damned* (1919), *New Lands* (1923), *Lo!* (1931), and *Wild Talents* (1932)—in an attempt to disturb what he believed was the dogmatism of conventional scientists. Lovecraft found his work scientifically valueless but imaginatively stimulating: "Fort scraped up all sorts of press anecdotes of a certain type—which in turn were typical misstatements, misinterpretations, exaggerations, & distortions of actually observed things, or else hallucinations or fabrications. Track down any one of them to its reported place of occurrence, & the marvel evaporates" (SL V.173). Fort is mentioned in the fragment "The Descendant" (1927?; D 361).

12. This imaginary paper was first cited in "The Dunwich Horror" (1928) and would be mentioned again in *At the Mountains of Madness* (1931). It is perhaps meant to correspond to the *Salem* [MA] *Advertiser* (founded 1832), a leading paper in Salem at the time.

13. *Rutland Herald:* Properly, the *Rutland Daily Herald,* founded 1861.

14. *Brattleboro Reformer:* Properly, the *Brattleboro Daily Reformer.* "The Pendrifter" was the pseudonym of Charles Crane, who conducted the "Pen-Drift" column for the paper. Vrest Orton contributed an article on Lovecraft, entitled "A Weird Writer Is in Our Midst," for the column of June 16, 1928. Lovecraft met Crane on June 21.

15. The name, and certain facets of the character, are manifestly derived from a reclusive painter named Bert G. Akley, living in a cabin outside of Brattleboro, whom Lovecraft met in the summer of 1928. Lovecraft writes on a postcard: "Akeley [*sic*]—who lives alone in the ancient farmhouse shewn on the other side of this card, turned out to be a highly remarkable rustic genius. His paintings—covering every field, but specialising in the local scenery, are of a remarkable degree of excellence; yet he has never taken a lesson in his life. . . . In other fields, too, he is a veritable jack-of-all-trades. Through it all he retains the primitiveness of the agrestic yeoman, & lives in unbelievable heaps & piles of disorder." (Lovecraft to Lillian D. Clark, [c. 24 June 1928]; ms., JHL).

16. Wilmarth is a prominent family in Rhode Island. Nelson Wilmarth Aldrich (1841–1915) was U.S. Senator from Rhode Island (1881–1911) and a leading Republican politician of his day.

17. Saltonstall is an ancient and distinguished name throughout New England. Sir Richard Saltonstall (1586–1661) came to the region in 1630 on the *Arbella* and founded the town of Watertown in Massachusetts.

18. An impressive array of anthropologists, although some of them did their best work in the later nineteenth century:

Sir Edward Burnett Tylor (British; 1832–1917) was author of *Primitive Culture* (1871), a landmark in the study of folklore and primitive religion.

John Lubbock, Baron Avebury (British; 1834–1913) was a naturalist and author of *Prehistoric Times* (1865), *The Origin of Civilization* (1870), and other works.

For Sir James George Frazer see n. 11 to "The Call of Cthulhu."

Armand de Quatrefages de Bréau (French; 1810–1892) wrote *L'Espèce humaine* (1877; translated as *The Human Species*).

For Margaret Murray see introductory note to "The Festival."

Henry Fairfield Osborn (American; 1857–1935) was president of the American Museum of Natural History and author of *Origin and Evolution of Life* (1917) and many other works.

Sir Arthur Keith (British; 1866–1915) wrote *The Antiquity of Man* (1915), *Nationality and Race* (1920), and other works.

[Pierre] Marcellin Boule (French; 1842–1942) was the author of *Les Hommes fossiles* (1921; translated as *Fossil Man*).

Sir G[rafton] Elliot Smith (British; 1871–1937) wrote *The Evolution of Man* (1924), *Human History* (1929), and other works.

19. "I once owned an Edison machine of the primitive type, with recorder and blanks; and I made many vocal records in imitation of the renowned vocalists of the was cylinder" (SL I.44). And, more amusingly: "Something over a decade ago [c. 1908] I conceived the idea of displacing Sig. Caruso as the world's greatest lyric vocalist, and accordingly inflicted some weird and wondrous ululations upon a perfectly innocent Edison blank. My mother actually liked the results—mothers are not always unbiased critics—but I saw to it that an accident soon removed the incriminating evidence. Later I tried something less ambitious; a simple, touching, plaintive, ballad sort of thing a la John McCormack. This was a better success, but reminded me so much of the wail of a dying fox-terrier that I very carelessly happened to drop it soon after it was made" (SL I.60).

20. *Ex nihilo nihil fit:* "From nothing comes nothing," an enunciation of the principle that matter cannot be created or destroyed; here used figuratively. The phrase is often thought to have come from Lucretius' *De Rerum Natura*, but Lucretius uses only the form *nil*, never *nihil;* the closest parallel in his poem is: *nil igitur fieri de nilo posse fatendumst* (1.205).

21. The ether is a conception of pre-Einsteinian physics—"an extremely attenuated medium, filling the whole of space outside of ponderable matter" (Ernst Haeckel, *The Riddle of the Universe* [New York: Harper & Brothers, 1900], p. 225)—to which physicists had to resort as a result of their inability to imagine how light or matter could travel through empty space without a medium to convey it.

22. Cf. Zadok Allen's comment in "The Shadow over Innsmouth": ". . . they [the fish-creatures] cud wipe aout the hull brood o' humans ef they was willin' to bother" (p. 299).

23. The Great Race in "The Shadow out of Time" (1934–35) perform mind-exchange with intelligent entities throughout the universe for much the same purpose, although more benignly.

24. Yog-Sothoth was first cited, nebulously, in *The Case of Charles Dexter Ward* (1927), in the letters of the seventeenth-century wizard Joseph Curwen: "I laste Night strucke on yᵉ Wordes that bringe up YOGGE-

SOTHOTHE . . . " (MM 151). The entity occupies a central role only in "The Dunwich Horror," and is otherwise only mentioned in passing in Lovecraft's tales. For Cthulhu see "The Call of Cthulhu."

25. Cf. Charles Dexter Ward's exculpatory letter in *The Case of Charles Dexter Ward*: "I have brought to light a monstrous abnormality, but I did it for the sake of knowledge" (MM 182).

26. Cf. *At the Mountains of Madness*: "The hitherto withheld photographs . . . will count in my favour; for they are damnably vivid and graphic. Still, they will be doubted because of the great lengths to which clever fakery can be carried" (MM 3).

27. These standing stones, or megaliths, are scattered throughout New England; most of them were probably built by the Indians for ritual purposes. They figure prominently in "The Dunwich Horror." See Andrew E. Rothovius, "Lovecraft and the New England Megaliths," in *The Dark Brotherhood and Other Pieces* (Sauk City, WI: Arkham House, 1966), pp. 179–97. Rothovius, however, perhaps exaggerates Lovecraft's familiarity with the megaliths.

28. The black stone is clearly borrowed from the "black seal" featured in Machen's "Novel of the Black Seal" (a chapter of the episodic novel, *The Three Impostors*). "I had possessed for many years an extraordinary stone seal—a piece of dull, black stone, two inches long from the handle to the stamp, and the stamping end a rough hexagon an inch and a quarter in diameter. Altogether, it presented the appearance of an enlarged tobacco-stopper of an old-fashioned make. It had been sent to me by an agent in the east, who informed me that it had been found near the site of the ancient Babylon. But the characters engraved on the seal were to me an intolerable puzzle. Somewhat of the cuneiform pattern, there were yet striking differences, which I detected at the first glance, and all efforts to read the inscription on the hypothesis that the rules for deciphering the arrow-headed writing would apply proved futile." *The Three Impostors* (London: John Lane; Boston: Roberts Brothers, 1895), pp. 146–47.

29. Lovecraft himself owned a bust of Milton, although it was not kept on his desk but rather on top of one of his bookcases. It can be seen in a photograph of Lovecraft's study reproduced in *Marginalia* (Sauk City, WI: Arkham House, 1944), facing p. 214.

30. A celebrated catalogue of weird names—some invented by Lovecraft himself, others borrowed from the writings of his predecessors or colleagues.

Yuggoth: Invented in the sonnet cycle *Fungi from Yuggoth* (1929–30); see such lines as: "I knew this strange, grey world was not my own, / But Yuggoth, past the starry voids" (AT 66). Later in the story it is identified with the newly discovered planet Pluto (see p. 262).

Tsathoggua: An entity invented by Clark Ashton Smith in "The Return of Satampra Zeiros" (written 1929; published *Weird Tales*, November 1931), where it is described as follows: "He was very squat and pot-bellied, his head was more like that of a monstrous toad than a deity, and his whole body was covered with an imitation of short fur, giving somehow a vague suggestion of both the bat and the sloth." *A Ren-*

dezvous in Averoigne (Sauk City, WI: Arkham House, 1988), p. 156. Lovecraft borrowed the entity in his revision of Zealia Bishop's tale "The Mound" (1929–30) and in many later stories.

R'lyeh: See "The Call of Cthulhu" (p. 155 and note 29).

Nyarlathotep: See "Nyarlathotep" (p. 31).

Azathoth: See n. 21 to "The Festival."

Hastur: An entity (described as a god of the shepherds) invented by Ambrose Bierce in the story "Haïta the Shepherd" (in *Tales of Soldiers and Civilians* [1891]) and borrowed by Robert W. Chambers in *The King in Yellow* (1895), where it is apparently a constellation ("When from Carcosa, the Hyades, Hastur, and Aldebaran . . . "). This is its only mention in Lovecraft.

Yian: Borrowed from Robert W. Chambers's *The Maker of Moons* (1896), where we find this dialogue: " 'We lived in Yian until I was sixteen years old.' . . . 'Where is Yian, Ysonde?' I asked with deadly calmness. 'Yian? I don't know. . . . It is across seven oceans and the great river which is longer than from the earth to the moon.' " Yian is never again mentioned in Lovecraft's stories, but Yian-Ho is cited in "Through the Gates of the Silver Key" (1933–34) and in Lovecraft's revision of William Lumley's "The Diary of Alonzo Typer" (1936).

Leng: See "The Hound" (p. 86).

the Lake of Hali: Hali, a prophet, was an invention of Ambrose Bierce, cited in "An Inhabitant of Carcosa" (1886; in *Tales of Soldiers and Civilians* [1891]) and "The Death of Halpin Frayser" (1891; in *Can Such Things Be?* [1893]).

Bethmoora: Invented by Lord Dunsany in the story "Bethmoora," in *A Dreamer's Tales* (1910). It is a city somewhere in the East that is mysteriously wiped out.

the Yellow Sign: Invented by Robert W. Chambers in the story "The Yellow Sign" in *The King in Yellow* (1895).

L'mur-Kathulos: Adapted from Robert E. Howard's Kathulos in the story "Skull-Face" (*Weird Tales*, October–December 1929), where it is described as a preternatural Egyptian entity.

Bran: Presumably derived from Robert E. Howard's stories about Bran Mak Morn (a king of the Picts in their battles with Rome in Britain).

Magnum Innominandum: "The Great Not-to-Be-Named," the "unknown, unnamable deity" of the strange tribe in the hills of Spain, cited in Lovecraft's great "Roman dream" of 1927 (SL II.189–97).

31. Dexter is a prominent family name in Providence. See Lovecraft's short novel, *The Case of Charles Dexter Ward* (1927).

32. *Lee's Swamp:* A tip of the hat to the neighbors of Vrest Orton (Charley Lee and his three sons), whom Lovecraft met frequently during his Vermont stay of 1928. For a photograph of them see MW 306.

33. *Shub-Niggurath:* First cited, oddly, in Lovecraft's revision of Adolphe de Castro's "The Last Test" (1927; HM 47), and later in many of Lovecraft's stories. In a late letter he whimsically notes: "Yog-Sothoth's wife is the hellish cloud-like entity Shub-Niggurath, in whose honour nameless cults hold the rite of the Goat with a Thousand Young" (SL V.303).

34. Cf. *At the Mountains of Madness*, where the fungi from Yuggoth are depicted as battling the Old Ones in Antarctica millions of years ago: "They were able to undergo transformations and reintegrations impossible for their adversaries, and seem therefore to have originally come from even remoter gulfs of cosmic space" (MM 68).

35. Note that the misspelling of Akeley's name here by the fungi parallels Lovecraft's own initial misspelling of the name of Bert G. Akley (as *Akeley*) (see n. 15 above). Burleson (p. 12) notes that the two spellings Akley and Akeley are legitimate variants of the family name in Vermont.

36. The typed note by the fungi anticipates the forged note that was sent to Wilmarth in the next chapter (p. 234).

37. A nod to Arthur Goodenough, the amateur poet from Vermont whom Lovecraft visited in 1927 and 1928.

38. Cf. the attempt to classify the Old Ones in *At the Mountains of Madness*: "It was partly vegetable, but had three-fourths of the essentials of animal structure" (MM 25).

39. Cf. Lovecraft's own goals in writing as expressed in "Notes on Writing Weird Fiction" (1933): "I choose weird stories because they suit my inclination best—one of my strongest and most persistent wishes being to achieve, momentarily, the illusion of some strange suspension or violation of the galling limitations of time, space, and natural law which forever imprison us and frustrate our curiosity about the infinite cosmic spaces beyond the radius of our sight and analysis" (MW 113). The "limitations" are of course our own sensory limitations, not any inherent limitations in space or time.

40. The above paragraph is a reworking of the first paragraph of "Vermont—A First Impression" (1927; MW 293).

41. Daylight saving time was first utilized in the U.S. during the later stages of World War I as a measure to conserve energy, but was repealed in 1919, largely because of opposition by farmers who did not want their work schedules disrupted. Thereafter it was adopted randomly by decisions of individual municipalities and state legislatures. It did not become uniform throughout the U.S. until 1967.

42. Wantastiquet Mountain rises to an elevation of 1335 feet in the southwestern corner of Chesterfield County in New Hampshire, just across the Connecticut River from Brattleboro.

43. The above paragraph is a reworking of the second paragraph of "Vermont—A First Impression" (MW 293–94).

44. The above two paragraphs are a considerable reworking of the fourth paragraph of "Vermont—A First Impression" (MW 295).

45. *Italian primitives:* A now outmoded term for Italian tempera painters of the thirteenth and fourteenth centuries who broke from medieval traditions of painting and helped to usher in the Renaissance. Giovanni Antonio Bazzi Sodoma (1477–1549) was an Italian painter, in part influenced by Leonardo da Vinci (1452–1519).

46. The above paragraph borrows extensively from the fourth paragraph of "Vermont—A First Impression" (MW 295).

47. The remark may have been suggested by Frank Belknap Long's "The

Hounds of Tindalos" (*Weird Tales*, March 1929), where the protagonist notes: "What do we know of time, really? Einstein believes that it is relative, that it can be interpreted in terms of space, of *curved* space. But why must we stop there? . . . With . . . the aid of my mathematical knowledge I believe that I can *go back through time.*" Long was one of Lovecraft's closest associates and probably sent the story to Lovecraft in manuscript well in advance of its publication.

48. In *At the Mountains of Madness* Lovecraft dates the advent of the fungi to earth as "during the Jurassic age" (MM 68).

49. These realms were invented in Lovecraft's revision of Zealia Bishop's "The Mound" (written 1929–30; first published *Weird Tales*, November 1940). K'n-yan is an underground region somewhere in Oklahoma; Yoth lies below K'n-yan; and N'kai is below Yoth (see HM 133, 140).

50. The Pnakotic Manuscripts had been first cited in "Polaris" (1918), thereby being the earliest "mythical book" created by Lovecraft. In *The Dream-Quest of Unknown Kadath* it is stated that they were "made by waking men in forgotten boreal kingdoms and borne into the land of dreams when the hairy cannibal Gnophkehs overcame many-templed Olathoë and slew all the heroes of the land of Lomar" (MM 310). Klarkash-Ton is a playful reference to Lovecraft's longtime colleague, the poet and fiction writer Clark Ashton Smith, whom he frequented addressed as "Klarkash-Ton" in letters (see also the poem "To Klarkash-Ton, Lord of Averoigne" [1936]). "Commoriom" is a city in the land of Hyberborea, cited in several of Smith's tales.

51. The meal is a typical one for Lovecraft, who was exceptionally fond of cheese, sweets, and heavily sugared coffee. He does not seem to have eaten sandwiches regularly, but they are cited here presumably to obviate the need for cooking.

52. One of these temporary stars—sighted on February 22, 1901, near Algol—is the subject of Lovecraft's early story "Beyond the Wall of Sleep" (1919).

53. Tao ("the Way") is the basic principle of the universe as enunciated in the Chinese philosophical/religious system known as Taoism. By tradition it was established by the philosopher Lao Tzu (sixth century BCE) in the work *Tao-te-Ching*. Cf. Frank Belknap Long's "The Hounds of Tindalos": "I have here five pellets of the drug Liao. It was used by the Chinese philosopher Lao Tze, and while under its influence he visioned Tao. Tao is the most mysterious force in the world, it surrounds and pervades all things; it contains the visible universe and everything that we call reality. He who apprehends the mysteries of Tao sees clearly all that was and will be."

54. The Doels are borrowed directly from Long's "The Hounds of Tindalos" ("In my room at night I have talked with the Doels"), although Long himself may have adapted them from the "Dôls" mentioned in Arthur Machen's "The White People."

55. Yig was a snake-god invented by Lovecraft in his revision of Zealia Bishop's "The Curse of Yig" (1928).

56. The narrator of "The Shadow Over Innsmouth" does the same when he senses the foreboding atmosphere at the Gilman House (see p. 311).

57. Pluto was discovered on January 23, 1930, by C. W. Tombaugh at the Lowell Observatory in Flagstaff, Arizona. But the discovery was not broadcast to the public until it was announced on the front page of *The New York Times* for March 14, three weeks after Lovecraft had begun writing this story. A day after the announcement, Lovecraft wrote in a letter: "Whatcha thinka the NEW PLANET? HOT STUFF!!! It is probably Yuggoth" (Lovecraft to James F. Morton, 15 March 1930; ms., private collection). The comment "hideous appropriateness" alludes to the fact that in Greek mythology Pluto is the god of the underworld.

58. It appears that the voices following belong to these characters: Speech-Machine = the brain of Akeley; First Buzzing Voice = Pseudo-Akeley (= Nyarlathotep?); Second Buzzing Voice = one of the fungi from Yuggoth.

59. Arthur Rimbaud (1854–1891), revolutionary French poet whose work is filled with references to alchemy, cabbalism, and occult mysticism.

THE SHADOW OVER INNSMOUTH

"The Shadow Over Innsmouth" was written in November and December of 1931. Lovecraft was so unsatisfied with the tale that he refused to submit it anywhere; but in early 1933 August Derleth, to whom Lovecraft had lent the typescript, submitted it—without Lovecraft's knowledge or permission—to Farnsworth Wright of *Weird Tales*. Wright rejected it on the ground that it was too long and could not be conveniently serialized without destroying the tale's unity. It was finally published in 1936 as a separate booklet, *The Shadow Over Innsmouth*, by William L. Crawford's Visionary Press—the only book of Lovecraft's fiction to be published in his lifetime.

The topographical inspiration for the story is Lovecraft's visit in the autumn of 1931 to the decaying seaport of Newburyport, Massachusetts (he had first seen the town in 1923). The tale is Lovecraft's richest evocation of the mingled terror and wonder of the New England landscape. In its warning on the dangers of miscegenation it may be considered an expansion and subtilization of the plot of "Facts Concerning the Late Arthur Jermyn and His Family" (1920). An examination of the literary influences upon the story can clarify how Lovecraft has enriched a conception that was by no means his own invention. Aside from Irvin S. Cobb's "Fishhead," which had probably influenced his earlier tale, "The Shadow Over Innsmouth" owes something to Robert W. Chambers's "The Harbor-Master," a short story later included as the first five chapters of the episodic novel *In Search of the Unknown* (1904). But in both these stories we are dealing with a *single* case of hybridism, not an entire community or civilization; it is only the latter that creates the sense of worldwide menace that we find in Lovecraft's tale.

The narrator is never named in the story, but in the surviving notes he is named Robert Olmstead. He reflects many of Lovecraft's own parsimonious traveling habits. Almost as important a character is Zadok Allen, whose monologue is Lovecraft's most exhaustive utilization of backwoods New England dialect. There seem to be two dominant influences upon the creation of Zadok Allen, one real and the other fictional. The lifespan of Lovecraft's aged amateur friend, Jonathan E. Hoag (1831–1927), coincides exactly with that of Zadok. More substantially, Zadok seems loosely based upon the figure of Humphrey Lathrop, an elderly doctor in Herbert Gorman's *The Place Called Dagon* (1927), which Lovecraft read in March 1928. Like Zadok, Lathrop is the repository for the secret history of the Massachusetts town in which he resides (Leominster, in the north-central part of Massachusetts); and, like Zadok, he is partial to spirits—in his case apple-jack!

In the end, "The Shadow Over Innsmouth" is about the inexorable call of heredity. In 1929 Lovecraft the antiquarian made the poignant utterance: "The past is *real*—it is *all there is*" (SL III.31). This tale is perhaps his finest meditation on that conception.

Further Reading

T. G. L. Cockcroft, "Some Notes on 'The Shadow Over Innsmouth,'" *Lovecraft Studies* No. 3 (Fall 1980): 3–4.

Sam Gafford, "'The Shadow Over Innsmouth': Lovecraft's Melting Pot," *Lovecraft Studies* No. 24 (Spring 1991): 6–13.

1. The name Innsmouth had been invented in "Celephaïs" (see p. 30), but is clearly in England there. It was resurrected in two sonnets ("The Port" [VIII] and "The Bells" [XIX]) of *Fungi from Yuggoth*, where the location is unspecified, although a New England setting seems likely. The suffix *-mouth* refers to the city's location at the mouth of a river.
2. Although the most notorious use of concentration camps occurred under the Nazis in the late 1930s, extending through World War II, the detention of individuals—usually in wartime—in camps dates to the later nineteenth century. It was used, for example, by the British in South Africa during the Boer War (1899–1902).
3. Cf. "The Picture in the House": "I had been travelling for some time amongst the people of the Miskatonic Valley in quest of certain genealogical data" (p. 36).
4. *Newburyport:* A city in northeastern Massachusetts, at the mouth of the Merrimack River; it was settled in 1635, incorporated as a town in 1764, and incorporated as a city in 1851. It was formerly known for shipbuilding. Lovecraft first visited the city in April 1923 with the young amateur writer Edgar J. Davis; he visited it again in late October 1931 (SL III.435).
5. *Manuxet:* Mythical; presumably based upon the Merrimack River, which flows through Newburyport. There is also a town named Manomet and a Manomet River in Plymouth County, emptying into Buzzard's Bay.
6. *B. & M.:* Boston & Maine Railroad, incorporated in 1835. It was initially designed to provide rail service between Boston and Portland, Maine. There were indeed branch lines to Rowley and Ipswich.
7. *Croesus:* Latinized form of Kroisos, King of Lydia (c. 560–546 BCE), a region in Asia Minor (Turkey); known in antiquity both for his magnanimity and his wealth.

8. Cf. "Facts Concerning the Late Arthur Jermyn and His Family," where Sir Wade Jermyn is said to have married "the daughter of a Portuguese trader whom he had met in Africa" (p. 15). This wife was, of course, a white ape.

9. A town on the east coast of Lake Champlain; founded c. 1770.

10. Cf. an entry in Lovecraft's commonplace book: "Lonely bleak islands off N.E. coast. Horrors they harbour—outpost of cosmic influences" (MW 99).

11. Cf. Lovecraft to Lillian D. Clark, 15–16 August 1930: "Our drive to Onset [on Cape Cod] was uneventful—though it was interesting to have [Frank] Belknap [Long] point out a colony of *Fiji-Islanders* near Onset" (ms., JHL).

12. Cf. "The Outsider": "I stretched out my fingers . . . and touched *a cold and unyielding surface of polished glass*" (p. 50).

13. Although Gilman is a common New England name, it is here also a pun (gill-man).

14. *Casey:* Around 1928 Lovecraft discovered that he had an Irish strain of Caseys in his own ancestry. See SL II.322–24.

15. Cf. "Beyond the Wall of Sleep" (1919): "Among these odd folk [in the Catskill mountains], who correspond exactly to the decadent element of 'white trash' in the South, law and morals are non-existent" (D 26).

16. The city of Danvers, about 5 miles northwest of Salem, was originally founded as Salem-Village in 1636 by members of the original Salem settlement of 1626. The State Hospital for the Insane was built in 1874.

17. The library was built in 1864–65 and opened on January 1, 1866. In 1905 its head librarian was Helen E. Tilton (John C. Currier, *History of Newburyport, Mass., 1764–1905* [Newburyport: Published by the Author, 1906], p. 528); cf. the presumably fictitious Anna Tilton, head of the Newburyport Historical Society.

18. As Lovecraft frequently visited on his various journeys.

19. Poles and Portuguese were significant minorities throughout New England. Cf. "The Terrible Old Man" (1920), where two of the three criminals in the tale—Joe Czanek and Manuel Silva—are, respectively, Polish and Portuguese.

20. An actual institution, officially called the Historical Society of Old Newbury, situated in Lovecraft's day at the Pettingell-Fowler House at 164 High Street (currently at the Cushing House at 98 High Street). Lovecraft had himself visited it (Lovecraft to Lillian D. Clark, August 1927; ms., JHL).

21. Cf. a similar passage in "The Call of Cthulhu" (pp. 150–151 and n. 20).

22. *Freemasonry:* A fellowship evolving out of medieval guilds. It is not a secret society, as frequently claimed, since there was no attempt at secrecy; nor is it a religion or church, although it stressed the fatherhood of God and the brotherhood of mankind. The first masonic lodge in England was established in 1717; the first in the U.S. in 1730. Lovecraft's grandfather Whipple Van Buren Phillips (1833–1904) was a freemason, having founded the Masonic lodge in Foster in 1869.

23. *Levantine:* Jewish; derived from the Levant, an archaic term for the lands of the eastern Mediterranean.

24. *Plum Island:* A long, narrow island off the coast of Massachusetts facing Newburyport.

25. For Kingsport see n. 4 to "The Festival." Kingsport Head seems to refer to a cliff, bluff, or headland that looks out to sea. Cf. *At the Mountains of Madness:* "The ship's outfit . . . was to convey press reports to the *Arkham Advertiser*'s powerful wireless station on Kingsport Head, Mass." (MM 8). Cape Ann is the designation for the northern portion of the peninsula on which Gloucester and Rockport are situated.

26. This house is the focal point of "The Strange High House in the Mist" (1926).

27. Cf. the recurring line in "St. Toad's" (sonnet XXV of *Fungi from Yuggoth):* "Beware St. Toad's cracked chimes!" (AT 74).

28. *Gothic:* i.e., the Victorian Gothic architecture of the middle nineteenth century that sought to imitate medieval Gothic architecture.

29. Cf. the "processions of blear-eyed and pockmarked young men" in the Red Hook district of Brooklyn, as described in "The Horror at Red Hook" (1925): "One saw groups of these youths incesssantly . . . in leering vigils on street corners" (D 248).

30. An actual chain once very common throughout New England. It was founded around 1900 by two Irishmen who received a loan from the First National Bank of Boston, from which they took the name. In the 1970s the name was changed to Finast, but most of the stores have now been purchased by other chains.

31. I.e., May-Eve and Hallowmass, the two most important festivals of the Witches' Sabbath.

32. For the possible influence of Herbert Gorman's novel *The Place Called Dagon* (New York: George H. Doran Co., 1927) on the figure of Zadok Allen, see the introductory note. In the Old Testament, Zadok is a priest of Israel in the reigns of kings David and Solomon.

33. Cf. Lovecraft's description of Oscar Wilde: "As a man, however, Wilde admits of absolutely no defence. His character, notwithstanding a daintiness of manners which imposed an exterior shell of decorative decency & decorum, was as thoroughly rotten & contemptible as it is possible for a human character to be. . . . It is an ironic circumstance that he who succeeded for a time in being the Prince of Dandies, was never in any basic sense what one likes to call a gentleman" (Lovecraft to August Derleth, 20 January 1927; ms., State Historical Society of Wisconsin). Lovecraft is perhaps suggesting that Obed Marsh's miscegenation and Wilde's homosexuality are equally aberrant. Wilde (1854–1900) died, of course, just before the commencement of the Edwardian age (the reign of Edward VII, 1901–10).

34. Two of Lovecraft's favorite edibles, both because of his fondness for cheese and sweets and because they were inexpensive.

35. A clear reference to Poe's poem "The Conqueror Worm" (included in "Ligeia").

36. Another nod to Poe, this time to his tale "The Imp of the Perverse," which introduced this idiom into the language.

37. Cf. "The Well" (sonnet XI of *Fungi from Yuggoth):* "And yet we put the

bricks back—for we found / The hole too deep for any line to sound"
(AT 69).

38. *snow:* Not an error for *scow,* but "A small sailing-vessel resembling a brig, carrying a main and fore mast and a supplementary trysail mast close behind the mainmast; formerly employed as a warship" (OED).

39. An archaic name for the island of Tahiti, in the South Pacific (17° 38' S. Latitude, 149° 30' W. Longitude). The island was discovered in 1767 by the British navigator Samuel Wallis.

40. Ponape is an island located at 6° 50' N. Latitude, 158° 10' E. Longitude in the Pacific. The Caroline Islands encompass a widely scattered array of islands in the western Pacific north of New Guinea. Cf. A. Merritt, "The Moon Pool" (1918): "I shall first recapitulate what has actually been known of the Throckmorton expedition to the island of Ponape in the Carolines . . ." (*Under the Moons of Mars,* ed. Sam Moskowitz [New York: Holt, Rinehart & Winston, 1970], p. 138).

41. For the Kanakas see n. 42 to "The Call of Cthulhu."

42. Perhaps an echo of the myth of Minos, who exacted a tribute of seven young men and women every year from the Athenians until Theseus defeated him by slaying the Minotaur.

43. The first part of the sentence brings to mind Lovecraft's early story "The Temple" (1920), about an underwater city in the Atlantic; the second part of the sentence appears to allude to "Dagon" and "The Call of Cthulhu."

44. The mention of Old Ones is one of the several subtle hints that this tale is an indirect sequel to *At the Mountains of Madness,* written earlier in 1931. The Old Ones are the extraterrestrial entities who, as described in that novel, came to earth millions of years ago; the "signs" that they used were presumably some kind of weapon that held the Deep Ones in check. See also the later mention of "shoggoth" (p. 308).

45. This would mean that Zadok was born in 1831, the same year that Lovecraft's aged friend, the poet Jonathan E. Hoag (1831–1927), was born; and since Zadok is presumably killed by the Innsmouth denizens shortly after speaking with the narrator, his death date coincides with Hoag's as well.

46. The swastika is a symbol (generally thought to represent the sun or fire) found in Polynesian and North American Indian cultures, and also in Norse mythology. Adolf Hitler's belief that it was Aryan in origin led to his adoption of it in 1919 as the emblem for his National Socialist (Nazi) party.

47. Ashtoreth is an intentional Hebrew mispronunciation of the Canaanite fertility goddess Astarte. For Belial see n. 13 to "The Hound." Beelzebub is a name used interchangeably with Satan in the New Testament (e.g., Matthew 12:24–27). The Golden Calf was a gold-plated figure of a young bull used in a variety of Israelite rituals as cited in the Old Testament (e.g., I Kings 12:28) and later condemned as idolatry. Canaan is the name of the area in the Middle East now occupied by Israel and Lebanon. The Canaanites' religious rituals were full of sensuality and were regarded as dangerous and sacrilegious by the Israelites (cf. Exodus 23:24: "Thou shalt not bow downe to their gods, nor serve them, nor

doe after their workes: but thou shalt utterly overthrowe them, and quite breake downe their images"). For the Philistines, see n. 11 to "Dagon." *Mene, mene, tekel, upharsin* is the so-called "writing on the wall," i.e., the words that magically appeared on a wall during Belshazzar's feast in Babylon. The prophet Daniel interpreted the words for Belshazzar as follows: "*MENE*, God hath numbered thy kingdome, and finished it. *TEKEL*, thou art weighed in the balances, and art found wanting. *PERES*, thy kingdome is divided, and given to the Medes and Persians" (Daniel 5:26–28). Belshazzar was slain that night.

48. Commandery is the name for a local branch or lodge of an order or brotherhood, such as the Freemasons (see n. 22).

49. A selectman is an executive officer in New England towns that are run by the town-meeting form of government.

50. Repeated from "The Call of Cthulhu" (p. 152).

51. Cf. "Facts Concerning the Late Arthur Jermyn and His Family," where the "Oriental seclusion in which [Sir Wade Jermyn] kept his wife" is noted: "No one had ever seen her closely, not even the servants; for her disposition had been violent and singular" (p. 15). She was, of course, a white ape.

52. *shoggoth:* First cited in "Night-Gaunts" (sonnet XX of *Fungi from Yuggoth*): "Where the puffed shoggoths splash in doubtful sleep" (AT 72); later described in *At the Mountains of Madness* as protoplasmic monsters created by the Old Ones as slave labor, who overthrew their civilization in Antarctica.

53. The price was not unusual for inexpensive hotels of the period. During his trip to Florida in the summer of 1931, Lovecraft secured lodgings at the Rio Vista Hotel in St. Augustine for as little as $4.00 per week.

54. Lovecraft on his travels often ate frugally in this manner, largely from economic necessity.

55. A Eunice Babson of Innsmouth is a minor character in "The Thing on the Doorstep" (DH 296).

56. *at grade:* "on the same level" (OED, noting that the idiom is restricted to the U.S.).

57. Recall Dr. Armitage's comment on Wilbur Whateley's monstrous twin brother in "The Dunwich Horror": "*it looked more like the father* [Yog-Sothoth] *than he did*" (DH 198).

58. The narrator of "Under the Pyramids" (1924) witnesses a similarly cataclysmic sight in an underground chamber beneath the Great Pyramid: "*their crazy torches began to cast shadows on the surface of those stupendous columns. . . . Hippopotami should not have human hands and carry torches . . . men should not have the heads of crocodiles . . .* " (D 240).

59. Peabody is a prominent name throughout New England: cf. the Peabody Museum in Salem. Lovecraft used a variant spelling for a character (Frank H. Pabodie) in *At the Mountains of Madness*.

60. Cf. Simon Orne in *The Case of Charles Dexter Ward* (MM 112f.). A Granny Orne is mentioned in "The Strange High House in the Mist" (1926; D 279); and an Orne's Gangway is cited in "The Dreams in the Witch House" (MM 288). There is an Orne's Rock north of Marblehead.

61. Lovecraft had visited Alfred Galpin and Samuel Loveman in Cleveland in August 1922—his only trip to the Midwest.
62. In Massillon, a city about 5 miles west of Canton, a Massillon State Hospital for the insane opened in 1899.
63. A parody of Psalm 23:6: "Surely goodness and mercy shall follow me all the days of my life: and I will dwell in the house of the Lord for ever."

THE HAUNTER OF THE DARK

The genesis of this story is almost as celebrated as the story itself. Lovecraft wrote it on November 5–9, 1935, almost immediately after hearing of the nearly simultaneous selling of *At the Mountains of Madness* and "The Shadow Out of Time" to *Astounding Stories*, for a net total of $630 (minus a $35 agenting fee for the former tale).

This last original story by Lovecraft was written almost on a whim. Robert Bloch had written a story, "The Shambler from the Stars," in the spring of 1935, in which a character—never named, but clearly meant to be Lovecraft—is killed off. Lovecraft was taken with the story, and when it was published in *Weird Tales* (September 1935), a reader, B. M. Reynolds, praised it and wrote to the magazine's letter column with a suggestion: "Contrary to previous criticism, Robert Bloch deserves plenty of praise for *The Shambler from the Stars*. Now why doesn't Mr. Lovecraft return the compliment, and dedicate a story to the author?" Lovecraft took up the offer, and his story tells of one Robert Blake who ends up a glassy-eyed corpse staring out his study window.

But if Blake, a young writer of weird fiction from Milwaukee, is meant to be Bloch, the setting owes much to Lovecraft's own circumstances. The view down Providence's College Hill that Blake's study commands, looking out over the Italian district of Federal Hill, is nothing more than what Lovecraft saw out of his own study at 66 College Street. The church that figures so prominently in the tale is also real—St. John's Catholic Church on Atwell's Avenue (now destroyed). This church was in fact situated on a raised plot of ground, as in the story, although there was (at least in recent years) no metal fence around it. It was, in Lovecraft's day, very much a going concern, being the principal Catholic church in the area. The description of the interior and belfry of the church is quite accurate. Lovecraft heard that the steeple had been destroyed by lightning in late June of 1935 (he was not there at the time, being in Florida visiting R. H. Barlow); instead of rebuilding the steeple, the church authorities decided merely to put a conical cap on the brick tower. This incident no doubt started Lovecraft's imagination working.

Some of the surface details of the plot were taken directly from Hanns Heinz Ewers's "The Spider," which Lovecraft read in Dashiell Hammett's anthology *Creeps by Night* (1931). This story involves a man who becomes fascinated with a strange woman he sees through his window in a building across from his own, until finally he seems to lose hold of his own personality. The entire story is told in the form of the man's diary, and at the end he writes: "My name—Richard Bracquemont, Richard Bracquemont, Richard—oh, I can't get any farther . . ."

Further Reading
Steven J. Mariconda, "Some Antecedents of the Shining Trapezohedron," in Mariconda's *On the Emergence of "Cthulhu" and Other Observations* (West Warwick, RI: Necronomicon Press, 1995), pp. 66–71.

1. The epigraph is from Lovecraft's own poem, "Nemesis," written "in the sinister small hours of the black morning after Hallowe'en [1917]" (SL I.51) and first published in the *Vagrant* for June 1918.
2. St. John's Catholic Church on Atwell's Avenue in Providence; built in 1871 and torn down in 1992.
3. Lovecraft reports that St. John's "lost its steeple in a storm last summer [i.e., the summer of 1935] while I was away [in Florida]" (Lovecraft to Duane W. Rimel, 12 November 1935; ms., JHL).
4. The John Hay Library (College and Prospect Streets), erected in 1910, was named after John Hay (1838–1905), Secretary of State under McKinley and Theodore Roosevelt and a Brown graduate (class of 1858). At this time it was the main library for the university; it now houses rare books and manuscripts, including the extensive H. P. Lovecraft Papers.
5. Lovecraft believed the Samuel B. Mumford house at 66 College Street to have been built around 1800 (see SL IV.187), but a more probable date is c. 1825. It was moved in 1959 to 65 Prospect Street.
6. The titles are representative of Lovecraft's own work, as well as of the work that Bloch was writing under Lovecraft's tutelage. "The Burrowers Beneath" may allude to an early (non-extant) tale by Bloch, "The Blasphemy Beneath," which Lovecraft read in manuscript in June 1933. "In the Vale of Pnath" is an allusion to several Lovecraft stories: Pnath is first cited in "The Doom That Came to Sarnath" (1919; D 48), and the vale of Pnath is mentioned frequently in *The Dream-Quest of Unknown Kadath* (MM 336f.). "The Feaster from the Stars" is a nod to "The Shambler from the Stars," the story by Bloch that inspired "The Haunter of the Dark."
7. Memorial Hall is the main building on the campus of the Rhode Island School of Design, on Benefit Street. The "Georgian court-house belfry" is the neo-Georgian Providence County Court House at 30 Main Street, built in 1927–33.
8. The Industrial Trust Building at 55 Exchange Place was built in 1926–28. At twenty-six stories it was the tallest building in the city at this time.
9. *Walpurgisnacht* ("the night of St. Walpurga") corresponds with May Eve (April 30). It is traditionally the time when witches were thought to congregate. The relation to St. Walpurga derives from one of the feasts held in commemoration of the saint on May Day; she then came to be regarded as a protector against the witches' magic.
10. Cf. "Hesperia" (sonnet XIII of *Fungi from Yuggoth*): "It is the land where beauty's meaning flowers; / . . . Dreams bring us close—but ancient lore repeats / That human tread has never soiled these streets" (AT 69).
11. Presumably a reference to what Lovecraft elsewhere terms the Elder

Sign, a cryptic hand gesture made by denizens of both the real and the dream worlds as a means of protection from supernatural forces. Cf. *The Dream-Quest of Unknown Kadath*: "At another house . . . [Randolph Carter] asked questions about the gods . . . but the farmer and his wife would only make the Elder Sign . . ." (MM 311).

12. Cf. "St. Toad's" (sonnet XXV of *Fungi from Yuggoth*), where a character is similarly both eager and afraid to come upon a church: "And growing weak, / I paused, when a third greybeard croaked in fear: / 'Beware St. Toad's cracked chimes!' Aghast, I fled— / Till suddenly that black spire loomed ahead" (AT 74).

13. Lovecraft here presents an implied monologue by the Irish policeman, with his typical modes of pronunciation ("ould") and syntax.

14. The *crux ansata* is a cross in the shape of the letter *tau* (symbolizing life) surmounted by a circle (symbolizing eternity). It was used by the ancient Egyptians to convey the idea of divine life and secret wisdom.

15. Another collection of mythical books:

> For the *Necronomicon* see n. 7 to "The Hound."
>
> *Liber Ivonis* is Lovecraft's Latinized title for *The Book of Eibon* or *Livre d'Eibon*, a title invented by Clark Ashton Smith, first cited in "Ubbo-Sathla" (*Weird Tales*, July 1933). Eibon was, in Smith's tales, a Hyperborean wizard. His work was translated into medieval Latin by Gaspard du Nord of Averoigne.
>
> *Cultes des Goules* ("Ghoul Cults") by the comte d'Erlette was invented by Bloch, apparently in "The Grinning Ghoul" (*Weird Tales*, June 1936), which Lovecraft read in manuscript in November 1934. Bloch derived the author's name, however, from Lovecraft, who frequently referred to August Derleth (1909–1971) by the whimsical name "Auguste-Guillaume, Comte d'Erlette."
>
> *Unaussprechlichen Kulten* ("Nameless Cults") by Friedrich von Junzt is a complicated matter. Von Juntz was invented by Robert E. Howard (1906–1936) in "The Black Stone" (*Weird Tales*, November 1931), although Lovecraft supplies von Junzt's first name in a 1933 letter to Bloch (see *Letters to Robert Bloch* [West Warwick, RI: Necronomicon Press, 1993], p. 23). Howard cites von Junzt's work variously as "the Black Book" or *Nameless Cults*. On Lovecraft's request, August Derleth supplied a German title for the work, although later a debate arose as to whether *unaussprechlich* meant "nameless" or merely "unpronounceable." It is, however, erroneous German, and should either be *Die unaussprechlichen Kulten* or *Unaussprechliche Kulten*. Lovecraft first cited it in print in "The Dreams in the Witch House" (*Weird Tales*, July 1933).
>
> Ludvig Prinn's *De Vermis Mysteriis* ("Mysteries of the Worm") is a joint invention by Lovecraft and Bloch. Bloch had cited the author and the English title of his work in "The Secret in the Tomb" (*Weird Tales*, May 1935), but Lovecraft supplied the Latin title when he read the ms. of "The Shambler from the Stars" in April 1935 (*Letters to Robert Bloch*, p. 65).
>
> For the Pnakotic Manuscripts see n. 50 to "The Whisperer in Darkness."
> For *The Book of Dzyan* see n. 4 to "The Call of Cthulhu."

16. Easter Island is cited in several Lovecraft stories as a locus of mystery. It is located at 27° 08´ S. Latitude, 109° 26´ W. Longitude. It is 1100 miles east of Pitcairn Island and 2200 miles west of Chile. It was discovered by Europeans in 1722; Captain James Cook landed there in 1774. Lovecraft saw several Easter Island statues in the Smithsonian Museum in Washington, DC, in 1929: ". . . last mute and terrible survivors of an unknown elder age when the towers of weird Lemurian cities clawed at the sky where now only the trackless waters roll" ("Travels in the Provinces of America" [1929; MW 345]).

   In 1932 Lovecraft's friend Donald Wandrei wrote a novel, *Dead Titans, Waken!*, in which the climactic scene is laid on Easter Island. Lovecraft read the work in manuscript in early 1933. In revised form it was published as *The Web of Easter Island* (1948).

17. For the literary prototypes of this object (the shining trapezohedron), ranging from the *Arabian Nights* to H. G. Wells's "The Crystal Egg," see Steven J. Mariconda's "Some Antecedents of the Shining Trapezohedron" (cited above).

18. *Providence Telegram:* Properly, the *Evening Telegram,* founded in 1880. In 1906 it became the *Evening Tribune and Telegram,* and in this incarnation it published monthly astronomical columns by Lovecraft in 1906–08.

19. The pastor at St. John's Catholic Church when Lovecraft wrote this story was Francis J. Feeney.

20. *Orrin B. Eddy:* A nod to Lovecraft's longtime Providence associate Clifford M. Eddy (1896–1971), for whom he ghostwrote some stories in *Weird Tales* in 1923–24.

21. Thomas A. Doyle was mayor of Providence in 1864–69, 1870–81, and 1884–86.

22. "Aklo letters" were invented by Arthur Machen in "The White People" (1904). Lovecraft borrowed the term first in "The Dunwich Horror" (Wilbur Whateley writes in his diary: "Today learned the Aklo for the Sabaoth" [DH 184]).

23. The "serpent-men of Valusia" is a nod to Robert E. Howard, who cited the mythical prehistoric realm of Valusia in many tales, notably "The Shadow Kingdom" (*Weird Tales*, August 1929), where "snake-people" are mentioned as the rulers of Valusia before human beings drove them out.

   Lemuria is a purportedly "lost" continent that sank in the Indian Ocean. It was conjectured by the naturalist Ernst Haeckel (see n. 3 to "Herbert West—Reanimator") as a means of accounting for the existence of lemurs and other plants and animals in southern Africa and the Malay Peninsula. See also n. 10 to "The Call of Cthulhu."

24. Khem ("black") is the native ancient name for Egypt, corresponding linguistically with the Hebrew Ham (cf. Psalms 78:51, where Ham is a poetic metaphor for Egypt).

25. For Nephren-Ka see n. 2 to "The Outsider."

26. *The Providence Journal,* founded in 1829, was and is the leading paper in Providence.

27. Cf. "Nemesis," l. 5: "And I struggle and shriek ere the daybreak, being driven to madness with fright."
28. *Bulletin:* Properly, the *Evening Bulletin,* founded in 1863. In 1976 it merged with the *Journal* to form the *Providence Journal-Bulletin.* Lovecraft subscribed to this paper for most of his life, including the time when he was in New York (1924–26).
29. See n. 21 to "The Festival."
30. *Spirito Santo Church:* mythical.
31. The fraternity houses at Brown University were in fact located on College Street at this time, near Lovecraft's residence.
32. Yaddith is a mythical planet devised by Lovecraft; first cited in "Alienation" (sonnet XXXII of *Fungi from Yuggoth*) ("He had seen Yaddith, yet retained his mind" [AT 77]), and extensively mentioned in "Through the Gates of the Silver Key" (1932–33; MM 447f.).
33. The reference to Roderick Usher relates to Lovecraft's interpretation of the central theme of Poe's "The Fall of the House of Usher" as enunciated in "Supernatural Horror in Literature": "[the story] displays an abnormally linked trinity of entities at the end of a long and isolated family history—a brother, his twin sister, and their incredibly ancient house all sharing a single soul and meeting one common dissolution at the same moment" (D 399). The suggestion is that Blake and the Haunter of the Dark share the same soul at this moment.